What could be m[...]ress or the *Train Bleu*? T[...] [...]llowing steam from the engine, the slamming of carriage doors . . . they all recall a time of mystery and the excitement of travel by train. But do these sounds mask something more sinister? Did the engine's whistle hide the scream of a victim? Did the noise of the wheels and the bustle of the passengers cover the sound of a violent struggle? And who *really* are your fellow passengers: innocent travellers – or potential killers?

Peter Haining has put together an outstanding collection of tales featuring such famous writers as Agatha Christie, Ruth Rendell, Roald Dahl, Maeve Binchy, Elmore Leonard and Dorothy L. Sayers. *Murder on the Railways* – a nerve-tingling journey into the unknown . . .

Peter Haining is an internationally-known anthologist and writer on crime fiction whose books have been published in over a dozen languages. He was a 1992 Edgar nominee by the Mystery Writers of America for his Centenary study of Agatha Christie's work on stage, film, radio and TV, *Murder in Four Acts* and was recently featured in BBC TV's 'Bookmark' programme. Peter Haining is married with three grown-up children and lives in rural Suffolk.

Also edited by Peter Haining

The Armchair Detective
The Television Crimebusters Omnibus
The Armchair Horror Collection
The Frankenstein Omnibus
The Vampire Omnibus
Murder At The Races
The Orion Books of Murder

MURDER

ON THE RAILWAYS

edited by
PETER HAINING

ORION

An Orion paperback
First published in Great Britain by Orion in 1996
This paperback edition published in 1997 by Orion Books Ltd,
Orion House, 5 Upper St Martin's Lane, London WC2H 9EA

A CIP catalogue record for this book
is available from the British Library

ISBN 0 75280 873 7

Typeset by Deltatype Ltd, Birkenhead, Merseyside
Printed and bound in Great Britain by
Clays Ltd, St Ives plc

For
JOHN KENT
Steam Buff – and man
in the driver's seat!

Murders committed in a train have always excited great public interest – because nearly everybody at some time or other travels by train.

CANON J. A. R. BROOKES

Contents

Introduction

Trains have inspired authors to make the
wheels of fear spin in their readers' minds
as no other mode of transport could.

HUGH DOUGLAS

The sun was just beginning to rise into a clear blue sky over
the Chihuahua mountains on the border between Texas
and Mexico when the train came into view. A long, snaking
line of carriages, it travelled slowly over the parched desert
scrubland, heading in an easterly direction. At first
glimpse, the sight was a normal enough one on this stretch
of the Southern Pacific Railroad linking America's Gulf
coast with the Pacific Ocean.

Suddenly, however, the stillness of the morning air was
broken by the screeching of the huge locomotive's brakes
as it juddered to a halt. Immediately the sound was
accompanied by gun shots as about a dozen armed bandits
broke from the cover of some mesquite bushes in a dusty
ravine close to the track, and ran towards the train. A few
stumbled as they ran, suggesting that the whole gang had
probably been waiting in hiding for much of the night.

No sign of resistance came from the driver's cabin of the
locomotive as two of the raiders climbed aboard, while
further down the train more of the men scrambled quickly
up into the carriages. Then a voice, speaking unmistakably
in Spanish, was heard raised in anger in the guard's wagon
at the rear of the train. For a moment there was the sound
of a scuffle and then the harsh crack of a pistol being fired.
An eerie stillness gripped the railroad for several seconds,
followed by shouting and the sight of boxes being thrown
out of the train to where some of the men waited beside the
track. The pile of loot grew quickly in the brightening
sunshine . . .

This scene is not, as you might expect, from a typical Western novel or movie. It occurred only last year just ten miles from El Paso, and was, in fact, just one of a whole series of similar raids that have been carried out in recent years on the Southern Pacific Railroad. The bandits were Mexicans from shanty towns just over the border who had been crossing under the cover of darkness to hold up trains at first light and seize boxes of television sets and videos, cases of wines and spirits, and all manner of consumer goods bound for the cities in the east. Because of the sheer length of these freight trains – as many as a hundred carriages are not unusual, with each holding up to ten containers – they move slowly and are easy to board. With only a driver and guard in attendance there is also little chance of resistance, although several brave employees of the railroad have lost their lives in hold-ups.

The Texan authorities believe that a number of Mexican gangs are making a good living from these hit-and-run raids on trains which are very difficult to police. Raiders have been arrested, usually as the result of a tip-off, enabling officers to catch them red-handed while they are filling trucks brought across the border with their spoils. Once over the border into Mexico, however, the men are soon swallowed up by the desert terrain or by the maze of shacks which make up the shanty towns. Crime pays, it is ruefully admitted by the Texas patrolmen, for these modern-day train robbers . . .

It is a well-documented fact that crime has been associated with the railways almost since the opening of the very first railroad, the Stockton and Darlington line in September 1825, when George Stephenson's engine, *Locomotion*, coupled to coaches full of passengers and goods, steamed ceremonially before a large, wide-eyed audience (many of whom, it was said, had only come in the hope of 'seeing the travelling machine fired by the Devil blow itself up!'). Indeed, records show that the first murder on the railways was committed just a little over twenty years later. I quote from the *Swiss National Gazette* of 27 February 1847, under the heading: MYSTERIOUS MURDER IN A RAILROAD CARRIAGE.

> A person whose name is unknown took his seat at Mannheim in a railroad carriage with a ticket for Karlsruhe. Three other individuals of respectable appearance shortly afterwards placed themselves in the same carriage, strangled the first, rifled his pockets, and quitted the carriage at Heidelberg. The crime was not discovered until the train arrived at Karlsruhe, when the man was found in the corner of the carriage dead and already cold. This crime appears to be unique in the annals of the railroads.

Unique it may well have been *then*, but it has become almost commonplace in fact and fiction ever since.

In his excellent *History of the Railways* (1964), Erwin Berghaus draws our attention to a grisly incident that took place on a track near Phoci in ancient Greece. I quote again:

> It all began with the track. Even in Ancient Greece the heavy carts and two-wheeled coaches ran in ruts – a practical necessity in wet weather. When one vehicle met another along the path of this single pair of stone ruts unpleasant scenes would sometimes take place. When Oedipus, in a sunken road by Phoci, was met by another wagon carrying an old man and his driver-servant, a dispute arose as to who had right of way, and Oedipus slew the driver and then killed the old man who had sprung to avenge his servant's death.

This, Berghaus suggests, may well qualify as the first 'railway' murder – but the story does not end there. For with a twist of fate worthy of the best crime novels, it transpires that the old man Oedipus killed was actually someone he should have recognised, even though he had not seen him for years: his own father, Laios.

But history apart, the train has featured large in the crime novel since the genre was born in the middle of the last century. Trains of every kind, from the continental express crossing international frontiers to the local commuter special and subway train, have proved to be a popular setting with writers of crime and mystery stories. The simple truth is that probably no other form of transport – the car, the boat or the aircraft – has quite the same allure as the train, nor its unique environment. The railway train is virtually a world of its own. It is isolated from the outside world, yet still a part of it. The real world passes by, but it cannot affect the traveller one way or another. It is a confined environment, certainly, but a comfortable one. There is no escape until journey's end.

Within the closed doors of the carriages, as the miles pass by and the scenery constantly changes, there exists another even more important element: the other passengers. Who are they? What are their intentions? Are they innocent travellers or potential criminals? When the eyes of strangers meet and then hastily avoid each glance, is this out of embarrassment or perhaps because they hide a guilty secret? This sense of a *frisson* of tension can be heightened by the monotonous clickety-clack of the train's wheels lulling the unsuspecting to sleep . . . the sudden approach of tunnels, plunging the compartment into darkness . . . or the unexpected shriek of the engine's whistle which can sound so like a victim's scream of terror . . . Is there any wonder that the railway should have proved such an ideal setting for the murder story?

The short stories I have selected for this volume cover a wide spectrum. To begin with there are a group of tales by famous authors whose names are inextricably linked with the railway murder story such as Agatha Christie (*Murder on the Orient Express*), Ethel Lina White (*The Lady*

Vanishes), Patricia Highsmith (*Strangers on a Train*), Georges Simenon (*The Man Who Watched the Trains Go By*), and Elmore Leonard (*Three-Ten to Yuma*). These are followed by a selection of stories about the railway detectives including Sherlock Holmes, Godfrey Page, Calvin Sprague and Commissioner John Appleby. The third section concentrates on the Underground with some tense dramas by Baroness Orczy, Cornell Woolrich, Ken Follett, Maeve Binchy and others. To complete the picture, there is a selection devoted to the dramas that even the ordinary commuter can face by such respected writers as Stanley Ellin, Roald Dahl, William F. Nolan and Ruth Rendell. All are introduced with information about the writers and the backgrounds to their stories which, in some cases, I think, are almost as intriguing as the mysteries they have created.

In these pages the reader will find the nostalgic smell of the steam locomotive mingling with the roar of modern high-speed electric trains; here, too, the days of luxury carriages when three classes of compartments were a common feature, contrast with the crush of commuter trains and tube travel. All, though, are alike in providing a unique environment for murder and mystery in which the perpetrator and the victim are confined in the same place until the train reaches its destination.

It was Shakespeare, I believe, writing in an age long before the advent of the railways, who remarked in one of his plays that 'The wheel is come full circle'. My journey through the mystery genre to compile this book of crime on wheels is now at an end – yours is just about to begin. I hope the excursion will prove an enjoyable one, and if you are tempted to read this book on a train remember the adage: 'The man who cannot sleep in a sleeping car is the loneliest man on earth.'

PETER HAINING
Boxford, Suffolk

Murder in the Railway Train

Listen to my song, and I will not detain you long,
   And then I will tell you of what I've heard.
Of a murder that's been done, by some wicked one,
   And the place where it all occurred;
Between Stepney and Bow they struck the fatal blow,
   To resist he tried all in vain,
Murdered by some prigs was poor Mr Briggs
   Whilst riding in a railway train.

Muller is accused, at present we cannot refuse
   To believe that he is the very one,
But all his actions, you see, have been so very free,
   Ever since the murder it was done;
From his home he never went, but such a happy time he
     spent,
   He never looked troubled on the brain,
If he'd been the guilty man, he would have hid all he can,
   From the murder in the railway train.

Muller he did state that he was going to emigrate
   Long before this dreadful tragedy;
He often used to talk, about travelling to New York,
   In the *Victoria*, that was going to sea.
Mr Death, the jeweller, said, he was very much afraid,
   He might not know the same man again,
When he heard of the reward, he started out abroad,
   About the murder in the railway train.

If it's Muller, we can't deny, on the cabman keep your eye,
   Remember what he said the other day,
That Muller a ticket sold for money, which seems so very
     funny,
   When he had no expenses for to pay.
They say his money he took, and his name entered on the
     book,

Long before this tragedy he came;
Like Muller, the cabman had a hat, and it may be his, perhaps
That was found in the railway train.

Would a murderer have forgot, to have destroyed the jeweller's box,
Or burnt up the sleeve of his coat,
Would he the chain ticket have sold, and himself exposed so bold,
And to all his friends a letter wrote,
Before Muller went away, why did not the cabman say,
And not give him so much start on the main
If the cabman knew – it's very wrong – to keep the secret up so long,
About the murder in the railway train.

When Muller does arrive, we shall not be much surprised,
To hear that that's him on the trial;
Give him time to repent, though he is not innocent,
To hear the evidence give no denial.
Muller's got the watch, you see, so it proves that he is guilty,
But like Townley don't prove that he's insane;
For if it should be him, on the gallows let him swing,
For the murder on the railway train.

Now Muller's caught at last, tho' he's been so very fast,
And on him they found the watch and hat,
Tho' across the ocean he did roam, he had better stayed at home,
And hid himself in some little crack,
Tho' he pleads his innocence, but that is all nonsense,
For they'll hang him as sure as he's a man,
For he got up to his rigs, and murdered Mr Briggs
While riding in a railway train.

Penny Broadsheet
c. 1870

I

MURDER EXPRESS

Classic Journeys into Fear

If criminals would always schedule their
movements like railway trains, it would
certainly be more convenient for all of us.

SIR ARTHUR CONAN DOYLE

Express to Stamboul

AGATHA CHRISTIE

The Orient Express is, beyond argument, the most famous train in the world. Since the two-thousand-mile, de luxe service from Paris to Istanbul's Sirkeci station was inaugurated in 1883 by George Nagelmackers, a wealthy Belgian banker who was also a steam enthusiast (the further leg from London was added in 1889), it has become *the* rail journey: a five-day experience forever associated with opulence, spectacular scenery . . . and murder. Except for the two world wars, the train continued to run until May 1977 when it was felt it could no longer compete with aviation. But feelings of nostalgia were so strong about the journey that bridges East and West and provides a gateway to Asia – in particular those of another rail enthusiast, the American James B. Sherwood, who tracked down and refurbished all the original carriages – that in November 1983 the Orient Express set out once again to the sound of popping champagne corks and the excited chatter of passengers over their smoked salmon on railway's finest 'time machine'. One traveller, so legend has it, when seen furiously scribbling postcards was asked if they were for friends; 'No,' she replied, 'all my enemies.' (Bizarrely, in February 1992 on the journey to mark the 150th anniversary of the birth of Thomas Cook, the Orient Express was actually delayed by the discovery of a corpse on the line between London's Victoria station and Folkestone. The police suspected murder.)

The allure of the Orient Express has been evocatively captured by the great railway historian Erwin Berghaus, who wrote in 1964: 'It is the fulfilment of dreams of adventure. The travelling scene of countless pleasantly frightening film dramas from the early days of the cinema. There they sat in their luxurious seats, the rich, the pleasure-seekers, the diplomats and the mysteriously attractive smuggler of secret documents.' Small wonder, then, that this journey should have captivated the imagination of Agatha Christie (1890–1976), the world's most popular and still biggest selling author of crime fiction. In fact, she took her first journey on the Orient Express in the autumn of 1928, preferring rails to a sea journey to the East, which usually made her seasick. 'Trains have always been one of my favourite things,' she was to write years later in her *Autobiography*. 'All my life I had wanted to go on the Orient Express. Whenever I had travelled to France or Spain or Italy, the Orient Express had often been standing at Calais and I longed to climb up into it.'

Christie realised her ambition in 1928, catching the Simplon–Orient Express at Calais, and quickly found that her expectations were not disappointed. She travelled the route several times, her quick and ingenious mind taking in everything she saw and heard. Then in January 1929, the train's infamous journey in appalling weather conditions which brought it to a halt in an impassable snowdrift near the Turkish border provided her with the inspiration that, five years later, would be turned into probably the most famous of all her mysteries, *Murder on the Orient Express* (also known as *Murder in the Calais Coach*), complete with Hercule Poirot's masterly exposure of the crime. It was, of course, memorably filmed in 1974 with Albert Finney. Trains feature in a number of her other works, too, including the Miss Marple novel, *4.50 from Paddington* (1957), also filmed with Margaret Rutherford (1962) and Joan Hickson (1987); and short stories such as 'The Plymouth Express' (later enlarged into the full-length novel *The Mystery of the Blue Train*, 1928), 'The Fourth Man'

(1933), and 'Express to Stamboul', which was also published in 1933 as 'Have You Got Everything You Want?'

The story is something of a landmark in Agatha Christie's career: firstly, because of its setting, which makes it a precursor to the famous Poirot novel; and secondly because it does not feature the little Belgian, but her other rather neglected though equally fastidious and perceptive detective, Parker Pyne. It concerns a deadly threat to a young wife who is travelling on the Simplon–Orient Express where she enlists the help of fellow passenger Pyne, and makes for a perfect opening to this collection . . .

* * *

'Par ici, madame.'

A tall woman in a mink coat followed her heavily encumbered porter along the platform of the Gare de Lyon. She wore a dark-brown knitted hat pulled down over one eye and ear. The other side revealed a charming tip-tilted profile and little golden curls clustering over a shell-like ear. Typically an American, she was altogether a very charming-looking creature and more than one man turned to look at her as she walked past the high carriages of the waiting train.

Large plates were stuck in holders on the sides of the carriages.

PARIS – ATHÈNES
PARIS – BUCHAREST
PARIS – STAMBOUL

At the last named the porter came to an abrupt halt. He undid the strap which held the suitcases together and they slipped heavily to the ground. 'Voici, madame.'

The *wagon-lit* conductor was standing beside the steps. He came forward, remarking, 'Bonsoir, madame,' with an *empressement* perhaps due to the richness and perfection

13

of the mink coat. The woman handed him her sleeping-car ticket of flimsy paper.

'Number Six,' he said. 'This way.'

He sprang nimbly into the train, the woman following him. As she hurried down the corridor after him, she nearly collided with a portly gentleman who was emerging from the compartment next to hers. She had a momentary glimpse of a large bland face with benevolent eyes.

'Voici, madame.' The conductor displayed the compartment. He threw up the window and signalled to the porter. A lesser employee took in the baggage and put it up in the racks. The woman sat down.

Beside her on the seat she had placed a small scarlet case and her handbag. The carriage was hot, but it did not seem to occur to her to take off her coat. She stared out of the window with unseeing eyes.

People were hurrying up and down the platform. There were sellers of newspapers, pillows, chocolate, fruit, mineral waters. They held up their wares to her, but her eyes looked blankly through them. The Gare de Lyon had faded from her sight. On her face were sadness and anxiety.

'If madame will give me her passport?'

The words made no impression on her. The conductor, standing in the doorway, repeated them. Elsie Jeffries roused herself with a start.

'I beg your pardon?'

'Your passport, madame.'

She opened her bag, took out the passport, and gave it to him.

'That will be all right, madame, I will attend to everything.' A slight significant pause. 'I shall be going with madame as far as Stamboul.'

Elsie drew out a fifty-franc note and handed it to him. He accepted it in a businesslike manner, and enquired when she would like her bed made up and whether she was taking dinner. These matters settled, he withdrew and almost immediately the restaurant man came rushing down the corridor ringing his little bell frantically, and calling out, 'Premier service. Premier service.'

Elsie rose, divested herself of the heavy fur coat, took a brief glance at herself in the little mirror, and picking up her handbag and jewel case, stepped out into the corridor. She had gone only a few steps when the restaurant man came pushing along on his return journey. To avoid him, Elsie stepped back for a moment into the doorway of the adjoining compartment, which was now empty.

As the restaurant man passed and she prepared to continue her journey to the dining car, her glance fell idly on the label of a suitcase which was lying on the seat. It was a stout pigskin case, somewhat worn. On the label were the words, 'J. Parker Pyne, passenger to Stamboul'. The suitcase itself bore the intials 'P.P.'

A startled expression came over the girl's face. She hesitated a moment in the corridor, then going back to her own compartment she picked up a copy of *The Times* which she had laid down on the table with some magazines and books. She ran her eye down the advertisement columns on the front page, but what she was looking for was not there. A slight frown on her face, she made her way to the dining car.

The attendant allotted her a seat at a small table already tenanted by one person – the man with whom she had nearly collided in the corridor. In fact, the owner of the pigskin suitcase.

Elsie looked at him without appearing to do so. He seemed very bland, very benevolent, and in some way impossible to explain, delightfully reassuring. He behaved in reserved British fashion, and it was not till the fruit was on the table that he spoke.

'They keep these places terribly hot,' he said.

'I know,' said Elsie. 'I wish one could have the window open.'

He gave a rueful smile. 'Impossible! Every person present except ourselves would protest.'

She gave an answering smile. Neither said any more.

Coffee was brought and the usual indecipherable bill. Having laid some notes on it, Elsie suddenly took her courage in both hands.

'Excuse me,' she murmured. 'I saw your name on your suitcase – Parker Pyne. Are you – are you, by any chance—?'

She hesitated and he came quickly to her rescue.

'I believe I am. That is,' he quoted from the advertisement which Elsie had noticed more than once in *The Times*, and for which she had searched vainly just now, ' "Are you happy? If not, consult Mr Parker Pyne." Yes, I'm that one, all right.'

'I see,' said Elsie. 'How – how extraordinary!'

He shook his head. 'Not really. Extraordinary from your point of view, but not from mine.' He smiled reassuringly, then leaned forward. Most of the other diners had left the car. 'So you are unhappy?' he said.

'I—' began Elsie, and stopped.

'You would not have said "How extraordinary" otherwise,' he pointed out.

Elsie was silent a minute. She felt strangely soothed by the mere presence of Mr Parker Pyne. 'Ye-es,' she admitted at last. 'I am – unhappy. At least, I am worried.'

He nodded sympathetically.

'You see,' she continued, 'a very curious thing has happened – and I don't know in the least what to make of it.'

'Suppose you tell me about it,' suggested Mr Pyne.

Else thought of the advertisement. She and Edward had often commented on it and laughed. She had never thought that she . . . perhaps she had better not? . . . If Mr Parker Pyne were a charlatan . . . But he looked so nice!

Elsie made her decision. Anything to get this worry off her mind.

'I'll tell you. I'm going to Constantinople to join my husband. He does a lot of Oriental business, and this year he found it necessary to go there. He went a fortnight ago. He was to get things ready for me to join him. I've been very excited at the thought of it. You see, I've never been abroad before. We've been in England six months.'

'You and your husband are both American?'

'Yes.'

'And you have not, perhaps, been married very long?'

'We've been married a year and a half.'

'Happily?'

'Oh, yes! Edward's a perfect angel.' She hesitated. 'Not, perhaps, very much go to him. Just a little – well, I'd call it strait-laced. Lot of Puritan ancestry and all that. But he's a *dear*,' she added hastily.

Mr Parker Pyne looked at her thoughtfully for a moment or two, then he said, 'Go on.'

'It was about a week after Edward had started. I was writing a letter in his study, and I noticed that the blotting paper was all new and clean, except for a few lines of writing across it. I'd just been reading a detective story with a clue in a blotter and so, just for fun, I held it up to a mirror. It really *was* just fun, Mr Pyne – I mean, I wasn't spying on Edward or anything like that. I mean, he's such a mild lamb one wouldn't dream of anything of that kind.'

'Yes, yes. I quite understand.'

'The thing was quite easy to read. First there was the word "wife", then "Simplon Express", and lower down, "just before Venice would be the best time".' She stopped.

'Curious,' said Mr Pyne. 'Distinctly curious. It was your husband's handwriting?'

'Oh, yes. But I've cudgelled my brains and I cannot see under what circumstances he would write a letter with just those words in it.'

' "Just before Venice would be the best time," ' repeated Mr Parker Pyne. 'Distinctly curious.'

Mrs Jeffries was leaning forward looking at him with a flattering hopefulness. 'What shall I do?' she asked simply.

'I am afraid,' said Mr Parker Pyne, 'that we shall have to wait until just before Venice.' He took up a folder from the table. 'Here is the schedule time of our train. It arrives at Venice at two twenty-seven tomorrow afternoon.'

They looked at each other.

'Leave it to me,' said Parker Pyne.

It was five minutes past two. The Simplon Express was eleven minutes late. It had passed Mestre about a quarter of an hour before.

Mr Parker Pyne was sitting with Mrs Jeffries in her compartment. So far the journey had been pleasant and uneventful. But now the moment had arrived when, if anything was going to happen, it presumably would happen.

Mr Parker Pyne and Elsie faced each other. Her heart was beating fast, and her eyes sought his in a kind of anguished appeal for reassurance.

'Keep perfectly calm,' he said. 'You are quite safe. I am here.'

Suddenly a scream broke out from the corridor.

'Oh, look – look! The train is on fire!'

With a bound Elsie and Mr Parker Pyne were in the corridor. An agitated woman with a Slav countenance was pointing a dramatic finger. Out of one of the front compartments smoke was pouring in a cloud.

Mr Parker Pyne and Elsie ran along the corridor. Others joined them. The compartment in question was full of smoke. The first comers drew back, coughing. The conductor appeared.

'The compartment is empty!' he cried. 'Do not alarm

yourselves, messieurs et dames. Le feu, it will be controlled.'

A dozen excited questions and answers broke out. The train was running over the bridge that joins Venice to the mainland.

Suddenly Mr Parker Pyne turned, forced his way through the little pack of people behind him, and hurried down the corridor to Elsie's compartment. The lady with the Slav face was seated in it, drawing deep breaths from the open window.

'Excuse me, madame,' said Parker Pyne. 'But this is not your compartment.'

'I know. I know,' said the Slav lady. '*Pardon*. It is the shock, the emotion – my heart.' She sank back on the seat and indicated the open window. She drew her breath in great gasps.

Mr Parker Pyne stood in the doorway. His voice was fatherly and reassuring. 'You must not be afraid,' he said. 'I do not think for a moment that the fire is serious.'

'Not? Ah, what a mercy! I feel restored.' She half rose. 'I will return to my own compartment.'

'Not just yet.' Mr Parker Pyne's hand pressed her gently back. 'I will ask you to wait a moment, madame.'

'Monsieur, this is an outrage!'

'Madame, you will remain.'

His voice rang out coldly. The woman sat still looking at him when Elsie joined them.

'It seems it was a smoke bomb,' she said breathlessly. 'Some ridiculous practical joke. The conductor is furious. He is asking everybody—' She broke off, staring at the second occupant of the carriage.

'Mrs Jeffries,' said Mr Parker Pyne, 'what do you carry in your little scarlet case?'

'My jewellery.'

'Perhaps you would be kind enough to look and see that everything is there.'

19

There was immediately a torrent of words from the Slav lady. She broke into French, the better to do justice to her feelings. In the meantime Elsie had picked up the jewel case. 'Oh!' she cried. 'It's unlocked.'

'. . . Et je porterai plainte à la Compagnie des Wagons-Lits,' finished the Slav lady.

'They're gone!' cried Elsie. 'Everything! My diamond bracelet. And the necklace Papa gave me. And the emerald and ruby rings. And some lovely diamond brooches. Thank goodness I was wearing my pearls. Oh, Mr Pyne, what shall we do?'

'If you will fetch the conductor,' said Mr Parker Pyne, 'I will see that this woman does not leave this compartment till he comes.'

'Scélérat! Monstre!' shrieked the Slav lady. She went on to further insults. The train drew in to Venice.

The events of the next half-hour may be briefly summarised. Mr Parker Pyne dealt with several different officials in several different languages – and suffered defeat. The suspected lady consented to be searched – and emerged without a stain on her character. The jewels were not on her.

Between Venice and Trieste, Mr Parker Pyne and Elsie discussed the case.

'When was the last time you actually saw your jewels?'

'This morning. I put away some sapphire earrings I was wearing yesterday and took out a pair of plain pearl ones.'

'And all the jewellery was there intact?'

'Well, I didn't go through it all, naturally. But it looked the same as usual. A ring or something like that might have been missing, but not more.'

Mr Parker Pyne nodded. 'Now, when the conductor made up the compartment this morning.'

'I had the case with me – in the dining car. I always take it with me. I've never left it except when I ran out just now.'

'Therefore,' said Mr Parker Pyne, 'that injured innocent,

Madame Subayska, or whatever she calls herself, *must* have been the thief. But what the devil did she do with the things? She was only in here a minute and a half – just time to open the case with a duplicate key and take out the stuff – yes, but what next?'

'Could she have handed them to anyone?'

'Hardly. I had turned back and was forcing my way along the corridor. If anyone had come out of this compartment I should have seen them.'

'Perhaps she threw them out of the window to someone.'

'An excellent suggestion – only, as it happens, we were passing over the sea at that moment. We were on the bridge.'

'Then she must have hidden them in the carriage.'

'Let's hunt for them.'

With true transatlantic energy Elsie began to look about. Mr Parker Pyne participated in the search in a somewhat absent fashion. Reproached for not trying, he excused himself.

'I'm thinking that I must send a rather important telegram at Trieste,' he explained.

Elsie received the explanation coldly. Mr Parker Pyne had fallen heavily in her estimation.

'I'm afraid you're annoyed with me, Mrs Jeffries,' he said meekly.

'Well, you've not been very successful,' she retorted.

'But, my dear lady, you must remember I am not a detective. Theft and crime are not in my line at all. The human heart is my province.'

'Well, I was a bit unhappy when I got on this train,' said Elsie, 'but nothing to what I am now! I could just cry buckets. My lovely, lovely bracelet – and the emerald ring Edward gave me when we were engaged.'

'But surely you are insured against theft?' Mr Parker Pyne asked.

'Am I? I don't know. Yes, I suppose I am. But it's the *sentiment* of the thing, Mr Pyne.'

The train slackened speed. Mr Parker Pyne peered out of the window. 'Trieste,' he said. 'I must send my telegram.'

'Edward!' Elsie's face lit up as she saw her husband hurrying to meet her on the platform at Stamboul. For the moment even the loss of her jewellery faded from her mind. She forgot the curious words she had found on the blotter. She forgot everything except that it was a fortnight since she had seen her husband last, and that in spite of being sober and strait-laced he was really a most attractive person.

They were just leaving the station when Elsie felt a friendly tap on the shoulder and turned to see Mr Parker Pyne. His bland face was beaming good-naturedly.

'Mrs Jeffries,' he said, 'will you come to see me at the Hotel Tokatlian in half an hour? I think I may have good news for you.'

Elsie looked uncertainly at Edward. Then she made the introduction. 'This – er – is my husband – Mr Parker Pyne.'

'As I believe your wife wired you, her jewels have been stolen,' said Mr Parker Pyne. 'I have been doing what I can to help her recover them. I think I may have news for her in about half an hour.'

Elsie looked enquiringly at Edward. He replied promptly, 'You'd better go, dear. The Tokatlian, you said, Mr Pyne? Right. I'll see she makes it.'

It was just half an hour later that Elsie was shown into Mr Parker Pyne's private sitting-room. He rose to receive her.

'You've been disappointed in me, Mrs Jeffries,' he said. 'Now, don't deny it. Well, I don't pretend to be a magician, but I do what I can. Take a look inside here.'

He passed along the table a small stout cardboard box.

Elsie opened it. Rings, brooches, bracelet, necklace – they were all there.

'Mr Pyne, how marvellous! How – how wonderful!'

Mr Parker Pyne smiled modestly. 'I am glad not to have failed you, my dear young lady.'

'Oh Mr Pyne, you make me feel just mean! Ever since Trieste I've been horrid to you. And now – this. But how did you get hold of them? When? Where?'

Mr Parker Pyne shook his head thoughtfully. 'It's a long story,' he said. 'You may hear it one day. In fact, you may hear it quite soon.'

'Why can't I hear it now?'

'There are reasons,' said Mr Parker Pyne.

And Elsie had to depart with her curiosity unsatisfied.

When she had gone, Mr Parker Pyne took up his hat and stick and went out into the streets of Pera. He walked along smiling to himself, coming at last to a little café, deserted at the moment, which overlooked the Golden Horn. On the other side, the mosques of Stamboul showed slender minarets against the afternoon sky. It was very beautiful. Mr Pyne sat down and ordered two coffees. They came thick and sweet. He had just begun to sip his when a man slipped into the seat opposite. It was Edward Jeffries.

'I have ordered some coffee for you,' said Mr Parker Pyne, indicating the little cup.

Edward pushed the coffee aside. He leaned forward across the table. 'How did you know?' he asked.

Mr Parker Pyne sipped his coffee dreamily. 'Your wife will have told you about her discovery on the blotter? No? Oh, but she will tell you – it has slipped her mind for the moment.'

He mentioned Elsie's discovery.

'Very well. That linked up perfectly with the curious incident that happened just before Venice. For some reason or other you were engineering the theft of your wife's jewels. But why the phrase "just before Venice would be

23

the best time"? Why did you not leave it to your – agent – to choose her own time and place?

'And then, suddenly, I saw the point. *Your wife's jewels were stolen before you yourself left London and were replaced by paste duplicates.* But that solution did not satisfy you. You were a high-minded, conscientious young man. You have a horror of some servant or other innocent person being suspected. A theft must actually occur – at a place and in a manner which will leave no suspicion attached to anybody of your acquaintance or household.

'Your accomplice is provided with a key to the jewel box and a smoke bomb. At the correct moment she gives the alarm, darts into your wife's compartment, unlocks the jewel case, and flings the paste duplicates into the sea. She may be suspected and searched, but nothing can be proved against her, since the jewels are not in her possession.

'And now the significance of the place chosen becomes apparent. If the jewels had merely been thrown out by the side of the line, they might have been found. Hence the importance of the one moment when the train is passing over the sea.

'In the meantime you make your arrangements for selling the jewellery here. You have only to hand over the stones when the robbery has actually taken place. My wire, however, reached you in time. You obeyed my instructions and deposited the box of jewellery at the Tokatlian to await my arrival, knowing that otherwise I should keep my threat of placing the matter in the hands of the police. You also obeyed my instructions in joining me here.'

Edward Jeffries looked at Mr Parker Pyne appealingly. He was a good-looking young man, tall and fair, with a round chin and very round eyes. 'How can I make you understand?' he said hopelessly. 'To you I must seem just a common thief.'

'Not at all,' said Mr Parker Pyne. 'On the contrary, I

should say you are almost painfully honest. I am accustomed to the classification of types. You, my dear sir, fall naturally into the category of victims. Now, tell me the whole story.'

'I can tell you that in one word – blackmail.'

'Yes?'

'You've seen my wife. You realise what an innocent creature she is – without thought or knowledge of evil.'

'Yes, yes.'

'She has the most marvellously pure ideals. If she were to find out about – about anything I had done, she would leave me.'

'I wonder. But that is not the point. What *have* you done, my young friend? I presume this is some affair with a woman?'

Edward Jeffries nodded.

'Since your marriage – or before?'

'Before – oh, before.'

'Well, what happened?'

'Nothing – nothing at all. That is the cruel part of it. It was at a hotel in the West Indies. There was a very attractive woman – a Mrs Rossiter – staying there. Her husband was a violent man – he had the most savage fits of temper. One night he threatened her with a revolver. She escaped from him and came to my room. She was half crazy with terror. She – she asked me to let her stay there till morning. I – what else could I do?'

Mr Parker Pyne gazed at the young man, and the young man gazed back with conscious rectitude. Mr Parker Pyne sighed. 'In other words, to put it plainly, you were had for a mug, Mr Jeffries.'

'Really—'

'Yes, yes. A very old trick – but it often comes off successfully with quixotic young men. I suppose, when your approaching marriage was announced, the screw was turned?'

'Yes. I received a letter. If I did not send a certain sum of money, everything would be disclosed to my prospective father-in-law. How I had – had alienated this young woman's affection from her husband; how she had been seen coming to my room. The husband would bring a suit for divorce. Really, Mr Pyne, the whole thing made me out the most utter blackguard.' He wiped his brow in a harassed manner.

'Yes, yes, I know. And so you paid. And from time to time the screw has been put on again.'

'Yes. This was the last straw. Our business has been badly hit by the slump. I simply could not lay my hands on any ready money. I hit on this plan.' He picked up his cup of cold coffee, looked at it absently, and drank it. 'What am I to do now?' he demanded pathetically. 'What *am* I to do, Mr Pyne?'

'You will be guided by me,' said Parker Pyne firmly. 'I will deal with your tormentors. As to your wife, you will go straight back to her and tell her the truth – or at least a portion of it. The only point where you will deviate from the truth is concerning the actual facts in the West Indies. You must conceal from her the fact that you were – well, had for a mug, as I said before.'

'But—'

'My dear Mr Jeffries, you do not understand women. If a woman has to choose between a mug and a Don Juan, she will choose Don every time. Your wife, Mr Jeffries, is a charming, innocent, high-minded girl, and the only way she is going to get any kick out of her life with you is to believe that she has reformed a rake.'

Edward Jeffries was staring at him open-mouthed.

'I mean what I say,' said Mr Parker Pyne. 'At the present moment your wife is in love with you, but I see signs that she may not remain so if you continue to present to her a picture of such goodness and rectitude that it is almost synonymous with dullness.'

Edward winced.

'Go to her, my boy,' said Mr Parker Pyne kindly. 'Confess everything – that is, as many things as you can think of. Then explain that from the moment you met her you gave up all that life. You even stole so that it might not come to her ears. She will forgive you enthusiastically.'

'But when there's nothing really to forgive—'

'What is truth?' said Mr Parker Pyne. 'In my experience it is usually the thing that upsets the apple cart! It is a fundamental axiom of married life that you *must* lie to a woman. She likes it! Go and be forgiven, my boy. And live happily ever afterwards. I dare say your wife will keep a wary eye on you in future whenever a pretty woman comes along. Some men would mind that, but I don't think you will.'

'I never want to look at any woman but Elsie,' said Mr Jeffries simply.

'Splendid, my boy,' said Mr Parker Pyne. 'But I shouldn't let her know that if I were you. No woman likes to feel she's taken on too soft a job.'

Edward Jeffries rose. 'You really think—?'

'I *know*,' said Mr Parker Pyne, with force.

Crime on the Footplate

FREEMAN WILLS CROFTS

The most glamorous name among British trains is undoubtedly the *Flying Scotsman*. From 1862, for almost a hundred years, the train ran on the UK's main line to the north – the London & North Eastern Railway – and rapidly became the subject of legends. According to the English railway historian O. S. Nock, in 1938 the *Flying Scotsman* 'had the most beautiful interior decoration ever applied to British railway carriages in its restaurant cars', while a decade later it was still making 'the longest regular non-stop run the world had ever seen – 393 miles from London King's Cross to Edinburgh in seven hours'.

During the years of its greatest fame, the *Scotsman* also attracted a certain notoriety for having provided the means of escape for a number of criminals including three murderers (though all were subsequently caught), and on 21 January 1876 was involved in a disastrous crash. The night was one of very heavy snow, and the intense cold froze the signals at Abbots Ripton and caused the express to run into a coal train, killing thirteen people and injuring twenty-four. The train's fame was such that it featured in one of the earliest novels about crime on the railways, *My Adventure in the Flying Scotsman* by Eden Phillpots (1862–1960), the Devonshire author who is remembered for encouraging the early literary efforts of a young neighbour, Agatha Christie. It was also the subject of the first important British railway mystery movie, *The Flying Scotsman* (1930), about the conflict between a driver and a fireman on the train. The picture was partly inspired by the following story which was written by the man who acted as technical adviser on the film.

Freeman Wills Crofts (1879–1957) is famous today as the railwayman who turned crime writer and produced some of the most authentic mystery stories ever written around steam trains. Born in Dublin, he became an apprentice engineer on the Belfast and Northern Counties Railway. By 1899 he was a junior construction engineer and within another ten years had risen to become chief assistant engineer in Belfast. His career was halted in 1912 when he was struck down by illness, and while confined to bed he wrote a mystery novel, *The Cask* (1920), which made clever use of railway timetables in establishing the clues. The novel was soon being hailed as the first mystery story to use step-by-step methods of police routine and went on to sell over 100,000 copies; subsequently, Freeman Wills Crofts had no need to return to a life on the railways. Instead, he started putting his intimate knowledge of the running of rail systems into fair but complex detective novels with titles that speak for themselves: *The 12.30 from Croydon* (1934), *Death of a Train* (1946) and *The Mystery of the Sleeping Car Express* (1956). His work is credited along with that of Agatha Christie and several other crime writers with beginning what is known as the 'Golden Age' of the detective story.

Crofts's knowledge of the railways was frequently called upon by the radio (he wrote over thirty plays for the BBC) and by film companies. *The Flying Scotsman*, which was made by British International Pictures to capitalise on the fame of the train, made full use of Crofts's expertise when filming the track scenes on the main line between King's Cross and Edinburgh. The director, Castleton Knight, insisted on using the locomotive then pulling the *Flying Scotsman* – LNER Gresley 'Pacific' No. 4472 – for all the big action scenes which were filmed on the Hertford Loop. Interestingly, too, the picture, which co-starred Moore

Marriott and Ray Milland, was initially to be a silent, but with the advent of the talkies while it was in production, a soundtrack was hastily added. Despite some faults, the film is now regarded as a classic and the following story serves as a reminder of how steam in the shape of Britain's most famous train and a tale of mystery were first combined on the screen.

***

The August day was stifling as the 11.55 a.m. express from Leeds beat heavily up the grade towards the summit in the foothills of the Pennines. From there the run down to Carlisle would be easy and rapid. The train was on time and travelling at the full thirty miles an hour customary at the place.

On the footplate Driver Deane sat watching the line ahead and occasionally casting an eye over the faceplate, with its maze of dials and gauges and handles. For Fireman Grover, on the other hand, this was the busy time of the run. With a heavy train on a grade like this, firing was practically continuous.

The engine, while a splendid machine, was of one of the older types. The cab was more open than is now usual, having no side windows, an advantage on this day when the heat of the sun vied with that pouring from the steel endplate of the boiler. It was fitted with small doors at each side between engine and tender, and was driven from the right side of the cab.

All seemed well with the train, yet all was not well. On this footplate, as in the great world beyond, human passions were aflame. For many weeks evil had been festering in Fireman Grover's heart. He had not expelled it while he could, and now he was held in its grip. On this very run and before they had gone a dozen miles further he intended to murder his driver, William Deane.

The story of the madness which had overtaken him was commonplace enough. Some three months earlier he had visited his driver's Leeds home on some railway business. There he had met the driver's wife and immediately had fallen for her. He contrived to meet her again and found out that his feeling was returned.

Rosie Deane was a well-meaning young woman who had made an unwise marriage. She had an unhappy home and accepted Deane, who was many years her senior, as a means of escape. But she had not deceived him. Admitting the truth, she had added that while she liked and respected him, she did not love him, though she would do her best to make him happy. Deane had not hesitated and the marriage had taken place.

For several years she had kept her word. But during this time Deane had suffered an increasing disappointment. He had believed that his wife would gradually come to love him, and when he found that, instead of this, the very opposite was taking place he grew bitter. He became sharp-tongued and suspicious. Rosie resented it and her feeling came out in her manner. Relations between the two went from bad to worse.

It was then that Grover had appeared. His love gave him insight and he soon guessed Rosie's unhappiness. Hatred of his driver grew fanatical when he realised that he was at once the cause of her misery and the bar to its alleviation. The thought of murder had not at first entered his mind, but as he brooded the idea became more and more insistent. He began to consider methods, and when he found one which would infallibly guarantee his own safety, Deane's fate was sealed.

One of Grover's friends was a male nurse in a mental home and the two had frequently discussed inmates and work in such places. Among other things Grover had learned that a certain harmless drug was used to calm patients if they became over-excited. His friend had told him about a dose of this being given to the wrong man, with the result that for some time he had become moody, depressed and ill-tempered. Grover had not forgotten the name of the drug.

During a spare hour in London when they were on the St Pancras link, he had changed into his ordinary clothes, which he had taken up in a parcel, and had purchased a small quantity of the drug at a busy chemist's. No interest had been aroused. Thus his first hurdle was taken.

The second depended on the fact that Deane wore a short beard. The man had been a good deal ragged about it, but Grover had learnt that it was to cover a deep scar on his chin. After getting the drug, Grover had gone on to a theatrical supplies shop and bought a false beard of the correct colour 'to amuse the children'. In the security of his room he trimmed it to the shape of Deane's, and practised putting it on till he could do it quickly and without the aid of a mirror.

His third and last essential was to choose a suitable run for the deed. It must be through sparsely populated country, where observation of what took place on the engine would be unlikely. Also as much time as possible was desirable between block posts. This climb up the bleak Pennine foothills exactly met the conditions.

Grover began operations by doctoring the driver's tea. Before taking their engine out Deane went round it, oiling moving parts and looking out for defects. During this time Grover was alone on the footplate, working at the fire. To slip a daily drop or two of the drug into the other's can was simplicity itself.

When by experiment he had learnt the right amount to use, he was overjoyed with the result. Deane reacted perfectly, growing more bitter and morose, while his temper became a byword among the men.

Some six weeks later Grover decided to strike, and now this was the run which was to free Rosie and open a new door of happiness for himself. On the previous day he had given Deane a specially large dose of the drug, and the effect had been clear to all.

They were approaching what might be called the last outpost of civilisation, the little town of Sleet, for here the railway left the green, well-cultivated valley and entered on the open moor. As they laboured through the small station, the powerful beat echoing from the buildings, Grover began firing. By the time this was finished they had passed the signal cabin and sidings. That all was well on the footplate would have been noted by the signalman. Now they were out into the open. On these bare slopes figures stood out clearly. Grover glanced carefully around. There were none.

He laid down his shovel and picked up a heavy spanner which he had secreted in the coal. Stepping over to Driver Deane, he bent down. 'I think I hear a blowing gasket,' he shouted, for the noise was considerable.

Deane sat still, obviously listening. Grover immediately brought his spanner down with force on the man's head. Deane made no sound. He remained for a moment motionless, then pitched slowly forward. He fell on his knees against the end of the boiler, rolled partially back, and lay with head and arms hunched up in the corner of the cab.

Grover was breathless and trembling, but he forced himself to stoop and examine him. That the man was dead there could be no doubt, for the top of the head was driven down, though owing to the cap the skin was not broken. Moreover, the body's position was admirable. It had to be well forward, so as to be screened by the cab from the next signal cabin, and also to leave space on the congested footplate for the act by which Grover intended to secure his safety.

Haste was now the prime essential, for before they reached the next station, Ottershaw, already less than two miles distant, he must be ready to put on his act. Quickly he adjusted the false beard, checking its position in a mirror from his pocket. Then he twisted up his cap to the angle Deane affected and glanced ahead through the cab window.

They were just passing the Ottershaw distant signal, off as it always was. As they approached the platform and signal cabin Grover began dancing, waving his arms and singing drunkenly. While he did so he kept a keen eye on the cabin, some twenty yards away across the sidings. What happened thrilled him. His plan was working out.

He saw the signalman stare at the engine, then swing round and pick something up, slide open his window, lean out, and begin frantically waving a red flag.

For Grover it was a moment of sickening anxiety. If the guard saw the flag and applied the brakes, only the most speedy and skilful action could save him. He danced on lest someone else should see him, but in a cold sweat of fear.

The advanced starting signal had gone to danger in front of him, but he took no notice. It was only another attempt of the signalman to attract the guard's attention. As they left it behind without an application of the brakes, Grover experienced a relief so intense that he feared his nerve would crack. Then he rallied himself fiercely. Though the worst was over, the job was not finished. The least weakness and he was as good as hanged.

Haste again was the ruling factor. He tore off the beard and threw it into the firebox, making sure with his mirror that no traces remained. Then came a horrible part of the affair. With the flat of the spanner he struck a heavy blow on his own left shoulder. It hurt so much that he feared he had done damage. So much the better, he told himself grimly. He dropped the spanner and threw himself forcibly down against the tender. Then taking off his cap, he knocked his head back against the steel plating, again and again till he could endure no more.

Struggling unsteadily to his feet, he glanced once more through the cab window. In a little over a mile they would reach Grammond block post, a signal cabin without any station. At this he was sure they would be checked, as the Ottershaw signalman would certainly have wired on 'Stop and examine train'. This, and the fact that the post was approached by a wide left-hand curve from which cabin and signals could be seen for nearly a mile across the bend of the valley, were features of his plan.

A few seconds later they entered on the curve. Yes, there were the signals, all at danger. Things certainly were going as he had hoped. He had only to carry out one remaining essential and the whole ghastly affair would be done.

Once again he glanced carefully round. Here also no spectator was in sight. He now stooped and pulled off Deane's cap, then seizing the body beneath the armpits, dragged it painfully back to the rear of the footplate. The doors between engine and tender were shut, and using all his strength, he laid the body over the left door, with the head and trunk hanging down outside and the legs within.

He was just in time, for the body was scarcely in position when they passed the Grammond distant signal. Now was the moment! He heaved up the legs and the body shot out, crashed on its head on the ground and rolled on partly down the embankment. The cap he dropped at the same moment. Then, gasping, he staggered back to the faceplate.

By this time they were approaching the home signal and cabin. Grover passed the former without action, intending that his efforts to stop should be seen by the signalman. But just before they reached the cabin the vacuum disappeared on his gauge and the brakes went on. The guard this time had noticed the adverse signal and used his emergency handle. Grover therefore shut off steam, a little earlier than he had intended. Automatically he closed the firebox door and damper and put on the injector, then sank down, shaken and trembling, on one of the cab seats.

The train ground to a standstill, having overshot the home signal by some quarter of a mile. Grover remained seated where he was. No acting was needed to give the impression he desired, for the shock of what he had done added to the blow on his head had left him really weak and dazed. He sat on till a flustered guard climbed on to the footplate. Others followed. To them Grover outlined the story he had prepared. Everyone was sympathetic. His head was bandaged and he was sent home by the first available train.

Next day the police called for a fuller statement. They began by warning him. 'We have to do it, you know,' they told him. 'Matter of form mostly.'

Grover nodded. He had heard that this was their custom. Then he repeated his story: again and again he had polished its every detail. 'Deane had been a bit queer for a few weeks,' he explained. 'Seemed to have something on his mind and was getting worse. You couldn't hardly speak to him about anything: he'd snap the head off you.'

It was a good beginning. To the police the statement had already been attested by many witnesses.

'On this trip he was worse than ever,' went on Grover. 'I was beginning to wonder if I could get a shift to another driver. I signed to him shortly after we left Leeds that the Riglett distant signal was on, and he went off the deep end good and proper: wanted to know if I thought he was blind and that. It never occurred to me his mind was touched, but it settled mine for me. I decided I'd ask for the change.'

The police made encouraging sounds.

'After a while he quieted down. Just sat there and looked ahead same as usual. Then when we got to Sleet the thing happened. I was firing going through the station, but just after we passed it he turned round and threw up his hands and began laughing fit to burst his sides. It was sort of uncanny, him roaring with laughter, but it didn't seem funny to me. At first I didn't interfere, then I asked him what the joke was. That about put the lid on: he jumped up and yelled at me. He looked sort of wild. I knew then that he was mad and I don't deny I was scared stiff. Suddenly he let fly at my head. I twisted and got it on my shoulder. It knocked me back and I hit my head against the tender. Then he went off his rocker altogether. He began to sing and shout and dance about the footplate while I lay there half stunned.'

Grover's belief that the police would have had confirmation of this statement from the Ottershaw signalman was not misplaced. They begged him to continue, and he did so with increasing confidence.

'I can tell you, gentlemen, I was in a proper fix. We're not often checked by signals on this run, but you have to be prepared for it. If we got a check he wouldn't stop and I couldn't.

'Then, easing up on my elbow, I got a peep over the cab door. We were on the big curve coming into Grammond and you can see the signals a mile away across country. They were against us. Well, I had the train to think of as well as my own life, and I hadn't much time to do it in. I don't know whether I was right or wrong, but I gripped a spanner out of the box, and when Deane turned his back, I nipped up and hit him over the head. I only meant to knock him out, but he staggered forward against the door and overbalanced. Before I could catch him he was out over it.'

For this also there was a reasonable amount of corroboration. The signals *could* be seen as described, and they *were* against the train. The place where the body was found worked in with the time element of the story, and Grover bore the bruises which it demanded. Yes, it was a good tale and had confirmation on nearly every point. Grover's self-satisfaction became impressive when the police thanked him politely and withdrew.

He got his first shock, a terrible numbing shock, when the inquest was adjourned. Then for several days nothing happened. But one night the police returned. They were curt and businesslike. Stunned and incredulous, he heard the inconceivable words, 'Arrest . . . charge with murder . . . anything you say . . .'

Though the exact nature of his mistake did not in a way matter, Grover raged against himself in speechless fury when he learned what it was. His scheme was good, indeed masterly, and it would have worked perfectly but for one quite trivial oversight. He had not examined with sufficient care the position into which Deane had fallen. The driver's shoulders and arms were clear of the boiler, but Grover had been in such a hurry that he had looked no further. On the dead man's leg was a huge scorched wound. Some ghastly experiments showed that at least six minutes' contact with the hot steel plate would have been necessary to produce it.

This gave the police something to think about. When the train was passing Sleet, Deane was alive and well: the signalman had seen that conditions on the footplate were normal. Therefore the man could not at that time have received this crippling injury. Some eight minutes later his body fell from the engine near Grammond. For six of those eight minutes, therefore, he must have been lying with his leg against the boiler: and during that time a bearded man was dancing on the footplate. Only impersonation by Grover could explain it.

At the trial the doctor testified to the finding of a debilitating drug in the remains, though the prisoner's responsibility for this could not be proved. But the whole story of Grover's friendship with Rosie Deane came out, together with the purchase of the false beard. The prisoner's failure to account for the latter on legitimate grounds was the factor which finally swayed the jury.

The Man With No Face

DOROTHY L. SAYERS

The popularity of *The Flying Scotsman* with cinemagoers
led to several more classic railway mysteries being adapted
for the screen by British film makers in the following
decade including Graham Greene's *Orient Express* (Fox,
1934) with Norman Foster and Heather Angel; Alfred
Hitchcock's *The Lady Vanishes* (Gainsborough, 1938)
based on a novel by Ethel Lina White, of which more later;
and *Background to Danger* from Eric Ambler's novel
which starred George Raft, Sydney Greenstreet and Peter
Lorre (Warner Brothers, 1943). Also released at this time
was *The Silent Passenger* made by Associated British in
1935 based on a storyline by Dorothy L. Sayers
(1893–1957), the advertising copywriter turned crime
novelist, who was another of the authors responsible for
the genre's 'Golden Age'. Like Agatha Christie, Dorothy
Sayers had been fascinated by steam trains ever since her
childhood and a number of her mysteries are either set on
express trains or feature train journeys – amongst the best
known being the novel *Five Red Herrings* (1931), a murder
story featuring the Scottish railways in Galloway, and the
short stories 'The Article in Question' (trains in Paris), 'A
Matter of Taste' (a journey across France), and 'The Man
With No Face', all of which are cases featuring her famous
detective Lord Peter Wimsey, an inveterate train traveller
both in Britain and on the Continent.

The huge success of Sayers's first two mysteries, *Whose
Body?* (1923) and *Clouds of Witness* (1926), led to her
signing an agreement with Associated British in the late

thirties to provide ideas for films, the most successful of which was *The Silent Passenger*. The action takes place mainly on a boat train where the body of a murdered blackmailer, hidden in a trunk, is being taken to France for disposal by the husband of one of the man's victims. Also on the train is Lord Peter who ultimately solves the real mystery behind the killing. The picture was directed by Reginald Denham and starred Peter Haddon (as the noble sleuth), John Loder and Mary Newland. Some of the most dramatic scenes in the picture were shot at Liverpool Street station where a big LNER N7 Class 0–6–2T was used for a fight sequence on the footplate which resulted in a dramatic climax with the train smashing through some shed doors. Lord Peter Wimsey also solves a crime on a train in the following short story written in 1928 some years before *The Silent Passenger*. There are certain similarities in the way the plot is worked out that suggest to me the story could well have been at the back of Sayers's mind as she devised the movie . . .

* * *

'And what would *you* say, sir,' said the stout man, 'to this here business of the bloke what's been found down on the beach at East Felpham?'

The rush of travellers after the bank holiday had caused an overflow of third class passengers into the firsts, and the stout man was anxious to seem at ease in his surroundings. The youngish gentleman whom he addressed had obviously paid full fare for a seclusion which he was fated to forgo. He took the matter amiably enough, however, and replied in a courteous tone:

'I'm afraid I haven't read more than the headlines. Murdered, I suppose, wasn't he?'

'It's murder, right enough,' said the stout man, with relish. 'Cut about he was, something shocking.'

'More like as if a wild beast had done it,' chimed in the thin, elderly man opposite. 'No face at all he hadn't got, by what my paper says. It'll be one of these maniacs, I shouldn't be surprised, what goes about killing children.'

'I wish you wouldn't talk about such things,' said his wife, with a shudder. 'I lays awake at nights thinking what might 'appen to Lizzie's girls, till my head feels regular in a fever, and I has such a sinking in my inside I has to get up and eat biscuits. They didn't ought to put such dreadful things in the papers.'

'It's better they should, ma'am,' said the stout man, 'then we're warned, so to speak, and can take our measures accordingly. Now, from what I can make out, this unfortunate gentleman had gone bathing all by himself in a lonely spot. Now, quite apart from cramps, as is a thing that might 'appen to the best of us, that's a very foolish thing to do.'

'Just what I'm always telling my husband,' said the young wife. The young husband frowned and fidgeted. 'Well, dear, it really isn't safe, and you with your heart not strong—' Her hand sought his under the newspaper. He drew away, self-consciously, saying, 'That'll do, Kitty.'

'The way I look at it is this,' pursued the stout man. 'Here we've been and had a war, what has left 'undreds o' men in what you might call a state of unstable ekilibrium. They've seen all their friends blown up or shot to pieces. They've been through five years of 'orrors and bloodshed, and it's given 'em what you might call a twist in the mind towards 'orrors. They may seem to forget it and go along as peaceable as anybody to all outward appearance, but it's all artificial, if you get my meaning. Then, one day something 'appens to upset them – they 'as words with the wife, or the weather's extra hot, as it is today – and something goes pop inside their brains and makes raving monsters of them. It's all in the books. I do a good bit of

41

reading myself of an evening, being a bachelor without encumbrances.'

'That's all very true,' said a prim little man, looking up from his magazine, 'very true indeed – too true. But do you think it applies in the present case? I've studied the literature of crime a good deal – I may say I make it my hobby – and it's my opinion there's more in this than meets the eye. If you will compare this murder with some of the most mysterious crimes of late years – crimes which, mind you, have never been solved, and, in my opinion, never will be – what do you find?' He paused and looked round. 'You will find many features in common with this case. But especially you will find that the face – and the face only, mark you – has been disfigured, as though to prevent recognition. As though to blot out the victim's personality from the world. And you will find that, in spite of the most thorough investigation, the criminal is never discovered. Now what does all that point to? To organisation. Organisation. To an immensely powerful influence at work behind the scenes. In this very magazine that I'm reading now' – he tapped the page impressively – 'there's an account – not a faked-up story, but an account extracted from the annals of the police – of the organisation of one of these secret societies, which mark down men against whom they bear a grudge, and destroy them. And, when they do this, they disfigure their faces with the mark of the Secret Society, and they cover up the track of the assassin so completely – having money and resources at their disposal – that nobody is ever able to get at them.'

'I've read of such things, of course,' admitted the stout man, 'but I thought as they mostly belonged to the medeevial days. They had a thing like that in Italy once. What did they call it now? A Gomorrah, was it? Are there any Gomorrahs nowadays?'

'You spoke a true word, sir, when you said Italy,' replied the prim man. 'The Italian mind is made for intrigue.

There's the Fascisti. That's come to the surface now, of course, but it started by being a secret society. And, if you were to look below the surface, you would be amazed at the way in which that country is honeycombed with hidden organisations of all sorts. Don't you agree with me, sir?' he added, addressing the first-class passenger.

'Ah!' said the stout man, 'no doubt this gentleman has been in Italy and knows all about it. Should you say this murder was the work of a Gomorrah, sir?'

'I hope not, I'm sure,' said the first-class passenger. 'I mean, it rather destroys the interest, don't you think? I like a nice, quiet, domestic murder myself, with the millionaire found dead in the library. The minute I open a detective story and find a Camorra in it, my interest seems to dry up and turn to dust and ashes – a sort of Sodom and Camorra, as you might say.'

'I agree with you there,' said the young husband, 'from what you might call the artistic standpoint. But in this particular case I think there may be something to be said for this gentleman's point of view.'

'Well,' admitted the first-class passenger, 'not having read the details—'

'The details are clear enough,' said the prim man. 'This poor creature was found lying dead on the beach at East Felpham early this morning, with his face cut about in the most dreadful manner. He had nothing on him but his bathing-dress—'

'Stop a minute. Who was he, to begin with?'

'They haven't identified him yet. His clothes had been taken—'

'That looks more like robbery, doesn't it?' suggested Kitty.

'If it was just robbery,' retorted the prim man, 'why should his face have been cut up in that way? No – the clothes were taken away, as I said, to prevent identification. That's what these societies always try to do.'

'Was he stabbed?' demanded the first-class passenger.

'No,' said the stout man. 'He wasn't. He was strangled.'

'Not a characteristically Italian method of killing,' observed the first-class passenger.

'No more it is,' said the stout man. The prim man seemed a little disconcerted.

'And if he went down there to bathe,' said the thin, elderly man, 'how did he get there? Surely somebody must have missed him before now, if he was staying at Felpham. It's a busy spot for visitors in the holiday season.'

'No,' said the stout man, 'not East Felpham. You're thinking of West Felpham, where the yacht club is. East Felpham is one of the loneliest spots on the coast. There's no house near except a little pub all by itself at the end of a long road, and after that you have to go through three fields to get to the sea. There's no real road, only a cart-track, but you can take a car through. I've been there.'

'He came in a car,' said the prim man. 'They found the track of the wheels. But it had been driven away again.'

'It looks as though the two men had come there together,' suggested Kitty.

'I think they did,' said the prim man. 'The victim was probably gagged and bound and taken along in the car to the place, and then he was taken out and strangled and—'

'But why should they have troubled to put on his bathing-dress?' said the first-class passenger.

'Because,' said the prim man, 'as I said, they didn't want to leave any clothes to reveal his identity.'

'Quite; but why not leave him naked? A bathing-dress seems to indicate an almost excessive regard for decorum, under the circumstances.'

'Yes, yes,' said the stout man impatiently, 'but you 'aven't read the paper carefully. The two men couldn't have come there in company, and for why? There was only one set of footprints found, and they belonged to the murdered man.'

He looked round triumphantly.

'Only one set of footprints, eh?' said the first-class passenger quickly. 'This looks interesting. Are you sure?'

'It says so in the paper. A single set of footprints, it says, made by bare feet, which by a careful comparison 'ave been shown to be those of the murdered man, lead from the position occupied by the car to the place where the body was found. What do you make of that?'

'Why,' said the first-class passenger, 'that tells one quite a lot, don't you know. It gives one a sort of a bird's eye view of the place, and it tells one the time of the murder, besides castin' quite a good bit of light on the character and circumstances of the murderer – or murderers.'

'How do you make that out, sir?' demanded the elderly man.

'Well, to begin with – though I've never been near the place, there is obviously a sandy beach from which one can bathe.'

'That's right,' said the stout man.

'There is also, I fancy, in the neighbourhood, a spur of rock running out into the sea, quite possibly with a handy diving-pool. It must run out pretty far; at any rate, one can bathe there before it is high water on the beach.'

'I don't know how you know that, sir, but it's a fact. There's rocks and a bathing-pool, exactly as you describe, about a hundred yards further along. Many's the time I've had a dip off the end of them.'

'And the rocks run right back inland, where they are covered with short grass.'

'That's right.'

'The murder took place shortly before high tide, I fancy, and the body lay just about at high-tide mark.'

'Why so?'

'Well, you say there were footsteps leading right up to the body. That means that the water hadn't been up beyond the body. But there were no other marks. Therefore the murderer's footprints must have been washed away by the tide. The only explanation is that the two men were standing together just below the tide-mark. The murderer came up out of the sea. He attacked the other man – maybe he forced him back a little on his own tracks – and there he killed him. Then the water came up and washed out any marks the murderer may have left. One can imagine him squatting there, wondering if the sea was going to come up high enough.'

'Ow!' said Kitty, 'you make me creep all over.'

'Now, as to these marks on the face,' pursued the first-class passenger. 'The murderer, according to the idea I get of the thing, was already in the sea when the victim came along. You see the idea?'

'I get you,' said the stout man. 'You think as he went in off them rocks what we was speaking of, and came up through the water, and that's why there weren't no footprints.'

'Exactly. And since the water is deep round those rocks, as you say, he was presumably in a bathing-dress too.'

'Looks like it.'

'Quite so. Well, now – what was the face-slashing done with? People don't usually take knives out with them when they go for a morning dip.'

'That's a puzzle,' said the stout man.

'Not altogether. Let's say, either the murderer had a knife with him or he had not. If he had—'

'If he had,' put in the prim man eagerly, 'he must have laid wait for the deceased on purpose. And, to my mind, that bears out my idea of a deep and cunning plot.'

'Yes. But, if he was waiting there with the knife, why didn't he stab the man and have done with it? Why strangle him, when he had a perfectly good weapon there to hand? No – I think he came unprovided, and, when he saw his enemy there, he made for him with his hands in the characteristic British way.'

'But the slashing?'

'Well, I think that when he had got his man down, dead before him, he was filled with a pretty grim sort of fury and wanted to do more damage. He caught up something that was lying near him on the sand – it might be a bit of old iron, or even one of those sharp shells you sometimes see about, or a bit of glass – and he went for him with that in a desperate rage of jealousy or hatred.'

'Dreadful, dreadful!' said the elderly woman.

'Of course, one can only guess in the dark, not having seen the wounds. It's quite possible that the murderer dropped his knife in the struggle and had to do the actual killing with his hands, picking the knife up afterwards. If the wounds were clean knife-wounds, that is probably what happened, and the murder was premeditated. But if they were rough, jagged gashes, made by an impromptu weapon, then I should say it was a chance encounter, and that the murderer was either mad or—'

'Or?'

'Or had suddenly come upon somebody whom he hated very much.'

'What do you think happened afterwards?'

'That's pretty clear. The murderer, having waited, as I said, to see that all his footprints were cleaned up by the tide, waded or swam back to the rock where he had left his clothes, taking the weapon with him. The sea would wash away any blood from his bathing-dress or body. He then climbed out upon the rocks, walked, with bare feet, so as to leave no tracks on any seaweed or anything, to the short grass of the shore, dressed, went along to the murdered man's car, and drove it away.'

'Why did he do that?'

'Yes, why? He may have wanted to get somewhere in a hurry. Or he may have been afraid that if the murdered man were identified too soon it would cast suspicion on him. Or it may have been a mixture of motives. The point is, where did he come from? How did he come to be bathing at that remote spot, early in the morning? He didn't get there by car, or there would be a second car to be accounted for. He may have been camping near the spot; but it would have taken him a long time to strike camp and pack all his belongings into the car, and he might have been seen. I am rather inclined to think he had bicycled there, and that he hoisted the bicycle into the back of the car and took it away with him.'

'But, in that case, why take the car?'

'Because he had been down at East Felpham longer than he expected, and he was afraid of being late. Either he had to get back to breakfast at some house, where his absence would be noticed, or else he lived some distance off, and had only just time enough for the journey home. I think, though, he had to be back to breakfast.'

'Why?'

'Because, if it was merely a question of making up time on the road, all he had to do was to put himself and his bicycle on the train for part of the way. No; I fancy he was staying in a smallish hotel somewhere. Not a large hotel, because there nobody would notice whether he came in or not. And not, I think, in lodgings, or somebody would have mentioned before now that they had had a lodger who went bathing at East Felpham. Either he lives in the neighbourhood, in which case he should be easy to trace, or was staying with friends who have an interest in concealing his movements. Or else – which I think is more likely – he was in a smallish hotel, where he would be missed from the breakfast-table, but where his favourite bathing-place was not a matter of common knowledge.'

'That seems feasible,' said the stout man.

'In any case,' went on the first-class passenger, 'he must have been staying within easy bicycling distance of East Felpham, so it shouldn't be too hard to trace him. And then there is the car.'

'Yes. Where is the car, on your theory?' demanded the prim man, who obviously still had hankerings after the Camorra theory.

'In a garage, waiting to be called for,' said the first-class passenger promptly.

'Where?' persisted the prim man.

'Oh! somewhere on the other side of wherever it was the murderer was staying. If you have a particular reason for not wanting it to be known that you were in a certain place at a specified time, it's not a bad idea to come back from the opposite direction. I rather think I should look for the car at West Felpham, and the hotel in the nearest town on the main road beyond where the two roads to East and West Felpham join. When you've found the car, you've found the name of the victim, naturally. As for the murderer, you will have to look for an active man, a good swimmer and ardent bicyclist – probably not very well off, since he cannot afford to have a car – who has been taking a holiday in the neighbourhood of the Felphams, and who has a good reason for disliking the victim, whoever he may be.'

'Well, I never,' said the elderly woman admiringly. 'How beautiful you do put it all together. Like Sherlock Holmes, I do declare.'

'It's a very pretty theory,' said the prim man, 'but, all the same, you'll find it's a secret society. Mark my words. Dear me! We're just running in. Only twenty minutes late. I call that very good for holiday-time. Will you excuse me? My bag is just under your feet.'

There was an eighth person in the compartment, who had remained throughout the conversation apparently buried in a newspaper. As the passengers decanted themselves upon the platform, this man touched the first-class passenger upon the arm.

'Excuse me, sir,' he said. 'That was a very interesting suggestion of yours. My name is Winterbottom, and I am investigating the case. Do you mind giving me your name? I might wish to communicate with you later on.'

'Certainly,' said the first-class passenger. 'Always delighted to have a finger in any pie, don't you know. Here is my card. Look me up any time you like.'

Detective Inspector Winterbottom took the card and read the name: LORD PETER WIMSEY, 110A Piccadilly.

The *Evening Views* vendor outside Piccadilly tube station arranged his placard with some care. It looked very well, he thought: MAN WITH NO FACE IDENTIFIED. It was, in his opinion, considerably more striking than that displayed by a rival organ, which announced, unimaginatively: BEACH MURDER VICTIM IDENTIFIED. A youngish gentleman in a grey suit who emerged at that moment from the Criterion Bar appeared to think so too, for he exchanged a copper for the *Evening Views*, and at once plunged into its perusal with such concentrated interest that he bumped into a hurried man outside the station and had to apologise.

The *Evening Views*, grateful to murderer and victim alike for providing so useful a sensation in the dead days after the bank holiday, had torn Messrs Negretti & Zambra's rocketing thermometrical statistics from the 'banner' position which they had occupied in the lunch edition, and substituted:

FACELESS VICTIM OF BEACH OUTRAGE IDENTIFIED
MURDER OF PROMINENT PUBLICITY ARTIST
POLICE CLUES

The body of a middle-aged man who was discovered, attired only in a bathing-costume and with his face horribly disfigured by some jagged instrument, on the beach at East Felpham last Monday morning, has been identified as that of Mr Coreggio Plant, studio manager of Messrs Crichton Ltd, the well-known publicity experts of Holborn.

Mr Plant, who was forty-five years of age and a

bachelor, was spending his annual holiday in making a motoring tour along the West Coast. He had no companion with him and had left no address for the forwarding of letters, so that, without the smart work of Detective Inspector Winterbottom of the Westshire police, his disappearance might not in the ordinary way have been noticed until he became due to return to his place in three weeks' time. The murderer had no doubt counted on this, and had removed the motor-car, containing the belongings of his victim, in the hope of covering up all traces of this dastardly outrage so as to gain time for escape.

A rigorous search for the missing car, however, eventuated in its discovery in a garage at West Felpham, where it had been left for decarbonisation and repairs to the magneto. Mr Spiller, the garage proprietor, himself saw the man who left the car, and has furnished a description of him to the police. He is said to be a small, dark man of foreign appearance. The police hold a clue to his identity, and an arrest is confidently expected in the near future.

Mr Plant was for fifteen years in the employment of Messrs Crichton, being appointed Studio Manager in the latter years of the war. He was greatly liked by all his colleagues, and his skill in the layout and designing of advertisements did much to justify the truth of Messrs Crichton's well-known slogan: 'Crichton's for Admirable Advertising'.

The funeral of the victim will take place tomorrow at Golders Green Cemetery. (Pictures on Back Page.)

Lord Peter Wimsey turned to the back page. The portrait of the victim did not detain him long; it was one of those characterless studio photographs which establish nothing except that the sitter has a tolerable set of features. He noted that Mr Plant had been thin rather than fat, commercial in appearance rather than artistic, and that the photographer had chosen to show him serious rather than smiling. A picture of East Felpham beach, marked with a cross where the body was found, seemed to arouse in him rather more than a casual interest. He studied it intently for some time, making little surprised noises. There was no obvious reason why he should have been surprised, for the photograph bore out in every detail the deductions he had made in the train. There was the curved line of sand, with a long spur of rock stretching out behind it into deep water, and running back till it mingled with the short, dry turf. Nevertheless, he looked at it for several minutes with close attention, before folding the newspaper and hailing a taxi; and when he was in the taxi he unfolded the paper and looked at it again.

'Your lordship having been kind enough,' said Inspector Winterbottom, emptying his glass rather too rapidly for true connoisseurship, 'to suggest I should look you up in town, I made bold to give you a call in passing. Thank you, I won't say no. Well, as you've seen in the papers by now, we found that car all right.'

Wimsey expressed his gratification at this result.

'And very much obliged I was to your lordship for the hint,' went on the inspector generously, 'not but what I wouldn't say but I should have come to the same conclusion myself, given a little more time. And, what's more, we're on the track of the man.'

'I see he's supposed to be foreign-looking. Don't say he's going to turn out to be a Camorrist after all!'

'No, my lord.' The inspector winked. 'Our friend in the corner had got his magazine stories a bit on the brain, if you ask me. And *you* were a bit out too, my lord, with your bicyclist idea.'

'Was I? That's a blow.'

'Well, my lord, these here theories *sound* all right, but half the time they're too fine-spun altogether. Go for the facts – that's our motto in the Force – facts and motive, and you won't go far wrong.'

'Oh! you've discovered the motive, then?'

The inspector winked again.

'There's not many motives for doing a man in,' said he. 'Women or money – or women *and* money – it mostly comes down to one or the other. This fellow Plant went in for being a bit of a lad, you see. He kept a little cottage down Felpham way, with a nice little skirt to furnish it and keep the love-nest warm for him – see?'

'Oh! I thought he was doing a motor-tour.'

'Motor-tour your foot!' said the inspector, with more energy than politeness. 'That's what the old [epithet] told 'em at the office. Handy reason, don't you see, for leaving no address behind him. No, no. There was a lady in it all right. I've seen her. A very taking piece too, if you like 'em skinny, which I don't. I prefer 'em better upholstered myself.'

'That chair is really more comfortable with a cushion,' put in Wimsey, with anxious solicitude. 'Allow me.'

'Thanks, my lord, thanks. I'm doing very well. It seems that this woman – by the way, we're speaking in confidence, you understand. I don't want this to go further till I've got my man under lock and key.'

Wimsey promised discretion.

'That's all right, my lord, that's all right. I know I can rely on you. Well, the long and the short is, this young woman had another fancy man – a sort of an Italiano, whom she'd chucked for Plant, and this same dago got wind of the business and came down to East Felpham on the Sunday night, looking for her. He's one of these professional partners in a Palais de Danse up Cricklewood way, and that's where the girl comes from, too. I suppose she thought Plant was a cut above him. Anyway, down he comes, and busts in upon them Sunday night when they were having a bit of supper – and that's when the row started.'

'Didn't you know about this cottage and the goings-on there?'

'Well, you know, there's such a lot of these weekenders nowadays. We can't keep tabs on all of them, so long as they behave themselves and don't make a disturbance. The woman's been there – so they tell me – since last June, with him coming down Saturday to Monday; but it's a lonely spot, and the constable didn't take much notice. He came in the evenings, so there wasn't anybody much to recognise him, except the old girl who did the slops and things, and she's half-blind. And of course, when they found him, he hadn't any face to recognise. It'd be thought he'd just gone off in the ordinary way. I dare say the dago fellow reckoned on that. As I was saying, there was a big row, and the dago was kicked out. He must have lain in wait for Plant down by the bathing-place, and done him in.'

'By strangling?'

'Well, he *was* strangled.'

'Was his face cut up with a knife, then?'

'Well, no – I don't think it was a knife. More like a broken bottle, I should say, if you ask me. There's plenty of them come in with the tide.'

'But then we're brought back to our old problem. If this Italian was lying in wait to murder Plant, why didn't he take a weapon with him, instead of trusting to the chance of his hands and a broken bottle?'

The inspector shook his head.

'Flighty,' he said. 'All these foreigners are flighty. No headpiece. But there's our man and there's our motive, plain as a pikestaff. You don't want more.'

'And where is the Italian fellow now?'

'Run away. That's pretty good proof of guilt in itself. But we'll have him before long. That's what I've come to town about. He can't get out of the country. I've had an all-stations call sent out to stop him. The dance-hall people were able to supply us with a photo and a good description. I'm expecting a report in now any minute. In fact, I'd best be getting along. Thank you very much for your hospitality, my lord.'

'The pleasure is mine,' said Wimpsey, ringing the bell to have the visitor shown out. 'I have enjoyed our little chat immensely.'

Sauntering into the Falstaff at twelve o'clock the following morning, Wimsey, as he had expected, found Salcombe Hardy supporting his rather plump contours against the bar. The reporter greeted his arrival with a heartiness amounting almost to enthusiasm, and called for two large scotches immediately. When the usual skirmish as to who should pay had been honourably settled by the prompt disposal of the drinks and the standing of two more, Wimsey pulled from his pocket the copy of last night's *Evening Views*.

'I wish you'd ask the people over at your place to get hold of a decent print of this for me,' he said, indicating the picture of East Felpham beach.

Salcombe Hardy gazed limpid enquiry at him from eyes like drowned violets.

'See here, you old sleuth,' he said, 'does this mean you've got a theory about the thing? I'm wanting a story badly. Must keep up the excitement, you know. The police don't seem to have got any further since last night.'

'No; I'm interested in this from another point of view altogether. I did have a theory – of sorts – but it seems it's all wrong. Bally old Homer nodding, I suppose. But I'd like a copy of the thing.'

'I'll get Warren to get you one when we come back. I'm just taking him down with me to Crichton's. We're going to have a look at a picture. I say, I wish you'd come too. Tell me what to say about the damned thing.'

'Good God! I don't know anything about commercial art.'

' 'Tisn't commercial art. It's supposed to be a portrait of this blighter Plant. Done by one of the chaps in his studio or something. Kid who told me about it says it's clever. I don't know. Don't suppose she knows, either. You go in for being artistic, don't you?'

'I wish you wouldn't use such filthy expressions, Sally. Artistic! Who is this girl?'

'Typist in the copy department.'

'Oh, Sally!'

'Nothing of that sort. I've never met her. Name's Gladys Twitterton. I'm sure that's beastly enough to put anybody off. Rang us up last night and told us there was a bloke there who'd done old Plant in oils and was it any use to us? Drummer thought it might be worth looking into. Make a change from that everlasting syndicated photograph.'

'I see. If you haven't got an exclusive story, an exclusive picture's better than nothing. The girl seems to have her wits about her. Friend of the artist's?'

'No – said he'd probably be frightfully annoyed at her having told me. But I can wangle that. Only I wish you'd come and have a look at it. Tell me whether I ought to say it's an unknown masterpiece or merely a striking likeness.'

'How the devil can I say if it's a striking likeness of a bloke I've never seen?'

'I'll say it's that, in any case. But I want to know if it's well painted.'

'Curse it, Sally, what's it matter whether it is or not? I've got other things to do. Who's the artist, by the way? Anybody one's ever heard of?'

'Dunno. I've got the name here somewhere.' Sally rooted in his hip-pocket and produced a mass of dirty correspondence, its angles blunted by constant attrition. 'Some comic name like Buggle or Snagtooth – wait a bit – here it is.

Crowder. Thomas Crowder. I knew it was something out of the way.'

'Singularly like Buggle or Snagtooth. All right, Sally. I'll make a martyr of myself. Lead me to it.'

'We'll have another quick one. Here's Warren. This is Lord Peter Wimsey. This is on me.'

'On me,' corrected the photographer, a jaded young man with a disillusioned manner. 'Three large White Labels, please. Well, here's all the best. Are you fit, Sally? Because we'd better make tracks. I've got to be up at Golders Green by two for the funeral.'

Mr Crowder of Crichton's appeared to have had the news broken to him already by Miss Twitterton, for he received the embassy in a spirit of gloomy asquiescence.

'The directors won't like it,' he said, 'but they've had to put up with such a lot that I suppose one irregularity more or less won't give 'em apoplexy.' He had a small, anxious, yellow face like a monkey. Wimsey put him down as being in his late thirties. He noticed his fine, capable hands, one of which was disfigured by a strip of sticking-plaster.

'Damaged yourself?' said Wimsey pleasantly, as they made their way upstairs to the studio. 'Mustn't make a practice of that, what? An artist's hands are his livelihood – except, of course, for Armless Wonders and people of that kind! Awkward job, painting with your toes.'

'Oh, it's nothing much,' said Crowder, 'but it's best to keep the paint out of surface scratches. There's such a thing as lead-poisoning. Well, here's this dud portrait, such as it is. I don't mind telling you that it didn't please the sitter. In fact, he wouldn't have it at any price.'

'Not flattering enough?' asked Hardy.

'As you say.' The painter pulled out a four by three canvas from its hiding-place behind a stack of poster cartoons, and heaved it up on to the easel.

'Oh!' said Hardy, a little surprised. Not that there was any reason for surprise as far as the painting itself was concerned. It was a straightforward handling enough; the skill and originality of the brushwork being of the kind that interests the painter without shocking the ignorant.

'Oh!' said Hardy. 'Was he really like that?'

He moved closer to the canvas, peering into it as he might have peered into the face of the living man, hoping to get something out of him. Under this microscopic scrutiny, the portrait, as is the way of portraits, dislimned, and became no more than a conglomeration of painted spots and streaks. He made the discovery that, to the painter's eye, the human face is full of green and purple patches.

He moved back again, and altered the form of his question: 'So that's what he was like, was he?'

He pulled out the photograph of Plant from his pocket, and compared it with the portrait. The portrait seemed to sneer at his surprise.

'Of course, they touch these things up at these fashionable photographers,' he said. 'Anyway, that's not my business. This thing will make a jolly good eye-catcher, don't you think so, Wimsey? Wonder if they'd give us a two-column spread on the front page? Well, Warren, you'd better get down to it.'

The photographer, bleakly unmoved by artistic or journalistic considerations, took silent charge of the canvas, mentally resolving it into a question of pan-chromatic plates and coloured screens. Crowder gave him a hand in shifting the easel into a better light. Two or three people from other departments, passing through the studio on their lawful occasions stopped, and lingered in the neighbourhood of the disturbance, as though it were a street accident. A melancholy, grey-haired man, temporary head of the studio, vice Coreggio Plant, deceased, took Crowder aside, with a muttered apology, to give him some instructions about adapting a whole quad to an eleven-inch treble. Hardy turned to Lord Peter.

'It's damned ugly,' he said. 'Is it good?'

'Brilliant,' said Wimsey. 'You can go all out. Say what you like about it.'

'Oh, splendid! Could we discover one of our neglected British masters?'

'Yes; why not? You'll probably make the man the fashion and ruin him as an artist, but that's his pigeon.'

'But, I say – do you think it's a good likeness? He's made him look a most sinister sort of fellow. After all, Plant thought it was so bad he wouldn't have it.'

'The more fool he. Ever heard of the portrait of a certain statesman that was so revealing of his inner emptiness that he hurriedly bought it up and hid it to prevent people like you from getting hold of it?'

Crowder came back.

'I say,' said Wimsey, 'whom does that picture belong to? You? Or the heirs of the deceased, or what?'

'I suppose it's back on my hands,' said the painter. 'Plant – well, he more or less commissioned it, you see, but—'

'How more or less?'

'Well, he kept on hinting, don't you know, that he would like me to do him, and, as he was my boss, I thought I'd better. No price actually mentioned. When he saw it, he didn't like it, and told me later to alter it.'

'But you didn't.'

'Oh – well, I put it aside and said I'd see what I could do with it. I thought he'd perhaps forget about it.'

'I see. Then presumably it's yours to dispose of.'

'I should think so. Why?'

'You have a very individual technique, haven't you?' pursued Wimsey. 'Do you exhibit much?'

'Here and there. I've never had a show in London.'

'I fancy I once saw a couple of small seascapes of yours somewhere. Manchester, was it? or Liverpool? I wasn't sure of your name, but I recognised the technique immediately.'

'I dare say. I did send a few things to Manchester about two years ago.'

'Yes – I felt sure I couldn't be mistaken. I want to buy the portrait. Here's my card, by the way. I'm not a journalist; I collect things.'

Crowder looked from the card to Wimsey and from Wimsey to the card, a little reluctantly.

'If you want to exhibit it, of course,' said Lord Peter, 'I should be delighted to leave it with you as long as you liked.'

'Oh, it's not that,' said Crowder. 'The fact is, I'm not altogether keen on the thing. I should like to – that is to say, it's not really finished.'

'My dear man, it's a bally masterpiece.'

'Oh, the painting's all right. But it's not altogether satisfactory as a likeness.'

'What the devil does the likeness matter? I don't know what the late Plant looked like and I don't care. As I look at the thing it's a damn fine bit of brushwork, and if you tinker about with it you'll spoil it. You know that as well as I do. What's biting you? It isn't the price, is it? You know I shan't boggle about that. I can afford my modest pleasures, even in these thin and piping times. You don't want me to have it? Come now – what's the real reason?'

'There's no reason at all why you shouldn't have it if you really want it, I suppose,' said the painter, still a little sullenly. 'If it's really the painting that interests you.'

'What do you suppose it is? The notoriety? I can have all I want of *that* commodity, you know, for the asking – or even without asking. Well, anyhow, think it over, and when you've decided, send me a line and name your price.'

Crowder nodded without speaking, and the photographer having by this time finished his job, the party took their leave.

As they left the building, they became involved in the stream of Crichton's staff going out to lunch. A girl, who seemed to have been loitering in a semi-intentional way in the lower hall, caught them as the lift descended.

'Are you the *Evening Views* people? Did you get your picture all right?'

'Miss Twitterton?' said Hardy interrogatively. 'Yes, rather – thank you so much for giving us the tip. You'll see it on the front page this evening.'

'Oh! that's splendid! I'm frightfully thrilled. It has made an excitement here – all this business. Do they know anything yet about who murdered Mr Plant? Or am I being horribly indiscreet?'

'We're expecting news of an arrest any minute now,' said Hardy. 'As a matter of fact, I shall have to buzz back to the office as fast as I can, to sit with one ear glued to the telephone. You will excuse me, won't you? And, look here – will you let me come round another day, when things aren't as busy, and take you out to lunch?'

'Of course. I should love to,' Miss Twitterton giggled. 'I do so want to hear about all the murder cases.'

'Then here's the man to tell you about them, Miss Twitterton,' said Hardy, with mischief in his eye. 'Allow me to introduce Lord Peter Wimsey.'

Miss Twitterton offered her hand in an ecstasy of excitement which almost robbed her of speech.

'How do you do?' said Wimsey. 'As this blighter is in such a hurry to get back to his gossip-shop, what do you say to having a spot of lunch with me?'

'Well, really—' began Miss Twitterton.

'He's all right,' said Hardy, 'he won't lure you into any gilded dens of infamy. If you look at him, you will see he has a kind, innocent face.'

'I'm sure I never thought of such a thing,' said Miss Twitterton. 'But you know – really – I've only got my old things on. It's no good wearing anything decent in this dusty old place.'

'Oh, nonsense!' said Wimsey. 'You couldn't possibly

look nicer. It isn't the frock that matters – it's the person who wears it. *That's* all right, then. See you later, Sally! Taxi! Where shall we go? What time do you have to be back, by the way?'

'Two o'clock,' said Miss Twitterton regretfully.

'Then we'll make the Savoy do,' said Wimsey, 'it's reasonably handy.'

Miss Twitterton hopped into the waiting taxi with a little squeak of agitation.

'Did you see Mr Crichton?' she said. 'He went by just as we were talking. However, I dare say he doesn't really know me by sight. I hope not – or he'll think I'm getting too grand to need a salary.' She rooted in her handbag. 'I'm sure my face is getting all shiny with excitement. What a silly taxi. It hasn't got a mirror – and I've bust mine.'

Wimsey solemnly produced a small looking-glass from his pocket.

'How wonderfully competent of you!' exclaimed Miss Twitterton. 'I'm afraid, Lord Peter, you are used to taking girls about.'

'Moderately so,' said Wimsey. He did not think it necessary to mention that the last time he had used that mirror it had been to examine the back teeth of a murdered man.

'Of course,' said Miss Twitterton, 'they had to say he was popular with his colleagues. Haven't you noticed that murdered people are always well dressed and popular?'

'They have to be,' said Wimsey. 'It makes it more mysterious and pathetic. Just as girls who disappear are always bright and home-loving and have no men friends.'

'Silly, isn't it?' said Miss Twitterton, with her mouth full of roast duck and green peas. 'I should think everybody was only too glad to get rid of Plant – nasty, rude creature. So mean, too, always taking credit for other people's work. All those poor things in the studio, with all the spirit squashed out of them. I always say, Lord Peter, you can tell if a head of a department's fitted for his job by noticing the atmosphere of the place as you go into it. Take the copy-room, now. We're all as cheerful and friendly as you like, though I must say the language that goes on there is something awful, but these writing fellows are like that, and they don't mean anything by it. But then, Mr Ormerod is a real gentleman – that's our copy-chief, you know – and he makes them all take an interest in the work, for all they grumble about the cheese-bills and the department-store bilge they have to turn out. But it's quite different in the studio. A sort of dead-and-alive feeling about it, if you understand what I mean. We girls notice things like that more than some of the high-up people think. Of course, I am very sensitive to these feelings – almost psychic, I've been told.'

Lord Peter said there was nobody like a woman for sizing up character at a glance. Women, he thought, were remarkably intuitive.

'That's a fact,' said Miss Twitterton. 'I've often said, if I could have a few frank words with Mr Crichton, I could tell him a thing or two. There are wheels within wheels beneath the surface of a place like this that these brass-hats have no idea of.'

Lord Peter said he felt sure of it.

'The way Mr Plant treated people he thought were beneath him,' went on Miss Twitterton, 'I'm sure it was enough to make your blood boil. I'm sure, if Mr Ormerod sent me with a message to him, I was glad to get out of the room again. Humiliating, it was, the way he'd speak to you. I don't care if he's dead or not; being dead doesn't make a person's past behaviour any better, Lord Peter. It wasn't so much the rude things he said. There's Mr Birkett, for example; *he's* rude enough, but nobody minds him. He's just like a big, blundering puppy – rather a lamb, really. It was Mr Plant's nasty sneering way we all hated so. And he was always running people down.'

'How about this portrait?' asked Wimsey. 'Was it like him at all?'

'It was a lot too like him,' said Miss Twitterton emphatically. 'That's why he hated it so. He didn't like Crowder, either. But, of course, he knew he could paint, and he made him do it, because he thought he'd be getting a valuable thing cheap. And Crowder couldn't very well refuse, or Plant would have got him sacked.'

'I shouldn't have thought that would have mattered much to a man of Crowder's ability.'

'Poor Mr Crowder! I don't think he's ever had much luck. Good artists don't always seem able to sell their pictures. And I know he wanted to get married – otherwise he'd never have taken up this commercial work. He's told me a good bit about himself. I don't know why – but I'm one of the people men seem to tell things to.'

Lord Peter filled Miss Twitterton's glass.

'Oh, please! No, really! Not a drop more! I'm talking a lot too much as it is. I don't know what Mr Ormerod will say when I go in to take his letters. I shall be writing down all kinds of funny things. Ooh! I really must be getting back. Just look at the time!'

'It's not really late. Have a black coffee – just as a corrective.' Wimsey smiled. 'You haven't been talking at all too much. I've enjoyed your picture of office life enormously. You have a very vivid way of putting things, you know. I see now why Mr Plant was not altogether a popular character.'

'Not in the office, anyway – whatever he may have been elsewhere,' said Miss Twitterton darkly.

'Oh?'

'Oh! he was a one,' said Miss Twitterton. 'He certainly was a one. Some friends of mine met him one evening up in the West End, and they came back with some nice stories. It was quite a joke in the office – old Plant and his rosebuds, you know. Mr Cowley – he's *the* Cowley, you know, who rides in the motor-cycle races – he always said he knew what to think of Mr Plant and his motor-tours. That time Mr Plant pretended he'd gone touring in Wales, Mr Cowley was asking him about the roads, and he didn't know a thing about them. Because Mr Cowley really had been touring there, and he knew quite well Mr Plant hadn't been where he said he had; and, as a matter of fact, Mr Cowley knew he'd been staying the whole time in a hotel at Aberystwyth, in very attactive company.'

Miss Twitterton finished her coffee and slapped the cup down defiantly.

'And now I really *must* run away, or I shall be most dreadfully late. And thank you ever so much.'

'Hullo!' said Inspector Winterbottom, 'you've bought that portrait, then?'

'Yes,' said Wimsey. 'It's a fine bit of work.' He gazed thoughtfully at the canvas. 'Sit down, inspector; I want to tell you a story.'

'And I want to tell *you* a story,' replied the inspector.

'Let's have yours first,' said Wimsey, with an air of flattering eagerness.

'No, no, my lord. You take precedence. Go ahead.'

He snuggled down with a chuckle into his armchair.

'Well!' said Wimsey. 'Mine's a sort of a fairy-story. And, mind you, I haven't verified it.'

'Go ahead, my lord, go ahead.'

'Once upon a time—' said Wimsey, sighing.

'That's the good old-fashioned way to begin a fairy-story,' said Inspector Winterbottom.

'Once upon a time,' repeated Wimsey, 'there was a painter. He was a good painter, but the bad fairy of Financial Success had not been asked to his christening – what?'

'That's often the way with painters,' agreed the inspector.

'So he had to take up a job as a commercial artist, because nobody would buy his pictures and, like so many people in fairy-tales, he wanted to marry a goose-girl.'

'There's many people want to do the same,' said the inspector.

'The head of his department,' went on Wimsey, 'was a man with a mean, sneering soul. He wasn't even good at his job, but he had been pushed into authority during the war, when better men went to the Front. Mind you, I'm rather sorry for the man. He suffered from an inferiority complex' – the inspector snorted – 'and he thought the only way to keep his end up was to keep other people's end down. So he became a little tin tyrant and a bully. He took all the credit for the work of the men under his charge, and he sneered and harassed them till they got inferiority complexes even worse than his own.'

'I've known that sort,' said the inspector, 'and the marvel to me is how they get away with it.'

'Just so,' said Wimsey. 'Well, I dare say this man would have gone on getting away with it all right, if he hadn't thought of getting this painter to paint his portrait.'

'Damn silly thing to do,' said the inspector. 'It was only making the painter-fellow conceited with himself.'

'True. But, you see, this tin tyrant person had a fascinating female in tow, and he wanted the portrait for the lady. He thought that, by making the painter do it, he would get a good portrait at starvation price. But unhappily he'd forgotten that, however much an artist will put up with in the ordinary way, he is bound to be sincere with his art. That's the one thing a genuine artist won't muck about with.'

'I dare say,' said the inspector. 'I don't know much about artists.'

'Well, you can take it from me. So the painter painted the

portrait as he saw it, and he put the man's whole creeping, sneering, paltry soul on the canvas for everybody to see.'

Inspector Winterbottom stared at the portrait, and the portrait sneered back at him.

'It's not what you'd call a flattering picture, certainly,' he admitted.

'Now, when a painter paints a portrait of anybody,' went on Wimsey, 'that person's face is never the same to him again. It's like – what shall I say? Well, it's like the way a gunner, say, looks at a landscape where he happens to be posted. He doesn't see it as a landscape. He doesn't see it as a thing of magic beauty, full of sweeping lines and lovely colour. He sees it as so much cover, so many landmarks to aim by, so many gun-emplacements. And when the war is over and he goes back to it, he will still see it as cover and landmarks and gun-emplacements. It isn't a landscape any more. It's a war map.'

'I know that,' said Inspector Winterbottom. 'I was a gunner myself.'

'A painter gets just the same feeling of deadly familiarity with every line of a face he's once painted,' pursued Wimsey. 'And, if it's a face he hates, he hates it with a new and more irritable hatred. It's like a defective barrel organ, everlastingly grinding out the same old maddening tune, and making the same damned awful wrong note every time the barrel goes round.'

'Lord! how you can talk!' ejaculated the inspector.

'That was the way the painter felt about this man's hateful face. All day and every day he had to see it. He couldn't get away because he was tied to his job, you see.'

'He ought to have cut loose,' said the inspector. 'It's no good going on like that, trying to work with uncongenial people.'

'Well, anyway, he said to himself, he could escape for a bit during his holidays. There was a beautiful little quiet spot he knew on the west coast, where nobody ever came.

He'd been there before and painted it. Oh! by the way, that reminds me – I've got another picture to show you.'

He went to a bureau and extracted a small panel in oils from a drawer.

'I saw that two years ago at a show in Manchester, and I happened to remember the name of the dealer who bought it.'

Inspector Winterbottom gaped at the panel.

'But that's East Felpham!' he exclaimed.

'Yes. It's only signed T.C., but the technique is rather unmistakable don't you think?'

The inspector knew little about technique, but initials he understood. He looked from the portrait to the panel and back at Lord Peter.

'The painter—'

'Crowder?'

'If it's all the same to you, I'd rather go on calling him the painter. He packed up his traps on his push-bike carrier, and took his tormented nerves down to this beloved and secret spot for a quiet weekend. He stayed at a quiet little hotel in the neighbourhood, and each morning he cycled off to this lovely little beach to bathe. He never told anybody at the hotel where he went, because it was *his* place, and he didn't want other people to find it out.'

Inspector Winterbottom set the panel down on the table, and helped himself to whisky.

'One morning – it happened to be the Monday morning' – Wimsey's voice became slower and more reluctant – 'he went down as usual. The tide was not yet fully in, but he ran out over the rocks to where he knew there was a deep bathing-pool. He plunged in and swam about, and let the small noise of his jangling troubles be swallowed up in the innumerable laughter of the sea.'

'Eh?'

'κυμάτων ἀνήριθμον γέλασμα – quotation from the classics. Some people say it means the dimpled surface of the waves in the sunlight – but how could Prometheus, bound upon his rock, have seen it? Surely it was the chuckle of the incoming tide among the stones that came up to his ears on the lonely peak where the vulture fretted at his heart. I remember arguing about it with old Philpotts in class, and getting rapped over the knuckles for contradicting him. I didn't know at the time that he was engaged in producing a translation on his own account, or doubtless I should have contradicted him more rudely and been told to take my trousers down. Dear old Philpotts!'

'I don't know anything about that,' said the inspector.

'I beg your pardon. Shocking way I have of wandering. The painter – well! he swam round the end of the rocks, for the tide was nearly in by that time; and, as he came up from the sea, he saw a man standing on the beach – that beloved beach, remember, which he thought was his own sacred haven of peace. He came wading towards it, cursing the bank holiday rabble who must needs swarm about everywhere with their cigarette packets and their Kodaks and their gramophones – and then he saw that it was a face he knew. He knew every hated line in it, on that clear sunny morning. And, early as it was, the heat was coming up over the sea like a haze.'

'It was hot weekend,' said the inspector.

'And then the man hailed him, in his smug, mincing voice. "Hullo!" he said, "you here? How did you find my little bathing-place?" And that was too much for the painter. He felt as if his last sanctuary had been invaded. He leapt at the lean throat – it's rather a stringy one, you may notice, with a prominent Adam's apple – an irritating throat. The water chuckled round their feet as they swayed to and fro. He felt his thumbs sink into the flesh he had painted. He saw, and laughed to see, the hateful familiarity of the features change and swell into an unrecognisable purple. He watched the sunken eyes bulge out and the thin mouth distort itself as the blackened tongue thrust through it – I am not unnerving you, I hope?'

The inspector laughed.

'Not a bit. It's wonderful, the way you describe things. You ought to write a book.'

> 'I sing but as the throstle sings,
> Amid the branches dwelling,'

replied his lordship negligently, and went on without further comment.

'The painter throttled him. He flung him back on the sand. He looked at him, and his heart crowed within him. He stretched out his hand, and found a broken bottle, with a good jagged edge. He went to work with a will, stamping and tearing away every trace of the face he knew and loathed. He blotted it out and destroyed it utterly.

'He sat beside the thing he had made. He began to be frightened. They had staggered back beyond the edge of the water, and there were the marks of his feet on the sand. He had blood on his face and on his bathing-suit, and he had cut his hand with the bottle. But the blessed sea was still coming in. He watched it pass over the bloodstains and the footprints and wipe the story of his madness away. He remembered that this man had gone from his place, leaving no address behind him. He went back, step by step, into the water, and, as it came up to his breast, he saw the red stains smoke away like a faint mist in the brown-blueness of the tide. He went – wading and swimming and plunging his face and arms deep in the water, looking back from time to time to see what he had left behind him. I think that when he got back to the point and drew himself out, clean and cool, upon the rocks, he remembered that he ought to have taken the body back with him and let the tide carry it away, but it was too late. He was clean, and he could not bear to go back for the thing. Besides, he was late, and they would wonder at the hotel if he was not back in time for breakfast.

He ran lightly over the bare rocks and the grass that showed no footprint. He dressed himself, taking care to leave no trace of his presence. He took the car, which would have told a story. He put his bicycle in the back seat, under the rugs, and he went – but you know as well as I do where he went.'

Lord Peter got up with an impatient movement, and went over to the picture, rubbing his thumb meditatively over the texture of the painting.

'You may say, if he hated the face so much, why didn't he destroy the picture? He couldn't. It was the best thing he'd ever done. He took a hundred guineas for it. It was cheap at a hundred guineas. But then – I think he was afraid to refuse me. My name is rather well known. It was a sort of blackmail, I suppose. But I wanted that picture.'

Inspector Winterbottom laughed again.

'Did you take any steps, my lord, to find out if Crowder has really been staying at East Felpham?'

'No.' Wimsey swung round abruptly. 'I have taken no steps at all. That's your business. I have told you the story, and, on my soul, I'd rather have stood by and said nothing.'

'You needn't worry.' The inspector laughed for the third time. 'It's a good story, my lord, and you told it well. But you're right when you say it's a fairy-story. We've found this Italian fellow – Francesco, he called himself, and he's the man all right.'

'How do you know? Has he confessed?'

'Practically. He's dead. Killed himself. He left a letter to the woman, begging her forgiveness, and saying that when he saw her with Plant he felt murder come into his heart. "I have revenged myself," he says, "on him who dared to love you." I suppose he got the wind up when he saw we were after him – I wish these newspapers wouldn't be always putting these criminals on their guard – so he did away with himself to cheat the gallows. I may say it's been a disappointment to me.'

'It must have been,' said Wimsey. 'Very unsatisfactory, of course. But I'm glad my story turned out to be only a fairy-tale after all. You're not going?'

'Got to get back to my duty,' said the inspector, heaving himself to his feet. 'Very pleased to have met you, my lord. And I mean what I say – you ought to take to literature.'

Wimsey remained after he had gone, still looking at the portrait.

' "What is Truth?" said jesting Pilate. No wonder, since it is so completely unbelievable . . . I could prove it . . . if I liked . . . but the man had a villainous face, and there are few good painters in the world.'

Dead Man

JAMES M. CAIN

American crime and mystery writers have also produced a number of classic stories featuring the railways, several of which have been made into movies. Among those that spring to mind are *The Man in Lower Ten* by Mary Roberts Rinehart (1909), *Bombay Mail* by Lawrence G. Blochman (1934), *Grand Central Murder* by Sue MacVeigh (1939), and Ross Macdonald's *Trouble Follows Me* (1946). One of the earliest railway crime novels to become a critical and public success both as a book and film was James M. Cain's *Double Indemnity* (1943), the gritty story of an insurance salesman who falls in love with a scheming wife and plots with her to murder her husband in a train accident. The film adaptation was made by the great Hollywood director Billy Wilder and starred Fred MacMurray, Barbara Stanwyck and Edward G. Robinson. A lot of the picture was shot in Paramount Pictures' own back lot where the studio actually had its own rail track and a pair of steam engines! These scenes were also augmented with location shots of the AT&SF Railway lines and rolling stock in and around Los Angeles.

James Mallahan Cain (1892–1977) was one of America's premier 'hard-boiled' crime writers and is deservedly compared with Raymond Chandler and Dashiell Hammett. Born in Annapolis, Maryland, Cain initially wanted to follow the career of his mother who had been an opera singer. But after being told that he did not have the voice, he settled instead for the life of a reporter on the *Baltimore Sun* where he soon encountered the crime and vice that would become the staple ingredients of his literary career. He became a bestselling author overnight with his very first book, *The Postman Always Rings Twice* (1934) which was filmed and provided him with an entrée to Hollywood. Subsequent successes with *Mildred Pierce* (1941) and *Double Indemnity* assured him fame and financial security, although he continued writing well into his eighties.

'Dead Man', written in 1944, is one of his most powerful short stories and again returns to the world of the railways. It tells the story of a hobo, one of the drifters who have been riding on US trains for a hundred years and more. These men, some criminals on the run, others too poor to pay for a ticket, were first immortalised in Jack London's *The Road* (1907) based on his own experiences, and then became almost commonplace in the thirties when the era of the Depression caused many more to risk this highly dangerous form of transport. Deaths by falling off the axle rods beneath the freight wagons or from the couplings of passenger trains occurred almost daily, and some of the railway companies became so worried by the problem that they hired special teams of detectives – nicknamed 'bulls' – to try and put a stop to the rail-roading hobos. 'Dead Man' not only conjures up the world of these drifters but, in the style that is uniquely James Cain, gets deep inside the mind of a murderer.

***

He felt the train check, knew what it meant. In a moment, from up toward the engine, came the chant of the railroad detective: 'Rise and shine, boys, rise and shine.' The hoboes began dropping off. He could hear them out there in the dark, cursing as the train went by. That was what they always did on these freights: let the hoboes climb on in the yards, making no effort to dislodge them there, for that would have meant a foolish game of hide-and-seek between two or three detectives and two or three hundred hoboes, with the hoboes swarming on as fast as the detectives put them off. What they did was let the hoboes alone until the train was several miles under way; then they pulled down to a speed slow enough for men to drop off, but too fast for them to climb back on. Then the detective went down the line, brushing them off like caterpillars from a twig. In two minutes they would all be ditched, a crowd of bitter men in a lonely spot; but they always cursed, always seemed surprised.

He crouched in the coal gondola and waited. He hadn't boarded a flat or a refrigerator with the others back in the Los Angeles yards, tempting though this comfort was. He wasn't long on the road, and he still didn't like to mix with the other hoboes, admit he was one of them. Also, he couldn't shake off a notion that he was sharper than they were, that playing a lone hand he might think of some magnificent trick that would defeat the detective, and thus, even at this ignoble trade, give him a sense of accomplishment, of being good at it. He had slipped into the gond not in spite of its harshness, but because of it; it was blacky and would give him a chance to hide, and the detective, not expecting him there, might pass him by. He was nineteen years old and was proud of the nickname they had given him in the poolroom back home. They called him Lucky.

'Rise and shine, boys, rise and shine.'

Three dropped off the tank car ahead, and the detective climbed into the gond. The flashlight shot around, and Lucky held his breath. He had curled into one of the three chutes for unloading coal. The trick worked. These chutes were dangerous, for if you stepped into one and the bottom dropped, it would dump you under the train. The detective took no chances. He first shot the flash, then held on to the side while he climbed over the chutes. When he came to the last one, where Lucky lay, he shot the flash, but carelessly, and not squarely into the hole, so that he saw nothing.

Stepping over, he went on, climbed to the boxcar behind, and resumed his chant; there were more curses, more feet sliding on ballast on the roadbed outside. Soon the train picked up speed. That meant the detective had reached the caboose, that all the hoboes were cleared.

Lucky stood up, looked around. There was nothing to see except hot-dog stands along the highway, but it was pleasant to poke your head up, let the wind whip your hair, and reflect how you had outwitted the detective. When the click of the rails slowed and station lights showed ahead, he squatted down again, dropped his feet into the chute. As soon as lights flashed alongside, he braced against the opposite side of the chute: that was one thing he had learned, the crazy way they shot the brakes on these freights. When the train jerked to a shrieking stop, he was ready, and didn't get slammed. The bell tolled; the engine pulled away; there was an interval of silence. That meant they had cut the train and would be picking up more cars. Soon they would be going on.

'Ah-ha! Hiding out on me, hey?'

The flashlight shot down from the boxcar. Lucky jumped, seized the side of the gond, scrambled up, vaulted. When he hit the roadbed his ankles stung from the impact, and he staggered for footing. The detective was on him, grappling. He broke away and ran down the track, past the caboose into the dark. The detective followed, but he was a big man and began to lose ground. Lucky was clear, when all of a sudden his foot drove against a switch bar and he went flat on his face, panting from the hysteria of shock.

The detective didn't grapple this time. He let go with a barrage of kicks.

'Hide out on me, will you? Treat you right, give you a break, and you hide out on me. I'll learn you to hide out on me.'

Lucky tried to get up, couldn't. He was jerked to his feet, rushed up the track on the run. He pulled back, but couldn't get set. He sat down, dug in with his sliding heels. The detective kicked and jerked in fury. Lucky clawed for something to hold on to; his hand caught the rail. The detective stamped on it. He pulled it back in pain, clawed again. This time his fingers closed on a spike sticking an inch or two out of the tie. The detective jerked, the spike pulled out of the hole, and Lucky resumed his unwilling run.

'Lemme go! Why don't you lemme go?'

'Come on! Hide out on me, will you? I'll learn you to hide out on Larry Nott!'

'Lemme go! Lemme—'

Lucky pulled back, braced with his heels, got himself stopped. Then his whole body coiled like a spring and let go in one convulsive, passionate lunge. The spike, still in his hand, came down on the detective's head, and he felt it crush. He stood there, looking down at something dark and formless lying across the rails.

Hurrying down the track, he became aware of the spike, gave it a toss, heard it splash in the ditch. Soon he realised that his steps on the ties were being telegraphed by the listening rail, and he plunged across the ditch to the highway. There he resumed his rapid walk, trying not to run. But every time a car overtook him, his heels lifted queerly, and his breath first stopped, then came in gasps as he listened for the car to stop. He came to a crossroads, turned quickly to his right. He let himself run here, for the road wasn't lit, as the main highway was, and there weren't many cars. The running tired him, but it eased the sick feeling in his stomach. He came to a sign that told him Los Angeles was seventeen miles, and to his left. He turned, walked, ran, stooped down sometimes, panting, to rest. After a while it came to him why he had to get to Los Angeles, and so soon. The soup kitchen opened at seven o'clock. He had to be there, in that same soup kitchen where he had had supper, so it would look as though he had never been away.

When the lights went off and it came broad daylight with the suddenness of southern California, he was in the city, and a clock told him it was ten minutes after five. He thought he had time. He pressed on, exhausted, but never relaxing his rapid, half-shuffling walk.

It was ten minutes to seven when he got to the soup kitchen, and he quickly walked past it. He wanted to be clear at the end of the line, so he could have a word with Shorty, the man who dished out the soup, without impatient shoves from behind and growls to keep moving.

Shorty remembered him. 'Still here, hey?'

'Still here.'

'Three in a row for you. Holy smoke, they ought to be collecting for you by the month.'

'Thought you'd be off.'

'Who, me?'

'Sunday, ain't it?'

'Sunday? Wake up. This is Saturday.'

'Saturday? You're kidding.'

'Kidding my eye, this is Saturday, and a big day in this town, too.'

'One day looks like another to me.'

'Not this one. Parade.'

'Yeah?'

'Shriners. You get that free.'

'Well, that's my name, Lucky.'

'My name's Shorty, but I'm over six feet.'

'Nothing like that with me. I really got luck.'

'You sure?'

'Like, for instance, getting a hunk of meat.'

'I didn't give you no meat.'

'Ain't you going to?'

'Shove your plate over quick. Don't let nobody see you.'

'Thanks.'

'Okay, Lucky. Don't miss the parade.'

'I won't.'

He sat at the rough table with the others, dipped his bread in the soup, tried to eat, but his throat kept contracting from excitement, and he made slow work of it. He had what he wanted from Shorty. He had fixed the day, and not only the day but the date, for it would be the same date as the big Shriners' parade. He had fixed his name, with a little gag. Shorty wouldn't forget him. His throat relaxed, and he wolfed the piece of meat.

Near the soup kitchen he saw signs: LINCOLN PARK PHARMACY, LINCOLN PARK CAFETERIA.

'Which way is the park, Buddy?' If it was a big park, he might find a thicket where he could lie down, rest his aching legs.

'Straight down; you'll see it.'

There was a fence around it, but he found a gate, opened it, slipped in. Ahead of him was a thicket, but the ground was wet from a stream that ran through it. He crossed a small bridge, followed a path. He came to a stable, peeped in. It was empty, but the floor was thickly covered with new hay. He went in, made for a dark corner, burrowed under the hay, closed his eyes. For a few moments everything slipped away, except warmth, relaxation, ease. But then something began to drill into the back of his mind: Where did he spend last night? Where would he tell them he spent last night? He tried to think, but nothing would come to him. He would have said that he spent it where he spent the night before, but he hadn't spent it in Los Angeles. He had spent it in Santa Barbara and come down in the morning on a truck. He had never spent a night in Los Angeles. He didn't know the places. He had no answers to the questions that were now pounding at him like sledgehammers:

'What's that? Where you say you was?'

'In a flophouse.'

'Which flophouse?'

'I didn't pay attention which flophouse. It was just a flophouse.'

'Where was this flophouse at?'

'I don't know where it was. I never been to Los Angeles before. I don't know the names of no streets.'

'What this flophouse look like?'

'Looked like a flophouse.'

'Come on, don't give us no gags. What this flophouse look like? Ain't you got eyes? Can't you say what this here place looked like? What's the matter, can't you talk?'

Something gripped his arm, and he felt himself being lifted. Something of terrible strength had hold of him, and he was going straight up in the air. He squirmed to get loose, then was plopped on his feet and released. He turned, terrified.

An elephant was standing there, exploring his clothes with its trunk. He knew then that he had been asleep. But when he backed away, he bumped into another elephant. He slipped between the two elephants, slithered past a third to the door, which was open about a foot. Out in the sunlight, he made his way back across the little bridge, saw what he hadn't noticed before: pens with deer in them, and ostriches, and mountain sheep, that told him he had stumbled into a zoo. It was after four o'clock, so he must have slept a long time in the hay. Back on the street, he felt a sobbing laugh rise in his throat. *That* was where he had spent the night. 'In the elephant house at Lincoln Park.'

'*What*?'

'That's right. In the elephant house.'

'What you giving us? A stall?'

'It ain't no stall. I was in the elephant house.'

'With them elephants?'

'That's right.'

'How you get in there?'

'Just went in. The door was open.'

'Just went in there, seen the elephants, and bedded down with them?'

'I thought they was horses.'

'You thought them elephants was horses?'

'It was dark. I dug in under the hay. I never knowed they was elephants till morning.'

'How come you went in this place?'

'I left the soup kitchen, and in a couple of minutes I came to the park. I went in there, looking for some grass to lie down on. Then I come to this here place, looked to me like a stable, I peeped in, seen the hay, and hit it.'

'And you wasn't scared of them elephants?'

'It was dark, I tell you, and I could hear them eating the hay, but I thought they was horses. I was tired, and wanted some place to sleep.'

'Then what?'

'Then when it got light, and I seen they was elephants, I run out of there, and beat it.'

'Couldn't you tell them elephants by the smell?'

'I never noticed no smell.'

'How many elephants was there?'

'Three.'

He brushed wisps of hay off his denims. They had been fairly new, but now they were black with the grime of the coal gond. Suddenly his heart stopped; a suffocating feeling swept over him. The questions started again, hammered at him, beat into his brain.

'Where that coal dust come from?'

'I don't know. The freights, I guess.'

'Don't you know it ain't no coal ever shipped into this part of the state? Don't you know that here all they burn is gas? Don't you know it ain't only been one coal car shipped in here in six months, and that come in by a misread train order? Don't you know that car was part of the train this here detective was riding that got killed? *Don't you know that*? Come on, out with it: WHERE THAT COAL DUST COME FROM?'

Getting rid of the denims instantly became an obsession. He felt that people were looking at him on the street, spying the coal dust, waiting till he got by, then running into drugstores to phone the police that he had just passed by. It was like those dreams he sometimes had, where he was walking through crowds naked, except that this was no dream, and he wasn't naked: he was wearing these denims, these telltale denims with coal dust all over them. He clenched his hands, had a moment of terrible concentration, headed into a filling station.

'Hello.'

'Hello.'

'What's the chances on a job?'

'No chances.'

'Why not?'

'Don't need anybody.'

'That's not the only reason.'

'There's about forty-two other reasons – one of them is I can't even make a living myself – but it's all the reason that concerns you. Here's a dime, kid. Better luck somewhere else.'

'I don't want your dime. I want a job. If the clothes were better, that might help, mightn't it?'

'If the clothes were good enough for Clark Gable in the swell gambling house scene, that wouldn't help a bit. Not a bit. I just don't need anybody, that's all.'

'Suppose I got getter clothes. Would you talk to me?'

'Talk to you any time, but I don't need anybody.'

'I'll be back when I get the clothes.'

'Just taking a walk for nothing.'

'What's your name?'

'Hook's my name. Oscar Hook.'

'Thanks, Mr Hook. But I'm coming back. I just got a idea I can talk myself into a job. I'm some talker.'

'You're all of that, kid. But don't waste your time. I don't need anybody.'

'Okay. Just the same, I'll be back.'

He headed for the centre of town, asked the way to the cheap clothing stores. At Los Angeles and Temple, after an hour's trudge, he came to a succession of small stores in a Mexican quarter that were what he wanted. He went into one. The storekeeper was a Mexican, and two or three other Mexicans were standing around, smoking.

'Mister, will you trust me for a pair of white pants and a shirt?'

'No trust. Hey, scram.'

'Look. I can have a job Monday morning if I can show up in that outfit. White pants and a white shirt. That's all.'

'No trust. What you think this is, anyway?'

'Well, I got to get that outfit somewhere. If I get that, they'll let me go to work Monday. I'll pay you as soon as I get paid off Saturday night.'

'No trust. Sell for cash.'

He stood there. The Mexicans stood there, smoked, looked out at the street. Presently one of them looked at him. 'What kind of job, hey? What you mean, got to have white pants a white shirt a hold a job?'

'Filling station. They got a rule you got to have white clothes before you can work there.'

'Oh. Sure. Filling station.'

After a while the storekeeper spoke. 'Ha! Is a joke. Job in filling station, must have a white pants, white shirt. Ha! Is a joke.'

'What else would I want them for? Holy smoke, these are better for the road, ain't they? Say, a guy don't want white pants to ride freights, does he?'

'What filling station? Tell me that?'

'Guy name of Hook, Oscar Hook, got a Acme station, Main near Twentieth. You don't believe me, call him up.'

'You go to work there, hey?'

'I'm *supposed* to go to work. I *told* him I'd get the white pants and white shirt, somehow. Well – if I don't get them I don't go to work.'

'Why you come to me, hey?'

'Where else would I go? If it's not you, it's another guy down the street. No place else I can dig up the stuff over Sunday, is there?'

'Oh.'

He stood around. They all stood around. Then once again the storekeeper looked up. 'What size you wear, hey?'

He had a wash at a tap in the back yard, then changed there, between piled-up boxes and crates. The storekeeper gave him a white shirt, white pants, necktie, a suit of thick underwear, and a pair of shoes to replace his badly worn brogans. 'Is pretty cold, night-time, now. A thick underwear feel better.'

'Okay. Much obliged.'

'Can roll this other stuff up.'

'I don't want it. Can you throw it away for me?'

'Is pretty dirty.'

'Plenty dirty.'

'You no want?'

'No.'

His heart leaped as the storekeeper dropped the whole pile into a rubbish brazier and touched a match to some papers at the bottom of it. In a few minutes, the denims and everything else he had worn were ashes.

He followed the storekeeper inside. 'Okay, here is a bill. I put all a stuff on a bill, no charge you more than anybody else. Is six dollar ninety-eight cents, then is a service charge one dollar.'

All of them laughed. He took the 'service charge' to be a gyp overcharge to cover the trust. He nodded. 'Okay on the service charge.'

The storekeeper hesitated. 'Well, six ninety-eight. We no make a service charge.'

'Thanks.'

'See you keep a white pants clean till Monday morning.'

'I'll do that. See you Saturday night.'

'Adios.'

Out in the street, he stuck his hand in his pocket, felt something, pulled it out. It was a $1 bill. Then he understood about the 'service charge', and why the Mexicans had laughed. He went back, kissed the $1 bill, waved a cheery salute into the store. They all waved back.

He rode a streetcar down to Mr Hook's, got turned down for the job, rode a streetcar back. In his mind, he tried to check over everything. He had an alibi, fantastic and plausible. So far as he could recall, nobody on the train had seen him, not even the other hoboes, for he had stood apart from them in the yards and had done nothing to attract the attention of any of them. The denims were burned, and he had a story to account for the whites. It even looked pretty good, this thing with Mr Hook, for anybody who had committed a murder would be most unlikely to make a serious effort to land a job.

But the questions lurked there, ready to spring at him, check and recheck as he would. He saw a sign, '5-Course Dinner, 35 Cents'. He still had ninety cents, and went in, ordered steak and fried potatoes, the hungry man's dream of heaven. He ate, put a ten-cent tip under the plate. He ordered cigarettes, lit one, inhaled. He got up to go. A newspaper was lying on the table.

He froze as he saw the headline: L. R. NOTT, R. R. MAN, KILLED.

On the street, he bought a paper, tried to open it under a street light, couldn't, tucked it under his arm. He found Highway 101, caught a hay truck bound for San Francisco. Going out Sunset Boulevard, it unexpectedly pulled over to the curb and stopped. He looked warily around. Down a side street, about a block away, were the two red lights of a police station. He was tightening to jump and run, but the driver wasn't looking at the lights. 'I told them bums that air hose was leaking. They set you nuts. Supposed to keep the stuff in shape, and all they ever do is sit around and play blackjack.'

The driver fished a roll of black tape from his pocket and got out. Lucky sat where he was a few minutes, then climbed down, walked to the glare of the headlights, opened his paper. There it was:

L. R. NOTT, R. R. MAN, KILLED

The decapitated body of L. R. Nott, 1327 De Soto Street, a detective assigned to a northbound freight, was found early this morning on the track near San Fernando station. It is believed he lost his balance while the train was shunting cars at the San Fernando siding and fell beneath the wheels. Funeral services will be held tomorrow from the De Soto Street Methodist Church.

Mr Nott is survived by a widow, formerly Miss Elsie Snowden of Mannerheim, and a son, L. R. Nott, Jr, 5.

He stared at it, refolded the paper, tucked it under his arm, walked back to where the driver was tapping the air hose. He was clear, and he knew it. 'Boy, do they call you Lucky? Is your name Lucky? I'll say it is.'

He leaned against the trailer, let his eye wander down the street. He saw the two red lights of the police station – glowing. He looked away quickly. A queer feeling began to stir inside him. He wished the driver would hurry up.

Presently he went back to the headlights again, found the notice, reread it. He recognised that feeling now; it was the old Sunday-night feeling that he used to have back home, when the bells would ring and he would have to stop playing hide in the twilight, go to church, and hear about the necessity for being saved. It shot through his mind, the time he had played hookey from church and hid in the livery stable; and how lonely he had felt, because there was nobody to play hide with; and how he had sneaked into church and stood in the rear to listen to the necessity for being saved.

His eyes twitched back to the red lights, and slowly, shakily, but unswervingly he found himself walking toward them.

'I want to give myself up.'

'Yeah, I know, you're wanted for grand larceny in Hackensack, New Jersey.'

'No, I—'

'We quit giving them rides when the New Deal come in. Beat it.'

'I killed a man.'

'You—? . . . When was it you done this?'

'Last night.'

'Where?'

'Near here. San Fernando. It was like this—'

'Hey, wait till I get a card . . . Okay, what's your name?'

'Ben Fuller.'

'No middle name?'

'They call me Lucky.'

'Lucky like in good luck?'

'Yes, sir . . . Lucky like in good luck.'

Cheese

ETHEL LINA WHITE

The Lady Vanishes is another landmark in railway mystery
fiction. Published originally in 1936 by the prestigious
Crime Club of London under the title *The Wheel Spins*,
Ethel Lina White's macabre story of Iris Carr and her eerie
journey on a continental express was filmed in 1938 by
Alfred Hitchcock and is today recognised as one of the
films that helped to make his reputation. The British-born
director put a lot of time and effort into filming the story.
Apart from location shots of a PLM Express, a Southern
Railway boat train and several French 231 locomotives
racing across the European countryside, Hitchcock had
two complete stations built in the Gainsborough Studios at
Twickenham and even set up a large, immobile studio
locomotive. A number of Bassett Lowke o-gauge models
were also used to help generate the feeling of atmosphere
and tension which was then rapidly becoming the hallmark
of Hitchcock's films. Indeed, the stars of the picture –
Margaret Lockwood, Michael Redgrave and Paul Lukas –
almost became secondary to the railway elements! Forty
years later, the film was remade by Hammer Films
although this time it was filmed almost entirely on location
in Austria along a single-track line between Klangenfurt
and Rosenbach. An OBB 2-10-0 locomotive with six
coaches was used for this version which co-starred Cybill
Shepherd and Elliott Gould.

The success of the novel and film confirmed that the
decision of Ethel Lina White (1884–1944) to give up her
job in the Ministry of Pensions to write fiction had been the

right one. Born on a small farm in Abergavenny on the Welsh border, she was one of a family of twelve and had to leave home to find employment in Cardiff. In her spare time, however, she pursued her ambition to write detective novels, and her first published novel, *Fear Stalks the Village* (1932), earned her the praise from one critic of being 'the new Edgar Allan Poe'. She wrote over a dozen more novels, two of which followed *The Wheel Spins* into the cinema. *Midnight House* (1942) was filmed as *The Unseen* by Paramount in 1942 directed by Lewis Allen with Gail Russell, Joel McCrea and Herbert Marshall; while *Some Must Watch* (1934) became *The Spiral Staircase* when Robert Siodmak directed it for RKO with Dorothy McGuire, George Brent and Ethel Barrymore in 1946.

Although trains featured in several of Ethel Lina White's books, she only once made a railway station the location in the following rare short story, 'Cheese', published in 1941 when *The Lady Vanishes* was still being screened for British audiences starved of new productions because of the Second World War. Do not be misled by the innocuous title: this is a tale of murder by a skilled practitioner of the crime story and may well leave the reader with a sense of unease about visiting London's Victoria station.

***

This story begins with a murder. It ends with a mouse-trap.

The murder can be disposed of in a paragraph. An attractive girl, carefully reared and educated for a future which held only a twisted throat. At the end of seven months, an unsolved mystery and a reward of £500.

It is a long way from a murder to a mouse-trap – and one with no finger-posts; but the police knew every inch of the way. In spite of a prestige punctured by the press and public, they had solved the identity of the killer. There remained the problem of tracking this wary and treacherous rodent from his unknown sewer in the underworld into their trap.

They failed repeatedly for lack of the right bait.

And unexpectedly, one spring evening, the bait turned up in the person of a young girl.

Cheese.

Inspector Angus Duncan was alone in his office when her message was brought up. He was a red-haired Scot, handsome in a dour fashion, with the chin of a prize-fighter and keen blue eyes.

He nodded.

'I'll see her.'

It was between the lights. River, government offices and factories were all deeply dyed with the blue stain of dusk. Even in the city, the lilac bushes showed green tips and an occasional crocus cropped through the grass of the public-gardens, like strewn orange-peel. The evening star was a jewel in the pale green sky.

Duncan was impervious to the romance of the hour. He knew that twilight was but the prelude to night and that darkness was a shield for crime.

He looked up sharply when his visitor was admitted. She was young and flower-faced – her faint freckles already fading away into pallor. Her black suit was shabby, but her hat was garnished for the spring with a cheap cowslip wreath.

As she raised her blue eyes, he saw that they still carried the memory of country sweets . . . Thereupon he looked at her more sharply for he knew that of all poses, innocence is easiest to counterfeit.

'You say Roper sent you?' he enquired.

'Yes, Maggie Roper.'

He nodded. Maggie Roper – Sergeant Roper's niece –

was already shaping as a promising young Stores' detective.

'Where did you meet her?'

'At the Girls' Hostel where I'm staying.'

'Your name?'

'Jenny Morgan.'

'From the country?'

'Yes. But I'm up now for good.'

For good? . . . He wondered.

'Alone?'

'Yes.'

'How's that?' He looked at her mourning. 'People all dead?'

She nodded. From the lightning sweep of her lashes, he knew that she had put in some rough work with a tear. It prejudiced him in her favour. His voice grew more genial as his lips relaxed.

'Well, what's it all about?'

She drew a letter from her bag.

'I'm looking for work and I advertised in the paper. I got this answer. I'm to be companion-secretary to a lady, to travel with her and be treated as her daughter – if she likes me. I sent my photograph and my references and she's fixed an appointment.'

'When and where?'

'The day after tomorrow, in the First Room in the National Gallery. But as she's elderly, she is sending her nephew to drive me to her house.'

'Where's that?'

She looked troubled.

'That's what Maggie Roper is making the fuss about. First, she said I must see if Mrs Harper – that's the lady's name – had taken up my references. And then she insisted on ringing up the Ritz where the letter was written from. The address was *printed*, so it was bound to be genuine, wasn't it?'

'Was it? What happened then?'

'They said no Mrs Harper had stayed there. But I'm sure it must be a mistake.' Her voice trembled. 'One must risk something to get such a good job.'

His face darkened. He was beginning to accept Jenny as the genuine article.

'Tell me,' he asked, 'have you had any experience of life?'

'Well, I've always lived in the country with Auntie. But I've read all sorts of novels and the newspapers.'

'Murders?'

'Oh, I love those.'

He could tell by the note in her childish voice that she ate up the newspaper accounts merely as exciting fiction, without the slightest realisation that the printed page was grim fact. He could see the picture: a sheltered childhood passed amid green spongy meadows. She could hardly cull sophistication from clover and cows.

'Did you read about the Bell murder?' he asked abruptly.

'Auntie wouldn't let me.' She added in the same breath, 'Every word.'

'Why did your aunt forbid you?'

'She said it must be a specially bad one, because they'd left all the bad parts out of the paper.'

'Well, didn't you notice the fact that that poor girl – Emmeline Bell – a well-bred girl of about your own age, was lured to her death through answering a newspaper advertisement?'

'I – I suppose so. But those things don't happen to oneself.'

'Why? What's there to prevent your falling into a similar trap?'

'I can't explain. But if there was something wrong, I should know it.'

'How? D'you expect a bell to ring or a red light to flash "Danger"?'

'Of course not. But if you believe in right and wrong, surely there must be some warning.'

He looked sceptical. That innocence bore a lily in its hand, was to him a beautiful phrase and nothing more. His own position in the sorry scheme of affairs was, to him, proof positive of the official failure of guardian angels.

'Let me see that letter, please,' he said.

She studied his face anxiously as he read, but his expression remained inscrutable. Twisting her fingers in her suspense, she glanced around the room, noting vaguely the three telephones on the desk and the stacked files in the pigeon-holes. A Great Dane snored before the red-caked fire. She wanted to cross the room and pat him, but lacked the courage to stir from her place.

The room was warm, for the windows were opened only a couple of inches at the top. In view of Duncan's weather-tanned colour, the fact struck her as odd.

Mercifully, the future is veiled. She had no inkling of the fateful part that Great Dane was to play in her own drama, nor was there anything to tell her that a closed window would have been a barrier between her and the yawning mouth of hell.

She started as Duncan spoke.

'I want to hold this letter for a bit. Will you call about this time tomorrow? Meantime, I must impress upon you the need of utmost caution. Don't take one step on your own. Should anything fresh crop up, 'phone me immediately. Here's my number.'

When she had gone, Duncan walked to the window. The blue dusk had deepened into a darkness pricked with lights. Across the river, advertisement-signs wrote themselves intermittently in coloured beads.

He still glowed with the thrill of the hunter on the first spoor of the quarry. Although he had to await the report of the expert test, he was confident that the letter which he held had been penned by the murderer of poor ill-starred Emmeline Bell.

Then his elation vanished at a recollection of Jenny's wistful face. In this city were scores of other girls, frail as windflowers too – blossom-sweet and country-raw – forced through economic pressure into positions fraught with deadly peril.

The darkness drew down overhead like a dark shadow pregnant with crime. And out from their holes and sewers stole the rats . . .

At last Duncan had the trap baited for his rat.

A young and pretty girl – ignorant and unprotected. Cheese.

When Jenny, punctual to the minute, entered his office, the following evening, he instantly appraised her as his prospective decoy. His first feeling was one of disappointment. Either she had shrunk in the night or her eyes had grown bigger. She looked such a frail scrap as she stared at him, her lips bitten to a thin line, that it seemed hopeless to credit her with the necessary nerve for his project.

'Oh, please tell me it's all perfectly right about that letter.'

'Anything but right.'

For a moment, he thought she was about to faint. He wondered uneasily whether she had eaten that day. It was obvious from the keenness of her disappointment that she was at the end of her resources.

'Are you sure?' she insisted. 'It's – very important to me. Perhaps I'd better keep the appointment. If I didn't like the look of things, I needn't go on with it.'

'I tell you, it's not a genuine job,' he repeated. 'But I've something to put to you that is the goods. Would you like to have a shot at £500?'

Her flushed face, her eager eyes, her trembling lips, all answered him.

'Yes, please,' was all she said.

He searched for reassuring terms.

'It's like this. We've tested your letter and know it is written, from a bad motive, by an undesirable character.'

'You mean a criminal?' she asked quickly.

'Um. His record is not good. We want to get hold of him.'

'Then why don't you?'

He suppressed a smile.

'Because he doesn't confide in us. But if you have the courage to keep your appointment tomorrow and let his messenger take you to the house of the suppositious Mrs Harper, I'll guarantee it's the hiding-place of the man we want. We get him – you get the reward. Question is – have you the nerve?'

She was silent. Presently she spoke in a small voice.

'Will I be in great danger?'

'None. I wouldn't risk your safety for any consideration. From first to last, you'll be under the protection of the Force.'

'You mean I'll be watched over by detectives in disguise?'

'From the moment you enter the National Gallery, you'll be covered doubly and trebly. You'll be followed every step of the way and directly we've located the house, the place will be raided by the police.'

'All the same, for a minute or so, just before you can get into the house, I'll be alone with – *him*?'

'The briefest interval. You'll be safe at first. He'll begin with overtures. Stall him off with questions. Don't let him see you suspect – or show you're frightened.'

Duncan frowned as he spoke. It was his duty to society to rid it of a dangerous pest and in order to do so, Jenny's co-operation was vital. Yet, to his own surprise, he disliked the necessity in the case of this especial girl.

'Remember we'll be at hand,' he said. 'But if your nerve goes, just whistle and we'll break cover immediately.'

'Will *you* be there?' she asked suddenly.

'Not exactly in the foreground. But I'll be there.'

'Then I'll do it.' She smiled for the first time. 'You laughed at me when I said there was something inside me which told me – things. But I just know I can trust *you*.'

'Good.' His voice was rough. 'Wait a bit. You've been put to expense coming over here. This will cover your fares and so on.'

He thrust a note into her hand and hustled her out, protesting. It was a satisfaction to feel that she would eat that night. As he seated himself at his desk, preparatory to work, his frozen face was no index of the emotions raised by Jenny's parting words.

Hitherto, he had thought of women merely as 'skirts'. He had regarded a saucepan with an angry woman at the business end of it, merely as a weapon. For the first time he had a domestic vision of a country girl – creamy and fragrant as meadowsweet – in a nice womanly setting of saucepans.

Jenny experienced a thrill which was almost akin to exhilaration when she entered Victoria station, the following day. At the last moment, the place for meeting had been altered in a telegram from 'Mrs Harper'.

Immediately she had received the message, Jenny had gone to the telephone-box in the hostel and duly reported the change of plan, with a request that her message should be repeated to her, to obviate any risk of mistake.

And now – the incredible adventure was actually begun.

The station seemed filled with hurrying crowds as she walked slowly towards the clock. Her feet rather lagged on the way. She wondered if the sinister messenger had already marked the yellow wreath in her hat which she had named as her mark of identification.

Then she remembered her guards. At this moment they

were here, unknown, watching over her slightest movement. It was a curious sensation to feel that she was spied upon by unseen eyes. Yet it helped to brace the muscles of her knees when she took up her station under the clock with the sensation of having exposed herself as a target for gunfire.

Nothing happened. No one spoke to her. She was encouraged to gaze around her . . .

A few yards away, a pleasant-faced smartly dressed young man was covertly regarding her. He carried a yellowish sample-bag which proclaimed him a drummer.

Suddenly Jenny felt positive that this was one of her guards. There was a quality about his keen clean-shaven face – a hint of the eagle in his eye – which reminded her of Duncan. She gave him the beginnings of a smile and was thrilled when, almost imperceptibly, he fluttered one eyelid. She read it as a signal for caution. Alarmed by her indiscretion, she looked fixedly in another direction.

Still – it helped her to know that even if she could not see him, he was there.

The minutes dragged slowly by. She began to grow anxious as to whether the affair were not some hoax. It would be not only a tame ending to the adventure but a positive disappointment. She would miss the chance of a sum which – to her – was a little fortune. Her need was so vital that she would have undertaken the venture for five pounds. Morever, after her years of green country solitude, she felt a thrill at the mere thought of her temporary link with the underworld. This was life in the raw; while screening her as she aided him, she worked with Angus Duncan.

She smiled – then started as though stung.

Someone had touched her on the arm.

'Have I the honour, happiness and felicity of addressing

Miss Jenny Morgan? Yellow wreath in the lady's hat. Red Flower in the gent's buttonhole, as per arrangement.'

The man who addressed her was young and bull-necked, with florid colouring which ran into blotches. He wore a red carnation in the buttonhole of his check overcoat.

'Yes, I'm Jenny Morgan.'

As she spoke, she looked into his eyes. She felt a sharp revulsion – an instinctive recoil of her whole being.

'Are you Mrs Harper's nephew?' she faltered.

'That's right. Excuse a gent keeping a lady waiting, but I just slipped into the bar for a glass of milk. I've a taxi waiting if you'll just hop outside.'

Jenny's mind worked rapidly as she followed him. She was forewarned and protected. But – were it not for Maggie Roper's intervention – she would have kept this appointment in very different circumstances. She wondered whether she would have heeded that instinctive warning and refused to follow the stranger.

She shook her head. Her need was so urgent that, in her wish to believe the best, she knew that she would have summoned up her courage and flouted her fears as nerves. She would have done exactly what she was doing – accompanying an unknown man to an unknown destination.

She shivered at the realisation. It might have been herself. Poor defenceless Jenny – going to her doom.

At that moment she encountered the grave scrutiny of a stout clergyman who was standing by the book-stall. He was ruddy, wore horn-rimmed spectacles and carried the *Church Times*.

His look of understanding was almost as eloquent as a vocal message. It filled her with gratitude. Again she was certain that this was a second guard. Turning to see if the young commercial traveller were following her, she was thrilled to discover that he had preceded her into the station yard. He got into a taxi at the exact moment that her companion flung open the door of a cab which was waiting. It was only this knowledge that Duncan was thus making good his promise which induced her to enter the vehicle. Once again her nerves rebelled and she was rent with sick forebodings.

As they moved off, she had an overpowering impulse to scream aloud for help to the porters – just because all this might have happened to some poor girl who had not her own good fortune.

Her companion nudged her.

'Bit of all right, joy-riding, eh?'

She stiffened, but managed to force a smile.

'Is it a long ride?'

'Ah, now you're asking.'

'Where does Mrs Harper live?'

'Ah, that's telling.'

She shrank away, seized with disgust of his blotched face so near her own.

'Please give me more room. It's stifling here.'

'Now, don't you go taking no liberties with me. A married man I am, with four wives all on the dole.' All the same, to her relief, he moved further away. 'From the country, aren't you? Nice place. Lots of milk. Suit me a treat. Any objection to a gent smoking?'

'I wish you would. The cab reeks of whisky.'

They were passing St Paul's which was the last landmark in her limited knowledge of London. Girls from offices passed on the pavement, laughing and chatting together, or hurrying by intent on business. A group was scattering crumbs to the pigeons which fluttered on the steps of the cathedral.

She watched them with a stab of envy. Safe happy girls.

Then she remembered that somewhere, in the press of traffic, a taxi was shadowing her own. She took fresh courage.

The drive passed like an interminable nightmare in

which she was always on guard to stem the advances of her disagreeable companion. Something seemed always on the point of happening – something unpleasant, just out of sight and round the corner – and then, somehow she staved it off.

The taxi bore her through a congested maze of streets. Shops and offices were succeeded by regions of warehouses and factories, which in turn gave way to areas of dun squalor where gas-works rubbed shoulders with grimed laundries which bore such alluring signs as DEWDROP or WHITE ROSE.

From the shrilling of sirens, Jenny judged that they were in the neighbourhood of the river, when they turned into a quiet square. The tall lean houses wore an air of drab respectability. Lace curtains hung at every window. Plaster pineapples crowned the pillared porches.

'Here's our "destitution".'

As her guide inserted his key in the door of No. 17, Jenny glanced eagerly down the street, in time to see a taxi turn the corner.

'Hop in, dearie.'

On the threshold Jenny shrank back.

Evil.

Never before had she felt its presence. But she knew. Like the fumes creeping upwards from the grating of a sewer, it poisoned the air.

Had she embarked on this enterprise in her former ignorance, she was certain that at this point, her instinct would have triumphed.

'I would never have passed through this door.'

She was wrong. Volition was swept off the board. Her arm was gripped and before she could struggle, she was pulled inside.

She heard the slam of the door.

'Never loiter on the doorstep, dearie. Gives the house a

bad name. This way. Up the stairs. All the nearer to heaven.'

Her heart heavy with dread, Jenny followed him. She had entered on the crux of her adventure – the dangerous few minutes when she would be quite alone.

The place was horrible – with no visible reason for horror. It was no filthy East-end rookery, but a technically clean apartment-house. The stairs were covered with brown linoleum. The mottled yellow wallpaper was intact. Each landing had its marble-topped table, adorned with a forlorn aspidistra – its moulting rug at every door. The air was dead and smelt chiefly of dust.

They climbed four flights of stairs without meeting anyone. Only faint rustlings and whispers within the rooms told of other tenants. Then the blotched-faced man threw open a door.

'Young lady come to see Mrs Harper about the sitooation. Too-tel-oo, dearie. Hope you strike lucky.'

He pushed her inside and she heard his step upon the stairs.

In that moment, Jenny longed for anyone – even her late companion.

She was vaguely aware of the figure of a man seated in a chair. Too terrified to look at him, her eyes flickered around the room.

Like the rest of the house, it struck the note of parodied respectability. Yellowish lace curtains hung at the windows which were blocked by pots of leggy geraniums. A walnut-wood suite was upholstered in faded bottle-green rep with burst padding. A gilt-framed mirror surmounted a stained marble mantelpiece which was decorated with a clock – permanently stopped under its glass case – and a bottle of whisky. On a small table by the door rested a filthy cage, containing a grey parrot, its eyes mere slits of wicked eld between wrinkled lids.

It had to come. With an effort, she looked at the man.

He was tall and slender and wrapped in a once-gorgeous dressing-gown of frayed crimson quilted silk. At first sight, his features were not only handsome but bore some air of breeding. But the whole face was blurred – as though it were a waxen mask half-melted by the sun and over which the Fiend – in passing – had lightly drawn a hand. His eyes drew her own. Large and brilliant, they were of so light a blue as to appear almost white. The lashes were unusually long and matted into spikes.

The blood froze at Jenny's heart. The girl was no fool. Despite Duncan's cautious statements, she had drawn her own deduction which linked an unsolved murder mystery and a reward of £500.

She knew that she was alone with a homicidal maniac – the murderer of ill-starred Emmeline Bell.

In that moment, she realised the full horror of a crime which, a few months ago, had been nothing but an exciting newspaper-story. It sickened her to reflect that a girl – much like herself – whose pretty face smiled fearlessly upon the world from the printed page, had walked into this same trap, in all the blindness of her youthful confidence. No one to hear her cries. No one to guess the agony of those last terrible moments.

Jenny at least understood that first rending shock of realisation. She fought for self-control. At sight of that smiling marred face, she wanted to do what she knew instinctively that other girl had done – precipitating her doom. With a desperate effort she suppressed the impulse to rush madly round the room like a snared creature, beating her hands against the locked door and crying for help. Help which would never come.

Luckily, common sense triumphed. In a few minutes' time, she would not be alone. Even then a taxi was speeding on its mission; wires were humming; behind her was the protection of the Force.

She remembered Duncan's advice to temporise. It was

true that she was not dealing with a beast of the jungle which sprang on its prey at sight.

'Oh, please.' She hardly recognised the tiny pipe. 'I've come to see Mrs Harper about her situation.'

'Yes.' The man did not remove his eyes from her face. 'So you are Jenny?'

'Yes, Jenny Morgan. Is – is Mrs Harper in?'

'She'll be in presently. Sit down. Make yourself at home. What are you scared for?'

'I'm not scared.'

Her words were true. Her strained ears had detected faintest sounds outside – dulled footsteps, the cautious fastening of a door.

The man, for his part, also noticed the stir. For a few seconds he listened intently. Then to her relief, he relaxed his attention.

She snatched again at the fiction of her future employer.

'I hope Mrs Harper will soon come in.'

'What's your hurry? Come closer. I can't see you properly.'

They were face to face. It reminded her of the old nursery story of 'Little Red Riding Hood'.

'What big eyes you've got, Grandmother.'

The words swam into her brain.

Terrible eyes. Like white glass cracked in distorting facets. She was looking into the depths of a blasted soul. Down, down . . . That poor girl. But she must not think of *her*. She must be brave – give him back look for look.

Her lids fell . . . She could bear it no longer.

She gave an involuntary start at the sight of his hands. They were beyond the usual size – unhuman – with long knotted fingers.

'What big hands you've got.'

Before she could control her tongue, the words slipped out.

The man stopped smiling.

But Jenny was not frightened now. Her guards were near. She thought of the detective who carried the bag of samples. She thought of the stout clergyman. She thought of Duncan.

At that moment, the commercial traveller was in an upper room of a wholesale drapery house in the city, holding the fashionable blonde lady buyer with his magnetic blue eye, while he displayed his stock of crêpe-de-Chine underwear.

At that moment, the clergyman was seated in a third-class railway carriage, watching the hollows of the Downs fill with heliotrope shadows. He was not quite at ease. His thoughts persisted on dwelling on the frightened face of a little country girl as she drifted by in the wake of a human vulture.

'I did wrong. I should have risked speaking to her.'

But – at that moment – Duncan was thinking of her.

Jenny's message had been received over the telephone wire, repeated and duly written down by Mr Herbert Yates, shorthand-typist – who, during the absence of Duncan's own secretary, was filling the gap for one morning. At the sound of his chief's step in the corridor outside, he rammed on his hat, for he was already overdue for a lunch appointment with one of the numerous 'only girls in the world'.

At the door he met Duncan.

'May I go to lunch now, sir?'

Duncan nodded assent. He stopped for a minute in the passage while he gave Yates his instructions for the afternoon.

'Any message?' he enquired.

'One come this instant, sir. It's under the weight.'

Duncan entered the office. But in that brief interval, the disaster had occurred.

Yates could not be held to blame for what happened. It

was true that he had taken advantage of Duncan's absence to open a window wide, but he was ignorant of any breach of rules. In his hurry he had also written down Jenny's message on the nearest loose-leaf to hand, but he had taken the precaution to place it under a heavy paper-weight.

It was Duncan's Great Dane which worked the mischief. He was accustomed at this hour to be regaled with a biscuit by Duncan's secretary who was an abject dog-lover. As his dole had not been forthcoming he went in search of it. His great paws on the table, he rooted among the papers, making nothing of a trifle of a letter-weight. Over it went. Out of the window – at the next gust – went Jenny's message. Back to his rug went the dog.

The instant Duncan was aware of what had happened, a frantic search was made for Yates. But that wily and athletic youth, wise to the whims of his official superiors, had disappeared. They raked every place of refreshment within a wide radius. It was not until Duncan's men rang up to report that they had drawn a blank at the National Gallery, that Yates was discovered in an underground dive, drinking coffee and smoking cigarettes with his charmer.

Duncan arrived at Victoria forty minutes after the appointed time.

It was the bitterest hour of his life. He was haunted by the sight of Jenny's flower-face upturned to his. She had *trusted* him. And in his ambition to track the man he had taken advantage of her necessity to use her as a pawn in his game.

He had played her – and lost her.

The thought drove him to madness. Steeled though he was to face reality, he dared not to let himself think of the end. Jenny – country-raw and blossom-sweet – even then struggling in the grip of murderous fingers.

Even then.

Jenny panted as she fought, her brain on fire. The thing had rushed upon her so swiftly that her chief feeling was of sheer incredulity. What had gone before was already burning itself up in a red mist. She had no clear memory afterwards of those tense minutes of fencing. There was only an interlude filled with a dimly comprehended menace – and then this.

And still Duncan had not intervened.

Her strength was failing. Hell cracked, revealing glimpses of unguessed horror.

With a supreme effort she wrenched herself free. It was but a momentary respite, but it sufficed for her signal – a broken tremulous whistle.

The response was immediate. Somewhere outside the door a gruff voice was heard in warning.

'Perlice.'

The killer stiffened, his ears pricked, every nerve astrain. His eyes flickered to the ceiling which was broken by the outline of a trap-door.

Then his glance fell upon the parrot.

His fingers on Jenny's throat, he paused. The bird rocked on its perch, its eyes slits of malicious eld.

Time stood still. The killer stared at the parrot. Which of the gang had given the warning? Whose voice? Not Glass-eye. Not Mexican Joe. The sound had seemed to be within the room.

That parrot.

He laughed. His fingers tightened. Tightened to relax.

For a day and a half he had been in Mother Bargery's room. During that time the bird had been dumb. Did it talk?

The warning echoed in his brain. Every moment of delay was fraught with peril. At that moment his enemies were here, stealing upwards to catch him in their trap. The instinct of the human rodent, enemy of mankind – eternally hunted and harried – prevailed. With an oath, he flung Jenny aside and jumping on the table, wormed through the trap of the door.

Jenny was alone. She was too stunned to think. There was still a roaring in her ears, shooting lights before her eyes. In a vague way, she knew that some hitch had occurred in the plan. The police were here – yet they had let their prey escape.

She put on her hat, straightened her hair. Very slowly she walked down the stairs. There was no sign of Duncan or of his men.

As she reached the hall, a door opened and a white puffed face looked at her. Had she quickened her pace or shown the least sign of fear she would never have left that place alive. Her very nonchalance proved her salvation as she unbarred the door with the deliberation bred of custom.

The street was deserted, save for an empty taxi which she hailed.

'Where to, miss?' asked the driver.

Involuntarily she glanced back at the drab house, squeezed into its strait-waistcoat of grimed bricks. She had a momentary vision of a white blurred face flattened against the glass. At the sight, realisation swept over her in wave upon wave of sick terror.

There had been no guards. She had taken every step of that perilous journey – alone.

Her very terror sharpened her wits to action. If her eyesight had not deceived her, the killer had already discovered that the alarm was false. It was obvious that he would not run the risk of remaining in his present quarters. But it was possible that he might not anticipate a lightning swoop; there was nothing to connect a raw country girl with a preconcerted alliance with a Force.

'The nearest telephone-office,' she panted. 'Quick.'

A few minutes later, Duncan was electrified by Jenny's voice gasping down the wire.

'He's at 17 Jamaica Square, SE. No time to lose. He'll go out through the roof . . . Quick, quick.'

'Right. Jenny, where'll you be?'

'At your house. I mean, Scot – Quick.'

As the taxi bore Jenny swiftly away from the dun outskirts, a shrivelled hag pattered into the upper room of that drab house. Taking no notice of its raging occupant, she approached the parrot's cage.

'Talk for mother, dearie.'

She held out a bit of dirty sugar. As she whistled, the parrot opened its eyes.

'Perlice.'

It was more than two hours later when Duncan entered his private room at Scotland Yard.

His eyes sought Jenny.

A little wan, but otherwise none the worse for her adventure, she presided over a teapot which had been provided by the resourceful Yates. The Great Dane – unmindful of a little incident of a letter-weight – accepted her biscuits and caresses with deep sighs of protest.

Yates sprang up eagerly.

'Did the cop come off, chief?'

Duncan nodded twice – the second time towards the door, in dismissal.

Jenny looked at him in some alarm when they were alone together. There was little trace left of the machine-made martinet of the Yard. The lines in his face appeared freshly re-tooled and there were dark pouches under his eyes.

'Jenny,' he said slowly, 'I've – sweated – blood.'

'Oh, was he so very difficult to capture? Did he fight?'

'Who? That rat? He ran into our net just as he was about to bolt. He'll lose his footing all right. No.'

'Then why are you—'

'*You.*'

Jenny threw him a swift glance. She had just been half-murdered after a short course of semi-starvation, but she commanded the situation like a lion tamer.

'Sit down,' she said, 'and don't say one word until you've drunk this.'

He started to gulp obediently and then knocked over his cup.

'Jenny, you don't know the hell I've been through. You don't understand what you ran into. That man—'

'He was a murderer, of course. I knew that all along.'

'But you were in deadliest peril—'

'I wasn't frightened, so it didn't matter. I knew I could trust you.'

'Don't Jenny. Don't turn the knife. I failed you. There was a ghastly blunder.'

'But it *was* all right, for it ended beautifully. You see, something told me to trust you. I always know.'

During his career, Duncan had known cases of love at first sight. So, although he could not rule them out, he always argued along Jenny's lines.

Those things did not happen to him.

He realised now that it had happened to him – cautious Scot though he was.

'Jenny,' he said, 'it strikes me that I want someone to watch *me*.'

'I'm quite sure you do. Have I won the reward?'

His rapture was dashed.

'Yes.'

'I'm so glad. I'm rich.' She smiled happily. 'So this can't be pity for me.'

'Pity? Oh, Jenny—'

Click. The mouse-trap was set for the confirmed bachelor with the right bait.

A young and friendless girl – homely and blossom-sweet.

Cheese.

A Curious Suicide

PATRICIA HIGHSMITH

For many aficionados of the railway mystery, Patricia Highsmith's *Strangers on a Train* (1950) is equalled only by Agatha Christie's *Murder on the Orient Express*. Certainly, Highsmith's drama about a passenger who is approached by a psychotic to 'swap' murders, each removing an obstacle from the other's life with no visible connection between killer and victim, was one of the most unusual plot devices ever encountered in the genre. And when Alfred Hitchcock followed the success of *The Lady Vanishes* with a second train crime story based on High-smith's novel he created a truly memorable picture that is reshown on television with thoroughly deserved regularity. In making this film, however, Hitchcock used fewer location shots than for its predecessor – primarily of Grand Central station in New York where the journey begins – although he did order the building of an authentic and impressive-looking dining car in Warner Brothers' Holly-wood studios in which the two protagonists, played by Farley Granger and Robert Walker, acted out their bizarre bargain with death. In 1969 the novel was reworked again by the same studios as *Once You Kiss a Stranger* in which the two potential murderers became a young female and a man. The girl offered to murder the rival of her fellow traveller, a professional golfer, if he would kill her psychiatrist. The picture, directed by Robert Sparr and starring Paul Burke and Carol Lynley, was, sadly, nothing like the classic original.

Patricia Highsmith (1921–1995) has been described as

the writer who 'reinvented the crime novel as a whydunit in which an interest in the criminal psychology replaces the puzzle'. Born in Fort Worth, Texas, she came to public attention with her first short story, 'The Heroine', which was published in *Harper's Bazaar* in 1945 and was selected as one of the best short stories of the year. *Strangers on a Train* was her first full-length novel and at once established her as a wholly new voice in the suspense genre. Over twenty novels and seven collections of short stories followed including five adventures of the charming psychopath Tom Ripley, who finds confidence only when acting out a criminal role – which earned her the epithet of 'the high priestess of the nasty'. Reclusive by nature, she moved home from America to Europe, with periods in England and Paris, before spending her final years in Switzerland. When she died in February 1995, *The Times* devoted a leader column to her in which it mourned that her passing 'impoverishes the public stock of shuddering pleasure'. Patricia Highsmith was perhaps at her best in short stories, especially in tales like 'A Curious Suicide' where once again a passenger bent on a crime is using the passing hours to plan what he hopes will be the perfect murder.

***

Dr Stephen McCullough had a first-class compartment to himself on the express from Paris to Geneva. He sat browsing in one of the medical quarterlies he had brought from America, but he was not concentrating. He was toying with the idea of murder. That was why he had taken the train instead of flying, to give himself time to think or perhaps merely dream.

He was a serious man of forty-five, a little overweight, with a prominent and spreading nose, a brown moustache, brown-rimmed glasses, a receding hairline. His eyebrows were tense with an inward anxiety, which his patients often thought a concern with their problems. Actually, he was unhappily married, and though he refused to quarrel with Lillian – that meant answer her back – there was discord between them. In Paris yesterday he had answered Lillian back, and on a ridiculous matter about whether he or she would take back to a shop on the Rue Royale an evening bag that Lillian had decided she did not want. He had been angry not because he had had to return the bag, but because he had agreed, in a weak moment fifteen minutes before, to visit Roger Fane in Geneva.

'Go and see him, Steve,' Lillian had said yesterday morning. 'You're so close to Geneva now, why not? Think of the pleasure it'd give Roger.'

What pleasure? Why? But Dr McCullough had rung Roger at the American Embassy in Geneva, and Roger had been very friendly, much too friendly, of course, and had said that he must come and stay a few days and that he had plenty of room to put him up. Dr McCullough had agreed to spend one night. Then he was going to fly to Rome to join Lillian.

Dr McCullough detested Roger Fane. It was the kind of hatred that time does nothing to diminish. Roger Fane, seventeen years ago, had married the woman Dr McCullough loved. Margaret. Margaret had died a year ago in an automobile accident on an Alpine road. Roger Fane was smug, cautious, mightily pleased with himself and not very intelligent. Seventeen years ago, Roger Fane had told Margaret that he, Stephen McCullough, was having a secret affair with another girl. Nothing was further from the truth, but before Stephen could prove anything, Margaret had married Roger. Dr McCullough had not expected the marriage to last, but it had, and finally Dr McCullough had married Lillian whose face resembled Margaret's a little, but that was the only similarity. In the past seventeen years, Dr McCullough had seen Roger and Margaret perhaps three times when they had come to New

York on short trips. He had not seen Roger since Margaret's death.

Now as the train shot through the French countryside, Dr McCullough reflected on the satisfaction that murdering Roger Fane might give him. He had never before thought of murdering anybody, but yesterday evening while he was taking a bath in the Paris hotel, after the telephone conversation with Roger, a thought had come to him in regard to murder: most murderers were caught because they left some clue, despite their efforts to erase all the clues. Many murderers wanted to be caught, the doctor realised, and unconsciously planted a clue that led the police straight to them. In the Leopold and Loeb case, one of them had dropped his glasses at the scene, for instance. But suppose a murderer deliberately left a dozen clues, practically down to his calling card? It seemed to Dr McCullough that the very obviousness of it would throw suspicion off. Especially if the person were a man like himself, well thought of, a non-violent type. Also, there'd be no motive that anyone could see, because Dr McCullough had never even told Lillian that he had loved the woman Roger Fane had married. Of course, a few of his old friends knew it, but Dr McCullough hadn't mentioned Margaret or Roger Fane in a decade.

He imagined Roger's apartment formal and gloomy, perhaps with a servant prowling about full time, a servant who slept in. A servant would complicate things. Let's say there wasn't a servant who slept in, that he and Roger would be having a nightcap in the living room or in Roger's study, and then just before saying good night, Dr McCullough would pick up a heavy paperweight or a big vase and . . . Then he would calmly take his leave. Of course, the bed should be slept in, since he was supposed to stay the night, so perhaps the morning would be better for the crime than the evening. The essential thing was to leave quietly and at the time he was supposed to leave. But the doctor found himself unable to plot in much detail after all.

Roger Fane's street in Geneva looked just as Dr McCullough had imagined it – a narrow, curving street that combined business establishments with old private dwellings – and it was not too well lit when Dr McCullough's taxi entered it at 9 p.m., yet in law-abiding Switzerland, the doctor supposed, dark streets held few dangers for anyone. The front door buzzed in response to his ring, and Dr McCullough opened it. The door was heavy as a bank vault's door.

'Hullo!' Roger's voice called cheerily down the stairwell. 'Come up! I'm on the third floor. Fourth to you, I suppose.'

'Be right there!' Dr McCullough said, shy about raising his voice in the presence of the closed doors on either side of the hall. He had telephoned Roger a few moments ago from the railway station, because Roger had said he would meet him. Roger had apologised and said he had been held up at a meeting in his office, and would Steve mind hopping into a taxi and coming right over? Dr McCullough suspected that Roger had not been held up at all, but simply hadn't wanted to show him the courtesy of being at the station.

'Well, well, Steve!' said Roger, pumping Dr McCullough's hand. 'It's great to see you again. Come in, come in. Is that thing heavy?' Roger made a pass at the doctor's suitcase, but the doctor caught it up first.

'Not at all. Good to see you again, Roger.' He went into the apartment.

There were oriental rugs, ornate lamps that gave off dim light. It was even stuffier than Dr McCullough had anticipated. Roger looked a trifle thinner. He was shorter than the doctor, and had sparse blond hair. His weak face perpetually smiled. Both had eaten dinner, so they drank scotch in the living room.

'So you're joining Lillian in Rome tomorrow,' said Roger. 'Sorry you won't be staying longer. I'd intended to drive you out to the country tomorrow evening to meet a friend of mine. A woman,' Roger added with a smile.

'Oh? Too bad. Yes, I'll be off on the one o'clock plane tomorrow afternoon. I made the reservation from Paris.' Dr McCullough found himself speaking automatically. Strangely, he felt a little drunk, though he'd taken only a couple of sips of his scotch. It was because of the falsity of the situation, he thought, the falsity of his being here at all, of his pretending friendship or at least friendliness. Roger's smile irked him, so merry and yet so forced. Roger hadn't referred to Margaret, though Dr McCullough had not seen him since she died. But then, neither had the doctor referred to her, even to give a word of condolence. And already, it seemed, Roger had another female interest. Roger was just over forty, still trim of figure and bright of eye. And Margaret, that jewel among women, was just something that had come his way, stayed a while, and departed, Dr McCullough supposed. Roger looked not at all bereaved.

The doctor detested Roger fully as much as he had on the train, but the reality of Roger Fane was somewhat dismaying. If he killed him, he would have to touch him, feel the resistance of his flesh at any rate with the object he hit him with. And what was the servant situation? As if Roger read his mind, he said:

'I've a girl who comes in to clean every morning at ten and leaves at twelve. If you want her to do anything for you, wash and iron a shirt or something like that, don't hesitate. She's very fast, or can be if you ask her. Her name's Yvonne.'

Then the telephone rang. Roger spoke in French. His face fell slightly as he agreed to do something that the other person was asking him to do. Roger said to the doctor:

'Of all irritating things. I've got to catch the seven o'clock plane to Zurich tomorrow. Some visiting fireman's being welcomed at a breakfast. So, old man, I suppose I'll be gone before you're out of bed.'

'Oh!' Dr McCullough found himself chuckling. 'You think doctors aren't used to early calls? Of course I'll get up to tell you goodbye – see you off.'

Roger's smile widened slightly. 'Well, we'll see. I certainly won't wake you for it. Make yourself at home and I'll leave a note for Yvonne to prepare coffee and rolls. Or would you like a more substantial brunch around eleven?'

Dr McCullough was not thinking about what Roger was saying. He had just noticed a rectangular marble pen and pencil holder on the desk where the telephone stood. He was looking at Roger's high and faintly pink forehead. 'Oh, brunch,' said the doctor vaguely. 'No, no, for goodness' sake. They feed you enough on the plane.' And then his thoughts leapt to Lillian and the quarrel yesterday in Paris. Hostility smouldered in him. Had Roger ever quarrelled with Margaret? Dr McCullough could not imagine Margaret being unfair, being mean. It was no wonder Roger's face looked relaxed and untroubled.

'A penny for your thoughts,' said Roger, getting up to replenish his glass.

The doctor's glass was still half full.

'I suppose I'm a bit tired,' said Dr McCullough, and passed his hand across his forehead. When he lifted his head again, he saw a photograph of Margaret which he had not noticed before on top of the highboy on his right. Margaret in her twenties, as she had looked when Roger married her, as she had looked when the doctor had so loved her. Dr McCullough looked suddenly at Roger. His hatred returned in a wave that left him physically weak. 'I suppose I'd better turn in,' he said, setting his glass carefully on the little table in front of him, standing up. Roger had showed him his bedroom.

'Sure you wouldn't like a spot of brandy?' asked Roger. 'You look all in.' Roger smiled cockily, standing very straight.

The tide of the doctor's anger flowed back. He picked up

the marble slab with one hand, and before Roger could step back, smashed him in the forehead with its base. It was a blow that would kill, the doctor knew. Roger fell and without even a last twitch lay still and limp. The doctor set the marble back where it had been, picked up the pen and pencil which had fallen, and replaced them in their holders, then wiped the marble with his handkerchief where his fingers had touched it and also the pen and pencil. Roger's forehead was bleeding slightly. He felt Roger's still warm wrist and found no pulse. Then he went out the door and down the hall to his own room.

He awakened the next morning at 8.15, after a not very sound night's sleep. He showered in the bathroom between his room and Roger's bedroom, shaved, dressed and left the house at a quarter past nine. A hall went from his room past the kitchen to the flat's door; it had not been necessary to cross the living room, and even if he had glanced into the living room through the door he had not closed, Roger's body would have been out of sight to him. Dr McCullough had not glanced in.

At 5.30 p.m. he was in Rome, riding in a taxi from the airport to the Hotel Majestic where Lillian awaited him. Lillian was out, however. The doctor had some coffee sent up, and it was then that he noticed his briefcase was missing. He had wanted to lie on the bed and drink coffee and read his medical quarterlies. Now he remembered distinctly: he had for some reason carried his briefcase into the living room last evening. This did not disturb him at all. It was exactly what he should have done on purpose if he had thought of it. His name and his New York address were written in the slot of the briefcase. And Dr McCullough supposed that Roger had written his name in full in some engagement book along with the time of his arrival.

He found Lillian in good humour. She had bought a lot of things in the Via Condotti. They had dinner and then took a carozza ride through the Villa Borghese, to the

Piazza di Spagna and the Piazza del Populo. If there were anything in the papers about Roger, Dr McCullough was ignorant of it. He bought only the Paris *Herald-Tribune* which was a morning paper.

The news came the next morning as he and Lillian were breakfasting at Donay's in the Via Veneto. It was in the Paris *Herald-Tribune*, and there was a picture of Roger Fane on the front page, a serious official picture of him in a wing collar.

'Good Lord!' said Lillian. 'Why – it happened the night you were there!

Looking over her shoulder, Dr McCullough pretended surprise. ' "... died some time between eight p.m. and three a.m.",' the doctor read. 'I said good night to him about eleven, I think. Went into my room.'

'You didn't *hear* anything?'

'No. My room was down a hall. I closed my door.'

'And the next morning. You didn't—'

'I told you, Roger had to catch a seven o'clock plane. I assumed he was gone. I left the house around nine.'

'And all the time he was in the living room!' Lillian said with a gasp. 'Steve! Why, this is terrible!'

Was it, Dr McCullough wondered. Was it so terrible for her? Her voice did not sound really concerned. He looked into her wide eyes. 'It's certainly terrible – but I'm not responsible, God knows. Don't worry, Lillian.'

The police were at the Hotel Majestic when they returned, waiting for Dr McCullough in the lobby. They were both plainclothes Swiss police, and they spoke English. They interviewed Dr McCullough at a table in a corner of the lobby. Lillian had, at Dr McCullough's insistence, gone up to their room. Dr McCullough had wondered why the police had not come for him hours earlier than this – it was so simple to check the passenger list of planes leaving Geneva – but he soon found out why. The maid Yvonne had not come to clean yesterday morning, so Roger Fane's body had not been discovered until 6 p.m. yesterday, when his office had become alarmed by his absence and sent someone around to his apartment to investigate.

'This is your briefcase, I think,' said the slender blond officer with a smile, opening a large manila envelope he had been carrying under his arm.

'Yes, thank you very much. I realised today that I'd left it.' The doctor took it and laid it on his lap.

The two Swiss watched him quietly.

'This is very shocking,' Dr McCullough said. 'It's hard for me to realise.' He was impatient for them to make their charge – if they were going to – and ask him to return to Geneva with them. They both seemed almost in awe of him.

'How well did you know Mr Fane?' asked the other officer.

'Not too well. I've known him many years, but we were never close friends. I hadn't seen him in five years, I think.' Dr McCullough spoke steadily and in his usual tone.

'Mr Fane was still fully dressed, so he had not gone to bed. You are sure you heard no disturbance that night?'

'I did not,' the doctor answered for the second time. A silence. 'Have you any clues as to who might have done it?'

'Oh, yes, yes,' the blond man said matter of factly. 'We suspect the brother of the maid Yvonne. He was drunk that night and hasn't an alibi for the time of the crime. He and his sister live together and that night he went off with his sister's batch of keys – among which were the keys to Mr Fane's apartment. He didn't come back until nearly noon yesterday. Yvonne was worried about him, which is why she didn't go to Mr Fane's apartment yesterday – that plus the fact she couldn't have got in. She tried to telephone at eight-thirty yesterday morning to say she wouldn't be coming, but she got no answer. We've questioned the brother Anton. He's a ne'er-do-well.' The man shrugged.

Dr McCullough remembered hearing the telephone ring at eight-thirty. 'But – what was the motive?'

'Oh – resentment. Robbery maybe if he'd been sober enough to find anything to take. He's a case for a psychiatrist or an alcoholic ward. Mr Fane knew him, so he might have let him into the apartment, or he could have walked in, since he had the keys. Yvonne said that Mr Fane had been trying for months to get her to live apart from her brother. Her brother beats her and takes her money. Mr Fane had spoken to the brother a couple of times, and it's on our record that Mr Fane once had to call the police to get Anton out of the apartment when he came there looking for his sister. That incident happened at nine in the evening, an hour when his sister is never there. You see how off his head he is.'

Dr McCullough cleared his throat and asked, 'Has Anton confessed to it?'

'Oh, the same as. Poor chap, I really don't think he knows what he's doing half the time. But at least in Switzerland there's no capital punishment. He'll have enough time to dry out in jail, all right.' He glanced at his colleague and they both stood up. 'Thank you very much, Dr McCullough.'

'You're very welcome,' said the doctor. 'Thank you for the briefcase.'

Dr McCullough went upstairs with his briefcase to his room.

'What did they say?' Lillian asked as he came in.

'They think the brother of the maid did it,' said Dr McCullough. 'Fellow who's an alcoholic and who seems to have had it in for Roger. Some ne'er-do-well.' Frowning, he went into the bathroom to wash his hands. He suddenly detested himself, detested Lillian's long sigh, an 'Ah-h' of relief and joy.

'Thank God, thank God!' Lillian said. 'Do you know what this would have meant if they'd – if they'd have accused *you*?' she asked in a softer voice, as if the walls had ears, and she came closer to the bathroom door.

'Certainly,' Dr McCullough said, and felt a burst of anger in his blood. 'I'd have had a hell of a time proving I was innocent, since I was right there at the time.'

'Exactly. You couldn't have proved you were innocent. Thank God for this Anton, whoever he is.' Her small face glowed, her eyes twinkled. 'A ne'er-do-well. Ha! He did us some good!' She laughed shrilly and turned on one heel.

'I don't see why you have to gloat,' he said, drying his hands carefully. 'It's a sad story.'

'Sadder than if they'd blamed you? Don't be so – so altruistic, dear. Or rather, think of us. Husband kills old rival-in-love after – let's see – seventeen years, isn't it? And after eleven years of marriage to another woman. The torch still burns high. Do you think I'd like that?'

'Lillian, what're you talking about?' He came out of the bathroom scowling.

'You know exactly. You think I don't know you were in love with Margaret? *Still* are? You think I don't know you killed Roger?' Her grey eyes looked at him with a wild challenge. Her head was tipped to one side, her hands on her lips.

He felt tongue-tied, paralysed. They stared at each other for perhaps fifteen seconds, while his mind moved tentatively over the abyss her words had just spread before him. He hadn't known that she still thought of Margaret. Of course she'd known about Margaret. But who had kept the story alive in her mind? Perhaps himself by his silence, the doctor realised. But the future was what mattered. Now she had something to hold over his head, something by which she could control him for ever. 'My dear, you are mistaken.'

But Lillian with a toss of her head turned and walked away, and the doctor knew he had not won.

Absolutely nothing was said about the matter for the rest

of the day. They lunched, spent a leisurely hour in the Vatican museum, but Dr McCullough's mind was on other things than Michelangelo's paintings. He was going to go to Geneva and confess the thing, not for decency's sake or because his conscience bothered him, but because Lillian's attitude was insupportable. It was less supportable than a stretch in prison. He managed to get away long enough to make a telephone call at 5 p.m. There was a plane to Geneva at 7.20 p.m. A 6.15 p.m., he left their hotel room empty-handed and took a taxi to Ciampino airport. He had his passport and traveller's cheques.

He arrived in Geneva before eleven that evening, and called the police. At first, they were not willing to tell him the whereabouts of the man accused of murdering Roger Fane, but Dr McCullough gave his name and said he had some important information, and then the Swiss police told him where Anton Carpeau was being held. Dr McCullough took a taxi to what seemed the outskirts of Geneva. It was a new white building, not at all like a prison.

Here he was greeted by one of the plainclothes officers who had come to see him, the blond one. 'Dr McCullough,' he said with a faint smile. 'You have some information, you say? I am afraid it is a little late.'

'Oh? Why?'

'Anton Carpeau has just killed himself – by bashing his head against the wall of his cell. Just twenty minutes ago.' The man gave a hopeless shrug.

'Good God,' Dr McCullough said softly.

'But what was your information?'

The doctor hesitated. The words wouldn't come. And then he realised that it was cowardice and shame that kept him silent. He had never felt so worthless in his life, and he felt infinitely lower than the drunken ne'er-do-well who had killed himself. 'I'd rather not. In this case – I mean – it's so all over, isn't it? It was something else against Anton, I thought – and what's the use now? It's bad enough—' The words stopped.

'Yes, I suppose so,' said the Swiss.

'So – I'll say good night.'

'Good night, Dr McCullough.'

Then the doctor walked on into the night, aimlessly. He felt a curious emptiness, a nothingness in himself that was not like any mood he had ever known. His plan for murder had succeeded, but it had dragged worse tragedies in its wake. Anton Carpeau. And *Lillian*. In a strange way, he had killed himself just as much as he had killed Roger Fane. He was now a dead man, a walking dead man.

Half an hour later, he stood on a formal bridge looking down at the black water of Lake Leman. He stared down a long while, and imagined his body toppling over and over, striking the water with not much of a splash, sinking. He stared hard at the blackness that looked so solid but would be so yielding, so willing to swallow him into death. But he hadn't even the courage or the despair as yet for suicide. One day, however, he would, he knew. One day when the planes of cowardice and courage met at the proper angle. And that day would be a surprise to him and to everyone else who knew him. Then his hands that gripped the stone parapet pushed him back, and the doctor walked on heavily. He would see about a hotel for tonight, and then tomorrow arrange to get back to Rome.

Jeumont: 51 Minutes' Wait

GEORGES SIMENON

Several major French writers have added important works to the railway mystery field including Maurice Dekobra with his million-seller, *The Madonna of the Sleeping Cars* (1927); Sebastien Japrisot with *The Sleeping Car Murders*, written in 1965; and, foremost of all, the prodigious Georges Simenon with his *The Man Who Watched the Trains Go By*. The French cinema can also lay claim to having filmed the very first railway picture in 1895, although it was not a mystery. This was a short, silent movie entitled *Arrival of a Train at La Ciotat Station* made by the Lumière brothers which apparently so startled the first-night audience as the train steamed towards the camera and appeared about to break into the auditorium that a number ran screaming from the place! The classic French movie in the genre is *La Bête Humaine*, made in 1938 from Emile Zola's dark and brooding novel about a doomed engine driver, which was directed by Jean Renoir, starred Jean Gabin and Simone Simon, and was superbly filmed with a number of SNCF 231 Pacifics in the steam yards around Paris. In 1954, the story was relocated to America for a new version entitled *Human Desire* directed by Fritz Lang. Locomotives and track belonging to Southern Pacific formed the background to the Columbia movie which starred Glenn Ford and Gloria Graham.

The Man Who Watched the Trains Go By, written in 1938, was one of the first major works by Georges Simenon (1903–1989), the Belgian-born novelist whose total of over 200 books have sold almost as many copies worldwide as those of Agatha Christie. The story concerns a bank clerk who has embezzled his firm's money, killed a cabaret dancer, and then fled Paris by train hoping to escape justice. It had been inspired by Simenon's lifelong interest in trains, a love affair that enabled him to use the railways to great effect in two of his early pseudonymous serial stories as well as to make them the focal point in a number of his later novels including *Newhaven-Dieppe* (1942) – which was filmed in 1947 as *Temptation Harbour* with Robert Newton, Simone Simon and William Hartnell – and *The Negro* (1959). Curiously, *The Man Who Watched the Trains Go By* was actually made by a British company, Compton, although the producer, Raymond Stross, was determined to use Dutch and French electric trains for the pursuit scenes. However, a dramatic suicide attempt by an onlooker during the first week of filming made Stross decide to switch to steam locomotives instead. As a result primary location shooting took place on a stretch of SNCF track on the approach to Paris. The film, retitled *Paris Express* in the USA, was directed by Harold French and starred Claude Rains, Anouk Aimée, Herbert Lom and Marius Goring.

Although *The Man Who Watched the Trains Go By* did not feature Simenon's famous detective, Inspector Maigret, the pipe-smoking policeman has been featured in various films and several TV series – notably played by Jean Gabin, Rupert Davies and Michael Gambon – and has occasionally had cause to board an express train or take a city local while investigating crime. One such instance is 'Jeumont: 51 Minutes' Wait' which was first published in 1944 and adapted in 1960 as *Unscheduled Departure* for the BBC TV series with Rupert Davies. It is a superb tale of murder on board a European express travelling from Berlin to Paris and reveals Maigret at his most painstaking as he brings a clever killer to justice.

Dimly through a deep sleep Maigret heard a ringing sound, but he was not aware that it was the telephone bell and that his wife was leaning over him to answer.

'It's Paulie,' she said, shaking her husband. 'He wants to speak to you.'

'You, Paulie?' Maigret growled, half awake.

'Is that you, Nunk?' came from the other end of the wire.

It was three in the morning. The bed was warm but the windowpanes were covered with frost flowers, for it was freezing outside. It was freezing even harder up at Jeumont, from where Paulie was telephoning.

'What's that you say? . . . Wait – I'll take the names . . . Otto . . . Yes, spell it, it's safer.'

Madame Maigret, watching her husband, had only one question in her mind; whether he would have to get up or not. And, of course, he did, grumbling away. 'Something very odd has happened,' he explained, 'over at Jeumont, and Paulie has taken it upon himself to detain an entire carriage . . .'

Paulie was Maigret's nephew, Paul Vinchon, and he was an inspector at the Belgian frontier.

'Where are you going?' Madame Maigret asked.

'First to Headquarters to get some information. Then I'll probably hop on the first train . . .'

When anything happens it is always on the 106 – a train that leaves Berlin at 11 a.m. with one or two carriages from Warsaw, reaches Liège at 11.44 p.m., when the station is empty – it closes as soon as the train leaves – and finally gets to Erquelinnes at 1.57.

That evening the carriage steps were white with frost and slippery. At Erquelinnes the Belgian customs officials, who had virtually nothing to do as the train was on its way out, passed down the corridors, looking into a compartment here and there, before hurrying off back to the warmth of the station stove.

By 2.14 the train got under way again to cross the frontier, and reached Jeumont at 2.17.

'Jeumont!' came the cry of a porter running along the platform with a lamp. 'Fifty-one minutes' wait!'

In most of the compartments the passengers were still asleep, the lights were dimmed and the curtains drawn.

'Second- and third-class passengers off the train for customs,' echoed down the train.

And Inspector Paul Vinchon stood frowning at the number of curtains that were drawn back and lights turned up. He went up to the conductor. 'Why are there so many travelling first today?' he asked.

'Some international congress of dentists that starts in Paris tomorrow. We have at least twenty-five of them as well as the ordinary passengers.'

Vinchon climbed into the compartment at the head of the train, opened the doors one after the other, growling out mechanically, 'Have your passports ready, please.'

When the passengers had not wakened and the light was still dimmed, he turned it up; faces rose out of the shadows, swollen with fatigue.

Five minutes later, on his way back up the corridor, he passed the customs men who were going through the first-class compartments, clearing the passengers into the corridor, while they examined the seats and searched every cranny.

'Passports, identity cards . . .'

He was in one of the red-upholstered German carriages. Usually these compartments held only four passengers, but because of the invasion of dentists this one had six. Paulie threw an admiring glance at the pretty woman with the Austrian passport in the left corner seat by the corridor. The others he hardly looked at until he reached the far side of the compartment, where a man, covered with a thick rug, still had not moved.

'Passport,' he said, touching him on the shoulder.

The other passengers were beginning to open their cases for the customs officials, who were arriving. Vinchon shook his sleeping traveller harder; the man slid over on his side. A moment later Vinchon had ascertained he was dead . . .

The scene was chaotic. The compartment was too narrow for all the people who crowded in, and when a stretcher was brought in, there was some difficulty in placing the extremely heavy body on it.

'Take him to the first-aid post,' Vinchon ordered. A little later he found a German doctor on the train.

At the same time he put a customs official on guard over the compartment. The young Austrian woman was the only one who wanted to leave the train to get some fresh air. When she was stopped, she gave a contemptuous shrug.

'Can you tell me what he died of?' Vinchon asked the doctor.

The doctor seemed puzzled; in the end, with Vinchon's help, he undressed the dead man. Even then there was no immediate sign of a wound; it took a good moment before the German pointed out, on the fleshy chest, a mark that could hardly be seen. 'Someone stuck a needle in his heart,' he said.

The train had still twelve or thirteen minutes before leaving again. The special inspector was absent. Vinchon, feverish with excitement, had to make a snap decision: he ran to the stationmaster and gave orders for the carriage to be uncoupled.

The passengers were not sure what was happening. Those in the adjoining compartments protested when they were told that the carriage was staying at Jeumont and that they would have to find seats elsewhere. Those who had been travelling with the dead man protested even more when Vinchon told them he was obliged to keep them there till the next day.

However, there was nothing else for it, seeing that there was a murderer among them. All the same, once the train had left, one carriage and six passengers short, Vinchon began to feel weak at the knees, and rang up his uncle.

At a quarter to four in the morning Maigret was at the Quai des Orfèvres; only a few lights were burning and he asked a sergeant on duty to make him some coffee. By four o'clock, with his office already clouded with pipe-smoke, he had Berlin on the line, and was dictating to a German colleague the names and addresses his nephew had given him. Afterwards he asked for Vienna, as one of the passengers in the compartment came from there, and then he wrote out a telegram for Warsaw, for there had also been a lady from Vilna by name of Irvitch.

Meanwhile, in the inspector's office at the station at Jeumont, Paul Vinchon was taking a firm line with his five victims, whose reactions varied according to their temperaments. At least there was a good fire on – one of those large station stoves that swallows up bucket after bucket of coal. Vinchon had chairs brought in from the neighbouring offices, and good old administrative seats they were, too, with turned legs and shabby velvet upholstery.

'I assure you I am doing everything I can to speed things up, but in the circumstances I have no choice but to detain you here . . .'

He had not a minute to lose if he wanted to draw up anything like a suitable report for the morning. The passports were on his desk. The body of Otto Braun – the victim's name, according to the passport found in his pocket – was still at the first-aid post.

'I can, if you like, get you something to drink. But you

will have to make up your minds quickly – the buffet is about to close.'

At ten past four Vinchon was disturbed by a ring on the telephone. 'Hullo? Aulnoye? What's that? Of course. There's probably some connection, yes. Well, send him over by the first train. And the documents, too, of course.'

Vinchon went into an adjoining office to put through his call to Maigret unheard.

'Is that you, Nunk? . . . Something else, this time . . . A few minutes ago, as the train was drawing into the station at Aulnoye, a man was seen getting out from under a carriage . . . There was a bit of a chase, but they managed to get him in the end . . . He was carrying a waxed-paper packet of bearer bonds, mostly oil securities, for quite an amount . . . The man gave his name as Jef Bebelmans, native of Antwerp, and he gave his profession as acrobat . . . Yes . . . They're bringing him over on the first train . . . You'll be on that one, too? . . . No? . . . At ten-twenty? . . . Thanks, Nunk.'

And he returned to his flock of sheep and goats, as he called them.

When day broke, the frosty light made it seem even colder than the night before. Passengers for a local train started to arrive, and Vinchon worked on, deaf to the protests of his clients, who eventually subsided, overwhelmed with fatigue.

No time was lost. This was essential, for it was the kind of business that could bring diplomatic complications. One could not go on indefinitely detaining five travellers of different nationalities, all with their papers in order, just because a man had been killed in their railway compartment.

Maigret arrived at 10.20, as he had said he would. At 11, on a siding where the carriage had been shunted, the reconstruction of the crime took place. It was a little ghostly, with the grey light, the cold, and the general weariness. Twice a nervous laugh rang out, proving that one of the lady passengers had helped herself too freely to the drinks to warm herself.

'First of all put the dead man in his seat,' Maigret ordered. 'I suppose the curtains on the outside window were drawn?'

'Nothing's been touched,' said his nephew.

Of course, it would have been better to wait until night, until the exact time of the affair. But as that was impossible . . .

Otto Braun, according to his passport, was fifty-eight, born at Bremen, and formerly a banker at Stuttgart. He certainly looked the part, neatly dressed, with his comfortable, heavy build, close-cropped hair, and fairly pronounced Jewish features. The information that had just arrived from Berlin stated: *Had to stop his financial activities after the National Socialist revolution, but gave an undertaking of loyalty to the government, and has never been disturbed. Said to be very rich. Contributed one million marks to party funds.* In one of his pockets Maigret found a hotel bill from the Kaiserhof, in Berlin, where Otto Braun had stayed three days on his way from Stuttgart.

Meanwhile the five passengers were standing in the corridor, watching, some dismally and others angrily, the comings and goings of Chief Inspector Maigret. Pointing to the luggage rack above Braun, he asked, 'Are those his cases?'

'They're mine,' came the sharp voice of Lena Leinbach, the Austrian.

'Will you take the seat you had last night?'

She did so reluctantly, and her unsteady movements betrayed the effects of the drinks. She was beautifully dressed, and wore a mink coat, and a ring on every finger. The report on her that was telegraphed from Vienna said: *Courtesan of the luxury class, who has had numerous affaires in the capitals of central Europe, but has never come to the attention of the police. Was for a long time the mistress of a German prince . . .*

'Which of you got on at Berlin?' Maigret asked, turning to the others.

'If you will allow me,' someone said in excellent French. And, in fact, it turned out to be a Frenchman, Adolphe Bonvoisin, from Lille. 'I can perhaps be of some help to you as I was on the train from Warsaw. There were two of us. I myself came from Lvov, where my firm – a textile concern – has a Polish subsidiary. Madame boarded the train at Warsaw at the same time as I did.' He indicated a middle-aged woman in an astrakhan coat, Jewish like Otto Braun, dark and heavily built, with swollen legs.

'Madame Irvitch of Vilna?'

As she spoke no French, the interview was conducted in German. Madame Irvitch, the wife of a wholesale furrier, was coming to Paris to consult a specialist, and she wished to lodge a protest . . .

'Sit down in the place you were occupying last night.'

Two passengers remained, two men.

'Name?' Maigret asked the first, a tall, thin, distinguished man with an officer's bearing.

'Thomas Hauke, of Hamburg.'

On Hauke, Berlin had had plenty to say: *Sentenced in 1924 to two years' imprisonment for dealing in stolen jewellery . . . closely watched since . . . frequents the pleasure spots of various European capitals . . . suspected of engaging in cocaine and morphine smuggling.*

Finally, the last one, a man of thirty-five, bespectacled, shaven-headed, severe. 'Dr Gellhorn,' he said, 'from Cologne.'

A silly misunderstanding arose. Maigret asked him why, when his fellow passenger was discovered unconscious, he had done nothing about it.

'Because I'm not a doctor of medicine. I'm an archaeologist.'

By now the compartment was occupied as it had been the previous night:

Otto Braun	Adolphe Bonvoisin	Madame Irvitch
Thomas Hauke	Dr Gellhorn	Lena Leinbach

Naturally, except for Otto Braun, henceforth incapable of giving evidence one way or another, each one protested entire innocence. And each one claimed to know nothing.

Maigret had already spent a quarter of an hour in another room with Jef Bebelmans, the acrobat from Antwerp who had appeared from under a carriage at Aulnoye carrying two to three million in bearer bonds. At first, when confronted with the corpse, Bebelmans had betrayed no emotion, merely asking, 'Who is it?' Then he had been found to be in possession of a third-class ticket from Berlin to Paris, although that had not prevented him spending part of the journey clinging to the bogies, no doubt to avoid declaring his bonds at the frontier.

Bebelmans, however, was not a talkative fellow. His one observation revealed a touch of humour: 'It's your business to ask questions. Unfortunately, I have absolutely nothing to tell you.' The information on him was not too helpful, either: *Formerly an acrobat, he had since been a nightclub waiter in Brussels, and later in Berlin.*

'Well now,' Maigret began, puffing away at his pipe despite the presence of the two women, 'you, Bonvoisin, and Madame Irvitch were already in the train at Warsaw. Who got in at Berlin?'

'Madame was first,' Bonvoisin said, indicating Lena Leinbach.

'And your cases, madame?'

She pointed to the rack above the dead man, where there were three luxurious crocodile cases, each in a fawn cover.

'So you put your luggage over this seat, and you sat down in the other corner. Diagonally opposite . . .'

'The dead man – I mean, that gentleman – came in next.' Bonvoisin asked nothing better than to go on talking.

'Without luggage?'

'All he had with him was a travelling-rug.'

Cue for consultation between Maigret and his nephew. New inventory of the dead man's wallet, in which a luggage slip was found. As the heavy luggage had by then reached Paris, Maigret sent telephone instructions that these pieces should be opened post-haste.

'Good! Now, this gentleman—' He motioned towards Hauke.

'He got in at Cologne.'

'Is that right, Monsieur Hauke?'

'To be precise, I changed compartments at Cologne. I was in a non-smoker.'

Dr Gellhorn, too, had got on at Cologne, where he lived. While Maigret, hands in pockets, was putting his questions, muttering away to himself, watching each of them in turn, Paul Vinchon, like a good secretary, was taking notes at a rapid rate. These notes read: *Bonvoisin: Until the German frontier, no one seemed to know anyone else, except for Madame Irvitch and myself. After the customs we all settled down to sleep as best we could, and the light was dimmed. At Liège I saw the lady opposite (Lena Leinbach) try to go out into the corridor. Immediately the gentleman in the other corner (Otto Braun) got up and asked her in German what she was doing. 'I want a breath of air,' she said. And I'm sure I heard him say, 'Stay where you are.'*

Later in his statement Bonvoisin returned to this point: *At Namur she tried once more to get out of the train, but Otto Braun, who seemed to be asleep, suddenly moved, and she stayed where she was. At Charleroi they spoke to each other again, but I was falling asleep and have only a hazy recollection.*

So, somewhere between Charleroi and Jeumont, in that

hour and a half or so, one of the passengers must have made the fatal move, must have got up, approached Otto Braun, and plunged a needle into his heart. Only Bonvoisin would not have needed to get up. He had only to move to the right to reach the German. Hauke's position, opposite the victim, was the next best, then came Dr Gellhorn, and finally the two women.

Despite the cold, Maigret's forehead was bathed with sweat. Lena Leinbach watched him furiously, while Madame Irvitch complained of rheumatism and consoled herself by talking Polish to Bonvoisin. Thomas Hauke was the most dignified of them all, and the most aloof, while Gellhorn claimed that he was missing an important appointment at the Louvre.

To return to Vinchon's notes, the following dialogue appears:

Maigret, to Lena: Where were you living in Berlin?
Lena: I was only there for a week. I was staying as usual at the Kaiserhof.
M: Did you know Otto Braun?
L: No. I may have run across him in the hall or the lift . . .
M: Why, then, after the German frontier did he start talking to you as if he knew you?
L: (dryly) Perhaps because he grew bolder away from home. In Germany a Jew is not allowed to make approaches to an Aryan woman.
M: Was that why he forbade you to get off the train at Liège and Namur?
L: He merely said I'd catch cold.

The questioning was still going on when there was a telephone call from Paris. Otto Braun's luggage – there were eight pieces – contained a great amount of clothing, and so much linen and personal stuff that one might have assumed the ex-banker was going off on a long trip, if not for ever. But no money – only four hundred marks in the notecase. As for the other passengers: Lena Leinbach was carrying 500 French francs, 50 marks, 30 crowns; Dr Gellhorn 700 marks; Thomas Hauke 40 marks and 20 French francs; Madame Irvitch 30 marks, 100 francs, and letters of credit on a Polish bank in Paris; Bonvoisin 12 zloty, 10 marks, 5,000 francs.

They still had to search the hand luggage that was in the compartment. Hauke's dressing-case held only one change of clothes, a dinner-jacket, and some underwear. In Bonvoisin's there were two marked packs of cards. But the real find came in Lena Leinbach's cases which, under the crystal-and-gold bottles, the fragile lingerie, and the gowns, had beautifully contrived false bottoms.

But the concealed compartments were empty. When questioned, all Lena Leinbach said was, 'I bought these cases from a lady who went in for smuggling. They were a great bargain. *I've* never used them for anything like that.'

Who had killed Otto Braun in the bluish half light of the compartment between Charleroi and Jeumont?

Paris was beginning to get worried. Maigret was summoned to the telephone. This business was going to cause a stir, and there would be complications. The numbers of the bonds found on Jef Bebelmans had been transmitted to the leading banks, and they seemed to be in order.

It was eleven o'clock when they started this laborious reconstruction in the railway carriage. It was two o'clock before they got out, and then only because Madame Irvitch fainted after declaring in Polish she could no longer bear the smell of the corpse.

Paul Vinchon was pale, for it seemed to him that his uncle was not showing his usual composure, that he was, in fact, dithering.

'It's not going well, Nunk?' he said in a low voice as they were crossing the tracks.

Maigret's only response was to sigh, 'I wish I could find the needle. Hold them all another hour.'

'But Madame Irvitch is ill!'

'What's that to do with me?'

'Dr Gellhorn claims—'

'Let him,' the chief inspector cut him short.

And he went off to lunch on his own at the station bar.

'Be quiet, I tell you!' Maigret snapped, an hour later. His nephew hardly knew where to look. 'All you do is bring me trouble. I'm going to tell you my conclusions. After that, I warn you, you can get yourself out of this mess, and if you don't, you needn't bother to ring up your nunk. Nunk's had enough . . .'

Then, changing his tone, he went on, 'Now! I've been looking for the one logical explanation of the facts. It's up to you to prove it, or to obtain a confession. Try to follow me.

'First, Otto Braun, with all his wealth, would not have come to France with eight cases and goodness knows how many suits – and, on the other hand, with precisely four hundred marks.

'Second, there must have been some reason for him to pretend during the German part of the journey not to know Lena Leinbach, and then as soon as they were over the Belgian border for them to be on the most familiar terms.

'Third, he refused to let her get out of the train at Liège, at Namur, and at Charleroi.

'Fourth, in spite of that she made several desperate attempts to get out.

'Fifth, a certain Jef Bebelmans, a passenger from Berlin who had never seen Braun – or he would have shown some sign on seeing the corpse – was found carrying two or three million in bonds.'

And, still in a very bad temper, Maigret rumbled on, 'Now I'll explain. Otto Braun, as a Jew, would like to see his fortune, or part of it, outside Germany. Knowing that his luggage will be minutely searched, he comes to an agreement with a *demi-mondaine* in Berlin, and has double-bottomed suitcases made for her, knowing that they stand less chance of being closely examined, being full of feminine articles.

'But Lena Leinbach, like all self-respecting members of her calling, has one real love: Thomas Hauke. Hauke, who is a specialist in this line, arranges with Lena in Berlin – perhaps even in the Kaiserhof – that he will make off with the bonds hidden in her cases.

'She gets on the train first, and puts the cases where Braun, still suspicious, has told her to put them. She sits down in the opposite corner, for they are not supposed to know each other.

'At Cologne Hauke, to keep an eye on things, comes to take his place in the compartment. Meanwhile another accomplice, probably a professional burglar, Jef Bebelmans, is travelling third with the bonds, and at each frontier has orders to get down for a spell underneath the carriage.

'Once the Belgian frontier is crossed, Otto Braun obviously runs no further risk. He could at any moment take it into his head to open his companion's cases and remove his bonds. That is why, first at Liège, then at Namur, and again at Charleroi, Lena Leinbach tries to get off the train and take French leave.

'Is Braun mistrustful? Does he suspect something? Or is he just in love with her? Whichever it is, he watches Lena closely, and she begins to panic, for in Paris he will inevitably discover the theft. He may even notice it at the French frontier where, having no reason to hide the bonds, he will want to open the concealed compartment. Thomas Hauke, too, must be aware of the situation—'

'And it's he who kills Braun?' Vinchon asked.

'I'm certain it is not. If Hauke had got up to do that, one or other of his travelling companions would have seen him.

In my opinion, Braun was killed when you went past the first time, calling, "Have your passports ready, please."

'At that moment everyone got up, in the dark, still half asleep. Only Lena Leinbach had a reason to go over to Braun, press close to him to take down her cases, and I am convinced that it was at that moment—'

'But the needle?'

'Look for it!' Maigret grunted. 'A brooch pin will do. If this woman had not happened on someone like you, who insisted on undressing the corpse, for a long time it would have seemed to be death from natural causes. It's all your fault that we're in this mess. Now draw up your plan. Make Lena think Bebelmans has talked, make Bebelmans think Hauke has been caught out – all the old dodges, eh?'

And he went off to have a beer while Vinchon did what his uncle had told him. Old dodges are good dodges because they work. In this case they worked because Lena Leinbach was wearing an enormous arrow-shaped pin of brilliants in her hat, and because Paulie, as Madame Maigret called him, pointing at it, said to her, 'You can't deny it. There's blood on the pin!'

It wasn't true. But, for all that, she had a fit of hysterics and made a full confession.

Three-Ten to Yuma

ELMORE LEONARD

The Wild West and railways are forever linked in popular imagination, the one having ultimately been won over by the other. Here again a constant flow of novels and movies has featured the violence and lawlessness of the old West where the gun ruled and the job of the lawman was an unenviable task. It is a fact, too, that the very first *story* film of the cinema was a tale of crime set in the West, *The Great Train Robbery*, made in 1903 with 'Bronco Billy' Anderson as the first of countless lawmen who have set out in pursuit of train robbers. The picture featured three Baldwin 4-4-0 locomotives and was shot on the Delaware and Lackawanna Western Railroad near Paterson, New Jersey. By 1952, when *High Noon*, one of the most famous Western movies of all time, was released, the Sierra Railroad, not far from Hollywood, had become a familiar location for railway scenes and was used in this classic story of a marshal played by Gary Cooper who resolutely defends his own town against outlaws. A Rogers 4-6-0, number 4493, built originally in 1891, which had also been used almost as frequently as the railroad by film makers, made an impressive appearance. Several other Westerns made in the fifties and featuring the railroad set standards of excellence that have never been surpassed: in particular *Bad Day at Black Rock* starring Spencer Tracy and Robert Ryan (1954); *Man of the West* featuring Gary Cooper again with Lee J. Cobb (1956); and this next story adapted for the movies in 1957.

Three-Ten to Yuma, shot in black and white, was based

on a short story by Elmore John Leonard (1925–), the New Orleans-born novelist now regarded as one of the finest writers of crime and suspense novels in the world. It was published originally in 1953 in *Dime Western Magazine*, to which he had been contributing short stories for the previous two years as a diversion from his day job as an advertising copywriter in Detroit. Publication of the story also coincided with the appearance of Leonard's first novel, *The Bounty Hunters*, and it was to be several years before he would switch from Westerns to the crime stories that have earned him his enduring fame. 'Three-Ten to Yuma' is about a hard-up farmer who is holding a notorious outlaw in a hotel waiting for the train to take him to prison. It was adapted for the screen by Halsted Welles and directed with great panache by Delmar Daves who drew outstanding performances from Van Heflin as the farmer and Glenn Ford as his prisoner. Much of the location shooting was done around the Warnerville station on the Sierra Railroad and the atmosphere was wonderfully evoked by a stirring theme tune by Frankie Laine.

Despite the success of this movie, Elmore Leonard remained in advertising until 1961 when he became a writer of industrial and educational films. In 1963 he opened his own advertising agency and it was to be another four years before he finally became a full-time author. To date he has written thirty-two novels, the more recent ones featuring the hoods, low-lifes and con artists of Florida which has become his favourite locale – and the stamping ground of his most regular character, Marshal Raylan Givens, the law officer with a penchant for cowboy boots and shooting bad guys. The story which brings this section of classics to a close is both a reminder of a famous railway movie as well as an early example of the talent of the man who was named Grandmaster of the Mystery Writers of America in 1992 – the organisation's highest honour – and of whom Martin Amis wrote recently in the *New York*

Times, 'Elmore Leonard is a literary genius who just happens to write thrillers.'

* * *

He had picked up his prisoner at Fort Huachuca shortly after midnight and now, in a silent early morning mist, they approached Contention. The two riders moved slowly, one behind the other.

Entering Stockman Street, Paul Scallen glanced back at the open country with the wet haze blanketing its flatness, thinking of the long night ride from Huachuca, relieved that this much was over. When his body turned again, his hand moved over the sawed-off shotgun that was across his lap and he kept his eyes on the man ahead of him until they were near the end of the second block, opposite the side entrance of the Republic Hotel.

He said just above a whisper, though it was clear in the silence, 'End of the line.'

The man turned in his saddle, looking at Scallen curiously, 'The jail's around on Commercial.'

'I want you to be comfortable.'

Scallen stepped out of the saddle, lifting a Winchester from the boot, and walked toward the hotel's side door. A figure stood in the gloom of the doorway, behind the screen, and as Scallen reached the steps the screen door opened.

'Are you the marshal?'

'Yes, sir.' Scallen's voice was soft and without emotion. 'Deputy, from Bisbee.'

'We're ready for you. Two-oh-seven. A corner . . . fronts on Commercial.' He sounded proud of the accommodation.

'You're Mr Timpey?'

The man in the doorway looked surprised. 'Yeah, Wells Fargo. Who'd you expect?'

'You might have got a back room, Mr Timpey. One with no windows.' He swung the shotgun on the man still mounted. 'Step down easy, Jim.'

The man, who was in his early twenties, a few years younger than Scallen, sat with one hand over the other on the saddle horn. Now he gripped the horn and swung down. When he was on the ground his hands were still close together, iron manacles holding them three chain lengths apart. Scallen motioned him toward the door with the stubby barrel of the shotgun.

'Anyone in the lobby?'

'The desk clerk,' Timpey answered him, 'and a man in a chair by the front door.'

'Who is he?'

'I don't know. He's asleep . . . got his brim down over his eyes.'

'Did you see anyone out on Commercial?'

'No . . . I haven't been out there.' At first he had seemed nervous, but now he was irritated, and a frown made his face pout childishly.

Scallen said calmly, 'Mr Timpey, it was your line this man robbed. You want to see him go all the way to Yuma, don't you?'

'Certainly I do.' His eyes went to the outlaw, Jim Kidd, then back to Scallen hurriedly. 'But why all the melodrama? The man's under arrest – already been sentenced.'

'But he's not in jail till he walks through the gates at Yuma,' Scallen said. 'I'm only one man, Mr Timpey, and I've got to get him there.'

'Well, dammit . . . I'm not the law! Why didn't you bring men with you? All I know is I got a wire from our Bisbee office to get a hotel room and meet you here in the morning of November third. There weren't any instructions that I had to get myself deputised a marshal. That's your job.'

'I know it is, Mr Timpey,' Scallen said, and smiled, though it was an effort. 'But I want to make sure no one knows Jim Kidd's in Contention until after train time this afternoon.'

Jim Kidd had been looking from one to the other with a faintly amused grin. Now he said to Timpey, 'He means he's afraid somebody's going to jump him.' He smiled at Scallen. 'That marshal must've really sold you a bill of goods.'

'What's he talking about?' Timpey said.

Kidd went on before Scallen could answer. 'They hid me in the Huachuca lockup 'cause they knew nobody could get at me there . . . and finally the Bisbee marshal gets a plan. He and some others hopped the train in Benson last night, heading for Yuma with an army prisoner passed off as me.' Kidd laughed, as if the idea were ridiculous.

'Is that right?' Timpey said.

Scallen nodded. 'Pretty much right.'

'How does he know all about it?'

'He's got ears and ten fingers to add with.'

'I don't like it. Why just one man?'

'Every deputy from here down to Bisbee is out trying to scare up the rest of them. Jim here's the only one we caught,' Scallen explained – then added, 'Alive.'

Timpey shot a glance at the outlaw. 'Is he the one who killed Dick Moons?'

'One of the passengers swears he saw who did it . . . and he didn't identify Kidd at the trial.'

Timpey shook his head. 'Dick drove for us a long time. You know his brother lives here in Contention. When he heard about it he almost went crazy.' He hesitated, and then said again, 'I don't like it.'

Scallen felt his patience wearing away, but he kept his voice even when he said, 'Maybe I don't either . . . but what you like and what I like aren't going to matter a whole lot, with the marshal past Tucson by now. You can grumble about it all you want, Mr Timpey, as long as you keep it under your breath. Jim's got friends . . . and since I have to haul him clear across this territory, I'd just as soon they didn't know about it.'

Timpey fidgeted nervously. 'I don't see why I have to get dragged into this. My job's got nothing to do with law enforcement . . .'

'You have the room key?'

'In the door. All I'm responsible for is the stage run between here and Tucson—'

Scallen shoved the Winchester at him. 'If you'll take care of this and the horses till I get back, I'll be obliged to you . . . and I know I don't have to ask you not to mention we're at the hotel.'

He waved the shotgun and nodded and Jim Kidd went ahead of him through the side door into the hotel lobby. Scallen was a stride behind him, holding the stubby shotgun close to his leg. 'Up the stairs on the right, Jim.'

Kidd started up, but Scallen paused to glance at the figure in the armchair near the front. He was sitting on his spine with limp hands folded on his stomach and, as Timpey had described, his hat low over the upper part of his face. You've seen people sleeping in hotel lobbies before, Scallen told himself, and followed Kidd up the stairs. He couldn't stand and wonder about it.

Room 207 was narrow and high-ceilinged, with a single window looking down on Commercial Street. An iron bed was placed the long way against one wall and extended to the right side of the window, and along the opposite wall was a dresser with wash basin and pitcher and next to it a rough-board wardrobe. An unpainted table and two straight chairs took up most of the remaining space.

'Lay down on the bed if you want to,' Scallen said.

'Why don't you sleep?' Kidd asked. 'I'll hold the shotgun.'

The deputy moved one of the straight chairs near to the door and the other to the side of the table opposite the bed. Then he sat down, resting the shotgun on the table so that it pointed directly at Jim Kidd sitting on the edge of the bed near the window.

He gazed vacantly outside. A patch of dismal sky showed above the frame buildings across the way, but he was not sitting close enough to look directly down on to the street. He said, indifferently, 'I think it's going to rain.'

There was a silence, and then Scallen said, 'Jim, I don't have anything against you personally . . . this is what I get paid for, but I just want it understood that if you start across the seven feet between us, I'm going to pull both triggers at once – without first asking you to stop. That clear?'

Kidd looked at the deputy marshal, then his eyes drifted out the window again. 'It's kinda cold, too.' He rubbed his hands together and the three chain links rattled against each other. 'The window's open a crack. Can I close it?'

Scallen's grip tightened on the shotgun and he brought the barrel up, though he wasn't sure of it. 'If you can reach it from where you're sitting.'

Kidd looked at the window sill and said without reaching toward it, 'Too far.'

'All right,' Scallen said, rising. 'Lay back on the bed.' He worked his gun belt around so that now the Colt was on his left hip.

Kidd went back slowly, smiling. 'You don't take any chances, do you? Where's your sporting blood?'

'Down in Bisbee with my wife and three youngsters,' Scallen told him without smiling, and moved around the table.

There were no grips on the window frame. Standing with his side to the window, facing the man on the bed, he put the heel of his hand on the bottom ledge of the frame and shoved down hard. The window banged shut and with the slam he saw Jim Kidd kicking up off his back, his body straining to rise without his hands to help. Momentarily, Scallen hesitated and his finger tensed on the triggers.

Kidd's feet were on the floor, his body swinging up and his head down to lunge from the bed. Scallen took one step and brought his knee up hard against Kidd's face.

The outlaw went back across the bed, his head striking the wall. He lay there with his eyes open looking at Scallen.

'Feel better now, Jim?'

Kidd brought his hands up to his mouth, working the jaw around. 'Well, I had to try you out,' he said. 'I didn't think you'd shoot.'

'But you know I will the next time.'

For a few minutes Kidd remained motionless. Then he began to pull himself straight. 'I just want to sit up.'

Behind the table, Scallen said, 'Help yourself.' He watched Kidd stare out the window.

Then, 'How much do you make, marshal?' Kidd asked the question abruptly.

'I don't think it's any of your business.'

'What difference does it make?'

Scallen hesitated. 'A hundred and fifty a month,' he said, finally, 'some expenses, and a dollar bounty for every arrest against a Bisbee ordinance in the town limits.'

Kidd shook his head sympathetically. 'And you got a wife and three kids.'

'Well, it's more than a cowhand makes.'

'But you're not a cowhand.'

'I've worked my share of beef.'

'Forty a month and keep, huh?' Kidd laughed.

'That's right, forty a month,' Scallen said. He felt awkward. 'How much do you make?'

Kidd grinned. When he smiled he looked very young, hardly out of his teens. 'Name a month,' he said. 'It varies.'

'But you've made a lot of money.'

'Enough. I can buy what I want.'

'What are you going to be wanting the next five years?'

'You're pretty sure we're going to Yuma.'

'And you're pretty sure we're not,' Scallen said. 'Well,

I've got two train passes and a shotgun that says we are. What've you got?'

Kidd smiled. 'You'll see.' Then he said right after it, his tone changing. 'What made you join the law?'

'The money,' Scallen answered, and felt foolish as he said it. But he went on, 'I was working for a spread over by the Pantano Wash when Old Nana broke loose and raised hell up the Santa Rosa Valley. The army was going around in circles, so the Pima County marshal got up a bunch to help out and we tracked Apaches almost all spring. The marshal and I got along fine, so he offered me a deputy job if I wanted it.' He wanted to say that he had started for seventy-five and worked up to the one hundred and fifty, but he didn't.

'And then someday you'll get to be marshal and make two hundred.'

'Maybe.'

'And then one night a drunk cowhand you've never seen will be tearing up somebody's saloon and you'll go in to arrest him and he'll drill you with a lucky shot before you get your gun out.'

'So you're telling me I'm crazy.'

'If you don't already know it.'

Scallen took his hand off the shotgun and pulled tobacco and paper from his shirt pocket and began rolling a cigarette. 'Have you figured out yet what my price is?'

Kidd looked startled, momentarily, but the grin returned. 'No, I haven't. Maybe you come higher than I thought.'

Scallen scratched a match across the table, lit the cigarette, then threw it to the floor, between Kidd's boots. 'You don't have enough money, Jim.'

Kidd shrugged, then reached down for the cigarette. 'You've treated me pretty good. I just wanted to make it easy on you.'

The sun came into the room after a while. Weakly at first,

cold and hazy. Then it warmed and brightened and cast an oblong patch of light between the bed and the table. The morning wore on slowly because there was nothing to do and each man sat restlessly thinking about somewhere else, though it was a restlessness within and it showed on neither of them.

The deputy rolled cigarettes for the outlaw and himself and most of the time they smoked in silence. Once Kidd asked him what time the train left. He told him shortly after three, but Kidd made no comment.

Scallen went to the window and looked out at the narrow rutted road that was Commercial Street. He pulled a watch from his vest pocket and looked at it. It was almost noon, yet there were few people about. He wondered about this and asked himself if it was unnaturally quiet for a Saturday noon in Contention . . . or if it were just his nerves . . .

He studied the man standing under the wooden awning across the street, leaning idly against a support post with his thumbs hooked in his belt and his flat-crowned hat on the back of his head. There was something familiar about him. And each time Scallen had gone to the window – a few times during the past hour – the man had been there.

He glanced at Jim Kidd lying across the bed, then looked out the window in time to see another man moving up next to the one at the post. They stood together for the space of a minute before the second man turned a horse from the tie rail, swung up and rode off down the street. The man at the post watched him go and tilted his hat against the sun glare. And then it registered. With the hat low on his forehead Scallen saw him again as he had that morning. The man lying in the armchair . . . as if asleep.

He saw his wife, then, and the three youngsters and he could almost feel the little girl sitting on his lap where she had climbed up to kiss him goodbye, and he had promised to bring her something from Tucson. He didn't know why they had come to him all of a sudden. And after he had put them out of his mind, since there was no room now, there was an upset feeling inside as if he had swallowed something that would not go down all the way. It made his heart beat a little faster.

Jim Kidd was smiling up at him. 'Anybody I know?'

'I didn't think it showed.'

'Like the sun going down.'

Scallen glanced at the man across the street and then to Jim Kidd. 'Come here.' He nodded to the window. 'Tell me who your friend is over there.'

Kidd half rose and leaned over looking out the window, then sat down again. 'Charlie Prince.'

'Somebody else just went for help.'

'Charlie doesn't need help.'

'How did you know you were going to be in Contention?'

'You told the Wells Fargo man I had friends ... and about the posses chasing around in the hills. Figure it out for yourself. You could be looking out a window in Benson and seeing the same thing.'

'They're not going to do you any good.'

'I don't know any man who'd get himself killed for a hundred and fifty dollars.' Kidd paused. 'Especially a man with a wife and young ones ...'

Men rode to town in something less than an hour later. Scallen heard the horses coming up Commercial, and went to the window to see the six riders pull to a stop and range themselves in a line in the middle of the street facing the hotel. Charlie Prince stood behind them, leaning against the post. Then he moved away from it, leisurely, and stepped down into the street. He walked between the horses and stopped in front of them just below the window. He cupped his hands to his mouth and shouted, 'Jim!'

In the quiet street it was like a pistol shot.

Scallen looked at Kidd, seeing the smile that softened his

face and was even in his eyes. Confidence. It was all over him. And even with the manacles on you would believe that it was Jim Kidd who was holding the shotgun.

'What do you want me to tell him?' Kidd said.

'Tell him you'll write every day.'

Kidd laughed and went to the window, pushing it up by the top of the frame. It raised a few inches. Then he moved his hands under the window and it slid up all the way.

'Charlie, you go buy the boys a drink. We'll be down shortly.'

'Are you all right?'

'Sure I'm all right.'

Charlie Prince hesitated. 'What if you don't come down? He could kill you and say you tried to break . . . Jim you tell him what'll happen if we hear a gun go off.'

'He knows,' Kidd said, and closed the window. He looked at Scallen standing motionless with the shotgun under his arm. 'Your turn, marshal.'

'What do you expect me to say?'

'Something that makes sense. You said before I didn't mean a thing to you personally – what you're doing is just a job. Well, you figure out if it's worth getting killed for. All you have to do is throw your guns on the bed and let me walk out the door and you can go back to Bisbee and arrest all the drunks you want. Nobody's going to blame you with the odds stacked seven to one. You know your wife's not going to complain . . .'

'You should have been a lawyer, Jim.'

The smile began to fade from Kidd's face. 'Come on – what's it going to be?'

The door rattled with three knocks in quick succession. Abruptly the room was silent. The two men looked at each other and now the smile disappeared from Kidd's face completely.

Scallen moved to the side of the door, tiptoeing in his

high-heeled boots, then pointed his shotgun toward the bed. Kidd sat down.

'Who is it?'

For a moment there was no answer. Then he heard, 'Timpey.'

He glanced at Kidd who was watching him. 'What do you want?'

'I've got a pot of coffee for you.'

Scallen hesitated. 'You alone?'

'Of course I am. Hurry up, it's hot!'

He drew the key from his coat pocket, then held the shotgun in the crook of his arm as he inserted the key with one hand and turned the knob with the other. The door opened – and slammed against him, knocking him back against the dresser. He went off balance, sliding into the wardrobe, going down on his hands and knees, and the shotgun clattered across the floor to the window. He saw Jim Kidd drop to the floor for the gun . . .

'Hold it!'

A heavyset man stood in the doorway with a Colt pointing out past the thick bulge of his stomach. 'Leave that shotgun where it is.' Timpey stood next to him with the coffeepot in his hand. There was coffee down the front of his suit, on the door and on the flooring. He brushed at the front of his coat feebly, looking from Scallen to the man with the pistol.

'I couldn't help it, marshal – he made me do it. He threatened to do something to me if I didn't.'

'Who is he?'

'Bob Moons . . . you know, Dick's brother . . .'

The heavyset man glanced at Timpey angrily. 'Shut your damn whining.' His eyes went to Jim Kidd and held there. 'You know who I am, don't you?'

Kidd looked uninterested. 'You don't resemble anybody I know.'

'You didn't have to know Dick to shoot him!'

'I didn't shoot that messenger.'

Scallen got to his feet, looking at Timpey. 'What the hell's wrong with you?'

'I couldn't help it. He forced me.'

'How did he know we were here?'

'He came in this morning talking about Dick and I felt he needed some cheering up, so I told them Jim Kidd had been tried and was being taken to Yuma and was here in town . . . on his way. Bob didn't say anything and went out, and a little later he came back with the gun.'

'You damn fool.' Scallen shook his head wearily.

'Never mind all the talk.' Moons kept the pistol on Kidd. 'I would've found him sooner or later. This way, everybody gets saved a long train ride.'

'You pull that trigger,' Scallen said, 'and you'll hang for murder.'

'Like he did for killing Dick . . .'

'A jury said he didn't do it.' Scallen took a step toward the big man. 'And I'm damned if I'm going to let you pass another sentence.'

'You stay put or I'll pass sentence on you!'

Scallen moved a slow step nearer. 'Hand me the gun, Bob.'

'I'm warning you – get the hell out of the way and let me do what I came for.'

'Bob, hand me the gun or I swear I'll beat you through that wall.'

Scallen tensed to take another step, another slow one. He saw Moons's eyes dart from him to Kidd and in that instant he knew it would be his only chance. He lunged, swinging his coat aside with his hand and when the hand came up it was holding a Colt. All in one motion. The pistol went up and chopped an arc across Moons's head before the big man could bring his own gun around. His hat flew off as the barrel swiped his skull and he went back against the wall heavily, then sank to the floor.

Scallen wheeled to face the window, thumbing the hammer back. But Kidd was still sitting on the edge of the bed with the shotgun at his feet.

The deputy relaxed, letting the hammer ease down. 'You might have made it, that time.'

Kidd shook head. 'I wouldn't have got off the bed.' There was a note of surprise in his voice. 'You know, you're pretty good . . .'

At 2.15 Scallen looked at his watch, then stood up, pushing the chair back. The shotgun was under his arms. In less than an hour they would leave the hotel, walk over Commercial to Stockman and then up Stockman to the station. Three blocks. He wanted to go all the way. He wanted to get Jim Kidd on that train . . . but he was afraid.

He was afraid of what he might do once they were on the street. Even now his breath was short and occasionally he would inhale and let the air out slowly to calm himself. And he kept asking himself if it was worth it.

People would be in the windows and the doors though you wouldn't see them. They'd have their own feelings and most of their hearts would be pounding . . . and they'd edge back of the door frames a little more. The man out on the street was something without a human nature or a personality of its own. He was on a stage. The street was another world.

Timpey sat on the chair in front of the door and next to him, squatting on the floor with his back against the wall, was Moons. Scallen had unloaded Moons's pistol and placed it in the pitcher behind him. Kidd was on the bed.

Most of the time he stared at Scallen. His face bore a puzzled expression, making his eyes frown, and sometimes he would cock his head as if studying the deputy from a different angle.

Scallen stepped to the window now. Charlie Prince and another man were under the awning. The others were not in sight.

'You haven't changed your mind?' Kidd asked him seriously.

Scallen shook his head.

'I don't understand you. You risk your neck to save my life, now you'll risk it again to send me to prison.'

Scallen looked at Kidd and suddenly felt closer to him than any man he knew. 'Don't ask me, Jim,' he said, and sat down again.

After that he looked at his watch every few minutes.

At five minutes to three he walked to the door, motioning Timpey aside, and turned the key in the lock. 'Let's go, Jim.' When Kidd was next to him he prodded Moons with the gun barrel. 'Over on the bed, mister, if I see or hear about you on the street before train time, you'll face an attempted murder charge.' He motioned Kidd past him, then stepped into the hall and locked the door.

They went down the stairs and crossed the lobby to the front door, Scallen a stride behind with the shotgun barrel almost touching Kidd's back. Passing through the doorway he said as calmly as he could, 'Turn left on Stockman and keep walking. No matter what you hear, keep walking.'

As they stepped out into Commercial, Scallen glanced at the ramada where Charlie Prince had been standing, but now the saloon porch was an empty shadow. Near the corner, two horses stood under a sign that said EAT in red letters; and on the other side of Stockman the signs continued, lining the rutted main street to make it seem narrower. And beneath the signs, in the shadows, nothing moved. There was a whisper of wind along the ramadas. It whipped sand specks from the street and rattled them against clapboard, and the sound was hollow and lifeless. Somewhere a screen door banged, far away.

They passed the café, turning on to Stockman. Ahead, the deserted street narrowed with distance to a dead end at the rail station – a single-storey building standing by itself, low and sprawling with most of the platform in shadow.

The westbound was there, along the platform, but the engine and most of the cars were hidden by the station house. White steam lifted above the roof to be lost in the sun's glare.

They were almost to the platform when Kidd said over his shoulder, 'Run like hell while you're still able.'

'Where are they?'

Kidd grinned, because he knew Scallen was afraid. 'How should I know?'

'Tell them to come out in the open!'

'Tell them yourself.'

'Dammit, *tell* them!' Scallen clenched his jaw and jabbed the short barrel into Kidd's back. 'I'm not fooling. If they don't come out, I'll kill you!'

Kidd felt the gun barrel hard against his spine and suddenly he shouted, 'Charlie!'

It echoed in the street, but after there was only the silence. Kidd's eyes darted over the shadowed porches. 'Dammit, Charlie – hold on!'

Scallen prodded him up the warped plank steps to the shade of the platform and suddenly he could feel them near. 'Tell them again!'

'Don't shoot, Charlie!' Kidd screamed the words.

From the other side of the station they heard the trainsman's call trailing off, '. . . Gila Bend, Sentinel, Yuma!'

The whistle sounded loud, wailing, as they passed into the shade of the platform, then out again to the naked glare of the open side. Scallen squinted, glancing toward the station office, but the train dispatcher was not in sight. Nor was anyone. 'It's the mail car,' he said to Kidd. 'The second to last one.' Steam hissed from the iron cylinder of the engine, clouding that end of the platform. 'Hurry it up!' he snapped, pushing Kidd along.

Then, from behind, hurried footsteps on the planking, and, as the hiss of steam died away – 'Stand where you are!'

The locomotive's main rods strained back, rising like the legs of a grotesque grasshopper, and the wheels moved. The connecting rods stopped on an upward swing and couplings clanged down the line of cars.

'Throw the gun away, brother!'

Charlie Prince stood at the corner of the station house with a pistol in each hand. Then he moved around carefully between the two men and the train. 'Throw it far away, and unhitch your belt,' he said.

'Do what he says,' Kidd said. 'They've got you.'

The others, six of them, were strung out in the dimness of the platform shed. Grim-faced, stubbles of beard, hat brims low. The man nearest Prince spat tobacco lazily.

Scallen knew fear at that moment as fear had never gripped him before; but he kept the shotgun hard against Kidd's spine. He said, just above a whisper, 'Jim – I'll cut you in half!'

Kidd's body was stiff, his shoulders drawn up tightly. 'Wait a minute . . .' he said. He held his palms out to Charlie Prince, though he could have been speaking to Scallen.

Suddenly Prince shouted, 'Go down!'

There was a fraction of a moment of dead silence that seemed longer. Kidd hesitated. Scallen was looking at the gunman over Kidd's shoulder, seeing the two pistols. Then Kidd was gone, rolling on the planking, and the pistols were coming up, one ahead of the other. Without moving, Scallen squeezed both triggers of the scatter gun.

Charlie Prince was going down, holding his hands tight to his chest, as Scallen dropped the shotgun and swung around drawing his Colt. He fired hurriedly. *Wait for a target!* Words in his mind. He saw the men under the platform shed, three of them breaking for the station office, two going full length to the planks . . . one crouching, his pistol up. *That one! Get him quick!* Scallen aimed and

157

squeezed the heavy revolver and the man went down. *Now get the hell out!*

Charlie Prince was face down. Kidd was crawling, crawling frantically and coming to his feet when Scallen reached him. He grabbed Kidd by the collar savagely, pushing him on and dug the pistol into his back. 'Run, damn you!'

Gunfire erupted from the shed and thudded into the wooden caboose as they ran past it. The train was moving slowly. Just in front of them a bullet smashed a window of the mail car. Someone screamed, 'You'll hit Jim!' There was another shot, then it was too late. Scallen and Kidd leaped up on the car platform and were in the mail car as it rumbled past the end of the station platform.

Kidd was on the floor, stretched out along a row of mail sacks. He rubbed his shoulder awkwardly with his manacled hands and watched Scallen who stood against the wall next to the open door.

Kidd studied the deputy for some minutes. Finally he said, 'You know, you really earn your hundred and a half.'

Scallen heard him, though the iron rhythm of the train wheels and his breathing were loud in his temples. He felt as if all his strength had been sapped, but he couldn't help smiling at Jim Kidd. He was thinking pretty much the same thing.

2
TRACKED DOWN
The Railway Detectives

A detective, if he is wise, takes pains to make and keep as many friends as possible among transfer company, express company and railroad employees.

DASHIELL HAMMETT

The Adventure of the
First-Class Carriage

RONALD A. KNOX,
after SIR ARTHUR CONAN DOYLE

Probably no other fictional detective is more closely associated with the railways than Sherlock Holmes. The great sleuth of Baker Street not only used the train on numerous occasions when involved in criminal investigations – mostly dramatically in 'The Final Problem' when he was fleeing to the Continent from his arch-enemy, Professor Moriarty, for what was ostensibly to be their final confrontation at the Reichenbach Falls – but also put his knowledge of schedules and the operating of the railway systems to use in solving particularly baffling cases. During Holmes's era the railways offered the fastest, most efficient and reliable means of transport, and a detective could, if he required and had the resources, hire a 'Special' – an engine and its own carriage: cost five shillings or thirty pence per mile! – to chase a villain. And it is fact that no self-respecting investigator of the Victorian era and early twentieth century would ever set out without first consulting his copy of *Bradshaw's Railway Guide*.

In Holmes's adventures written by Sir Arthur Conan Doyle (1859–1930), he solved one case, 'Silver Blaze', through working out the speed of a train by counting telegraph posts as they sped by the window of his compartment; surmised that the jerky writing of a letter in 'The Norwood Builder' had resulted from its being undertaken in a moving train; and spent a considerable amount of time on the London Underground during the case of 'The Bruce-Partington Plans', which resulted from the discovery of a body near Aldgate station. Apart from his express journeys to distant parts of England including the West Country, the Midlands, Birmingham and even further north, Holmes was equally at home on the suburban lines and took numerous trips with Dr Watson to places like Woolwich, Norbury, Streatham, Croydon, Beckenham and Chislehurst – always travelling first class, of course, and in a smoking compartment. Cries from Holmes such as, 'Look up the trains, Watson!' – 'There is one at 5.20 from Liverpool Street' ('The Retired Colourman') echo throughout the pages of many of the investigations and still have a familiar ring about them today. Even Holmes, though, was capable of mistakes – as in 'The Dancing Man' where the pair found themselves stranded in the wilds of East Anglia after missing the last train from North Walsham.

Ronald Knox (1888–1957) was a detective story writer and Catholic priest who in 1930 instituted the study of the Sherlock Holmes stories which has since become a world-wide 'industry'. One of his earliest investigations was to query the Birmingham trip by 'The Stockbroker's Clerk' which apparently began at Paddington but ended at New Street instead of Snow Hill as it should have done. His lifelong interest in railways had, in fact, inspired his own first mystery novel, *The Viaduct Murder* (1925), and later prompted the following Sherlockian pastiche published in the February 1947 issue of the *Strand Magazine* (where, of course, the Sherlock Holmes cases had first appeared) which is so faithful to the style of the originals that it might easily have come from the pen of Conan Doyle himself. Judge for yourself as we join the master and Dr Watson on a journey from Paddington to try and solve a particularly difficult crime.

***

The general encouragement extended to my efforts by the public is my excuse, if excuse were needed, for continuing to act as chronicler of my friend Sherlock Holmes. But even if I confine myself to those cases in which I have had the honour of being personally associated with him, I find it difficult to make a selection among the large amount of matter at my disposal.

As I turn over my records, I find that some of them deal with events of national or even international importance; but the time has not yet come when it would be safe to disclose (for instance) the true facts about the recent change of government in Paraguay. Others (like the case of the Missing Omnibus) would do more to gratify the modern craving for sensation; but I am well aware that my friend himself is the first to deplore it when I indulge what is, in his own view, a weakness.

My preference is for recording incidents whose bizarre features gave special opportunity for the exercise of that analytical talent which he possessed in such a marked degree. Of these, the case of the Tattooed Nurseryman and that of the Luminous Cigar-Box naturally suggest themselves to the mind. But perhaps my friend's gifts were even more signally displayed when he had occasion to investigate the disappearance of Mr Nathaniel Swithinbank, which provoked so much speculation in the early days of September, five years back.

Mr Sherlock Holmes was, of all men, the least influenced by what are called class distinctions. To him the rank was but the guinea stamp; a client was a client. And it did not surprise me, one evening when I was sitting over the familiar fire in Baker Street – the days were sunny but the evenings were already falling chill – to be told that he was expecting a visit from a domestic servant, a woman who 'did' for a well-to-do, childless couple in the southern Midlands.

'My last visit,' he explained, 'was from a countess. Her

mind was uninteresting, and she had no great regard for the truth; the problem she brought was quite elementary. I fancy Mrs John Hennessy will have something more important to communicate.'

'You have met her already, then?'

'No, I have not had the privilege. But anyone who is in the habit of receiving letters from strangers will tell you the same – handwriting is often a better form of introduction than hand-shaking. You will find Mrs Hennessy's letter on the mantelpiece; and if you care to look at her j's and her w's, in particular, I think you will agree that it is no ordinary woman we have to deal with. Dear me, there is the bell ringing already; in a moment or two, if I mistake not, we shall know what Mrs Hennessy, of the Cottage, Guiseborough St Martin, wants of Sherlock Holmes.'

There was nothing in the appearance of the old dame who was shown up, a few minutes later, by the faithful Mrs Hudson to justify Holmes's estimate. To the outward view she was a typical representative of her class; from the bugles on her bonnet to her elastic-sided boots everything suggested the old-fashioned caretaker such as you may see polishing the front doorsteps of a hundred office buildings any spring morning in the city of London. Her voice, when she spoke, was articulated with unnecessary care, as that of the respectable working-class woman is apt to be. But there was something precise and businesslike about the statement of her case which made you feel that this was a mind which could easily have profited by greater educational advantages.

'I have read of you, Mr Holmes,' she began, 'and when things began to go wrong up at the Hall it wasn't long before I thought to myself, if there's one man in England who will be able to see light here, it's Mr Sherlock Holmes. My husband was in good employment, till lately, on the railway at Chester; but the time came when the rheumatism got hold of him, and after that nothing seemed to go well with us until he had thrown up his job, and we went to live in a country village not far from Banbury, looking out for any odd work that might come our way.

'We had only been living there a week when a Mr Swithinbank and his wife took the old Hall, that had long been standing empty. They were newcomers to the district, and their needs were not great, having neither chick nor child to fend for; so they engaged me and Mr Hennessy to come and live in the lodge, close by the house, and do all the work of it for them. The pay was good and the duties light, so we were glad enough to get the billet.'

'One moment!' said Holmes. 'Did they advertise, or were you indebted to some private recommendation for the appointment?'

'They came at short notice, Mr Holmes, and were directed to us for temporary help. But they soon saw that our ways suited them, and they kept us on. They were people who kept very much to themselves, and perhaps they did not want a set of maids who would have followers, and spread gossip in the village.'

'That is suggestive. You state your case with admirable clearness. Pray proceed.'

'All this was no longer ago than last July. Since then they have once been away in London, but for the most part they have lived at Guiseborough, seeing very little of the folk round about. Parson called, but he is not a man to put his nose in where he is not wanted, and I think they must have made it clear they would sooner have his room than his company. So there was more guessing than gossiping about them in the countryside. But, sir, you can't be in domestic employment without finding out a good deal about how the land lies; and it wasn't long before my husband and I were certain of two things. One was that Mr and Mrs Swithinbank were deep in debt. And the other was that they got on badly together.'

'Debts have a way of reflecting themselves in a man's

correspondence,' said Holmes, 'and whoever has the clearing of his waste-paper basket will necessarily be conscious of them. But the relations between man and wife? Surely they must have gone very wrong indeed before there is quarrelling in public.'

'That's as may be, Mr Holmes, but quarrel in public they did. Why, it was only last week I came in with the blancmange, and he was saying, "The fact is, no one would be better pleased than you to see me in my coffin." To be sure, he held his tongue after that, and looked a bit confused; and she tried to put a brave face on it. But I've lived long enough, Mr Holmes, to know when a woman's been crying. Then last Monday, when I'd been in drawing the curtains, he burst out just before I'd closed the door behind me, "The world isn't big enough for both of us." That was all I heard, and right glad I'd have been to hear less. But I've not come round here just to repeat servants'-hall gossip.

'Today, when I was cleaning out the waste-paper basket, I came across a scrap of a letter that tells the same story, in his own handwriting. Cast your eye over that, Mr Holmes, and tell me whether a Christian woman has the right to sit by and do nothing about it.'

She had dived her hand into a capacious reticule and brought out, with a triumphant flourish, her documentary evidence. Holmes knitted his brow over it, and then passed it on to me. It ran: 'Being of sound mind, whatever the numbskulls on the jury may say of it.'

'Can you identify the writing?' my friend said.

'It was my master's,' replied Mrs Hennessy. 'I know it well enough; the bank, I am sure, will tell you the same.'

'Mrs Hennessy, let us make no bones about it. Curiosity is a well-marked instinct of the human species. Your eye having lighted on this document, no doubt inadvertently, I will wager you took a look round the basket for any other fragments it might contain.'

'That I did, sir; my husband and I went through it carefully together, for who knew but the life of a fellow-creature might depend on it? But only one other piece could we find written by the same hand, and on the same note-paper. Here it is.' And she smoothed out on her knee a second fragment, to all appearances part of the same sheet, yet strangely different in its tenor. It seemed to have been torn away from the middle of a sentence; nothing survived but the words 'in the reeds by the lake, taking a bearing at the point where the old tower hides both the middle first-floor windows'.

'Come,' I said, 'this at least gives us something to go upon. Mrs Hennessy will surely be able to tell us whether there are any landmarks in Guiseborough answering to this description.'

'Indeed there are, sir; the directions are plain as a pikestaff. There is an old ruined building which juts out upon the little lake at the bottom of the garden, and it would be easy enough to hit on the place mentioned. I daresay you gentlemen are wondering why we haven't been down to the lake-side ourselves to see what we could find there. Well, the plain fact is, we were scared. My master is a quiet-spoken man enough at ordinary times, but there's a wild look in his eye when he's roused, and I for one should be sorry to cross him. So I thought I'd come to you, Mr Holmes, and put the whole thing in your hands.'

'I shall be interested to look into your little difficulty. To speak frankly, Mrs Hennessy, the story you have told me runs on such familiar lines that I should have been tempted to dismiss the whole case from my mind. Dr Watson here will tell you that I am a busy man, and the affairs of the Bank of Mauritius urgently require my presence in London. But this last detail about the reeds by the lake-side is piquant, decidedly piquant, and the whole matter shall be gone into. The only difficulty is a practical one. How are we to explain my presence at Guiseborough without betraying to your employers the fact that you and your husband have been intruding on their family affairs?'

'I have thought of that, sir,' replied the old dame, 'and I think we can find a way out. I slipped away today easily enough because my mistress is going abroad to visit her aunt, near Dieppe, and Mr Swithinbank has come up to town with her to see her off. I must go back by the evening train, and had half thought of asking you to accompany me. But no, he would get to hear of it if a stranger visited the place in his absence. It would be better if you came down by the quarter past ten train tomorrow, and passed yourself off for a stranger who was coming to look at the house. They have taken it on a short lease, and plenty of folks come to see it without troubling to obtain an order-to-view.'

'Will your employer be back so early?'

'That is the very train he means to take; and to speak truth, sir, I should be the better for knowing that he was being watched. This wicked talk of making away with himself is enough to make anyone anxious about him. You cannot mistake him, Mr Holmes,' she went on; 'what chiefly marks him out is a scar on the left-hand side of his chin, where a dog bit him when he was a youngster.'

'Excellent, Mrs Hennessy; you have thought of everything. Tomorrow, then, on the quarter past ten for Banbury without fail. You will oblige me by ordering the station fly to be in readiness. Country walks may be good for health, but time is more precious. I will drive straight to your cottage, and you or your husband shall escort me on my visit to this desirable country residence and its mysterious tenant.' With a wave of his hand, he cut short her protestations of gratitude.

'Well, Watson, what did you make of her?' asked my companion when the door had closed on our visitor.

'She seemed typical of that noble army of women whose hard scrubbing makes life easy for the leisured classes. I could not see her well because she sat between us and the window, and her veil was lowered over her eyes. But her manner was enough to convince me that she was telling the truth, and that she is sincere in her anxiety to avert what may be an appalling tragedy. As to its nature, I confess I am in the dark. Like yourself, I was particularly struck by the reference to the reeds by the lake-side. What can it mean? An assignation?'

'Hardly, my dear Watson. At this time of the year a man runs enough risk of cold without standing about in a reed-bed. A hiding-place, more probably, but for what? And why should a man take the trouble to hide something, and then obligingly litter his waste-paper basket with clues to its whereabouts? No, these are deep waters, Watson, and we must have more data before we begin to theorise. You will come with me?'

'Certainly, if I may. Shall I bring my revolver?'

'I do not apprehend any danger, but perhaps it is as well to be on the safe side. Mr Swithinbank seems to strike his neighbours as a formidable person. And now, if you will be good enough to hand me the more peaceful instrument which hangs beside you, I will try out that air of Scarlatti's, and leave the affairs of Guiseborough St Martin to look after themselves.'

I often had occasion to deprecate Sherlock Holmes's habit of catching trains with just half a minute to spare. But on the morning after our interview with Mrs Hennessy we arrived at Paddington station no later than ten o'clock – to find a stranger, with a pronounced scar on the left side of his chin, gazing out at us languidly from the window of a first-class carriage.

'Do you mean to travel with him?' I asked, when we were out of earshot.

'Scarcely feasible, I think. If he is the man I take him for, he has secured solitude all the way to Banbury by the simple process of slipping half a crown into the guard's hand.'

And, sure enough, a few minutes later we saw that functionary shepherd a fussy-looking gentleman, who had been vigorously assaulting the locked door, to a compartment further on. For ourselves, we took up our post in the carriage next but one behind Mr Swithinbank. This, like the other first-class compartments, was duly locked when we had entered it; behind us the less fortunate passengers accommodated themselves in seconds.

'The case is not without its interest,' observed Holmes, laying down his paper as we steamed through Burnham Beeches. 'It presents features which recall the affairs of James Phillimore, whose disappearance (though your loyalty may tempt you to forget it) we investigated without success. But this Swithinbank mystery, if I mistake not, cuts even deeper. Why, for example, is the man so anxious to parade his intention of suicide, or fictitious suicide, in the presence of his domestic staff? It can hardly fail to strike you that he chose the moment when the good Mrs Hennessy was just entering the room, or just leaving it, to make those remarkable confidences to his wife. Not content with that, he must leave evidence of his intentions lying about in the waste-paper basket. And yet this involved the risk of having his plans foiled by good-natured interference. Time enough for his disappearance to become public when it became effective! And why, in the name of fortune, does he hide something only to tell us where he has hidden it?'

Amid a maze of railway tracks, we came to a standstill at Reading. Holmes craned his neck out of the window, but reported that all the doors had been left locked. We were not destined to learn anything about our elusive travelling companion until, just as we were passing the pretty hamlet of Tilehurst, a little shower of paper fragments fluttered past the window on the right-hand side of the compartment, and two of them actually sailed in through the space we had dedicated to ventilation on that bright morning of autumn. It may easily be guessed with what avidity we pounced on them.

The messages were in the same handwriting with which Mrs Hennessy's find had made us familiar; they ran, respectively, 'Mean to make an end of it all' and 'This is the only way out.' Holmes sat over them with knitted brows, till I fairly danced with impatience.

'Should we not pull the communication cord?' I asked.

'Hardly,' answered my companion, 'unless five pound notes are more plentiful with you than they used to be. I will even anticipate your next suggestion, which is that we should look out of the windows on either side of the carriage. Either we have a lunatic two doors off, in which case there is no use in trying to foresee his next move, or he intends suicide, in which case he will not be deterred by the presence of spectators, or he is a man with a scheming brain who is sending us these messages in order to make us behave in a particular way. Quite probably, he wants to make us lean out of the windows, which seems to me an excellent reason for not leaning out of the windows. At Oxford we shall be able to read the guard a lesson on the danger of locking passengers in.'

So indeed it proved; for when the train stopped at Oxford there was no passenger to be found in Mr Swithinbank's carriage. His overcoat remained, and his wide-awake hat; his portmanteau was duly identified in the guard's van. The door on the right-hand side of the compartment, away from the platform, had swung open; nor did Holmes's lens bring to light any details about the way in which the elusive passenger had made his exit.

It was an impatient horse and an injured cabman that awaited us at Banbury, when we drove through golden woodlands to the little village of Guiseborough St Martin, nestling under the shadow of Edge Hill. Mrs Hennessy met us at the door of her cottage, dropping an old-fashioned curtsy; and it may easily be imagined what wringing of hands, what wiping of eyes with her apron, greeted the announcement of her master's disappearance. Mr Hennessy, it seemed, had gone off to a neighbouring farm upon some errand, and it was the old dame herself who escorted us up to the Hall.

'There's a gentleman there already, Mr Holmes,' she informed us. 'Arrived early this morning and would take no denial; and not a word to say what business he came on.'

'That is unfortunate,' said Holmes. 'I particularly wanted a free field to make some investigation. Let us hope that he will be good enough to clear off when he is told that there is no chance of an interview with Mr Swithinbank.'

Guiseborough Hall stands in its own grounds a little way outside the village, the residence of a squire unmistakably, but with no airs of baronial grandeur. The old, rough walls have been refaced with pointed stone, the mullioned windows exchanged for a generous expanse of plate-glass, to suit a more recent taste, and a portico has been thrown out from the front door to welcome the traveller with its shelter. The garden descends at a precipitous slope from the main terrace, and a little lake fringes it at the bottom, dominated by a ruined eminence that serves the modern owner for a gazebo.

Within the house, furniture was of the scantiest, the Swithinbanks having evidently rented it with what fittings it had, and introduced little of their own. As Mrs Hennessy ushered us into the drawing-room, we were not a little surprised to be greeted by the wiry figure and melancholy features of our old rival, Inspector Lestrade.

'I knew you were quick off the mark, Mr Holmes,' he said, 'but it beats me how you ever heard of Mr Swithinbank's little goings-on; let alone that I didn't think you took much stock in cases of common fraud like this.'

'Common fraud?' repeated my companion. 'Why, what has he been up to?'

'Drawing cheques, and big ones, Mr Holmes, when he

knew that his bank wouldn't honour them; only little things of that sort. But if you're on his track I don't suppose he's far off, and I'll be grateful for any help you can give me to lay my hands on him.'

'My dear Lestrade, if you follow out your usual systematic methods, you will have to patrol the Great Western line all the way from Reading to Oxford. I trust you have brought a drag-net with you, for the line crossed the river no less than four times in the course of the journey.' And he regaled the astonished inspector with a brief summary of our investigations.

Our information worked like a charm on the little detective. He was off in a moment to find the nearest telegraph office and put himself in touch with Scotland Yard, with the Great Western Railway authorities, with the Thames Conservancy. He promised, however, a speedy return, and I fancy Holmes cursed himself for not having dismissed the jarvey who had brought us from the station, an undeserved windfall for our rival.

'Now, Watson!' he cried, as the sound of the wheels faded away into the distance.

'Our way lies to the lake-side, I presume.'

'How often am I to remind you that the place where the criminal tells you to look is the place not to look? No, the clue to the mystery lies, somehow, in the house, and we must hurry up if we are to find it.'

Quick as a thought, he began turning out shelves, cupboards, escritoires, while I, at his direction, went through the various rooms of the house to ascertain whether all was in order, and whether anything suggested the anticipation of a hasty flight. By the time I returned to him, having found nothing amiss, he was seated in the most comfortable of the drawing-room armchairs, reading a book he had picked out of the shelves – it dealt, if I remember right, with the aborigines of Borneo.

'The mystery, Holmes!' I cried.

'I have solved it. If you will look on the bureau yonder, you will find the household books which Mrs Swithinbank has obligingly left behind. Extraordinary how these people always make some elementary mistake. You are a man of the world, Watson; take a look at them and tell me what strikes you as curious.'

It was not long before the salient feature occurred to me. 'Why, Holmes,' I exclaimed, 'there is no record of the Hennessys being paid any wages at all!'

'Bravo, Watson! And if you will go into the figures a little more closely, you will find that the Hennessys apparently lived on air. So now the whole facts of the story are plain to you.'

'I confess,' I replied, somewhat crestfallen, 'that the whole case is as dark to me as ever.'

'Why, then, take a look at that newspaper I have left on the occasional table; I have marked the important paragraph in blue pencil.'

It was a copy of an Australian paper, issued some weeks previously. The paragraph to which Holmes had drawn my attention ran thus:

ROMANCE OF RICH MAN'S WILL

The recent lamented death of Mr John Macready, the well-known sheep-farming magnate, has had an unexpected sequel in the circumstance that the dead man, apparently, left no will. His son, Mr Alexander Macready, left for England some years back, owing to a misunderstanding with his father – it was said – because he announced his intention of marrying a lady from the stage. The young man has completely disappeared, and energetic steps are being taken by the lawyers to trace his whereabouts. It is estimated that the fortunate heirs, whoever they be, will be the richer by not far short of a hundred thousand pounds sterling.

Horse-hoofs echoed under the archway, and in another

minute Lestrade was again of our party. Seldom have I seen the little detective looking so baffled and ill at ease.

'They'll have the laugh of me at the Yard over this,' he said. 'We had word that Swithinbank was in London, but I made sure it was only a feint, and I came racing up here by the early train, instead of catching the quarter past ten and my man in it. He's a slippery devil, and he may be half-way to the Continent by this time.'

'Don't be downhearted about it, Lestrade. Come and interview Mr and Mrs Hennessy, at the lodge; we may get news of your man down there.'

A coarse-looking fellow in a bushy red beard sat sharing his tea with our friend of the evening before. His greasy waistcoat and corduroy trousers proclaimed him a manual worker. He rose to meet us with something of a defiant air; his wife was all affability.

'Have you heard any news of the poor gentleman?' she asked.

'We may have some before long,' answered Holmes. 'Lestrade, you might arrest John Hennessy for stealing that porter's cap you see on the dresser, the property of the Great Western Railway Company. Or, if you prefer an alternative charge, you might arrest him as Alexander Macready, alias Nathaniel Swithinbank.' And while we stood there literally thunder-struck, he tore off the red beard from a chin marked with a scar on the left-hand side.

'The case was difficult,' he said to me afterwards, 'only because we had no clue to the motive. Swithinbank's debts would almost have swallowed up Macready's legacy; so it was necessary for the couple to disappear, and take up the claim under a fresh alias. This meant a duplication of personalities, but it was not really difficult. She had been an actress; he had really been a railway porter in his hard-up days. When he got out at Reading, and passed along the six-foot way to take his place in a third-class carriage, nobody marked the circumstance, because on the way from London he had changed into a porter's clothes; he had the cap, no doubt, in his pocket. On the sill of the door he left open, he had made a little pile of suicide messages, hoping that when it swung open these would be shaken out and flutter into the carriages behind.'

'But why the visit to London? And, above all, why the visit to Baker Street?'

'That is the most amusing part of the story; we should have seen through it at once. He wanted Nathaniel Swithinbank to disappear finally, beyond all hope of tracing him. And who would hope to trace him, when Mr Sherlock Holmes, who was travelling only two carriages behind, had given up the attempt? Their only fear was that I should find the case uninteresting; hence the random reference to a hiding-place among the reeds, which so intrigued you. Come to think of it, they nearly had Inspector Lestrade in the same train as well. I hear he has won golden opinions with his superiors by cornering his man so neatly. *Sic vos non vobis*, as Virgil said of the bees; only they tell us nowadays the lines are not by Virgil.'

The Murder on the Okehampton Line

VICTOR L. WHITECHURCH

Victor Whitechurch, the creator of Godfrey Page, the first specialist railway detective, was like Ronald Knox a man of the church and began writing his cases about an astute crime solver in 1903 hard on the heels of Sherlock Holmes. Unlike Holmes, however, the stories about the pioneer railway sleuth did not appear in the *Strand*, but in its great rival publication, *Pearson's Weekly*. An even bigger mystery surrounds Whitechurch and Page, for until recently it was widely accepted that another of Victor Whitechurch's characters, Thorpe Hazell, whose adventures he contributed to the *Strand* from 1912 onwards, was actually the first railway detective; *vide* this entry by Ellery Queen in his definitive study of the detective–crime novel, *Queen's Quorum* (1969): 'Thorpe Hazell is a fanatical devotee of vegetarianism and setting-up exercises; more significant historically, he is the earliest short-story specialist in railway detection, antedating by four months Francis Lynde's "Scientific" Sprague.' (Of whom more next.)

Yet research into the files of *Pearson's* magazine by bibliographer George Locke has brought to light 'The Investigations of Godfrey Page, Railwayac' who himself predates Hazell by no less than six years, having made his debut in the December 1903 issue. Here, Victor Whitechurch introduces his character in these words: 'Godfrey Page takes the most intense interest – amounting almost to madness – in anything and everything connected with railways, and for this reason I have termed him a "railwayac" which is a shortened form of "railway maniac". By profession he is an architect, but being possessed of ample means, only works occasionally, spending his leisure in solving railway mysteries.'

Sadly, time has not dealt kindly with Godfrey Page. None of his cases were ever collected into a book, while those of his successor, Thorpe Hazell, were not only published in volume form immediately after their magazine appearances as *Thrilling Stories of the Railways* (1912), but have been reprinted as recently as 1977. The publication of Page's murder enquiry hereunder is therefore something of a landmark and one which further emphasises the claim of Victor Whitechurch to be regarded as a major figure in the detective story genre.

Whitechurch (1868–1933), a canon in the Anglican church, managed to combine the task of a busy minister in Didcot, Berkshire with writing stories of crime and mystery for *Harmsworth's Magazine*, *The Strand* and *Pearson's*. He was also one of the first contributors to the *Railway Magazine* founded in 1897. Like Ronald Knox, he had been fascinated by the railways ever since his childhood in East Anglia, and according to one of his biographers, Bryan Morgan, was a practical railwayman long before he began to write. 'He knew how to scotch a point,' says Morgan, 'what was the loading-gauge of the Great Northern and how long an engine took to re-water.' Whitechurch's first railway crime stories were written in the closing years of the nineteenth century – 'Donald Penstone's Escape' (*Pearson's*, October 1897) and 'Saved by a Train Wrecker' (*Strand*, August 1899) are two typical examples – but it was with Thorpe Hazell and, more particularly, with Godfrey Page that he added a new dimension to the railway mystery story. 'The Murder on the Okehampton Line' was the 'railwayac's' very first case.

* * *

The solution of the murder on the Okehampton line was, at best, only partial, and yet there can be no doubt whatever that Godfrey Page penetrated the mystery as deeply as it could be penetrated and that his theory was correct; in fact, though some links in the chain of evidence were missing, there was quite sufficient to prove that my brother-in-law had fathomed the leading points.

He was not pressed into the investigation, but took it up out of sheer curiosity.

I had been dining at his house one night and he had sent out for the last edition of the evening paper. I think there was a railway strike or something of the kind going on that interested him. But however that might be, his attention was caught directly he opened the paper with the following paragraph, which he handed me to read:

MURDER ON THE OKEHAMPTON LINE!
(A Railway Mystery)

On the arrival of the last train from Exeter to Okehampton at the latter station last night, a gruesome discovery was made. A porter on the platform noticed a gentleman seated in the corner of a third-class compartment and, as he made no attempt to get out of the carriage, opened the door to wake him, thinking he might be asleep. To his horror he discovered that the man was dead and a subsequent examination revealed the fact that he had been stabbed in the heart with some sharp instrument. There were signs of a struggle in the carriage.

The murdered man was dressed in a dark blue suit with a soft felt hat, but there was absolutely nothing on him to lead to his identification – not a scrap of paper of any sort.

That robbery was not the object is proved by the fact that some five or six pounds in gold and silver and his watch and chain were still on him.

Although the police were communicated with at once

nothing further has been ascertained up to going to press. The body has been removed to the White Hart Hotel and there awaits identification.

'Here's a mystery if you like,' said Godfrey Page. 'Let me see, the last down train arrives at Okehampton at ten-fifty. It's the one that leaves Waterloo at five-fifty and Exeter, St David's, at ten-thirty. Of course, the great question is – where did he get into the train and whereabouts on the journey was he murdered?'

'And who he was?' I added.

'Exactly. Do you know, I've half a mind to run down tomorrow and have a look at things. Would you care to come?'

'Well,' I said, 'I think I could spare the day.'

'It means two days. We'll go down tomorrow morning by the ten-thirty express from Paddington. I've been wanting to have a run on that train for a long time.'

'But Okehampton is on the L & SW Railway,' I ventured to suggest.

'I fancy I'm aware of that,' he replied snappishly, 'but I tell you I want a run on the Great Western. I've got a friend at Paddington, too, who'll give me a leg up. I'll write to him tonight. Meet me at Paddington at ten-fifteen under the clock.'

I found him waiting for me when I arrived, holding in his hand a newspaper and a letter.

'It's all right,' he said; 'I've got a line of introduction to the officials at St David's in case I want information. And there's a whole column about the case in this morning's paper. We'll read it as we go down.'

He spent the rest of the time before starting in noting the name of the engine, the number of the coaches, and other details of the express, and then we found ourselves in a comfortable carriage, speeding westward.

'Now,' he said, when we had read the paper, 'you see,

there are several new points in the case. Let's try and sum them up.

'First of all, the identity of the murdered man is still unknown. Secondly, you see, the crime must have been committed between Exeter and Okehampton, because the guard of the train remembers speaking to the man at Exeter. It appears that the guard put his head in the window just before the train started and said: "Where are you for, sir?" To which the man made a singular reply. He answered: "Where does this train go to?" Upon the guard saying "Okehampton," he simply replied, "All right." Now this seems to show that he was in a train *the destination of which he didn't know*.'

'And the next point evidently touches the murderer,' I said.

'Yes; I think so, too. Two men got off the train at Yeoford junction, telling the ticket-collector that there had been no time for them to get a ticket at St David's and paying him the fare. These two men seem to have disappeared. They could not have got away by train, for that was the last one at the junction that night. But it's only a seven or eight miles' walk back to Exeter, and that's probably how they've eluded search.

'Now, you see, this gives us two more points. First, if these two men committed the crime, they did it between Exeter and Yeoford; and secondly, the fact of their having no tickets proves our theory correct that the murdered man was in a train that was strange to him.'

'How so?'

'Because *they* didn't know where they were going either. They must have been following him. They saw him get into the Okehampton train and they got in after him.'

'But the guard said he was alone when he saw him at St David's and spoke to him.'

'Very likely. But the train had not quite started. There was time for them to get in – if not in his compartment in another one. And there *is* such a thing as walking along the footboard of a train in motion, and getting into another compartment. I've done it lots of times.

'Now,' he went on, 'acting on these theories, the next question is – what made the murdered man get into the Okehampton train, and where was he before he got in? Perhaps our good friend Bradshaw will help us.' He opened the book and consulted its pages carefully. 'I won't say what I think yet,' he remarked presently, 'but I've a sort of an idea. There's an island platform at St David's.'

'What on earth's that?'

He looked at me scornfully.

'An island platform is one between two lines, so that trains run on either side of it. But now I'm going to enjoy the run.'

I scarcely saw where the enjoyment came in. He was not still for five minutes together. At every station his head went out of the window, once or twice when we slowed down he grew impatient, but brightened up when he timed a mile in fifty-seven and three-fifths seconds. He made notes of all sorts of things and generally fidgeted during the whole journey.

'It's been a glorious run,' he exclaimed as we drew up at St David's. 'One hundred and ninety-four miles without a stop, and a minute ahead of scheduled time in spite of that signal against us at Taunton and the slowing down for the PW operations.'

'What's "PW"?' I asked.

'Permanent way, you ignoramus. Stop a minute. I want to speak to the driver.'

He was back in a few minutes.

'Our train leaves for Okehampton at three twenty-five,' he said. 'Now, we'll just have a chat with one of the officials here to begin with.'

We found our way to one of the officials, and Godfrey Page presented the letter of introduction.

'Ah, I've heard of you, Mr Page,' he said. 'You unearthed that strange affair at Warchester, didn't you? Well, I see you've come down to have a look at this Okehampton mystery. Can I do anything for you?'

'Not at present,' said my brother-in-law, 'except to tell me if the train in which the murder took place wasn't a bit late in starting from St David's.'

'Aha,' laughed the other, 'we Great Western men always like to get a rise out of the South-Western, you know. Yes, she *was* three or four minutes late.'

'That's all I want to know. It confirms me in a little theory, though. If I find out anything further at Okehampton I shall trouble you again.'

'Certainly. Anything we can do for you, please ask me. But it seems to me that it is a South-Western job, Mr Page.'

'Ah! I'm not so sure that your line isn't mixed up in it!'

Arrived at Okehampton we quickly found our way to the hotel. Godfrey Page made himself known to the detective-inspector on the premises and we were ushered by him into the room where the body of the murdered man had been taken. He lay in the bed, quiet and serene, with quite a smile upon his face.

He was a man of some five and thirty years of age, with very dark moustache and beard and a bronzed countenance which even death had not been able to stamp with pallor.

'Are there no marks about him?' asked Godfrey Page of the inspector.

'Only this,' and he turned down the sheet and showed the man's right arm, on which a small dragon was tattooed in black and red.

'Hm!' said my brother-in-law, 'looks as if he'd been in the Far East. Only a Chinese or Japanese artist could have done that.'

'Yes,' said the inspector, 'there was a silver dollar along with his money, too, which corroborates that.'

'Were there no marks on his clothes?'

'No.'

'May I look at them?'

'Here they are.'

The inspector narrowly watched Godfrey Page as he turned over garment after garment till he arrived at the shirt. It was an ordinary white one, but with a nasty red stain upon it that told its own tale.

'It's no use,' said the inspector, 'there's no name upon it.'

'By George, though, there's something else. Look, have you noticed this?'

And he pointed to a faint pencilling inside the starched linen cuff.

'What is it?' asked the inspector. 'Looks like a pencilled note. Strange we never noticed it.'

'You gentlemen don't always look everywhere. But I'll just jot that down, please. It's interesting.'

And he entered the following in his notebook, a copy of what had been scrawled on the dead man's shirt cuff: 242, E3 Great Marlow.

'I'll wire to Great Marlow at once,' said the inspector; 'it looks like a clue. It may be he's known there. It might even be the number of a street he knows, or something of that kind.'

'It might be,' returned Godfrey Page dryly. 'I'll only detain you one moment. Was anything else found on him besides money?'

'Only this knife.'

It was an ordinary, rather large, clasp knife. My brother-in-law opened it.

'The big blade's broken,' he said, 'and freshly done, too. Ah, and see how loose it is.'

'Now, sir,' said the inspector impatiently, 'if you've quite finished we'll go. I hope you won't mention what you've seen.'

'Not I. And you're really going to investigate at Great Marlow?'

'Certainly!'

'Ah! Perhaps the bit of blade broken off that knife lies somewhere by Great Marlow.'

The inspector stared at him with astonishment.

'I've heard of you as a sort of private detective where railways are concerned,' he said, 'but, if you'll excuse my saying so, you don't seem to know much about this kind of thing.'

'And perhaps you are as strangely ignorant of railways,' retorted Godfrey Page, 'but I don't bear you any malice. If I'm ever in a position to help you, I will.'

'Now,' he said to me, as we regained the street, 'there's just time for us to make a little purchase, and then we'll catch the five-twelve train back to Exeter.'

And, taking me into an ironmonger's shop, he bought a small screwdriver and put it into his pocket.

Arrived at Exeter we sought out the friendly GW official, and my brother-in-law at once began:

'I'm going to ask you for some rather curious information. We shall stay the night at Exeter, and if you can get it by tomorrow I shall be much obliged.'

'What is it, Mr Page?'

'Find out on what train the third-class coach numbered 242 was running the night before last, and where it is to be found tomorrow.'

The official promised to do so.

Godfrey Page refused to say another word on the subject that night. The next morning we went to St David's and sought out our friend.

'Well?' asked the 'railwayac'.

'I've got you the information, but I don't see how it will help you. Number 242 third coach is one that at present is kept at Plymouth as a spare carriage in case there is an abnormal number of passengers for the Paddington express. The night to which you refer it ran—'

'On the eight-twenty p.m. from North Road, Plymouth, arriving here at 10.03.'

'How on earth did you know that, for it's quite true?'

'It was only my little theory,' said Page, with a smile, 'but go on.'

'It was put on to the up-corridor express at Plymouth because some passengers, arriving by a P&O steamer, increased the demand for room on that train. You know, perhaps, that if we have over twenty-four P&O passengers we run a "boat special", but not if we take them by ordinary express. On this occasion only sixteen travelled to London.'

'And where is number 242 now?' asked Page impatiently.

'Here.'

'Here?'

'Yes. It was running back to Plymouth last night and I took the liberty of detaining it here because you seemed interested in it.'

Godfrey Page was jubilant.

'Let's go and see it at once,' he said, drawing the screwdriver out of his pocket.

'What do you want that for?' asked the official.

'You'll see,' was the only reply he would make.

We very soon reached the siding where the third-class carriage was standing. Page counted down the fifth compartment and climbed in. We followed.

'Now,' said he to me, 'what do you see? Notice that!' And he pointed above the door. There I read as follows: 242, E. 'All the compartments are lettered, you see,' went on Page, 'and E, of course, is the fifth compartment from the end, commencing with A. Now look at those photographs!'

As is customary in Great Western carriages there were

photographs of places of interest along the line over the seats.

'Great Scott!' I exclaimed.

'Great Marlow! you mean,' said my brother-in-law triumphantly, for there, before me, was a photograph of that picturesque Thames town.

'Now,' said Godfrey Page, 'I'll give you my theory, and then we'll see if it's correct.

'A man, travelling in a train the destination of which he is seemingly ignorant of, is found murdered. Not a single scrap of paper of any kind remains upon him to prove his identity. His money being left proves that robbery of *that* was not an object. The two men whom we assume committed the crime were following him, and he was flying from them. He was evidently acquainted with China or Japan, and his bronzed face suggested a recent return from abroad.

'Let us assume that he landed at Plymouth from the P&O boat and took the eight-twenty express to Paddington, travelling alone in this compartment. Let us further assume that he discovered that his enemies were on board the same train, having watched for his arrival at Plymouth, and further that he had in his possession some very important paper or letter that it was their object to obtain.

'He knows he is watched and is in danger. First, then, he hides the paper and scribbles the key to finding it again on his wristband. Then, as the train draws up at 10.03 on the left-hand side of the island platform, here he sees another train, the Okehampton one, which ought to have been starting at that very moment, standing on the other side of the platform. Thinking to escape, he rushes across and takes a seat in it. But he is observed by his followers, and they do the same. Then the murder takes place, and they search in vain for the hidden paper.'

'But where did he hide it?'

'Behind this picture of Great Marlow,' said Godfrey

Page, commencing to unscrew the panel of it. 'He broke the blade of his knife in doing what I'm doing now.'

Breathlessly we waited while the four screws were withdrawn. Then the panel was removed, and out dropped a large sheet of thin tracing paper, many times folded. We undid it carefully.

'A map,' exclaimed the railway official.

'Yes, but what a map! Look, Tom!'

'A plan of a fortress apparently,' I said.

'A plan of Port Arthur!' cried Godfrey Page.

There, sure enough, was the map of a fortress, with guns and other points marked out with care, and brief explanations in French.

'I'll tell you what,' said Godfrey Page, as he commenced screwing up the panel, 'it's my opinion that we three had better keep this little discovery to ourselves. For, depend upon it, even if we handed this over to the police, the murderers would never be discovered.'

'Why not?'

'Because in all probability they are police themselves.'

'Russians?'

'Exactly so. He met with a spy's fate.'

'But who was this map intended for?'

'My dear fellow, our government would have paid well for it, eh?'

On further consultation we agreed to say nothing to the police. Just before we took the train back to Paddington, Godfrey Page said to our friend the official: 'By the way, they take tickets at Reading from the passengers in the eight-twenty p.m. from Plymouth? You might try and find out if three fewer tickets than were issued at Plymouth were collected that night?'

'All right, Mr Page, I'll drop you a line.'

On our way home my brother-in-law was much puzzled how to act. He had retained the map in his possession, and he was talking of destroying it when suddenly an idea occurred to him.

'Tom,' he said, 'do you ever come across Colonel Sylvester now?'

'Occasionally I meet him at the club.'

'Ah! Isn't he something to do with the Secret Service?'

'Yes.'

'Good. Let's sound him. Ask me to meet him at your place to dinner and leave the rest to me.'

A few days later the dinner came off. We three men were lazily smoking our cigars afterwards when Godfrey Page exlaimed: 'Mysterious affair that at Okehampton the other night.'

'Very,' said the Colonel, with a quick look at him.

'I was down there a day or two afterwards.'

'Indeed!'

'I made an interesting discovery.'

'What?'

'I found a curious thing in a railway carriage.'

'May I ask what?'

'This map,' replied Godfrey Page, taking it out of his pocket.

The Colonel seized it eagerly.

'Good heavens!' he said. 'Have you told anyone of this?'

'Only two beside ourselves know it.'

'For goodness' sake say nothing, Mr Page. If the Russian police knew you had that map, they'd – they'd—'

'Murder me as they did the man who brought it to England, eh?'

The Colonel was pale and trembling as he laid a hand on Godfrey Page's arm.

'Tell me,' he said, 'the police know nothing of this?'

'Nothing.'

'What do you propose to do with it?'

'I thought *you* might find it more useful than I should,' he said significantly.

The Colonel put it in his breast-pocket with a sigh of satisfaction.

'You are a wise man, Mr Page,' he said. 'I am extremely obliged to you.'

'I wonder,' remarked my brother-in-law a day or two later, 'how the inspector got on at Great Marlow? By the way, I've had a letter from Exeter. There *were* three tickets from Plymouth to London missing at the collection at Reading!'

The Mystery of the
Black Blight

FRANCIS LYNDE

America's first railway detective was Calvin Sprague, a
hulking man possessed of the same ability to analyse the
characters of people and employ scientific experiments to
solve cases as Sherlock Holmes. He made his first appearance in *Scribner's Magazine* in 1911 where he was referred
to by the sobriquet 'Scientific' Sprague. Sprague is actually
a federal agent, but poses as a chemist employed by the
Department of Agriculture in Washington, DC in order to
allay the suspicions of criminals. Most of Sprague's cases
occur not on the nation's major railroads but on small,
independent lines such as the Nevada Short Line run by his
friend, Richard Maxwell, which operates through the
picturesque mountains and harsh deserts of that state. The
targets of his investigation are frequently 'stock-jobbing
gangs' from New York out to wreck the small lines, or else
the 'big money crooks' trying to take them over. Sprague
disparagingly refers to these men on one occasion as
'buccaneers neatly labelled with the dollar-mark instead of
the skull and crossbones'.

The creator of 'Scientific' Sprague, Francis Lynde
(1856–1930), had actually been involved in the development of the American railway system and was very well
aware of the history of fraud, corruption, violence and
murder that had prevailed during its construction. His
sense of outrage on hearing that four directors of the
Central Pacific Railroad had cheated their line of more than
$60 million is said to have given him the idea for an
undercover detective with a mission to root out crime on

the nation's tracks. Lynde was born and grew up in Lewiston, in New York state, but as part of his job travelled extensively on the nation's railways, particularly in the Midwest, before settling down to become a writer. His success with the tales of Calvin Sprague, which were immediately praised for their authentic knowledge of the railroads and railway men, enabled him to make a living as a writer and a novelist. Despite the fact that many of his later works were also about the American West – such as *The Taming of Red Butte Western* (1925) and *Young Blood* (1929) – none enjoyed the success of those featuring the pioneer railway detective. The following case clearly demonstrates Francis Lynde's knowledge of the early days of railroading, and in it Sprague investigates a series of mysterious train wrecks that are threatening the future of a small line. 'The Mystery of the Black Blight' has not been in print for seventy-five years.

***

The wreck at Lobo Cut, half-way between Angels and the upper portal of Timanyoni Canyon, was a pretty bad one. Train Six, known in the advertising folders as 'The Fast Mail,' had collided in the early-morning darkness with the first section of a westbound freight which, though it was an hour and fifty minutes off its schedule time, had run past Angels without heeding the 'stop for orders' signal plainly displayed.

Ten minutes after the crash, the second section of the freight had shot around the hill curve to hurl itself, a six-thousand-ton, steel-pointed projectile, into the rear end of the first section, and the disaster was complete. Somewhere under the smoking mountain of wreckage marking the spot where the Mail and first-section locomotives had locked themselves together, reared, and fallen over into the ditch, two firemen and an engineer were buried. Out of one of the crushed mail-cars two postal clerks were taken; one of them to die a few minutes after his rescue, and the other bruised and broken, with an arm and a leg dangling, as he was carried out to safety.

At the other point of impact there had been no loss of life, though the material damage was almost as great. The engine of the second section had split its way sheer through the first-section caboose – which, in the nature of things, had no one in it to be killed – and through two of the three merchandise-cars next in its plunging path. With a mixed chaos of groceries, farming implements, and splintered timbers for its monument, the big mogul had burrowed into the soft side bank of the cutting as if in some blind attempt to bury itself out of sight of the havoc it had wrought.

On the Thursday morning of this, the worst of a series of accidents thickly bestudding that fateful month of August, Maxwell, the general superintendent, chanced to be two hundred miles away to the eastward. His service-car was in the Copah yards, and he was asleep in it when the nightwatchman came down from the despatcher's office to rouse him with the bad news.

What could be done at such long range was done instantly and with good generalship. The wires were working with Brewster, the division headquarters in Timanyoni Park. With his own hand Maxwell sent the orders to Connolly, the despatcher, to Fordyce, the train-master, and to Bascom, the master mechanic. A relief train was to be made up with all haste to take the doctors to the wreck, and to convey the passengers of Number Six back to Brewster. Following the relief train, but giving it precedence, should go the wrecking-train. The superintendent even went so far as to specify the equipment which should be taken: the heavier of the two wrecking-cranes, a car-load of rails for temporary tracking, and two or three water-cars for the extinguishing of the fire.

These things done, and the arrangements made to start his own special immediately for the scene of disaster, the superintendent had the fine courage, in the face of this last and most unnerving of many disheartenments, to return to his car and to go back to bed. He had been up very late in conference with his president, Ford, and he knew that the demands awaiting him at the end of the five-hour run to Lobo Cut would call for all the reserves of strength and energy he could hope to store up during the distance-covering interval.

Much good work had already been accomplished when Maxwell's special, feeling its way past the four long freights and the midnight passenger, all held up at Angels, came upon the scene of destruction among the foothills at an early hour in the forenoon. The relief train had come and gone, bearing away the unhurt, the injured, and the dead. A temporary working-track had been laid through the cut, and the mighty one-hundred-and-fifty-ton steam crane, its movements directed by a big, rather flashily dressed man with an accurately creased brown hat pulled down over his brows, was reaching its steel finger here and there in the debris and plucking the derelict freight-cars out of the way.

Up at the other end Fordyce, the trainmaster, was working with another crew, using a mammoth block-and-tackle, with a detached locomotive for its pulling power. When Maxwell came on the ground, Fordyce, a gnarled little man with a twist in his jaw and a temper like the sparks from an emery wheel, was alternately cajoling and cursing his men in a praiseworthy attempt to make his block-and-tackle outheave the master mechanic's powerful crane.

'Yank 'em – yank 'em, men! Get that rail under there and heave! Wig it – *wig it*! Now get that grab-hook in here – lively! Don't let them fellows at the other end snake two to our ONE!'

Maxwell stopped to exchange a word or two with the sweating trainmaster and then passed on down the wreck-strewn line. At the master mechanic's end of things he came upon Benson, chief of construction, who had accompanied the wrecking-train from Brewster only because he had happened to be on the way to Angels and saw no other probable means of reaching his destination.

'Pretty bad medicine – the worst of the lot,' commented the young chief of construction, when, tramping soberly, they came to the place where the two great locomotives, locked in their death grapple, were nuzzling the clay bank of the cutting.

Maxwell's teeth came together with a savage little click.

'A few weeks ago, Jack, we were scared stiff for fear the "Big-Nine" crowd of stock-jobbers would succeed in doing something to put us on the panic-slide. Now we are doing it ourselves, just about as fast as we can. Is it true that there were four killed?'

'Yes; both firemen, and Bamberg, the engineer of the freight. The other man was a postal clerk; and his mate had an arm and a leg broken.'

'Many injuries?'

'Astonishingly few, when there was such a good chance for a general massacre. Both men on the second-section engine jumped, and both were hurt, though not badly. There was nobody in the split caboose when it was hit. On the Mail, Cargill, who was running, got off with a pretty bad scalp wound. An express messenger had his foot jammed; and the train baggageman had a lot of trunks shaken down on him. In the coaches there were a few people thrown out of their seats and hurt by the sudden stop; but in the sleepers there were a good many who slept straight through it, incredible as that may sound.'

'I know,' said Maxwell; 'I've seen that happen more than once, when the Pullmans stayed on the rails.' Then, with a slight backward nod of his head he changed the subject abruptly. 'Bascom – has he been handling it all right?'

'He's a dandy!' said Benson. 'Personally, I'd about as soon associate with any one of a dozen Copah tin-horns that I could name as to foregather with Mr Judson Bascom. But he's on to his job, all right. He laid this temporary track himself; I haven't butted in at all, either here or at Fordyce's end.'

'How did you happen to get here? I thought you were up Red Butte way,' said the superintendent.

'I was; but I came down to Brewster on Six last night, meaning to go through to Angels. While we were changing engines I ran upstairs to get some maps and papers out of my office, and took too long about it; the train got away from me and I chased out with the wreck-wagons. That's how near I came to being mixed up in this thing myself.'

'And you want to go on to Angels now?'

'Yes; when I get a chance. Those irrigation people in Mesquite Valley are howling to have an unloading spur built up from the old copper-mine track, and I thought I'd go and look the ground over.'

The superintendent's frown was expressive of impatient dissatisfaction.

'That Mesquite project is another of the grafts that are continually giving this country a black eye, Jack. It's "bunk", pure and simple. Everybody who has ever been in the Mesquite knows that you couldn't raise little white beans in that disintegrated sandstone!'

'It'll do for an excuse to rake in a few hundred thousand Eastern shekels,' Benson remarked. 'There will be plenty of "come-ons" to buy the land when the dam is built.'

Bascom's great crane was poising a crushed and mangled box-car in air, and when the crooking steel finger swung its burden aside and dropped it with a crash out of the way, Maxwell turned upon his heel.

'I have my car here, and I'm going back to Angels to do

some wiring,' he said. 'Come along, if you want to see those irrigation people. But I'll tell you right now, I won't approve any recommendation for more track-laying for them.'

They had walked possibly half the length of the long blockade when a noisy automobile, dust-covered and filled with men, drew up on the mesa flat above the wreck. Benson looked up with a scowl.

'There's another gang of those newspaper ghouls!' he commented, as two of the three men in the tonneau got out and began to unlimber their cameras and tripods. 'It's no picnic to drive a car from Brewster over the range, to say nothing of the danger; and this is the second squad since daylight. There have been enough pictures taken of this wreck to fill all the newspapers between New York and San Francisco for a week!'

Maxwell's smile was a mere teeth-baring.

'Yes; we're getting the advertising all right,' he said. 'We've been getting it for a month or more.' Then, as they tramped on out of the wreck raffle and headed for the waiting office-car: 'I had a talk with Ford last night; that is what took me to Copah. We're in bad, Benson. Ford says they've taken to calling us "the sick railroad" on the Stock Exchange, and our securities are simply going to the puppies. Another month like this one we've just stumbled through will either wipe us from the map or clean us up definitely and put us into the hands of a receiver.'

'Does Ford say that?' gasped the young chief engineer.

'He said a good bit more than that. He still insists that these troubles of ours are helped along from the outside; that they are in reality just so many moves in the game that a certain Wall Street pool is playing to get control of our road. I tried to show him how impossible it was; how the entire slump in discipline which causes all the trouble is merely one of those crazy epidemics that now and then sweep over the length of the best-managed railroads on earth.'

'And he wouldn't believe it?' queried Benson.

'No; the last thing he said to me as his train was pulling out proved that he didn't. He intimated that there wasn't any "act-of-God" verdict to be brought in, in our case, and told me to go back to Brewster and dig until I found the real cause.'

By this time they had reached the service-car special, and Maxwell passed the word to his engineer to back up the line to Angels. When the wreck and the wreckers had vanished beyond the hill curves, Benson filled his short pipe and at the lighting of it asked another question.

'I've been wondering if we couldn't get a little expert help on this thing, Maxwell. Have you tried to interest Mr Sprague in this discipline business?'

The superintendent shook his head.

'Sprague isn't going around doing odd jobs in psychology for anybody and everybody,' he deprecated. 'He is a government chemist, and he is out here on the government's business. Besides, it isn't a case for a detective; even for the best amateur detective in the bunch – which is easily what Sprague might claim to be, you'd say. You see, there isn't anything special to detect. What we need is a doctor; not a plainclothes man.'

Benson's left eye closed itself slowly in qualified dissent.

'What does Mr Sprague himself have to say about it?' he queried.

'He hasn't said anything. In fact, I haven't seen him for over two weeks. He's been out with Billy Starbuck, gathering soil specimens; they are still out somewhere, I don't know just where.'

Neither of the two men riding the rear platform of the backing service-car spoke again until the car stopped with a jerk at the edge-of-the-desert station with the celestial name, which had once been the headquarters of the original Red Butte Western Railroad. Then Benson summed up the situation in a couple of terse sentences.

'If we don't do something, and do it quick, there is a bunch of us so-called railroad bosses on this high-line who may as well pack our dufflebags and fade away into the landscape. Three wrecks within a week; and this last one will cost a hundred thousand cold iron dollars before we're through with the lawyers; I'll be hanged if I wouldn't call in the doctor – some doctor – any doctor, Maxwell. That's my ante. So long; see you a little later about this Mesquite business, if you're still here.' And he put a leg over the platform railing and went away.

Three minutes later, when the superintendent had crossed the station platform and was on his way around to the door opening into the operator's office, two men mounted upon wiry range horses rode down the single remaining street of the dead-alive former railroad town, pointing for the station.

One of them, a good-looking youngish man with a preternaturally grave face and the shrewd, thoughtful eyes that tell of days and nights spent afield and alone with the desert immensities, was the superintendent's brother-in-law by courtesy. The other, a gigantic athlete of a man, whose weight fairly bowed the back of the stout horse he rode, was Mr Calvin Sprague.

Maxwell paused when he saw and recognised the two horsemen. But when they came up, the weight of the recent disaster made his greeting a rather dismal attempt at friendly jocularity.

'Well, well!' he said, gripping hands with the athlete; 'Billy certainly had it in for you this time! Rode you over the range, did he? I'll bet you'll never have the nerve to look a horse in the face again, after this. Where on top of earth have you two been keeping yourselves for the last fortnight?'

'Oh, just sashayin' round on the edges,' drawled Starbuck, replying for both; 'gettin' acquainted with the luminous landscape, and chewin' off chunks of the scenery, and layin' awake nights to soak up some of the good old ozone.'

'Ozone!' chuckled the big man; 'I'm jammed gullet-full of it, Dick, and I have a hunch that it's going to settle somewhere below the waist line and make me bow-legged for life. King David said that a horse is a vain thing for safety, but I can go him one better and say that it's the vainest possible thing for just plain, ordinary, everyday comfort. I'm a living parenthesis-mark – or a pair of 'em, if you like that better.' Then without warning and almost without a break: 'Where is the wreck, this time?'

Maxwell's frown was a little brow-wrinkling of curious perplexity.

'You've just ridden down from the hills, haven't you? How do you know there is a wreck?'

'That's too easy,' laughed the expert, waving a Samsonic arm toward the five side-tracked trains held up in the Angels yard. 'If you didn't have your track cluttered up somewhere, those trains wouldn't be hanging up here, I'm sure. Is it a bad one? – but you needn't answer that; I can see at least one dead man in your eyes.'

'There are four of them,' said the superintendent soberly, 'and some others desperately hurt. We're in a bad way, Sprague. This is the third smash within a week.'

Sprague dismounted stiffly and secured his saddle-bags containing the soil specimens gathered at the price of so much discomfort.

'Starbuck,' he said whimsically, 'I'm willing to pay the price of a hundred-dollar guinea-pig, if necessary, to have this razor-back mustang shipped home in a palace stock-car to his stable in Brewster. Mr Maxwell's office-car is good enough for me from this on.'

Starbuck smiled grimly and took the abandoned horse in

charge. 'I'll take care of the bronc',' he agreed; and the big man limped around the station to board the service-car while Maxwell went into the office to do his telegraphing.

When the superintendent returned half an hour later he found his self-invited guest lounging luxuriously in the easiest of the big wicker chairs in the open compartment of the car, smoking the fattest of black cigars and reading a two-days-old Denver paper.

'This is something like,' he said. 'I was never cut out for a pioneer, Richard; Starbuck has proved that to my entire satisfaction in these last two weeks. But that's enough of me and my knockings. Sit down and tell me your troubles. I see the papers are making space-fillers out of your railroad to beat the band. Are you ready to come around to my point of view yet?'

Maxwell sat down like a man who was both worried and wearied.

'The Lord knows, I wish I could come around to your point of view, Calvin. If I could see any possibility of charging these things to outside influences . . . But there isn't any. The trouble is purely local and internal – and as unaccountable as the breaking out of an epidemic when the strictest kind of quarantine has been maintained.'

Sprague smiled incredulously.

'There never was a case of typhoid yet without its germ to account for it, Dick,' he asserted dogmatically.

'I know; but that theory doesn't hold good in the psychological field. We've got a good set of men, Sprague. To a degree which you don't often find in modern railroad consolidations, we've had that precious thing called *esprit de corps*. We've never had any labour troubles since Lidgerwood's time, and there are no grievances in the air to account for the present let-down. Yet the let-down is with us. Almost every day some man who has hitherto proved trustworthy falls down on his job, and there you are.'

'You've tried all the usual remedies, I suppose?'

'I should say I had! I've stormed and cursed and pleaded and reasoned until I'm worn out! If I fire a bunch of them, I have to hire a new bunch, and inside of a week the new men have caught the disease for themselves. One bad wreck will make a hundred trainmen uncertain and jumpy, and a second one will turn half of the hundred into irresponsible lunatics. You'd have to mix and mingle with the force as I do to understand the condition things have gotten into. It's horrible, Calvin. It is like the black blight that you have seen spread through a well-kept orchard.'

'There is a cause,' said the expert, settling himself solidly in his chair. 'I tell you, Dick, there's a germ in the air, and that second mentality of mine that you are so fond of poking fun at tells me that in the case of your railroad orchard the germ has been deliberately planted. You say it's impossible: I've a good notion to let the soil-testing rest for a few minutes and show you.'

'If I thought there was the least chance in the world that you could show me—'

'Is that a challenge? By Jove! I'll take you. When can you get me back to Brewster?'

'As soon as the track is cleared. We ought to be able to get through by noon.'

The expert got up, shook the riding kinks out of his legs, and threw the newspaper aside.

'I'm going out to walk around for a bit, and after a while I'll ask you to take me down to this wreck,' he said; and Maxwell, who had a deskful of work awaiting him, nodded.

'Say, in an hour?'

'An hour will do; I'll show up within that time.'

Later, the superintendent, wading through the files of business correspondence which always accompanied him in his goings to and fro on the line, had window glimpses of Sprague strolling up and down beside the waiting trains in the yard or standing to chat with some member of the loafing crews.

The glimpses were provocative of good-natured incredulity on the part of the desk-worker. Thrice during the summer of warfare Sprague had been able to step into the breach, each time with signal success. But in each of the three former instances there had been tangible causes with which to grapple; flesh-and-blood criminals to be ferreted out and apprehended. Maxwell, glancing out of the window again, shook his head despondently. What could the keenest intelligence avail in the case of an entire railroad suffering from an acute attack of nervous disintegration and recklessness? Nothing, the superintendent decided; there was nothing for it but to settle down upon a grim determination to outlive and worry through the period of disaster; and he was still grinding away at his desk with that thought in the back part of his mind when Sprague came in and announced his willingness to be taken on to the wreck.

Maxwell gave the necessary order, and in due time the one-car special had repassed the few miles intervening between Angels and Lobo Cut, to come to a stand on the curve of hazard. Sprague was lighting a fresh cigar preparatory to a plunge into the track-clearing activities, and Maxwell looked up from his work.

'Want me to get off with you?' he asked.

'No; it's the very thing I don't want,' declared the expert briefly; and therewith he went out to drop from the car-step and to take the plunge alone.

In the two hours which had elapsed since the departure of the superintendent's car the track-clearers at both ends of the wreck had made astonishingly good progress. Step by step the master mechanic had worked his big crane up the line, tossing the derelicts aside or righting them upon the rails, as their condition warranted; and further along

Fordyce, with his huge tackle and its pulling locomotive, had been equally enthusiastic.

It was Sprague's boast that his methods of investigation, in the field of his hobby, as in all others, were purely scientific; and he insisted that the true scientist and the most successful is the one who can best qualify as a shrewd and wholly impartial observer.

Where another man might have asked questions, he stood aside and looked on and listened. In the fierce toil of track-clearing no one seemed to pay any attention to him, and the picture which presented itself was a life-sketch of the railroad force *in petto* and in the raw. The big onlooker took his time and made his mental jottings thoughtfully, strolling from one group to another and lingering longest near the hot boiler-cab of the great crane where a wizened human automaton in dirty overalls and jumper jerked the levers and spun the wheels of the hoist in obedience to the signals given by the flashily dressed master mechanic.

It wanted less than a quarter of an hour of noon when the final obstruction was heaved aside, and the track gang, which had been following the wreckers, trued and spiked the distorted rails of the main line into place. Sprague closed his mental notebook and went back to join Maxwell.

In the office-car the porter-cook had laid the table for the midday meal; and the superintendent and his guest ate it in transit, the office-car special being the first of the halted trains to pass westward over the newly cleared line.

'Well?' said Maxwell interrogatively, when the meal had progressed to the meat and vegetables without comment on the part of the one who had lifted the challenge.

'You've got the disease, all right; it's with you, and in the epidemic form, too. Its expression came out emphatically every now and then in that track-clearing hustle. One little snappy, snarly fellow lying under a box-car to make the hoisting-hitch voiced it precisely when his mate yelled at him to come out, that the hitch might slip. He yapped back, "Who the hell and blinkety-blank blankation cares!" That's one form your disease is taking, and you'd say it would account for a good many of the smashes.'

'Well?' queried the superintendent again. 'You didn't stop at that?'

'No; I made a few other preliminary observations which may or may not prove up. Give me a little time; and when we get back to Brewster, detail that ex-cowboy "relief operator" of yours, Tarbell, to run errands for me. If I can't show you good, tangible results within the next forty-eight hours or so, you may discharge me and hire a Pinkerton.'

'You'll fail,' said Maxwell gloomily. 'I've been through a sickness of this kind before. There's no cure for it. It has simply got to run its course and wear itself out.'

'That's what they used to say about cholera and the plague and yellow-fever, and all those things,' laughed the man from Washington; but he did not go any further into the matter of theories.

The run of the special train to Brewster was made without incident, and from the station Sprague went directly across to his hotel.

'I'm going over to clean up,' he announced. 'By and by, when you get around to it, send Tarbell over and tell him to wait in the lobby for me.'

It was possibly an hour later when the young man who resembled William Starbuck sufficiently to pass for the mine owner's younger brother, got out of his chair in the quietest corner of the Hotel Topaz lobby and crossed to the elevators to meet the government chemist.

'How are you, Archer?' was the renovated soil-gatherer's greeting. And then, as he led the way back to the quiet corner from which the young man had been keeping his watch upon the elevators: 'We're up against it good and hard, this time, young man. Your boss has stumped us to prove a thing which he says can't be proved. Sit down and let's see if we can't start the thin edge of a wedge. I'll do the hammering and let you hold the wedge, and you can squeal if I strike off and hit you. How long has this case of bad railroading, which is smashing things right and left, been going on?'

The young fellow who was on the railroad payrolls as a 'relief operator' took time to consider.

'A month or better.'

'How did it begin?'

'I don't know. One way 'r another, the boys've just seemed to be gettin' sort o' careless and losin' their grip. After two or three wrecks had happened, it was all off. Half o' the men've taken to runnin' on their nerve, and the other half act like they don't care a durn.'

'Is it only in the train service?'

'Lord, no; it's mighty near everywhere. It's sort of a dry rot; cars go without repairin', engines burn out, and twice within the last week the roundhouse has caught fire. You'd think every man on the road had just turned loose all holts and didn't give a cuss whether he ever got 'em again or not.'

'What do the men themselves say about it?'

'There's a heap o' kickin' and knockin'. Some say it's Mr Maxwell. When he gets good and mad and fires a bunch of 'em, they raise a rookus about it; and when he lets the next bunch down easy, they kick the other way.'

Sprague sat back in the big leather-upholstered lobby chair and for a time seemed to be absorbed in a study of the rather over-massive beam arrangement of the ceiling. Suddenly he turned to ask: 'How much of a prohibition country is this, Archer?'

Tarbell laughed.

'I reckon you don't need to ask that, with three saloons in every block in Brewster. We haven't got the water-wagon bug much out here. They say it don't breed well this side o' the main range.'

'Much drinking among the railroad men?'

'Well – m – m – not so you could notice it. There's a rule against it.'

'While they're on duty, you mean?'

'Any old time.'

'Is that rule enforced?'

'Mr Maxwell allows it is. He's sure some Ranahan when it comes to buckin' the booze-fighters.'

'Still, there is more or less drinking among the men; you know there is, don't you, Archer?'

The young man grinned soberly.

'I ain't tellin' no tales out o' school, Mr Sprague, not me,' he drawled.

'Get rid of that notion,' said the big man sharply. 'You are working for Mr Maxwell and his rules are your law and gospel. I'll tell you what I've seen, and then you can tell me what you've seen. I counted sixteen men in one place on this railroad today who, within the half-hour that I was looking on, stopped work either to hit or to pass a pocket-flask. Now go on.'

'If you hold me up that-away, I reckon maybe there *is* a good many empty bottles layin' round on the right-o'-way – more'n what the passengers throw out o' the car windows,' was the reluctant admission.

'And more than there used to be, say, two or three months ago?'

'Yes; right smart more.'

'I thought so. We don't need to look any further, Archer, for the disease itself. Your "dry rot" is very pointedly a wet rot. Booze and the running of a railroad are two things that won't mix. Now we'll come to the nib of it. Why is there more drinking now than there used to be?'

The younger man took time to think about it before he said: 'You got me goin'; I don't know the answer to that.'

'I didn't suppose you did,' was the curt rejoinder. 'But you are going to learn the answer, Archer, my son. It is now four o'clock; by half past seven this evening I want you to be back here prepared to tell me who has been letting down the fences for the railroad men in this matter of drinking.'

'Holy Smoke!' exclaimed the ex-cowboy, jarred for once out of his plainsman calm, 'how am I goin' to do that, Mr Sprague?'

'That is for you to find out, my boy. If you don't use your brain you'll never know whether or no you've got any. That's all – until half past seven. You'll find me here at the hotel.'

It was an even hour before the time appointed for Tarbell's return when Maxwell joined the chemistry expert at the table in the Topaz café where they usually sat when they could dine together.

At the unfolding of the napkins Sprague said: 'I've found your germ, Dick, and things are beginning to develop. What do you think of that?' – passing a bit of dingy coarse-fibred paper across the table.

Maxwell opened the paper and read the ill-spelled typewritten note it bore.

Mr Spraig:
    Weer onto you with both feet. keep youre fingers out ov the geers or maybe youll git em mashed.
    A well-Wishur.

'Where did that come from?' asked the superintendent, plainly amused.

'It was pushed under the door of my room upstairs about half an hour ago. The man who left it was short, thick-set, smooth-shaven, and he wore a pepper-and-salt suit and a slouch hat. Also, his breath smelled of whiskey.'

'You expect me to recognise the description?'

'I didn't know but you might.'

'I don't,' Maxwell denied. Then his smile of amusement changed to one of amazement. 'How could you know all these things about this man if you were on the other side of a closed door, Calvin?'

Sprague laughed. 'See how easy it is to jump to conclusions,' he derided. 'I wasn't on the other side of a closed door; I was in the corridor when the fellow passed me, looking for the number on the door. I saw him leave the note. I'll ask one question, and then we'll dismiss that phase of the case. Is the wrecking-train back from Lobo yet?'

'Yes; it came in about four o'clock with the string of crippled cars. But you say you have found the germ; does that mean that you are going to prove up on your assertion about the epidemic?'

'I can't tell what it means yet; but I can tell you the name of the germ. It's whiskey.'

'Drinking among the men?'

'Worse than that; drunkenness among the men. Enough of it, I should say, to account for all of your troubles and then some.'

'Oh, you're off – way off!' objected the harassed one irritably. 'I know there is some drinking; in a wide-open country like this it is almost impossible to stamp it out entirely. But to account for the epidemic in that way, you'd have to imagine every other man in the service carrying a pocket-pistol on the job!'

'And you think that couldn't happen without your knowing it, eh? A little further along I may have some statistics to show you; but just now I'm looking not so much for the germ as for the germ-carrier.'

Maxwell smiled wearily.

'Still sticking to the theory that the blight is imported, are you? It's the only time I've ever known you to be "yellow", Calvin. I can imagine some wild-eyed newspaper reporter hatching such an idea, but not you. Think of the absurdity of a bunch of Wall Street stock-jobbers trying to get at us in any such indirect way as that – shipping whiskey in here to demoralise our working force! Pshaw! When these fellows get busy and go to work, they want action – quick action.'

The expert put down his knife and fork and sat back in his chair.

'You are so close to the thing that you are continually losing the perspective, Dick,' he said earnestly. 'You are going on the supposition that those New York looters are trying first one thing and then another. That doesn't follow at all. For all you know, they may be gunning for you in half a dozen different ways this blessed minute – as they probably are. Assume, for the sake of the argument, that this whiskey scheme could be worked; I know you say it can't, but suppose it could: can you conceive of any expedient that would be more certain to kill your traffic, wipe out your earnings, smash your securities, and put you on the toboggan slide generally?'

'Oh, no; if it could be worked.' Maxwell's answer this time was less confidently derisive.

'All right; now that you've come that far, I'll say this: it can be worked, and I'm here to tell you that it has been worked. Your railroad is practically an inebriate asylum in the making, right now, Richard. Half of your force has already fallen off the water chariot, and the other half is scared to death at the thought of what the drunken half may do.'

Maxwell pushed away his dessert untasted.

'You have the proof of this, Calvin?' he broke out.

'I have some proof, and Tarbell is getting more. You've been blind. You didn't want to admit that your house of discipline was tumbling about your ears, and you've been shutting your eyes to the plain facts. For example: you may or may not be the only man in the service who doesn't know that those two freight engineers – the one who was killed and the other who overran their orders and smashed into the passenger at Lobo Cut this morning were just plain drunk!'

'What's that? It – it can't be, Calvin!'

'But it *is*,' insisted the big man across the table. 'It is common talk among your own men; so common that it reached out and hit me – an outsider.'

The superintendent drank his small coffee at a single gulp and flung his napkin aside.

'I'll get 'em!' he gritted savagely. 'I'll get the last damned booze-fighter in the bunch!' And then: 'Good God, Sprague; how could anything like this go on without my knowing it?'

'You would have found it out, sooner or later, of course. But you're a railroad man yourself, and you ought to know railroad men well enough to take into consideration that sort of loyalty among them which keeps them from "peaching" on one another. Even Tarbell had to be jarred before he would admit that he knew about it. I can imagine that there has been a sort of generous conspiracy among the men to keep you from finding out.'

'That's all right; I know now, and I'll sift them out; I'll go through the whole blamed outfit with a club! I'll—'

The man who had called out this upbubbling of righteous wrath was chuckling softly.

'You won't do anything that you say you will,' he interrupted good-naturedly. 'You stumped me to take the case, and I've taken it; which means that you're under the doctor's orders. When you have cooled down a bit, you'll see very clearly that the worst thing you could do at this particular crisis would be to start a division-wide scrap with the rank and file.'

'But, good Lord, Sprague; I've got to do something, haven't I?'

'You surely have; and that something is to help me find the germ-carrier. Somebody has been taking down the bars for your men; who is it?'

'I don't know any more than a goat. I can't yet believe that it is the work of any one man.'

'Possibly it isn't; there may be a good many. But I'll chance a guess that someone in authority is setting the pace.

Leave that for a moment and we'll take up something else. You have two daily papers here in Brewster: I've noticed that one of them, *The Tribune*, is friendly to your road. How about the other, *The Times-Record*?'

'It is supposed to be independent, with a slant against corporations and "the system", whatever that may be.'

'Um,' said the scientist. 'Before I went out on this last trip with Billy, I remarked that this other paper was giving a good bit of space to your road troubles in its news columns, and a good bit of its editorial space to criticisms of the Ford management. It occurred to me then that there might be a reason. How is the paper organised?'

'It is owned by one of our near-millionaires; a retired ranchman named Parker Higginson, who has dabbled in real estate, in mines, and latterly in politics. His grouch against the railroad is purely personal. He has asked favours that I couldn't legally grant; and on one occasion he took offence because I told him that a newspaper man should be the last person in the world to invite us to become law-breakers.'

'And his editor?' queried the expert.

'Is a bird of the same feather; a rather "yellow" little fice named Healy.'

Sprague looked rather dubiously at the two cigars which the waiter was tendering on a server. 'No, I think not, George,' he said, waving the cigars aside and feeling for his own pocket-case of stronger ones. And then to Maxwell: 'This is all very nourishing. It may help out more than you suspect. Later in the evening I may ask you to call with me at the office of *The Times-Record* – though we may not have to go that far up the ladder to find what we are looking for. In the meantime, Tarbell is waiting for us out yonder in the lobby. Suppose we go and see what he wants.'

They found the young man, who looked like a younger brother to Starbuck, and who had made his record chasing cattle thieves in Montana, methodically rolling a cigarette in the loggia alcove, and Sprague began on him briskly.

'Spit it out, Archer; what have you found?'

'I didn't make out to find what you sent me after,' was the half-evasive reply.

'All right; tell us what you did find.'

The young man dropped his cigarette and looked up with a glint of stubbornness in his stone-grey eyes.

'If it's just the same to you, Mr Sprague, I'd a heap ruther not,' he said.

Sprague reached out and turned the lapel of Tarbell's coat, exposing the small silver star of a deputy sheriff.

'You took an oath when you got that, Archer; and Mr Maxwell pays you for wearing it.'

Tarbell threw up his head defiantly. 'Deputy or no deputy, I ain't goin' to name no names,' he began slowly. 'But here's what I found out: I been in twenty-three saloons and dives since you told me to go chase, and I counted thirty-one railroad men in 'em. Not all of 'em was drinkin' or gamblin', but some of 'em was.'

Sprague turned to Maxwell.

'You see, I knew what I was talking about.'

The superintendent was shaking his head.

'As openly as that!' he exclaimed. 'I must have been the blindest fool in all this hill country!'

Tarbell chipped in quickly. 'It ain't been that bad for very long. But it's just as Mr Sprague says; it's spreadin' like murrain on a dry range. I saw men in them places this evenin' that I'd a swore never got off the water-wagon. I ain't namin' no names.'

'Mr Maxwell isn't asking you to give anybody away,' the expert qualified. And then: 'Had your supper?'

Tarbell nodded. 'I had a hand-out in one o' the saloons.'

'Good. Then I'll give you another job. Look around town for a man about Mr Maxwell's build, only about twenty pounds heavier. He is between twenty-five and thirty years old, wears a slouch hat soft grey in colour, dresses in pepper-and-salt, is clean-shaven, red-faced, blue-eyed, and walks with a little hitch to his left leg which isn't quite a limp. When you catch up with him, find out who he is and come and tell me. I'll be over at Mr Maxwell's office.'

Tarbell vanished, rolling a fresh cigarette as he went, and Sprague thrust his arm in Maxwell's.

'I'll go over to your shop with you,' he said. 'I know you're anxious to climb back into the working saddle. I'm not going to bore you; I merely want to have a little talk with that irreproachable chief clerk of yours, Harvey Calmaine.'

A little later they climbed the stair to the office floor of the railroad building together, and Maxwell went on down the corridor to the despatcher's room. When he came back to his own office a half-hour later and found Sprague and young Calmaine figuring together at the chief clerk's desk in the outer room, he went on to his own inner sanctum without disturbing them.

It was perhaps another half-hour further along when the expert, who had been patiently going over a mass of statistics with the alert, well-groomed young fellow who served as the superintendent's right hand, sat back in his chair and relit the fat black cigar which had been suffered to go out many times during the figuring process.

'It seems that a good many things besides wrecks have been happening in the past few weeks, Mr Calmaine,' he suggested musingly. 'In that short interval you have had many changes in the force, especially in the motive-power department. I don't know whether you have remarked it, but fully half of the men in the shops and roundhouses are new men. And that is the department in which the sickness seems to be the worst. Your maintenance costs have increased three hundred per cent over the same period last year.'

'I know it,' admitted the chief clerk. 'It is the more marked because Dawson, our former master mechanic, made such phenomenally good records.'

'I remember Dawson,' said the big man, slipping easily from the statistics into the humanities. 'He was here the first time I came over the road, early in the summer. Has he left the Short Line?'

'He has been promoted. He is superintendent of motive power on the east end of the South-western.'

'That is recent, isn't it?'

'Yes; it was only a few weeks ago.'

'And you have a new man as department chief?'

'We have – Judson Bascom. You may remember him as the man who ran the special train for you and Mr Maxwell the day you made the blind trip to Tunnel Number Three. He is a sort of slave-driver and seems to have a good deal of trouble with his men – is continually hiring and firing, you'd say, from the appearance of his payrolls.'

The big expert's eyes narrowed.

'Was he also promoted from some other place on the sytem?' he asked.

'No; he is a new man. I don't know where he got his experience; somewhere in the East, I suppose.'

'Another question,' put in Sprague. 'Does Mr Maxwell have the appointment of his own motive-power chief?'

'No; this appointment was made in New York – by the executive committee, I imagine.'

'Somebody's nephew or brother-in-law?' queried the chemist, with a twinkle in his eye.

'I don't know about that. I guess it happens that way, once in a while, on any railroad. But Bascom is all kinds of capable.'

Sprague shook his head. 'The true test of capability is always in the final result, my son,' he said reflectively; adding, 'and results nowadays are usually measured in dollars and cents. As an outsider, I should say that this Mr

Bascom is a pretty expensive man to have around, judging from his cost sheets. He drinks some, doesn't he?'

The young chief clerk closed one eye gravely.

'I'm not supposed to know anything about that, Mr Sprague.'

'No, of course not. As you might say, it's nobody's business but Mr Bascom's. By the way, what is that whistle blowing so persistently for?'

Calmaine leaped out of his chair as if it had been suddenly connected with the grounding wire of a forty-kilowatt generator.

'By George! It's a fire!' he exclaimed; and the sound of hurrying feet in the corridor confirmed the surmise. Maxwell's door opened at the same instant, and the three rushed out to join the crowd which was already streaming across the yard tracks toward the company's shops.

The fire was in the shops, originating in the boiler-room; and, thanks to the timely alarm and the comparative earliness of the hour, it was soon extinguished. Investigation, promptly instituted on the spot by the superintendent, proved that it was the result of pure carelessness. Some of the mechanics had washed their overalls and had hung them too near the sheet-iron stack in the fire-room; that was all.

Sprague lingered at Maxwell's elbow while the investigation was going on, and he appeared to be a more or less perfunctory listener when Bascom, oozing wrathful profanity at every pore, told the superintendent what he would do to the careless clothes-driers when they should show up in the morning. But later, after the return to the headquarters offices, the man from Washington sat for a long time in Maxwell's easiest chair, smoking steadily and with his gaze fixed upon the disused gas chandelier marking the exact centre of the ceiling.

It was not until after Maxwell had finished his quota of night work and was closing his desk that Tarbell came in to make a whispered report to the big man apparently dreaming in the easy-chair.

Sprague listened, nodded, and rose to join the office-closing retreat.

'That is about what I thought, Archer,' he said soberly. 'Now I have one more little job for you, and when it is done we'll call it a go for tonight. Come around to my laboratory with me and I'll explain it to you.' And when the four of them reached the plaza-fronting street he excused himself to Maxwell and the chief clerk and went, with Tarbell at his elbow, to the little second-floor den in the Kinzie Building where his experiments in soil analysis were conducted.

Reaching the back room which served as the laboratory proper, Sprague provided his follower with half a dozen small bottles, empty and tightly corked.

'There you are,' he said, from which it may be inferred that the nature of the remaining 'job' had been explained on the way up from the railroad headquarters. 'Do it neatly, Archer, and don't let them catch you at it. Everything will have quieted down by this time, and you shouldn't have any trouble. I'll wait for you here.'

Tarbell was gone possibly half an hour, and when he returned the bottles they were filled, two of them with a black-brown liquid, thick and viscous, and four with what appeared to be specimens of more or less dirty water. Each bottle was carefully marked on the blank label pasted upon it. Sprague stood them in a row on the laboratory working-table.

'I shall be busy here for twenty or thirty minutes,' he said. 'I don't want to ride a willing horse to death, but I'd be glad if you'd go by the hotel and ask Mr Maxwell to wait up for me. I want to see him before he goes to bed.'

Tarbell nodded, but he hesitated about going.

'I got a hunch that we ain't doin' all the shadow work by our little lonesomes, Mr Sprague,' he ventured to say. But before he could go on, Sprague lifted a finger for silence, made a whirling half-turn with a swiftness marvellous in so huge a body, and flung himself through the open door into the unlit outer office-room to which the laboratory was an inner extension.

There were sounds of a collision, a fall, and a brief struggle before Tarbell could get action. At the end of it Sprague came back into the laboratory, dragging a thick-set, square-shouldered man in pepper-and-salt clothes; a man with a clean-shaven red face down the side of which a thin line of blood was trickling.

'You were eminently correct, Archer,' said the expert, slamming his unresisting burden into a corner of the room after he had deftly gone through the pepper-and-salt pockets for weapons with the result of turning out a cheap revolver, and a wicked-looking knife. 'I'm sorry I can't keep my word and let you go to bed, but the plot has thickened a little too rapidly. Go around to the Topaz and ask Mr Maxwell to wait. Then come back here and keep this fellow quiet while I do my work.'

When Tarbell went out, Sprague quickly stripped his coat and went to work at his laboratory table. For some little time the man in the corner lay as he had been cast, and the worker at the table paid no attention to him. But a few minutes before Tarbell's return, the red-faced man gasped, gurgled, and sat up to hold his head in his hands as one trying to remember what had happened to him. Presently he looked up, and after a long stare at the big figure of the man at the work table, he found his voice.

'Say, guv'ner, wot am I doin' here?' he asked huskily.

Sprague, who was skilfully dropping a fuming yellow liquor from a glass-stoppered bottle into a beaker, replied without turning his head.

'If anybody should ask, I should say you are waiting for an officer to come and take you to jail.'

'Who, me? Wot have I been doin'?' queried the husky

one, in the anxious rasp of a deeply aggrieved victim of circumstances.

'You've been shoving threatening letters under my door in the Hotel Topaz, for one thing,' said Sprague, still busy with his experiment.

'Who me? My Gawd – just lissen to 'im!' wheezed the red-faced man, as if appealing to some third person invisible.

A silence followed during which the crouching man's feet drew themselves by imperceptible fractions of an inch at a time into position for a tackling spring. Sprague did not look aside, but when the leg muscles of the man began to bulge as if testing themselves for the leap, the worker at the table spoke again.

'I shouldn't try it if I were you. This stuff that I am fooling with is nitric acid, ninety-eight per cent pure. If any of it should happen to get spilled on you, there wouldn't be sweet oil enough in this town to put the fire out.'

'My Gawd!' gasped the red-faced one, suddenly sticking his feet out in front of him again; and just then Tarbell came in.

'I'll be through in a minute, Archer,' said the experimenter at the work-table, still without looking around. 'Did you find your man?'

'Yes; and Starbuck is with him. What do you want me to do with this geezer?'

'Nothing. I'll fix him when we're ready to go.'

'I've got a pair of handcuffs,' Tarbell suggested.

'They won't be needed – not for this one.'

Tarbell dragged out a chair and sat down, tilting comfortably against the wall and staring half-absently at the man in the corner. 'Before I'd let any bare-handed man take my arsenal away from me and slam me around like that,' he murmured, quite impersonally.

The man on the floor lifted the challenge promptly.

'Lemmie git up and gimme half a chanst,' he croaked. 'I

won't hurt you none if you don't git in the way o' that door.'

'Not this evenin',' said Tarbell succinctly; and there the matter rested until Sprague put his beakers and test-tubes aside, and, resuming his coat, took a flat black box from a shelf and slipped it into his pocket.

'Now we're ready,' he announced; and then he turned to the captured spy. 'We're going to leave you here in the dark for a little while, and there will be nothing between you and a get-away but a small matter of fear. After we turn the lights off I shall leave a few bottles of stuff around where they will do the most good. If you should happen to upset one of them in moving about, it's goodbye. If it doesn't burn you to death, you'll stifle.'

'My Gawd!' said the captive; and he was still saying it over softly to himself when they switched off the lights, shut the office doors, and went away.

'There is a good example of the power of matter over mind, Archer,' said Sprague whimsically, when they reached the street. 'If that fellow would use his reason even a little bit he'd know that I hadn't made any very elaborate preparations to hold him; there wasn't time between the turning off of the lights and our leaving. Yet I'll bet a small chicken worth twenty-five dollars that we find him still crouching in his corner and afraid to move when we go back. He saw me using acid in my little experiment; saw the fumes and probably got a whiff of them. That was enough.'

They found Maxwell and Starbuck sitting on the hotel porch, smoking. Sprague took the superintendent aside.

'It's rather worse than I thought it was, Dick,' he began, when they had drawn their chairs a little apart. 'That is my excuse for keeping you up so late. We have one of the conspirators under a sort of mental lock and key over at my place in the Kinzie Building, but he is only a hired striker, and I'd like to flush the big game. Are you good for a watch-meeting – you and Starbuck? It may last all night, and nothing may come of it, but it's worth trying.'

Maxwell spread his hands.

'Whatever you say, Calvin,' he acquiesced. 'After the jolt you've given me tonight, I can only get into the harness and pull when you give the word.'

'All right. We'll take Tarbell for a guide. Tarbell, you know your way around in the shops pretty well, don't you?'

'I reckon so,' was the young man's reply.

'We want to go to the foundry, or to some place near by where we can keep an eye on the pickle shed. Can you get us there without arousing curiosity?'

'Sure,' said Tarbell.

'Good. Pitch out,' was the curt command, and the four of them left the hotel to make a circuit through ill-lit streets and around the lower end of the eastern railroad yard to come at the long line of shop buildings from the rear.

On the way Maxwell enquired curiously: 'What do you know about pickling-sheds, Calvin?'

'I know that every well-regulated foundry has one where castings which are to be machined are treated with acid to take the hard sand-scale off.'

'And why, just why, are you anxious to get a near-hand view of ours, at this time of night?'

'I'm hoping we shall find the answer to that in your foundry yard, Dick. If we don't, the joke will be on me.'

The approach to the locomotive-repairing section of the railroad plant was made through a riverbank yard littered with slag dumps, piled flasks, and heaps of scrap iron. There was no moon, and when they got among the lumber sheds in the rear of the car-shops the darkness was almost tangible. But Tarbell knew the ground, and when he finally called a halt the twin cupola stacks of the foundry loomed before them in the darkness and the acrid smell of the warm, moist moulding sand was in the air.

When the pickling-shed had been located for him, Sprague chose the waiting-place under a flask shelter directly opposite and the silent watch began. For a weary half-hour nothing happened. Though the month was August, a cool wind crept down from the Timanyoni snow peaks, and the splash and gurgle of the nearby river added its suggestion of chill to the moonless night. Over in the western yards the night crew was making up the midnight freights; but with the buildings of the plant intervening, the noises of the shifter's exhaust and the clankings and crashings of the shunted cars came faintly to the ears of the watchers.

On the even hour of one the watchman made his round. They could see his lantern twinkling through the windows of the shops, and later he made a circuit of the outbuildings. His route led him finally through the foundry, and as he came out the light of his lantern fell upon the piled castings and the pickling-troughs, and on the carboys of vitriol. There were four of the boxed acid-holders standing under the shed. Sprague drew down his left cuff and made pencil marks on it in the darkness when the watchman passed on.

It was possibly fifteen minutes after the watchman had disappeared when Maxwell broke the strained silence with a whisper.

'Duck!' he said to Starbuck, who was standing up. 'Dunkell's coming back – without his lantern!'

Sprague spread his arms and crushed the other three back into the shadows. 'It isn't the watchman this time – be ready!' he whispered; and as he said it the figure of a man appeared coming down the littered roadway from the blacksmith shop.

Though he walked in darkness there was no incertitude about the man's movements. Turning abruptly out of the material-road he went straight to the foundry shed. A moment later a beam of white light played steadily upon the acid carboys, a sheltered beam which seemed to come from a tiny electric searchlight. Plainly they saw a pair of hands place a large bottle on the ground, remove the stopper, and fix a tin funnel in the neck. Then one of the carboys was tilted, presumably by the same pair of hands, though the hands were invisible now, and a thin stream of the yellow acid gurgled through the funnel.

When the bottle was filled the carboy slowly righted itself; the hands came in view again to remove the funnel and to replace the stopper; and then the searchlight went out with the faint snap of an electric switch. Almost at the same instant the watchers saw the figure of the man fading away into the inner and darker blackness of the foundry.

'We've got to follow him, Tarbell,' said Sprague, hurriedly; 'and we lose out if he discovers us. Can you pilot us?'

'I can,' asserted Maxwell, and under the superintendent's lead the shadow race was begun.

Happily, there was a noisy diversion to make the secret pursuit feasible. The train-making clamour had come down from the western yards, and for the moment the yard crew was working on the freight-house tracks opposite the shops. Under cover of the outdoor clamour the four pursuers were able to close up on the bottle-carrier until they were treading almost in his footsteps. The route led through the foundry floor to the machine shop. On the erecting pits were two locomotives, apparently ready to be hauled out and put into service after their period of back-shop repairs.

Into the cab of one of the engines the bottle-bearer climbed, first placing his burden carefully in the gangway. A little later they heard him climbing over the coal in the tender, heard him remove the cover of the water manhole, and heard the glug-glug of liquid issuing from a bottle-neck.

Sprague silently drew a small square object from his pocket, the little flat black box he had caught up as he was leaving his office in the Kinzie Building. Then he whispered to Tarbell: 'Cover him, Archer, and don't hesitate to shoot if you need to: ready!' At the word there was a blinding burst of illumination and the report of a flashlight cartridge, followed instantly by the crash of the breaking bottle, silence, and black darkness. Then Sprague's mellow voice boomed into the stillness.

'Come down, Mr Bascom. We've got your picture, and a man who doesn't often miss what he shoots at is covering you with his gun.'

It was a grim little group of five which gathered in the master mechanic's room in the office wing of the machine shop a few minutes after the flashlight photograph had been taken in the erecting shop. Bascom's ruddy flush was gone when he sat down heavily in his desk chair; but his natty brown crush hat was pushed back, and the gleam in his small, lynx-like eyes was not of fear.

'Just name the kind of a hand-spring you'd like to have me turn, gentlemen,' he said, half-sardonically, when Tarbell had switched on the second circuit of incandescents. 'I'm not much of an acrobat, but I'll do the best I can to amuse you.'

It was Sprague who did the talking for the prosecution.

'We want to know first who is with you in this job of inside worm-eating, Mr Bascom,' he said coolly.

'Nobody,' came the prompt lie.

Sprague's smile was affable. 'I'm sure you'll make one exception,' he urged; 'a man named Murtagh, who was for a little time one of your shop machinists and who is now a press-repairer on *The Times-Record*.'

Bascom sat up and swore a savage oath.

'So that damned scab has welshed, has he?' he grated.

Sprague branched off and began again, this time in the straitly criminal field.

'How many locomotives have you treated with the acid cure, first and last, Mr Bascom?'

'Enough so you'll still be resetting flues in 'em a year from now.'

This time it was Maxwell's turn to swear, and for a minute or two the air of the office was sulphurous. When the atmosphere had cleared again, Sprague went on.

'I presume that your defence in court will be that you were trying an experiment to neutralise the effect of the alkaline water of this region?'

Bascom grinned appreciatively. 'You're an expert chemist yourself, Mr Sprague. The water in this country, outside of the Park, *is* pretty badly alkaline, as you probably know.'

'But that defence will scarcely explain why you put acid in the oil which is used for lubricating the internal parts of the engines – cylinders and valves,' Sprague cut in quietly.

The master mechanic's chair righted itself with a crash, and the crash punctuated another blast of bad language directed at the man who had been left crouching in the corner in Sprague's uptown laboratory.

'So Murtagh gave you that, too, did he?' Bascom finished. 'It's your lead, Mr Sprague; what do you want me to play?'

'Names,' said the expert curtly.

'But if I say I was playing a lone hand?'

'We should know you were lying. This acid business may be all your own; but there are other things. You've had plenty of help in the drink-fest and the demoralisation game, Bascom.'

The big master mechanic's lips shut like the jaws of a steel trap. But after a time he said: 'What do I get if I spout on the others?'

'A chance to get out of the country – eh, Maxwell?'

The superintendent nodded. 'Yes; if he can get away before I can find a gun to kill him with.'

Bascom reached into his desk, found a scratch-pad and tossed it over to Starbuck. 'Take 'em down,' he said briefly;

and then followed a blacklist that was simply heart-breaking to Richard Maxwell, a man who had built his reputation as a railroad executive, and would have staked it instantly, upon the loyalty of his rank and file. Shop foremen, roundhouse bosses, bridge men, yard foremen, section bosses, a travelling engineer, a clerk here and a telegraph operator there – the list seemed endless.

When Bascom paused, Sprague began again.

'What was the plan, Bascom, as it was outlined to these others?'

The master mechanic's smile showed his fine even teeth.

'To make this jerk-water railroad a little easier to work for,' he sneered. 'When we found the right kind of a man we made him believe that the discipline was keyed up too damned tight and showed him how he could loosen up a little, if he felt like it. Murtagh was barkeep' and handed out the bug-juice. That's all there was to it.'

'Not quite all,' said Sprague evenly. 'You got Murtagh his job on *The Times-Record* in order to have him handy without being too much in the way or too much in evidence. How much do the *Times-Record* people know about the scheme for smashing the Nevada Short Line securities from the inside?'

Bascom laughed hardily.

'You'll never catch a newspaper man,' he said. 'But I'll tell you this: Parker Higginson is a pretty smooth politician, and he's got a mighty long arm when it comes to reaching for the thing he wants. He was the man who got me my job here, and I'll bet those New York people who appointed me don't know yet why they did it. Another thing: when I'm gone, Higginson will still be here – don't you forget that!'

'We'll try to remember it,' Sprague promised. Then he looked at his watch. 'The overland passenger, westbound, will be here in a few minutes, and when it goes, you may go with it, Mr Bascom. But first we want a few more names, the names of the New York people who are behind both you and Mr Higginson.'

Bascom got up, went to a wardrobe in one corner of the office, and dragged out two heavy suitcases.

'I've been fixed for this for some little time,' he volunteered. 'Send Murtagh to the stone-pile for splitting on us, and I won't make any claim for the half-month's salary that's due me. As to the names of the big fellows, I only wish I knew them, Mr Sprague. If I did, I'd go east instead of west and make somebody come across with big money. As it is, I guess it's South America for mine. Good night, all. I wish you luck with the booze-fighters, Mr Maxwell. You'll have a bully good time loading some of them back on to the water-automobile.' And he went out into the night with a suitcase in either hand.

'Talk about cold gall!' said Starbuck, when the door closed behind the retreating figure of the big master mechanic; 'Great Cat! That fellow's got enough to swim in.' Then he turned to Sprague. 'Is the show over?'

The man from Washington laughed genially.

'That is for Maxwell to say. We might go uptown and give those newspaper people a bad quarter of an hour, though I doubt if we'd make any money at it.'

Maxwell looked up quickly.

'You think they're in it, Calvin? Bascom wasn't lying about that part of it?'

'Yes; they are in it up to their necks. I suppose it's politics for Higginson. Haven't I heard somewhere that he is one of the State bosses?'

'You might have,' drawled Starbuck. 'He's It, all right.'

Sprague stood up, and yawned sleepily.

'Perhaps, a little later on, we can throw a scare into this Mr Parker Higginson,' he suggested. 'Just now, I'm for the hotel and a few winks of much-needed sleep. Tarbell, you go up to my office and get Murtagh. Have him locked up on a charge of – oh, any old charge will do; breaking into my office tonight, if you can't think of anything better. If we can manage to hold on to him for a while, we may be able to keep this Mr Higginson quiet while Maxwell is straightening out his booze-fighters. Let's go.'

'Hold on, just a minute,' pleaded Maxwell. 'There are three of us here who have seen the wheels go round, and I don't forget that I was the one who said there weren't any wheels. How in the name of all that is wonderful have you been able to work this puzzle out in less than twelve hours, Sprague?'

The big chemistry expert sat down again and locked his hands behind his head.

'My gosh!' he said; 'have I got to open up a kindergarten for you fellows when I'm so sleepy that I don't know what I'm going to have for breakfast tomorrow morning? It was easy, dead easy. Half an hour with those delayed train crews at Angels this morning showed me that the discipline strings were all off; one of the freight conductors even offered me a nip out of his pocket-flask when I intimated that I was thirsty. With that for a pointer, I had my eyes open at the wreck, and what I saw there you all know. Moreover, I noticed that the pocket-flasks were all alike, as if they'd all been handed out over the same bar. All straight, so far?'

'Go on,' said Maxwell.

'I got my first pointer on Bascom at the wreck, too. I saw that the men in the trainmaster's gang didn't drink when the boss was looking, a condition which didn't apply in the other crew. Again, I noticed that Bascom took his track-clearing privilege with a large and handsome disregard for the salvage. He didn't care how much property was destroyed in the process, and once I saw him give the signal to the crane engineer to drop a car loaded with automobiles – which was promptly done and the autos properly smashed.'

'The cold-blooded devil!' growled the superintendent.

'When we reached town, Tarbell here promptly confirmed my guess about the whiskey; and in the evening Calmaine helped some more by going with me over the payrolls for new names, and over the cost-sheets for increases. Naturally, we dwelt longest upon the motive-power and repair department, with its huge increases, and it so happened that my eye fell upon the various charges for vitriol in carboys. I asked Calmaine what use a railroad shop had for so much sulphuric acid, and he told me it was used to pickle castings. Afterward I sent Tarbell out to bring me samples of water from the tanks of the crippled locomotives on the shop-track and of the oil in their cylinder-cups. Analyses of both, which I made on the spot, showed the presence of sulphuric acid in the water, and also in the oil.'

'Still, you didn't have any cinch on Bascom,' Starbuck put in.

'No, but things were leaning pretty heavily his way. Tarbell had traced Murtagh for me and had found out the one thing that I needed to know; namely, that Murtagh had been "placed" on *The Times-Record* by Bascom's recommendation. Murtagh was the man who put the threatening note under my door; the note was printed on a scrap of scratch-paper – copy paper – of the sort that you rarely find outside of a newspaper office. Here I simply put two and two together. Bascom had been conferring with Higginson, or his editor, or both of them, and telling them of my rubber-necking at the wreck. They had agreed among themselves that I'd better be warned off the grass, and they took about the stupidest possible way they could think of to do it.'

'Still, you didn't have Bascom,' reiterated Starbuck.

'No; but he was the man who had been signing the requisitions for the big purchases of acid, and I was far enough along to chance a jump at him. I knew that if he were the man who was poisoning the locomotives, he wasn't trusting anybody else; he was doing it himself, often and by littles. I wasn't at all sure of catching him tonight, of course; but we saw him down here at the fire, and I thought there was an even chance that he might stay and do a little more devilment.'

Maxwell stood up and shook himself into his coat.

'I'm on to you now, Sprague,' he chuckled, in a brave attempt to jolly himself out of the depressive nightmare which had been weighing him down for weeks. 'You're a guesser – a bold, bad four-flusher, with a perfectly miraculous knack of drawing the other card you need when you reach for it. Now, if you could only guess me out some way in which I can straighten up these poor fellows of mine who have been pulled neck and heels off of the water-wagon—'

'Pshaw! That's a cinch,' said the big man, yawning sleepily again. 'We'll just put our heads together and get out a little circular letter, talking to the boys just as you'd talk to a bunch of them in your office. Tell 'em it's all off, and the bar is closed and padlocked, and you'll have 'em all eating out of your hand again, same as they used to. You don't believe it can be done? You let me write the letter and I'll show you. All you have to do is to apply the scientific principle; surround the whole subject and look at it calmly and dispassionately, and – ye-ow! Say, I'm going to chance another guess – the last in the box. If you don't head me over to the hotel and my room, you'll have to carry me over and put me to bed. And that's no joke, with a man of my size. Let's go.'

The Knight's Cross Signal Problem

ERNEST BRAMAH

Undoubtedly the most unusual detective ever to have tackled a crime on the railways is Max Carrados, the hero of this next story. Max is completely blind, yet this has not stopped him earning the accolade of being 'the first and best blind detective in literature' from Chris Steinbrunner and Otto Penzler in their *Encyclopedia of Mystery and Detection* (1976). Despite having suffered amaurosis as a result of an accident, Max has developed his other senses to an extraordinary degree – he can, for example, 'read' the type on the pages of a newspaper with his fingers – and now devotes his time to solving crimes. A handsome, wealthy bachelor, Carrados has a personal attendant named Parkinson who serves as his 'eyes' whenever the need arises. The amateur detective also works with an old friend named Louis Carlyle, a disgraced former solicitor who has become a private investigator. The adventures of this trio began in 1914 in *Max Carrados* which Ellery Queen (rightly this time!) has called 'one of the ten best volumes of detective shorts ever written', and they continued for twenty years when the final novel about Max called *The Bravo of London* was published in 1934.

Ernest Bramah (1862–1942), born Ernest Smith in Manchester, was for some years a farmer before turning to journalism and then becoming the editor of a short-lived magazine, *The Minister*. While searching for another job he began writing crime stories, creating two very different but equally successful characters: a jocular Chinese investigator, Kai Lung, and Max Carrados. The fame which ensued rather unsettled Bramah who was by nature a very shy and retiring man, and he became something of a recluse, so much so that for a time a rumour persisted that the name Ernest Bramah was actually the pen-name of another well-known literary figure. Eventually driven to distraction by the persistence of this story, Bramah issued a photograph of himself, in which he appeared rather like a jovial clergyman, along with a brief statement: 'Either I am to have no existence, or I am to have decidedly too much. On the one hand banished into space as a mythical creation, on the other regarded askance as the leader of a double (literary) life.' Recently, several of the Kai Lung titles have been reprinted and it is to be hoped that the extraordinary Max Carrados might enjoy the same attention. In the meantime, here is one of his finest cases in which all of his other senses are at their most highly tuned as he sets out to solve the mystery of the first collision in England between a steam engine and an electric train.

* * *

'Louis,' exclaimed Mr Carrados, with the air of genial gaiety that Carlyle had found so incongruous to his conception of a blind man, 'you have a mystery somewhere about you! I know it by your step.'

Nearly a month had passed since the incident of the false Dionysius had led to the two men meeting. It was now December. Whatever Mr Carlyle's step might indicate to the inner eye it betokened to the casual observer the manner of a crisp, alert, self-possessed man of business. Carlyle, in truth, betrayed nothing of the pessimism and despondency that had marked him on the earlier occasion.

'You have only yourself to thank that it is a very poor one,' he retorted. 'If you hadn't held me to a hasty promise—'

'To give me an option on the next case that baffled you, no matter what it was—'

'Just so. The consequence is that you get a very unsatisfactory affair that has no special interest to an amateur and is only baffling because it is – well—'

'Well, baffling?'

'Exactly, Max. Your would-be jest has discovered the proverbial truth. I need hardly tell you that it is only the insoluble that is finally baffling and this is very probably insoluble. You remember the awful smash on the Central and Suburban at Knight's Cross station a few weeks ago?'

'Yes,' replied Carrados, with interest. 'I read the whole ghastly details at the time.'

'You read?' exclaimed his friend suspiciously.

'I still use the familiar phrases,' explained Carrados, with a smile. 'As a matter of fact, my secretary reads to me. I mark what I want to hear and when he comes at ten o'clock we clear off the morning papers in no time.'

'And how do you know what to mark?' demanded Mr Carlyle cunningly.

Carrados's right hand, lying idly on the table, moved to a newspaper near. He ran his finger along a column heading, his eyes still turned towards his visitor.

' "The Money Market. Continued from page two. British Railways",' he announced.

'Extraordinary,' murmured Carlyle.

'Not very,' said Carrados. 'If someone dipped a stick in treacle and wrote "Rats" across a marble slab you would probably be able to distinguish what was there, blindfold.'

'Probably,' admitted Mr Carlyle. 'At all events we will not test the experiment.'

'The difference to you of treacle on a marble background is scarcely greater than that of printers' ink on newspaper to me. But anything smaller than pica I do not read with comfort, and below long primer I cannot read at all. Hence the secretary. Now the accident, Louis.'

'The accident: well, you remember all about that. An ordinary Central and Suburban passenger train, non-stop at Knight's Cross, ran past the signal and crashed into a crowded electric train that was just beginning to move out. It was like sending a garden roller down a row of handlights. Two carriages of the electric train were flattened out of existence; the next two were broken up. For the first time on an English railway there was a good stand-up smash between a heavy steam engine and a train of light cars, and it was "bad for the coo".'

'Twenty-seven killed, forty something injured, eight died since,' commented Carrados.

'That was bad for the Co.,' said Carlyle. 'Well, the main fact was plain enough. The heavy train was in the wrong. But was the engine-driver responsible? He claimed, and he claimed vehemently from the first and he never varied one iota, that he had a "clear" signal – that is to say, the green light, it being dark. The signalman concerned was equally dogged that he never pulled off the signal – that it was at "danger" when the accident happened and that it had been for five minutes before. Obviously, they could not both be right.'

'Why, Louis?' asked Mr Carrados smoothly.

'The signal must either have been up or down – red or green.'

'Did you ever notice the signals on the Great Northern Railway, Louis?'

'Not particularly. Why?'

'One wintery day, about the year when you and I were concerned in being born, the engine driver of a Scotch express received the "clear" from a signal near a little Huntingdon station called Abbots Ripton. He went on and crashed into a goods train and into the thick of the smash a down express mowed its way. Thirteen killed and the usual tale of injured. He was positive that the signal gave him a "clear"; the signalman was equally confident that he had never pulled it off the "danger". Both were right, and yet the signal was in working order. As I said, it was a wintery day; it had been snowing hard and the snow froze and accumulated on the upper edge of the signal arm until its weight bore it down. That is a fact that no fiction writer dare have invented, but to this day every signal on the Great Northern pivots from the centre of the arm instead of from the end, in memory of that snowstorm.'

'That came out at the inquest, I presume?' said Mr Carlyle. 'We have had the Board of Trade inquiry and the inquest here and no explanation is forthcoming. Everything was in perfect order. It rests between the word of the signalman and the word of the engine driver – not a jot of direct evidence either way. Which is right?'

'That is what you are going to find out, Louis?' suggested Carrados.

'It is what I am being paid for finding out,' admitted Mr Carlyle frankly. 'But so far we are just where the inquest left it, and, between ourselves, I candidly can't see an inch in front of my face in the matter.'

'Nor can I,' said the blind man, with a rather wry smile. 'Never mind. The engine driver is your client, of course?'

'Yes,' admitted Carlyle. 'But how the deuce did you know?'

'Let us say that your sympathies are enlisted on his behalf. The jury were inclined to exonerate the signalman, weren't they? What has the company done with your man?'

'Both are suspended. Hutchins, the driver, hears that he may probably be given charge of a lavatory at one of the stations. He is a decent, bluff, short-spoken old chap, with his heart in his work. Just now you'll find him at his worst – bitter and suspicious. The thought of swabbing down a lavatory and taking pennies all day is poisoning him.'

'Naturally. Well, there we have honest Hutchins: taciturn, a little touchy perhaps, grown grey in the service of the company, and manifesting quite a bulldog-like devotion to his favourite 538.'

'Why, that actually was the number of his engine – how do you know it?' demanded Carlyle sharply.

'It was mentioned two or three times at the inquest, Louis,' replied Carrados mildly.

'And you remembered – with no reason to?'

'You can generally trust a blind man's memory; especially if he has taken the trouble to develop it.'

'Then you will remember that Hutchins did not make a very good impression at the time. He was surly and irritable under the ordeal. I want you to see the case from all sides.'

'He called the signalman – Mead – a "lying young dog", across the room, I believe. Now, Mead, what is he like? You have seen him, of course?'

'Yes. He does not impress me favourably. He is glib, ingratiating, and distinctly "greasy". He has a ready answer for everything almost before the question is out of your mouth. He has thought of everything.'

'And now you are going to tell me something, Louis,' said Carrados encouragingly.

Mr Carlyle laughed a little to cover an involuntary movement of surprise.

'There is a suggestive line that was not touched at the inquiries,' he admitted. 'Hutchins has been a saving man all his life, and he has received good wages. Among his class he is regarded as wealthy. I daresay that he has five hundred pounds in the bank. He is a widower with one daughter, a very nice-mannered girl of about twenty. Mead is a young man, and he and the girl are sweethearts – have been informally engaged for some time. But old Hutchins would not hear of it; he seems to have taken a dislike to the signalman from the first and latterly he had forbidden him to come to his house or his daughter to speak to him.'

'Excellent, Louis,' cried Carrados in great delight. 'We

shall clear your man in a blaze of red and green lights yet and hang the glib, "greasy" signalman from his own signal-post.'

'It is a significant fact, seriously?'

'It is absolutely convincing.'

'It may have been a slip, a mental lapse on Mead's part which he discovered the moment it was too late, and then, being too cowardly to admit his fault, and having so much at stake, he took care to make detection impossible. It may have been that, but my idea is rather that probably it was neither quite pure accident nor pure design. I can imagine Mead meanly pluming himself over the fact that the life of this man who stands in his way, and whom he must cordially dislike, lies in his power. I can imagine the idea becoming an obsession as he dwells on it. A dozen times with his hand on the lever he lets his mind explore the possibilities of a moment's defection. Then one day he puts the signal off in sheer bravado – and hastily puts it at danger again. He may have done it once or he may have done it oftener before he was caught in a fatal moment of irresolution. The chances are about even that the engine driver would be killed. In any case he would be disgraced, for it is easier on the face of it to believe that a man might run past a danger signal in absentmindedness, without noticing it, than that a man should pull off a signal and replace it without being conscious of his actions.'

'The fireman was killed. Does your theory involve the certainty of the fireman being killed, Louis?'

'No,' said Carlyle. 'The fireman is a difficulty; but looking at it from Mead's point of view – whether he has been guilty of an error or a crime – it resolves itself into this: First, the fireman may be killed. Second, he may not notice the signal at all. Third, in any case he will loyally corroborate his driver and the good old jury will discount that.'

Carrados smoked thoughtfully, his open, sightless eyes

merely appearing to be set in a tranquil gaze across the room.

'It would not be an improbable explanation,' he said presently. 'Ninety-nine men out of a hundred would say: "People do not do these things." But you and I, who have in our different ways studied criminology, know that they sometimes do, or else there would be no curious crimes. What have you done on that line?'

To anyone who could see, Mr Carlyle's expression conveyed an answer.

'You are behind the scenes, Max. What was there for me to do? Still I must do something for my money. Well, I have had a very close inquiry made confidentially among the men. There might be a whisper of one of them knowing more than had come out – a man restrained by friendship, or enmity, or even grade jealousy. Nothing came of that. Then there was the remote chance that some private person had noticed the signal without attaching any importance to it then, one who would be able to identify it still by something associated with the time. I went over the line myself. Opposite the signal the line on one side is shut in by a high blank wall; on the other side are houses, but coming below the butt-end of a scullery the signal does not happen to be visible from any road or from any window.'

'My poor Louis!' said Carrados, in friendly ridicule. 'You were at the end of your tether?'

'I was,' admitted Carlyle. 'And now that you know the sort of job it is I don't suppose that you are keen on wasting your time over it.'

'That would hardly be fair, would it?' said Carrados reasonably. 'No, Louis, I will take over your honest old driver and your greasy young signalman and your fatal signal that cannot be seen from anywhere.'

'But it is an important point for you to remember, Max, that although the signal cannot be seen from the box, if the mechanism had gone wrong, or anyone tampered with the arm, the automatic indicator would at once have told Mead that the green light was showing. Oh, I have gone very thoroughly into the technical points, I assure you.'

'I must do so too,' commented Mr Carrados gravely.

'For that matter, if there is anything you want to know, I dare say that I can tell you,' suggested his visitor. 'It might save your time.'

'True,' acquiesced Carrados. 'I should like to know whether anyone belonging to the houses that bound the line there came of age or got married on the twenty-sixth of November.'

Mr Carlyle looked across curiously at his host.

'I really do not know, Max,' he replied, in his crisp, precise way. 'What on earth has that got to do with it, may I enquire?'

'The only explanation of the Pont St Lin swing-bridge disaster of '75 was the reflection of a green Bengal light on a cottage window.'

Mr Carlyle smiled his indulgence privately.

'My dear chap, you mustn't let your retentive memory of obscure happenings run away with you,' he remarked wisely. 'In nine cases out of ten the obvious explanation is the true one. The difficulty, as here, lies in proving it. Now, you would like to see these men?'

'I expect so; in any case, I will see Hutchins first.'

'Both live in Holloway. Shall I ask Hutchins to come here to see you – say tomorrow? He is doing nothing.'

'No,' replied Carrados. 'Tomorrow I must call on my brokers and my time may be filled up.'

'Quite right; you mustn't neglect your own affairs for this – experiment,' assented Carlyle.

'Besides, I should prefer to drop in on Hutchins at his own home. Now, Louis, enough of the honest old man for one night. I have a lovely thing by Eumenes that I want to show you. Today is – Tuesday. Come to dinner on Sunday and pour the vials of your ridicule on my want of success.'

'That's an amiable way of putting it,' replied Carlyle. 'All right, I will.'

Two hours later Carrados was again in his study, apparently, for a wonder, sitting idle. Sometimes he smiled to himself, and once or twice he laughed a little, but for the most part his pleasant, impassive face reflected no emotion and he sat with his useless eyes tranquilly fixed on an unseen distance. It was a fantastic caprice of the man to mock his sightlessness by a parade of light, and under the soft brilliance of a dozen electric brackets the room was as bright as day. At length he stood up and rang the bell.

'I suppose Mr Greatorex isn't still here by any chance, Parkinson?' he asked, referring to his secretary.

'I think not, sir, but I will ascertain,' replied the man.

'Never mind. Go to his room and bring me the last two files of *The Times*. Now' – when he returned – 'turn to the earliest you have there. The date?'

'November the second.'

'That will do. Find the Money Market; it will be in the Supplement. Now look down the columns until you come to British Railways.'

'I have it, sir.'

'Central and Suburban. Read the closing price and the change.'

'Central and Suburban Ordinary, $66\frac{1}{2}$–$67\frac{1}{2}$, fall of an eighth. Preferred Ordinary, 81–$81\frac{1}{2}$, no change. Deferred Ordinary $27\frac{1}{2}$–$27\frac{3}{4}$, fall of a quarter. That is all, sir.'

'Now take a paper about a week on. Read the Deferred only.'

'27–$27\frac{1}{4}$, no change.'

'Another week.'

'$29\frac{1}{2}$–30, rise of five-eighths.'

'Another.'

'$31\frac{1}{2}$–$32\frac{1}{2}$, rise of one.'

'Very good. Now on Tuesday the twenty-seventh November.'

'3 $1\frac{7}{8}$–3 $2\frac{3}{4}$, rise of a half.'

'Yes. The next day.'

'$24\frac{1}{2}$–$23\frac{1}{2}$, fall of nine.'

'Quite so, Parkinson. There had been an accident, you see.'

'Yes, sir. Very unpleasant accident. Jane knows a person whose sister's young man has a cousin who had his arm torn off in it – torn off at the socket, she says, sir. It seems to bring it home to one, sir.'

'That is all. Stay – in the paper you have, look down the first money column and see if there is any reference to the Central and Suburban.'

'Yes, sir. "City and Suburbans, which after their late depression on the projected extension of the motor bus service, had been steadily creeping up on the abandonment of the scheme, and as a result of their own excellent traffic returns, suffered a heavy slump through the lamentable accident of Thursday night. The Deferred in particular at one time fell eleven points as it was felt that the possible dividend, with which rumour has of late been busy, was now out of the question." '

'Yes; that is all. Now you can take the papers back. And let it be a warning to you, Parkinson, not to invest your savings in speculative railway deferreds.'

'Yes, sir. Thank you, sir, I will endeavour to remember.' He lingered for a moment as he shook the file of papers level. 'I may say, sir, that I have my eye on a small block of cottage property at Acton. But even cottage property scarcely seems safe from legislative depredation now, sir.'

The next day Mr Carrados called on his brokers in the city. It is to be presumed that he got through his private business quicker than he expected, for after leaving Austin Friars he continued his journey to Holloway, where he found Hutchins at home and sitting morosely before his kitchen fire. Rightly assuming that his luxuriant car would involve him in a certain amount of public attention in

Klondyke Street, the blind man dismissed it some distance from the house, and walked the rest of the way, guided by the almost imperceptible touch of Parkinson's arm.

'Here is a gentleman to see you, father,' explained Miss Hutchins, who had come to the door. She divined the relative positions of the two visitors at a glance.

'Then why don't you take him into the parlour?' grumbled the ex-driver. His face was a testimonial of hard work and general sobriety but at the moment one might hazard from his voice and manner that he had been drinking earlier in the day.

'I don't think that the gentleman would be impressed by the difference between our parlour and our kitchen,' replied the girl quaintly, 'and it is warmer here.'

'What's the matter with the parlour now?' demanded her father sourly. 'It was good enough for your mother and me. It used to be good enough for you.'

'There is nothing the matter with it, nor with the kitchen either.' She turned impassively to the two who had followed her along the narrow passage. 'Will you go in, sir?'

'I don't want to see no gentleman,' cried Hutchins noisily. 'Unless' – his manner suddenly changed to one of pitiable anxiety – 'unless you're from the Company, sir, to – to—'

'No; I have come on Mr Carlyle's behalf,' replied Carrados, walking to a chair as though he moved by a kind of instinct.

Hutchins laughed his wry contempt.

'Mr Carlyle!' he reiterated; 'Mr Carlyle! Fat lot of good he's been. Why don't he *do* something for his money?'

'He has,' replied Carrados, with imperturbable good humour; 'he has sent me. Now, I want to ask you a few questions.'

'A few questions!' roared the irate man. 'Why, blast it, I have done nothing else but answer questions for a month. I didn't pay Mr Carlyle to ask me questions; I can get enough of that for nixes. Why don't you go and ask Mr Herbert Ananias Mead your few questions – then you might find out something.'

There was a slight movement by the door and Carrados knew that the girl had quietly left the room.

'You saw that, sir?' demanded the father, diverted to a new line of bitterness. 'You saw that girl – my own daughter, that I've worked for all her life?'

'No,' replied Carrados.

'The girl that's just gone out – she's my daughter,' explained Hutchins.

'I know, but I did not see her. I see nothing. I am blind.'

'Blind!' exclaimed the old fellow, sitting up in startled wonderment. 'You mean it, sir? You walk all right and you look at me as if you saw me. You're kidding surely.'

'No,' smiled Carrados. 'It's quite right.'

'Then it's a funny business, sir – you what are blind expecting to find something that those with their eyes couldn't,' ruminated Hutchins sagely.

'There are things that you can't see with your eyes, Hutchins.'

'Perhaps you are right, sir. Well, what is it you want to know?'

'Light a cigar first,' said the blind man, holding out his case and waiting until the various sounds told him that his host was smoking contentedly. 'The train you were driving at the time of the accident was the six-twenty-seven from Notcliff. It stopped everywhere until it reached Lambeth Bridge, the chief London station of your line. There it became something of an express, and leaving Lambeth Bridge at seven-eleven, should not stop again until it fetched Swanstead on Thames, eleven miles out, at seven-thirty-four. Then it stopped on and off from Swanstead to Ingerfield, the terminus of that branch, which it reached at eight-five.'

Hutchins nodded, and then, remembering, said: 'That's right, sir.'

'That was your business all day – running between Notcliff and Ingerfield?'

'Yes, sir. Three journeys up and three down mostly.'

'With the same stops on all the down journeys?'

'No. The seven-eleven is the only one that does a run from the Bridge to Swanstead. You see, it is just on the close of the evening rush, as they call it. A good many late business gentlemen living at Swanstead use the seven-eleven regular. The other journeys we stop at every station to Lambeth Bridge, and then here and there beyond.'

'There are, of course, other trains doing exactly the same journey – a service, in fact?'

'Yes, sir. About six.'

'And do any of those – say, during the rush – do any of those run non-stop from Lambeth to Swanstead?'

Hutchins reflected a moment. All the choler and restlessness had melted out of the man's face. He was again the excellent artisan, slow but capable and self-reliant.

'That I couldn't definitely say, sir. Very few short-distance trains pass the junction, but some of those may. A guide would show us in a minute but I haven't got one.'

'Never mind. You said at the inquest that it was no uncommon thing for you to be pulled up at the "stop" signal east of Knight's Cross station. How often would that happen – only with the seven-eleven, mind.'

'Perhaps three times a week; perhaps twice.'

'The accident was on a Thursday. Have you noticed that you were pulled up oftener on a Thursday than on any other day?'

A smile crossed the driver's face at the question.

'You don't happen to live at Swanstead yourself, sir?' he asked in reply.

'No,' admitted Carrados. 'Why?'

'Well, sir, we were *always* pulled up on Thursday;

244

practically always, you may say. It got to be quite a saying among those who used the train regular; they used to look out for it.'

Carrados's sightless eyes had the one quality of concealing emotion supremely. 'Oh,' he commented softly, 'always; and it was quite a saying, was it? And *why* was it always so on Thursday?'

'It had to do with the early closing, I'm told. The suburban traffic was a bit different. By rights we ought to have been set back two minutes for that day, but I suppose it wasn't thought worth while to alter us in the timetable, so we most always had to wait outside Three Deep tunnel for a westbound electric to make good.'

'You were prepared for it then?'

'Yes, sir, I was,' said Hutchins, reddening at some recollection, 'and very down about it was one of the jury over that. But, mayhap once in three months, I did get through even on a Thursday, and it's not for me to question whether things are right or wrong just because they are not what I may expect. The signals are my orders, sir – stop! go on! and it's for me to obey, as you would a general on the field of battle. What would happen otherwise! It was nonsense what they said about going cautious; and the man who started it was a barber who didn't know the difference between a "distance" and a "stop" signal down to the minute they gave their verdict. My orders, sir, given me by that signal, was "Go right ahead and keep to your running time!"'

Carrados nodded a soothing assent. 'That is all, I think,' he remarked.

'All!' exclaimed Hutchins in surprise. 'Why, sir, you can't have got much idea of it yet.'

'Quite enough. And I know it isn't pleasant for you to be taken along the same ground over and over again.'

The man moved awkwardly in his chair and pulled nervously at his grizzled beard.

'You mustn't take any notice of what I said just now, sir,' he apologised. 'You somehow make me feel that something may come of it; but I've been badgered about and accused and cross-examined from one to another of them these weeks till it's fairly made me bitter against everything. And now they talk of putting me in a lavatory – me that has been with the company for five and forty years and on the footplate thirty-two – a man suspected of running past a danger signal.'

'You have had a rough time, Hutchins; you will have to exercise your patience a little longer yet,' said Carrados sympathetically.

'You think something may come of it, sir? You think you will be able to clear me? Believe me, sir, if you could give me something to look forward to it might save me from—' He pulled himself up and shook his head sorrowfully. 'I've been near it,' he added simply.

Carrados reflected and took his resolution.

'Today is Wednesday. I think you may hope to hear something from your general manager towards the middle of next week.'

'Good God, sir! You really mean that?'

'In the interval show your good sense by behaving reasonably. Keep civilly to yourself and don't talk. Above all' – he nodded towards a quart jug that stood on the table between them, an incident that filled the simple-minded engineer with boundless wonder when he recalled it afterwards – 'above all, leave that alone.'

Hutchins snatched up the vessel and brought it crashing down on the hearthstone, his face shining with a set resolution.

'I've done with it, sir. It was the bitterness and despair that drove me to that. Now I can do without it.'

The door was hastily opened and Miss Hutchins looked anxiously from her father to the visitors and back again.

'Oh, whatever is the matter?' she exclaimed. 'I heard a great crash.'

'This gentleman is going to clear me, Meg, my dear,' blurted out the old man irrepressibly. 'And I've done with the drink for ever.'

'Hutchins! Hutchins!' said Carrados warningly.

'My daughter, sir; you wouldn't have her not know?' pleaded Hutchins, rather crestfallen. 'It won't go any further.'

Carrados laughed quietly to himself as he felt Margaret Hutchins's startled and questioning eyes attempting to read his mind. He shook hands with the engine driver without further comment, however, and walked out into the commonplace little street under Parkinson's unobtrusive guidance.

'Very nice of Miss Hutchins to go into half-mourning, Parkinson,' he remarked as they went along. 'Thoughtful, and yet not ostentatious.'

'Yes, sir,' agreed Parkinson, who had long ceased to wonder at his master's perceptions.

'The Romans, Parkinson, had a saying to the effect that gold carries no smell. That is a pity sometimes. What jewellery did Miss Hutchins wear?'

'Very little, sir. A plain gold brooch representing a merry-thought – the merry-thought of a sparrow, I should say, sir. The only other article was a smooth-backed gun-metal watch, suspended from a gun-metal bow.'

'Nothing showy or expensive, eh?'

'Oh dear no, sir. Quite appropriate for a young person of her position.'

'Just what I should have expected.' He slackened his pace. 'We are passing a hoarding, are we not?'

'Yes, sir.'

'We will stand here a moment. Read me the letter-press of the poster before us.'

'This "Oxo" one, sir?'

'Yes.'

' "Oxo", sir.'

Carrados was convulsed with silent laughter. Parkinson had infinitely more dignity and conceded merely a tolerant recognition of the ludicrous.

'That was a bad shot, Parkinson,' remarked his master when he could speak. 'We will try another.'

For three minutes, with scrupulous conscientiousness on the part of the reader and every appearance of keen interest on the part of the hearer, there were set forth the particulars of a sale by auction of superfluous timber and builders' material.

'That will do,' said Carrados, when the last detail had been reached. 'We can be seen from the door of No. 107 still?'

'Yes, sir.'

'No indication of anyone coming to us from there?'

'No, sir.'

Carrados walked thoughtfully on again. In the Holloway Road they rejoined the waiting motor car. 'Lambeth Bridge station,' was the order the driver received.

From the station the car was sent on home and Parkinson was instructed to take two first-class singles for Richmond, which could be reached by changing at Stafford Road. The 'evening rush' had not yet commenced and they had no difficulty in finding an empty carriage when the train came in.

Parkinson was kept busy that journey describing what he saw at various points between Lambeth Bridge and Knight's Cross. For a quarter of a mile Carrados's demands on the eyes and the memory of his remarkable servant were wide and incessant. Then his questions ceased. They had passed the 'stop' signal, east of Knight's Cross station.

The following afternoon they made the return journey as far as Knight's Cross. This time, however, the surroundings failed to interest Carrados. 'We are going to look at some rooms,' was the information he offered on the subject, and an imperturbable 'Yes, sir' had been the extent of Parkinson's comment on the unusual proceeding. After leaving the station they turned sharply along a road that ran parallel with the line, a dull thoroughfare of substantial, elderly houses that were beginning to sink into decrepitude. Here and there a corner residence displayed the brass plate of a professional occupant, but for the most part they were given up to the various branches of second-rate apartment letting.

'The third house after the one with the flagstaff,' said Carrados.

Parkinson rang the bell, which was answered by a young servant, who took an early opportunity of assuring them that she was not tidy as it was rather early in the afternoon. She informed Carrados, in reply to his enquiry, that Miss Chubb was at home, and showed them into a melancholy little sitting-room to await her appearance.

'I shall be "almost" blind here, Parkinson,' remarked Carrados, walking about the room. 'It saves explanation.'

'Very good, sir,' replied Parkinson.

Five minutes later, an interval suggesting that Miss Chubb also found it rather early in the afternoon, Carrados was arranging to take rooms for his attendant and himself for the short time that he would be in London, seeing an oculist.

'One bedroom, mine, must face north,' he stipulated. 'It has to do with the light.'

Miss Chubb replied that she quite understood. Some gentlemen, she added, had their requirements, others their fancies. She endeavoured to suit all. The bedroom she had in view from the first *did* face north. She would not have known, only the last gentleman, curiously enough, had made the same request.

'A sufferer like myself?' enquired Carrados affably.

Miss Chubb did not think so. In his case she regarded it

merely as a fancy. She had had to turn out of her own room to accommodate him, but if one kept an apartment-house one had to be adaptable; and Mr Ghoosh was certainly very liberal in his ideas.

'Ghoosh? An Indian gentleman, I presume?' hazarded Carrados.

It appeared that Mr Ghoosh was an Indian. Miss Chubb confided that at first she had been rather perturbed at the idea of taking in 'a black man', as she confessed to regarding him. She reiterated, however, that Mr Ghoosh proved to be 'quite the gentleman'. Five minutes of affability put Carrados in full possession of Mr Ghoosh's manner of life and movements – the dates of his arrival and departure, his solitariness and his daily habits.

'This would be the best bedroom,' said Miss Chubb.

It was a fair-sized room on the first floor. The window looked out on to the roof of an outbuilding; beyond, the deep cutting of the railway line. Opposite stood the dead wall that Mr Carlyle had spoken of.

Carrados 'looked' round the room with the discriminating glance that sometimes proved so embarrassing to those who knew him.

'I have to take a little daily exercise,' he remarked, walking to the window and running his hand up the woodwork. 'You will not mind my fixing a "developer" here, Miss Chubb – a few small screws?'

Miss Chubb thought not. Then she was sure not. Finally she ridiculed the idea of minding with scorn.

'If there is width enough,' mused Carrados, spanning the upright critically. 'Do you happen to have a wooden foot-rule convenient?'

'Well, to be sure!' exclaimed Miss Chubb, opening a rapid succession of drawers until she produced the required article. 'When we did out this room after Mr Ghoosh, there was this very ruler among the things that he hadn't thought worth taking. This is what you require, sir?'

'Yes,' replied Carrados, accepting it, 'I think this is exactly what I require.' It was a common new whitewood rule, such as one might buy at any small stationer's for a penny. He carelessly took off the width of the upright, reading the figures with a touch; and then continued to run a finger-tip delicately up and down the edges of the instrument.

'Four and seven-eighths,' was his unspoken conclusion.

'I hope it will do, sir.'

'Admirably,' replied Carrados. 'But I haven't reached the end of my requirements yet, Miss Chubb.'

'No, sir?' said the landlady, feeling that it would be a pleasure to oblige so agreeable a gentleman. 'What else might there be?'

'Although I can see very little I like to have a light, but not any kind of light. Gas I cannot do with. Do you think that you would be able to find me an oil lamp?'

'Certainly, sir. I got out a very nice brass lamp that I have specially for Mr Ghoosh. He read a good deal of an evening and he preferred a lamp.'

'That is very convenient. I suppose it is large enough to burn for a whole evening?'

'Yes, indeed. And very particular he was always to have it filled every day.'

'A lamp without oil is not very useful,' smiled Carrados, following her towards another room, and absentmindedly slipping the foot-rule into his pocket.

Whatever Parkinson thought of the arrangement of going into second-rate apartments in an obscure street it is to be inferred that his devotion to his master was sufficient to overcome his private emotions as a self-respecting 'man'. At all events, as they were approaching the station he asked, and without a trace of feeling, whether there were any orders for him with reference to the proposed migration.

'None, Parkinson,' replied his master. 'We must be satisfied with our present quarters.'

'I beg your pardon, sir,' said Parkinson, with some constraint. 'I understood that you had taken the rooms for a week certain.'

'I am afraid that Miss Chubb will be under the same impression. Unforeseen circumstances will prevent our going, however. Mr Greatorex must write tomorrow, enclosing a cheque, with my regrets, and adding a penny for this ruler which I seem to have brought away with me. It, at least, is something for the money.'

Parkinson may be excused for not attempting to understand the course of events.

'Here is your train coming in, sir,' he merely said.

'We will let it go and wait for another. Is there a signal at either end of the platform?'

'Yes, sir; at the further end.'

'Let us walk towards it. Are there any of the porters or officials about here?'

'No, sir; none.'

'Take this ruler. I want you to go up the steps – there are steps up the signal, by the way?'

'Yes, sir.'

'I want you to measure the glass of the lamp. Do not go up any higher than is necessary, but if you have to stretch be careful not to mark off the measurement with your nail, although the impulse is a natural one. That has been done already.'

Parkinson looked apprehensively around and about. Fortunately the part was a dark and unfrequented spot and everyone else was moving towards the exit at the other end of the platform. Fortunately, also, the signal was not a high one.

'As near as I can judge on the rounded surface, the glass is four and seven-eighths across,' reported Parkinson.

'Thank you,' replied Carrados, returning the measure to

his pocket, 'four and seven-eighths is quite near enough. Now we will take the next train back.'

Sunday evening came, and with it Mr Carlyle to The Turrets at the appointed hour. He brought to the situation a mind poised for any eventuality and a trenchant eye. As the time went on and the impenetrable Carrados made no allusion to the case, Carlyle's manner inclined to a waggish commiseration of his host's position. Actually, he said little, but the crisp precision of his voice when the path lay open to a remark of any significance left little to be said.

It was not until they had finished dinner and returned to the library that Carrados gave the slightest hint of anything unusual being in the air. His first indication of coming events was to remove the key from the outside to the inside of the door.

'What are you doing, Max?' demanded Mr Carlyle, his curiosity overcoming the indirect attitude.

'You have been very entertaining, Louis,' replied his friend, 'but Parkinson should be back very soon now and it is as well to be prepared. Do you happen to carry a revolver?'

'Not when I come to dine with you, Max,' replied Carlyle, with all the aplomb he could muster. 'Is it unusual?'

Carrados smiled affectionately at his guest's agile recovery and touched the secret spring of a drawer in an antique bureau by his side. The little hidden receptacle shot smoothly out, disclosing a pair of dull-blued pistols.

'Tonight, at all events, it might be prudent,' he replied, handing one to Carlyle and putting the other into his own pocket. 'Our man may be here at any minute, and we do not know in what temper he will come.'

'Our man!' exclaimed Carlyle, craning forward in excitement. 'Max! you don't mean to say that you have got Mead to admit it?'

'No one has admitted it,' said Carrados. 'And it is not Mead.'

'Not Mead . . . Do you mean that Hutchins—?'

'Neither Mead nor Hutchins. The man who tampered with the signal – for Hutchins was right and a green light *was* exhibited – is a young Indian from Bengal. His name is Drishna and he lives at Swanstead.'

Mr Carlyle stared at his friend between sheer surprise and blank incredulity.

'You really mean this, Carrados?' he said.

'My fatal reputation for humour!' smiled Carrados. 'If I am wrong, Louis, the next hour will expose it.'

'But why – why – why? The colossal villainy, the unparalleled audacity!' Mr Carlyle lost himself among incredulous superlatives and could only stare.

'Chiefly to get himself out of a disastrous speculation,' replied Carrados, answering the question. 'If there was another motive – or at least an incentive – which I suspect, doubtless we shall hear of it.'

'All the same, Max, I don't think that you have treated me quite fairly,' protested Carlyle, getting over his first surprise and passing to a sense of injury. 'Here we are and I know nothing, absolutely nothing, of the whole affair.'

'We both have our ideas of pleasantry, Louis,' replied Carrados genially. 'But I dare say you are right and perhaps there is still time to atone.' In the fewest possible words he outlined the course of his investigations. 'And now you know all that is to be known until Drishna arrives.'

'But will he come?' questioned Carlyle doubtfully. 'He may be suspicious.'

'Yes, he will be suspicious.'

'Then he will not come.'

'On the contrary, Louis, he will come because my letter will make him suspicious. He *is* coming; otherwise Parkinson would have telephoned me at once and we should have had to take other measures.'

'What did you say, Max?' asked Carlyle curiously.

'I wrote that I was anxious to discuss an Indo-Scythian inscription with him, and sent my car in the hope that he would be able to oblige me.'

'But is he interested in Indo-Scythian inscriptions?'

'I haven't the faintest idea,' admitted Carrados, and Mr Carlyle was throwing up his hands in despair when the sound of motor-car wheels softly kissing the gravel surface of the drive outside brought him to his feet.

'By gad, you are right, Max!' he exclaimed, peeping through the curtains. 'There is a man inside.'

'Mr Drishna,' announced Parkinson, a minute later.

The visitor came into the room with leisurely self-possession that might have been real or a desperate assumption. He was a slightly built young man of about twenty-five, with black hair and eyes, a small, carefully trained moustache, and a dark olive skin. His physiognomy was not displeasing, but his expression had a harsh and supercilious tinge. In attire he erred towards the immaculately spruce.

'Mr Carrados?' he said enquiringly.

Carrados, who had risen, bowed slightly without offering his hand.

'This gentleman,' he said, indicating his friend, 'is Mr Carlyle, the celebrated private detective.'

The Indian shot a very sharp glance at the object of this description. Then he sat down.

'You wrote me a letter, Mr Carrados,' he remarked, in English that scarcely betrayed any foreign origin, 'a rather curious letter, I may say. You asked me about an ancient inscription. I know nothing of antiquities; but I thought, as you had sent, that it would be more courteous if I came and explained this to you.'

'That was the object of my letter,' replied Carrados.

'You wished to see me?' said Drishna, unable to stand

the ordeal of the silence that Carrados imposed after his remark.

'When you left Miss Chubb's house you left a ruler behind.' One lay on the desk by Carrados and he took it up as he spoke.

'I don't understand what you are talking about,' said Drishna guardedly. 'You are making some mistake.'

'The ruler was marked at four and seven-eighths inches – the measure of the glass of the signal lamp outside.'

The unfortunate young man was unable to repress a start. His face lost its healthy tone. Then, with a sudden impulse, he made a step forward and snatched the object from Carrados's hand.

'If it is mine I have a right to it,' he exclaimed, snapping the ruler in two and throwing it on to the back of the blazing fire. 'It is nothing.'

'Pardon me, I did not say that the one you have so impetuously disposed of was yours. As a matter of fact, it was mine. Yours is – elsewhere.'

'Wherever it is you have no right to it if it is mine,' panted Drishna, with rising excitement. 'You are a thief, Mr Carrados. I will not stay any longer here.'

He jumped up and turned towards the door. Carlyle made a step forward, but the precaution was unnecessary.

'One moment, Mr Drishna,' interposed Carrados, in his smoothest tones. 'It is a pity, after you have come so far, to leave without hearing of my investigations in the neighbourhood of Shaftesbury Avenue.'

Drishna sat down again.

'As you like,' he muttered. 'It does not interest me.'

'I wanted to obtain a lamp of a certain pattern,' continued Carrados. 'It seemed to me that the simplest explanation would be to say that I wanted it for a motor-car. Naturally I went to Long Acre. At the first shop I said: "Wasn't it here that a friend of mine, an Indian gentleman, recently had a lamp made with a green glass that was nearly five inches across?" No, it was not there but they could make me one. At the next shop the same; at the third, and fourth, and so on. Finally my persistence was rewarded. I found the place where the lamp had been made, and at the cost of ordering another I obtained all the details I wanted. It was news to them, the shopman informed me, that in some parts of India green was the danger colour and therefore tail lamps had to show a green light. The incident made some impression on him and he would be able to identify their customer – who paid in advance and gave no address – among a thousand of his countrymen. Do I succeed in interesting you, Mr Drishna?'

'Do you?' replied Drishna, with a languid yawn. 'Do I look interested?'

'You must make allowance for my unfortunate blindness,' apologised Carrados, with grim irony.

'Blindness!' exclaimed Drishna, dropping his affectation of unconcern as though electrified by the word. 'Do you mean – really blind – that you do not see me?'

'Alas, no,' admitted Carrados.

The Indian withdrew his right hand from his coat pocket and with a tragic gesture flung a heavy revolver down on the table between them.

'I have had you covered all the time, Mr Carrados, and if I had wished to go and you or your friend had raised a hand to stop me, it would have been at the peril of your lives,' he said, in a voice of melancholy triumph. 'But what is the use of defying fate, and who successfully evades his destiny? A month ago I went to see one of our people who reads the future and sought to know the course of certain events. "You need fear no human eye," was the message given to me. Then she added: "But when the sightless sees the unseen, make your peace with Yama." And I thought she spoke of the Great Hereafter!'

'This amounts to an admission of your guilt,' exclaimed Mr Carlyle practically.

'I bow to the decree of fate,' replied Drishna. 'And it is fitting to the universal irony of existence that a blind man should be the instrument. I don't imagine, Mr Carlyle,' he added maliciously, 'that you, with your eyes, would ever have brought that result about.'

'You are a very cold-blooded young scoundrel, sir!' retorted Mr Carlyle. 'Good heavens! Do you realise that you are responsible for the death of scores of innocent men and women?'

'Do *you* realise, Mr Carlyle, that you and your government and your soldiers are responsible for the death of thousands of innocent men and women in my country every day? If England was occupied by the Germans who quartered an army and an administration with their wives and their families and all their expensive paraphernalia on the unfortunate country until the whole nation was reduced to the verge of famine, and the appointment of every new official meant the callous death sentence on a thousand men and women to pay his salary, then if you went to Berlin and wrecked a train you would be hailed a patriot. What Boadicea did and – and Samson, so have I. If they were heroes, so am I.'

'Well, upon my word!' cried the highly scandalised Carlyle, 'what next! Boadicea was a – er – semi-legendary person, whom we may possibly admire at a distance. Personally, I do not profess to express an opinion. But Samson, I would remind you, is a biblical character. Samson was mocked as an enemy. You, I do not doubt, have been entertained as a friend.'

'And haven't I been mocked and despised and sneered at every day of my life here by your supercilious, superior, empty-headed men?' flashed back Drishna, his eyes leaping into malignity and his voice trembling with sudden passion. 'Oh! how I hated them as I passed them in the street and recognised by a thousand petty insults their lordly English contempt for me as an inferior being – a nigger.

How I longed with Caligula that a nation had a single neck that I might destroy it at one blow. I loathe you in your complacent hypocrisy, Mr Carlyle, despise and utterly abominate you from an eminence of superiority that you can never even understand.'

'I think we are getting rather away from the point, Mr Drishna,' interposed Carrados, with the impartiality of a judge. 'Unless I am misinformed, you are not so ungallant as to include everyone you have met here in your execration?'

'Ah, no,' admitted Drishna, descending into a quite ingenuous frankness. 'Much as I hate your men I love your women. How is it possible that a nation should be so divided – its men so dull-witted and offensive, its women so quick, sympathetic and capable of appreciating?'

'But a little expensive, too, at times?' suggested Carrados.

Drishna sighed heavily.

'Yes; it is incredible. It is the generosity of their large nature. My allowance, though what most of you would call noble, has proved quite inadequate. I was compelled to borrow money and the interest became overwhelming. Bankruptcy was impracticable because I should have then been recalled by my people, and much as I detest England a certain reason made the thought of leaving it unbearable.'

'Connected with the Arcady Theatre?'

'You know? Well, do not let us introduce the lady's name. In order to restore myself I speculated on the Stock Exchange. My credit was good through my father's position and the standing of the firm to which I am attached. I heard on reliable authority, and very early, that the Central and Suburban, and the Deferred especially, was safe to fall heavily, through a motor bus amalgamation that was then a secret. I opened a bear account and sold largely. The shares fell, but only fractionally, and I waited. Then, unfortunately, they began to go up. Adverse forces were at work and rumours were put about. I could not stand the settlement, and in order to carry over an account I was literally compelled to deal temporarily with some securities that were not technically my own property.'

'Embezzlement, sir,' commented Mr Carlyle icily. 'But what is embezzlement on the top of wholesale murder!'

'That is what it is called. In my case, however, it was only to be temporary. Unfortunately, the rise continued. Then, at the height of my despair, I chanced to be returning to Swanstead rather earlier than usual one evening, and the train was stopped at a certain signal to let another pass. There was conversation in the carriage and I learned certain details. One said that there would be an accident some day, and so forth. In a flash – as by an inspiration – I saw how the circumstance might be turned to account. A bad accident and the shares would certainly fall and my position would be retrieved. I think Mr Carrados has somehow learned the rest.'

'Max,' said Mr Carlyle, with emotion, 'is there any reason why you should not send your man for a police officer and have this monster arrested on his own confession without further delay?'

'Pray do so, Mr Carrados,' acquiesced Drishna. 'I shall certainly be hanged, but the speech I shall prepare will ring from one end of India to the other; my memory will be venerated as that of a martyr; and the emancipation of my motherland will be hastened by my sacrifice.'

'In other words,' commented Carrados, 'there will be disturbances at half-a-dozen disaffected places, a few unfortunate police will be clubbed to death, and possibly worse things may happen. That does not suit us, Mr Drishna.'

'And how do you propose to prevent it?' asked Drishna, with cool assurance.

'It is very unpleasant being hanged on a dark winter morning; very cold, very friendless, very inhuman. The long trial, the solitude and the confinement, the thoughts of the long sleepless night before, the hangman and the pinioning and the noosing of the rope, are apt to prey on the imagination. Only a very stupid man can take hanging easily.'

'What do you want me to do instead, Mr Carrados?' asked Drishna shrewdly.

Carrados's hand closed on the weapon that still lay on the table between them. Without a word he pushed it across.

'I see,' commented Drishna, with a short laugh and a gleaming eye. 'Shoot myself and hush it up to suit your purpose. Withhold my message to save the exposures of a trial, and keep the flame from the torch of insurrectionary freedom.'

'Also,' interposed Carrados mildly, 'to save your worthy people a good deal of shame, and to save the lady who is nameless the unpleasant necessity of relinquishing the house and the income which you have just settled on her. She certainly would not then venerate your memory.'

'What is that?'

'The transaction which you carried through was based on a felony and could not be upheld. The firm you dealt with will go to the courts, and the money, being directly traceable, will be held forfeit as no good consideration passed.'

'Max!' cried Mr Carlyle hotly, 'you are not going to let this scoundrel cheat the gallows after all?'

'The best use you can make of the gallows is to cheat it, Louis,' replied Carrados. 'Have you ever reflected what human beings will think of us a hundred years hence?'

'Oh, of course I'm not really in favour of hanging,' admitted Mr Carlyle.

'Nobody really is. But we go on hanging. Mr Drishna is a dangerous animal who for the sake of pacific animals must cease to exist. Let his barbarous exploit pass into oblivion with him. The disadvantages of spreading it broadcast immeasurably outweigh the benefits.'

'I have considered,' announced Drishna. 'I will do as you wish.'

'Very well,' said Carrados. 'Here is some plain note-paper. You had better write a letter to someone saying that the financial difficulties in which you are involved make life unbearable.'

'But there are no financial difficulties – now.'

'That does not matter in the least. It will be put down to an hallucination and taken as showing the state of your mind.'

'But what guarantee have we that he will not escape?' whispered Mr Carlyle.

'He cannot escape,' replied Carrados tranquilly. 'His identity is too clear.'

'I have no intention of trying to escape,' put in Drishna, as he wrote. 'You hardly imagine that I have not considered this eventuality, do you?'

'All the same,' murmured the ex-lawyer, 'I should like to have a jury behind me. It is one thing to execute a man morally; it is another to do it almost literally.'

'Is that all right?' asked Drishna, passing across the letter he had written.

Carrados smiled at this tribute to his perception.

'Quite excellent,' he replied courteously. 'There is a train at nine-forty. Will that suit you?'

Drishna nodded and stood up. Mr Carlyle had a very uneasy feeling that he ought to do something but could not suggest to himself what.

The next moment he heard his friend heartily thanking the visitor for the assistance he had been in the matter of the Indo-Scythian inscription, as they walked across the hall together. Then a door closed.

'I believe that there is something positively uncanny

about Max at times,' murmured the perturbed gentleman to himself.

Once Upon a Train

CRAIG RICE AND STUART PALMER

Apart from being an excellent murder mystery set on the Super-Century Express bound from Chicago to New York, this next tale is also the very first in detective story history in which two authors brought their chief characters together on a case. For herein Craig Rice's whiskey-loving Chicago lawyer, John J. Malone, and Stuart Palmer's retired New York spinster detective Hildegarde Withers are unexpectedly thrown together in order to solve the murders of several passengers on the train, whose bodies mysteriously disappear. The combination – which Stuart Palmer himself confessed was 'as contrasty as oil and vinegar, and the two go just about as well together!' – startled detective story readers all over America when the case was first published in 1949 as 'The Loco Motive'. But such was its quality that the tale won that year's *Ellery Queen Mystery Magazine* prize as best story of the year, and at the same time was snapped up for a movie by MGM. The magazine, however, promptly retitled it 'Once Upon a Train' for its issue of October 1950, while MGM did the same thing with the picture – directed by Norman Taurog and starring Marjorie Main, James Whitmore and Ann Dvorak – by calling it *Mrs O'Malley and Mr Malone*. (The Mrs O'Malley of the title is the winner of a radio quiz contest whose prize is a trip to New York.)

The individual cases featuring John J. Malone and Hildegarde Withers owed a lot of their early popularity to being published in *Ellery Queen's Mystery Magazine*. Former journalist and scriptwriter Stuart Palmer

(1905–1968) launched the career of his thin, horse-faced amateur detective Miss Withers in 1931 in *The Penguin Pool Murder*, but by far the best of her exploits are those that subsequently appeared in short story form. The eccentric and acerbic sleuth was actually based on Palmer's high school English teacher, but the enduring image of her was that created by actress Edna May Oliver in a series of RKO films released in the thirties. Craig Rice (the pseudonym of Georgiana Ann Randolph, 1908–1957) worked as a public relations officer in Chicago before publishing several mystery novels in the early forties and thereafter being signed to work in Hollywood on the *The Falcon* mystery series which starred George Sanders. Here she ghosted a mystery novel under Sanders's name, *Crime on My Hands* (1944), as well as two for Gypsy Rose Lee which similarly carried the famous burlesque star's name on the title pages: *The G-String Murders* (1941) and *Mother Finds a Body* (1942). She created the bibulous lawyer John J. Malone in *Eight Faces at Three* (1939), and he thereafter appeared in a dozen more bestselling novels and collections of short stories during the next three decades. It was while she was working in Hollywood that Craig Rice was hired to collaborate on one of the *Falcon* movies with Stuart Palmer, and it was their happy working relationship that led to the landmark story which follows.

***

'It was nothing, really,' said John J. Malone with weary modesty. 'After all, I never lost a client yet.'

The party in Chicago's famed Pump Room was being held to celebrate the miraculous acquittal of Stephen Larsen, a machine politician accused of dipping some thirty thousand dollars out of the municipal till. Malone had proved to the jury and to himself that his client was innocent – at least, innocent of that particular charge.

It was going to be a nice party, the little lawyer kept telling himself. By the way Larsen's so-called friends were bending their elbows, the tab would be colossal. Malone hoped fervently that his fee for services rendered would be taken care of today, before Larsen's guests bankrupted him. Because there was the matter of two months' back office rent . . .

'Thank you, I will,' Malone said, as the waiter picked up his empty glass. He wondered how he could meet the redhead at the next table, who looked sultry and bored in the midst of a dull family party. As soon as he got his money from Larsen he would start a rescue operation. The quickest way to make friends, he always said, was to break a hundred-dollar bill in a bar, and that applied even to curvaceous redheads in Fath models.

But where *was* Steve Larsen? Lolly was here, wearing her most angelic expression and a slinky gown which she overflowed considerably at the top. She was hinting that the party also celebrated a reconciliation between herself and Stevie; that the divorce was off. She had hocked her bracelet again, and Malone remembered hearing that her last show had closed after six performances. If she got her hand back into Steve's pocket, Malone reflected, goodbye to his fee of three grand.

He'd made elaborate plans for that money. They not only included the trip to Bermuda which he'd been promising himself for twenty years, but also the redhead he'd been promising himself for twenty minutes.

Others at the table were worrying too. 'Steve is late, even for him!' spoke up Allen Roth suddenly.

Malone glanced at the porcine paving-contractor who was rumoured to be Larsen's secret partner, and murmured, 'Maybe he got his dates mixed.'

'He'd *better* show,' Roth said, in a voice as cold as a grave-digger's shovel.

The little lawyer shivered, and realised that he wasn't the

only guest who had come here to make a collection. But he simply had to have that money. $3,000 – $30,000. He wondered, half-musing, if he shouldn't have made his contingent fee, say, $2,995. This way it almost looked like . . .

'What did you say about ten per cent, counsellor?' Bert Glick spoke up wisely.

Malone recovered himself. 'You misunderstood me. I merely said, "When on pleasure bent, never muzzle the ox when he treadeth out the corn." I mean rye.' He turned to look for the waiter, not solely from thirst. The little lawyer would often have been very glad to buy back his introduction to Bert Glick.

True, the city-hall hanger-on had been helpful during the trial. In fact, it had been his testimony as a prosecution witness that cinched the acquittal, for he had made a surprise switch on several moot points of the indictment. Glick was a private detective turned bail-bondsman, clever at tapping wires and dipping his spoon into any gravy that was being passed.

Glick slapped Malone on the back and said, 'If you knew what I know, you wouldn't be looking at your watch all the time. Because this ain't a coming-out party, it's a surprise party. And the surprise is that the host ain't gonna be here!'

Malone went cold – as cold as Allen Roth's grey eyes across the table. 'Keep talking,' he said, adding in a whisper a few facts which Glick might not care to have brought to the attention of the district attorney.

'You don't need to be so nasty,' Glick said. He rose suddenly to his feet, lifting his glass. 'A toast! A toast to good ol' Stevie, our pal, who's taking the Super-Century for New York tonight, next stop Paris or Rio. And with him, my fine feathered friends, he's taking the dough he owes most of us, and a lot more too. Bon voyage!' The man absorbed the contents of his glass and slowly collapsed in his chair.

There was a sudden hullaballoo around the table. Malone closed his eyes for just five seconds, resigning himself to the certainty that his worst suspicions were true. When he opened his eyes again, the redhead was gone. He looked at his watch. There was still a chance of catching that New York train, with a quick stop at Joe the Angel's bar to borrow the price of a ticket. Malone rushed out of the place, wasting no time in farewells. Everybody else was leaving too. Finally, Bert Glick was alone, alone with the waiter and with the check.

As Malone had expected, Joe the Angel took a very dim view of the project, pointing out that it was probably only throwing good money after bad. But he handed over enough for a round trip, plus Pullman. By the time his cab had dumped him at the IC station, Malone had decided to settle for one-way. He needed spending money for the trip. There were poker games on trains.

Suddenly he saw the redhead! She was jammed in a crowd at the gate, crushed between old ladies, noisy sailors, and a bearded patriarch in the robes of the Greek Orthodox Church. She struggled with a mink coat, a yowling cat in a travelling case, and a caged parrot.

Malone leapt gallantly to her rescue, and for a brief moment was allowed to hold the menagerie, before a Redcap took over. The moment was just long enough for the lawyer to have his hand clawed by the irate cat, and for him and the parrot to develop a lifelong dislike. But he did hear the girl say, 'Compartment B in Car Ten, please.' And her warm grateful smile sent him racing off in search of the Pullman conductor.

Considerable eloquence, some trifling liberties with the truth, and a ten-dollar bill got him possession of the drawing-room next to a certain compartment. That settled, he paused to make a quick deal with a roving Western Union boy, and more money changed hands. When he finally swung aboard the already-moving train, he felt fairly confident that the trip would be pleasant and eventful. And lucrative, of course. The minute he got his hands on Steve Larsen . . .

Once established in the drawing-room, Malone studied himself in the mirror, whistling a few bars of 'On the Wabash Cannonball'. For the moment the primary target could wait. He was glad he was wearing his favourite Finchley suit, and his new green and lavender Sulka tie.

'A man of distinction,' he thought. True, his hair was slightly mussed, a few cigar ashes peppered his vest, and the Sulka tie was beginning to creep toward one ear, but the total effect was good. Inspired, he sat down to compose a note to Operation Redhead, in the next compartment. He knew it was the right compartment, for the parrot was already giving out with imitations of a boiler factory, assisted by the cat.

He wrote: *Lovely lady, let's not fight Fate. We were destined to have dinner together. I am holding my breath for your eyes. Your unknown admirer, JJM.* He poked the note under the connecting door, rapped lightly, and waited.

After a long moment the note came back, with an addition in a surprisingly precise hand. *Sir, you have picked the wrong girl. Besides, I had dinner in the Pump Room over an hour ago, and so I believe did you.*

Undaunted, Malone whistled another bar of the song. Just getting any answer at all was half the battle. So she'd noticed him in the Pump Room! He sat down and wrote swiftly, *Please, an after-dinner liqueur with me, then?*

This time the answer was: *My dear sir: MY DEAR SIR!* But the little lawyer thought he heard sounds of feminine laughter, though of course it might have been the parrot. He sat back, lit a fresh cigar, and waited. They were almost to Gary now, and if the telegram had got through . . .

It had, and a messenger finally came aboard with an armful of luscious *Gruss von Teplitz* roses. Malone intercepted him long enough to add a note which really should be the clincher. *To the Rose of Tralee, who makes all other women look like withered dandelions. I'll be waiting in the club car. Faithfully, John J. Malone.* That was the way, he told himself happily. Don't give her a chance to say No again.

After a long and somewhat bruising trip through lurching Pullman cars, made longer still because he first headed fore instead of aft, Malone finally sank into a chair in the club-car lounge, facing the door. Of course, she would take time to arrange the roses, make a corsage out of a couple of buds, and probably shift into an even more startling gown. It might be quite a wait. He waved at the bar steward and say, 'Rye, please, with a rye chaser.'

'You mean rye with a beer chaser, Mista Malone?'

'If you know my name, you know enough not to confuse me. I mean beer with a rye chaser!' When the drink arrived Malone put it where it would do the most good, and then for lack of anything better to do fell to staring in awed fascination at the lady who had just settled down across the aisle.

She was a tall, angular person who somehow suggested a fairly well-dressed scarecrow. Her face seemed faintly familiar, and Malone wondered if they'd met before. Then he decided that she reminded him of a three-year-old who had winked at him in the paddock at Washington Park one Saturday and then run out of the money.

Topping the face – as if anything could – was an incredible headpiece consisting of a grass-green crown surrounded by a brim of nodding flowers, wreaths, and ivy. All it seemed to need was a nice marble tombstone.

She looked up suddenly from her magazine. 'Pardon me, but did you say something about a well-kept grave?' Her voice reminded Malone of a certain Miss Hackett who had talked him out of quitting second-year high school. Somehow he found himself strangely unable to lie to her.

'Madam, do you read minds?'

'Not minds, Mr Malone. *Lips*, sometimes.' She smiled. 'Are you really *the* John J. Malone?'

He blinked. 'How in the – oh, of course! The *magazine*! Those fact detective sheets *will* keep writing up my old cases. Are you a crime-story fan, Mrs—?'

'Miss Hildegarde Withers, schoolteacher by profession and meddlesome old snoop by avocation, at least according to the police. Yes, I've read about you. You solve crimes and right wrongs, but usually by pure accident while chasing through saloons after some young woman who is no better than she should be. Are you on a case now?'

'Working my way through the second bottle,' he muttered, suddenly desperate. It would never do for the redhead to come in and find him tied up with this character.

'I didn't mean that kind of a case,' Miss Withers explained. 'I gather that even though you've never lost a client, you have mislaid one at the moment?'

Malone shivered. The woman had second sight, at least. He decided that it would be better if he went back through the train and met the Rose of Tralee, who must certainly be on her way here by this time. He could also keep an eye open for Steve Larsen. With a hasty apology he got out of the club car, pausing only to purchase a handy pint of rye from the bar steward, and started on a long slow prowl of mile after mile of wobbling, jerking cars. The rye, blending not unpleasantly with the champagne he had taken on earlier, made everything a little hazy and unreal. He kept getting turned around and blundering into the long-deserted diner. Two or three times he bumped into the Greek Orthodox priest with the whiskers, and similarly kept interrupting four sailors shooting craps in a men's lounge.

But – no redhead. And no Larsen. Finally the train stopped – could it be Toledo already? Malone dashed to the vestibule and hung over the step, to make sure that Steve didn't disembark. When they were moving again he resumed his pilgrimage, though by this time he had resigned himself to the fact that he was being stood up by the Rose of Tralee. At last, he turned mournfully back toward where his own lonesome cubicle ought to be – and then suddenly found himself back in the club car!

No redheaded Rose. Even The Hat had departed, taking her copy of *Official Fact Detective Stories* with her. The car was deserted except for a bridge game going on in one corner and a sailor – obviously half-seas over – who was drowsing in a big chair with a newspaper over his face.

The pint was empty. Malone told the steward to have it buried with full military honours, and to fetch him a cheese on rye. 'On second thought, skip the cheese and make it just straight rye, please.'

The drink arrived, and with it a whispered message. There was a lady waiting down the corridor.

Malone emptied his glass and followed the steward, trying to slip him five dollars. It slipped right back. 'Thanks, Mister Malone, but I can't take money from an old classmate. Remember, we went through the last two years of Kent College of Law together?'

Malone gasped. 'Class of '25. And you're Homer – no *Horace* Lee Randolph. But—'

'What am I doing here? The old story. Didn't know my place, and got into Chicago southside politics. Bumped up against the machine, and got disbarred on a phoney charge of subornation of perjury. It could have been squared by handing a grand to a certain sharper at City Hall, but I didn't have the money.' Horace shrugged. 'This pays better than law, anyway. For instance, that lady handed me five dollars just to unlock the private lounge and tell you she's waiting to see you there.'

The little lawyer winced. 'She – was she a queer old maid in a hat that looked like she'd made it herself?'

'Oh, no. No hat.'

Malone breathed easier. 'Was she young and lovely?'

'My weakness is the Numbers game, but I should say the description is accurate.'

Humming 'But 'twas not her beauty alone that won me, oh, no, 'twas the truth', Malone straightened his tie and opened the door.

Lolly Larsen exploded in his face with all the power of a firecracker under a tin can. She grabbed his lapels and yelped: 'Well, where is the dirty—'

'Be more specific. Which dirty—?' Malone said, pulling himself loose.

'*Steve*, of course!'

'I don't know, but I still hope he's somewhere on this train. You joining me in the search? Nice to have your pretty face among us.'

Lolly had the face of a homesick angel. Her hair was exactly the colour of a twist of lemon peel in a glass of champagne brut, her mouth was an overripe strawberry, and her figure might have inspired the french bathing-suit, but her eyes were cold and strange as a mermaid's. 'Are you in this with Steve?' she demanded.

Malone said: 'In simple, one-syllable words that even you can understand – No!'

Lolly suddenly relaxed, swaying against him so that he got a good whiff of brandy, nail polish, and Chanel Number Five. 'I'm sorry. I guess I'm just upset. I feel so terribly helpless.' For Malone's money, she was as helpless as an eight-button rattlesnake. 'You see,' Lolly murmured, 'I'm partly to blame for Steve's running away. I should have stood by him at the trial, but I hadn't the courage. Even afterward – I didn't actually promise to come back to him, I just said I'd come to his party. I meant to tell him – in the Pump Room. So, please, please help me find him – so I can make him see how much we really *need* each other!'

Malone said, 'Try it again, and flick the eyelashes a little bit more when you come to "need each other".'

Lolly jerked away and called him a number of things, of which 'dirty little shyster' was the most complimentary. 'All right,' she finally said in a matter-of-fact tone. 'Steve's carrying a hundred grand, and you can guess how he got it. I happen to know – Glick isn't the *only* one who's been spying on him since he got out of jail yesterday. I don't want Steve back, but I do want a fat slice for keeping my mouth shut. One word from me to the DA or the papers, and not even you can get him off.'

'Go on,' Malone said wearily. 'But you interest me in less ways than one.'

'Find Steve!' she told him. 'Make a deal and I'll give you ten per cent of the take. But work fast, because we're not the only ones looking for him. Steve doublecrossed everybody who was at that party this afternoon. He's somewhere on this train, but he's probably shaved off his moustache, or put on a fright-wig, or—'

Malone yawned and said, 'Where can I get in touch with you?'

'I couldn't get a reservation of any kind.' Her strange eyes warmed hopefully. 'But I hear you have a drawing-room?'

'Don't look at me in that tone of voice,' Malone said hastily. 'Besides, I snore. Maybe there'll be something available for you at the next stop.'

He was out of there and back in the club car before Lolly could turn on any more of the charm. He decided to have one for the road – the New York Central Road, and one for the Pennsy too. The sensible thing was to find Steve Larsen, collect his own hard-earned fee, and let Lolly alone. Her offer of ten per cent of the blackmail take touched on a sore spot.

Malone began to work his way through the train again, this time desperately questioning porters. The worst of it was, there was nothing remarkable about Larsen's appearance except curly hair, which he'd probably had straightened and dyed, a moustache that could have been shaved off, and a briefcase full of money, which he'd probably hidden. In fact, the man was undoubtedly laughing at everybody from behind a false set of whiskers.

Such were Malone's thoughts as he suddenly came face to face again with the Greek Orthodox priest, who stared past him through thick, tinted spectacles. The little lawyer hesitated and was lost. Throwing caution to the winds, he yanked vigorously at the beard. But it was an orthodox beard, attached in the orthodox manner. Its owner let loose a blast which just possibly might have been an orthodox Greek blessing. Malone didn't wait to find out.

His ears were still burning when he stepped into a vestibule and ran head on into Miss Hildegarde Withers. He nodded coldly and started past her.

'Ah, go soak your fat head!'

Malone gasped.

'It's the parrot,' Miss Withers explained, holding up the caged monstrosity. 'It's been making such a racket that I'm taking it to the baggage car for the night.'

'Where – where did you get that – bird?' Malone asked weakly.

'Why, Sinbad is a legacy from the aunt whose funeral I just went back to attend. I'm taking him back to New York with me.'

'New York!' Malone moaned. 'We'll be there before I find that—'

'You mean that Mr Larsen?' As he stood speechless, she went briskly on. 'You see, I happened to be at a family farewell party at the table next to yours in the Pump Room, and my hearing is very acute. So, for that matter, is my eyesight. Has it occurred to you that Larsen may be wearing a disguise of some sort?'

'That it has,' admitted Malone sadly, thinking of the Greek priest.

The schoolteacher lowered her voice. 'You remember that when we had our little chat in the club car some time ago, there was an obviously inebriated sailor dozing behind a newspaper?'

'There's one on every train,' Malone said. 'One or more.'

'Exactly. Like Chesterton's postman, you never notice them. But somehow that particular sailor managed to stay intoxicated without ordering a single drink or nipping at a private bottle. More than that, when you suddenly left he poked his head out from behind the paper and stared after you with a very odd expression, rather as if he suspected you had leprosy. I couldn't help noticing—'

'Madam, I love you,' the lawyer said fervently. 'I love you because you remind me of Miss Hackett back in Dorchester High, and because of your hat, and because you are sharper than a tack.'

Miss Withers sniffed, but it was a mollified sniff. 'Sorry to interrupt, but that same sailor entered our car just as I left it with the parrot. I just happened to look back, and I rather think he was trying the door of your drawing-room.'

Malone clasped her hand fondly. Unfortunately it was the hand that held the cage, and the parrot took advantage of the long-awaited opportunity to nip viciously at his thumb. 'Thank you so very much – some day I'll wring your silly neck,' was Malone's sincere but somewhat garbled exit-line.

'Go boil your head in lard,' the bird screamed after him.

The maiden schoolteacher sighed. 'Come on, Sinbad, you're going into durance vile. And I'm going to retire to my lonely couch, drat it all.' She looked wistfully over her shoulder. 'Some people have all the fun!'

But twelve cars, ten minutes, and four drinks later, Malone was lost again. A worried porter was saying, 'If you could only remember your car number, sah?' A much-harassed Pullman conductor added, 'If you'd just show us your ticket stub, we'd locate you.'

'You don't need to locate *me*,' Malone insisted. 'I'm right here.'

'Maybe you haven't got a stub.'

'I have so a stub. It's in my hatband.' Crafty as an Indian guide, Malone backtracked them unerringly to his drawing-room. 'Here's the stub – now where am I?'

The porter looked out the window and said, 'Just coming into Altoona, sah.'

'They lay in the wreck when they found them, they had died when the engine had fell . . .' sang Malone happily. But the conductor winced and said they'd be going.

'You might as well,' Malone told him. 'If neither of you can sing baritone.'

The door closed behind them, and a moment later a soft voice called, 'Mr Malone?'

He stared at the connecting door. The Rose of Tralee, Malone told himself happily. He adjusted his tie, and tried the door. Miraculously, it opened. Then he saw that it was Miss Hildegarde Withers, looking very worried, who stared back at him.

Malone said, 'What have you done with my redhead?'

'If you refer to my niece Joannie,' the schoolteacher said sharply, 'she only helped me get my stuff aboard and rode as far as Englewood. But never mind that now. I'm in trouble.'

'I knew there couldn't be two parrots like that on one train,' Malone groaned. 'Or even in one world.'

'There's worse than parrots on this train,' snapped Miss Withers. 'This man Larsen you were looking for—'

The little lawyer's eyes narrowed. 'Just what is your interest in Larsen?'

'None whatever, except that he's here in my compartment. It's very embarrassing, because he's not only dead, he's *undressed*!'

'Holy St Vitus!' gulped Malone. 'Quiet! Keep *calm*. Lock your door and *don't* talk!'

'My door is locked, and who's talking?' the school-teacher stepped aside and Malone peered gingerly past her. The speed with which he was sobering up probably established a new record. It was Larsen, all right. He was face down on the floor, dressed only in black shoes, blue socks, and a suit of long underwear. There was also a moderate amount of blood.

At last Malone said hoarsely, 'I suspect foul play!'

'Knife job,' said Miss Withers with professional cool-ness. 'From the back, through the *latissimus dorsi*. Within the last twenty minutes, I'd say. If I hadn't had some difficulty in convincing the baggage men that Sinbad should be theirs for the night, I might have walked in on the murderer at work.' She gave Malone a searching glance. 'It wasn't *you*, by any chance?'

'Do you think I'd murder a man who owed me $3,000?' Malone demanded indignantly. He scowled. 'But a lot of people are going to jump to that conclusion. Nice of you not to raise an alarm.'

She sniffed. 'You didn't think I'd care to have a man – even a dead man – found in my room in this state of undress? Obviously, he hasn't your money on his person. So – what is to be done about it?'

'I'll defend you for nothing,' John J. Malone promised. 'Justifiable homicide. Besides, you were framed. He burst in upon you and you stabbed him in defence of your honour . . .'

'*Just* a minute! The corpse was *your* client. You've been publicly asking for him all through the train. I'm only an innocent bystander.' She paused. 'In my opinion, Larsen was lured to your room purposely by someone who had penetrated his disguise. He was stabbed, and dumped here. Very clever, because if the body had been left in your room, you could have got rid of it or claimed that you were framed. But this way, to the police mind at least, it would be obvious that you did the job and then tried to palm it off on the nearest neighbour.'

Malone sagged weakly against the berth. His hand brushed against the leather case, and something slashed viciously at his fingers. 'But I thought you got rid of that parrot!' he cried.

'I did,' Miss Withers assured him. 'That's Precious in his case. A twenty-pound Siamese, also part of my recent legacy. Don't get too close, the creature dislikes train travel and is in a foul temper.'

Malone stared through the wire window and said, 'It's father must have been either a bobcat or a buzz saw.'

'My aunt left me her mink coat, on condition that I take both her pets,' Miss Withers explained wearily. 'But I'm beginning to think it would be better to shiver through these cold winters. And speaking of cold – I'm a patient woman, but not very. You have one minute, Mr Malone, to get your dead friend out of here!'

'He's no friend of mine, dead or alive,' Malone began. 'And I suggest—'

There was a heavy knocking on the corridor door. 'Open up in there!'

'Say something!' whispered Malone. 'Say you're un-dressed!'

'You're undressed – I mean, I'm undressed,' she cried obediently.

'Sorry, ma'am,' a masculine voice said on the other side of the door. 'But we're searching this train for a fugitive from justice. Hurry, please.'

'Just a minute,' sang out the schoolteacher, making frantic gestures at Malone.

The little lawyer shuddered, then grabbed the late Steve Larsen and tugged him through the connecting door into his drawing-room. Meanwhile, Miss Withers cast aside maidenly modesty and tore pins from her hair, the dress from her shoulders. Clutching a robe around her, she opened the door a crack and announced, 'This is an *outrage!*'

The train conductor, a Pullman conductor, and two Altoona police detectives crowded in, ignoring her protest. They pawed through the wardrobe, peered into every nook and cranny.

Miss Withers stood rooted to the spot, in more ways than one. There was a damp brownish-red spot on the carpet, and she had one foot firmly holding it down. At last the delegation backed out, with apologies. Then she heard a feeble, imploring tapping on the connecting door, and John J. Malone's voice whispering, 'Help!'

The maiden schoolteacher stuck her head out into the corridor again, where the search-party was already waiting for Malone to open up. 'Oh, officer!' she cried tremulously, 'is there any danger?'

'No, ma'am.'

'Was the man you're looking for a burly, dark-complexioned cut-throat with dark glasses and a pronounced limp in the left leg?'

'No, lady. Get lost, please, lady.'

'Because on my way back from the diner I saw a man like that. He leered, and then followed me through three cars.'

'The man we're looking for is an embezzler, not a mental case.' They hammered on Malone's door again. 'Open up in there!'

Over her shoulder Miss Withers could see the pale, perspiring face of John J. Malone as he dragged Steve Larsen back into her compartment again.

'But, officer,' she improvised desperately, 'I'm sure that the awful dark man who followed me was a distinct criminal type—' There was a reassuring whisper of 'Okay' from behind her, and the sound of a softly closing door. Miss Withers backed into her compartment, closed and locked the connecting door, and then sank down on the edge of her berth, trying to avoid the blankly staring eyes of the dead man.

Next door there was a rumble of voices, and then suddenly Malone's high tenor doing rough justice to 'Did Your Mother Come from Ireland?' The schoolteacher heard no more than the first line of the chorus before the jello in her knees melted completely. When she opened her eyes again, she saw Malone holding a dagger before her, and she very nearly fainted again.

'You were so right,' the little lawyer told her admiringly. 'It was a frame-up all right – but meant for me. *This* was tucked into the upholstery of my room. I sat on it while they were searching, and had to burst into song to cover my howl of anguish.'

'Oh, dear!' said Miss Withers.

He sat down beside her, patted her comfortingly on the shoulder, and said, 'Maybe I can shove the body out the window!'

'We're still in the station,' she reminded him crisply. 'And from what experience I've had with train windows, it would be easier to solve the murder than open one. Why don't we start searching for clues?'

Malone stood up so quickly that he rapped his head on the bottom of the upper berth. 'Never mind *clues*. Let's just find the murderer!'

'Just as easy as that?'

'Look,' he said. 'This train was searched at the request of the Chicago police because somebody – probably Bert Glick – tipped them off that Larsen and a lot of stolen money are on board. The word has got around. Obviously, somebody else knew – somebody who caught the train and did the dirty work. It's reasonable to assume that whoever has the money is the killer.'

There was a new glint in Miss Withers' blue-grey eyes. 'Go on.'

'Also, Larsen's ex-wife – or do I mean ex-widow? – is

aboard. I saw her. She is a lovely girl whose many friends agree that she would eat her young or sell her old mother down the river into slavery for a fast buck.' He took out a cigar. 'I'll go next door and have a smoke while you change, and then we'll go look for Lolly Larsen.'

'I'm practically ready now,' the schoolteacher agreed. 'But take *that* with you!'

Malone hesitated, and then with a deep sigh reached down and took a firm grasp of all that was mortal of his late client. 'Here we go again!'

A few minutes later Miss Hildegarde Withers was following Malone through the now-darkened train. The fact that this was somebody else's problem never occurred to her. Murder, according to her tenets, was everybody's business.

Malone touched her arm as they came at last to the door of the club car. 'Here is where I saw Lolly last,' he whispered. 'She only got aboard at the last minute, and didn't have a reservation.' He pointed down the corridor. 'See that door, just this side of the pantry? It's a private lounge, used only for railroad officials or big-shots like governors or senators. Lolly bribed the steward to let her use it when she wanted to have a private talk with me. It just occurred to me that she might have talked him into letting her have it for the rest of the night. If she's still there—'

'Say no more,' Miss Withers cut in. 'I am a fellow-passenger, also without a berth, seeking only a place to rest my weary head After all, I have as much right in there as she has. But you will be within call, won't you?'

'If you need help, just holler,' he promised. Malone watched as the schoolteacher marched down the corridor, tried the lounge door gently, and then knocked. The door opened and she vanished inside.

The little lawyer had an argument with his conscience. It wasn't just that she reminded him of Miss Hackett, it was that she had become a sort of partner. Besides, he was getting almost fond of that equine face.

Oh, well, he'd be within earshot. And if there was anything in the inspiration which had just come to him, she wasn't in any real danger anyway. He went on into the bar. It was half-dark and empty now, except for a little group of men in Navy uniforms at the far end, who were sleeping sprawled and entangled like a litter of puppies.

'Sorry, Mister Malone, but the bar is closed,' a voice spoke up behind him. It was Horace Lee Randoph, looking drawn and exhausted. He caught Malone's glance toward the sleeping sailors and added, 'Against the rules, but the conductor said don't bother 'em.'

Malone nodded, and then said, 'Horace, we're old friends and classmates. You know me of old, and you know you can trust me. *Where did you hide it?*'

'Where did I hide what?'

'You know what!' Malone fixed the man with the cold and baleful eye he used on prosecution witnesses. 'Let me have it before it's too late, and I'll do my best for you.'

The eyes rolled. 'Oh, Lawdy! I knew I shouldn't a done it, Mista Malone! I'll show you!' Horace hurried on down through the car and unlocked a small closet filled with mops and brooms. From a box labelled Soap Flakes he came up with a paper sack. It was a very small sack to hold a hundred thousand dollars, Malone thought, even if the money was in big bills. Horace fumbled inside the sack.

'What's *that*?' Malone demanded.

'What would it be but the bottle of gin I sneaked from the bar? Join me?'

The breath went out of John J. Malone like air out of a busted balloon. He caught the doorknob for support, swaying like an aspen in the wind. It was just at that moment that they both heard the screams.

The rush of self-confidence with which Miss Hildegarde

Withers had pushed her way into the lounge ebbed somewhat as she came face to face with Lolly Larsen. Appeals to sympathy, as from one supposedly stranded fellow passenger to another, failed utterly. It was not until the schoolteacher played her last card, reminding Lolly sharply that if there was any commotion the Pullman conductor would undoubtedly have them both evicted, that she succeeded in getting a toe-hold.

'Oh, *all right*!' snarled Lolly ungraciously. 'Only shut up and go to sleep.'

During the few minutes before the room went dark again, Miss Withers made a mental snapshot of everything in it. No toilet, no wardrobe, no closet. A small suitcase, a coat, and a handbag were on the only chair. The money must be somewhere in this room, the schoolteacher thought. There was a way to find out.

As the train flashed through the moonlit night, Miss Withers busily wriggled out of her petticoat and ripped it into shreds. Using a bit of paper from her handbag for tinder – and inwardly praying it wasn't a ten-dollar bill – she did what had to be done. A few minutes later she burst out into the corridor, holding her handkerchief to her mouth.

She almost bumped into one of the sailors who came lurching toward her along the narrow passage, and gasped, 'What do you want?'

He stared at her with heavy eyes, 'If it's any of your business, I'm looking for the latrine,' he said dryly.

When he was out of sight, Miss Withers turned and peeked back into the lounge. A burst of acrid smoke struck her in the face. Now was the time. '*Fire!*' she shrieked.

Thick billows of greasy smoke flooded out through the half-open door. Inside, little tongues of red flame ran greedily along the edge of the seat where Miss Withers had tucked the burning rags and paper.

Down the corridor came Malone and Horace Lee

Randolph, and a couple of startled bluejackets appeared from the other direction. Somebody tore an extinguisher from the wall.

Miss Winters grabbed Malone's arm. 'Watch her! She'll go for the money—'

The fire extinguisher sent a stream of foaming chemicals into the doorway just as Lolly Larsen burst out. Her mascara streaked down her face, already blackened by smoke, and her yellow hair was plastered unflatteringly to her skull. But she clutched a small leather case.

Somehow she tripped over Miss Withers' outstretched foot. The leather case flew across the corridor to smash against the wall, where it flew open, disclosing a multitude of creams, oils, and tiny bottles – a portable beauty parlour.

'She must have gone to sleep smoking a cigarette!' put in Miss Withers in loud clear tones. 'A lucky thing I was there to smell the smoke and give the alarm—'

But John J. Malone seized her firmly by the arm and propelled her back through the train. 'It was a good try, but you can stop acting now. She doesn't have the money.' Back in her own compartment he confessed about Horace. 'I had a wonderful idea, but it didn't pay off. The poor guy's career as a lawyer was busted by a City Hall chiseller. If Larsen was the one, Horace might have spotted him on the train and decided to get even.'

'You were holding out on me,' said Miss Withers, slightly miffed.

Malone unwrapped a cigar and said, 'If anybody finds that money, I want it to be me. Because I've got to get my fee out of it or I can't even get back to Chicago.'

'Perhaps you'll learn to like Manhattan,' she told him brightly.

Malone said grimly, 'If something isn't done soon, I'm going to see Manhattan through those cold iron bars.'

'We're in the same boat. Except,' she added honestly,

'that I don't think the inspector would go so far as to lock me up. But he does take a dim view of anybody who finds a body and doesn't report it.' She sighed. 'Do you think we *could* get one of these windows open?'

Malone smothered a yawn and said, 'Not in my present condition of exhaustion.'

'Let's begin at the beginning,' the schoolteacher said. 'Larsen invited a number of people to a party he didn't plan to attend. He sneaked on this train, presumably disguised in a Navy enlisted man's uniform. How he got hold of it—'

'He was in the Service for a while,' said the little lawyer.

'The murderer made a date to meet his victim in your drawing-room, hoping to set *you* up as the goat. He stuck a knife in him and then stripped him, looking for a money-belt or something.'

'You don't have to undress a man to find a money-belt,' Malone murmured.

'Really? I wouldn't know.' Miss Withers sniffed. 'The knife was then hidden in your room, but the body was moved in here. The money—' She paused and studied him searchingly. 'Mr Malone, are you sure you didn't—?'

'We plead not guilty and not guilty by reason of insanity,' Malone muttered. He closed his eyes for just five seconds' much-needed rest, and when he opened them a dirty-looking dawn was glaring in at him through the window.

'Good morning,' Miss Withers greeted him, entirely too cheerfully. 'Did you get any ideas while you were in dreamland?' She put away her toothbrush and added, 'You know, I've sometimes found that if a problem seems insoluble, you can sleep on it and sometimes your subconscious comes up with the answer. Sometimes it's even happened to me in a dream.'

'It does? It *has*?' Malone sat up suddenly. 'Okay. Burglars can't be choosers. Sleep and the world sleeps – I mean, I'll just stand watch for a while and you try taking a nap. Maybe you can dream up an answer out of your subconscious. But dream fast, lady, because we get in about two hours from now.'

But when Miss Withers had finally been comfortably settled against the pillows, she found that her eyelids stubbornly refused to stay shut.

'Try once more,' John J. Malone said soothingly. She closed her eyes obediently, and his high, whispering tenor filled the little compartment, singing a fine old song. It was probably the first time in history, Miss Withers thought, that anyone had tried to use 'Throw Him Down, McCluskey' as a lullaby, but she found herself drifting off . . .

Malone passed the time by trying to imagine what he would do with a hundred grand if he were the murderer. There must have been a desperate need for haste – at any moment, someone might come back to the murder room. The money would have to be put somewhere handy – some obvious place where nobody would ever think of looking, and where it could be quickly and easily retrieved when all was clear.

There was an angry growl from Precious in his cage. 'If you could only say something besides "Meeerow" and "Fssst"!' Malone murmured wistfully. 'Because you're the only witness. Now if it had been the parrot . . .'

At last he touched Miss Withers apologetically on the shoulder. 'Wake up, ma'am, we're coming into New York. Quick, what did you dream?'

She blinked, sniffed, and came wide awake. 'My dream? Why – I was buying a hat, a darling little sailor hat, only it had to be exchanged because the ribbon was yellow. But first I wore it out to dinner with Inspector Piper, who took me to a Greek restaurant and the proprietor was so glad to see us that he said dinner was on the house. But naturally we didn't eat anything because you have to beware of the Greeks when they come bearing gifts. His name was Mr Roberts. That's all I remember.'

'Oh, *brother*!' said John J. Malone.

'And there wasn't anyone named Roberts mixed up in this case, or anyone of Greek extraction, was there?' She sighed. 'Pure nonsense. I guess a watched subconscious never boils.'

The train was crawling laboriously up an elevated platform. 'A drowning man will grasp at a strawberry,' Malone said suddenly. 'I've got a sort of an idea. Greeks bearing gifts – that means look out for somebody who wants to give you something for nothing. And that something could include gratuitous information.'

She nodded. 'Perhaps someone planned to murder Larsen aboard this train and wanted you aboard to be the obvious suspect.'

The train shuddered to a stop. Malone leapt up, startled, but the schoolteacher told him it was only 125th Street. 'Perhaps we should check and see who gets off.' She glanced out the window and said, 'On second thought, let's not. The platform is swarming with police.'

They were interrupted by the porter, who brushed off Miss Withers, accepted a dollar from the gallant Malone, and then lugged her suitcases and the pet container down to the vestibule. 'He'll be in your room next,' she whispered to Malone. 'What do we do now?'

'We think fast,' Malone said. 'The rest of your dream! The sailor hat with the wrong ribbon! And Mr Roberts—'

The door burst open and suddenly they were surrounded by detectives, led by a grizzled sergeant in plain clothes. Lolly Larsen was with them. She had removed most of the traces of the holocaust, her face was lovely and her hair was gleaming, but her mood was that of a dyspeptic cobra. She breathlessly accused Miss Withers of assaulting her and trying to burn her alive, and Malone of engineering Steve Larsen's successful disappearance.

'So,' said Malone. 'You wired ahead from Albany, crying copper?'

'Maybe she did,' said the sergeant. 'But we'd already been contacted by the Chicago police. Somebody out there swore a warrant for Steve Larsen's arrest . . .'

'Glick, maybe?'

'A Mr Allen Roth, according to the teletype. Now, folks—'

But Malone was trying to pretend that Lolly, the sergeant, and the whole police department didn't exist. He faced Miss Withers and said, 'About that dream! It must mean a sailor under false colours. We already know that Larsen was disguised in Navy uniform . . .'

'Shaddap!' said the sergeant. 'Maybe you don't know, mister, that helping an embezzler to escape makes you an assessory after the fact.'

'*Acc*essory,' corrected Miss Withers firmly.

'If you want Larsen,' Malone said easily, 'he's next door in my drawing-room, wrapped up in the blankets.'

'Sure, sure,' said the sergeant, mopping his face. 'Wise guy, eh?'

'Somebody helped Larsen escape – escape out of this world, with a shiv through the – through the—?' Malone looked hopefully at Miss Withers.

'The *latissimus dorsi*,' she prompted.

The sergeant barked, 'Never mind the double-talk. Where is this Larsen?'

Then Lolly, who had pushed open the connecting door, let out a thin scream like tearing silk. 'It *is* Steve!' she cried. 'It's Steve, and he's dead!'

Momentarily the attention of the Law was drawn elsewhere. 'Now or never,' said Miss Withers coolly. 'About the Mr Roberts thing – I just remembered that there was a play by that name a while back. All about sailors in the last war. I saw it, and was somewhat shocked at certain scenes. Their language – but anyway, I ran into a sailor just after I started that fire, and he said he was looking for the *latrine*. Sailors don't use Army talk – in "Mr Roberts" they called it *the head*!'

Suddenly the Law was back, very direct and grim about everything. Miss Withers gasped with indignation as she found herself suddenly handcuffed to John J. Malone. But stone walls do not a prison make, as she pointed out to her companion-in-crime. 'And don't you see? It means—'

'Madam, I am ahead of you. There was a *wrong* sailor aboard this train even after Larsen got his. The murderer must have taken a plane from Chicago and caught this train at Toledo. I was watching to see who got off, not who got on. The man penetrated Larsen's disguise—'

'In more ways than one,' the schoolteacher put in grimly.

'And then after he'd murdered his victim, he took Larsen's sailor suit and got rid of his own clothes, realising that nobody notices a sailor on a train! Madam, I salute your subconscious!' Malone waved his hand, magnificent even in chains. 'The defence rests! Officer, call a cop!'

The train was crawling into one of the tunnels beneath Grand Central station, and the harried sergeant was beside himself. 'You listen to Mr Malone,' Miss Withers told their captor firmly, 'or I'll hint to my old friend Inspector Oscar Piper that you would look well on a bicycle beat way out in Brooklyn!'

'Oh, no!' the unhappy officer moaned. 'Not *that* Miss Withers!'

'That Miss Withers,' she snapped. 'My good man, all we ask is that you find the real murderer, who must still be on this train. He's wearing a Navy uniform . . .'

'Lady,' the sergeant said sincerely, 'you ask the impossible. The train is full of sailors. Grand Central is full of sailors.'

'But this particular sailor,' Malone put in, 'is wearing the uniform of the man he killed. *There will be a slit in the back of the jumper* – just under the shoulder blade!'

'When the knife went in,' Miss Withers added. 'Hurry, man! The train is stopping.'

It might still have been a lost cause had not Lolly put in her five cents. 'Don't listen to that old witch!' she cried. 'Officer, you do your duty!'

The sergeant disliked being yelled at, even by blondes. 'Hold all of 'em – her too,' he ordered, and leapt out on the platform. He seized upon a railroad dick, who listened and then grabbed a telephone attached to a nearby pillar. Somewhere far off an alarm began to ring, and an emotionless voice spoke over the public address system . . .

In less than two minutes the vast labyrinth of Grand Central was alerted, and men in Navy uniforms were suddenly intercepted by polite but firm railroad detectives who sprang up out of nowhere. Only one of the sailors, a somewhat older man who was lugging a pet container that wasn't his, had any real difficulty. He alone had a narrow slit in the back of his jumper.

Bert Glick flung the leather case down the track and tried vainly to run, but there was no place to go. The container flew open, and Precious scooted. Only a dumb Siamese cat, as Malone commented later, would have abandoned a lair that had a hundred grand tucked under its carpet of old newspapers.

'And to think that I spent the night within reach of that dough, and didn't grab my fee!' said Malone.

But it developed that there was a comfortable reward for the apprehension of Steve Larson, alive or dead. Before John J. Malone took off for Chicago, he accepted an invitation for dinner at Miss Withers' modest little apartment on West 74th Street, arriving with four dozen roses. It was a good dinner, and Malone cheerfully put up with the screamed insults of Sinbad and the well-meant attentions of Talley, the apricot poodle. 'Just as long as the cat stays lost!' he said.

'Yes, isn't it odd that nobody has seen hide nor hair of

Precious! It's my idea that he's waxing fat in the caverns beneath Grand Central, preying on the rats who are rumoured to flourish there. Would you care for another piece of pie, Mr Malone?'

'All I really want,' said the little lawyer hopefully, 'is an introduction to your redheaded niece.'

'Oh, yes, Joannie. Her husband played guard for Southern California, and he even made all-American,' Miss Withers tactfully explained.

'On second thought, I'll settle for coffee,' said John J. Malone.

Miss Withers sniffed, not unsympathetically.

The Rhine Maiden

LESLIE CHARTERIS

Just like detectives, spies and secret agents have also been making use of trains in fiction almost as long as the railways have been in existence. From some of Victor Whitechurch's very early stories such as 'The Affair of the German Dispatch Box' (1912) to John Jakes's 'Cloak and Dagger' (1965) by way of Eric Ambler's novel, *Background to Disaster* (1937), and Ian Fleming's famous James Bond escapade, *From Russia With Love* (1957), these undercover agents of the law have made dramatic and daring escapes from the most perilous situations thanks to steam power. Simon Templar, better known as The Saint, has had better reasons than most to be grateful to the express trains of Britain, Europe and even America. In a number of the forty-six books written about him by Leslie Charteris, the 'Robin Hood of Modern Crime' has taken to the rails in pursuit of criminals – especially in books such as *Enter the Saint* (1930), *The Saint in New York* (1935) and *The Saint in Europe* (1953).

The Saint's creator, Leslie Charteris (1907–1993), modelled his charismatic law-enforcer on an idealised view of himself, which made Simon Templar's love of good food and wine, smart clothes and luxury train travel all the more understandable. Charteris's love of adventure took him travelling to various parts of the world and inspired one of his most popular non-Saint books, *Lady on a Train* (1945), which was filmed that same year by Charles David for Universal Pictures. The story of a baffling murder on a 4-6-4 Streamliner on the New York central system, it starred

Deanna Durbin as a detective story fan who encourages her favourite crime story writer, played by David Bruce, to solve the crime ahead of the police. With its atmospheric score and Elwood Bredell's lustrous black-and-white photography, *Lady on a Train* has been described as 'a convincing suspenser as well as a send-up of the *noir* thriller' by critic William K. Everson.

The story included here, 'The Rhine Maiden', does feature The Saint, however, and was written by the author after what he described as an eventful train journey through France and Germany in 1954. In 1965 it was adapted for the long-running ITC television series, *The Saint*, starring Roger Moore with Nigel Davenport, Victor Beaumont and Stephanie Randall. Because of financial restrictions, however, the production was much more studio-bound than Charteris's original story of crime and punishment which, as the reader will now discover, takes place entirely in the carriages of a train speeding alongside the Rhine from Stuttgart to Mainz.

***

Simon Templar always thought of her as the Rhine Maiden for the simple reason that he met her on his way down the Rhine. He had never found the time or the inclination to sit through Wagner's epic on the subject, but he surmised that the Rhine Maidens of the operas would probably have been in keeping with the usual run of half-pint Siegfrieds and 200-pound Brunnhildes. The girl on the train was what Simon, in a mood of poetic fancy, would have liked a Rhine Maiden to be; and he didn't care whether she could sing top F or not.

Simon took the train because he had made the trip from Cologne to Mainz by boat before, and had announced himself a Philistine unimpressed. Reluctantly, he had summarised that much-advertised river as an enormous quantity of muddy water flowing northwards at tremendous speed under a litter of black barges and tugboats and pleasure steamers, with a few crumbling ruins on its banks smouldering awkwardly between clumps of factory chimneys. Scenically, it had been scanned and found wanting by the keen and gay blue eyes that had reflected every great river in the world from the Nile to the Amazon, even though he found the ruins a little pitiful, as if they had only asked to be left in the peace of years and had been refused. Also Simon took the train because it was quicker, and he had unlawful business to conclude in Stuttgart; which was perhaps the best reason of all.

For the saga of any adventurer take this: an idea, a scheme, action, danger, escape, and perhaps a surprise somewhere. Repeat indefinitely, with irregular interludes of quiet. Flavour it with the eternal discontent of unattainable horizons, and the everlasting content of an eagle's freedom. That had been Simon Templar's life since the day when he was first nicknamed the Saint; and it was his one prayer that he might be spared many years more in which to demonstrate the peculiar brand of saintliness which he had made his own. With valuable property burgled from an unsavoury ex-collaborationist's house near Paris in his valise, and his fare paid out of a wallet picked from the pocket of a waiter who had made the mistake of being rude to him, the Saint lit a cigarette and leaned back in his corner to be innocently glad that the lottery of travel could still shuffle a girl like that into the compartment chosen by the voyaging buccaneer.

She was very young – about seventeen or eighteen, he guessed – and her eyes were the bright greenish-blue that the waters of the Rhine ought to have been. She had pulled off her hat when she sat down, so that the unstudied symmetry of her curving honey-blonde hair framed her face in a careless aureole. She was beautiful. But there was something more to her than her mere unspoiled young beauty, something strange and startling that he could not define. She was the fairy princess that no man ever meets except in his most youthful dreams, the Cinderella that every man looks for all his life and knows he will never find. She was the woman that each man marries, only to find that he saw nothing but the mirror of his own hopes. And even when he had said that, the Saint knew that he had touched only a crude outline – that there was still something more which he might never be able to say. But because there seemed to be nothing of immediate importance in the newspaper he had bought at the station, and because even a lawless adventurer may find his own pleasure in the enjoyment of simple loveliness, Simon Templar leaned back with the smoke drifting past his eyes and wove romantic fantasies about the Rhine Maiden and the old man who was with her.

'This is der most vonderful river of der whole vorld, Greta,' said the old man, gazing out of the window. 'For der Danube der is a valtz; but this id der only river in der vorld dot has four operas written about it. Some day you shall see it all properly, Gretchen – die Lorelei, und Ehrenbreitstein, und all kinds of vonderful places—'

An adventurer lives on impulse, riding the crest of life only because he takes the wave in the split second where others hesitate. The Saint said, quietly and naturally, with a slight movement of his hand: 'I think there's some better stuff over that way. Over around the Eifel.'

The other two both looked at him; and the happy eyes of the solid old man lighted up.

'Ach, so you know your Chermany!'

Simon wondered what they would have said if he had explained that the police of two nations had once hunted him up from Innsbruck through Munich to Treuchtlingen and beyond, on a certain adventure that was one of his blithest memories; but he only smiled.

'I've been here before.'

'I know dot country, too,' said the old man eagerly, with his soft German-American accent faltering a little in his throat. 'When I vos a boy we used to try and catch fish in der river at Gemund; and vonce I got lost by myself in her voods going over to Heimbach. Now I hear der is a great *Thalsperre*, a big dam dot makes all der valley into a great lake. So maybe der is some more fish there now.'

It was if he had suddenly met an old friend; the sluice-gates of memory were opened at a touch, and the old man let them flow, stumbling through his words with the same naïve happiness as he must have stumbled through the woods and streams he spoke of as a boy. There were many places that the Saint also knew; and a nod of recognition here and there was almost as much encouragement as the old man needed. His whole life story, commonplace as it was, came pattering out with a childish zest that was almost frightening in its godlike simplicity. Simon listened, and was queerly moved.

' . . . Und so I vork and vork, und I safe money and look after my little Greta, und she looks after me, und we are very happy. Und then at last I can retire mit a little money, not much, but plenty for us; und Greta is grown up.'

The eyes of the old man shone with a serenity that was blinding, the eyes of a man who had never known the doubts and the fretfulness of his age, whose humble faith had passed utterly and incredibly unscathed through the squalid brawl of civilisation perhaps because he had never been aware of it.

'So now we come back to der Faderland to see my brother dot is a policeman in Mainz. Und Greta is going to see der vorld, und buy herself pretty clothes, und do all kinds of vonderful things. Isn't dot all we could vant, Gretchen?'

Simon glanced at the girl again. He knew that she had been studying his face ever since he had first spoken, but his clear gaze turned on her with its hint of the knowledge veiled down almost to invisibility. Even so, it took her by surprise.

'Why – yes,' she stammered; and then in an instant her confusion was gone. She slipped her hand under the old man's arm and rested her cheek on his shoulder. 'But I suppose it's all very ordinary to you.'

The Saint shook his head.

'No,' he said gently. 'I've known what it is to feel just like that.'

And in that moment, in one of those throat-catching flashes of vision where a man looks back and sees for the first time what he has left behind, Simon Templar knew how far he and the rest of the world had travelled when such a contented and unassuming honesty could have such a strange pathos.

'I know,' said the Saint. 'That's when the earth's at your feet, and you look at it out of an enchanted castle. How does the line go? – "Magic casements opening on the foam of perilous seas in faery lands forlorn . . ." '

'There's music in that,' she said softly.

But he wondered how much she understood. One never knows how magical the casements were until after the magic has been lost.

She had her composure back – even Rhine Maidens must have been born with that defensive armour of the eternal woman. She returned his gaze calmly enough, liking the reckless cut of his lean face and the quick smile that could be cynical and sad and mocking at the same time. There was a boyishness there that spoke to her own youth; but with it there were the deep-etched lines of many dangerous years which she was too young to read.

'I expect you know lots of marvellous places,' she said.

The Saint smiled.

'Wherever you went now would be marvellous. It's only tired and disillusioned people who have to look for sensations.'

'I'm spoiled,' she said. 'Ever since we left home I've been living in a dream. First there was New York, and then the boat, and then Paris, and Cologne – and we've scarcely started yet. I haven't done anything to deserve it. Daddy did it all by himself.'

The old man shook his head.

'No, Gretchen, I didn't do it all by myself. There was dot great man who helped me. You know?' He looked at the Saint. 'Und he is on this train himself!'

'Who's that?' asked the Saint cheerfully.

'Mr Voyson. Mr Bruce Voyson. He has der big factory where I vork. When I safe a little money I put it in his company because they pay so big dividends, und so there is always much more money; und I invest dot also, and so it all helps us. All my money I have in his company.'

Simon hardly moved.

'Sometimes I see him in der factory, und he has alvays something to say to me,' said the old man almost reverently. 'Now today I see him on der platform at Cologne. You remember, Greta? I think he is very tired with all the vork he does to look after the factory, because he is vearing dark glasses und he is very stooped like he never was before und his hair is gone quite white. But I recognise him because I have seen him so often, und besides he has a scar on his hand dot I remember so vell and I see it when he takes off his glove. So I go up und speak to him und thank him, und at first he does not recognise me. Of course he has so many employees in der big factory, how can he remember every one of them all der time? But I tell him, "You are Mr Voyson und I vork in your factory fifteen years und I invest all my money in your company, und I vant to thank you that now I can retire and go home." So he shakes hands with me, und then he is so busy that he has to go away. But he is on der train, too.'

'You put all your money in Voyson's company?' repeated the Saint, with a sudden weariness.

The old man nodded.

'Dot is how I mean, I didn't do it all by myself. If I hadn't done that I should've had to vork some more years.'

Simon Templar's eyes fell to the newspaper on his knee. For it was on that day that the collapse of the Voyson Plastics Company was exposed by the sudden disappearance of the president, and ruined investors learned for the first time that the rock on which they had been lured to found their fortunes was nothing but a quicksand. Even the local sheet which the Saint had bought devoted an entire column to the first revelations of the crack-up.

Simon drew a slow breath as if he had received a physical blow. There was nothing very novel about the story; there never will be anything very novel about these things, except for the scale of the disaster; and certainly there was nothing very novel about it in the Saint's experience. But his heart went oddly heavy. For a second he thought that he would rather anyone but himself should bring the tragedy – anyone who hadn't seen what he had seen, who hadn't been taken into the warmth and radiance of the enchanted castle that had been opened to him. But he knew that the old man would have to know, sooner or later. And the girl would have to know.

He held out the paper.

'Maybe you haven't read any news lately,' he said quietly, and turned away to the window because he preferred not to see.

The lottery of travel had done a good job. It reached out into the world and threw lives and stories together, shuffled them in a brief instant, and then left them altered for ever. An adventurer, a Rhine Maiden, an old man. Hope, romance, a crooked company promoter, a scrap of cheap newsprint, tragedy. Perhaps every route that carries human freight is the same, only one doesn't often see the working of it. Human beings conquering and falling and rising again, each in his own trivial little play, in the inscrutable loneliness which everything human makes for itself wherever crowds mingle and never know each other's names. Simon Templar had loved the lottery for its own sake, because it was a gamble where such infinitely exciting things could happen; but now he thought that it looked on its handiwork and sneered. He could have punched it on the nose.

After a long time the old man was speaking to him.

'It isn't true. It couldn't be true. Der great big company like dot couldn't break down!'

Simon looked into the dazed honest eyes.

'I'm afraid it must be true,' he said steadily.

'But I spoke to him only a little while ago. I thanked him. Und he shook hands with me.' The old man's voice was pleading, pleading tremulously for the light that wasn't there. 'No man could have acted a lie like dot . . . Vait! I go to him myself, and he'll tell me it isn't true.'

He stood up and dragged himself shakily to the door, holding the luggage rack to support himself.

Simon filled his lungs.

He fell back into the reality of it with a jolt like a plunge into cold water, which left him braced and tingling. Mentally, he shook himself like a dog. He realised that the fragment of drama which had been flung before him had temporarily obscured everything else; that because the tragedy had struck two people who had given him a glimpse of a rare loveliness that he had forgotten for many years, he had taken their catastrophe for his own. But they were only two of many thousands. One never feels the emotion of these things, except academically, until it touches the links of one's own existence. Life was life. It had happened before, and it would happen again. Of the many crooked financiers whom the Saint had known to their loss, there was scarcely one whose victims he had ever considered. But Bruce Voyson was actually on the train, and he must have been carrying some wealth with him, and the old man knew what he looked like.

The girl was rising to follow, but Simon put his hands on her shoulders and held her back.

'I'll look after him,' he said. 'Perhaps you'd better stay here.'

He swung himself through the door and went wafting down the corridor, long-limbed and alert. A man like Bruce Voyson would be fair game for any adventurer; and it was in things like that that the Saint was most at home. The fact that he could be steered straight to his target by a man who could really recognise the financier when he saw him, in spite of his disguise, was a miracle too good to miss. Action, swift and spontaneous and masterly, was more in the Saint's line than a contemplation of the brutal ironies of Fate; and the prospect of it took his mind resiliently away from gloom.

He followed the old man along the train at a leisured distance. At each pause where the old man stopped to peer into a compartment the Saint stopped also and lounged against the side, patient as a stalking tiger. Some time later he pushed into another carriage and found himself in the dining-car, for it was an early train with provision for the breakfasts of late-rising travellers. The old man was standing over a table half-way down; and one glance was enough to show that he had found his quarry.

Simon sank unnoticed into the adjoining booth. In a panel of mirror on the opposite side he could see the man who must have been Bruce Voyson – a thin dowdily dressed man with the almost white hair and tinted glasses which the old German had described. The glasses seemed to hide most of the sallow face, so that the line of the thin straight mouth was the only expressive feature to be seen.

The old German was speaking.

'Mr Voyson, I'm asking you a question und I vant an answer. Is it true dot your company is smashed?'

Voyson hesitated for a moment, as if he was not quite sure whether he had heard the question correctly. And then, as he seemed to make up his mind, his gloved fingers twisted together on the table in front of him.

'Absolute nonsense,' he said shortly. 'I don't know what you're talking about.'

The old man swallowed.

'Then vhy is it, Mr Voyson, dot der paper here says dot it is all smashed, und everyone vants to know where you are?'

'What paper is that?' demanded Voyson; but there was a harsh twitch in his voice.

The old man dropped it on the table.

'Dot's der paper. If you don't understand Cherman I translate it for you. It says: "Von of der biggest swindle in history was yesterday in Maxton, Ohio, exposed—" '

Voyson bit the corner of his mouth, then swung round.

'Well, what about it?'

'But Mr Voyson, you cannot speak of it like dot. You cannot realise vat it means. If it is true dot der money is all gone . . . You don't understand. All my life I vork and vork, und I safe money, und I put it all in your company. It cannot be true dot all my money is gone – dot all my life I have vork for nothing—'

'Suppose it is gone?' snapped Voyson. 'There are plenty of others in the same boat.' He sighed. 'It's all in the luck of the game.'

The old man swayed and steadied himself heavily.

'Luck?' he said hoarsely. 'You talk to me of luck? When I am ruined, und it says here dot it vas all a swindle – dot you are nodding but a criminal—'

Voyson's fist hit the table.

'Now you listen to me,' he rasped. 'We're not in America now – either of of us. If you've got any complaints you can take me back to Ohio first and then go ahead and prove I swindled you. That'll be soon enough for you to start shooting off your mouth about criminals. Now, what d'you think you're going to do about it? Think it over. And get the hell out of here while you do your thinking, or I'll call the guard and have you thrown off the train!'

The Saint's muscles hardened, and relaxed slowly. His dark head settled back almost peacefully on the upholstery behind him; but the wraith of a smile on his lips had the grim glitter of polished steel. A steward hovered over him, and he ordered a sandwich which he did not want without turning his head.

Minutes later, or it might have been hours, he saw his travelling acquaintance going past him. The old man looked neither to right nor left. His faded eyes stared sightlessly ahead, glazed with a terrible stony emptiness. His big toil-worn hands, which could have picked Voyson up and broken him across one knee, hung listlessly at his sides. His feet slouched leadenly, as if they were moved by a conscious effort of will.

Simon sat on. After another few minutes Voyson paid his bill and went past, walking jerkily. His coat was rucked up on one side, and Simon saw the tell-tale bulge on the right hip before it was straightened.

The Saint spread coins thoughtfully on the table to cover the price of his sandwich. His eyes ran over the selection of condiments which had come with it, and almost absent-mindedly he dropped the pepper-pot into his pocket. Then he picked up the sandwich as he stood up, took a bite from it, and sauntered out with it in his hand.

At the entrance of the next coach something caught at the tail of his eye, and he stopped abruptly. The door at the side was open, and the bowed figure of the old German stood framed in the oblong, looking out. The broad, rounded shoulders had a deathly rigidity. While Simon looked, the gnarled hands tightened on the handrails by which the figure held itself upright, stretching the skin white over the knuckles; then they let go.

Simon covered the distance in two lightning strides and

dragged him back. A train passing in the opposite direction blasted his ears with its sudden crashing clamour, and went clattering by in a gale of acrid wind. The old man fought him blindly, but Simon's lean strength pinned him against the bulkhead. The noise outside whisked by and vanished again as suddenly as it had come, giving place to the subdued rhythmic mutter of their own passage.

'Don't be a fool!' snapped the Saint metallically. 'What sort of help is that going to be to Greta?'

The old man's struggling arms went limp gradually. He gazed dumbly back, trying to understand. His throat moved twice, convulsively, before his voice came.

'Dot's right . . . Dot's right . . . I must look after Greta. Und she is so young . . .'

Simon let him go, and he went weakly past, around the corner into the main corridor.

The Saint lit a cigarette and inhaled deeply. It had been close enough . . . And once again he gave himself that mental shake, feathering himself down to that ice-cold clarity of purpose in which any adventurer's best work must be done. It was a tough break for the old Dutchman, but Simon couldn't keep his mind solely on that. He didn't want to. Such distractions as the rescuing of potential damn-fool suicides from sticky ends disturbed the even course of buccaneering. Voyson was on the train; and the ungodly prospered only that a modern pirate might loot them.

A little way further down the carriage Simon found the financier sitting in a first-class compartment by himself. The Saint eased back the door and stepped through, sliding it shut behind him. He stood with his sandwich in one hand and his cigarette in the other, balancing himself lightly against the sway.

'A word with you,' he said.

Voyson looked up.

'Who are you?' he demanded irritably.

'*New York Herald Tribune*, European editor,' said the Saint coolly and mendaciously. 'I want an interview. Mind if I sit down?'

He took a seat next to the financier as if he had never considered the possibility of a refusal.

'Why do you think I should have anything to tell you?'

The Saint smiled.

'You're Bruce Voyson, aren't you?' He touched the man's head, then looked at his finger-tips. 'Yes, I thought so. It's wonderful what a difference a little powder will make. And those dark glasses help a lot, too.' His fingers patted one of Voyson's hands. 'Besides, if there's going to be any argument, there ought to be a scar here which would settle it. Take that glove off and show me that you haven't got a scar, and I'll apologise and go home.'

'I've no statement to make,' said Voyson coldly, though the ragged edge of his nerves showed in the shift of his eyes and the flabby movement of his hands. 'When I have, you'll get it. Now, d'you mind getting out?'

'A bad line,' murmured the Saint reprovingly. 'Very bad. Always give the papers a break, and then they'll see you get a good seat when the fireworks go off.' He put his left arm round the financier's shoulders, and patted the man's chest in a brotherly manner with his right hand. 'Come along, now, Mr Voyson – let's have the dope. What's the inside story about your company?'

Voyson shook him off savagely.

'I've got no statement to make, I tell you! The whole story's a rigmarole of lies. When I get back I'll sue every paper that's printed it – and that goes for yours, too! Now get out – d'you hear?'

'Spoken like a man,' drawled the Saint appreciatively. 'We ought to have had a newsreel here to record it. Now, about this trip of ours—'

'Where did you get that?' whispered Voyson.

His eyes were frozen on the booklet of coloured papers

which the Saint was skimming through. Simon glanced up and back to them again.

'Out of your pocket,' he answered calmly. 'Just put me down as inquisitive.'

He turned the leaflets interestedly, examining them one by one until he came to the end. Then he replaced them in their neat folder, snapped the elastic, and stowed it away in his own pocket.

'Destination Batavia, I see,' he remarked genially. 'Well, I'm sure you'll be able to straighten everything out when you get back to Maxton. Putting duty before everything else and going home by the shortest route, too. Indonesia is on the direct line to Ohio from here – via Australia. Are you taking in Australia? You oughtn't to miss the wallabies . . . You certainly are going to have a nice long voyage to recover from the strain of trying to save your shareholders' money. And by the way, there are quite a lot of extradition difficulties from Indonesia to the United States when a guy is wanted for your particular kind of nastiness, aren't there?'

Voyson rubbed his chin with a shaking hand. His gaze was fixed on the Saint with the quivering intensity of a guinea-pig hypnotised by a snake.

'Picked my pocket, eh?' he got out harshly. 'I'll see your editor hears about that. I'll have you arrested!'

He reached for the communication cord. Simon tilted his head back and half-closed his eyes.

'What a story!' he breathed ecstatically. 'Of course it'll delay you a bit having to stay on in Germany to make the charge and see it all through. But if you think it's worth it, I do. It'd be front-page stuff!'

Voyson sank down again.

'Will you get out of my compartment?' he grated. 'I've stood as much from you as I intend to—'

'But you haven't stood as much from me as I've got waiting for you, brother,' said the Saint.

His eyes opened suddenly, very clear and blue and reckless, like sapphires with steel rapier-points behind them. He smiled.

'I'm here on business, Bruce,' he said in the same gentle voice with the tang of bared sword-blades behind its melting smoothness. 'I won't deceive you any longer – the *Herald Tribune* only knows me from the comic section. And I don't like you, brother. I never have cared much for your line of business, anyway, and the way you spoke to that poor old man in the dining-car annoyed me. Remember him? He was on the point of chucking himself off this train under another one just now when I happened along. Somehow, my pet, I don't think it would have distressed me nearly so much if you'd had the same idea.'

'Who are you?' asked Voyson huskily.

'I am the Saint – you may have heard of me. Just a twentieth-century privateer. In my small way I try to put right a few of the things that are wrong with this cock-eyed world, and clean up some of the excrescences I come across. You come into the category, comrade. You must be carrying quite a tidy bit of boodle along to comfort you in your exile, and I think I could spend it much more amusingly than you—'

Voyson's lips whitened. His hand slipped behind him, and Simon looked down at the barrel of an automatic, levelled into the centre of his chest. Only the Saint's eyebrows moved.

'You've been getting notions from some of these gangster pictures,' he said. 'May I go on with my eating?'

He put the sandwich on his knee and lifted off the top slice of bread. Then he felt in his pocket for the pepper-pot. The perforations in the top seemed inadequate, and he unscrewed the cap.

Voyson squinted at him.

'That makes it easier to deal with you,' he said; and then a cloud of pepper struck him squarely in the face.

It came with a crisp upward fling that drove the powder straight up his nostrils and up under the shield of his glasses into his eyes. He choked and gasped, and in the same instant his gun was struck aside and detached skilfully from his fingers.

Minutes of streaming agony passed before his tortured vision returned. While he wept with the stinging pain of it his pockets were rifled again, this time without any attempt at stealth. Once he tried to rise, and was pushed back like a child. He huddled away and waited impotently for the blindness to wear off.

When he looked up the Saint was still there, sitting on the seat opposite him with a handkerchief over his face and a litter of papers sorted out on his lap and overflowing on either side. The window had been lowered so that the draught could clear the air.

'You crook!' Voyson moaned.

'Well, well, well!' murmured the Saint amiably. 'So the little man's come to the surface again. Bad business, that hay fever of yours. Speaking as one crook to another, Bruce, you ought to give up gun-play until you're cured. Sneezing spoils the aim.'

He removed the handkerchief from his face, sniffed the air cautiously and tucked the silk square back in his pocket. Then he began to gather up the papers he had been investigating.

'I can only find ninety thousand dollars in cash,' he said. 'That's not a lot of booty out of a five-million-dollar swindle. But I see there are notes of two-million-dollar transfers to the Asiatic Bank in Batavia; so maybe you didn't do so badly out of it. I wish we could touch some of that bank account, though.'

He enveloped the documents deliberately in the wallet from which he had taken them, and tossed it back. Voyson's bloodshot glare steadied itself.

'I'll see that you don't get away with this,' he snarled.

'Tell me how,' invited the Saint, but his smile was still a glitter of clean-cut marble.

'Wait till we get to Mainz. There are plenty of people on this train. What are you going to do – walk me out of the station under that gun in broad daylight? I'd like to see you do it. I'll call your bluff!'

'Still hankering for that publicity?'

'I've got to have those tickets,' said Voyson, with his chest labouring. 'And my money. I've got to get to Batavia. You won't stop me! I shan't have to stay behind to make any charges. Your having a gun will be enough – and my money and tickets on you. I know the number of all those bills, and the tickets are signed with my name. The police'll be glad to see you!' Voyson's hands were clenching and twitching spasmodically. 'I think I read about you being in trouble here some time ago, didn't I?'

Simon said nothing, and Voyson's voice picked up. It grew louder than it need have done, almost as if the financier was trying to bolster up his own confidence with the sound of it.

'The German police wanted you pretty badly then! You're the Saint, eh? It's a good thing you told me.'

'You make things very difficult, brother,' said the Saint.

His quietness was unruffled, almost reflective; yet to any man in his senses that very quietness should have flared with warnings. Voyson was beyond seeing them. He leaned forward with the red pin-points in his stare glittering.

'I want to do it,' he raved. 'You've come to the wrong man with your nonsense. I'll give you thirty seconds to hand back my tickets—'

'One moment,' said the Saint.

His soft incisiveness floated like a white-hot filament across the other's babble of speech; and suddenly Voyson saw the coldness of his eyes and went silent.

'You're reminding me of things that I haven't remembered for a long time,' said the Saint soberly.

His cigarette-end dropped beside his heel, and was trodden out. The blue eyes never looked down at it.

'You're right – the Saint has been something of a crook sometimes, even if that didn't hurt anybody but specimens like you. And since I reformed I've become rather sophisticated. Maybe it's a pity. One loses sight of some simple elementary things that were very good. It wasn't always like that. Since you know my name so well, you may remember that I once had only one cure for creatures like you. I was judge and executioner.'

The train thundered south, perfected machinery roaring on its unswerving lines through a world of logic and materialism forged into wheels. And in one compartment of it Bruce Voyson sat mute, clutched in an eerie spell that drove like a clammy wind through the logic on which he had based his life.

'Romantic, wasn't it?' went on that incredible voice. 'But the law has so many loopholes. Before it can hang you for murder you've got to beat your victim's brains out with a club. And yet you are a murderer, aren't you? Just a few minutes ago a friend of ours would have committed suicide on your account if I hadn't spotted him in the nick of time. For all I know, others may have done the same thing already. Certainly some of your victims will. And while that's going on, you're on your way to Batavia to enjoy at least two million dollars of their money – two million which would do a little towards helping them to a fresh start. And all those dollars would be available for the receivers if you met with an unfortunate accident. There doesn't seem to be any obvious reason why you should go on living, does there?'

Simon Templar put his hand in his pocket and took out the folder of tickets. Deliberately he tore it across twice and scattered the pieces out of the window. Voyson started forward with a strangled gasp, and looked into the muzzle of his own gun.

'You've reminded me of days that I like to remember,' said the Saint. 'There is a justice above the law; and it seems just that a man like you should die.'

Voyson's red-rimmed eyes narrowed, and then he flung himself across the short space.

Simon took out a handkerchief and wiped the gun carefully all over. It was a small-calibre weapon, and the single crack of it should not have alarmed anyone who heard it among the other noises of the train.

Still holding it in his handkerchief, he folded Voyson's fingers around the butt, taking care to impress their prints on the shiny surface. Voyson slumped in the corner, with the bullet puncture in his right temple showing the centre of a shaded circle of burnt cordite. Working with dispassionate speed, the Saint dropped his sandwich and pepper-pot out of the window, picked up a couple of crumbs, and erased his fingerprints from the handle. He wiped the inside catch of the door in the same way, slid it back, and brushed his handkerchief over the outside as he closed it again. There was no flaw in the scene; nothing could have seemed more natural than that a man in Voyson's position should have lost his nerve and taken the easy way out. Simon was without pity or regret.

But as he went back to his own compartment he felt happy. He had always known that the old days were good; and the return had its own emotion.

He saw his fellow-travellers again with a sense of surprise and unreality. For a while he had almost forgotten them. But the old German caught his hand as he sat down, holding it in a kind of tremulous eagerness, with a pathetic brilliance awake in his dulled eyes.

'I vant to thank you,' he said. 'You safe me from doing something very foolish. I vas a coward – a traitor. I run away.'

'Don't we all?' said the Saint.

The old man shook his head.

'Dot vould have been a wicked thing to do. But I am not like dot now. Perhaps it isn't so bad. I am used to vork, und at my age I have so much experience, I am a better vorkman than any young man. So I say I go back und vork again. Does a few more years matter so much?'

'And I'm going to work too,' said the girl. 'Between us, we'll get it all back twice as quickly.'

Simon looked at them both for a long time.

There were ninety thousand dollars in his pocket, which was money in any man's life. He could have enjoyed every cent of it. He didn't want to see what he was seeing.

And yet, half against his will, against the resentful primitive selfishness which is rooted in every man, adventurer or not, he found himself looking at something grand and indestructible. Even the enigma of the Rhine Maiden baffled him no longer. He saw it only as the riddle of the ultimate woman waiting for life in the fearless faith of the enchanted castle, waiting for the knight in shining armour who must come riding down the hills of the morning with her name on his shield. And he did not want to see the magic dimmed.

'I don't think you'll have to do that,' he said.

He smiled, and held out the thin folds of bills he had taken. Life was still rich; he could take plenty more. And some things were cheap at any price.

'I had a word with Voyson myself. I think I made him see that he couldn't get away with what he was doing. Anyway, he changed his mind. He asked me to give you this.'

The train was slowing up; and a guard came down the corridor shouting 'Hier Mainz, alles umsteigen!' Simon stood up and took down his valise. Being human, he was aware that the girl's eyes were fixed on him with an odd breathlessness; and he thought that she could carry with her many worse ideals.

Murder on the 7.16

MICHAEL INNES

Sir John Appleby, the detective in this next story, is not only the most senior policeman in crime fiction – after a meteoric rise from the ranks by way of an inspectorship he has become Commissioner of the Metropolitan Police and the recipient of a knighthood – but he has also been referred to as one of the most erudite sleuths in the detective story genre. He is fully conversant with modern police techniques and has a formidable knowledge of forensic science. University educated, Appleby is at ease with people from all walks of life, be they criminals or nobility, and is as happy travelling by train as in an official car. Indeed, Appleby takes to the rails in several novels including *Stop Press* (1939) and *The Open House* (1972), as well as in a number of short stories including 'Dead Man's Shoes' and 'Murder on the 7.16' which, despite its rather prosaic title, is actually a tale of a brutal crime during the making of a railway movie.

Michael Innes was the pen-name of John Innes Mackintosh Stewart (1906–1995), the scholarly novelist and biographer who also published distinguished crime stories under his own name as J. I. M. Stewart, including the aptly titled *The Man Who Wrote Detective Stories* (1959). For much of his life he was a professor of English at universities in England and Australia, and it was during a sea voyage home in 1934 that he wrote the first of his mysteries about Appleby, *Death at the President's Lodgings*. Over thirty novels and short stories about the redoubtable commissioner have helped to make him one of the most popular characters in English crime fiction, a series which has now sadly come to an end with the author's recent death. Here, though, is a reminder of Sir John at his most perceptive *and* deceptive.

* * *

Appleby looked at the railway carriage for a moment in silence. 'You couldn't call it rolling-stock,' he said.

This was true. The carriage stood not on wheels but on trestles. And it had other peculiarities. On the far side of the corridor all was in order; sliding doors, plenty of plate glass, and compartments with what appeared to be comfortably upholstered seats. But the corridor itself was simply a broad platform ending in air. Mechanically propelled contrivances could manœuvre on it easily. That, of course, was the idea.

Appleby swung himself up and peered through one of the compartments at what lay beyond. He saw nothing but a large white concave surface. 'Monotonous view,' he murmured. 'Not for lovers of the picturesque.'

The producer laughed shortly. 'You should see it when we're shooting the damned thing. The diorama, you know. Project whole landscapes on that, we do. They hurtle past. And rock gently. It's terrific.' Realising that his enthusiasm was unseemly, he checked himself and frowned. 'Well, you'd better view the body. Several of your people on the job already, I may say.'

Appleby nodded, and moved along the hypertrophied corridor. 'What are you filming?' he asked.

'It's a thriller. I've no use for trains, if they're not in a thriller – or for thrillers, if there isn't a train.' The producer didn't pause on this generalisation. 'Just cast your mind back a bit, Sir John. Cast it back to September, 1955.'

Appleby considered. 'The tail end of a hot, dry summer.'

'Quite so. But there was something else. Do you

remember one of the evening papers running a series of short mystery stories, each called "Murder on the Seven-sixteen".'

'Yes. Oddly enough, I think I do.'

'We're filming one of them.'

'In fact, this *is* the seven-sixteen?' Appleby, although accustomed to bizarre occasions, was looking at the producer in some astonishment. 'And perhaps you're going to tell me that the murdered man is the fellow who wrote the story?'

'Good lord, no!' The producer was rather shocked. 'You don't imagine, Sir John, we'd insist on having you along to investigate the death of anyone like that. This corpse is important. Or was important, I suppose I should say. Our ace director. Lemuel Whale.'

'Fellow who does those utterly mad and freakish affairs?'

'That's him. Marvellous hand at putting across his own crazy vision of things. Brilliant – quite brilliant.'

It seemed that Whale was in the habit of letting himself into the studios at all hours, and wandering round the sets. He got his inspiration that way. Or he got part of it that way and part of it from a flask of brandy. If he was feeling sociable, and the brandy was holding out, he would pay a visit to Ferrett, the nightwatchman, before he left. They would have a drink together, and then Whale would clear out in his car.

This time Ferrett hadn't seen Whale – or not alive. That, at least, was his story. He had been aware that Whale was about, because quite early on this winter night he had seen lights going on here and there. But he hadn't received a visit. And when there was still a light on in this studio at 4 a.m. he went to turn it off. He supposed Whale had just forgotten about it. Everything seemed quite in order – but nevertheless something had prompted him to climb up and take a look at the 7.16. He liked trains, anyway. Had done ever since he was a kid. Whale was in the end compartment, quite dead. He had been bludgeoned.

Ferrett's was an unsupported story – and at the best it must be said that he took his duties lightly. He might have to be questioned very closely. But at present Appleby wanted to ask him only one thing. 'Just what was it that made you climb up and look through this so-called seven-sixteen?'

For a moment the man was silent. He looked stupid but not uneasy. 'I tell you, I always liked them. The sound of them. The smell of them. Excited me ever since I was a nipper.'

'But you've seen this affair in the studio often enough, haven't you? And, after all, it's *not* a train. There wasn't any sound or smell here?'

'There weren't no sound. But there was the smell, all right.'

'Rubbish, Ferrett. If there was any smell, it was of Whale's cursed brandy.' It was the producer who broke in. 'This place makes talkies – not feelies or tasties or smellies. *This* train just doesn't smell of train. And it never did.'

Appleby shook his head. 'As a matter of fact, you're wrong. I've got a very keen nose, as it happens. And that compartment – the one in which Whale died – does, very faintly, smell of trains. I'm going to have another look.' And Appleby returned to the compartment from which Whale's body had just been removed. When he reappeared he was frowning. 'At first one notices only the oceans of blood. Anything nasty happening to a scalp does that. But there's something else. That split-new upholstery on one side is slightly soiled. What it suggests to me is somebody in an oily boiler-suit.'

The producer was impatient. 'Nobody like that comes here. It just doesn't make sense.'

'Unsolved mysteries seldom do.' Appleby turned back to Ferrett. 'What lights were on when you came in here?'

'Only the line of lights in the seven-sixteen itself, sir. Not bright, they weren't. But enough for me to—'

Ferrett was interrupted by a shout from the centre of the studio. A man in shirt-sleeves was hurrying forward, gesticulating wrathfully. The producer turned on him. 'What the devil is wrong with you?'

'It's not merely Whale's flaming head that's suffering in this affair. It's my projector too. Somebody's taken a bleeding hammer to it. I call that beyond a joke.'

Appleby nodded gravely. 'This whole affair went beyond a joke, I agree. But I've a notion it certainly began in one.'

There was a moment's perplexed silence, and then another newcomer presented himself in the form of a uniformed sergeant of police. He walked straight up to Appleby. 'A fellow called Slack,' he murmured. 'Railway linesman. Turned up at the local station in a great state. Says he reckons he did something pretty bad somewhere round about here last night.'

Appleby nodded sombrely. 'I'm afraid, poor devil, he's right.'

'You didn't know,' Appleby asked next day, 'that there's a real seven-sixteen p.m. from your nearest railway station?'

The producer shook his head. 'Never travel on trains.'

'Well, there is. And Slack was straying along the road, muttering that he'd missed it, when Whale stopped his car and picked him up. Whale was already a bit tight, and he supposed that Slack was very tight indeed. Actually Slack has queer fits – loses his memory, wanders off, and so on – and this was one of them. That was why he was still in his oil-soaked work-clothes, and still carrying the long-handled hammer-affair he goes about tapping things with. There just wasn't any liquor in Slack at all. But Whale, in his own fuddled state, had no notion of what he was dealing with. And so he thought up his funny joke.'

'He always was a damned freakish fool over such things.' The producer spoke energetically. 'A funny joke with *our* seven-sixteen?'

'Precisely. It was the coincidence that put it in his head. He promised Slack to get him to his train at the next station. And then he drove him here. It was already dark, of course, and he found it enormous fun kidding this drunk – as he still thought him – that they were making it by the skin of their teeth. That sort of thing. No doubt there was a certain professional vanity involved. When he'd got Slack into that compartment, and turned on your gadget for setting scenery hurtling by, it was too amusing for words. Then he over-reached himself.'

'How do you mean?'

'If the doctors who've seen Slack have got it straight, it was like this. Whale suddenly took on the part of a homicidal maniac. His idea was to make Slack jump from what Slack believed to be a fast-moving train. Only Slack didn't jump. He struck.' Appleby paused. 'And you can imagine him afterwards – wandering in utter bewilderment and panic through this fantastic place. He had another fit of destruction – I suppose your diorama-gadget makes a noise that attracted him – and then he found a way out. He came to his senses – or part of them – early yesterday, and went straight to the police.'

The producer had brought out a handkerchief and was mopping his forehead. 'Slack won't be—?'

'No, no. Nothing like that. His story must be true, because he couldn't conceivably have invented it.'

'A plea of insanity?'

Appleby shook his head. 'You don't need to plead insanity if you defend yourself against a chap you have every reason to suppose insane. Whale's will be death by misadventure.'

The producer drew a deep breath. 'A ghastly business. But I'm glad it wasn't a real murder.'

Appleby smiled. 'That's only appropriate, I suppose. It wasn't a real train.'

Murder in the Tunnel

BRIAN HUNT

The opening of the Channel Tunnel railway link between Britain and France after over a hundred years of argument, feasibility studies and failed attempts has naturally provided novelists and short story writers with a new and unique background for their fiction. The Tunnel, which starts at Cheriton Park near Folkestone and emerges at Coquelles near Calais, actually consists of three tunnels: one in each direction and a third for maintenance, emergencies, etc. It offers two different services: Eurostar, the non-stop passenger service which runs between Waterloo station and Paris or Brussels; or Le Shuttle which is for cars and their passengers and provides drive-on and drive-off facilities at Cheriton and Coquelles. The first murder story to be set in the Tunnel is the following tale which was published in the *Daily Telegraph* of 17 December 1994, at the end of the project's first year of operation. It features a detective with the very familiar-sounding name of Ulysses Pierrot.

If she had still been alive today, few readers can doubt that Dame Agatha Christie would have been one of the first crime writers to utilise the Channel Tunnel in a murder story; and who more natural to feature in it than her little Belgian detective, Hercule Poirot, who was a European to the core and always fascinated by new technology. He would surely have been among the first passengers on Eurostar, and just as surely the man the authorities would have called upon in the event of a crime being committed! Ulysses Pierrot is not, however, the first time the name of

Christie's famous detective with his 'little grey cells' has been taken in vain. During the early years of his career his rivals in the pages of English and American magazines included Monsieur Poiret, a portly, retired Parisian police officer created by Frank Howel Evans; and a former French detective from the Paris Sûreté, Hercules Popeau, who appeared in three novels and several short stories by Marie Belloc Lowndes, the author of the famous and much-filmed Jack the Ripper novel, *The Lodger*. It was in the tradition of these authors that journalist and thriller writer Brian Hunt wrote 'Murder in the Tunnel' for the *Telegraph* which the paper invited readers to try and solve, offering a prize of a first-class trip on Eurostar to Paris for the first correct solution. 'With luck,' the paper added, 'the winner's journey will not be as eventful as this one!' (Brian Hunt's solution was published the following week; it is reprinted at the end of this section – but no looking first!) The story also leads neatly into the third part of this volume in which all the stories are set on the underground railways of Britain and America.

* * *

'**Y**ou spotted snakes with double tongue! Those trunks contain the keys to my kingdom? Damage them and you rot in Hell.' The last three words emerged as a low, slow growl, as the speaker drew his cloak around him and thrust out his tangled grey beard.

The porter nearest him, in whose hands the heavy trunk had slipped a matter of inches, turned his head. From the far end of the trunk, two more heads appeared. One was that of a second porter, the other belonged to Billy Gautier, Eurostar train manager.

'Don't worry, Sir Erskine,' said Billy. 'I'm personally supervising the loading of your luggage.' For a few seconds Sir Erskine Forret stood motionless on the platform. His black fedora cast a shadow across his face. His bulky form was wrapped in a black cloak buttoned high at the neck and reaching to the top of his black boots. In between hat and cloak was the bird's-nest of beard and moustache, and a glint of eyes.

The silence was broken by a loud belch; having delivered which, Sir Erskine swept round and marched off along the platform.

Some way along the train, Ulysses Pierrot was taking a seat in first class. 'Eat is very kind of you, Mr Down. But what 'ave I done to deserve thees honour?'

'The honour is mine,' replied Marcus Down. 'I never miss the opportunity to speak with a person distinguished in their own field. And no one is more distinguished a sleuth than yourself.'

'Forgive me, I do not know what is your own speciality,' said the dapper Frenchman.

'I'm a freelance publicist. I'm handling PR for the Paris Festival of English Drama. I chartered this compartment for festival VIPs and it's jolly that you can join us. May I introduce you to a few people? This is Mr Clapton Pond, the dramatist.'

'Why of course!' said Pierrot with sudden warmth. 'I saw *Absolute Murder* in the West End. The plot . . . I take my 'at off to you! You 'ave a suspiciously fine mind for crime.'

'Good lord,' said Pond, rising to shake the detective's hand, 'that is praise indeed.'

'And this is Shirley Knott-Mee, the theatrical agent,' said Down, indicating an elegant woman in late middle-age sitting opposite the playwright.

'Delighted,' she said huskily.

The public-address system crackled to life. 'Ladies and gentlemen, in a few minutes the doors will close and we will be departing for Paris.'

'Just think, in three hours we will be pulling into the Gare du Nord,' said Down as they settled into their seats.

'Check into our hotels, then off to enjoy the exquisite cuisine which only you French can offer!'

Pierrot wrinkled his nose with evident displeasure. 'I am sorry?' inquired Down. Then he, too, noticed a deeply unpleasant smell which had suddenly made itself known in the carriage.

'Oh God,' winced Clapton Pond, 'essence of Erskine.'

'Night and silence, who is here?' came a dark snarl from the other end of the compartment. Sir Erskine Forret stumbled sideways and teetered for a moment as he glared at his travelling companions. Then he swung on one heel to collapse out of sight in a seat at the far end of the compartment.

'This is the great Shakespearian actor?' whispered Pierrot incredulously.

Shirley Knott-Mee snorted. 'He was a great actor. And you needn't worry about lowering your voice. He'll be too drunk to know what's going on.'

'But what ees this odour?' queried Pierrot, preferring to keep to a half-whisper.

'Whisky plus sweat, I imagine,' said Knot-Mee. 'Since his personality dissuades anyone from getting near him, he thinks hygiene is irrelevant.'

'It isn't to his dressers,' said Clapton Pond sadly, 'though they have worse problems to contend with. He was in a play of mine several years ago. At least it started as my play. But by the time we transferred to the West End, dear Erskine had grown bored with my text and decided to embellish it. He made a nonsense of the plot and the reviews were so bad I thought he had single-handedly ended my career. I have never forgiven him and I never will.

'Anyway, the point is that he humiliated his dresser, William, so many times that the lad had a breakdown. I believe he recovered but not before the strain had wrecked his parents' marriage. That's the kind of trail of destruction he is renowned for.'

'Unfortunately, nothing has changed,' added Down. 'As *Visions of the Bard* is a one-man show and his dresser, Duncan, keeps the whole thing running, it seemed right for him to join us. But Sir Erskine refused and Duncan was only too glad not to be travelling with him. He's somewhere up at the front of the train.'

By now the Eurostar was gliding through the outskirts of London. The door towards the rear of the train slid open and a steward pushed a trolley though. In his wake came Billy the train manager. 'A small gift from Mr Down and Eurostar,' said Billy, as the steward produced several bottles of Grand Marnier Cordon Rouge. 'Do we have one for our guest, Monsieur Pierrot?' asked Down.

'The famous Monsieur Pierrot?' asked Billy. The Frenchman smiled modestly. Billy nodded to the steward who handed over a bottle. The passengers stowed the gifts away.

As the steward somewhat obsequiously offered the bottle, the thespian roared: 'How like a fawning publican he looks!' He refused the liqueur, and began swigging from his own bottle of whisky.

'Is he becoming too much?' asked Billy of the others in a low voice.

'Has been for years,' murmured Knott-Mee.

'We have a comfortable sin bin in the brake-van. Tip me the wink if you would like me to invite him there.'

'Don't I know you?' asked Clapton Pond, studying Billy hard. 'Were you ever involved in the theatre?'

'Not me,' said Billy, 'not my world at all. Wait a minute, where do you live?'

'Oxford,' said Pond.

'That's it then. I used to be a guard on the Oxford to London line,' said Billy.

'You've come up in the world,' said Marcus Down.

'Combination of charm and ambition,' said Billy. 'And my mother being French didn't do any harm for this job.'

He stood aside to let the steward pass before following him out of the compartment.

With a sound like an exhalation of breath, the train entered the Channel Tunnel. The background rumble was not enough to cover the grunts and occasional oaths from in front.

'Hard to think he was ever any good,' said Shirley Knott-Mee.

'You must admit there is no one who speaks Shakespearian verse like him,' said Down.

'Thank God,' said Knott-Mee.

'At least he has respect for Shakespeare's text,' said Clapton Pond. 'I wish he had shown the same regard for accuracy in my play.'

'You know why he won't allow any of the Shakespeare films he made to be shown until after his death?' asked Knott-Mee. 'He wouldn't stand comparison with his younger self. And I know what you are smiling at, Mr Down. Once he's gone, your investment in the film rights will pay off.'

'You won't do too badly for royalties yourself, Miss Knott-Mee. You play opposite him in two of them.'

'Oh yes, my brilliant first career. It was working with him that made me give it up.'

They were startled by a growl from in front. Sir Erskine stood up and shouted: 'Every tale condemns me for a villain! Must I suffer these slings and arrows of outrageous misfortune?' Then he slumped back out of sight.

'Just drunken ranting,' said Down. 'Clearly it's not Grand Marnier he's been drinking. That subtle blend of fine Cognac with essence of oranges wouldn't do that to him . . .'

'Bleeeuuuuch!' came an interruption from the front, followed by a dull thud.

Pierrot sprang to his feet and went forward. 'Sir Erskine 'as been poorly,' he reported.

'He is poorly, you say?' asked Down.

'Ee 'as already been poorly. All over 'is cloak.'

Sir Erskine half awoke from his slumber as Billy gently lifted him to his feet. 'Whaa . . . ? Where, pray, are we going?'

'Somewhere you will be more comfortable. A compartment all to yourself,' said Billy as he half-dragged, half-guided the fat actor towards the door at the rear of the compartment.

'Extraordinarily kind. Lead on Macduff!' came a mumble from somewhere beneath the fedora. The whisky bottle still swung from Sir Erskine's hand.

Five minutes later Pierrot and Knott-Mee were strolling in the direction of the buffet car, to the rear of the train, in search of a drink. 'I 'ope Sir Erskine will soon recover,' said Pierrot.

'Really?' said Knott-Mee. 'I think the world would be much better off without him.'

At that moment the train began a sudden deceleration. It ground to a controlled but jerky halt in the tunnel. There was an immediate hubbub. Pierrot peered out through the nearest window but could see nothing except the reflected interior lights. After half a minute Billy came through the doors to the rear of the compartment. As he passed he said: 'Not to worry. I think it is – literally – a false alarm. But we have to check.'

After he had gone Knott-Mee sighed. 'Well, I don't see that this little excitement should keep me from that drink.'

'Would you mind very much if I leave you for the moment? I am curious to see what is going on?'

'Of course not.'

Pierrot bowed and turned away. He had almost reached the front when he met Billy returning. 'No problem,' said the train manager. 'We'll be on our way again almost immediately.'

When he returned to the chartered compartment, Pierrot found that Pond had left to join Knott-Mee at the bar. He settled in opposite Down, just as the Eurostar moved off. Only to come to another immediate halt.

It was fifteen minutes before anyone in the festival party had any idea what was going on, by which time the agent and the playwright had returned to their seats.

Billy appeared, pale but self-possessed, through the rear connecting door. 'I'm afraid there has been a dreadful accident. Could you please tell me if any relative or close friend of Sir Erskine Forret is on this train?'

'The closest you will get is his dresser, Duncan. He's somewhere up at the front of the train,' said Marcus Down. 'But what sort of dreadful accident?'

'Thank you,' said Billy abruptly and continued up the train. He returned a minute or so later accompanied by a tall but slight blond youth wearing black trousers and T-shirt. The two of them, grim-faced, marched on to the rear of the train.

'Excuse me,' said Pierrot thoughtfully. He got up and followed them.

Close up, Sir Erskine Forret looked even more grotesque. He was laid out on the floor of the brake-van. He still wore the stained cape, though his hat was beside him. On his forehead was a fresh and ugly wound.

'This is all my fault,' said Billy, his head in his hands as he sat on the bench seat in the brake-van. Pierrot, standing opposite him, said: 'Tell me once more, please, as simply as possible, what 'appened.'

'Sir Erskine had already passed out by the time I got him here. I was trying to lower him into the seat when I saw a warning light indicating that someone had pressed the alarm in a carriage towards the front. Or at least I thought I did. Sir Erskine was masking the warning panel and the light was no longer showing when I'd put him down. Nevertheless, I decided to play safe and start the emergency braking procedure.

'I was pretty sure the signal had been just a blip, so I wasn't unduly worried. I was more concerned by the sickly odour, so when the train stopped I opened the side door – the one to the outside – to let the smell out. Sir Erskine was clearly dead to the world – sorry, that sounds terrible – and all the other doors were automatically sealed so it seemed safe. I'm the only one with a key to open the doors manually. I sealed the connecting door to the brake-van behind me, then checked all the carriages to the front. No one had sounded the alarm. I spoke to the driver on the internal phone and told him to await the signal to start again.

'I went back to the brake-van, closed the side door, gave the signal and then went to check on Sir Erskine. When I saw he had disappeared, I immediately initiated the emergency braking procedure again.

'And, as you know, we found him by the line. He must have woken up, stumbled out of the door and hit his head fatally as he fell. And it's all my fault.'

'I am certain it is not all your fault,' said Pierrot without emotion.

'The stewards helped me bring the body up. Then, as you all saw, I fetched his dresser from the front of the train.'

'Yes, we all saw that,' said the detective. 'Thank you, Mr Gautier. You told me earlier Sir Erskine's luggage is stored in this brake-van?'

'Right next door.'

'Per'aps I could look?'

While Billy opened the luggage compartment, Pierrot felt in the corpse's pockets. He used the keys he found to open the two trunks. Each was half-full with a jumble of costumes and props.

'Thank you. Zat is all,' said Pierrot. 'Perhaps you would be good enough to go forward to the compartment where the rest of us are sitting. I will 'ave a brief word with one of the stewards and then join you.'

'Monsieur Pierrot, may I please give the signal for us to move?' asked Billy with some impatience. He was sitting with Pond, Knott-Mee, Down and Duncan the dresser in the chartered compartment.

Pierrot stood in the aisle. 'We cannot leave yet,' he said calmly, 'for reasons which will soon become apparent. And I do not believe that, as you say, "a dreadful accident" 'as taken place. What 'as occurred is a murder and a conspiracy. Of the five people, excluding myself, 'oo 'ave sat in this carriage, I know that one 'as been an imposter and another less than truthful about personal 'istory.'

At that moment a steward appeared. 'Is this what you were looking for?' he asked Pierrot. 'It was lying some way back by the side of the track, just as you said.' Delicately using a handkerchief so as not to leave fingerprints, he held aloft a whisky bottle.

'Ah yes,' said Pierrot. 'The murder weapon.'

Solution opposite

Solution to:

Murder in the Tunnel

'Each of you,' said Ulysses Pierrot, strolling slowly along the aisle of the railway compartment, ''ad some motive, 'owever slight, for killing Sir Erskine. And each of you was out of my sight at some time during the few minutes in which the murder could 'ave taken place.

'But it is 'ard to explain 'ow any of you could 'ave got to the victim as 'e was apparently locked in the brake-van. True, the side door to this van was open but all the other doors were automatically sealed. And only Mr Gautier 'as keys to open them manually.

'But let me tell you 'ow I think the murder took place. Sir Erskine Forret was larger than life; 'e was a caricature of 'is former self; 'e was the very opposite of inimitable. The man in this compartment wore the cloak and 'at of Sir Erskine, but I now think 'is beard was false and 'e wore padding. His personal unpleasantness dissuaded anyone from taking a closer look.

'Though 'e seemed to be drunk and drinking 'eavily, this was also a deception. 'E 'ad himself removed to the brake-van, where, I believe, the real Sir Erskine Forret lay bound and gagged in 'is own locked trunk. When Mr Gautier and the impostor reached the brake van, they entered the luggage compartment, released Sir Erskine and struck 'im a fatal blow, probably with the whisky bottle.'

'Ridiculous!' gasped Billy Gautier. Pierrot went on.

'The two of you dressed the corpse in 'is own cloak and 'at. You distributed the costumes – including those the impostor used as padding – between the two trunks and locked them. Mr Gautier contrived the emergency stop, opened the side door and vacated the brake-van, sealing it behind 'im. He left 'is accomplice to 'eave the body out of the train. This accomplice then climbed out 'imself and ran alongside the track to the front of the train.'

'Wouldn't he have been spotted by other passengers?' asked Clapton Pond.

'The reflected light from inside the carriages made that unlikely. At the very front of the train Mr Gautier opened the carriage door and let in 'is fellow criminal. Thus, when Mr Gautier went to fetch Duncan the dresser from the front carriage, that is indeed where 'is co-conspirator was to be found.'

'You can't be serious,', said Duncan, leaping up.

'I do not joke about such matters,' said Pierrot quietly. 'Please sit down. I am per'aps the least qualified person 'ere to make such a judgment but I say you are a fine natural actor. Before you became the late gentleman's dresser, did you 'ave experience in the theatre?'

'None whatsoever,' said Duncan, 'and that can easily be proved.'

'I do not doubt you. I said you were a natural actor, not a trained one. You learned your lines well – those more obscure quotations from Shakespeare – but you tried to embellish the act with Shakespearian phrases everybody thinks they know. But although the man in the street might speak of the "slings and arrows of outrageous *mis*fortune", Sir Erskine, with 'is famed regard for the Bard's text, would know it is "outrageous fortune". And even if 'e were so reckless as to quote from the Scottish play, 'e would know it is "*Lay* on" and not "*Lead* on Macduff". So it is plain to me that it was you, Duncan, who impersonated Sir Erskine in this dastardly affair.

'If Duncan's weakness was too little knowledge, yours, Mr Gautier, was too much. When Mr Pond thought 'e recognised you, you denied you 'ad ever worked in the theatre. But you confirmed my suspicions when you told me Sir Erskine was "masking" the indicator panel. It is quaint and rare use of English – except in the theatre, where to mask a fellow actor is a crime in itself.

'Why did you kill Sir Erskine? At the moment I 'ave only

a strong 'unch but it will soon be checked. You said your mother was French; your surname is French. There are many reasons why a man may take 'is mother's surname but 'e may choose to take it when 'is father deserts the family. Mr Pond remembered "William" the dresser, whose parents 'ad separated. 'E thought 'e recognised "Billy" the train manager. You see where I am leading?

'Mr Gautier, forensic tests will prove that you and Duncan conspired to murder Sir Erskine Forret in the manner I 'ave described. But I would like to know now whether all my 'unches are correct. And 'ow you and Duncan met and planned all this. I will now pour myself a Grand Marnier and I invite you to take centre stage . . .'

All characters are entirely fictitious. The story should not be taken as a reflection of Eurostar's safety and security measures. Important details have been changed to frustrate would-be murderers.

3
TUNNEL VISIONS
Death on the Subway

The reality of the Underground is intimidating enough; but to the nervous it can be a fearsome place.

RONALD HOLMES

A Mystery of the
Underground

JOHN OXENHAM

On 9 January 1863 the Metropolitan Line was opened in London, the first underground railway in the world. This pioneer form of 'subway transportation' was the vision of a solicitor, Charles Pearson, who had got the idea from the opening of the Thames Tunnel in 1843. The four-mile-long track initially used steam engines, with the smoke mostly engulfing the carriages and those inside them, until the company's engineers had the idea of diverting the steam into tanks behind the locomotive. These noisy, dirty and uncomfortable pioneer trains were replaced in December 1890 when engines powered by electricity were introduced on the City and South London Railway – another first for the system. The man who masterminded this electrification was actually an American with a somewhat shady past: Charles Tyson Yerkes, who had served a term of imprisonment for embezzlement in his native Chicago before he came to London and took control of what is now known as the District Line. Conditions were still far from ideal, however: the passenger cars had no windows (except for ventilation slits high above the back of the seats) and travellers faced inwards because the manufacturers believed there was nothing to see in a tunnel. Not surprisingly, they were widely known as 'the padded cells'.

Today the 253 miles of track beneath the capital's streets which carry almost 500 trains to 274 stations comprise the largest underground or 'tube' system in the world, and though it may not be the most modern, reliable or clean it is still regarded as a necessary evil in the lives of millions of Londoners. And what with the gaping black mouths of the tunnels and the eerie sounds made by approaching trains, it is not surprising that the Underground should have provided the inspiration for quite a number of stories of murder and mystery during the past one hundred years.

There could be no more ideal story to open this section than 'A Mystery of the Underground' by John Oxenham (1853–1941) as it literally terrified many of its readers and made hundreds refuse to use the subway system. Published as a serial in the popular weekly magazine *To-Day*, beginning on Saturday, 27 February 1897, the story 'gave Londoners the jitters and earned the author notoriety' according to an account of the extraordinary events which followed. The tale was written in the style of newspaper reporting at the time and from the opening paragraphs revealed a detailed knowledge of the daily workings of the system. In terse sentences interspersed with seemingly genuine extracts from London papers, it described how a mysterious assassin was committing murders on the Underground every Tuesday night. Although *To-Day* was known to be edited by the well-known humorist Jerome K. Jerome, the weekly episodes about the punctilious 'serial killer' were soon the talking-point of Londoners, quite a few of whom evidently believed it was true.

Such indeed was the furore over the story – and so noticeably did the numbers of travellers drop each Tuesday evening – that after the publication of the fourth episode on 20 March, the underground authorities wrote a formal letter of protest to the magazine. Jerome K. Jerome, who had watched the circulation of his magazine soar during the past weeks, was naturally reluctant to stop such a popular serial, but before taking the final decision discussed the matter with the magazine's business manager. William Alfred Dunkerley was a quietly spoken, rather self-effacing former Manchester grocer who had joined the company because, he said, of his interest in print. And here the story of 'A Mystery on the Underground' takes an even stranger twist worthy of a classic mystery novel, for William Dunkerley was actually the author John Oxenham, though no one but he knew the fact. The episodes were, it seemed, being posted to the magazine from an address in Scotland by a writer who had insisted on anonymity. However, during their discussion Dunkerley persuaded Jerome that the serial was actually nearing its conclusion and, in any event, the locale of the events was about to switch dramatically from the subway to a boat bound for Australia. And so it did, with just three more instalments bringing events to a dramatic conclusion on 10 April.

It was not until two years later in 1898 when Dunkerley retired from the magazine that he at last revealed the truth about his subterfuge. Jerome, ever the humorist, was able to laugh at how he had been hoodwinked by his colleague just as the public had been fooled by his story of murder. The notoriety of 'A Mystery of the Underground' naturally propelled 'John Oxenham' to fame, and during the next forty years he wrote a total of over thirty novels as well as a number of books of poetry and works about religion. Subsequently, one of his daughters, Elsie, also became famous with generations of schoolgirls for her series of novels featuring the pupils and teachers of Abbey School. John Oxenham never achieved another *succès d'estime* like his notorious murder story, while the passing years have confined it to the pages of that long-dead magazine. Here, then, reprinted for the first time, slightly abridged, is the story that one hundred years ago very nearly frightened the London Underground to a standstill.

* * *

The underground station at Charing Cross was the scene of considerable excitement on the night of Tuesday, the fourth of November. As the 9.17 London and North-Western train rumbled up the platform, a lady was seen standing at the door of one of the first-class carriages, frantically endeavouring to get out, and screaming wildly.

The station inspector ran up to the carriage, and pulled open the door, when the lady literally sprang into his arms. She was in a state of violent hysterics, and it was with difficulty that he assisted her across the platform to a seat.

Meanwhile, a small crowd gathered round the open carriage door. The guard of the train had come up, elbowed his way through, and entered the carriage. The spectators could see a man sitting in the further corner, apparently asleep, his hat over his eyes, his head sunk forward.

'Drunken brute! he's frightened the lydy!'

'Pitch him out, guard, and we'll jump on 'im!'

The guard shook the man roughly, his hat rolled off, and the crowd jeered.

Then, suddenly, the guard came back to the door, waved his flag to a porter, and said hurriedly:

'Block the line behind – quick – and send the inspector.'

The porter hurried off, shouted to the inspector, and ran down the train to the signal-box.

The inspector left his charge in care of some ladies, and pushed his way into the carriage. The guard said a word to him, and they bent over the man in the corner. Then, with startled faces and compressed lips, after a momentary hesitation, they stopped and lifted him out of the carriage. The head fell back as they carried him awkwardly across the platform, and the crowd shrank away, silent and scared, at sight of the ghastly limpness and the stains of blood.

'Where to?' said the guard.

'Upstairs, I suppose,' said the inspector; and then added:

'Best thing would be to take him right on to Westminster. It's a Scotland Yard job, is this!'

'That's so!' said the guard. 'And her, too?' nodding towards the hysterical lady on the seat.

'Yes. Put him in again, and lock the door. I'll see to her. Tell Bob to keep the line blocked till they get the word from Westminster.'

They put the body back into the carriage, locked the door, and the guard went off to the signal-box, while the inspector took in hand the more difficult task of getting the lady, still in a state of hysterics, back into a carriage.

Finally, he had to have her carried in; he stepped in himself, and the train rolled off through the fog, past the line of scared faces on the platform, into the darkness which led towards Westminster; and the red stern light blinked ghoulishly back at the crowd, and tremulously disappeared up the tunnel like a great clot of blood.

Within seven minutes of the arrival of the train at Westminster, Scotland Yard was in possession of the facts, and of the chief factors in the case – the body – and the lady – by this time in a state of extreme nervous prostration. A couple of detectives were minutely examining the carriage as it sped on its journey, and the traffic on the Underground resumed its normal course.

The morning papers contained a brief announcement of the discovery. The evening papers imaginatively worked up all the details they had been able to obtain, and promoted the item to a prominent position among the day's news, in large type, well spaced out. But with the inquest, held next day, the excitement increased. Briefly, all that was learned was this:

From letters and papers found upon the deceased, the body was identified as that of Conrad Grosheim, a financier and speculator in the City. The identification was confirmed by Grosheim's clerk, and by the landlady of the room he occupied in King's Road, Chelsea.

The station inspector at Charing Cross and the guard of the train spoke to the finding of the body.

Maud Jones stated that she had had a race to catch the train at Temple station. She was running up towards the second-class carriages when the train started and the inspector flung open the door of a first-class and assisted her in, telling her to change at the next station. She had not noticed anything wrong with the gentleman in the corner – thought he was asleep – remembered his cigarette had slipped from his fingers, and was still smoking on the floor, when suddenly her eyes caught sight of blood dripping from his coat, and it flashed upon her that he was dead. She was so horrified that she nearly lost her senses. Was positive the cigarette on the floor was smoking when she got in. No, she did not smell anything like powder – nothing but the cigarette. The window next to the dead man was up. She touched nothing in the carriage, and got out of it as soon as she could. She was a waitress at Belloni's Restaurant, in the Strand. She had never seen the gentleman before, and was only sorry she had ever set eyes on him at all.

The inspector at Temple station confirmed Miss Jones's story as to her being put into the carriage.

The ticket porter at Temple station swore positively that no one whatever got out of the train. He had watched the young lady helped into the first-class carriage by the inspector, and there was not a single person on the platform when the train went out, except the inspector. Nobody could possibly have got up the stairs while he was watching. He had snapped the ingress gate as the lady passed through, and had not opened the egress one.

Dr Mortimer stated that he had examined the body, and was of the opinion that death had taken place not more than fifteen minutes, certainly not more than half an hour, before his examination. Cause of death was a bullet through the heart. It had entered the body level and straight, passed through the heart, causing instant death, and was found inside the ribs on the right side of the body. Bullet produced. It was of an unusually conical shape, and by impact with the ribs had been slightly flattened. In its natural shape it would be sharper, almost pointed. There were no signs of singeing or burning on deceased's clothing. The bullet made a clean cut through coat and vest, and did its work. If, as he understood, deceased was sitting in the corner of the carriage facing slightly towards the corner which Miss Jones occupied, the shot must have been fired from the seat exactly opposite where deceased sat.

'Or through the window?' queried the coroner.

'Or through the window,' granted the doctor. 'The exact spot from which the shot was fired would depend upon the angle at which deceased was sitting, but I understood the window was found closed.'

'Could the wound have been self-inflicted?'

'It could, of course, but not without singeing the clothing.'

'Could deceased have shot himself, thrown the revolver out of the window, and raised the window?'

'Absolutely impossible; death was instantaneous.'

Miss Jones, recalled, stated that the window was up when she entered the carriage. She was quite certain of that. It was a close, muggy night, and she felt half-suffocated. The window nearest her was jammed, and she could not let it down. She had looked across at the other, and thought of trying to open it. Then she saw the cigarette smoking on the floor, and then she saw the blood, and then she remembered screaming.

Detective-Sergeant Doane, of Scotland Yard, stated that the case had been placed in his hands; that he had taken possession of the carriage within a few minutes of the discovery of the body. It had been examined most minutely by himself and a colleague, both inside and out. Beyond the cigarette, trampled flat, probably in the removal of the body, and a few drops of blood on the floor, nothing whatever had been found. There was no weapon, no sign of a struggle. The contents of deceased's pockets, including a valuable watch and chain, had not been touched. He had questioned the passengers in the next compartments, but no one had heard a shot, or any sound whatever, except the screams of Miss Jones. Further stated that if Miss Jones was correct in stating that the cigarette was still burning on the floor when she entered, and he had no reason to doubt it, he judged that the deed was committed in the tunnel between Mansion House and Blackfriars, and he arrived at it thus. A cigarette of that brand would burn on the floor for five minutes; the train took one and a half minutes to travel from Temple to Charing Cross, half a minute's stoppage at Temple; two minutes from Blackfriars to Temple, half a minute's stoppage at Blackfriars took them into the tunnel between Mansion House and Blackfriars, and there the shot must have been fired. That tunnel had been searched inch by inch, so had the others, but nothing whatever had been found. He had his own ideas on the subject, but declined at present to make them public. Deceased's ticket was from Mansion House to Sloane Square.

The jury returned a verdict of wilful murder against some person or persons unknown; and so one more was added to the long list of undiscovered crimes of the Metropolis.

(From the *Link*, 12 November 1894)
ANOTHER MURDER ON THE UNDERGROUND
THE *LINK* MAN ON THE SPOT, AS USUAL

At 9.21 exactly, last night, as the weary *Link* man, having finished his appointed tasks, was patiently travelling in an Underground train to his humble abode at Chelsea, a piece of great good fortune befell him.

Great good fortune to one man generally means corresponding bad fortune to some other man, and so it was in this case. Without desiring to appear over-presumptuous, it does seem providential, that is, to the readers of the *Link*, that the *Link* man was right on the spot, and is therefore able to give an eye-witness's account of the very strange occurrence which took place at St James's Park station on the Underground railway last night.

Our contemporaries have published more or less garbled versions of the matter. They have done their best. The *Link*, however, was the only paper actually represented, and able, therefore, to give an absolutely exact account of what happened.

The *Link* man entered the train at Blackfriars, travelling third-class, as usual. He always travels third – not, as you might imagine, from necessity, but from choice. He thereby sees and feels, and, in every sense of the word, comes so much more in contact with his fellows, than is possible in the cold, refined, varnish-and-saddlebag atmosphere of the first-class. After standing patiently past three stations, the *Link* man had just managed to gently insinuate his person into the sixth place on a seat intended for five, and was jocularly remarking to his scowling neighbours, upon portions of whom he was sitting, that the tighter you sat the less you joggled, when a series of piercing screams from the next carriage forward rent the darkness of the tunnel, and heated all the *Link* man's professional instincts to boiling point. He sprang to the door. Something was happening – something untoward and out of the common. Such screams – off the stage – were an outrage, or implied one.

His first intention was to climb along the footboard till he arrived at the screams. But thoughts of Mrs *Link*-man and all the little *Link* men and women deterred him, and he decided not to risk his precious life, but to be first on the scene, all the same.

The screams had ceased. The silence seemed even more pregnant. While the screams continued something was happening. With their cessation, it – whatever it was – had happened. As the train slowed up at St James's Park, the *Link* man dashed forward to the next carriage – the rearmost first-class – and this is what he saw on opening the door – a lady lying apparently lifeless in the corner seat nearest the platform, and on the floor face downwards, the body of a man.

A crowd rushed to the door almost as soon as the *Link* man, but his were the first eyes that witnessed the scene. The station inspector came up, and was for ordering the *Link* man away, but, upon the latter disclosing his identity, became the courteous official the *Link* man has always found him, except upon that one unfortunate occasion when he (the inspector) found him (the *Link* man) riding first with a third-class ticket, and only let him off imprisonment for life with a reprimand, which still tingles in the *Link* man's ears, on the *Link* man's proving to him by ocular demonstration that every third-class carriage was carrying thirty per cent more humanity than it had any right to do.

The guard came up, too, and *ex officio*, the *Link* man was privileged to share the labours and cogitations of these officials.

By virtue of her sex, the lady claimed their first attention. She was in a dead faint, and was carefully carried through a double line of curious faces by the *Link* man and the guard to one of the station seats.

The *Link* man left the guard in charge, and hurried back to the carriage.

The inspector was stooping over the prostrate man, and as the *Link* man stepped in, he looked up with scared face, and said, 'It's another murder!'

'Good God!' said the *Link* man, involuntarily, for this was getting exciting. Then he saw blood on the inspector's hands.

'Better block the line behind, and wire to Scotland Yard, hadn't you?' he suggested.

'It blocks itself,' said the inspector; 'but we'll make doubly sure. Stop here in charge, will you, and I'll wire Scotland Yard at same time.' And he went off at a run, leaving the *Link* man in full charge.

Notebook and pencil came out of their own accord, with the following results: 'First-class carriage No. 32. London and North-Western train, St James's Park; time 9.25 p.m. Body dressed in dark grey overcoat with velvet collar – dark trousers – black diagonal coat and vest – patent leather shoes – Lincoln and Bennet hat, bruised from a fall. Face, so far as visible, dark and pale – age about forty-five – four-coil snake ring, with ruby and diamond in head, on third finger of left hand. In vest, exactly over heart, small, clean-cut hole, no singeing or burning, no smell of powder – no signs of struggle – window furthest from platform closed. Note – Exactly a week, to the minute almost, since discovery of the murder at Charing Cross last week. Is this accident or horrible intention?'

Link man acknowledges to creepy feeling. Door opens. Inspector returns, and a few minutes later, Scotland Yard, in the person of quiet, stern-faced Detective-Sergeant Doane, who has the previous case in hand, arrives with a colleague. They examine carriage minutely, inside and out, rear-side and off-side, under and over. They say little, but make many notes.

Carriage is locked up, and train sent on. *Link* man notices that most carriages are about half as full as when train came in, as though many had conceived sudden distaste for underground travel – that no single travellers are to be seen – general mistrustful gregariousness observable. *Link* man feels himself that sooner than travel in a carriage alone, or with only one other person, he would stop on the platform all night, and sleep on Smith's bookstall.

Body is carried to ambulance. Lady, now reviving, is placed in cab, and all drive off to Scotland Yard.

The unfortunate victim of this second outrage has since been identified as George Villars, commercial traveller, residing at West Kensington. The lady is Mrs Corbett, manageress of the ABC shop in Albert Street, Westminster.

Her account is simply that she entered the train at Westminster, and had barely got seated when the gentleman opposite lurched forward in his seat, presumably with the shaking of the carriage, and then fell prone on the floor. She saw blood on the floor, and screamed, and then fainted.

What may be the meaning of this exact repetition of the murder at Charing Cross exactly a week ago it is impossible to say. The time, the manner, the general conditions, are as nearly as possible identical.

Are both murders the act of the same hand; or is Number Two but one more proof of the epidemic nature of abnormal crimes – the result, in fact, of the action of Crime Number One on some weak intellect, with a morbid craving for notoriety?

One thing is certain: travel on the Underground is less attractive than of yore, and the homely 'bus is rising in public estimation.

(From the *Daily Telephone*, 19 November 1894)
A THIRD MURDER ON THE UNDERGROUND

The appalling discovery last night at Ealing Broadway station, on the District Railway, places beyond possibility of doubt the fact that a cold-blooded murderer is at large in our midst, and that travellers on that at all times depressing line are completely at his mercy. The police, we are willing to believe, are doing their best in the matter, but so far their efforts have apparently been fruitless. Every Tuesday night for the last three weeks, at, as near as can be told, exactly the same time to the minute, the mysterious death-dealer has chosen his victim, fired his fatal shot, and vanished. Whatever his motive and whatever his method, he has succeeded in instilling such a sense of dread into the public mind that the District Railway is beginning to be shunned by all persons of nervous temperament.

This curious state of things recalls to mind a similar series of crimes perpetrated on the Ceinture Railway, in Paris, about seven years ago. There, too, the victims were smitten down by an undiscoverable hand, and it was only when the seventh had fallen that the slaughter stopped. If it had not, the traffic on that line would have ceased, for the excitement was indescribable, and travellers shunned the Ceinture Railway as they would a pest-house.

Much the same feeling is growing in the minds of travellers by the District Railway, and especially so on Tuesday nights, which is the time fixed by the mysterious one for his horrible work. Last Tuesday night the trains ran nearly empty. Numbers of people, so curious is the hankering of the morbid mind after sensation, gathered in the stations most likely to afford the chance of a thrill. The platforms at Charing Cross, Westminster, St James's Park and Victoria were crowded with sensation-seekers, who had taken tickets which they had no intentions of using, but simply with the idea of being on the spot in case anything happened. And a very curious study those platforms were.

Throngs of people, waiting silently, in a damp fog, peering into carriage after carriage as the almost empty trains rolled slowly, like processions of funeral cars, in and out of the stations. In one carriage a party of young roughs had ensconced themselves, and endeavoured to make things lively by chaffing and jeering the silent crowds on the platforms as they passed through. They met with no encouragement, however, and had things all their own way. We wonder how those lively youths feel now when they know that, beyond a doubt, the mysterious murderer looked in on them, and could, had he so chosen, have launched his deadly bullet into their midst. But, as usual, his fatal choice fell upon a solitary wayfarer occupying a corner seat in a carriage by himself, and within three compartments of one occupied by the rowdy gang referred to.

Many of the crowd on the stations remarked on the temerity of the occupant of that corner seat. He might well sit so quiet. The fatal bullet was in his heart before he reached Victoria, at all events. But he journeyed peacefully on until he reached Ealing Broadway station, the terminus of the line. There, one of the principal duties of the porters is to arouse all the passengers who have succumbed to the monotony of the journey from the City and there John Small, the Ealing porter, tried in vain to arouse Carl Groeb, the occupant of the corner seat in the rear compartment of one of the first-class carriages, and found him dead – murdered, in the same way, and, beyond all doubt, by the same hand which struck down Conrad Grosheim, at, or about, 9.15 on the evening of Tuesday, the fourth inst., at Charing Cross, and which struck down George Villars, at 9.15 on the evening of Tuesday, the eleventh inst., at St James's Park.

The crowds at the stations up the line had dispersed with a sigh of disappointment, or let us take a charitable view, and say of relief. But the tragedy was there all the same, and the victim had passed beneath their eyes, though the public had to wait till Wednesday morning to get its thrill.

It is a terrible fact, but one that has to be faced that, in the greatest city in the world, in this year of grace 1894, such an appalling series of crimes can be perpetrated with impunity.

The police seem powerless. We give them credit for doing their utmost, but, up to now, nothing, so far as they let it be known, has resulted from their efforts.

One thing is certain, if the criminal cannot be brought to justice the directors of the District Railway can close up their line. It would pay them to run the electric light through every tunnel, and to line the route and sprinkle the carriages with detectives, in the style of an Imperial progress in Russia. The matter is really too gruesome for a jest, but *Punch* certainly hit the case off admirably in Bernard Partidge's clever sketch of the young City man attracting all the attentions of all the beauties in the drawing-room by the simple assertion that he had travelled from town by the District Railway, in a first-class carriage, *all by himself*, while the season's lions scowl at him from a distance, and twirl their moustaches, and growl in their neglected corners.

While, in another portion of the same journal, Mr Anstey's 'Voces Populi', describing the scene at Victoria station on Tuesday night, while the crowds waited for what they feared, and made simple bets on the basis of murder or no murder, and more complicated ones as to the age and nationality of the expected victim, the station where the discovery would be made, and so on, is immensely clever, but grim in the extreme. It proves the identity of one of the crowd at all events, and it will afford matter for much wondering comment on the part of readers of this year's *Punch* twenty years hence.

To return to the facts which confront us, however.

Murder, grim, cold, calculating, glides unchecked in our midst. No man's life is safe. You yourself, reading this, may be the next victim – that is, if you are so unwise as to trust yourself alone in a carriage on the District Railway. And this in London, AD 1894! What a satire on our boasted civilisation!

The official report of this latest crime is, with the necessary alterations of names, places, and dates, a mere duplication of the previous ones.

Carl Groeb took ticket at Mansion House for Victoria on the evening of Tuesday, the twenty-fifth inst., at 9.20. Before he reached Victoria he was dead – shot through the heart, in identically the same manner as the previous victims, and not a trace of the murderer is discoverable.

It is beyond belief, and yet it is horrible fact.

(From the *Daily Telephone*, 23 November 1894)

More light has been thrown on the dark corners of the Underground railway during the last few days than at any period of its existence, and yet the mystery remains unsolved. Travellers between 9 and 10.30 p.m. have been few and far between. Indeed, between those hours the service has been almost suspended, not more than one train in ten being run, and that running practically empty. But such hardy voyagers as have ventured, at risk of their lives, to run the passage from the City to Earl's Court, have travelled through a torchlight procession. Every tunnel has been filled with men with flare-lights, and the grotesque effects of the continuous blaze and the weird gigantic shadows are things to be remembered for a lifetime.

Not only is traffic on the Underground disorganised – business and pleasure alike are interrupted in their regular courses. Never, during the last twenty years, has London worked itself up into such a state of excitement as it has done over these mysterious crimes on the Underground. Suburban residents find words even of the most cerulean hue quite inadequate to express the annoyance and inconvenience they are being put to.

Scotland Yard has had a detective patrolling the footboard of every train. This, however, is to be stopped. The sensation of suddenly finding a strange face peering in at your ear as you sit harmlessly reading your evening paper in your favourite corner seat, is enough to startle any man. It has given rise to some most ludicrous scenes. Going home in a Richmond train last night, the writer sat opposite to a quiet, nervous-looking old gentleman. He happened to raise his eyes from his paper just as the patrol on the footboard passed the window. The old gentleman made up his mind at once that he had been selected as the murderer's next victim, and that the deadly bullet was just about to be launched. He instinctively sheltered his head behind his newspaper, and sank suddenly off his seat, and remained flat on the floor, nor could he be induced to rise till the next station was reached. Many ladies have been driven into hysterics in the same way, and the patrols are to be abolished.

In connection with the murder of Carl Groeb, it is now proved beyond doubt that the murderer has added to his other crime the meaner one of robbery. Groeb's pockets were empty when he was discovered – money, watch, chain, all were gone, though the evidence is conclusive that, when he left his office in Houndsditch, he carried a good round sum, and wore a good gold watch and chain. There is more hope of catching the murderer if he is driven by the exigencies of want, or the desire for gain, to unite the functions of footpad with those of self-constituted executioner. At all events, he descends from the sphere of the supernatural, into which popular credulity has been inclined to elevate him, and becomes a mere murderous thief.

(From the *Daily Telephone*, 25 November 1894)

We have received the following letter:

To the Editor of the *Daily Telephone*.

SIR, – You are wrong. I never touched the money or effects of Carl Groeb, or any other of my victims. I kill; I do not rob. – Yours truly,

The Underground Murderer.

The letter is post-marked 'London, SE, 24 November, 1894'. Is it a grim jest, or is it a genuine document? We give it for what it is worth.

(From the *Daily Telephone*, 26 November, 1894)

To the Editor of the *Daily Telephone*.

SIR, – The Underground Murderer has enough on his conscience. He did *not* rob Carl Groeb of his watch, chain and money. I did. I entered the carriage at Sloane Square. The attitude of the figure in the corner startled me. When we had passed South Kensington I spoke to him. He did not answer. I touched him. He did not move. I saw he was dead. I was stone-broke myself. I had bilked the ticket-man at Sloane Square, and intended doing the same at Earl's Court. The opportunity was too good to be missed. The man in the corner had no further use for his money. I had. I relieved him of it, and also of his watch and chain. The latter I pawned in Liverpool, and I enclose you the ticket. I am a bad lot, but, thank Heaven, I am

(Signed) Not the Underground Murderer.

The above letter was received by us two days ago, post-marked 'Liverpool'. We sent the pawn-ticket on to Liverpool. The watch and chain, recovered from the pawnbroker, have been sent to London, and have been identified beyond all doubt as Carl Groeb's!

Both letters are in possession of the police.

(From the *Daily Telephone*, 27 November 1894)

What, in Heaven's name, is this monstrous thing that is waging cruel, remorseless and indiscriminate warfare with that section of London that travels by the Underground? Is it against the Underground railway itself, as a system or as a corporation, that this foul fiend is fighting? Or is it some lunatic registering in this gruesome fashion his protest against the influx of foreigners into English business life? – for it is a noticeable fact that three out of the four victims have been foreigners.

Last night was 'Murder Night', as Tuesday night has come to be grimly dubbed on the Underground, and two more victims fell to the assassin's bullet – one in the usual neat and finished style to which we are becoming accustomed, but with a change of locality, necessitated, no doubt, by the close and incessant watch kept on every corner of the murderer's old haunts; the other was a gratuitous slap in the face – or, to be precise, bullet in the leg – of one of the guardians of the public safety in charge of the tunnel between Victoria and Sloane Square.

As the train which left Mansion House at 9.16, and left Victoria at 9.31, was running through the tunnel between Victoria and Sloane Square, it passed an up-line train proceeding to Mansion House.

The flare-light men are mostly concentrated between Victoria and Mansion House, in the tunnels of which section all the murders have hitherto been committed. As a precautionary measure, however, half a dozen men have been told off for duty each night in the tunnel between Victoria and Sloane Square. As the two trains passed, one of the flare-men standing in the six-foot fell to the ground, shot through the leg. No report was heard. Nothing but the rattle of the passing trains, which drowned the man's groans as he sank to the ground. His mate down the line saw a blaze of light as his flare fell over, and the oil caught fire and spread along the ground. Running up, he dragged the wounded man away from the flames, and yelled to the other men further down the tunnel.

Among them they carried this latest victim up to Victoria station, where their arrival caused a stampede of all except the officials.

The men's accounts of the matter are confused.

The bullet, of course, came from one of the passing trains, but which they cannot say. Even the wounded man is not certain how he was standing when the bullet struck him, but in any case only the very promptest action could have thrown any light on the matter. Had the men promptly wired to the next stations, both up and down the line, at which both trains would stop, strict search might have led to some discovery. But their wounded mate absorbed all their attention, and the chance, such as it was, was lost. We may, however, conclude, without doubt, that the shot came from the down train. That train reached Baker Street at 9.58, and four minutes later the murderer's fifth victim was discovered in a first-class carriage at Gower Street, in the person of John Stern, merchant, of Jewin Street, who was discovered shot through the heart, in exactly the same way as all the previous victims of the Underground fiend.

How much longer this state of matters is to continue depends, apparently, entirely on the will of the mysterious and bloodthirsty perpetrator of these atrocious crimes. The arm of the law seems powerless. It only remains now for the Underground fiend to shoot down an engine driver and his mate to bring about a catastrophe too horrible to contemplate. The bare possibility of an Underground train deprived of its natural controllers, and crashing madly along at its own sweet will, is enough to make one forswear for ever the delights of travel on that much-maligned line.

(From the *Link*, 4 December 1894)
ANOTHER OUTRAGE ON THE UNDERGROUND
THE *LINK* MAN THE SIXTH VICTIM

To all intents and purposes, I am a dead man.

To all intents and purposes, I am victim No. Six of the Underground Demon.

That I am here alive to tell the tale is no fault of his, but is due to a little precautionary measure of my own.

I have passed through a very strange experience.

I have done what no other man has done. I have looked Death in the face – the Death of the Underground. I have looked down the barrel of the weapon with which the Underground Death-dealer slaughters his victims.

I myself was the victim.

I am free to confess that I am shaken in nerves and sorely bruised in body.

After the detailed account given below of my experiences last 'Murder Night' I have done with the matter. I have had enough of it. My constitution cannot stand the exigencies of up-to-date travel on the Underground. The facts I am about to relate are so passing strange, that I may state at once that they are vouched for by the one man who has had more to do with the Underground Murders (except, of course, the chief actor of all) than anyone else – Detective-Sergeant Doane, of Scotland Yard. Sergeant Doane, into whose hands, from the first, has been entrusted the discovery of the mysterious murderer, has been greatly exercised by the failure of all the ingenious plans laid for his capture, and the apparent impossibility of coming to grips with the invisible one.

It is obviously impossible to have a detective on the step of every carriage of every train on the Underground railway. It is impossible to line the whole length of the system with flare-light men, even on 'Murder Night'. As a matter of fact, since the shooting of John Cran, the flare-man, in Sloane Square tunnel, it is not easy to induce the men to undertake the duty at all, for every one of them feels that he takes his life in his hand when he picks up his lamp. Every man of them knows that, as like as not, he may be the next victim.

I came into contact with Sergeant Doane over the second murder, the one at St James's Park, as readers of the *Link* will remember. I have met him many times since, and we have discussed the matter from many points of view.

On Saturday last I laid before him a scheme which seemed to me to offer at least the chance of a solution of the mystery.

My proposition was this: I offered to take my place, alone, in a first-class compartment in the train leaving Mansion House at 9.12 on 'Murder Night,' and to afford the Underground Fiend every facility for selecting me as his next victim. As a precaution, I was to wear inside my waistcoat a breastplate of solid steel; I was to have the company of an armed detective beneath the opposite seat within reach of a kick, and on top of the carriage, lying flat on the roof, directly over each window of my compartment, were to be two other detectives.

Sergeant Doane turned this idea over in his mind before cautiously venturing the remark that it might do – might do for me, in any case, he grimly added.

The idea was carried out precisely as given above, and 9.13 last Tuesday night found me comfortably ensconced, steel breastplate and all, in the rear first-class compartment of the London and North-Western train from Mansion House to Willesden, gliding through brilliant tunnel after tunnel into the comparative obscurity of the stations, and patiently waiting to be shot at. Beneath the opposite seat, within easy reach of my toe, was one of Doane's trusty followers, armed with a revolver. Flat on the roof, feet to engine, and head over my window, with the cold night wind ploughing up his back hair, was Sergeant Doane himself and over the opposite window another of his men, both armed with revolvers. A slight iron framework had been fixed to the top of the carriage to prevent their rolling off.

Now, a scheme of this kind – I speak from experience – is all very well in the heat of inception and preliminary discussion, but, in the carrying out of it, one's temperature is apt to fall.

I must confess to feeling distinctly nervous as I took my seat in the carriage, and, as the train rumbled along through the weird, irregular illumination of the flare-light men, an odd idea grew upon me that the compartment I was sitting in was somehow unpleasantly familiar to me.

The sensation grew, and the feelings of discomfort increased in proportion. It was likely enough I had ridden in that same carriage dozens of times, for I use the Underground freely, and occasionally go 'first' when, in my opinion, the 'thirds' are full. I was arguing myself into the idea that it was just the natural nervousness incidental to the job I had in hand, when my eye, roving around, caught the number of the carriage – No. 32 – on the small enamelled plate above the door, and I experienced all the sensation of a cold douche down the spine.

'Nonsense!' said I to myself. 'Don't be an idiot!'

But I sat and stared at that small enamelled plate till it began to hypnotise me.

To prove myself a fool, and disperse the blue devils, I hauled out my notebook, and turned over the pages till I came to what was in my mind. And then – I had a strong inclination to get out of the carriage, and have done with the business.

I was sitting in the exact spot of the very compartment of the very carriage in which George Villars was shot exactly five weeks ago to the day, and almost to the minute. As readers of the *Link* will remember, I was the first to discover his body at St James's Park station. It was distinctly unpleasant, but it could not be helped.

For companionship's sake, I landed a kick on a tender portion of the recumbent detective under the seat opposite, and he grunted wakefully. Then, feeling deucedly uncomfortable, I sank my head down into the pose of a tired man, drew my hat down over my brow, and turned my eyes almost upside down in the endeavour to keep a bright look-out from under the brim of it.

Blackfriars, Temple, Charing Cross, Westminster, St James's, Victoria, Sloane Square: I heaved a sigh of relief. We were through the original murder zone, and looked like drawing blank this time. Still, as the murderer had broken fresh ground at Baker Street last week, there was no knowing where he might strike this time. And so the train rumbled on.

Earl's Court, and tickets; Addison Road, Uxbridge Road, Shepherd's Bush, and we were rushing across the wilds of Wormwood Scrubs, when my eyes, wearied almost to blindness with the unnatural strain, closed for a moment's rest.

When I opened them, to my amazement, the window on my left, which I had carefully closed, was down, and wind and rain were pouring in. It sank to the bottom. Every drop of blood in me was tingling with excitement. My heart was going like a sledge-hammer. I wanted to kick the man under the seat, but could not move a toe.

As I glanced at the window, along the polished framework of the part that slides down, there came gently and silently into view a shining steel barrel, pointing straight for my heart. I caught just one vague glimpse of a face beyond it, then – without any report, or any warning, an awful shock – and – blank.

They tell me that I was lifted out at Willesden, and that I was unconscious for upwards of four hours.

I take their word for it; at present I will take anybody's word for anything. As far as I am personally concerned, I have done with the Underground Murders. I hold a season ticket on that abnormal line from Blackfriars to Sloane Square. Anyone who wants it, and will take it with all risks, including its non-transferability, is welcome to it. I would suggest that whoever takes it, should also take out a £10,000 Life Policy for the benefit of his widow and children.

For myself, as I said at the beginning. Underground travel is not adapted to my peculiar constitution. I now go home by 'bus.

As this story is passing strange, and may, in some quarters, be received with incredulity, Sergeant Doane has very kindly offered to add a few words concerning his experiences on Tuesday night.

If any of my fellow-journalists desire ocular demonstration of the truth of my story, and will call at St Bartholomew's Hospital, they can see for themselves the documents in the case, viz.: one steel shield, and one journalist, with a bruise, of the dimensions of a soup-plate, round about the spot where his heart is supposed to be.

Sergeant Doane's account is as follows:—

'I have read the foregoing statement, and endorse it in every particular which came under my own knowledge. Journeying on one's stomach, stern foremost, on top of the Underground train, is not a mode of locomotion that

I can recommend. The motion of the train, much more violent up there than in the body of the carriage, the peculiar position, and the horrible atmosphere, produced a feeling of nausea to such an extent that my colleague, on the other side of the roof, when he descended at Willesden, was white as a sheet, and was practically in the throes of sea-sickness.

'Nothing happened on our journey till we reached Wormwood Scrubs. It was blowing half a gale. The heavy rain stung like pellets, and, combined with the rattle of the train, drowned every other sound.

'Half-way between Wormwood Scrubs station and Willesden Junction, the gale seemed to seize the train and shake it, and it was all we could do to hang on by main force. It was at that moment that I heard a shout in the carriage below; then my colleague, Detective Trevor, who had been hidden under the seat, put his head through the window, shouting, "Doane, Doane, he is shot." Half a minute more, and we ran into Willesden station. Mr Lester was insensible from the impact of the bullet, which was flattened on the shield like a shilling. I heard no report, and feel sure there was none. Trevor confirms this fact. Beyond the "ping" of the bullet on the shield, he heard nothing. On hearing that, however, he crawled out, found Mr Lester with all the breath knocked out of him, and yelled for me.'

(From the *Daily Telephone*, 10 December 1894)

We feel like accessories before the fact – like partners in the horrible work of the Underground Murderer.

Ten days ago we hinted in these columns at the appalling catastrophe which might result from the massacre of an Underground engine driver and his mate by the Underground Murderer.

Last night, William Johnson, driver of the 9.1 Outer

Circle train, was shot at and wounded, fortunately not fatally, as the train ran through the tunnel beyond South Kensington station.

When the train steamed into Gloucester Road station, it was seen at once that something was wrong. Charles Jones, the fireman, was hanging on to the brake lever, white as a sheet, shouting for help. As the train came to a stand, and the inspectors and guard ran up, Driver Johnson was found lying in a heap on the floor of the cab.

Jones explained hurriedly that, as they ran through the tunnel Johnson suddenly clapped his hand to his side, and cried, 'My God! I'm shot!' and fell all of a heap.

'I'm off,' said Jones, when he had finished his story. I'll have no more o' this – a man's life isn't safe.' Neither threats nor persuasion availed to induce him to resume his place on the engine. Another driver and fireman were eventually procured from Mansion House, and traffic was resumed.

Matters, however, have come to a pretty pass when such an occurrence is possible, and something has got to be done, and at once, to put an end to this unheard-of state of affairs.

The following proclamation has been posted broadcast over the Metropolis. May it have some effect:—

£1,000 REWARD

WHEREAS, on the night of Tuesday, 4 November 1894, Conrad Grosheim was murdered in a first-class carriage on the Underground railway between Mansion House and Charing Cross stations; and

WHEREAS on the night of Tuesday, 11 November 1894, George Villars was murdered in a first-class carriage on the Underground railway between Mansion House and Westminster Stations; and

WHEREAS, on the night of Tuesday, 18 November Carl

Groeb was murdered in a first-class carriage on the Underground railway between Mansion House and Victoria stations; and

WHEREAS, on the night of Tuesday, 25 November John Cran was shot in the leg in the tunnel between Victoria and Sloane Square stations on the Underground railway; and, on the same night, John Stern was found murdered, in a first-class carriage at Baker Street station; and

WHEREAS, on the night of Tuesday, 2 December Charles Lester was shot at and wounded, with intent to murder, while travelling in a first-class carriage between Wormwood Scrubs and Willesden; and

WHEREAS, on the night of Tuesday, 9 December William Johnson, engine-driver, was shot at and wounded, with intent to murder, while travelling on his engine, between South Kensington and Gloucester Road station on the Underground railway:

The sum of ONE THOUSAND POUNDS (£1,000) will be paid to any person or persons (not being the actual murderer or murderers) who shall give such information as shall lead to the detection of the perpetrator of the above deeds.

The above emanated from Scotland Yard. The chairman of the District Railway Company authorises us to state that his company will double the government reward for information.

(From the *Link*. Third Edition. Wednesday,
12 December 1894)

The £1,000 reward seems to have had its effect. Last night was 'Murder Night' on the Underground, and, for the first time in six weeks, we have no murder to chronicle.

Is the Underground Fiend sated with blood – or,

having accomplished the magical number 'Seven', has he retired, satisfied with his work?

Time will show. The terrible chain, however, is broken, and from this we may draw some slight hope that the reign of terror on the Underground is over – until such time as the Death-dealer chooses to resume his self-imposed duties.

Receiving a tip-off that a man believed to be the Underground Murderer is about to flee the country on a boat sailing for Australia, the Link *man Charles Lester joins the vessel, the* Bendigo. *During the following weeks at sea two more murders are committed before Lester finally narrows down the suspects to the most unlikely passenger on board: an old man named Hood who is travelling with his pretty young grand-daughter. When the murderer strikes a third time, however, and tries to kill the ship's doctor, Shannon, who has also become increasingly suspicious of the old fellow, the medical man defends himself with an iron bar and causes his adversary to fall down a stairway to his death. As soon as the news of the old man's death is conveyed to his grand-daughter she is overwhelmed with relief, having apparently been an unwitting accomplice to the reign of terror on the London subway and at sea. After Hood's body has been committed to the ocean, Charles Lester is summoned by Miss Hood to the cabin that had been occupied by her grandfather and there he finally learns the secret of the Underground mystery . . .*

The girl was kneeling on the floor, amid piles of books, papers, clothing, etc., which she had taken from his boxes.

She beckoned me inside, and bade me close the door.

'You have a right to see some of these things, Mr Lester,' she said. 'When you have seen all you care to, will you help me to get rid of them? I only learned this morning from Captain Joram that you were the Mr Lester who—' She faltered, and the large eyes, turned pathetically up to mine, were swimming with tears.

'Try and forget all about it,' I said, 'and let me help you.'

She stooped hurriedly, and picked up a bundle of papers.

'Read those – and those – and look at these,' putting into my hand some strange steel instruments, quite unlike anything I had ever seen before. One had a horse-shoe clutch at the end, and, at the other extremity, it was pinned on to another long, thin steel rod, one end of which terminated in four fine sharp teeth, like the prongs of a fork.

I turned it over in my hand, but could make nothing of it, so proceeded to look over the papers. And, reading them, I arrived at old Hood's story.

A mechanical engineer, of quite unique powers, he had patented a number of inventions, and offered them to the District Railway Company, in whose employment he had spent the best part of his life. Nothing had come of them, however, and I gathered from some of the company's letters in reply that the old man had accused them of using his ideas, but giving him no benefit of them. Then he left the company's service, with his brain bursting with grievances, and it was easy to conceive that he determined to strike at them in a way that was as horribly effective as it was, for him, easy of accomplishment.

I was puzzling over the strange implements, and trying to get at their use. In thought, I went back to one of the murderer's journeys along the swinging footboards, and suddenly it all flashed upon me. A long steel rod, with curved top – that hitched on to the edge of the carriage roof, and had enabled him to pass rapidly along, without troubling to grasp each handle. That spidery implement, with the curved horse-shoe clutch and the pronged lever – I could see the sharp teeth inserted quietly into the window sash, the clutch fitted to the bottom outside frame, the pressing of the lever – and my closed window was sliding quietly down, the wind and rain of Wormwood Scrubs were beating in on me again, and my paralysed eyes were looking once more down the deadly death-tube. I could see myself lying bruised and stunned in the corner, and, in imagination, could follow the murderer as he rapidly made his way back to the carriage he had issued from, and, perhaps, concealed himself under the seat, or, riding between two carriages, dropped quietly off as the train began to slow up to the station.

There were other curious contrivances, whose meaning I could not fathom, but had no doubt they all tended to the same end – the boarding of, or hanging on to, trains in motion.

I looked up at the girl.

'What do you want me to do with all these things?'

'Throw them all overboard – clothes – books – papers – everything. I have kept the only papers I need. Please get rid of them all for me.'

I did. Shannon, however, claimed the air-gun, and certainly no one who wanted it had a better right to it.

It was a wonderful weapon, the only remaining monument to the old engineer's skill. With two twists it came into three pieces, and was easily stowed in one's ordinary pockets. The first day Shannon appeared on deck, Miss Hood being below, he tried that demon air-gun on the main-mast with a bullet of his own making. It buried itself out of sight, and a three-inch probe failed to reach it.

'No wonder it knocked the wind out of you, old man,' he said; 'if you hadn't had that breastplate on, you wouldn't be here now.'

We cleaned our memories of Old Man Hood as far as we could, as we had cleaned the ship of himself and his belongings, and Mary Hood grew brighter every day. Her burden lay behind her at the bottom of the Indian Ocean, and her sweet face was set bravely and hopefully towards the new life that awaited her in the unknown land that lay beneath the rising sun.

Death in the Air

CORNELL WOOLRICH

Because much of New York is built on solid rock, it was impossible for the Big Apple's authorities immediately to follow London's lead and build a subway system. Indeed, it was not until ten years later that the city got its own form of cheap transportation when the 'Elevated' railway was born. The tracks of the 'El', as it was soon christened, were raised on iron pillars which ran over the streets of Manhattan. The first section was opened in 1872 and in the next twenty-five years a total of thirty-six miles of track spread across the city like a giant spider's web. The passenger carriages were all pulled by 0-4-4 Tank Engines which steamed at approximately fifteen mph. The system quickly caught on with work-bound travellers, but those who lived in buildings beside the tracks found that the incessant noise and dirt of the trains which passed one every minute became increasingly difficult to bear. Pressure then began to build on the New York authorities to copy London and dig a subway.

It was between 1902 and 1905 that the city finally got its Rapid Transit Subway: fifteen miles of underground track which had been modelled on the London system and ran from South Ferry to 28th Street. The service was electrified from the outset, but improved on its predecessor across the Atlantic by offering two distinct services, the 'Express' and 'Local' trains. Despite the relief with which the RTS was greeted by those living alongside the rapidly ageing 'El', there was an initial reservation among travellers to go underground, and in the first year of operation the service carried only 300,000 passengers. This attitude soon began to change, however, and today the New York Subway is every bit as busy, not to mention as hot, crowded and dirty as its model in London.

Although the New York Subway has featured in numerous novels and short stories, there are very few about its predecessor, the 'El', of which this next story by Cornell Woolrich (1903–1968) is the only one I know featuring crime and murder. Woolrich was born in New York just as the elevated railway was beginning to run and the trains which rattled and banged overhead whenever he was on the street clearly stuck in his mind. Indeed when he became a writer, trains of all kinds turned up in a number of his stories, especially those which focused on the crime and low life in his birthplace.

Woolrich, who has been compared to Edgar Allan Poe for his ability to create tales of mounting tension and fear, combined this talent with a writing style not unlike that of Dashiell Hammett and Raymond Chandler to produce a whole body of unforgettable literature. The everyday world where loneliness and despair are always just around the corner is a persistent theme in his work, as is the late-night train ride which ends in death: *vide* the novel *I Married a Dead Man* (1948) with its horrendous train wreck, and short stories such as the tale of a subway killer, 'You Pays Your Nickel' (which has been frequently anthologised as 'Subway'), and the next selection, 'Death in the Air'.

The darkness of Cornell Woolrich's work reflects his own unhappy life. After the success of his first novel, a Jazz Age story, *Cover Charge* (1926), he worked for a short while in Hollywood where he had a brief, unconsummated marriage before hastily returning to New York. Here he settled in a hotel with his domineering mother, Claire, with whom he developed an intense relationship which may well have been his way of coping with his undoubted homosexuality. Woolrich barely left her side during the following years and supported them both through his prodigious output of crime novels and short stories. After Mrs Woolrich's death in 1957 he became a total recluse, declined swiftly into alcoholism, and as he also suffered from diabetes, allowed his health to deteriorate. Woolrich coped with his bitterness and frustration by pouring it all into his work, yet still received the highest accolades from fellow mystery writers and critics for the brilliance of his plots and his mastery of suspense. The passage of time has further enchanced the reputation of this tragic figure, with his novel *Phantom Lady* (1942) – which was only one of many of his books to be filmed – perhaps enjoying the greatest acclaim. 'Death in the Air', which appeared in *Detective Fiction Weekly* in 1936, is set during the Depression and apart from its almost cinematic evocation of a ride on the 'El' is also noteworthy because it features the use of marijuana, even though the drug is referred to in the hostile terms that represented the public attitude towards it in the thirties. It is no exaggeration to say that 'Death in the Air' may well be the most unusual trip the reader will take in this book.

***

Inspector Stephen Lively, off-duty and homeward-bound, stopped at the news-stand underneath the stairs leading up to the Elevated station and selected one of the following day's newspapers and one of the following month's magazines for purposes of relaxation. His nightly trip was not only lengthy, it was in two parts – from headquarters to South Ferry by 'El' and from there to Staten Island by ferry – hence the two separate items of reading-matter; one for each leg of the way.

Given a combination of two such names as his and, human nature being what it is, what else can you expect in the way of a nickname but – Step Lively? It had started at the age of seven or thereabouts when he stood up in school and pronounced his first name the wrong way; he finally quit struggling against it when it followed him on to the squad and he realised that he was stuck with it for the rest of his days, like it or not.

It wouldn't have been so bad, only it was altogether inappropriate. Step Lively had never made a quick motion in his life. To watch him was to think of an eight-times-slowed-down film or a deep-sea diver wading through seaweed on the ocean floor; he gave the impression of having been born lazy and getting more so all the time. And the nickname probably made this trait more glaring.

He was not, strangely enough, obese along with it – just the opposite, tall and spare, concave at the waist where others bulge. He carried his head habitually bent forward a little, as though it were too much trouble to hold it up straight. He not only walked slowly, he even talked slowly. What mattered chiefly was that he thought fast; as far as results went, his record on the force seemed to prove that the race isn't always to the swift. He'd been known to bring in some of the nimblest, most light-footed gentry on record.

Like a steam-roller pursuing a motorcycle; it can't keep up with it, but it can keep remorselessly after it, wear it down, slowly overtake it, and finally flatten it out. So Step's superiors didn't let it worry them too much that he was the despair of traffic-cops crossing a busy street, or that he sent people waiting on line behind him out of their minds. It takes more than that to spoil a good detective.

Step entered the lit stairway-shed and sighed at the sight of the climb that awaited him, as it did every night. An escalator, like some of the other stations had, would have been so much easier on a man.

The subway, which would have gotten him to the ferry considerably quicker, he eschewed for two very good reasons. One was that he'd have to walk a whole additional block eastward to get to it. And secondly, even though you descended to it instead of climbing at this end, you had to climb up out of it at the other end anyway; he preferred to get the hard work over with at the start, and have a nice restful climb down waiting for him when he got off.

He slowly poised one large, paddle-like foot on the bottom step and eight minutes later he was upstairs on the platform, the ordeal of the ascent safely behind him until tomorrow night. As he stepped out from behind the turnstile, a Sixth Avenue train was standing by with its gates in the act of closing. Step could have made it; a man who had come up behind him darted across and did. Step preferred not to. It would have meant hurrying. There'd be another one along in a minute. The old adage about cars and women was good common horse-sense.

This was 59th, and the trains alternated. The next would be a Ninth Avenue. They separated at 53rd, but both wound up together again at South Ferry, so it didn't matter which he took. More seats on the Ninth anyway. And so, because he refused to bestir himself – this story.

A three-car Ninth flashed in in due course. Step got up off the bench – it wouldn't have been like him to stand waiting – and leisurely strolled across to it. He yawned and tapped his mouth as he perambulated sluggishly down the aisle. The crabby, walrus-moustached conductor, who had had to hold the gate for him, felt a sudden unaccountable urge to stick a pin in him and see if he really could move fast or not, but wisely restrained the impulse, maybe because he had no pin.

The first car had a single occupant, sitting on one of the lengthwise seats, visible only up to the waist. The rest of him was buried behind an outspread newspaper, expanded to its full length. Step sprawled out directly opposite him with a grunt of satisfaction, opened his own paper, and got busy relaxing. All the windows were open on both sides of the car, and it was a pleasant, airy way to ride home on a warm night. Two pairs of legs and two tents of newsprint on opposite sides of the aisle were all that remained visible. The conductor, maybe because Step irritated him vaguely, retired to the second car, between stations, instead of this one.

The train coasted down Ninth Avenue sixty feet in the air, with the buildings that topped it by a storey or two set back at a respectable distance from its roadbed. But then at Twelfth Street, it veered off into Greenwich Street and a change in spacing took place. The old mangy tenements closed in on it on both sides, narrowing into a bottleneck and all but scraping the sides of the cars as they threaded through them. There was, at the most, a distance of three yards between the outer rail of the super-structure and their fourth-floor window-ledges, and where fire-escapes protruded only half that much.

What saved them from incessant burglarising in this way was simply that there was nothing to burglarise. They were not worth going after. Four out of five were tenantless, windows either boarded up or broken-glass cavities yawning at the night. Occasionally a dimly-lighted one floated by, so close it gave those on the train a startling impression of being right in the same room with those whose privacy they were cutting across in this way. A man in his underwear reading a paper by a lamp, a woman bent over a washtub in a steaming kitchen. Their heads never turned at the streaming, comet-like lights or the roar of the wheels going by. They were so used to it they never gave it a thought. It was just part of their surroundings. Nor did those on the train show any interest either, as a rule. The few there were at this hour had their papers up and their backs to the passing scene. There isn't anything pretty about the lower West Side of New York. The river a block over is blotted out by docks, and the connecting side-streets are roofed with produce-sheds.

In the front car, the two solitary occupants continued

immersed in their reading-matter. Christopher and Houston had gone by, and they pulled into Desbrosses Street. As they cleared it again a moment later, the train slackened briefly, slowed down without coming to a full halt, then almost immediately picked up speed once more. Perhaps some slight hitch on the part of a track-signal or a momentary break in the 'shoe' gripping the third rail. Step took his eyes off his paper and glanced around over his shoulder, not because of that, but to find out how near his destination he was.

There was an open window staring him in the face, flush with the car-window that framed him, and so close it was almost like a continuation of it, a connecting-tunnel into the tenement's front room. There was no light in the first room, but light shone feebly in from the room beyond through an open doorway. At the same time the train-lights swept in and washed across the walls like a sort of lantern-slide, from left to right.

In the double glare, fore and aft, two forms could be glimpsed, moving unsteadily about together. A man and woman dancing drunkenly in the dark, with exaggerated motions of their arms and heads. Lurching, reeling, pressed tightly together. 'Wonder what the big idea of that is?' Step thought tolerantly. 'Too warm for lights, I guess—' The noise of the cars drowned out whatever music was being supplied them for their strange activities.

Just as the two superimposed windows slipped apart out of perspective, the wheels of the train cracked loudly as though passing over a defect in the rails. At the same time, one of the shadow-dancers struck a match and it went right out again, just a stab of orange, and some water-borne insect or other winged into the car past Step's face. He slapped vaguely at it, went back to his newspaper. The train picked up speed and headed down the track for Franklin Street.

The party across the aisle had fallen asleep, Step noticed

when next he glanced over across the top of his paper. He grinned broadly at the sight he presented. There was a man after his own heart. Too much trouble even to fold up his paper and put it away. The breeze coming in on Step's side of the car had slapped it back against his face and shoulders; his hands were no longer holding it up, had dropped limply to his lap. His legs had sprawled apart, were wobbling loosely in and out like rubber with the motion of the car.

Step wondered how he could breathe with the layers of paper flattened that way across his nose and mouth, you could actually see the indentation his nose made through it. And that insect that had blown in – it looked like a large black beetle – was perched there on the paper just above it. Step thought of the innumerable comedy-gags he'd seen where someone tried to swat a fly on a sleeper's face, and of course the sleeper got the full impact of it. If he only knew the guy, he'd be tempted to try that now himself. Still, it was an awful lot of effort to reach across a car-aisle just to swat a horse-fly.

As they began drawing up for Franklin, the air-current of their own momentum rushed ahead, outdistanced them. It tugged loose the outside paper of the sleeper's outspread newspaper, no longer clamped down by his fingers, and sent it whirling up the aisle. Step blinked and went goggle-eyed. The black bug was still there, on the page underneath, as though it had bored its way through! A second sheet loosened, went skimming off. The damn thing was still there, as though it were leaping invisibly from one page to the other!

Step got to his feet, and though the motion was slow enough, there was a certain tenseness about him. He wasn't grinning any more. Just as he did so, the train came to a halt. The jolt threw the sleeper over on the side of his face, and all the rest of the newspaper went fluttering off, separating as it went. The black bug had leaped the last gap, was in the exact middle of the sleeper's forehead now, this time red-rimmed and with a thread of red leading down from it alongside his nose, like a weird eyeglass-string, to lose itself in the corner of his mouth. Step had seen too many of them not to know a bullet-hole when he saw one. The sleeper was dead. He didn't have to put his hand in under his coat, nor touch the splayed hand, caught under his body and dangling down over the aisle like a chicken-claw, to make sure of that. Death had leaped out at him from the very print he was reading. Such-and-such, then – period! A big black one, right into the brain. He'd never known what had hit him, had died instantly, sitting up. It wasn't the breeze that had slapped the paper up against him; it was the bullet. It wasn't an insect that had winged past Step's shoulder that time; it was the bullet.

Step reached up leisurely and tugged twice at the emergency-cord overhead. The gates had closed on Franklin, and the train had already made a false start ahead, checked immediately with a lurch. The handlebar-moustached conductor came running in from the platform, the motorman looked out from his booth at the upper end of the car.

'What's the idea? What's going on in here?' The conductor's words splattered like buckshot around the heedless Step.

'Hold the train,' he drawled almost casually. 'Here's a man been shot dead.' Then as the blue-coated one began panting down the back of his neck and elbowing him aside, he remonstrated mildly, 'Now don't crowd like that. There's nothing *you* can do. What y'getting so excited about? Just lemme try to find out who he is first—'

The motorman said from the other side of him, 'Get him off. We can't stand here all night. We're on a schedule; we'll tie up the whole line into a knot behind us.'

'Stand aside! Who do you think you are anyway?' the fiery conductor demanded.

Step said wearily, 'Oh, do I have to go through that again?' and absentmindedly palmed his badge to him, backhand, while he continued bending over the prostrate form. From then on there was nothing but a respectful silence all around while he went on going through the corpse's pockets with maddening deliberation.

His mind, however, was anything but sluggish, was crackling like a high-tension wire. The sound of the shot? There didn't necessarily have to be any in this case, but that crack of the car-wheels over a split in the rails had probably been it. And the match that one of those two tipsy dancers had struck in the darkened tenement-room back there hadn't been a match at all, hadn't glowed steadily enough nor lasted long enough, couldn't have been anything but the flash of the shot, the results of which he was now beholding.

Drinking, carousing, then entertaining themselves by taking pot-shots out the window at passing trains, were they? Well, a nice little manslaughter rap would take the high spirits out of them, for some time to come, whoever they were.

'Dudley Wall,' he said, reading from an envelope. 'Lives on Staten Island like me. Shame, poor fella. All right, take him by the feet and help me get him outside to the waiting-room.' And as the conductor moved backwards before him down the aisle, with the body between them, he rebuked: 'Don't walk so fast. He ain't going to get away from us!' They moved at a snail's pace thereafter, to suit Step, out through the gate and across the platform with their burden. Stretched him out on one of the benches inside by the change-booth, and then Step strolled inside with the agent and sent in his report over the latter's phone.

'That guy,' whispered the conductor darkly to the motorman on their way back to their posts, 'has sleeping sickness, you can't tell me different!'

'Maybe it's ringworm,' hazarded the motorman. They

pulled out, and the two or three other trains that had ganged up behind them flashed by one after the other without stopping, to make up for lost time.

'I gotta get back to Desbrosses Street,' Step remarked, coming out again. 'You keep an eye on him till they get here.' He felt sure he'd know the tenement window again when he saw it, whether they were still there or not.

'Well, you'll have to go down to the street, cross over, and then climb to the uptown side,' the agent explained, wondering what he was waiting for.

Step looked horrified. 'And then when I get there climb down again? And climb up four flights of stairs inside that building? Oh, golly, I'm just tuckered out. I couldn't make it. I'll walk back along the track, only way I can see. That's bad enough.'

He sighed deeply, took a tuck in his belt, and made his way to the far end of the platform. He descended the short ladder to the track-level and stuck out from there, trudging doggedly along with one hand trailing along beside him on the guard-rail.

'Watch the trains!' the agent shouted after him warningly.

Step didn't answer out loud, that was too much trouble, but to himself he muttered: 'This is one time I'm glad I'm good and thin!'

One of them caught him half-way between the two stations, and the sight of it looming up on him was fairly terrifying to one unused to track-walking. He began to wobble unsteadily on the cat-walk, which seemed only inches wide, and realising that he would either topple dizzily in front of it or fall down to the street if he kept looking at it head-on, he wisely turned his back to it, grabbed the guard-rail with both hands, and stared intently out at the roof-tops, ignoring it till it had hurtled by. Its velocity nearly seemed to pull the coat off his back.

He stared after it disapprovingly. 'Such a town. Everything always in a hurry to get somewhere else!' Then he resumed his laborious progress alongside the tracks, feeling sorry for his feet and hoping the sniper in the tenement had no firearms licence, so he could also tack a stiff Sullivan-Law charge on him.

The two lighted halves of the Desbrosses Street platform loomed toward him, lighted under the apron like the footlights of a stage. It ought to be about here. They'd already pulled out, he remembered, when he'd turned around to look. Dark-red brick it had been, but then the whole row was that. No fire-escape, either. Wait a minute, there'd been a sign up on the cornice of the building next door, but on which side of it, he couldn't recall. Nor what it had said, until suddenly it was staring him in the face once more, with that vague familiarity that only twice-seen things can have. Then he knew that was it. PICKLED AND SALTED FISH in tarnished metal capitals with rain-streaks under them, each letter separately clamped to the brickwork, in the style of the nineteenth-century advertiser. He stopped in front of the building next to it, on the Desbrosses side. This had almost certainly been it. There was the same wide-open window through which he'd seen them dancing. But no light was coming in from the other room now. It was dark and deserted, just a gap in the façade.

It looked near enough to touch, but actually was far more inaccessible from where he now was, than it had seemed from the train-window. The gap was just wide enough to fall to your death in without half-trying, and the ledge was just over his head, now that he was down at track-level.

Step Lively had the courage of his convictions. He was going to get in this way, without going all the way down to the street and climbing up inside that dump, if he died in the attempt. He looked around him vaguely but determinedly.

They had been repairing the track-bed near here some-where, and there was a neat, handy little stack of short planks piled-up, almost directly across the way from him – but with two third-rails in-between.

He didn't hesitate for a minute. What was a third-rail compared to climbing four flights of stairs and getting all out of breath? Besides, they had guards on top of them, like covered troughs. There wasn't anything coming on this side, so he started across on one of the ties, and arched respectfully over the deadly metal when he came to it. So much for the downtown track. An uptown train was pulling out of Franklin, but it wouldn't get here for a while yet. Plenty of time to get back and across.

He reached the opposite catwalk safely, picked up the top plank, and tucked it broadside under his arm. The oncoming train was still at a respectable distance, although its lights were getting brighter by the moment. He started back over, the plank swaying up and down in his grasp like a see-saw. It wasn't the actual weight of it that hampered him, it was that its length threw him off-balance. He was like a tightrope-walker with too long a pole. He didn't have it right in the middle, and it kept tipping him forward. The train was big as a barn by now, he hadn't calculated on how quickly it would cover the short distance between the two stations. You could already look right down the lit aisle of the first car, through the open vestibule-door. But this was no time for surveying. He lifted one foot clear of the contact-rail, set it down on the other side, then tried to bring the second one over after it. It wouldn't come. He must have given it just the wrong kind of a little half-turn. It was stuck between the two ties.

He didn't do anything at all for just a split-second, which is sometimes the wisest possible course – and came easiest to him, anyway. However, there weren't many of them left, split or otherwise. The roar of the train was rising to a crescendo. The first thing almost anyone else would have done in his fix would have been to yank and tug at the recalcitrant foot – and wedge it in irretrievably. Step Lively was a slow mover but a quick thinker. He used his split-second to turn his head and stare down one hip at the treacherous hoof. The heel had dipped down into the space between the two ties and jammed. It ought to come out again easy enough, if he did the right thing. And there wasn't time to do the wrong thing. So he started turning back again on it, as if he were going to step right in front of the train. That reversed whatever twist had originally trapped it; it came up free, smooth as pie, and he stepped backwards with it out of death's path, face turned toward the train as it rushed abreast of him, brakes that wouldn't have been in time to save him screeching. He had presence of mind enough to point the plank skyward, like a soldier presenting arms, so the train wouldn't sideswipe it and throw him. The cars seemed to take the skin off his nose.

The damn thing stopped a car-length away, but whether on his account or the station's he didn't know and didn't bother finding out. He got back the rest of the way to the other side of the tracks on knees that made him ashamed of them, they jogged so.

'Now just for that,' he growled unreasonably at the blank window, 'I'm gonna slap you up plenty for attempting to escape while under arrest, or something!'

The plank, when he paid it out, bridged the gap neatly, but at rather a steep incline, the window-ledge being higher than the guard-rail of the 'El' structure. The distance, however, was so short that this didn't worry him. He took the precaution of taking out his gun, to forestall any attempt to shake him off his perch before he could grab the window-sash, but so far there had been no sign of life from within the room. They were probably sleeping it off.

He got up on the bottom rail, put his knee on the plank, and a minute later was grovelling across it in mid-air, above the short but very deep chasm. It slipped diagonally downward toward the 'El' a little under his weight, but not enough to come off the ledge. The next minute he had his free hand hooked securely around the wooden window-frame and was over and in.

He took a deep breath of relief, but still wouldn't have been willing to admit that this was a lot of trouble to go to just to get out of climbing a flock of stairs. He was that way. Without looking down just now, he'd been dimly aware of people milling about on the street below him, shouting up. They'd taken him for crazy, he supposed.

A downtown train careened past just behind his back right then, and lit up the interior of the room for him nicely, better than a pocket-flash. It also did something else – as though all these trains tonight bore him a personal grudge. It struck the lower edge of the plank he had just used, which extended too far in past the rail, with a crack and sent it hurtling down to the street below. As long as he hadn't been on it at the time, being cut off like this didn't worry him particularly – he'd intended walking down anyway. He only hoped those on the sidewalk would see it coming in time to dodge. They ought to, looking up the way they had been.

But before he could give it another thought, the flickering train-lights washing across the walls showed him that he wasn't alone in the room after all.

One-half of his quarry was lying there face-down across the bed. It was the lady-souse, and judging by the way her arms hung down on one side and her feet on the other she was more soused than ladylike. Step took his eye off her and followed the phantom yellow-square the last car-window made as it travelled around three of the walls after its mates and then flickered out in the opposite direction from the train. It had shown him a switch by the door. So the place was wired for electricity, decrepit as it was. There was a moment of complete darkness, and then he had the room-light on.

He turned back to her. 'Hey, you!' he growled. 'Where's that guy that was in here with you a couple minutes ago? Get up offa there and answer me before I—'

But she wasn't answering anybody any more. The bullet-hole under her left eye answered for her, when he tilted her face. It said: *Finished!* The cheek was all pitted with powder-burns. There was a playing-card symbol, the crimson ace of diamonds, on the white counterpane where the wound had rested. His eye travelled around the room. That had been her death-struggle in his arms. The first shot had missed her, had killed the man named Wall in the first car of the 'El' instead; the second one must have come a split-second after Step's car-window passed beyond range. The same bullet hadn't killed both; hers was still in her head. There was no wound of egress.

Step didn't bother playing detective, snooping around, even examining the remaining rooms of the tawdry little flat. His technique would have astounded a layman, horrified a rookie, probably only have made his superior sigh resignedly and shrug. 'Well, that's Step for you.' What he did about getting after the culprit, in a murder that had been committed so recently it was still smoking, was to pull over a warped rocking-chair, sit down, and begin rolling a cigarette. His attitude implied that it had tired him plenty to walk the tracks all the way back here, and everything could wait until he'd rested up a little. An occasional flickering of the eyelids, however, betokened that all was not as quiet on the inside of his head as on the outside.

The woman's hands seemed to fascinate him. The tips of her fingers were touching the floor, as though she were trying to balance herself upside-down. He took them up in his own and looked more closely. The nails were polished and well cared for. He turned them palm-up. The skin was not coarse and reddened, by dishwashing and housework. 'You didn't belong here on Greenwich Street,' he remarked. 'Wonder who you were hiding from?'

A long spike of ash had formed on the end of his cigarette, and crummy as the place was, he looked around for something to park it in. No ashtrays in sight; evidently the dead lady hadn't been a smoker. He flicked the ash off into space, and as he did so, his eyes travelled down the seam between two of the unpainted floor-boards. Wedged into it was a butt. He got it out with the aid of a pin from his lapel. The mouth-end was still damp. Her lips, he had noticed, had been reddened fairly recently. But there wasn't a fleck of colour on this. Not hers, therefore.

He dropped the cigarette he had been smoking and crushed it out, then passed the other one back and forth under his nose a couple of times. An acrid odour immediately took the place of the aroma of his familiar Virginia tobacco. He went a step further, put a lit match to the end of it and tried to draw on it without actually touching it to his lips, still holding it on the pin. He had to suck mightily to start it glowing. Instantly there were results. His lungs smarted. And yet it wasn't the smoke of the burning paper he was getting, as in the case of an ordinary cigarette. That was escaping at both ends. It was the vapour of the weed that filled it.

Marijuana – crazy-weed. And unwittingly he'd gone about just the right way of smoking it, not letting it come into contact with his lips. A vacuous, boisterous laugh wrenched from him abruptly, over the slain woman's head. Nothing to laugh at, and here he was roaring. He dropped the damned thing precipitately, trod on it as though it were a snake, opened his mouth and fanned pure air into it. The booming laugh subsided to a chortle, ebbed away. He mopped his forehead, got up and went unsteadily toward the outer door of the flat.

The din down below in the street seemed to have increased a hundredfold, meanwhile; he couldn't be sure whether it actually had or it was just the after-effects of the drugged cigarette making it seem so. Sirens screeching, bells clanging, voices yelling – as though there were a whole crowd milling around out there.

He opened the flat door, and you couldn't see your hand in front of your face. No lights out in the hall. Then he saw a peculiar hazy blur just a few feet away, up overhead, and realised that there *were* lights – but the building was on fire. It wasn't darkness he'd stepped out into, but a solid wall of smoke.

He could possibly have gotten out, still made the street from where he was, by a quick dash down the stairs then and there. Step Lively plus several whiffs of a drugged cigarette, however, was no combination calculated to equal a quick dash in any direction, up or down. He turned around coughing and shuffled back into the flat he had just emerged from, closing the door on the inferno outside.

To do him justice, it wasn't simply inertia or laziness this time that kept him up there where he was. Hundreds of men in hundreds of fires have hung back to drag somebody living out with them. But very few have lingered to haul out somebody already dead. That, however, was precisely what Step had gone back for. The lady was his *corpus delicti* and he wasn't leaving her there to be cremated.

That a fire should start up here and now, in the very building where a murder had been committed, was too much of a coincidence. It was almost certainly a case of incendiarism on the murderer's part, perpetrated in hopes of obliterating all traces of his crime. 'And if he was smoking that devilish butt I picked up,' he said to himself, 'he wouldn't stop to worry about whether anybody else was living in the building or not!'

He retrieved it a second time, what there was left of it, and dropped it in his pocket, pin and all. Then he wrapped the counterpane with the ace-of-diamonds symbol on it around the woman, turning her into a bundle of laundry, and moved toward the door with her. The current failed just as he was fumbling at it with one hand, under her, and the room went black.

A dull red glow shone up the stairwell, though, when he got it open. It would have been all right to see by, but there wasn't anything to breathe out there any more, just blistering heat and strangling smoke. Spearheads of yellow started to shoot up through it from below, like an army with bayonets marching up the stairs. He got back inside again, hacking and with water pouring out of his eyes, but hanging on to her like grim death, as though she were some dear one instead of just a murdered stranger he had happened to find.

The room was all obliterated with haze now, like the hallway had been the first time, but he groped his way through it to the window. He didn't lose his head; didn't even get frightened. That was all right for women or slobs in suspenders, trapped on the top floor of a blazing tenement. 'I didn't come in through the door, anyway,' he growled. He was good and sore, though, about all this hectic activity he was having to go through. 'I should 'a' been home long ago, and had my shoes off—' he was thinking as he leaned out across the sill and tried to signal to the mob that he could hear, but no longer see, down on the street.

He was hidden from them, and they from him, by the smoke billowing out from the windows below him. It formed a regular blanket between – but not the kind that it paid to jump into. Still, the apparatus must be ganged up down there by this time. You'd think they'd do something about helping a fellow get down, whether they could see him or not. Somebody must have almost certainly spotted him climbing in . . .

Even if he still had the plank, he couldn't have made it across on that any more. He not only had *her* now, but his lungs and eyes were going all wacky with this damn black stuff; he'd have toppled off it in a minute. The crack he'd just made to himself about having his shoes off at home registered. He parked her across the sill, bunched one leg, and started unlacing. It took him about forty-five seconds to undo the knot and slip the oxford off – which for him was excellent time. He poised it and flung it down through the smoke. If it would only bean somebody now, they'd stop and think maybe that shoes don't come flying down out of a fire unless there's somebody up there in it alive.

It did. A section of ladder shot up out of the swirling murk just as it left his hand. The helmeted figure scampering up monkey-like met the shoe half-way, with the bridge of his nose, and nearly went off into space. He flailed wildly with one propeller-like arm, caught the ladder once more in the nick of time, and resumed his ascent – a brief nosebleed to add to his troubles. Such language Step had rarely heard before. 'Oops,' he murmured regretfully. 'Shows it never pays to be too hasty. What I've always said.'

The fireman wiped his mouth, growled: 'C'mon, step out and over, the roof's gonna go any minute.' He was on a level with Step's eyes now, outside the window. The room was about ready to burst with heat; you could hear the floor-boards cracking as they expanded.

Step reared the mummy-like figure, thrust it across the sill into the smoke-eater's arms. 'Take this stiff and be careful of her,' he coughed. 'She's valuable. I'll be right down on top of you.'

The fireman, hooked on to the ladder by his legs, slung the burden over his shoulder, clamped it fast with one arm, and started down. Step started to climb over the sill backwards. The smoke was worse out here than in the room, he couldn't see the ladder any more. A silvery lining to the smoke, like a halo all around him, showed they were training a searchlight up from below, but it couldn't get through the dense, boiling masses. He found a rung with his one stockinged foot, made passes at the air until he'd finally connected with one of the invisible shafts – and the rest was just a switch over. Try it sometime yourself.

Then he stayed where he was until he'd shrugged his coat half-off his shoulders and hooded it completely over his head. Then he went down slowly, blind, deaf, seared, and breathing into worsted a little at a time. He went down ten storeys, twenty, fifty – and still the ground wouldn't come up and meet him. He decided the place must have been the Empire State in disguise. One time he passed through a spattering of cool, grateful spray blown off one of the hose-lines and almost felt like sticking around in it, it felt so good. Just about the time he decided that the ladder must be slowly moving upward under him, like a belt-line or treadmill, and that was why he wasn't getting anywhere, hands grabbed him at the ankles and shoulders and he was hoisted to terra firma a yard below.

'Bud,' said the fire chief patiently, 'as long as you were in shape to climb down on your own, couldn't you have made it a *little* faster! I'm a very nervous man.'

Step disengaged his head from his coat, kissed himself on the knuckles, bent down and rapped them against the Greenwich Street sidewalk. Then he straightened up and remonstrated: 'I never was rushed so in my life as I been for the past half-hour!' He glanced upward at the haze-blurred building, whose outline was beginning to emerge here and there from the haze of smoke.

'The fire,' the chief enlightened him, turning away, 'was brought under control during the half-hour you were passing the third floor. We finally put it out during the, er, forty-five minutes it took you getting from there down. The assistant marshal's in there now conducting an investigation—' Which may have leaned more toward sarcasm than accuracy, but was a good example of the impression Step made upon people the very first time they encountered him.

'Tell him for me,' Step said, 'it was arson – nothing else,

but. He mayn't be able to find any evidence, but that doesn't alter the fact any.'

'A firebug, you think?'

'Something just a step worse. A murderer. A pyromaniac is irresponsible, afflicted, can't help himself. This dog knew just what he was doing, killed his conscience for both acts ahead of time with marijuana.' He pointed to the muffled figure on the stretcher. 'That woman was shot dead a good quarter of an hour before the fire was discovered. I was a witness to it. I'm Lively, of the —th Precinct, uptown.'

The fire chief muttered something that sounded like: 'You may be attached to that precinct, but you're not lively.' But he was diplomatic enough to keep it blurred. 'But if you were a witness,' he said aloud, 'how is it the guy—?'

'Powdered? I wasn't in the room with them, I glimpsed it from an "El" train that stalled for a minute opposite the window! You go in there and tell your marshal not to bother looking for gasoline cans or oil-soaked rags. He didn't have time for a set-up like that, must have just put a match to a newspaper running down the stairs. Where's the caretaker or janitor, or didn't the dump have one?"

'Over behind the ropes there, in the crowd across the street. Take him over and point out the guy to him, Marty.'

Step trailed the fireman whom he had clouted with his shoe – which incidentally had vanished – limping on his one unshod foot, and ducked under the rope beside a grizzled, perspiring little man. Palmed his badge at him to add to his terror, and asked, while his eyes roved the crowd that hemmed them in: 'Who was the woman top-floor front?'

'Insoorance?' whined the terrified one.

"No, police department. Well, come on—'

'Smiff. Miss Smiff.'

Step groaned. But he'd figure'd she'd been hiding out anyway, so it didn't really matter much. 'How long she been living up there in your house?'

'Ten day.'

'Who visited her, see anybody?'

'Nome-body. She done even go out; my wife bring food.'

Good and scared, reflected Step. Scared stiff, but it hadn't saved her. 'Did you hear anything tonight just before the fire? Were you in the building? Hear a couple shots? Hear any screams?'

'No hear no-thing, train make too much noise. Only hear fella laff coming downstairs, like somebody tell-im good joke. Laff, laff, laff, all the way out to street—'

The marijuana, of course. Just two drags had affected his own risibilities. The effects of a whole reefer ought to last hours, at that rate. Step shoved away from the futile janitor, flagged one of the patrolmen holding the crowd in check behind the rope-barrier, introduced himself. The excitement was tapering off, now that everyone was out of the house and the fire had been subdued, it was only a matter of minutes before they'd start melting away. Overhead the 'El' trains, which had been held back at Debrosses Street while the smoke had been at its thickest, were again being allowed through, although surface traffic was still being detoured.

'Who's on this job with you?'' Step asked the cop in a low voice.

'One other guy, down at the other end.'

'Think the two of you can keep 'em in like they are, another couple minutes?'

The cop looked insulted. 'That's what we been doing. You don't see anybody edging out into the middle of the street, do ya?'

'No, you don't understand what I mean. Can you put up another rope at each side, hem them in where they are, keep them from strolling off just a little while longer till I get a chance to take a careful look through them all?'

'I'm not authorised to keep people from going about

their business, as long as they don't hamper the fire apparatus—'

'I'll take the responsibility. There's someone I'm out to get, and I've got a very good hunch he's right here looking on. Firebugs are known to do that, murderers too when they think they're safe from discovery. When you've got a combination of both, the urge to stay and gloat ought to be twice as strong!

'Bawl me out,' he added abruptly, 'so it don't look too phoney, my standing talking to you like this.'

The cop swung his club at him, barked: 'Get back there! Whaddya think that rope's for? Get back there before I—'

Step cringed away from him, began to elbow his way deeper into the tightly packed crowd jamming the narrow sidewalk. He did this as slow as he did everything else, didn't seem like anyone who had a definite place to go, just a rubber-necker working his way toward a better vantage-point. From time to time he glanced over at the gutted building, or what could be seen of it under the shadowy 'El' structure that bisected the street vertically. Torches blinked deep within the front hallway of it, as firemen passed in and out, still veiled by the haze that clung to it.

There wasn't, however, enough smoke left in the air, certainly not this close to the ground, to send anyone into paroxysms of strangled coughing. Such as that individual just ahead was experiencing, handkerchief pressed to mouth. Step himself had inhaled as much smoke as anyone, and his lungs were back on the job again as good as ever. He kept facing the burned building from this point on, edging over sidewise to the afflicted one. The spasms would stop and he'd lower the handkerchief; then another one would come on and he'd raise it again and nearly spill himself into it. Step was unobtrusively at his elbow by now.

When a person is suffering from a coughing fit, two ways of assisting them will occur to almost anybody. Offer them a drink of water or slap them helpfully on the back. Step didn't have any water to offer, so he chose the second means of alleviation. Slapped the tormented one between the shoulder-blades: but just once, not several times, and not nearly forcefully enough to do any good. 'You're under arrest,' he said desultorily, 'come on.'

The concealing handkerchief dropped – this time all the way to the ground. 'What for? What're you talking about?'

'For two murders and an arson,' drawled the wearied Step. 'I'm talking about you. And don't be afraid to laugh right out. No need to muffle it with your handkerchief and try to change it into a cough any more. That was what gave you away to me. When you've been smoking marijuana, you've just gotta laugh or else. But watching fires isn't the right place to do your laughing. And if it had been real coughing, you wouldn't have stayed around where the smoke irritated you that much. Now show me where you dropped the gun before you came back here to watch, and then we'll get in a taxi. I wouldn't ask my feet to carry me another step tonight.'

His prisoner bayed uncontrollably with mirth, then panted: 'I never was in that building in my life—' Writhed convulsively.

'I saw you,' said Step, pushing him slowly before him through the crowd, 'through the window from an "El" train as I was going by.' He knew the soporific effect the drug was likely to have, its blunting of the judgment. 'She came to us and told us she was afraid of this happening to her, asked for protection, and we been giving it to her. Did you think you could get away with it?'

'Then what'd she rat on Plucky at his trial for? She knew what to expect. He sent out word—'

'Oh, that vice trial. And she was one of the witnesses? I see.' Step slammed the door of the cab on the two of them. 'Thanks for telling me; now I know who she was, who you are, and why it was done. There is something to be said for marijuana after all. Not much, but maybe just a little.'

When he stepped out of the cab with his handcuffed quarry at the foot of the Franklin Street station four blocks away, he directed the driver: 'Now sound your horn till they come down off of up there.' And when they did, his mates found Inspector Stephen Lively seated upon the bottom step of the station stairs, his prisoner at his side.

'Fellas,' he said apologetically, 'this is the guy. And if I gotta go up there again to the top, I wonder could you two make a saddle with your hands and hoist me between you. I'm just plumb tuckered out!'

The Mysterious Death on the Underground Railway

BARONESS EMMUSKA ORCZY

It was to be ten years after the furore that surrounded the publication of John Oxenham's controversial serial, before another crime writer decided to set a murder mystery on the London Underground and hope that it would not panic travellers. This time, however, the story was merely one of a series, but it did still represent another landmark in detective fiction because of featuring the first of the now familiar band of 'armchair detectives' who solve the most complex crimes without ever needing to go to the scene of the crime.

This pioneer was a curious, nondescript old fellow who spent much of his life in the corner of a London tea shop to which an enthusiastic young reporter on an evening paper brought details of crimes which were baffling the police. He was known simply as The Old Man in the Corner, while his pretty female associate was Polly Burton of the *Evening Observer*. Together, the pair who first appeared in the *Royal Magazine* in 1901 were to solve more than two dozen cases in the next twenty-five years. The Old Man was an appealing character to many readers who had grown used to a host of detectives in the Sherlock Holmes mould, for he not only solved his crimes by pure intellect from the facts as given to him, but often ended up feeling sympathetic towards the criminals he brought to justice.

The Old Man was the creation of the Hungarian-born novelist and playwright Baroness Emmuska Orczy (1865–1947), who came to England to study art and became so highly regarded that a number of her paintings were exhibited in the Royal Academy. Although her first venture into fiction was with crime stories, real fame came five years later with the start of her adventures of *The Scarlet Pimpernel* (1905) who would become a great public favourite in novels, plays, and later in numerous films. The Old Man in the Corner was also featured in a series of twelve British movies from 1924 starring Rolf Leslie; then almost fifty years later he reappeared in the Thames TV series *The Rivals of Sherlock Holmes*, when the case of 'The Mysterious Death on the Underground Railway' was dramatised with John Savident and Judy Geeson as the eager Polly. The story is certainly one of the most ingenious about the Old Man and concerns the discovery of an attractive young woman's body in a carriage on the Metropolitan railway which at first appears to be a case of suicide, but soon turns into a murder hunt.

***

It was all very well for Mr Richard Frobisher (of the *London Mail*) to cut up rough about it. Polly did not altogether blame him.

She liked him all the better for that frank outburst of manlike ill-temper which, after all said and done, was only a very flattering form of masculine jealousy.

Moreover, Polly distinctly felt guilty about the whole thing. She had promised to meet Dickie – that is Mr Richard Frobisher – at two o'clock sharp outside the Palace Theatre, because she wanted to go to a Maud Allan matinée, and because he naturally wished to go with her.

But at two o'clock sharp she was still in Norfolk Street, Strand, inside an ABC shop, sipping cold coffee opposite a grotesque old man who was fiddling with a bit of string.

How could she be expected to remember Maud Allan or the Palace Theatre, or Dickie himself for a matter of that? The man in the corner had begun to talk of that mysterious death on the Underground railway, and Polly had lost count of time, of place, and circumstance.

She had gone to lunch quite early, for she was looking forward to the matinée at the Palace. The old scarecrow was sitting in his accustomed place when she came into the ABC shop, but he had made no remark all the time that the young girl was munching her scone and butter. She was just busy thinking how rude he was not even to have said 'Good morning', when an abrupt remark from him caused her to look up.

'Will you be good enough,' he said suddenly, 'to give me a description of the man who sat next to you just now, while you were having your cup of coffee and scone.'

Involuntarily Polly turned her head towards the distant door, through which a man in a light overcoat was even now quickly passing. That man had certainly sat at the next table to hers, when she first sat down to her coffee and scone: he had finished his luncheon – whatever it was – a moment ago, had paid at the desk and gone out. The incident did not appear to Polly as being of the slightest consequence.

Therefore she did not reply to the rude old man, but shrugged her shoulders, and called to the waitress to bring her bill.

'Do you know if he was tall or short, dark or fair?' continued the man in the corner, seemingly not the least disconcerted by the young girl's indifference. 'Can you tell me at all what he was like?'

'Of course I can,' rejoined Polly impatiently, 'but I don't see that my description of one of the customers of an ABC shop can have the slightest importance.'

He was silent for a minute, while his nervous fingers fumbled about in his capacious pockets in search of the inevitable piece of string. When he had found this necessary 'adjunct to thought', he viewed the young girl again through his half-closed lids, and added maliciously:

'But supposing it were of paramount importance that you should give an accurate description of a man who sat next to you for half an hour today, how would you proceed?'

'I should say that he was of medium height—'

'Five foot eight, nine, or ten?' he interrupted quietly.

'How can one tell to an inch or two?' rejoined Polly crossly. 'He was between colours.'

'What's that?' he enquired blandly.

'Neither fair nor dark – his nose—'

'Well, what was his nose like? Will you sketch it?'

'I am not an artist. His nose was fairly straight – his eyes—'

'Were neither dark nor light – his hair had the same striking peculiarity – he was neither short nor tall – his nose was neither aquiline nor snub—' he recapitulated sarcastically.

'No,' she retorted; 'he was just ordinary-looking.'

'Would you know him again – say tomorrow, and among a number of other men who were "neither tall nor short, dark nor fair, aquiline nor snub-nosed", etc.?'

'I don't know – I might – he was certainly not striking enough to be specially remembered.'

'Exactly,' he said, while he leant forward excitedly, for all the world like a Jack-in-the-box let loose. 'Precisely; and you are a journalist – call yourself one, at least – and it should be part of your business to notice and describe people. I don't mean only the wonderful personage with the clear Saxon features, the fine blue eyes, the noble brow and classic face, but the ordinary person – the person who represents ninety out of every hundred of his own kind – the average Englishman, say, of the middle classes, who is neither very tall nor very short, who wears a moustache which is neither fair nor dark, but which masks his mouth, and a top hat which hides the shape of his head and brow, a man, in fact, who dresses like hundreds of his fellow-creatures, moves like them, speaks like them, has no peculiarity.

'Try to describe *him*, to recognise him, say a week hence, among his other eighty-nine doubles; worse still, to swear his life away, if he happened to be implicated in some crime, wherein *your* recognition of him would place the halter round his neck.

'Try that, I say, and having utterly failed you will more readily understand how one of the greatest scoundrels unhung is still at large, and why the mystery on the Underground railway was never cleared up.

'I think it was the only time in my life that I was seriously tempted to give the police the benefit of my own views upon the matter. You see, though I admire the brute for his cleverness, I did not see that his being unpunished could possibly benefit anyone.

'In these days of tubes and motor traction of all kinds, the old-fashioned "best, cheapest, and quickest route to City and West End" is often deserted, and the good old Metropolitan railway carriages cannot at any time be said to be overcrowded. Anyway, when that particular train steamed into Aldgate at about four p.m. on March eighteenth last, the first-class carriages were all but empty.

'The guard marched up and down the platform looking into all the carriages to see if anyone had left a halfpenny evening paper behind for him, and opening the door of one of the first-class compartments, he noticed a lady sitting in the further corner, with her head turned away towards the window, evidently oblivious of the fact that on this line Aldgate is the terminal station.

' "Where are you for, lady?" he said.

'The lady did not move, and the guard stepped into the carriage, thinking that perhaps the lady was asleep. He touched her arm lightly and looked into her face. In his own poetic language, he was "struck all of a 'eap". In the glassy eyes, the ashen colour of the cheeks, the rigidity of the head, there was the unmistakable look of death.

'Hastily the guard, having carefully locked the carriage door, summoned a couple of porters, and sent one of them off to the police station, and the other in search of the stationmaster.

'Fortunately at this time of day the up platform is not very crowded, all the traffic tending westward in the afternoon. It was only when an inspector and two police constables, accompanied by a detective in plain clothes and a medical officer, appeared upon the scene, and stood round a first-class railway compartment, that a few idlers realised that something unusual had occurred, and crowded round, eager and curious.

'Thus it was that the later editions of the evening papers, under the sensational heading, "Mysterious Suicide on the Underground Railway", had already an account of the extraordinary event. The medical officer had very soon come to the decision that the guard had not been mistaken, and that life was indeed extinct.

'The lady was young, and must have been very pretty before the look of fright and horror had so terribly distorted her features. She was very elegantly dressed, and the more frivolous papers were able to give their feminine readers a detailed account of the unfortunate woman's gown, her shoes, hat, and gloves.

'It appears that one of the latter, the one on the right hand, was partly off, leaving the thumb and wrist bare. That hand held a small satchel, which the police opened, with a view to the possible identification of the deceased, but which was found to contain only a little loose silver, some smelling-salts, and a small empty bottle, which was handed over to the medical officer for purposes of analysis.

'It was the presence of that small bottle which had caused the report to circulate freely that the mysterious case on the Underground railway was one of suicide. Certain it was that neither about the lady's person, nor in the appearance of the railway carriage, was there the slightest sign of struggle or even of resistance. Only the look in the poor woman's eyes spoke of sudden terror, of the rapid vision of an unexpected and violent death, which probably only lasted an infinitesimal fraction of a second, but which had left its indelible mark upon the face, otherwise so placid and so still.

'The body of the deceased was conveyed to the mortuary. So far, of course, not a soul had been able to identify her, or to throw the slightest light upon the mystery which hung around her death.

'Against that, quite a crowd of idlers – genuinely interested or not – obtained admission to view the body, on the pretext of having lost or mislaid a relative or a friend. At about eight-thirty p.m. a young man, very well dressed, drove up to the station in a hansom, and sent in his card to the superintendent. It was Mr Hazeldene, shipping agent, of 11, Crown Lane, EC, and No. 19, Addison Row, Kensington.

'The young man looked in a pitiable state of mental distress; his hand clutched nervously a copy of the *St James's Gazette* which contained the fatal news. He said very little to the superintendent except that a person who was very dear to him had not returned home that evening.

'He had not felt really anxious until half an hour ago, when suddenly he thought of looking at his paper. The description of the deceased lady, though vague, had terribly alarmed him. He had jumped into a hansom, and now begged permission to view the body, in order that his worst fears might be allayed.

'You know what followed, of course,' continued the man in the corner, 'the grief of the young man was truly pitiable. In the woman lying there in a public mortuary before him, Mr Hazeldene had recognised his wife.

'I am waxing melodramatic,' said the man in the corner,

who looked up at Polly with a mild and gentle smile, while his nervous fingers vainly endeavoured to add another knot on the scrappy bit of string with which he was continually playing, 'and I fear that the whole story savours of the penny novelette, but you must admit, and no doubt you remember, that it was an intensely pathetic and truly dramatic moment.

'The unfortunate young husband of the deceased lady was not much worried with questions that night. As a matter of fact, he was not in a fit condition to make any coherent statement. It was at the coroner's inquest on the following day that certain facts came to light, which for the time being seemed to clear up the mystery surrounding Mrs Hazeldene's death, only to plunge that same mystery, later on, into denser gloom than before.

'The first witness at the inquest was, of course, Mr Hazeldene himself. I think everyone's sympathy went out to the young man as he stood before the coroner and tried to throw what light he could upon the mystery. He was well dressed, as he had been the day before, but he looked terribly ill and worried, and no doubt the fact that he had not shaved gave his face a careworn and neglected air.

'It appears that he and the deceased had been married some six years or so, and that they had always been happy in their married life. They had no children. Mrs Hazeldene seemed to enjoy the best of health till lately, when she had had a slight attack of influenza, in which Dr Arthur Jones had attended her. The doctor was present at this moment, and would no doubt explain to the coroner and the jury whether he thought that Mrs Hazeldene had the slightest tendency to heart disease, which might have had a sudden and fatal ending.

'The coroner was, of course, very considerate to the bereaved husband. He tried by circumlocution to get at the point he wanted, namely, Mrs Hazeldene's mental condition lately. Mr Hazeldene seemed loath to talk about this.

No doubt he had been warned as to the existence of the small bottle found in his wife's satchel.

' "It certainly did seem to me at times," he at last reluctantly admitted, "that my wife did not seem quite herself. She used to be very gay and bright, and lately I often saw her in the evening sitting, as if brooding over some matters, which evidently she did not care to communicate to me."

'Still the coroner insisted, and suggested the small bottle.

' "I know, I know," replied the young man, with a short, heavy sigh. "You mean – the question of suicide – I cannot understand it at all – it seems so sudden and so terrible – she certainly had seemed listless and troubled lately – but only at times – and yesterday morning, when I went to business, she appeared quite herself again, and I suggested that we should go to the opera in the evening. She was delighted, I know, and told me she would do some shopping, and pay a few calls in the afternoon.

' "Do you know at all where she intended to go when she got into the Underground railway?"

' "Well, not with certainty. You see, she may have meant to get out at Baker Street, and go down to Bond Street to do her shopping. Then again, she sometimes goes to a shop in St Paul's Churchyard, in which case she would take a ticket to Aldersgate Street; but I cannot say."

' "Now, Mr Hazeldene," said the coroner at last very kindly, "will you try to tell me if there was anything in Mrs Hazeldene's life which you know of, and which might in some measure explain the cause of the distressed state of mind, which you yourself had noticed? Did there exist any financial difficulty which might have preyed upon Mrs Hazeldene's mind; was there any friend – to whose intercourse with Mrs Hazeldene – you – er – at any time took exception? In fact," added the coroner, as if thankful that he had got over an unpleasant moment, "can you give me the slightest indication which would tend to confirm the suspicion that the unfortunate lady, in a moment of mental anxiety or derangement, may have wished to take her own life?"

'There was silence in the court for a few moments. Mr Hazeldene seemed to everyone there present to be labouring under some terrible moral doubt. He looked very pale and wretched, and twice attempted to speak before he at last said in scarcely audible tones:

' "No; there were no financial difficulties of any sort. My wife had an independent fortune of her own – and she had no extravagant tastes—"

' "Nor any friend you at any time objected to?" insisted the coroner.

' "Nor any friend, I – at any time objected to," stammered the unfortunate young man, evidently speaking with an effort.

'I was present at the inquest,' resumed the man in the corner, after he had drunk a glass of milk and ordered another, 'and I can assure you that the most obtuse person there plainly realised that Mr Hazeldene was telling a lie. It was pretty plain to the meanest intelligence that the unfortunate lady had not fallen into a state of morbid dejection for nothing, and that perhaps there existed a third person who could throw more light on her strange and sudden death than the unhappy, bereaved young widower.

'That the death was more mysterious even than it had at first appeared became very soon apparent. You read the case at the time, no doubt, and must remember the excitement in the public mind caused by the evidence of the two doctors. Dr Arthur Jones, the lady's usual medical man, who had attended her in a last very slight illness, and who had seen her in a professional capacity fairly recently, declared most emphatically that Mrs Hazeldene suffered from no organic complaint which could possibly have been the cause of sudden death. Moreover, he had assisted Mr Andrew Thornton, the district medical officer, in making a post-mortem examination, and together they had come to the conclusion that death was due to the action of prussic acid, which had caused instantaneous failure of the heart, but how the drug had been administered neither he nor his colleague were at present able to state.

' "Do I understand, then, Dr Jones, that the deceased died, poisoned with prussic acid?"

' "Such is my opinion," replied the doctor.

' "Did the bottle found in her satchel contain prussic acid?"

' "It had contained some at one time, certainly."

' "In your opinion, then, the lady caused her own death by taking a dose of that drug?"

' "Pardon me, I never suggested such a thing; the lady died poisoned by the drug, but how the drug was administered we cannot say. By injection of some sort, certainly. The drug certainly was not swallowed; there was not a vestige of it in the stomach."

' "Yes," added the doctor in reply to another question from the coroner, "death had probably followed the injection in this case almost immediately; say within a couple of minutes, or perhaps three. It was quite possible that the body would not have more than one quick and sudden convulsion, perhaps not that; death in such cases is absolutely sudden and crushing."

'I don't think that at the time anyone in the room realised how important the doctor's statement was, a statement which, by the way, was confirmed in all its details by the district medical officer, who had conducted the post-mortem. Mrs Hazeldene had died suddenly from an injection of prussic acid, administered no one knew how or when. She had been travelling in a first-class railway carriage at a busy time of the day. That young and elegant woman must have had singular nerve and coolness to go through the process of a self-inflicted injection of a deadly poison in the presence of perhaps two or three other persons.

'Mind you, when I say that no one there realised the importance of the doctor's statement at that moment, I am wrong; there were three persons, who fully understood at once the gravity of the situation, and the astounding development which the case was beginning to assume.

'Of course, I should have put myself out of the question,' added the weird old man, with that inimitable self-conceit peculiar to himself. 'I guessed then and there in a moment where the police were going wrong, and where they would go on going wrong until the mysterious death on the Underground railway had sunk into oblivion, together with the other cases which they mismanage from time to time.

'I said there were three persons who understood the gravity of the two doctors' statements – the other two were, firstly, the detective who had originally examined the railway carriage, a young man of energy and plenty of misguided intelligence, the other was Mr Hazeldene.

'At this point the interesting element of the whole story was first introduced into the proceedings, and this was done through the humble channel of Emma Funnel, Mrs Hazeldene's maid, who, as far as was known then, was the last person who had seen the unfortunate lady alive and had spoken to her.

' "Mrs Hazeldene lunched at home," explained Emma, who was shy, and spoke almost in a whisper; "she seemed well and cheerful. She went out at about half-past three, and told me she was going to Spence's, in St Paul's Churchyard, to try on her new tailor-made gown. Mrs Hazeldene had meant to go there in the morning, but was prevented as Mr Errington called."

' "Mr Errington?" asked the coroner casually. "Who is Mr Errington?"

'But this Emma found difficult to explain. Mr Errington was – Mr Errington, that's all.

' "Mr Errington was a friend of the family. He lived in a flat in the Albert Mansions. He very often came to Addison Row, and generally stayed late."

'Pressed still further with questions, Emma at last stated that latterly Mrs Hazeldene had been to the theatre several times with Mr Errington, and that on those nights the master looked very gloomy, and was very cross.

'Recalled, the young widower was strangely reticent. He gave forth his answers very grudgingly, and the coroner was evidently absolutely satisfied with himself at the marvellous way in which, after a quarter of an hour of firm yet very kind questionings, he had elicited from the witness what information he wanted.

'Mr Errington was a friend of his wife. He was a gentleman of means, and seemed to have a great deal of time at his command. He himself did not particularly care about Mr Errington, but he certainly had never made any observations to his wife on the subject.

' "But who is Mr Errington?" repeated the coroner once more. "What does he do? What is his business or profession?"

' "He has no business or profession."

' "What is his occupation, then?"

' "He has no special occupation. He has ample private means. But he has a great and very absorbing hobby."

' "What is that?"

' "He spends all his time in chemical experiments, and is, I believe, as an amateur, a very distinguished toxicologist." '

'Did you ever see Mr Errington, the gentleman so closely connected with the mysterious death on the Underground railway?' asked the man in the corner as he placed one or two of his little snap-shot photos before Miss Polly Burton.

'There he is, to the very life. Fairly good-looking, a pleasant face enough, but ordinary, absolutely ordinary.

'It was this absence of any peculiarity which very nearly, but not quite, placed the halter round Mr Errington's neck.

'But I am going too fast, and you will lose the thread.

'The public, of course, never heard how it actually came about that Mr Errington, the wealthy bachelor of Albert Mansions, of the Grosvenor, and other young dandies' clubs, one fine day found himself before the magistrate at Bow Street, charged with being concerned in the death of Mary Beatrice Hazeldene, late of No. 19, Addison Row.

'I can assure you both press and public were literally flabbergasted. You see, Mr Errington was a well-known and very popular member of a certain smart section of London society. He was a constant visitor at the opera, the racecourse, the Park, and the Carlton, he had a great many friends, and there was consequently quite a large attendance at the police court that morning.

'What had transpired was this:

'After the very scrappy bits of evidence which came to light at the inquest, two gentlemen bethought themselves that perhaps they had some duty to perform towards the State and the public generally. Accordingly they had come forward, offering to throw what light they could upon the mysterious affair on the Underground railway.

'The police naturally felt that their information, such as it was, came rather late in the day, but as it proved of paramount importance, and the two gentlemen, moreover, were of undoubtedly good position in the world, they were thankful for what they could get, and acted accordingly; they accordingly brought Mr Errington up before the magistrate on a charge of murder.

'The accused looked pale and worried when I first caught sight of him in the court that day, which was not to be wondered at, considering the terrible position in which he found himself.

'He had been arrested at Marseilles, where he was preparing to start for Colombo. I don't think he realised how terrible his position really was until later in the proceedings, when all the evidence relating to the arrest had been heard, and Emma Funnel had repeated her statement as to Mr Errington's call at 19, Addison Row, in the morning, and Mrs Hazeldene starting off for St Paul's Churchyard at three-thirty in the afternoon.

'Mr Hazeldene had nothing to add to the statements he had made at the coroner's inquest. He had last seen his wife alive on the morning of the fatal day. She had seemed very well and cheerful.

'I think everyone present understood that he was trying to say as little as possible that could in any way couple his deceased wife's name with that of the accused.

'And yet, from the servant's evidence, it undoubtedly leaked out that Mrs Hazeldene, who was young, pretty, and evidently fond of admiration, had once or twice annoyed her husband by her somewhat open, yet perfectly innocent, flirtation with Mr Errington.

'I think everyone was most agreeably impressed by the widower's moderate and dignified attitude. You will see his photo there, among this bundle. That is just how he appeared in court. In deep black, of course, but without any sign of ostentation in his mourning. He had allowed his beard to grow lately, and wore it closely cut in a point.

'After his evidence, the sensation of the day occurred. A tall, dark-haired man, with the word "City" written metaphorically all over him, had kissed the book, and was waiting to tell the truth, and nothing but the truth.

'He gave his name as Andrew Campbell, head of the firm of Campbell & Co., brokers, of Throgmorton Street.

'In the afternoon of March eighteenth Mr Campbell, travelling on the Underground railway, had noticed a very pretty woman in the same carriage as himself. She had asked him if she was in the right train for Aldersgate. Mr

Campbell replied in the affirmative, and then buried himself in the Stock Exchange quotations of his evening paper.

'At Gower Street, a gentleman in a tweed suit and bowler hat got into the carriage, and took a seat opposite the lady. She seemed very much astonished at seeing him, but Mr Andrew Campbell did not recollect the exact words she said.

'The two talked to one another a good deal, and certainly the lady appeared animated and cheerful. Witness took no notice of them; he was very much engrossed in some calculations, and finally got out at Farringdon Street. He noticed that the man in the tweed suit also got out close behind him, having shaken hands with the lady, and said in a pleasant way: "Au revoir! Don't be late tonight." Mr Campbell did not hear the lady's reply, and soon lost sight of the man in the crowd.

'Everyone was on tenter-hooks, and eagerly waiting for the palpitating moment when witness would describe and identify the man who last had seen and spoken to the unfortunate woman, within five minutes probably of her strange and unaccountable death.

'Personally I knew what was coming before the Scots stockbroker spoke.

'I could have jotted down the graphic and lifelike description he would give of a probable murderer. It would have fitted equally well the man who sat and had luncheon at this table just now; it would certainly have described five out of every ten young Englishmen you know.

'The individual was of medium height, he wore a moustache which was not very fair nor yet very dark, his hair was between colours. He wore a bowler hat, and a tweed suit – and – and – that was all – Mr Campbell might perhaps know him again, but then again, he might not – he was not paying much attention – the gentleman was sitting on the same side of the carriage as himself – and he had his hat on all the time. He himself was busy with his newspaper – yes – he might know him again – but he really could not say.

'Mr Andrew Campbell's evidence was not worth very much, you will say. No, it was not in itself, and would not have justified any arrest were it not for the additional statements made by Mr James Verner, manager of Messrs Rodney & Co., colour printers.

'Mr Verner is a personal friend of Mr Andrew Campbell, and it appears that at Farringdon Street, where he was waiting for his train, he saw Mr Campbell get out of a first-class railway carriage. Mr Verner spoke to him for a second, and then, just as the train was moving off, he stepped into the same compartment which had just been vacated by the stockbroker and the man in the tweed suit. He vaguely recollects a lady sitting in the opposite corner to his own, with her face turned away from him, apparently asleep, but he paid no special attention to her. He was like nearly all businessmen when they are travelling – engrossed in his paper. Presently a special quotation interested him; he wished to make a note of it, took out a pencil from his waistcoat pocket, and seeing a clean piece of paste-board on the floor, he picked it up, and scribbled on it the memorandum, which he wished to keep. He then slipped the card into his pocket-book.

' "It was only two or three days later," added Mr Verner in the midst of breathless silence, "that I had occasion to refer to these same notes again.

' "In the meanwhile the papers had been full of the mysterious death on the Underground railway, and the names of those connected with it were pretty familiar to me. It was, therefore, with much astonishment that on looking at the paste-board which I had casually picked up in the railway carriage I saw the name on it, Frank Errington."

'There was no doubt that the sensation in court was

almost unprecedented. Never since the days of the Fenchurch Street mystery, and the trial of Smethurst, had I seen so much excitement. Mind you, I was not excited – I knew by now every detail of that crime as if I had committed it myself. In fact, I could not have done it better, although I have been a student of crime for many years now. Many people there – his friends, mostly – believed that Errington was doomed. I think he thought so, too, for I could see that his face was terribly white, and he now and then passed his tongue over his lips, as if they were parched.

'You see he was in the awful dilemma – a perfectly natural one, by the way – of being absolutely incapable of *proving* an alibi. The crime – if crime there was – had been committed three weeks ago. A man about town like Mr Frank Errington might remember that he spent certain hours of a special afternoon at his club, or in the Park, but it is very doubtful in nine cases out of ten if he can find a friend who could positively swear as to having seem him there. No! no! Mr Errington was in a tight corner, and he knew it. You see, there were – besides the evidence – two or three circumstances which did not improve matters for him. His hobby in the direction of toxicology, to begin with. The police had found in his room every description of poisonous susbtances, including prussic acid.

'Then, again, that journey to Marseilles, the start for Colombo, was, though perfectly innocent, a very unfortunate one. Mr Errington had gone on an aimless voyage, but the public thought that he had fled, terrified at his own crime. Sir Arthur Inglewood, however, here again displayed his marvellous skill on behalf of his client by the masterly way in which he literally turned all the witnesses for the Crown inside out.

'Having first got Mr Andrew Campbell to state positively that in the accused he certainly did *not* recognise the man in the tweed suit, the eminent lawyer, after twenty minutes' cross-examination, had so completely upset the stockbroker's equanimity that it is very likely he would not have recognised his own office-boy.

'But through all his flurry and all his annoyance Mr Andrew Campbell remained very sure of one thing; namely, that the lady was alive and cheerful, and talking pleasantly with the man in the tweed suit up to the moment when the latter, having shaken hands with her, left her with a pleasant "Au revoir! Don't be late tonight." He had heard neither scream nor struggle, and in his opinion, if the individual in the tweed suit had administered a dose of poison to his companion, it must have been with her own knowledge and free will; and the lady in the train most emphatically neither looked nor spoke like a woman prepared for a sudden and violent death.

'Mr James Verner, against that, swore equally positively that he had stood in full view of the carriage door from the moment that Mr Campbell got out until he himself stepped into the compartment, that there was no one else in that carriage between Farringdon Street and Aldgate, and that the lady, to the best of his belief, had made no movement during the whole of that journey.

'No; Frank Errington was *not* committed for trial on the capital charge,' said the man in the corner with one of his sardonic smiles, 'thanks to the cleverness of Sir Arthur Inglewood, his lawyer. He absolutely denied his identity with the man in the tweed suit, and swore he had not seen Mrs Hazeldene since eleven o'clock in the morning of that fatal day. There was no *proof* that he had; moreover, according to Mr Campbell's opinion, the man in the tweed suit was in all probability not the murderer. Common sense would not admit that a woman could have a deadly poison injected into her without her knowledge, while chatting pleasantly to her murderer.

'Mr Errington lives abroad now. He is about to marry. I don't think any of his real friends for a moment believed that he committed the dastardly crime. The police think they know better. They do know this much, that it could not have been a case of suicide, that if the man who undoubtedly travelled with Mrs Hazeldene on that fatal afternoon had no crime upon his conscience he would long ago have come forward and thrown what light he could upon the mystery.

'As to who that man was, the police in their blindness have not the faintest doubt. Under the unshakeable belief that Errington is guilty they have spent the last few months in unceasing labour to try and find further and stronger proofs of his guilt. But they won't find them, because there are none. There are no positive proofs against the actual murderer, for he was one of those clever blackguards who think of everything, foresee every eventuality, who know human nature well, and can foretell exactly what evidence will be brought against them, and act accordingly.

'This blackguard from the first kept the figure, the personality, of Frank Errington before his mind. Frank Errington was the dust which the scoundrel threw metaphorically in the eyes of the police, and you must admit that he succeeded in blinding them – to the extent even of making them entirely forget the one simple little sentence, overheard by Mr Andrew Campbell, and which was, of course, the clue to the whole thing – the only slip the cunning rogue made – "Au revoir! Don't be late tonight." Mrs Hazeldene was going that night to the opera with her husband—

'You are astonished?' he added with a shrug of the shoulders, 'you do not see the tragedy yet, as I have seen it before me all along. The frivolous young wife, the flirtation with the friend? – all a blind, all pretence. I took the trouble which the police should have taken immediately, of finding out something about the finances of the Hazeldene *ménage*. Money is in nine cases out of ten the keynote to a crime.

'I found that the will of Mary Beatrice Hazeldene had been proved by the husband, her sole executor, the estate being sworn at fifteen thousand pounds. I found out, moreover, that Mr Edward Sholto Hazeldene was a poor shipper's clerk when he married the daughter of a wealthy builder in Kensington – and then I made note of the fact that the disconsolate widower had allowed his beard to grow since the death of his wife.

'There's no doubt that he was a clever rogue,' added the strange creature, leaning excitedly over the table, and peering into Polly's face. 'Do you know how that deadly poison was injected into the poor woman's system? By the simplest of all means, one known to every scoundrel in southern Europe. A ring – yes! a ring, which has a tiny hollow needle capable of holding a sufficient quantity of prussic acid to have killed two persons instead of one. The man in the tweed suit shook hands with his fair companion – probably she hardly felt the prick, not sufficiently in any case to make her utter a scream. And, mind you, the scoundrel had every facility, through his friendship with Mr Errington, of procuring what poison he required, not to mention his friend's visiting card. We cannot gauge how many months ago he began to try and copy Frank Errington in his style of dress, the cut of his moustache, his general appearance, making the change probably so gradual, that no one in his own entourage would notice it. He selected for his model a man his own height and build, with the same coloured hair.'

'But there was the terrible risk of being identified by his fellow-traveller in the Underground,' suggested Polly.

'Yes, there certainly was that risk; he chose to take it, and he was wise. He reckoned that several days would in any case elapse before that person, who, by the way, was a businessman absorbed in his newspaper, would actually see him again. The great secret of successful crime is to study human nature,' added the man in the corner, as he began looking for his hat and coat. 'Edward Hazeldene knew it well.'

'But the ring?'

'He may have bought that when he was on his honeymoon,' he suggested with a grim chuckle; 'the tragedy was not planned in a week, it may have taken years to mature. But you will own that there goes a frightful scoundrel unhung. I have left you his photograph as he was a year ago, and as he is now. You will see he has shaved his beard again, but also his moustache. I fancy he is a friend now of Mr Andrew Campbell.'

He left Miss Polly Burton wondering, not knowing what to believe.

And that is why she missed her appointment with Mr Richard Frobisher (of the *London Mail*) to go and see Maud Allan dance at the Palace Theatre that afternoon.

Thubway Tham's
Bomb Scare

JOHNSTON MCCULLEY

It did not take American crime and mystery writers long to realise what a host of opportunities existed for villainy in the dark recesses of the subway where the gloom was only penetrated by the neon-lit carriages as they rattled and swayed between stations. Contributors to both the 'slick' and 'pulp' magazines of the first half of the century wrote dozens of stories about robbery and death on the RTS, but the first regular character to feature in crime stories set in the Subway was a man with the unlikely name of Thubway Tham: a lisping, nimble-fingered pickpocket who was forever exercising his nefarious art amongst unsuspecting rush-hour travellers.

The first of Tham's escapades appeared in 1919 in the *Detective Story Magazine* and thus was launched a hugely popular series that lasted for twenty years during which the little law-breaker always managed to keep just one step ahead of his arch enemy, Detective Craddock. Several years into Tham's career, Johnston McCulley explained how he had created such a curious figure: 'I was walking through New York one morning after having taken a shot of whiskey to ward off a cold, when I saw the usual bunch of nine-o'-clockers being spewed out of the subway. I suddenly thought to myself what a spot for a handy pickpocket to work! The plot began forming in my mind as I walked on and, needing a name for the character, I thought of Subway Sam. I said it aloud to hear how it sounded, but the drink made me lisp slightly, so it came out

"Thubway Tham".'

Fired up by the idea, McCulley rushed home and pounded out the story. However, as soon as he had finished and mailed off the manuscript to *Detective Story Magazine* he had reservations about the reception that the publication – which specialised in all-action heroes – might give to a character with a physical defect. He need not have worried: 'Thubway Tham' struck an immediate chord with the magazine's editor Frank Blackwell, who wrote back to McCulley, 'We've read your yarn about the little subway dip and all of us are laughing yet.' The readers of *Detective Story Magazine* also joined in the chorus of laughter when Thubway Tham made his debut in print two months later.

Despite the fame of the ubiquitous pickpocket during the first half of this century, Johnston McCulley (1886–1959), a former Midwest newspaper reporter who moved to New York to write for the booming market in cheap fiction, is little remembered today. And when he is, it is usually as the author of *Curse of Capistrano*, about an early nineteenth-century masked hero, Zorro, which was filmed as *The Mark of Zorro* in 1920 with Douglas Fairbanks and remade twenty years later with Tyrone Power. Yet from 1919 until the late forties, McCulley wrote a total of 182 short stories and novelettes about Thubway Tham, making him at the time as familiar to many New Yorkers as the stations through which they passed on their way to work. Of all these stories, 'Thubway Tham's Bomb Scare', which was written just a few years before Johnston McCulley's death, is typical of the canon as a whole, as well as having an immediacy about its theme which will not be lost on contemporary readers. Furthermore, it serves as a reminder of arguably the most famous literary character ever to have emerged from the subway.

***

When Thubway Tham finally decided to make his life work a career as a pickpocket he found an expert tutor in Jack Burle. Jack's advice was a thing born of experience, and he coached Tham thoroughly, and not for money or a percentage of the take. He had known Tham from young boyhood, felt sorry for him, believed Tham had talent along certain lines – and as a genuine artist in any cultural pursuit, creative or interpretative, generally will do, Jack Burle decided to develop the dormant talent, and made the future Thubway Tham his protégé.

Into Tham's ears, Jack Burle poured a torrent of words whenever they met – systems, warnings, injunctions. He was a success in the business himself, so Tham listened intently to every word, stored knowledge in his brain cells, prepared for his life work. It was something like going to college and working up to graduation with a bachelor degree, and then working for a master's degree, and finally going after a doctorate. This, naturally, would take some time. Tham had to become educated.

Jack Burle explained how a cop could easily take a man in if he had no visible means of support, and so make him a vag. Burle himself was prepared for that; he was a husky product of a semi-slum district, as was Tham, and early had hung around gyms. He began fighting amateur bouts for small sums, offered his services as a human punching-bag when fighters with records were training. Policemen saw him frequently with a battered face, black eyes and patches over cuts on his face, and considered him nothing but a third-degree pug.

Tham had his alibi all ready. In the lodging house on a side street, he got room rent and a small amount of money for doing janitor work each evening from eight to eleven. The rest of the time was for him to do as he pleased.

Bit by bit, Jack Burle taught him things to avoid, dangerous situations, and began instructing Tham in the best manners in which to extract wallets without being detected.

'Never get tangled with a gun gang,' Burle warned. 'A gangster is nothin' but a coward with a gun in his hand. He's the lowest of the low. Can't work except with a gang around him. A good dip is high class. He's what you call a specialist.'

'Yeah, thpecialitht,' Tham agreed.

'A good dip can travel faster and safer when he travels alone. Remember that, Tham.'

'Yeth, thir.'

'A gangster is always tangled up with girls, gun molls. And they get into trouble that way. The girls get jealous or the boys start stealing one another's girls, or some guy tries to take over the gang, when they're fightin' among themselves, and they wind up in the jail house or the morgue. Stay away from girls, Tham. Never trust a skirt.'

'I underthtand,' Tham said. 'Never trutht a thkirt.'

'And never forget that, boy! Now we're ready to go out and watch you begin your work. I'll go with you at first. You catch, and I'll carry.'

'Thir?'

'We'll nail a victim. You'll go after his wallet and I'll stand right behind you, but we'll act like we never saw each other before. When you get the wallet, slip it back to me. If you're grabbed, you won't have the leather on you, and you'll howl to the sky that you're being mistreated. I'll get the folding money out of the wallet and drop the leather on the floor under the crowd's feet.'

'Yeth, thir. That ith clever.'

'You always lift a leather when a subway car door opens and people crowd to get in and out. I'm a tall, husky man, so I bully my way out, thrusting people aside, elbowing them like a roughneck, and get a leather as I plough my way through and get to the platform.'

'Yeth, thir.'

'But you, Tham, are a little man, and you'll have to use a different manner. You can duck and lurch and squeeze up against a man and touch him, and squirm through the crowd almost without being noticed except as a nuisance and a guy who isn't polite.'

'Who,' Tham asked, 'ith ever polite in the thubway?'

'I get your point,' Burle admitted. 'Now, you must wear dark clothes and a cap, and baggy suit that looks like you'd slept in it for a month, the kind of a guy who won't stick out in a crowd and be noticed. The less a dip is noticed, the better.'

'Yeth, thir. I'll remember everything you have thaid.'

So, Tham started his career, and rapidly grew expert in his work. And finally he attracted the attention of a certain Detective Craddock, who watched Tham as much as he could, and who told Tham he knew the latter was a dip, and that he'd catch him some day and send him up to the Big House. Tham obeyed Jack Burle's instructions to the letter, and prospered.

He always remembered one of Burle's warnings as he developed skill in his work: 'Never trutht a thkirt!'

And then Tham became involved with a woman.

She was a little lady who worked as head waitress in a small restaurant where Tham generally ate his breakfast a little before the noon hour, because his janitor work kept him up until late at night. She began her show of interest by smiling sweetly at Tham, and commencing to put a little more food on the table than he had ordered without increasing the amount on his tab. Perhaps she had read or heard of the old legend that the closest way to a man's heart was through his stomach.

It was Tham's habit to sit at a table in the rear of the restaurant, the restaurant generally being crowded at the time of his arrival. Directly behind his table was the exit from the kitchen, and near it a large table where the waitresses assorted their various orders before taking them forward to the main tables. The head waitress always smiled at him as she stopped there.

In front of Tham's table was a screen about five feet high. You couldn't see through it, but you could hear what was being said by anyone at the table on the opposite side. Often the little head waitress whispered before going on forward, as she left something a little extra for Tham's meal. Her interest in Tham grew swiftly, and he felt himself drawn to her by what a bard might call invisible gossamer threads holding with the strength of steel, or something like that.

This reciprocal attachment, however, had not been brought about by the nude little rascal who is supposed to use a bow and arrow to shoot at hearts and make them palpitate until they get into a state where Hymen takes over the task and causes invisible gossamer threads to appear and show they really are steel.

The head waitress was a darling of a little lady with silvery hair. Tham had the appearance of a half-fed waif in a cast-off suit. Their attachment was that of a motherly woman making life a bit easier for an orphan with not a friend in the world. Jack Burle's injunction, 'Never trutht a thkirt,' did not apply in this case.

As far as Tham was concerned, the elderly waitress had a motherly fixation. She was known to everyone simply as Tillie. Her ancestors had come from Russia after the downfall of the Tsar's regime, and down through the years the family fortune had dwindled, also the family itself, until the last of them had reached America, there to continue dying off until Tillie was left alone. She told Tham all about herself. At intervals she encountered a Russian family and delighted in using the language again.

Before long, queried as to his source of eating money, he first told her he was a lowly janitor, then one day confessed that he was a pickpocket at times. He expected his confession to ruin his association with Tillie, that she would turn with abhorrence.

Her reaction to his confession was rather startling. 'Oh, that's wonderful!' Tillie declared. 'You are the one of those brave and dashing heroes who have passed through history. "Rob the rich and give to the poor! Balance the scales in the name of justice! Feed the hungry from the larders of those who have too much stored away!" Those have been their fighting songs.'

Tham felt a little abashed. It wasn't exactly like that, but he did not want to disillusion her when she seemed to be so happy about it.

Tham learned that Tillie had a little two-room apartment in a side street not far away, where another of the waitresses lived with her and shared the cost of upkeep. Tillie had good blood in her, and the ruination of her family had not soured her against the world. She loved her adopted country – she had become a citizen long before. She had educated herself in English while working for some years as a lady's maid in a Long Island mansion, had devoured books; and as she grew older she became unsuitable for maid's work, because she was not snappy enough to please the guests, not so fast in her actions as before, she did not consider it menial labour to work as the head waitress in a small restaurant, since she was the *head* waitress.

She and Tham continued their association, and a couple of times he strolled home with her on her day off. They talked of many things, and seemed to agree on most of the topics discussed. And they soon learned that both of them hated Communism and all it meant to the free world.

'Anybody who thtepth on the toeth of Uncle Tham ith in for thome thad trouble from me,' Tham declared to her with an amount of vehemence.

For that, Tillie squealed joyously a little and clasped Tham around the neck and gave him a motherly kiss. And only a few days later their joint hatred of what Tham called 'thoth thneaky red ratth' resulted in what a financial wizard could have called gigantic dividends.

Tham was busy with his breakfast when he heard two men at the table on the opposite side of the screen. One of the waitresses took their orders delivered in somewhat guttural tones. After they had been served, and the waitress was giving her attention to other customers, the two men began speaking in a language strange to Tham.

When Tillie emerged from the kitchen again and began arranging her trays, Tham had a mouth filled with food and was chewing it with the enthusiasm of a hungry man. He realised that Tillie was suddenly quiet, and glanced at her. She was listening to the men in front of the screen as they talked. She put a finger to her lips in an ancient gesture meaning Tham was not to speak. She bent closer to the screen, for the men were talking in lower tones.

Tham looked up at her. An expression of horror was in her face. She bent and whispered to Tham: 'Be very quiet. Come with me into the kitchen.'

Tham obeyed. The expression in her face startled him. Inside the kitchen, she clasped his hand and pulled him to a corner where there was a telephone booth for the use of the employees of the restaurant. Then she whispered to Tham again:

'Those men were Russians – Reds. They were talking about having placed two bombs in the big building across Madison Square, where the clock strikes. The bombs are set to explode, one on the second floor and another on the fifth floor, at exactly half past one. That's when all the secretaries and office girls will be going back into the building after eating lunch in the park or some place near. They'll be blown to pieces!'

'What you goin' to do?' Tham asked.

'We must act fast, Tham. I heard them talking about going out and watching from the Fifth Avenue side of the

Square. They'll get a laugh out of it, the devils. And they were talking about going back to Washington to report, and about having plenty of Washington money in their pockets and more coming when they got back to their big Red boss there.'

'You got any ideath?' Tham asked, gulping as he began visualising what might happen.

'I know Mike Malone, the desk sergeant at the police precinct station down the street. He and his wife live right near me, and they've had me to dinner several times on my day off. He'll know I'm not fooling, knows I know Russian and how I hate the Reds. He will know what to do.'

She went into the phone booth and closed the door, and Tham watched her dialling a number. The terror grew on him, and he tried to fight it back. This was a time to be calm and act naturally, he knew. It was not a time for panic.

Tillie emerged from the phone booth. 'Mike Malone will attend to everything,' she told Tham. 'He knows I'm not fooling. Tham, you watch them after they go out. See where they go and what they do, and keep close to them so you can point them out. In a few minutes, I'll pretend I don't feel well and want to go home. One of the other girls can take my place. Then I'll get to you, and we both can watch them until we can turn them over. When I come out, I'll look for you on the Fifth Avenue side of the Square.'

Tham picked up his tab and wandered slowly towards the cashier's cage, fighting to keep from showing excitement. He paid his bill and exchanged salutations with the fat cashier, who knew him well from several years of loyalty to the restaurant. He went out upon the street, ignited a cigarette, crossed over the street and stood on a corner.

It was a soft, beautiful day. Many from the office buildings around the Square had chosen to eat luncheons in the park, food gathered mostly from nearby sandwich carts. There seemed to Tham to be at least a couple of thousand out there in the open. By half past one, they would be getting back into the office buildings, and if the bombs caught them there it would be wholesale slaughter, also possibly wrecked buildings and fires.

He glanced back across the street. The two men had not left the restaurant to come his way, and he did not see Tillie leave the restaurant and come towards him. Tham told himself to act in ordinary fashion, that he was not supposed to know anything unusual was transpiring. His job was only to get close to the two men so he could point them out later to Tillie. She was the one to put the finger on them. If Tham gave the alarm, anyone who knew him, especially Detective Craddock if he happened to be loitering in the Square hoping to have his usual repartee with him, would not believe anything Tham might say.

With horror, Tham noticed that many of those in the Square were strolling back towards the buildings where they worked. And just then, as he turned, he saw the two men come out of the restaurant and saunter towards him. Tillie was not in sight.

He glanced in the other direction, and saw Detective Craddock approaching slowly, puffing at a gigantic cigar, his battered old derby hat cocked over one ear in a nonchalant manner. 'He ith thinkin' of thomething thmart to thay to me,' Tham muttered to himself.

And then it happened!

From all directions they came, dashing along the streets. Police cars, fire department apparatus, ambulances, cars holding the police bomb squad – they all converged around Madison Square. Extra police reserves came, scattering around to control the gathering crowd. Men rushed to the buildings and ordered an immediate evacuation.

Something Tillie had said had informed Tham of a certain touchy situation. What she had heard the two men say in the Russian language could have been serious. This could be a genuine bomb affair, or it could be a hoax. So, officially, no hand could be put upon the two unless it developed it was a real attempt at bombing. They could only be watched until the outcome; and then, with Tillie's testimony, they possibly would be given a short sentence for causing the scare.

At that instant, Tham and Detective Craddock came into contact. Craddock did not know the cause of the sudden confusion, and Tham decided not to inform him.

'Well, well!' Tham exclaimed. 'If it ithn't my old college chum. What ith all thith noithe about? Don't tell me – I know.'

'Oh, you do? Let me in on the secret,' Craddock said.

'Thertainly. It ith a great honour for me. All theth carth and thingth – copth and firemen and all – jutht to watch me and thee that I do not go down into the thubway and maybe attend to thome buthineth.'

'Don't flatter yourself,' Craddock growled. 'There's something big going on, and I'm cussed well going to learn what it is.' He whirled and headed for the police officer not far away, getting out his badge to identify himself and ask what was happening.

Tham glanced back again. The two men had come out of the restaurant and were sauntering towards him on the Fifth Avenue side of the Square. Tillie had not yet appeared, and Tham wondered what had happened to her. The two men stopped at the kerb within a few feet of Tham. A charge of policemen was coming towards them. 'Keep back by the kerb!' they were calling. 'Don't move forward into the park!'

Tham turned and glanced across the Square. The crowd was screaming, acting like cattle in a stampede, fighting to get as far away from the buildings as possible. The panic was on. Tham saw policemen threatening with their clubs, trying to herd the frantic men and women. Some of them had broken out of the mob and were racing down the side streets. Over near the scene of danger, Tham saw an important man he knew by sight – Inspector Allison, an official who generally appeared at scenes such as this, a man who gave command, who knew how to break up a riot or quell a panic to a certain extent.

Tham turned again, and found himself behind the two men who had caused all this. They were speaking in a guttural English. They looked ordinary, dressed a little like working men, their coats a little baggy. As Tham watched them, not seeming to do so, he saw one handling a roll of currency, and almost gulped when he saw the man thrust it into the left-hand hip pocket of his trousers.

'The thilly ath,' Tham muttered to himself. 'Theth Redth are not very thmart. A hick from the thtickth would know better than that. Good Uncle Tham money in their filthy handth. Um.'

He glanced around again, and saw Tillie approaching with a man beside her. Tham backed away a few feet to meet her, standing so the two men who were watching something across the Square, would not see Tillie's approach and possibly get suspicious.

A glance told Tham that the space in front of the building where the bombs were supposed to be had been cleared of everyone. The hour the men had mentioned was at hand. In a moment, it would be known whether this was the real thing or a foolish hoax.

Suddenly Tham saw a man appear in a window on the second floor of the building and toss something down into the street. There was a terrific explosion, and the frantic crowd still in the Square began fighting to get back.

It was no hoax.

The crowd surged back towards the Fifth Avenue kerb. Tham looked towards Tillie again. Three men were with her now, and they were rushing forward. From a window on the fifth floor of the building, another bomb was tossed out to explode with terrific force to make a hole in the pavement.

Tham guessed the bombs had been located by the squad, and that the time was so short there was nothing to do except toss them out. Now firemen and ambulance men, as well as police, rushed into the building. More of the mob were fighting their way into the side streets.

Tillie and the men with her were coming on faster now. Tham turned towards the two men again. A surge of the crowd engulfed them for a moment, and he found himself jammed against them. Then the crowd broke again, and Tham was tossed aside.

He could see Tillie pointing. The three men beckoned plainclothes men who had been standing around, and the Reds found themselves grasped roughly, slammed together, found handcuffs on them behind their backs.

'Those are the men,' Tham heard Tillie say, by way of legal identification.

Tham slipped away; this was Tillie's own game. He felt proud for her as he began realising all she had done. But for her, people could have been slaughtered, buildings set aflame. He watched as a police car drew up to the kerb. The Reds were protesting in loud guttural voices and demanding to know the meaning of the assault on them. Though manacled, they tried to fight when they were thrust towards the police car. The three officers gave them a rather rough treatment and got them into the car without further trouble.

As Tham watched, he saw Tillie escorted to another police car, which followed the first. He knew her presence would be needed at Police Headquarters, where her statement would be recorded. And he realised she might be in danger afterward, when the men had been sent to prison for a long term. This was only one incident as far as the Reds were concerned. But Tham knew they had ways of dealing with any person who had obstructed their nefarious work.

Gradually, order was restored. Those who had worked

in the building were told to go home for the remainder of the day and quiet their nerves. Places were roped off, and policemen stationed to restrain the mob of curious sightseers which undoubtedly would appear after the news got out. And trained plainclothes men undoubtedly would scatter through the crowd, eyes and ears open, listening for any hint of sympathy, any word that would identify them as persons to be watched.

Tham drifted away without meeting Craddock again. He strolled back to his lodging house, for he had some work to do there. He had been on the scene, but all he told anyone at the lodging house was that he had seen the mob and heard the crashing of the bombs.

He began thinking again of Tillie. 'What a thkirt!' he muttered.

In time, he got a telephone call, something he seldom received. It was from Tillie, asking him to come over to her place. It was only a short distance away, and Tham got there in record time. Tillie was alone, and she had prepared a luncheon for them after her ordeal at Police Headquarters.

'An officer told them at the restaurant to let me have the remainder of the day off,' she explained. 'I'm so glad I was able to help. I should be ashamed to say it, I suppose, but I'm a tiny bit proud of myself.' She giggled a little; she was still a little tense from what had happened.

'I thure am proud of you, too,' Tham told her. 'It wath a good day.' He reached in a pocket, and brought forth a wad of United States currency.

Tillie's eyes bulged. 'What's that, Tham?'

'It ith like thith – I thaw one of thoth men thtick all thith money in hith hip pocket. Tho I got it. It ith good Uncle Tham money, and thoth thneakin' apeth have no buthnith havin' it. Ain't I a nephew of my Uncle Tham? Thure I am! Tho I jutht took money. And I am goin' to give you an even thplit on it. You can buy yourthelf fanthy clotheth or thomethin'.'

Tillie giggled, and kissed him again on the cheek.

'Tomorrow for breakfast,' she told him, 'I'll have the chef build you the finest omelette you ever saw or tasted. As you said, Tham, it's been a good day.'

The Coulman Handicap

MICHAEL GILBERT

Passengers on the London Underground system do many
things as they travel from station to station: read, knit,
snooze or perhaps study the advertisements to avoid one
another's eyes. Michael Gilbert, the next contributor, for
many years used his time on the subway to write novels and
short stories in neat long-hand on pads of yellow legal
notepaper. For almost thirty years, in fact, he combined the
profession of a city lawyer with that of crime story author,
devising his plots or alternately working on his dialogue
while travelling from his home in Kent to his office in
Lincoln's Inn near Chancery Lane station on the Central
Line. Now widely acknowledged as one of England's finest
detective story writers of the past half century, Gilbert was
the recipient of the highest honour of the Crime Writers'
Association, the Cartier Diamond Dagger, in April 1994.

Michael Francis Gilbert (1912–) was born in rural
Lincolnshire, and was urged to take up the law by his uncle
who was the Lord Chief Justice of India. The inspiration to
write crime fiction came years later when he was a partner
in a London law firm and became the legal adviser to
Raymond Chandler. Gilbert combined his knowledge of
the law with his fertile imagination and quickly proved
himself to be a master of the short story. His first detective
novel, *Close Quarters* (1947), however, was not an
immediate success; but his reputation soared six years later
with *Fear to Tread* (1953), which revealed that his interest
in railways went deeper than just the timetables of the
service he used from Kent to London. This fast-paced

thriller concerned the activities of a group of gangsters committing daring robberies on British Railways and was named as one of the best novels of the year by *The Times Literary Supplement*.

After this success, rail travel featured in a number of Michael Gilbert's later stories, in particular the cases of his astute London policeman, Detective Sergeant Patrick Petrella. Two outstanding examples of this, both set on the Underground, are 'Mr Duckworth's Night Out', which has appeared in several crime anthologies and at least one collection of railway stories, and 'The Coulman Handicap' which has only previously been published in *Argosy* magazine of April 1958. It is the story of a particularly ingenious criminal who is making use of the London Underground to distribute stolen goods – and of the surprise that awaits Petrella and the other members of the force when they finally lay hands on the culprit.

***

The door of No. 35 Bond Road opened and a thick-set, middle-aged woman came out. She wore a long grey coat with a collar of alpaca wool buttoned to the neck, a light grey hat well forward on her head, and mid-grey gloves on her hands. Her sensible shoes, her stockings, and the large, fabric-covered suitcase, which she carried in her right hand, were brown.

She paused for a moment on the step. Women of her age are often near-sighted, but there was nothing in her attitude to suggest this. She had bold, brown, somewhat protuberant eyes, set far apart in her strong face. They were not unlike the eyes of an intelligent horse.

She looked carefully to left and to right. Bond Road was never a bustling thoroughfare. At twelve o'clock on that bright morning of early April it was almost empty. A roadman, sweeping the gutter; a grocer's delivery boy, pushing his bicycle blindly, nose down in a comic; the postman, on his mid-morning round. All of them were well known to her. She waited to see if the postman had brought her anything, and then set off up the pavement.

In the front parlour of No. 34, a lace curtain parted one inch and closed again. The man sitting on a chair in the bow window reached for the telephone which stood by his hand and dialled.

He heard a click as the receiver was lifted at the other end and said, 'She's off. Going west.' Then he replaced the receiver and lit himself a cigarette. The stubs in the tray beside the telephone suggested that he had been waiting for some time.

At that moment no fewer than twenty-four people, in one way or another, were concentrating their attention on Bond Road and on Mrs Coulman, who lived at No. 35.

'It's a carrier service,' said Superintendent Palance of S Division, who was in charge of the joint operation, 'and it's got to be stopped.' Jimmy Palance was known throughout the Metropolitan Police Force as a fine organiser, a teetotaller, a man entirely lacking in any sense of humour, who worked with a Pawnbrokers' List and the Holy Bible side by side on his tidy desk.

'The first problem of a thief who steals valuable and identifiable jewellery is to get rid of it. What does he do with it?'

'Flogs it?' suggested Superintendent Haxtell of Q Division.

'No fence'll touch it,' said Superintendent Farmer of X Division. 'Not while the heat's on.'

'Then he hides it,' said Haxtell. 'In a safe deposit, or a bank. Crooks do have bank accounts, you know.'

'Or a cloakroom, or a left-luggage office.'

'Or with a friend, or at an accommodation address.'

'Or sealed up in a tin, under the third tree from the corner.'

'No doubt,' said Superintendent Palance, raising his heavy black eyebrows, 'there are a great number of possible hiding-places. I myself have listed twenty-seven distinct types. There may be more. The difficulty is that by the time the thief wishes to recover his loot, he is as often as not himself under observation.'

Neither Haxtell nor Farmer questioned this statement. They knew well enough that it was true. A complicated system of informers almost always gave them the name of the perpetrator of any big and successful burglary. 'All we then have to arrange is to watch the thief. If he goes near the stuff we will be able to lay hands on the man himself and his cache, and his receiver.'

'True,' said Haxtell. 'So what does he do?'

'He gets in touch with Mrs Coulman. And informs her where he has placed the stuff. Gives her the key, or cloakroom ticket, and leaves the rest to her. It is not even necessary to give her the name of the receiver. She knows them all, and gets the best prices. She gets paid in cash, keeps a third, and hands over two-thirds to the author of the crime.'

'Just like a literary agent,' said Farmer, who had once written a short story.

'Sounds quite a woman,' said Haxtell.

'She has curious antecedents,' said Palance. 'She is German. And I believe, although I've not been able to check it, that she and her brothers were in the German Resistance.'

'The fact that she's alive proves she was clever,' agreed Haxtell. 'Now, I gather you want quite a few men for this. Tell us how you plan to tackle it.'

'It's going to be a complicated job,' said Palance. 'But here is the outline . . .'

At the end of the street, after turning into the main road, Mrs Coulman had a choice of transport. She could take a bus going south, or could cross the street and take a bus going north. Or she could walk two hundred yards down the hill to the Underground station, or an equal distance up it to another. Or she could take a taxi. She was a thick woman of ample Teutonic build, and experience, gained in the last month of observation, had suggested that she would not walk very far.

Near each bus stop a man and girl were talking. Opposite the Underground a pair of workmen sat, drinking endless cups of tea. In a side street two taxis waited, a driving glove over the meter indicating that they were not for hire. A small tradesman's van, parked in a cul-de-sac, acted as mobile headquarters to this part of the operation. It was backed half-way into a private garage, chosen because it was on the telephone.

Mrs Coulman proceeded placidly to the far end of Bond Road, waited for a gap in the traffic, crossed the main road, and turned up a side road beyond it.

An outburst of intense activity followed.

'Still going west,' said the controller in the van. 'Making for Highside Park. Details one to eight, switch in that direction. Number one car straight up London Road and stop. Number two car parallel. Details nine and ten, cover Highside tube station and the bus stops at the top of the hill.'

Mrs Coulman emerged, panting slightly, from the side road which gave on to the top of Highside Hill, paused, and caused consternation in the ranks of her pursuers by turning round and walking back the way she had come.

Control had just worked out the necessary orders to jerk the machine into reverse when it was seen that Mrs Coulman had retraced her steps to admire a flowering shrub in a front garden she had passed. Looking carefully about her to see that no one was watching, she nipped off a small spray and put it in her buttonhole. Then she turned back towards Highside Hill and made, without further check, for the tube station.

Details number nine and ten were Detective Sergeants Petrella and Wynne. They were waiting inside the station, at the head of the emergency stairs, and were already equipped with all-day tickets. When Mrs Coulman reached the station entrance, therefore, she found it deserted. She bought a ticket for Euston and took the lift. A young man in corduroys and a raincoat, and an older one in flannel trousers, a windcheater, and a club scarf were already on the platform, waiting for the train. They got into the coaches on either side of her.

Above their heads the machine jerked abruptly into top gear. A word was exchanged with the booking-office clerk and two taxis sped towards Euston.

Mrs Coulman, however, had disconcertingly changed her mind. Euston, Goodge Street, Tottenham Court Road – station after station came and went and still she sat on. Her seat had been chosen to command the exits of her own and the two neighbouring carriages. She seemed to take a close interest in the people who got on and off. But if she noticed that the men who had come from Highside were still with her, she gave no sign.

It was nearly half an hour later when she quitted the train at Clapham Common station and made for the moving staircase, looking neither to right nor to left.

Petrella had time for a quick word with Wynne. 'It's my belief the old bitch has rumbled us,' he said. 'Get on the blower and bring the rest of the gang down here, as quickly as possible. Meanwhile, I'll do my best to keep on her trail.'

This proved easy. Mrs Coulman walked down the street without so much as a backward glance, and disappeared into the saloon bar of The Admiral Keppel public house. Petrella made a detour of the place to ensure that it had no back entrance, and settled down to watch. It could hardly have been better situated for his purpose. The doors of its saloon and public bar opened side by side on to the same strip of pavement. Opposite them stood a sandwich bar, with a telephone.

'I don't think we ought to crowd the old girl,' said Petrella into the telephone. 'It's my impression she's got eyes in the back of her head. If you could send someone – not Wynne, she's seen too much of him already this morning – and put a man at either end of the street, so that *we* don't have to follow her immediately she goes—'

The voice at the other end approved these arrangements. Time passed. Petrella saw Detective Constable Mote ambling down the pavement, and he flagged him in.

'She's been there a long time,' he said. 'It must be nearly closing time.'

'Sure she hasn't come out?' said Mote.

Petrella looked at his little book. 'Two businessmen,' he said. 'One youth with a girlfriend, aged about seventeen and skinny. One sailor with a kitbag. That's the score to date.'

The door of the public bar opened and three men came out and stood talking to the landlord, who seemed to know them. The men went off down the road together, the landlord disappeared inside, and they heard the sound of bolts being shut.

'Hey,' said Petrella. 'What's all this?'

'It's all right. There's still someone in the saloon bar,' said Mote. 'I can see the shadow on the glass. Seems to be knocking her drink back.'

'Slip across and have a look,' said Petrella.

Mote crossed the road lower down and strolled up past the ground-glass window of the saloon bar.

'It's a woman,' he reported. 'Sitting in the corner, drinking. I think the landlord's trying to turn her out.'

As he spoke the door was flung open and the last of the customers appeared. She was the same shape as Mrs

Coulman, but she seemed to have changed her hat and coat, and to have done something to her face, which was now a mottled red.

She stood on the pavement for a moment, while the landlord bolted the door behind her. Then she ploughed off, straight and strong up the street, dipping very slightly as she progressed.

A thin woman coming out of a shop with a basket full of groceries was nearly run down. She saved herself by a quick side-step, and said, in reproof, 'Carnchew look where you're goin'?'

The massive woman halted, wheeled, and hit the thin woman in the eye. It was a beautiful, co-ordinated, unconscious movement, as full of grace and power as a backhand passing-shot by a tennis champion at the top of her form.

The thin woman went down, but was up again in a flash. She was no quitter. She kicked her opponent hard on the ankle. A uniformed policeman appeared, closely followed by Sergeant Gwilliam, who had been waiting round the corner and felt that it was time to intervene. The massive woman, thus beset, back-heeled at her first assailant, aimed a swinging blow with a carrier-bag full of bottles at the constable, missed him, and hit Sergeant Gwilliam.

Some hours later Superintendent Palance said coldly, to Superintendent Haxtell, 'I take it that Sergeant Petrella is a reliable officer.'

'I have always found him so,' said Haxtell, equally coldly.

'This woman, to whom he seems, at some point, to have transferred his attention, is certainly not Mrs Coulman.'

'Apparently not,' said Haxtell. 'In fact she is a well-known local character called Big Bertha. She is also believed to hold the women's drinking records for both draught and bottled beer south of the Thames.'

'Indeed?' Superintendent Palance considered the information carefully. 'There is no possibility, I suppose, that she and Mrs Coulman are leading a double life?'

'You mean,' said Haxtell, 'that the same woman is sometimes the respectable Mrs Coulman of Bond Road, Highside, and sometimes the alcoholic Bertha of Clapham? It's an attractive idea, but I'm afraid it won't wash. Bertha's prison record alone makes it an impossibility. During the month you've been watching Mrs Coulman, Bertha has, I'm afraid, appeared no less than four times in the Southwark Magistrates Court.'

'In that case,' said Palance reasonably, 'since the lady under observation was Mrs Coulman when she started, Sergeant Petrella must have slipped up at some point.'

'I agree,' said Haxtell. 'But where?'

'That is for him to explain.'

'It's a stark impossibility,' said Petrella, later that day. 'I *know* it was Mrs Coulman when she went into the pub. There's no back entrance. I mean that, literally. It's a sort of penthouse, built on to the front of the block. The landlord himself has to come out of one of the bar doors when he leaves. And our local people say he's perfectly reliable. They've got nothing against him at all.'

'Could she have done a quick-change act? Is there a ladies' lavatory, or some place like that?'

'Yes. There's a lavatory. And she could have gone into it, and changed into other clothes which she had ready in her suitcase. It's all right as a theory. It's when you try to turn it into fact that it gets difficult. I saw nine people coming out of that pub. The first two were business types from the saloon bar. The landlord didn't know them, but they seemed to know each other. And anyway they just dropped in for a whisky and out again. Then there was a boy and girl in the public bar. They held hands most of the time and didn't weigh much more than nine stone nothing apiece.'

'None of them sounds very likely,' agreed Haxtell. 'And

the three workmen were local characters, or so I gather. That leaves the woman and the sailor.'

'Right,' said Petrella. 'And since we know that the woman wasn't Mrs Coulman, it leaves the sailor. He was broadly the right size and shape and weight, and he was the only one carrying anything. Thinking it over, one can see that's significant. He had a kitbag over his shoulder.'

'Just how is a suitcase turned into a kitbag?'

'That part wouldn't be too difficult. The suitcase could easily be a sham. A fabric cover round a collapsible frame, which would fold up to almost nothing and go inside the kitbag with the wig and hat and coat and the rest of the stuff.'

'Where did the kitbag come from? Oh, I see. She would have had it inside the suitcase. One wave of the wand and a large woman with a large suitcase turns into a medium-sized sailor with a kitbag.'

'Right,' said Petrella. 'And there's only one drawback. The sailor was a man, not a woman at all.'

'You're sure?'

'Absolutely and completely sure,' said Petrella. 'He crossed the road and passed within a few feet of me. He was wearing bell-bottom trousers and a dark blue sweater. There are certain anatomical differences, you know. And Mrs Coulman was a very womanly woman.'

'A queenly figure,' agreed Haxtell. 'Yes, I see what you mean.'

'It's not only that,' said Petrella. 'A woman might get away with being dressed as a man on the stage. Or seen from a distance, or from behind. But not in broad daylight, face to face in the street. A man's hair grows in quite a different way, and his ears are bigger, and—'

'All right,' said Haxtell. 'I'll take your word for it.' He paused and added, 'Palance thinks you fell asleep on the job, and Mrs Coulman slipped out when you weren't looking.'

'I know,' said Petrella. An awkward silence ensued. Petrella said, 'Will they keep up the watch?'

'I should think they'd lay off her a bit,' said Haxtell. 'It's an expensive job, immobilising a couple of dozen men. And a dinosaur would be suspicious after yesterday's performance. I should think they'd let her run for a bit. There's no reason you shouldn't keep your eyes open, though – unofficially.'

Petralla devoted what time he could spare in the next six weeks to his self-appointed task. His landlady's married sister had a house in Bond Road, so he spent a lot of time in her front parlour and, after dark, prowling round No. 35, the end house on the other side of the road. He also made friends with the booking-clerks at Highside station and Pond End station; and spent an interesting afternoon in the German Section of the Foreign Office.

'One thing's clear enough,' he said to Haxtell. 'When she's on the job, she starts on the Underground. Taxis and buses are too easy to follow. If you go by Underground, the pursuit has got to come down with you. Or guard the exit of every Underground station in London simultaneously, which is a stark impossibility. Anyway, I know that's what she does. She's been seen half a dozen times leaving Highside station, carrying that trick suitcase. She books to any old station. She's only got to pay the difference at the other end. She's a bit more cautious, too, after that last fiasco. She won't get on to the train if there's any other passenger she can't account for on the platform. Sometimes she's let three or four trains go past.'

Haxtell reflected on all this, and said, 'It seems a pretty watertight system to me. How do you suggest we break in on it?'

'Well, I think we've got to take a chance,' said Petrella. 'In theory it'd be safer with a lot of people, but actually, I don't think it would work at all. That kind can always spot organised opposition. There's just a chance, if you'd let two or three of us try it, next time we get word that she's likely to be busy—'

'We'll see,' said Haxtell.

Three nights after these words were spoken, on a Saturday, the redoubtable twin brothers, Jack and Sidney Ponting, made entry into Messrs Alfrey's West End establishment by forcing the skylight of an adjacent building, picking three separate locks, cutting their way through an eighteen-inch brick wall, and blowing the lock neatly out of the door of the new Alfrey strong room. When the staff arrived on Monday they found a mess of brickwork and twisted steel. The losses included sixty-four large rough diamonds deposited by a Greek ship-owner. They were to have formed the nuptial head-dress of his South American bride.

'It's a Ponting job,' said Superintendent Palance. 'It's got their registered trademark all over it. Get after them quick. They're probably hiding up.'

But the Pontings were not hiding. They were at home, and in bed. They raised no objection to a search of their premises.

'It's irregular,' said Sidney. 'But what have we got to hide?'

'You boys have got your job to do,' said Jack. 'Get it finished, and we can get on with our breakfast.'

Palance came up to see Haxtell.

'They certainly did it. They most certainly did it. Equally certainly they've dumped the diamonds. And none of them has reached a receiver yet, I'm sure of that. And the Pontings use Mrs Coulman.'

'Yes,' said Haxtell. 'Well, we must hope to do better this time.'

'Are you set on trying it on your own?'

Palance held the same rank as Haxtell. But he was longer in service, and older in experience. Haxtell thought of these things, and paused. He was well aware of the responsibility he was shouldering, and which he could so easily evade. Then he said, 'I really think the only way is to try it ourselves, quietly.'

'All right,' said Palance. He didn't add, 'And on your own head be it.' He was never a man to waste words.

Four days followed, during which Petrella attended to his other duties as well as he could by day, and prowled round the curtilage of No. 35 Bond Road by night. Four days in which Sergeant Gwilliam, Wilmot, and Mote were never out of reach of a telephone; and Superintendent Haxtell sweated.

On the fifth night Petrella gave the signal: Tomorrow's the day. And at eleven o'clock next morning, sure enough, the front door opened and Mrs Coulman peered forth. She was wearing her travelling coat and hat, and grasped in her muscular right hand was the fabric-covered suitcase.

She walked ponderously down the road. However acute her suspicions may have been, there was nothing for them to feed on. For it is a fact that at that moment no one was watching her at all.

Ten minutes later she was purchasing a ticket at Highside station. The entrance to the station was deserted. She waited placidly for the lift.

The lift and Sergeant Gwilliam arrived simultaneously. He was dressed as a workman, and he seemed to be in a hurry. He bought a ticket to the Elephant and Castle and got into the lift beside Mrs Coulman. In silence, and avoiding each other's eye, they descended to platform level. In silence they waited for the train.

When the train arrived, Sergeant Gwilliam hesitated. He seemed to have an eye on Mrs Coulman's movements. They approached the train simultaneously. At the very last moment Mrs Coulman stopped. Sergeant Gwilliam went on, the doors closed, and the train disappeared bearing the sergeant with it.

Mrs Coulman returned to her seat on the platform and

waited placidly. By the time the next train arrived, the only other occupants of the platform were three schoolgirls. Mrs Coulman got into the train, followed by the schoolgirls. Two stations later the schoolgirls got off. Mrs Coulman, from her customary seat beside the door, watched them go.

Thereafter, as the train ran south, she observed a succession of people getting on and off. There were three people she did not see. Petrella, with Mote and Wilmot, had entered the train at the station before her. Sergeant Gwilliam's planned diversion had given them plenty of time to get there. Petrella was in the first and the other two were in the last carriages of the train.

It was at Balham that Mrs Coulman finally emerged. Two women with shopping-bags, who had joined her carriage at Leicester Square, went with her. Also a commercial traveller with samples, whom she had watched join the next carriage at the Oval.

Petrella, Mote, and Wilmot all saw her go, but it was no part of their plan to follow her, so they sat tight.

At the next stop, all three of them raced for the moving stairs, hurled themselves into the street, and found a taxi.

'I'm off duty,' said the taxi-driver.

'Now you're on again,' said Petrella, and showed him his warrant card. 'Get us back to Balham station, as quick as you can.'

The taxi-driver blinked, but complied. Petrella had his eye on his watch.

'She's had four minutes' start,' he said, as they bundled out. 'You know what to do. Take every pub in your sector. And get a move on.'

The three men separated. There is no lack of public houses in that part of South London, but Petrella calculated that if they worked outwards from the station, taking a sector each, they could cover most of them quite quickly. It was the riskiest part of the scheme, but he could think of no way to avoid it.

He himself found her.

She was sitting quietly in the corner of the saloon bar of The Gatehouse, a big, newish establishment at the junction of the High Street and Trinity Road.

There was no convenient snack bar this time; there was very little cover at all. The best he could find was a trolley-bus shelter. If he stood behind it, it did at least screen him from the door.

The minutes passed, and added up to a quarter of an hour. Then to half an hour. During that time two people had gone in, and three had come out, but none of them had aroused Petrella's interest. He knew, more or less, what he was looking for.

At last the door opened and a man emerged. He was a thick, well set-up man, dressed in a close-fitting flannel suit which was tight enough across the shoulders and round the chest to exhibit his athletic frame. And he was carrying a small canvas bag, of a type that athletes use to hold their sports gear.

He turned left, and swung off down the pavement with an unmistakable, aggressive masculine stride, a mature bull of the human herd, confident of his strength and purpose.

Petrella let him have the length of the street, and then trotted after him. This was where he had to be very careful. What he mostly needed was help. The chase swung back past the Underground and there he spotted Wilmot and signalled him across.

'In the grey flannel suit, carrying a bag,' he said. 'See him? Then get right after him, and remember, he's got eyes in the back of his head.'

Wilmot grinned all over his guttersnipe face. He was imaginatively dressed in a teddy-boy suit and he fitted into the South London streets as easily as a rabbit into a warren.

'Doanchew worry,' he said, 'I won't lose him.'

Petrella fell back until he was a hundred yards behind Wilmot. He kept his eyes open for Mote. The more of them the merrier. There was a long, hard chase ahead.

He noticed Wilmot signalling.

'Gone in there,' said Wilmot.

'Where?'

'Small shop. Bit of the way up the side street.'

Petrella considered. 'Walk past,' he said. 'Take a note of the name and number on the shop. Go straight on, out of sight, to the other end. If he goes that way, you can pick him up. If he comes back I'll take him.'

Ten minutes went by. Petrella thought anxiously about back exists. But you couldn't guard against everything.

Then the man reappeared. He was carrying the same bag, yet it looked different. Less bulky but, by the swing of it, heavier.

He's dumped the hat and coat and the remains of the suitcase at that accommodation address, thought Petrella. Even if we lose him, we know one of the Ponting hide-outs. But we mustn't lose him. That bag's got several thousand pounds' worth of stolen jewellery in it now.

Would it be best to arrest him, and give up any chance of tracing the receiver? The temptation was almost overmastering. Only one thing stopped him. His quarry was moving with much greater freedom, as if convinced that there was no danger. Near the end of the run he would get cautious again. For the moment there was nothing to do but follow.

The man plunged back in the Underground; emerged at Waterloo; joined the queue at the Suburban Booking-Office. Petrella kept well clear for he owned a ticket which enabled him to travel anywhere on the railway.

Waterloo was a station whose layout he knew well. By positioning himself at the central bookstall, he could watch all three exits. His quarry had bought, and was eating, a meat pie. Petrella was quite unconscious of hunger. His eyes were riveted on the little bag, swinging heavily from the man's large fist. Once he put it down, but it was only to get out more money to buy an orange, which he peeled and ate neatly, depositing the remains in one of the refuse bins. Then he picked up the bag again and made for his train.

It was the electric line for Staines and Windsor. He went through the barrier, and walked slowly up the train. There were very few passengers about, and it must have been near enough empty. He walked along the platform, and climbed into a carriage at the far end.

Some instinct restrained Petrella. There were still five minutes before the train left. He waited. Three minutes later the man emerged from the carriage, walked very slowly back down the train, glancing into each carriage as he passed, and got into the carriage nearest to the barrier. The guard blew his whistle.

Two girls who had been sauntering towards the barrier broke into a run – Petrella ran with them. They pushed through the gate. The guard blew his whistle again; they jerked open the door of the nearest carriage and tumbled in together.

'We nearly left that too late,' said one of the girls. Her friend agreed with her. Petrella thought that they couldn't have timed it better. But he didn't say so. He was prepared to agree with everything they said. It was the quickest way he knew of getting on with people.

The girls were prepared to enjoy his company too. The dark vivacious one was called Beryl and the quieter mousy one was Doreen. They lived at Staines.

'Where are you getting out?' asked Beryl. 'Or is that a secret?'

'I haven't made my mind up yet,' said Petrella.

Beryl said he was a case. Doreen agreed.

The train ambled through dim-forgotten places like Feltham and Ashford. No one got out and no one got in.

Petrella heard about a dance, and what had gone on afterwards in the car park. He said he was sorry he didn't live at Staines. It sounded quite a place.

'It's all right in summer,' said Doreen. 'It's a dump in winter. Here we are.'

The train drew up.

'Sure you won't change your mind?' said Beryl.

'Perhaps I will, at that,' said Petrella. Out of the corner of his eye he saw that his man had got out and was making his way along the platform.

'You'd better hurry up then. They'll take you on to Windsor.'

'That'd never do,' said Petrella. 'I forgot to warn her that I was coming.'

'Who?' said Doreen.

'The Queen.'

His man was safely past the ticket collector now.

'Come on,' said Beryl. They went past the collector together. 'Wouldn't you like some tea? There's a good place in the High Street.'

'There's nothing I'd like better, but I think I see my uncle waving to me.'

The girls stared at him. Petrella manoeuvred himself across the open yard, keeping the girls between him and his quarry. The man had set off up the road without, apparently, so much as a backward glance, but Petrella knew that the most difficult part of the chase was at hand.

'I don't see your uncle,' said Beryl.

'There he is. Sitting in that taxi.'

'That's just the taxi-driver. I don't believe he's your uncle at all.'

'Certainly he is. How are you keeping, uncle?'

'Very fit, thank you,' said the taxi-driver, a middle-aged man with a brown bald head.

'There you are,' said Petrella. 'I'll have to say goodbye now. We've got a lot to talk about. Family business.'

The girls hesitated, and then withdrew, baffled.

'You a policeman?' said the taxi-driver. 'A detective or something?'

'As a matter of fact, I am.'

'Following that man in the light suit? I thought as much. Very pretty, the way you got behind those girls. As good as a book.'

His quarry was now half-way up the long, straight empty road, which leads from Staines station to the riverside. He had stopped to light a cigarette, and in stopping he half turned.

'Keep behind my cab,' said the driver. 'That's right, well down. He's getting nervous. I'd say he's not far from wherever it is he's going to. Good as a book, isn't it? Do you read detective stories?'

The man was walking on again now. He was a full three hundred yards away.

'I don't want to lose him,' said Petrella. 'Not now. I've come a long way with him.'

'You leave it to me,' said the cab-driver. 'I've been driving round here for forty years. There isn't a footpath I don't know blindfold. Just watch which way he turns at the end.'

'Turning right,' said Petrella.

'All aboard.' The taxi shot out of the station yard, and the driver turned round in his seat to say, 'Might be making for the High Street, but if he wanted the High Street, why not take a bus from the other platform? Ten to one he's for the ferry.'

'I say, look out for that dog,' said Petrella.

The driver slewed back in his seat. Said, 'Effie Muggridge's poodle. Asking for trouble,' and accelerated. The dog shot to safety with a squeal of rage.

'Got to do this bit carefully,' said the driver as they reached the corner. 'Keep right down. Don't show so much as the tip of your nose, now.'

Petrella obeyed. The taxi rounded the corner, and over it, in a wave, flowed the unmistakable smell of the river on a hot day – weed and water and tar and boat varnish.

'He's in the ferry,' said the driver. 'Got his back to you. You can come up for air now.'

Petrella saw that a ferry punt ran from the steps beside a public house. There were three passengers on her, standing cheek by jowl, and the ferryman was untying and pushing out. He realised how hopeless he would have been on his own.

'What do we do?' he said.

'Over the road bridge, and back down the other side. Plenty of time, if we hurry.'

'What were we doing just now?'

The driver chuckled throatily. Petrella held his breath and counted ten, slowly. Then they were crossing Staines Bridge.

'Not much traffic just now,' said the driver. 'You ought to see it at weekends.' They did a skid turn to the left, and drew up in the yard of another riverside inn.

'There's two things he could do,' said the driver. 'Walk up the towpath to the bridge. There's no way off it. Or he could come down the path – you see the stile? – the one that comes out there. I'll watch the stile. You go through that gate and down the garden – I know the man who owns it. He won't mind. You can see the towpath from his summer-house. If you hear my horn, come back quick.'

With a feeling that some power much stronger than himself had taken charge, Petrella opened a gate and walked down a well-kept garden, full of pinks and roses and stone dwarfs with pointed hats. At the bottom was a summer-house. In the summer-house he found a small girl reading a book.

'Are you coming to tea?' she said.

'I'm not sure,' said Petrella. 'I might be going to the cinema.'

'You'll have to hurry then. The big film starts in five minutes.'

Behind him a hooter sounded off.

'I'll run then,' said Petrella. He scooted back up the garden. The girl never raised her eyes from her book.

'Just come out,' said the taxi-driver. 'Going nicely. We'll give him twenty yards. Can't afford too much leeway here. Tricky navigation.'

He drove slowly towards the turning, and stopped just short of it.

'Better hop out and look,' he said. 'But be careful. He's stopped twice already to blow his nose. We're getting pretty warm.'

Petrella inched up to the corner, and poked his head round the wall. The man was going away from him, walking along the pavement, but slowly. It was an area of bungalows, some on the road, some on the river bank, with a network of private ways between.

The taxi-driver had got out, and was breathing down the back of his neck.

'Got to take a chance,' he said. 'If we follow him, he'll spot us for sure. I'll stay here. If he turns right, I'll mark it. If he turns left he's for Riverside Drive. You nip down that path, and you can cut him off.'

Petrella took the path. It ran between high hedges of dusty bramble and thorn; hot and sweet-smelling in the sun. It was the dead middle of the afternoon, with hardly a dog stirring. Petrella broke into a jog trot, then slowed for the road ahead.

As he reached the corner, he heard footsteps on the pavement. Their beat was unmistakable. It was his man, and he was walking straight towards him.

Petrella looked round for cover and saw none. He thought for a moment of diving into the shallow ditch, but realised that he would merely be attracting attention. The footsteps had stopped. Petrella held his breath. He heard the click of a latch. Feet on flagstones. The sudden purring of an electric bell.

The chase was over.

'I'm not saying,' said Palance, 'that it wasn't a success. It was a success. Yes.'

Haxtell said nothing. He knew just how Palance was feeling and sympathised with him.

'We've got back the Alfrey diamonds, and we've got our hands on that man at Staines. An insurance broker, of all things, and quite unsuspected. Judging from what we found in the false bottom of a punt in his boat-house he's been receiving stolen goods for years. And we've stopped up one of the Ponting middlemen at that tobacconist's in Balham. A little more pressure and we may shop the Pontings, too.'

'Quite,' said Haxtell sympathetically.

'All the same, it was a mad way to do it. You can't get over that, Haxtell. How long have you known that Coulman was a man?'

'We realised that as soon as we started to think about it,' said Haxtell. 'It was obviously impossible for a real, middle-aged buxom woman to turn into a convincing man. But, conversely, it was easy enough for a man dressed as a woman, padded and powdered and wigged, to whip it all off and turn back quickly into his own self.'

'Then do you mean to say,' said Palance, 'that the Mrs Coulman my men were watching for a month – doing her shopping, gossiping, hanging out her washing, having tea with the vicar – was really a man all the time?'

'Certainly not,' said Haxtell. Observing symptoms of apoplexy, he said, 'That *was* Mrs Coulman. She had a brother – two, actually. One was killed by the Nazis. The other one got over to England. Whenever she had a big job on hand, her brother would come along at night. The house she lived in was at the end of the row. There was a way in at

453

the side. He could slip in late at night without anyone seeing him. Next day he'd dress up in his sister's coat and hat and go out and do the job. She stayed quietly at home.'

'When you realised this,' said Palance, 'wouldn't it have been better to do the job properly? You could have had a hundred men if necessary.'

'It wouldn't have worked. Not a chance. You can't beat a methodical man like Coulman by being more methodical. He'll outdo you every time. The Underground, the change of clothes, the careful train check before he started for Staines, the long straight road, and the ferry. What you want with a man like that is luck – and imagination.'

'Yes, but—' said Palance.

'Method, ingenuity, system,' said Superintendent Haxtell. 'You'll never beat a German at his own game. Look at the Gestapo. They tried for five years and even they couldn't pull it off. The one thing they lacked was imagination. Perhaps it was a good thing. A little imagination, and they might have caused a lot more bother.'

A Midnight Train to Nowhere

KEN FOLLETT

This is a mystery story of the London Underground which I have a special reason for including, because apart from its relevance to this collection it also brings back memories of travelling on the tube with the author, Ken Follett. This was some years before he became a bestselling author, however, when he was the editor of a small London publishing house for whom I produced three books. We discovered that we shared an interest in crime fiction and he told me he had already tried his hand at writing some mystery novels under the pen-name of Simon Myles. None had proved very successful, but he was nevertheless developing the storytelling skills which have since made him a worldwide success. If I remember correctly, our journeys were between the Elephant and Castle station close to his offices in Valentine Place and Holborn where I worked just off Fleet Street. The memory of those journeys added a special sense of *déjà vu* when I read 'A Midnight Train to Nowhere' which, Ken said, was inspired by a late-night journey on the Underground.

Kenneth Martin Follett (1949–) took a degree in philosophy and began his career in the early seventies as a reporter and rock music columnist on the *South Wales Echo*, Cardiff before moving to London in 1970. Here he worked as a journalist for the *Evening News* until 1973 when he went into publishing with Everest Books. The early Simon Myles novels written in his spare time are now rare collectors' items; and it is equally difficult to find copies of his two sexually charged novels of intrigue, *The Modigliani*

Scandal and *Paper Money*, which he wrote not long afterwards as 'Zachary Stone' for Collins Crime Club. In these, he demonstrated the thoroughness of his research which has since become a hallmark of his bestsellers that started with *Storm Island* (1978), retitled *Eye of the Needle* in America. His later blockbusters have established him as 'an expert in the art of ransacking history for thrills', to quote *Time* magazine. Follett's ability to generate thrills was, in fact, already in evidence when he contributed 'A Midnight Train to Nowhere' to the *Evening News*, which ran a short story every night and had already included tales by several other authors destined for fame including James Clavell, Herbert Harris and Leslie Thomas (who was also an *Evening News* reporter for several years). It is the account of a grim journey on the Underground, and it still brings back a little chill of recognition whenever I find myself travelling on the line it features.

***

The driver was thinking about winning the pools, champagne, early retirement, a holiday in Jamaica, girls in bikinis. Through the mist of his daydreams he saw a station and touched the brake.

The guard was reading a paperback about a milkman's 'confessions'. The milkman had just been invited into a bedsitter by two girls in negligées when the train jerked to a halt. Automatically, the guard pressed the button which opened the doors.

He looked up from the book and realised his mistake. He closed the doors quickly.

The driver came back from Jamaica with a lurch. He, too, realised his mistake. His brow creased in puzzlement.

The train pulled away.

Janet stood on the platform, rubbing her eyes. She had

wakened with a start and, realising that she was well past Euston, jumped out just as the doors closed.

She muttered a curse as the lights of the train vanished. She had fallen asleep over a book of horror stories – the last station she could remember was Hendon Central. It was midnight. There should be one more train back.

Her heels tut-tutted irritably on the concrete as she walked towards the Way Out sign. The station lights seemed very dim, and she had to peer into the distance to see the end of the platform.

She followed the rusty metal signs to the northbound side.

The wooden bench was thick with dust. Typical London Transport, she thought. She searched her handbag for a tissue and cleaned a little space on the seat, then screwed the paper into a ball and dropped it into a litter bin.

They never provided enough litter bins, she thought automatically. If only they did, the stations would not get so filthy. But oddly enough there was no litter on this platform; just the thick dust everywhere. The air smelt musty.

She shivered again and looked impatiently at her watch; it was about time that train came in.

Something small scuttled across her feet, and she jumped up with a squeal. She saw a mouse disappear into a tiny hole in the brickwork. 'Oh! You little horror!' she gasped.

She looked about in embarrassment, but there was nobody on the platform to hear her shriek. She could not sit down again. There was probably a nest of the vile creatures. Where was that wretched train?

She felt hungry. She found a coin in her purse and went in search of a chocolate machine. There was one at the far end of the platform but it was empty.

There were cobwebs round it. That showed how long it had been since the thing had been filled.

A slight breeze ruffled her blonde fringe. At last – the train was coming.

The breeze turned into a wind and the train clattered into the station. As it slowed, she could see into the brightly lit, almost empty carriages.

In one a couple were necking; in another a man had fallen asleep under an open newspaper. A third carriage was filled with a grey haze from an old gent contentedly puffing a pipe like a small furnace.

She stepped to the edge of the platform. The train began to speed up.

Janet was flabbergasted. 'No!' she shouted. 'You haven't stopped!' Her voice was drowned by the noise of the accelerating train. 'Stop!' she cried uselessly. The last carriage disappeared into the black throat of the tunnel and the noise died away.

Janet looked at the tunnel blankly. This sort of thing did not happen – even on the Northern Line. How could a driver simply forget to stop?

Suddenly the station seemed very creepy. Flyblown posters, dim lights, dusty seats, cobwebs – and now trains which did not stop. She fought down panic.

'I am not frightened,' she said aloud. 'I will simply go up the escalator, pay my excess fare, and take a taxi home. And I will write a very nasty letter to London Transport.'

She took out her ticket as she walked towards the exit. No, I won't pay the excess, she decided. They can sue me for it, and I'll tell the court about the Northern Line drivers who are in such a hurry to get home they can't be bothered to stop at stations. It will get in the papers and cause a fuss.

Bursting with indignation, she turned a corner and stalked down the passage. She was brought up short.

The corridor was boarded up with planks. I must have taken a wrong turn, she thought.

She retraced her steps, looking for a way out. She ended up back on the platform. Suddenly she was terrified.

She ran back to the blocked exit, and returned to the platform. It was impossible – was there such a thing as a ghost station, a place in the supernatural limbo where lost souls wandered for eternity, clutching their tube tickets in their hands, cursing the driver who had stopped by mistake and the guard who had opened the doors before realising the error . . . ?

She screamed, very loud, and very long. She no longer knew what she was doing. She sat against the wall by the bench and shut her eyes tight, hoping she would wake up in bed.

After a while the mouse came out and stared at her.

In a dream, she heard a West Indian voice say, 'Trains ain't s'posed to stop here.' A hand shook her shoulder. She looked up, saw a black face and staring white eyes, and screamed again.

The man said, 'Quiet! Lady, do me a favour!'

Janet said, 'I'm in hell, aren't I?'

The man took a tube map from the pocket of his dungarees, put down his broom and pointed to the map.

Janet read aloud, 'Station closed until June 1976.'

The man said, 'You ain't in hell, lady. You are in the Strand station.'

Oxford Circus

MAEVE BINCHY

The unique map of the London Underground system is deservedly famous all over the world. Created originally in 1931 by draughtsman Henry Beck who based his idea on an electrical wiring diagram, and for which he was paid the princely sum of five guineas (£5.25 in today's currency), it has since served as a model for tube maps all over the world and is as much an icon of London as the red bus. Thanks to this inspired design, the subway's different lines are much simpler for travellers to follow, while the names of stations like Marble Arch, Bond Street and Oxford Circus have earned a fame all of their own. To the novelist Maeve Binchy, who lives in central London, the map provided the inspiration and framework for a series of stories about London life, all of them named after specific stations, and ranging in themes from tales of family jealousy to petty crime and . . . murder.

Maeve Binchy (1940–) was born in Dublin and after taking a history degree taught in various girls' schools. During her holidays she began to write and in 1969 decided to leave education in favour of journalism and joined the *Irish Times*. Here she quickly made a name for herself with a weekly column full of humour and insight into the human condition. Binchy also began writing plays for the stage and television, but it was in 1982 that she came to international attention with the publication of *Light a Penny Candle* which the *Sunday Telegraph* reviewer described as 'the most enchanting book I have read since *Gone with the Wind*'. Binchy's success has subsequently turned her into one of the most-travelled of contemporary authors, and when she began to plan the series of stories about London there seemed no better way of linking them than with the names of various Underground stations. These have now been collected in three volumes as *Central Line* (1978), *Victoria Line* (1980), and *London Transports* (1983).

One of Binchy's great pleasures is taking return trips to Dublin, and in a recent interview she was asked what would be the first thing she would do if she became Minister of Transport. Her reply was direct: 'Start a Motorail service between London and Holyhead so that people like myself could get from London to Dublin without having to panic about lorries and motorways!' The journey which she invites the reader to accompany her on from 'Oxford Circus' is, however, rather different. For here we are in the company of two women who were once the rivals for the love of the same man, but now have a decidedly unpleasant plan for his future.

***

Once she had decided to write the letter, Joy thought that it would be easy. She had never found it difficult to express herself. She found her big box of simple, expensive writing-paper and began with a flourish: 'Dear Linda . . .' and then she came to a sudden stop.

Joy didn't want to use any clichés about Linda being surprised to hear from her, she didn't want to begin by explaining who she was, since Linda knew. She had no wish to start by asking a favour since that would put her in a subservient role, and Joy wanted to have the upper hand in this whole business. She didn't want it to seem like girlish intrigue; both she and Linda were long past the age when schoolgirl plots held any allure.

Eventually she wrote a very short note indeed and

regarded it with great pleasure before she put it into the envelope.

> Linda,
>
> I'm sure my name is familiar to you from the long distant past when Edward was both your friend and mine. There is something I would very much like to discuss with you, something that has little bearing on the past and certainly nothing to do with either nostalgia or recriminations! Perhaps if you are coming to London in the next few weeks, you could let me know and I can take you to lunch?
>
> Sincerely, Joy Martin.

Linda re-read the letter for the twentieth time. Everything, every single warning bell inside her told her to throw it away, to pretend she had never read it. Joy Martin must be mad to want to reopen all the hurts and deceptions and rivalries of ten years ago. They had never met, but she had read all Joy's passionate letters to Edward, she had sneaked a look at the photographs of Joy and Edward taken on their illicit weekends, the weekends when Edward had said he was visiting his elderly mother. Linda could feel her throat and chest constricting with the remembered humiliations and injustices of a previous decade. Throw it away, burn it. Don't bring it all back. It was destructive then, it can only be destructive again now.

> Dear Joy,
>
> How intriguing! I thought this kind of thing only happened in glorious old black and white movies. Yes, I do come to London fairly often and will most certainly take you up on your offer of lunch. Can we make it somewhere near Oxford Circus? That way it will leave me right in the middle of the shopping belt. Simply mystified to know what all this is about.
>
> Regards, Linda Grey.

Joy breathed a great happy sigh. She had been so afraid of rejection. A whole week had passed without acknowledgement, and she had almost given up hoping for the Hampshire postmark. Her first hurdle had been cleared. She knew now that Linda Grey must feel exactly as she did about Edward. She had not been wrong. There had been a huge amount of caring, almost passion, in her love letters to him – those letters which Joy had sneaked from his wallet to read. There had been purpose and serious intent in her threats of suicide. No, her fear that Edward might have been forgotten in Linda's cosy Hampshire life was ... unrealistic. Edward was never forgotten.

Linda came to London the night before this rendezvous. In her handbag she had Joy's card with the name of the restaurant: '. . . only a few minutes from Oxford Circus, as you requested.' She checked in at an inexpensive hotel and ordered a cup of tea to wash down her two sleeping pills. A night in London with the possibility of some showdown involving Edward on the morrow would keep her awake for hours, and she had no wish to arrive looking flustered. She had made appointments for hair and facials. She was going to buy herself some very expensive shoes and a handbag. Joy Martin could not sit elegantly and pity poor Linda who had lost Edward all those years ago. Still, she thought as her body began to relax with the mogadon. Still, Joy had lost him too. He had left Joy very shortly after he had left Linda.

She felt very guilty about Hugh. He had been concerned about her visit to London, and wanted to come with her. No, she assured him, just a check-up. She really thought she needed the little break as much as the check-up. She begged him not to come. She would telephone him tomorrow and tell him that she felt perfect and that the doctor had confirmed it. He would be pleased and relieved. He would arrange to meet her at the station and take her out to dinner. He was so kind and good. She didn't know why she was making this ridiculous pilgrimage to dig up the hate-filled ghost of Edward.

Joy woke with a headache and a feeling that something was wrong. Oh God! This was the day. Linda Grey would be getting on her train somewhere in the countryside telling her mouse-like husband that she was going to look at some fabrics in Oxford Street, and was on her way panting with excitement at the very mention of Edward's name. She made herself a health drink in the blender and a cup of china tea. But the headache didn't lift so she took some pain-killers very much against her will. Joy liked to believe that she didn't need drugs. Drugs were for weak people. Today that belief didn't seem so clear. She also thought that only weak people stayed away from work when they felt a little below par. But today that wasn't a theory that she could substantiate. She telephoned her secretary. No, of course she wasn't seriously ill, just a little below par. Her secretary was alarmed. Crisply Joy gave instructions, meetings to be rearranged, appointments to be cancelled, letter to be written. She would be back tomorrow morning. Perhaps even this afternoon.

She felt alarmed that it was all taking so much out of her. She had planned it so very carefully. She had allowed no emotion, no waverings. It was now absolutely foolproof. Why did her stomach feel like water? Why did she think she couldn't face her job at all during the day? Full of annoyance she put on her smart sheepskin coat and set out for a long healthy walk in Hyde Park.

As she walked she saw people with their dogs. She would have liked to have a dog; she didn't disapprove of people having dogs in London if they gave them enough exercise. When all this business was over, Joy thought to herself, she might get a dog. A beautiful red setter, and she could walk him for hours in the park on a bright cold morning like this.

It was five to one and Linda was determined not to be early. She gave herself another admiring look in a window. Her hair was splendid. What a pity that nobody in the village at home could do that sort of thing with scissors and a comb. They really only liked you to have rollers and a half-hour under the dryer. Linda smiled at herself with her newly painted lips. She looked in no way like a woman of nearly forty. She supposed that Joy Martin probably spent days in beauticians. After all, she had a very glamorous job running an art gallery and an art dealing business. Linda had even seen her photograph once talking to a royal person. Facials and expensive handbags would be no treat for Joy.

She forced her feet to go slowly and only when she saw that she was a nice casual six minutes late did she allow herself to enter the restaurant, take two deep breaths and enquire about a table for two booked by Miss Martin.

'You look smashing,' said Joy warmly. 'Really glamorous. Much younger than you did years ago actually, I always think we improve in our thirties really instead of going off.'

'How on earth did you know what I used to look like?' asked Linda settling herself into the corner chair.

'Oh I used to look at the pictures of you in Edward's wallet. Now, will we have a gin or would you prefer a sherry?'

'A gin,' gulped Linda.

'What do you think of me? Have I aged or gone off do you think?'

'No, in fact you look very unsophisticated, sort of wind-blown and young,' said Linda truthfully. 'I thought you'd be much more studied, obviously groomed, over made-up. A bit like me,' she giggled.

Joy laughed too. 'I expect you went to a beautician's just to impress me. I was so nervous at the thought of meeting you, I've been out walking all morning in the park. That's

465

why I'm so windswept and rosy. Normally I'm never like this.'

Linda smiled, 'Isn't it funny?' she said. 'After all these years, and we both find it very anxious-making and . . . and well . . . disturbing.'

'Yes,' said Joy. 'That's exactly what it is. Disturbing.'

'Then why did you suggest it, I mean if it's going to make us both anxious and act out of character, what's the point?' Linda's face looked troubled.

Joy paused to order two gin and tonics and to tell the waiter that they would like a little time before they made up their minds about the lunch menu.

'Well,' she said, 'I had to. You see I want you to help me. I want you and I together to murder Edward. Seriously. That's what I'm hoping you'll help me to do.'

Most of Linda's omelette aux fines herbes lay untouched. But Joy had managed to eat much of the whole-wheat pizza. Linda had managed one sip of the dry white wine but it had tasted very sour. The longer Joy talked the more Linda realised that she was indeed perfectly serious.

'Well, it stands to reason that he's a man the world would be much better off without. We all agree about that. Well, Linda, be reasonable. There was my divorce. I haven't seen my son for nine and a half years because of Edward. If it hadn't been for Edward I would have a perfectly normal and happy relationship with my son who is now sixteen. As it is I am not allowed to visit him at school; everyone agrees it is less distressing for Anthony if his mother is kept away. Later when he's an adult I shall have some ridiculous "civilised" meeting with him, where we will have nothing to say. So that was one thing Edward destroyed.'

'But you were willing to divorce your husband, to leave everything for Edward. Wasn't it your fault too?'

'No it was not my fault,' Joy was calm and unemotional. 'I was twenty-eight and bored with marriage and a demanding child and Edward lied to me, used me, filled my head with nonsenses, betrayed me and then would not stop by me after I had done what he begged and implored me to do – leave home, leave my husband and child and run away with him. He laughed at me.'

Linda said: 'I didn't know that.'

'And look what he did to you. A nervous breakdown. A serious two-year depression. Two years out of your life because you believed him, and couldn't accept his betrayals, his double life, his endless pointless lies.'

Linda said: 'I didn't think you knew that.'

'There were people before us, Linda, there were people after us. Mine wasn't the only divorce he caused, yours wasn't the only nervous illness. And nobody has punished him. Nobody has said this man is evil and he must be stopped. He mustn't be allowed to roam the world destroying, destroying, turning good to bad and dark, turning simple things to twisted and frightening.' Joy's voice hadn't raised itself a decibel but there was something in it that was a little like a preacher, like some Southern Baptist in a movie describing Satan. It chilled Linda and forced her to speak.

'But it's all over Joy, it's all done. It's all finished. Other people are being silly and foolish nowadays, like you and I once were stupid. They're making mistakes now. Not us.'

Joy interrupted her. 'We were not silly, we made no mistakes, neither do his women of today. We all behaved normally as if Edward were normal. When we said things we meant them. When we told him tales they were true, when we made promises they were sincere.'

Once more her voice was uncomfortably like a preacher. In the busy crowded restaurant Linda felt frightened.

'But you don't seriously want to . . . er . . . get rid of him?'

'Oh yes,' said Joy.

'But why now? Why not years ago, when it hurt more?'

'It hurts just as much now,' said Joy.

'Oh, but it can't,' Linda cried sympathetically. 'Not now.'

'Not for myself,' said Joy. 'But now he has gone too far. Now he has done something he can't be forgiven for. He's taken my niece to live with him. She is, of course, utterly besotted with him. She's given up her job for him like you gave up yours, she's given up her fiancé like I gave up my marriage. She will shortly give up her sanity like you did, and her happiness like I did.'

Linda felt a little faint. The smart restaurant seemed somehow claustrophobic.

'Are you very concerned about your niece?' she asked, her voice coming from a long way away. She wanted to keep Joy talking. She didn't want to have to say anything herself.

'Yes, she lives with me. She's all I've got. I've had her since she was seventeen, three years. I thought that if, well if I did a good job looking after her, they might let me have Anthony back too. Anyway, I'm very attached to Barbara, I've told her everything, she's learning the trade in our company, she's studying art history as well. The one thing I couldn't foresee in a city of twelve million people was that she might meet Edward.'

'Does she know? Does he know?' Linda's voice was still weak: there was a coldness in Joy's tone now that terrified her.

'Barbara doesn't know. I've never seen any reason to tell her about my relationship with Edward. And Edward doesn't remember me.'

'What?'

'He came to the house, to my house last month to collect Barbara, she introduced him to me proudly. His eyes rested on me easily. He doesn't remember me, Linda. He has forgotten me.'

Linda was swept by sympathy for the woman ten years previously she would have like to have killed.

'He pretended. It was another ploy. He *can't* have forgotten you. Joy, don't get hurt over it, you know what he was like. He's just trying to wound you. Don't let him.'

'He had forgotten me, Linda. I am certain he has forgotten you too, and Susan or whoever came after us. I will not let him use Barbara. She took her things last week and has gone to him!'

'She's twenty years of age Joy, these days that's old enough . . .'

'No day is anyone old enough for Edward, or cruel enough,' said Joy. 'Oh, Barbara is sure she is doing the right thing: "You know how it is, Auntie Joy. You were wild once they say, Auntie Joy. If you knew how he makes me need him, Auntie Joy." '

Linda looked across the table. 'Don't tell me what you want to do,' she said.

Joy reached for her hand. 'Please, please. It needs two. You know, you understand, you and I were the same age, we went through the same things. We know. No one else can do it.'

'Don't tell me. I don't want to hear,' said Linda.

'We need two. Nobody can ever connect you with it. You can come up to London for a day, just like today, to buy curtains or whatever. It's in two parts. You needn't even look at him I tell you. He'll be unconscious anyway. I shall have given him the tablets first.'

Linda stood up shakily. 'I beg you not to think about it any more. Do something, anything. Go away. Come and stay in the country with me. Just stop planning it.'

'It has been planned. It's all planned. You are to come to my house, I'll leave the key and the gun.'

'I won't listen,' said Linda. 'I can't listen. You don't want to kill him, you want him back. You don't give two damns about your niece. You want Edward. You want him dead if you can't have him. It gives you a wave of pleasure just thinking of his head on one side, dead. His mouth still, his eyes open but not seeing things, not darting . . .'

'How do you know? How can you know that it's like that?' Joy's eyes were bright.

'Because I planned to kill him ten years ago. Ten years ago when you went to live with him. I planned it, too. But I had to plan it on my own. I wasn't confident enough.'

'You what?' Joy looked at her in disbelief.

'I planned it all, I would tell him I needed to see him once. I would assure him there would be no scenes, I would ask him to my flat but in fact I would have some friends there and when he came I would pretend that he had attacked me and that I was fighting him off in self-defence. In the mêlée a knife would be used.'

'Why didn't you do it?' asked Joy.

'Because of you. I knew that you would have known it was murder. You would know Edward didn't care enough for me to attack me. You could have had me convicted.'

'How far had you got?' whispered Joy.

'As far as organising the knife, the friends in my flat, and asking him to come and see me.'

'And what happened?'

'Oh when he called, I told him I had changed my mind, I didn't want to see him after all. He stayed for one drink, long enough to bewitch Alexandra, my friend.'

'Alex. Oh God! She was your friend?'

'So you saved me from doing it. Let me save you.'

Joy pulled herself together. It was almost a visible thing. First her spine straightened. Then her brow became unlined. A small smile came to her mouth.

'We are being very dramatic, aren't we?' she said in a brittle voice.

'Very,' agreed Linda politely.

'Shall we have coffee, or are you in a hurry to get on with your shopping?'

'Rather a hurry actually,' said Linda.

'So you're off back to Hampshire then and the peaceful life,' said Joy waving for the bill.

'Yes, nothing much to do,' said Linda.

'Very quiet and tranquil I expect,' Joy said producing her credit card for the waiter.

'Only excitement I get is reading the papers, seeing who's saying what and doing what. Reading about the things that happen in London, sudden deaths, scandal. You know the kind of thing.'

A small and almost genuine smile came to Joy's eyes.

'I see,' she said.

Linda left, pausing to ask the waiter if there was a phone she could use. She told Hugh that she was very pleased with her check-up and she might catch the earlier train home. He sounded very pleased. And, for the first time in a long time, his pleasure gave her pleasure too.

Drink Entire: Against the Madness of Crowds

RAY BRADBURY

The image of the New York Subway as 'a screeching, smelly, squalid, mugger's paradise', to quote one recent newspaper account, may well be close to the truth. But this picture which is accepted all over the world by people who have never even ridden on the Transit Authority trains does owe a lot to the way the system has been depicted in several recent blockbuster movies, including *The French Connection* (1971) in which a crazed killer terrorised passengers, *The Taking of Pelham 123* (1974) about the hijacking of a subway car, and *Money Train* (1994), featuring a group of crooked policemen who rip off the subway. The RTA also continues to act as a magnet for writers of fact and fiction such as Paul Theroux ('The Underground Jungle', *Observer* magazine, February 1984), Garrison Keillor ('Solidarity Forever', *Independent* magazine, February 1991) and Ray Bradbury in the following story, which he wrote for *Gallery* magazine in 1975.

Raymond Douglas Bradbury (1920–) is the universally acclaimed American novelist and short story writer who has taken his readers to Mars and beyond, yet hates flying and will only travel by boat or train. Born in Waukegan, Illinois, Bradbury has an enduring affection for his upbringing in small-town America, yet his imagination has taken him all over the galaxy in *The Martian Chronicles* (1950), *Fahrenheit 451* (1953) and *The Machineries of Joy* (1964), not to mention a host of short stories. His refusal to use aircraft has, in fact, turned him into something of a train freak as articles like 'Any Friend of Trains is a Friend of Mine', written for *Life* magazine in August 1968, bear witness. Steam trains and modern trains also feature in his poetry, *vide* 'A Train Station Sign Viewed from an Ancient Locomotive Passing Through Long After Midnight' (*Orange County Illustrated*, March 1969), essays such as 'Night Travel on the Orient Express' (for *Strange Seas and Shores*, 1971), and a string of short tales of which 'My Perfect Murder', 'A Touch of Petulance' and 'Orient, North' spring readily to mind. One of his earliest, and still unpublished, stories, 'The Lady Up Ahead', is about a mysterious woman in black who lures unsuspecting commuters from trains to murder them; while his recent novel, *Death is a Lonely Business* (1985), has a memorable opening section which focuses on a traveller who knows a killer is sitting behind him, laughing, but dares not look back. There is something of this kind of fear in 'Drink Entire: Against the Madness of Crowds', a story full of Bradbury's unique verbal imagery, in which two men meet on the New York Subway late at night, are drawn into a terrible pact, and then one finds himself travelling unsuspectingly towards a date with terror and death.

***

It was one of those nights that are so damned hot you lie flat out lost until 2.00 a.m., then sway upright, baste yourself with your own sour brine, and stagger down into the great bake-oven subway where the lost trains shriek in.

'Hell,' whispered Will Morgan.

And hell it was, with a lost army of beast people wandering the night from the Bronx on out to Coney and back, hour on hour, searching for sudden inhalations of salt ocean wind that might make you gasp with Thanksgiving.

Somewhere, God, somewhere in Manhattan or beyond was a cool wind. By dawn, it *must* be found . . .

'Damn!'

Stunned, he saw maniac tides of advertisements squirt by with toothpaste smiles, his own advertising ideas pursuing him the whole length of the hot night island.

The train groaned and stopped.

Another train stood on the opposite track.

Incredible. There in the open train window across the way sat Old Ned Amminger. Old? They were the same age, forty, but . . .

Will Morgan threw his window up.

'Ned, you bastard. You ride late like this often?'

'Every damn hot night since 1946!'

'Me, too! Glad to see you!'

'Liar!'

Each vanished in a shriek of steel.

God, thought Will Morgan, two men who hate each other, who work not ten feet apart grinding their teeth over the next step up the ladder, knock together in Dante's Inferno here under a melting city at 3.00 a.m. Hear our voices echo, fading:

'Liar . . . !'

Half an hour later, in Washington Square, a cool wind touched his brow. He followed it into an alley where . . .

The temperature dropped ten degrees.

'Hold on,' he whispered.

The wind smelled of the Ice House when he was a boy and stole cold crystals to rub on his cheeks and stab inside his shirt with shrieks to kill the heat.

The cool wind led him down the alley to a small shop where a sign read:

MELISSA TOAD, WITCH
LAUNDRY SERVICE:
CHECK YOUR PROBLEMS HERE BY NINE A.M.
PICK THEM UP, FRESH-CLEANED, AT DUSK

There was a smaller sign:

SPELLS, PHILTRES AGAINST DREAD CLIMATES, HOT OR
COLD. POTIONS TO INSPIRE EMPLOYERS AND ASSURE
PROMOTIONS. SALVES, UNGUENTS & MUMMY-DUSTS
RENDERED DOWN FROM ANCIENT CORPORATION
HEADS. REMEDIES FOR NOISE. EMOLLIENTS FOR GAS-
EOUS OR POLLUTED AIRS. LOTIONS FOR PARANOID
TRUCK DRIVERS. MEDICINES TO BE TAKEN BEFORE
TRYING TO SWIM OFF THE NEW YORK DOCKS.

A few bottles were strewn in the display window,
labelled:

PERFECT MEMORY.
BREATH OF SWEET APRIL WIND.
SILENCE AND THE TREMOR OF FINE BIRDSONG.

He laughed and stopped.

For the wind blew cool and creaked a door. And again
there was the memory of frost from the white Ice House
grottoes of childhood, a world cut from winter dreams and
saved on into August.

'Come in,' a voice whispered.

The door glided back.

Inside, a cold funeral awaited him.

A six-foot-long block of clear dripping ice rested like a
giant February remembrance upon three sawhorses.

'Yes,' he murmured. In his hometown-hardware-store
window, a magician's wife, MISS I. SICKLE, had been
stashed in an immense rectangle of ice melted to fit her
calligraphy. There she slept the nights away, a Princess of
Snow. Midnights, he and other boys snuck out to see her
smile in her cold crystal sleep. They stood half the summer
nights staring, four or five fiery-furnace boys of some
fourteen years, hoping their red-hot gaze might melt the
ice . . .

The ice had never melted.

'Wait,' he whispered. 'Look . . .'

He took one more step within this dark night shop.

Lord, yes. There, in *this* ice! Weren't those the outlines where, only moments ago, a woman of snow napped away in cool night dreams? Yes. The ice was hollow and curved and lovely. But . . . the woman was gone. Where?

'Here,' whispered the voice.

Beyond the bright cold funeral, shadows moved in a far corner.

'Welcome. Shut the door.'

He sensed that she stood not far away in shadows. Her flesh, if you could touch it, would be cool, still fresh from her time within the dripping tomb of snow. If he just reached out his hand . . .

'What are you doing here?' her voice asked, gently.

'Hot night. Walking. Riding. Looking for a cool wind. I think I need help.'

'You've come to the right place.'

'But this is *mad*! I don't believe in psychiatrists. My friends hate me because I say Tinkerbell *and* Freud died twenty years back, with the circus. I don't believe in astrologers, numerologists, or palmistry quacks—'

'I don't read palms. But . . . give me your hand.'

He put his hand out into the soft darkness.

Her fingers trapped his. It felt like the hand of a small girl who had just rummaged an icebox. He said:

'Your sign reads MELISSA TOAD, WITCH. What would a witch be doing in New York in the summer of 1974?'

'You ever know a city needed a witch more than New York does this year?'

'Yes. We've gone mad. But, *you*?'

'A witch is born out of the true hungers of her time,' she said. 'I was born out of New York. The things that are most wrong here summoned me. Now you come, not knowing, to find me. Give me your other hand.'

Though her face was only a ghost of cool flesh in the shadows, he felt her eyes move over his trembling palm.

'Oh, why did you wait so *long*?' she mourned. 'It's almost too late.'

'Too late for what?'

'To be saved. To take the gift that I can give.'

His heart pounded. '*What* can you give me?'

'Peace,' she said. 'Serenity. Quietness in the midst of bedlam. I am a child of the poisonous wind that copulated with the East River on an oil-slick, garbage-infested midnight. I turn about on my own parentage. I inoculate against those very biles that brought me to light. I am a serum born of venoms. I am the antibody of all Time. I am the Cure. You die of the City, do you not? Manhattan is your punisher. Let me be your shield.'

'How?'

'You would be my pupil. My protection could encircle you, like an invisible pack of hounds. The subway train would never violate your ear. Smog would never blight your lung or nostril or fever your vision. I could teach your tongue, at lunch, to taste the rich fields of Eden in the merest cut-rate too-ripe frankfurter. Water, sipped from your office cooler, would be a rare wine of a fine family. Cops, when you called, would answer. Taxis, off-duty rushing nowhere, would stop if you so much as blinked one eye. Theatre tickets would appear if you stepped to a theatre window. Traffic signals would change, at high noon, mind you! if you dared to drive your car from fifty-eighth down to the Square, and not one light red. Green all the way, if you go with me.

'If you go with me, our apartment will be a shadowed jungle glade full of bird cries and love calls from the first hot sour day of June till the last hour after Labor Day when the living dead, heat-beat, go mad on stopped trains coming back from the sea. Our rooms will be filled with crystal chimes. Our kitchen an Eskimo hut in July where we might share out a provender of Popsicles made of Mumm's and Château-Lafite Rothschild. Our larder? – fresh apricots in

August or February. Fresh orange juice each morning, cold milk at breakfast, cool kisses at four in the afternoon, my mouth always the flavour of chilled peaches, my body the taste of rimed plums. The flavour begins at the elbow, as Edith Wharton said.

'Any time you want to come home from the office the middle of a dreadful day, I will call your boss and it will be so. Soon after, you will be the boss and come home, anyway, for cold chicken, fruit wine punch, and me. Summer in the Virgin Isles. Autumns so ripe with promise you will indeed go lunatic in the right way. Winters, of course, will be the reverse. I will be your hearth. Sweet dog, lie there. I will fall upon you like snowflakes.

'In sum, everything will be given you. I ask little in return. Only your soul.'

He stiffened and almost let go of her hand.

'Well, isn't that what you *expected* me to demand?' She laughed. 'But souls can't be sold. They can only be lost and never found again. Shall I tell you what I really want from you?'

'Tell.'

'Marry me,' she said.

Sell me your soul, he thought, and did not say it.

But she read his eyes. 'Oh, dear,' she said. 'Is that *so* much to ask? For all I give?'

'I've got to think it over!'

Without noticing, he had moved back one step.

Her voice was very sad. 'If you have to think a thing over, it will never be. When you finish a book you know if you like it, yes? At the end of a play you are awake or asleep, yes? Well, a beautiful woman is a beautiful woman, isn't she, and a good life a good life?'

'Why won't you come out in the light? How do I know you're beautiful?'

'You can't know unless you step into the dark. Can't you

tell by my voice? No? Poor man. If you don't trust me now, you can't have me, ever.'

'I need time to think! I'll come back tomorrow night! What can twenty-four hours mean?'

'To someone your age, everything.'

'I'm only forty!'

'I speak of your soul, and *that* is late.'

'Give me one more night!'

'You'll take it, anyway, at your own risk.'

'Oh, God, oh, God, oh, God, God,' he said, shutting his eyes.

'I wish He could help you right now. You'd better go. You're an ancient child. Pity. Pity. Is your mother alive?'

'Dead ten years.'

'No, alive,' she said.

He backed off toward the door and stopped, trying to still his confused heart, trying to move his leaden tongue:

'How long have you been in this place?'

She laughed, with the faintest touch of bitterness.

'Three summers now. And, in those three years, only six men have come into my shop. Two ran immediately. Two stayed awhile but left. One came back a second time, and vanished. The sixth man finally had to admit, after three visits, he didn't Believe. You see, no one Believes a really all-encompassing and protective love when they see it clear. A farmboy might have stayed for ever, in his simplicity, which is rain and wind and seed. A New Yorker? Suspects everything.

'Whoever, whatever, you are, O good sir, stay and milk the cow and put the fresh milk in the dim cooling shed under the shade of the oak tree which grows in my attic. Stay and pick the watercress to clean your teeth. Stay in the North Pantry with the scent of persimmons and kumquats and grapes. Stay and stop my tongue so I can cease talking this way. Stay and stop my mouth so I can't breathe. Stay, for I am weary of speech and must need love. Stay. Stay.'

So ardent was her voice, so tremulous, so gentle, so sweet, that he knew he was lost if he did not run.

'Tomorrow night!' he cried.

His shoe struck something. There on the floor lay a sharp icicle fallen from the long block of ice.

He bent, seized the icicle, and ran.

The door *slammed*. The lights blinked out. Rushing, he could not see the sign: MELISSA TOAD, WITCH.

Ugly, he thought, running. A beast, he thought, she *must* be a beast and ugly. Yes, that's it! Lies! All of it, lies! She—

He collided with someone.

In the midst of the street, they gripped, they held, they stared.

Ned Amminger! My God, it was Old Ned!

It was four in the morning, the air still white-hot. And here was Ned Amminger sleepwalking after cool winds, his clothes scrolled on his hot flesh in rosettes, his face dripping sweat, his eyes dead, his feet creaking in their hot baked leather shoes.

They swayed in the moment of collision.

A spasm of malice shook Will Morgan. He seized Old Ned Amminger, spun him about, and pointed him into the dark alley. Far off deep in there, had that shop-window light blinked *on* again? Yes!

'Ned! *That* way! Go *there*!'

Heat-blinded, dead-weary Old Ned Amminger stumbled off down the alley.

'Wait!' cried Will Morgan, regretting his malice.

But Amminger was gone.

In the subway, Will Morgan tasted the icicle.

It was Love. It was Delight. It was Woman.

By the time his train roared in, his hands were empty, his body rusted with perspiration. And the sweet taste in his mouth? Dust.

Seven a.m. and no sleep.

Somewhere a huge blast furnace opened its door and burned New York to ruins.

Get up, thought Will Morgan. Quick! Run to the Village! For he remembered that sign:

LAUNDRY SERVICE:
CHECK YOUR PROBLEMS HERE BY NINE A.M.
PICK THEM UP, FRESH-CLEANED, AT DUSK

He did not go to the Village. He rose, showered, and went off into the furnace to lose his job for ever.

He knew this as he rode up in the raving-hot elevator with Mr Binns, the sunburned and furious personnel manager. Binns's eyebrows were jumping, his mouth worked over his teeth with unspoken curses. Beneath his suit, you could feel porcupines of boiled hair needling to the surface. By the time they reached the fortieth floor, Binns was anthropoid.

Around them, employees wandered like an Italian army coming to attend a lost war.

'Where's Old Amminger?' asked Will Morgan, staring at an empty desk.

'Called in sick. Heat prostration. Be here at noon,' someone said.

Long before noon the water cooler was empty, and the air-conditioning system? – committed suicide at 11.32. Two hundred people became raw beasts chained to desks by windows which had been invented not to open.

At one minute to twelve, Mr Binns, over the intercom, told them to line up by their desks. They lined up. They waited, swaying. The temperature stood at ninety-seven. Slowly, Binns began to stalk down the long line. A white-hot sizzle of invisible flies hung about him.

'All right, ladies and gentlemen,' he said. 'You all know there is a recession, no matter how happily the President of the United States put it. I would rather knife you in the stomach than stab you in the back. Now, as I move down the line, I will nod and whisper, "You". To those of you who hear this single word, turn, clean out your desks, and be gone. Four weeks' severance pay awaits you on the way out. Hold on! Someone's missing!'

'Old Ned Amminger,' said Will Morgan, and bit his tongue.

'*Old* Ned?' said Mr Binns, glaring. 'Old? *Old*?'

Mr Binns and Ned Amminger were exactly the same age. Mr Binns waited, ticking.

'Ned,' said Will Morgan, strangling on self-curses, 'should be here—'

'Now,' said a voice.

They all turned.

At the far end of the line, in the door, stood Old Ned or Ned Amminger. He looked at the assembly of lost souls, read destruction in Binns's face, flinched, but then slunk into line next to Will Morgan.

'All right,' said Binns. 'Here goes.'

He began to move, whisper, move, whisper, move, whisper. Two people, four, then six turned to clean out their desks.

Will Morgan took a deep breath, held it, waited.

Binns came to a full stop in front of him.

Don't say it! thought Morgan. Don't!

'You,' whispered Binns.

Morgan spun about and caught hold of his heaving desk. *You*, the word cracked in his head, *you*!

Binns stepped to confront Ned Amminger.

'Well, *old* Ned,' he said.

Morgan, eyes shut, thought: Say it, say it to him, you're fired, Ned, *fired*!

'Old Ned,' said Binns, lovingly.

Morgan shrank at the strange, the friendly, the sweet sound of Binns's voice.

An idle South Seas wind passed softly on the air. Morgan

blinked and stood up, sniffing. The sun-blasted room was filled with scent of surf and cool white sand.

'Ned, why dear old Ned,' said Mr Binns, gently.

Stunned, Will Morgan waited. I am mad, he thought.

'Ned,' said Mr Binns, gently. 'Stay with us. Stay on.'

Then, swiftly: 'That's all, everyone. Lunch!'

And Binns was gone and the wounded and dying were leaving the field. And Will Morgan turned at last to look full at Old Ned Amminger, thinking, Why, God, *why*?

And got his answer . . .

Ned Amminger stood there, not old, not young, but somehow in-between. As he was not the Ned Amminger who had leaned crazily out a hot train window last midnight or shambled in Washington Square at four in the morning.

This Ned Amminger stood quietly, as if hearing far green country sounds, wind and leaves and an amiable time which wandered in a fresh lake breeze.

The perspiration had dried on his fresh pink face. His eyes were not bloodshot but steady, blue, and quiet. He was an island oasis in this dead and unmoving sea of desks and typewriters which might start up and scream like electric insects. He stood watching the walking-dead depart. And he cared not. He was kept in a splendid and beautiful isolation within his own calm cool beautiful skin.

'No!' cried Will Morgan, and fled.

He didn't know where he was going until he found himself in the men's room frantically digging in the wastebasket.

He found what he knew he would find, a small bottle with the label: DRINK ENTIRE: AGAINST THE MADNESS OF CROWDS. Trembling, he uncorked it. There was the merest cold blue drop left inside. Swaying by the shut hot window, he tapped it to his tongue.

In the instant, his body felt as if he had leapt into a tidal

483

wave of coolness. His breath gusted out in a fount of crushed and savoured clover.

He gripped the bottle so hard it broke. He gasped, watching the blood.

The door opened. Ned Amminger stood there, looking in. He stayed only a moment, then turned and went out. The door shut.

A few moments later, Morgan, with the junk from his desk rattling in his briefcase, went down in the elevator.

Stepping out, he turned to thank the operator.

His breath must have touched the operator's face.

The operator smiled.

A wild, an incomprehensible, a loving, a *beautiful* smile!

The lights were out at midnight in the little alley, in the little shop. There was no sign in the window which said MELISSA TOAD, WITCH. There were no bottles.

He beat on the door for a full five minutes, to no answer. He kicked the door for another two minutes.

And at last, with a sigh, not wanting to, the door opened.

A very tired voice said: 'Come in.'

Inside he found the air only slightly cool. The huge ice slab, in which he had seen the phantom shape of a lovely woman, had dwindled, had lost a good half of its weight, and now was dripping steadily to ruin.

Somewhere in the darkness, the woman waited for him. But he sensed that she was clothed now, dressed and packed, ready to leave. He opened his mouth to cry out, to reach, but her voice stopped him:

'I warned you. You're too late.'

'It's never too late!' he said.

'Last night it wouldn't have been. But in the last twenty hours, the last little thread snapped in you. I feel. I know. I tell. It's gone, gone, gone.'

'What's gone, God damn it?'

'Why, your soul, of course. Gone. Eaten up. Digested. Vanished. You're empty. Nothing there.'

He saw her hand reach out of darkness. It touched at his chest. Perhaps he imagined that her fingers passed through his ribs to probe about his lights, his lungs, his beating and pitiful heart.

'Oh, yes, gone,' she mourned. 'How sad. The city unwrapped you like a candy bar and ate you all up. You're nothing but a dusty milk bottle left on a tenement porch, a spider building a nest across the top. Traffic din pounded your marrow to dust. Subway sucked your breath like a cat sucks the soul of a babe. Vacuum cleaners got your brain. Alcohol dissolved the rest. Typewriters and computers took your final dregs in and out their tripes, printed you on paper, punched you in confettis, threw you down a sewer vent. TV scribbled you in nervous tics on old ghost screens. Your final bones will be carried off by a big angry bulldog crosstown bus holding you munched in its big rubber-lipped mouth door.'

'No!' he cried. 'I've changed my mind! Marry me! Marry—'

His voice cracked the ice tomb. It shattered on the floor behind him. The shape of the beautiful woman melted into the floor. Spinning about, he plunged into darkness.

He fell against the wall just as a panel slammed shut and locked.

It was no use screaming. He was alone.

At dusk in July, a year later, in the subway, he saw Ned Amminger for the first time in 365 days.

In all the grind and ricochet and pour of fiery lava as trains banged through, taking a billion souls to hell, Amminger stood as cool as mint leaves in green rain. Around him wax people melted. He waded in his own private trout stream.

'Ned!' cried Will Morgan, running up to seize his hand and pump it. 'Ned, Ned! The best friend I ever had!'

'Yes, that's true, isn't it?' said young Ned, smiling.

And oh God, how true it was! Dear Ned, fine Ned, friend of a lifetime! Breathe upon me, Ned! Give me your life's breath!

'You're president of the company, Ned! I heard!'

'Yes. Come along home for a drink?'

In the raging heat, a vapour of iced lemonade rose from his creamy fresh suit as they looked for a cab. In all the curses, yells, horns, Ned raised his hand.

A cab pulled up. They drove in serenity.

At the apartment house, in the dusk, a man with a gun stepped from the shadows.

'Give me everything,' he said.

'Later,' said Ned, smiling, breathing a scent of fresh summer apples upon the man.

'Later.' The man stepped back to let them pass. 'Later.'

On the way up in the elevator, Ned said, 'Did you know I'm married? Almost a year. Fine wife.'

'Is she,' said Will Morgan, and stopped, '. . . beautiful?'

'Oh, yes. You'll love her. You'll love the apartment.'

Yes, thought Morgan; a green glade, crystal chimes, cool grass for a carpet. I know, I know.

They stepped out into an apartment that was indeed a tropic isle. Young Ned poured huge goblets of iced champagne.

'What shall we drink to?'

'To you, Ned. To your wife. To me. To midnight, tonight.'

'Why midnight?'

'When I go back down to that man who is waiting downstairs with his gun. That man you said "later" to. And he agreed "later". I'll be there alone with him. Funny, ridiculous, funny. And *my* breath just ordinary breath, not smelling of melons or pears. And him waiting all those long hours with his sweaty gun, irritable with heat. What a grand joke. Well . . . a toast?'

'A toast!'

They drank.

At which moment, the wife entered. She heard each of them laughing in a different way, and joined in their laughter.

But her eyes, when she looked at Will Morgan, suddenly filled with tears.

And he knew whom she was weeping for.

4
END OF THE LINE
Commuter Crimes

There have been many murders committed in railway trains, particularly in the days before corridor coaches became common, for lonely people, sitting in boxed-up compartments through the hours of long journeys, were very much at the mercy of any ruffians out for robbery. But suburban lines where the trains stop every three or four minutes seemed safe enough . . .

ELIZABETH VILLIERS

The Riddle of the 5.28

THOMAS W. HANSHEW

The Brighton line from London to the south coast was the
pioneer railway line for commuter transport and cheap
travel in Britain. Built just over 150 years ago, it was one of
the earliest rail routes in the south-east, and unlike its few
northern predecessors, such as the Stockton–Darlington
line, was built specifically for passengers rather than
freight. When opened in 1841, the fifty-one-mile journey
took one hour and forty-five minutes, but nowadays
commuters can reach their destination in fifty-two minutes.
Its much-loved train, the *Brighton Belle*, was for years
famous for taking such distinguished 'commuters' as Noël
Coward and Sir Laurence Olivier from their homes in the
town to performances in the West End. But the Brighton
line is also infamous for its association with murder as
crime historian Jonathan Goodman has explained: 'In the
decade or so following the Great War, when the race course
and the town were infested by villains, the town's nick-
names – "Doctor Brighton", "London-by-the-Sea", "Old
Ocean's Bauble", and other chamber-of-commerce-nur-
tured sobriquets – were joined by "Soho-on-Sea" and "The
Queen of the Slaughtering Places". But the preposterous
coincidence of the town being the scene of three of the five
known trunk-murders in Great Britain made "Torso City"
perhaps the most deserved of all.' These horrendous crimes
all involved women whose butchered bodies, one of them
headless, were found stuffed into suitcases.

'The Riddle of the 5.28' by Thomas W. Hanshew
(1857–1914) is among several stories to draw on the

notoriety of the Brighton line, but as it was originally published in 1910 is almost certainly the earliest. It is also notable as being an exploit of Hamilton Cleek, the 'Man of Forty Faces', a notorious cracksman, whose adventures in *Short Stories* magazine in the first quarter of this century earned the reputation of being 'the most consistent and most convincing detective stories since Sherlock Holmes'. For years, in fact, the sales of the magazine whenever Cleek appeared showed the same rise in circulation that Holmes provided for *The Strand*; while the three volumes of short stories – *Cleek of Scotland Yard* (1914), *Cleek's Greatest Riddles* (1916), and *The Riddle of the Mysterious Light* (1921) – sold in huge numbers in both Britain and America. In the USA, the Edison Company produced a long-running series of films about Cleek featuring the famous silent star, Thomas Meighan. What made 'The Vanishing Cracksman', as he was also called, unique was his curiously flexible facial skin which enabled him to contort his features in a variety of ways. He had no need of make-up or disguise: he could simply contort his features into a living mask and outwit the law – especially the men of Scotland Yard. After several years on the wrong side of the law, however, Cleek fell in love, gave up crime, and put his unique capabilities to work as a detective.

Thomas Hanshew, Cleek's creator, was born in New York and as a child wanted to go on the stage, actually making his debut with Ellen Terry. In the late 1870s, however, he abandoned the theatre and instead became associated with the publishers Street & Smith for whom he wrote innumerable dime novels, including many of the Nick Carter novels. Towards the end of the century, Hanshew moved to England and settled in Anerley, on the outskirts of London, close to the main line to Brighton, where he continued to write novels, short stories, plays and film scripts. Despite this success, Hanshew 'acquired several fortunes from his writing, but lost them all through unfortunate investments', according to his obituary in the *New York Dramatic Mirror*. Hamilton Cleek, however, lived on after Hanshew, his cases being continued for several years by his wife, Mary, and then by his daughter, Hazel. 'The Riddle of the 5.28' is, though, by Thomas Hanshew and, as the reader will find, might almost have been written by the author from his study window overlooking the Brighton line.

***

It was exactly thirty-two minutes past five o'clock on the evening of Friday, 8 December when the stationmaster at Anerley – which, no doubt you know, lies but a gunshot from the Crystal Palace on the London, Brighton and South Coast railway – received the following communication by wire from the signal-box at Forest Hill: 'Five twenty-eight down from London Bridge just passed. One first-class compartment in total darkness. Investigate.'

As two stations – Sydenham and Penge – lie between Forest Hill and Anerley, in the ordinary course of events this signal-box message would have been dispatched to one or the other of these. But it so happens that the five twenty-eight from London Bridge to Croydon is a special train, which makes no stop short of Anerley station on the way down; consequently, the signalman had no choice but to act as he did.

Promptly at five forty-two – the scheduled time for its arrival – the train came pelting up the snow-covered metals from Penge, and made its first stop since starting. It was packed to the point of suffocation, as it always is, and in an instant the station was in a state of congestion. Far down the uncovered portion of the platform Webb, the porter, who had now joined the stationmaster, spied a gap in the long line of brightly lit windows, and the pair bore down upon it forthwith, each with a glowing lantern in his hand.

'Here she is – now then, let's see what's the difficulty,' said the stationmaster as they came abreast of the lightless compartment, where, much to his surprise, he found nobody leaning out and making a 'to do' over the matter. 'Looks as if the blessed thing was empty, though that's by no means likely in a packed train like the five twenty-eight. Hullo! door's locked. And here's an "Engaged" label on the window. What the dickens did I do with my key? Oh, here it is. Now, then, let's see what's amiss.'

A great deal was amiss, as he saw the instant he unlocked the door and pulled it open. For the first lifting of the lantern made the cause of the darkness startlingly plain. The shallow glass globe which should have been in the centre of the ceiling had been smashed – ragged fragments of it still clinging to their fastenings – and the three electric bulbs had been removed bodily. A downward glance showed him that both these and the fragments of the broken globe lay on one seat, partly wrapped in a wet cloth, and on the other . . . He gave a jump and a howl and retreated a step or two in a state of absolute panic. For there in a corner, with his face towards the engine, half sat, half leaned the figure of a dead man with a bullet hole between his eyes and a small nickel-plated revolver loosely clasped in the bent fingers of one limp and lifeless hand.

The body was that of a man whose age could not at the most have exceeded eight-and-thirty – a man who must, in life, have been more than ordinarily handsome. His hair and moustache were fair; his clothing was of extreme elegance in both material and fashioning. An evening paper lay between his feet – open, as though it had been read. The body was quite alone in the compartment, and there was not a scrap of luggage of any description.

'Suicide!' gulped the startled stationmaster, as soon as he could find strength to say anything; then he hastily slammed and relocked the door, set Webb on guard before it, and flew to notify the engine driver and to send word to the local police.

The news of the tragedy spread like wildfire, but the stationmaster, who had his wits about him, would allow nobody to leave the station until the authorities had arrived, and suffer no man or woman to come within a yard of the compartment where the dead man lay.

Someone has said that 'nothing comes by chance'; but whether that be true or not, it happened that Mr Maverick Narkom was among those who were standing on the opposite platform waiting for the train to Victoria, which train was to convey Cleek – whom he had promised to join at Anerley – returning from a day spent with Captain Morrison and his daughter in the beautiful home they had bought when the law decided that the captain was the legitimate heir of George Carboys and lawful successor to Abdul ben Meerza's money.

As soon as the news of the tragedy reached him, Mr Narkom crossed to the scene of action and made known his identity. He first looked to see if any name was attached, as is often the case, to the 'Engaged' label secured to the window of the compartment occupied by the dead man. There was. Written in pencil under the blue-printed 'Engaged' were the three words 'For Lord Stavornell'.

'By George!' he exclaimed as he read the name – which was one that half England had heard of at one time or another, and knew to belong to a man whose wild, dissipated life and violent temper had passed into a proverb. 'Come to the end at last, has he? Give me your lantern, porter, and open the door. Let's have a look and see if there's any mistake, or—' The whistle of the arriving train for Victoria cut in upon his words, and, putting the local police in charge, he ran for the tunnel, made for the up platform, and caught Cleek. They returned together.

'Mr George Headland, one of my best men,' he explained to the local inspector, who had just arrived. 'Let us have all the light you can, please. Mr Headland wishes to view the body. Crowd round, the rest of you, and keep the passengers back. Tell the engine driver he'll get his orders in a minute. Now, then, Cl— Headland: decide – it rests with you.'

Cleek opened the door of the compartment, stepped in, gave one glance at the dead man, and then spoke.

'Murder!' he said. 'Look how the pistol lies in his hand. Wait a moment, however, and let me make sure.' Then he took the revolver from the yielding fingers, smelt it, smiled, then 'broke' it and looked at the cylinder. 'Just as I supposed,' he added, turning to Narkom. 'One chamber has been fouled by a shot and one cartridge has been exploded. But not today – not even yesterday. That sour smell tells its own story, Mr Narkom. This revolver was discharged two or three days ago. The assassin had everything prepared for this little event. But he was a fool for all his cleverness, for you will observe that in his haste when he put the revolver in the dead hand to make it appear a case of suicide, he laid it down just as he himself took it from his pocket – with the butt towards the victim's body and the muzzle pointing outward between the thumb and forefinger – and with bottom of the cylinder instead of the top of the trigger touching the ball of the thumb! It is a clear case of murder, Mr Narkom.'

'But, sir,' interposed the stationmaster, overhearing this assertion and looking at Cleek with eyes of blank bewilderment, 'if somebody killed him, where has that "somebody" gone? Both doors were locked and both windows closed when we discovered the body.'

'Get your men to examine all tickets – both in the train and out of it – and if there's one that's not clipped as it passed the barrier at London Bridge, look out for it, and detain the holder,' answered Cleek. 'I'll take the gate here and examine all local tickets. Meantime, wire all up the road to every station from here to London Bridge and find out if any other signalman than the one at Forest Hill noticed this dark compartment when the train went past.'

Both suggestions were acted upon immediately. But every ticket, save, of course, the season tickets (and the holders of these were in every case identified), was found to be properly clipped; and, in the end, every signal-box from New Cross on wired back 'All compartments lighted when train passed here.'

'That narrows the search, Mr Narkom,' said Cleek, when he heard this. 'The lights were put out somewhere between Honor Oak Park and Forest Hill – and, somewhere between Honor Oak Park and Anerley, the murderer made his escape. Inspector' – he turned to the officer in command of the local police – 'do me a favour. Put your men in charge of this carriage and let the train proceed. Norwood Junction is the next station, I believe, and there's a side track there. Have the carriage shunted and keep close guard over it until Mr Narkom and I arrive.'

'Right you are, sir. Anything else?'

'Yes. Have the stationmaster at the junction equip a hand car with a searchlight, and send it here as expeditiously as possible. If anybody or anything has left this train between this point and Honor Oak Park, Mr Narkom, this thin coating of snow will betray the fact beyond the question of a doubt.'

Twenty minutes later the hand car put in an appearance, manned by a couple of linesmen from the junction, and, word having been wired up the line to hold back all trains for a period of half an hour in the interests of Scotland Yard, Cleek and Narkom boarded the vehicle and went whizzing up the metals in the direction of Honor Oak Park, the shifting searchlight sweeping the path from left to right and glaring brilliantly on the surface of the fallen snow.

Four lines of tracks gleamed steel-bright against its spotless level – the two outer ones being those employed by the local trains going to and fro between London and the suburbs, the two inner ones belonging to the main line, but not one footstep indented the thin surface of that broad expanse of snow from one end of the journey to the other.

'The murderer, whoever he is, or wherever he went, never set foot upon so much as one inch of this ground, that's certain,' said Narkom, as he gave the order to reverse the car and return. 'You feel satisfied of that, do you not, my dear fellow?'

'Thoroughly, Mr Narkom – there can't be two opinions upon that point. But at the same time he *did* leave the train, otherwise we should have found him in it.'

'Granted. But the question is, *when* did he get in and *how* did he get out? We know from the evidence of the passengers that the train never stopped for one instant between London Bridge station and Anerley; that all compartments were alight up to the time it passed Honor Oak Park; that nobody aboard of it heard a sound of a pistol shot; that the assassin could not have crept along the footboard and got into some other compartment, for *all* were so densely crowded that half a dozen people were standing in each. My dear chap, are you sure – are you really *sure* that it isn't a case of suicide after all?'

Cleek gave his shoulders a lurch and smiled indulgently.

'My dear Mr Narkom,' he said, 'the position of the revolver in the dead man's hand ought, as I pointed out to you, to settle that question, even if there were no other discrepancies. In the natural order of things, a man who had just put a bullet into his own brain would, if he were sitting erect – as Lord Stavornell *was* – drop the revolver in the spasmodic opening and shutting of the hands in the final convulsion; but, if he retained any sort of a hold upon it, be sure his forefinger would be in the loop of the trigger. Then – if you didn't remark it – there was no scorch of powder upon the face—' He stopped and laid a sharp, quick-shutting hand on the shoulder of one of the two men who were operating the car. 'Turn back!' he exclaimed. 'Reverse the action and go back a dozen yards or so.'

The car slowed down, stopped, and then began to back, scudding along the rail until Cleek again called it to a halt. They were within gunshot of the station at Sydenham when this occurred; the glaring searchlight was still playing on the metals and the thin layer of snow between, and Cleek's face seemed all eyes as he bent over and studied the ground over which they were gliding. Of a sudden, however, he gave a little satisfied grunt, jumped down and picked up a shining metal object about two and a half inches long which lay in the space between the tracks of the main and the local lines. It was a guard's key for the locking and unlocking of compartment doors – one of the small, T-shaped kind that you can buy of almost any ironmonger for sixpence or a shilling any day. It was wet from contact with the snow, but quite unrusted – showing that it had not been lying there long – and it needed but a glance to reveal the fact that it was brand-new and of recent purchase.

He held it out on his palm as he climbed back upon the car and rejoined Narkom.

'Wherever he got on, Mr Narkom, here is where the murderer got off, you see, and either dropped or flung away this key when he had relocked the compartment after him,' he said. 'And yet, as you see, there is not a footstep – beyond those I have myself just made – to be discovered anywhere. From the position in which this key was lying, one thing is certain, however: our man got out on the opposite side from the platform toward which the train was hastening, and in the *middle of the right of way*.'

'What a mad idea! If there had been a main line express passing at the time, the fellow ran the risk of being cut to pieces. About this spot they would be going like the wind.'

'Yes,' said Cleek. 'Going like the wind . . . and the suction would be enormous between two speeding trains. A step outside and he'd have been under the wheels in a wink. Yes; it would have been certain death, instant death, if there had been a main line train passing at the time; and – that he was not sucked down and ground under the wheels, proves that *there wasn't*! Let us get on.'

'Any idea, old chap?'

'Yes – bushels of them. But they all may be exploded in another half-hour.'

'Which means?'

'That I shall leave the hand car at Sydenham, Mr Narkom, and 'phone up to London Bridge station – there are one or two points I wish to ask some questions about. Afterwards, I'll hire a motor from some local garage and join you at Norwood Junction in an hour's time. One question, however: Is my memory at fault, or was it not Lord Stavornell who was mixed up in that little affair with the French dancer, Mademoiselle Fifi de Lesparre, who was such a rage in town about a year ago?'

'Yes; that's the chap,' said Narkom in reply. 'And a rare bad lot he has been all his life, I can tell you. I dare say that Fifi herself was no better than she ought to have been – chucking over her country-bred husband as soon as she came into popularity and had men of the Stavornell class tagging after her – but whether she was or was not, Stavornell broke up that home, and if that French husband had done the right thing, he would have thrashed him within an inch of his life instead of acting like a fool in a play and challenging him. Stavornell laughed at the challenge, of course, and if all that is said of him is true, he was at the bottom of the shabby trick which finally forced the poor devil to get out of the country. When his wife – Fifi – left him, the poor wretch nearly went off his head, and, as he hadn't fifty shillings in the world, he was in a dickens of a pickle when *somebody* induced a lot of milliners, dressmakers, and the like of whom it was said that Fifi owed bills, to put their accounts into the hands of a collecting agency and to proceed against him for settlement of his wife's accounts. That was why he got out of the country post-haste. The case made a great stir at the time, and the scandal of it was so great that, although the fact never got into the papers, Stavornell's wife left him, refusing to live another hour with such a man.'

'Oh, he had a wife, then?'

'Yes. One of the most beautiful women in the kingdom. They had been married only a year when the scandal of the Fifi affair arose. That was another of his dirty tricks – the forcing of that poor creature to marry him.'

'She did so against her will?'

'Yes. She was engaged to another fellow at the time – an army chap who was out in India. Her father, too, was an army man – a Colonel something or other – poor as the proverbial church mouse; addicted to hard drinking, card playing, horse racing, and about as selfish an old brute as they make 'em. The girl took a deep dislike to Lord Stavornell the minute she saw him – knew his reputation, and refused to receive him. That's the very reason he determined to marry her, humble her pride as it were, and repay her for her scorn of him. He got her father into his clutches – deliberately, of course – lent him money, took his IOUs for card debts, and all that sort of thing, until the old brute was up to his ears in debt, and with no prospect of paying it off. Of course, when he'd got him to that point, Stavornell demanded the money, but finally agreed to wipe the debt out entirely if the daughter married him. They went at her, poor creature, those two, with all the mercilessness of a couple of wolves. In the end she gave in; then Stavornell took out a special licence, and they were married. Of course, the man never cared for her; he led her a dog's life.'

'Poor creature!' said Cleek sympathetically. 'And what became of the other chap – the lover out in India?'

'Oh, they say he went on like a madman when he heard it. Swore he'd kill Stavornell, and all that, but quieted down after a time and accepted the inevitable with the best grace possible. Crawford is his name. He was a lieutenant at the time, but he's got his captaincy since, and I believe is on leave and in England at present – as madly and as hopelessly in love with the girl of his heart as ever.'

'Oho!' said Cleek, with a strong rising reflection. 'Then Fifi's husband isn't the only man with a grievance and – a cause? There's another eh?'

'Another? I expect there must be a dozen, if the truth were known. There's only one creature in the world I ever heard of as having a good word to say for the man.'

'And who might that be?'

'The Hon. Mrs Brinkworth, widow of his younger brother. You'd think the man was an angel to hear *her* sing his praises. But I suppose even the devil's got a good spot in him somewhere, if one only knows where to look for it. Evidently the Hon. Mrs Brinkworth does. *Her* husband, too, was a wild sort. Left her up to her ears in debt without a penny to bless herself, and with a boy of five to rear and educate. Stavornell seems always to have liked her. At any rate, he came to the rescue, paid off debts, settled an annuity upon her, and arranged to have the boy sent to Eton as soon as he was old enough. I expect the boy is at the bottom of this good streak in him if all is told; for, having no children of his own – I say! By George, old chap! Why, that nipper – being the heir in the direct line – is Lord Stavornell himself, now that the uncle is dead! A lucky stroke for *him*, by Jupiter!'

'Yes,' agreed Cleek. 'Lucky for him; lucky for Lady Stavornell; lucky for Captain Crawford, and *unlucky* for the Hon. Mrs Brinkworth and Mademoiselle Fifi de Lesparre. So, of course – Sydenham at last. Join you at Norwood Junction as soon as possible, and – I say, Mr Narkom!'

'Yes, old chap?'

'Wire through to the low-level station at Crystal Palace,

will you? and enquire if anybody has mislaid an ironing board or lost an Indian canoe. See you later. So long!'

Then he stepped up on to the station platform and went in quest of a telephone booth.

It was after nine o'clock when he turned up at Norwood Junction as calm, serene and imperturbable as ever, and found Narkom awaiting him in a small private room, which the station clerk had placed at his disposal.

'My dear fellow, I never was so glad!' exclaimed the superintendent, jumping up excitedly as Cleek entered. 'What kept you so long? I've been on thorns. Got bushels to tell you. First off, as Stavornell's identity is established beyond doubt, no time has been lost in writing the news of the murder to his relatives. Both Lady Stavornell and Mrs Brinkworth have wired back that they are coming on. I expect them at any minute now. And – Cleek! Here's a piece of news for you. Fifi's husband is in England. The Hon. Mrs Brinkworth has wired me to that effect. Says she has means of knowing that he came over from France the other day; and that she, herself, saw him in London this morning when she was up there shopping.'

'Oho!' commented Cleek. Then: 'Find anything at the Crystal Palace low level, Mr Narkom?'

'Yes. My dear Cleek, I can't conceive what reason you can have for making such an enquiry, but—'

'Which was it? Canoe or ironing board?'

'Neither, as it happens. But they've got a lady's folding cutting table – you know the sort: one of those that women use for dressmaking operations and which fold up flat so they can be tucked away. Nobody knows who left it, but it's there awaiting an owner, and it was found—'

'Oh, I can guess that,' interposed Cleek nonchalantly. 'It was in a first-class compartment of the five-eighteen from London Bridge, which reached the low level at five forty-three. No, never mind questions for a few minutes, please.

Let's go and have a look at the body. I want to satisfy myself regarding the point of what in the world Stavornell was doing on a suburban train at a time when he ought, properly, to be on his way home to his rooms at the Ritz preparing to dress for dinner; and I want to find out, if possible, what means that chap with the little dark moustache used to get him to go out of town, in his ordinary afternoon dress, and by that particular train.'

'Chap with the small dark moustache? Who do you mean by that?'

'Party that killed him. My 'phone to London Bridge station has cleared the way a bit. It seems that Lord Stavornell engaged that compartment in that particular train by telephone at three o'clock this afternoon. He arrived all alone, and was in no end of a temper because the carriage was dirty, had it swept out, and then the porter says that he found him laughing and talking with a dark-moustached little man – apparently of continental origin – dressed in a Norfolk suit and carrying a brown leather portmanteau. In that portmanteau was an air pistol for one thing: also a mallet or hammer, and that wet cloth we found, both of which were for the purpose of smashing the electric light globe without sound. And he went into that compartment with his victim!'

'Yes, but, man alive, how did he get *out*? Where did he go after that, and what became of the brown leather portmanteau?'

'I hope to be able to answer both questions before this night is over, Mr Narkom. Meantime, let us go and have a look at the body and settle one of the little points that bother me.'

The superintendent led the way to the siding where the shunted carriage stood, and Cleek was soon deep in his examination.

Aided by the better light, he now perceived something which, in the first hurried examination, had escaped him –

or, if it had not (which is, perhaps, open to question), he had made no comment upon it. It was a spot about the size of an ordinary dinner plate on the square of crimson carpet which covered the floor of the compartment. It was slightly darker than the rest of the surface, and was at the foot of the corner seat directly facing the dead man.

'I think we can fairly decide, Mr Narkom, on the evidence of that,' said Cleek, pointing to it, 'that Lord Stavornell did have a companion in this compartment, and that it *was* the little dark man with the false moustache. Put your hand on the spot. Damp, you see – the effect of someone who had walked through the snow sitting down on this particular seat. We've got past the point of "guesswork" now. We've *established* the presence of the second party beyond all question. We also know that he was a person with whom Stavornell felt at ease and was intimate enough with to feel no necessity for putting himself out by entertaining with those little courtesies one is naturally obliged to show a guest.'

'How do you make that out?'

'This newspaper. He was reading at the time he was shot. You can see for yourself where the bullet went through – this hole, here, close to the top of the paper. When a man *invites* another man to occupy with him a compartment which he has engaged and then proceeds to read the news instead of troubling himself to treat his companion as a guest, it is pretty safe to say that they are acquaintances of long standing and upon such terms of intimacy that the social amenities may be dispensed with inoffensively.

'Now look! No powder on the face, no smell of it in the compartment; and yet the pistol found in his hand is an ordinary American-made twenty-eight calibre revolver. We have an amateur assassin to deal with Mr Narkom, not a hardened criminal, and the witlessness of the fellow is enough to bring the case to an end before this night is over. Why didn't he discharge that revolver today and have enough sense to bring a thimbleful of powder to burn in this compartment after the work was done? One knows in an instant that the weapon used was an air pistol. I don't suppose that there are three places in all London that stock air pistols, and I don't suppose that they sell as many as two in a whole year. But if one has been sold or repaired at any of the shops in the past six months – well, Dollops will know that in less than no time. I 'phoned him to make enquiries.'

As he spoke he bent over the dead man and commenced to search the clothing. He slid his hand into the inner pocket of the creaseless morning coat and drew out a pocket notebook and two or three letters. All were addressed in the handwriting of women, but only one seemed to possess any interest for Cleek. It was written on pink notepaper, enclosed in a pink envelope, and was postmarked 'Croydon, 9 December, 2.30 p.m.', and bore those outward marks which betokened its delivery not in course of post, but by express messenger. One instant after Cleek had looked at it he knew he need seek no further for the information he desired.

'Piggy,' it read. 'Stupid boy, the ball of the dress-fancy is not for tomorrow, but tonight; I have made sudden discoverment. Come quick – by the train that shall leave London Bridge at the time of twenty-eight minutes after the hour of five. You shall not fail of this, or it shall make much difficulties for me, as I come to meet it on arrival. Do not bother of the costume – I will have one ready for you. I have one large joke of the somebody else that is coming which will make you scream of the laughter. Burn this. – FIFI.' And, at the bottom of the sheet: 'Do burn this. I have hurt the hand and must use the writing of my maid; and I do not want you to treasure that.'

'There's the explanation, Mr Narkom,' said Cleek as he held the letter out. 'That's why he came by this particular train. There's the snare. That's how he was lured.'

Narkom opened his lips to make some comment upon this, but closed them suddenly and said nothing. For, at that moment, one of the constables put in an appearance with news that 'Two ladies and two gentlemen have arrived, sir, and are asking permission to view the body for purposes of identification. Here are the names, sir, on this slip of paper.'

'Lady Stavornell, Colonel Murchison, Hon. Mrs Brinkworth, Captain James Crawford,' Narkom read aloud; then looked up enquiringly at Cleek.

'Yes,' he said. 'Let them come.'

Then he stood looking up at the shattered globe and rubbing his chin between his thumb and forefinger and wrinkling up his brows after the manner of a man who is trying to solve a problem in mental arithmetic. And Narkom – unwise in that direction for once – chose to interrupt his thoughts, for no greater reason than that he had thrice heard him mutter 'Suction – displacement – resistance.'

'Working out a problem, old chap?' he ventured. 'Can I help you? I used to be rather good at that sort of thing.'

'Were you?' said Cleek a trifle testily. 'Then tell me something: combating a suction power of about two pounds to the square inch, how much wind does it take to make a cutting table fly, with an unknown weight upon it, from the Sydenham switch to the Low Level station? When you've worked that out, you've got the murderer. And when you do get him – well, he won't be any man you ever saw or ever heard of in all the days of your life! But he will be light enough to hop like a bird, heavy enough to pull up a wire rope with about three hundred pounds on the end of it, and – there will be two holes of about an inch in diameter and a foot apart in one end of the table that flew.'

'My dear chap!' began Narkom in tones of blank bewilderment, then stopped suddenly and screwed round on his heel. For a familiar voice had sung out suddenly a yard or two distant – 'Ah, keep yer 'air on! Don't get to thinkin' you're Niagara Falls, just because yer got water on the brain!' And there, struggling in the grip of a constable, who had laid strong hands upon him, stood Dollops, with a kit-bag in one hand and a half-devoured bath bun in the other.

'All right there, constable – let the boy pass. He's one of us!' rapped out Cleek; and in an instant the detaining hand fell, and Dollops's chest went out like a pouter pigeon's.

'Catch on to that, *Suburbs?*' said he, giving the constable a look of blighting scorn and swaggering by like a mighty conqueror. 'Nailed it at the second rap, guv'ner,' he added in an undertone to Cleek. 'Fell down on Gamage's, picked myself up on Loader, Tottenham Court Road. Fourteen, twelve, seven, a – manufactured Stockholm. Valve tightened – old customer – day before yesterday in the afternoon.'

'Good boy! good boy!' said Cleek, patting him approvingly. 'Keep your tongue between your teeth. Scuttle off and find out where there's a garage, and then wait outside the station till I come.'

'Right you are, sir,' responded Dollops, bolting the remainder of the bun; then he ducked down and slipped away; and Cleek, stepping back into the shadow where his features might not be too clearly seen until he was ready that they should be, stood and watched narrowly the small procession which was being piloted to the scene of the tragedy. A moment later the four persons already announced passed under Cleek's watchful eye, and stood in the dead man's presence.

A moment he stood there silent – watching, listening, making neither movement nor sound – then of a sudden he put forth his hand and tapped Narkom's arm.

'Detain this party – every member of it – by any means – on any pretext, for another forty-five minutes,' he whispered. 'In three quarters of an hour the murderer will be here on this spot with me!' Then he screwed round on his heel and, before Narkom could speak, was gone: soundlessly and completely gone – just as he used to go in his vanishing cracksman's days – leaving just that promise behind him.

It wanted but thirteen minutes of being midnight when the gathering about the siding where the shunted carriage containing the body of the murdered man still stood received something in the nature of a shock when, on glancing round as a sharp whistle shrilled a warning note, they saw an engine, attached to one solitary carriage, backing along the metals and bearing down upon them.

'I say, Mr Knockem or Narkhim or whatever your name is,' blurted out Colonel Murchison, as he hastily caught the Hon. Mrs Brinkworth by the arm and whisked her back from the metals, leaving his daughter to be looked after by Captain Crawford, 'look out for your blessed bobbies. Somebody's shunting another coach in on top of us; and if the ass doesn't look what he's doing . . . There! I told you!' – as the coach in question settled with a slight jar against that containing the body of Lord Stavornell. 'Of all the blundering, pig-headed fools! Might have killed some of us. What next, I wonder?'

What next, as a matter of fact, gave him cause for even greater wonder; for, as the two carriages met, the door of the last compartment in the one which had just arrived opened briskly, and out of it stepped: first, a couple of uniformed policemen; next, a ginger-haired youth with a kit-bag in one hand and a saveloy in the other; then the trim figure of the lady who had so long and popularly been known in the music-hall world as Mlle Fifi de Lesparre, and last of all— 'Cleek!' blurted out Narkom, overcome with amazement, as he saw the serenely alighting figure. And 'Cleek?' went in a little rippling murmur throughout the entire gathering – civilians and local police alike.

'All right, Mr Narkom,' said Cleek himself, with a slight shrug of the shoulders. 'Even the best of us slip up sometimes; and since everybody knows now – well, we'll have to make the best of it. Gentlemen – ladies – you, too, my colleagues: my best respects. Now to business.' Then he stepped out of the shadow in which he had alighted into the full glow of the lanterns and the flare which had been lit close to the door of the dead man's carriage, conscious that every eye was fixed upon his face and that the members of the local force were silently and breathlessly 'spotting' him. But in that moment the weird birth-gift had been put into practice; and Narkom fetched a sort of sigh of relief as he saw that a sagging eyelid, a twisted lip, a queer blurred *something* about all the features, had set upon that face a living mask that hid effectually the face he knew too well.

'To business?' he repeated. 'Ah, yes, quite so, my dear Cleek. Shall I tell the ladies and gentlemen of your promise? Well, listen. Mr Cleek is more than a quarter of an hour beyond the time he set, but – he gave me his word that this riddle would be solved tonight – tonight, ladies and gentlemen – and that when I saw him here the murderer would be with him.'

'Oh, bless him! bless him!' burst forth Mrs Brinkworth impulsively. 'And he brings her – that wicked woman! Oh, I knew that she had something to do with it – I knew – I knew!'

'Your pardon, Mrs Brinkworth, but for once your woman's intuition is at fault,' said Cleek quietly. 'Mademoiselle Fifi is not here as a prisoner, but as a witness for the Crown. She has had nothing even in the remotest to do wtih the crime. Her name was used to trap Lord Stavornell to his death, but the lady is here to prove that she never heard of the note which was found on Lord Stavornell's body; to prove also that, although it is true she did expect to go to a fancy dress ball with his lordship, that fancy dress ball does not occur until next Friday, the sixteenth inst. –

not the ninth; and that she never even heard of any alteration in the date.'

'Ah, non! non! non! nevaire – I do swear!' chimed in Fifi herself, almost hysterical with fright. 'I know nossing – nossing!'

'That is true,' said Cleek quietly. 'There is not any question of Mademoiselle Fifi's complete innocence of any connection with this murder.'

'Then her husband?' ventured Captain Crawford agitatedly.

'It so happens that I know for a certainty M. Philippe de Lesparre had no more to do with it than did his wife.'

'But, my dear sir,' interposed the colonel. 'The – er – foreign person at the station – the little slim man in the Norfolk suit – the fellow with the little dark moustache? What of him?'

'A great deal of him. But – well, that the little dark man is a little dark fiction; in other words, he does not and never did exist!'

'What's that?' fairly gasped Narkom. 'Never existed? But, my dear Cleek, you told me that the porter at London Bridge saw him, and—'

'I told you what the porter told me – what the porter thought he saw, and what we shall, no doubt, find out in time at least fifty other people thought they saw, and what was, doubtless, the "good joke" alluded to in the forged note. The only man against whom we need direct our attention, the only man who had any hand in this murder, is a big, burly, strong-armed one like Colonel Murchison here.'

'What's that?' roared out the Colonel furiously. 'By the Lord Harry, do you dare to assert that I – I, sir, killed the man?'

'No, I do not. And for the best of reasons. You never put foot aboard the five twenty-eight from the moment it started to the one in which it stopped. And at that final moment, Colonel' – he reached round, took something from his pocket, and then held it out on the palm of his hand – 'at that final moment, Colonel, you were passing the barrier at the Crystal Palace Low Level with a lady whose ticket from London Bridge had never been clipped and with this air pistol, which she had restored to you, in your coat pocket!'

'W-w-what crazy nonsense is this, sir? I never saw the blessed thing in all my life.'

'Oh, yes, Colonel. Loader, of Tottenham Court Road, repaired the valve for you the day before yesterday, and I found it in your room just— Quick! nab him, Petrie! Well played! After the king, the trump – after the confederate the assassin! And so—' He sprang suddenly, like a jumping cat; there was a click of steel, a shrill, despairing cry, then the rustle of something falling; and when Captain Crawford and Lady Stavornell turned and looked he was standing, with both hands on his hips, looking frowningly down on the spot where the Hon. Mrs Brinkworth lay, curled up in a limp, unconscious heap with a pair of handcuffs locked on her folded wrists.

'I said that when the murderer was found, Mr Narkom,' he said as the superintendent moved toward him, 'that it would be no man you ever saw or ever heard of in all your life. I knew it was a woman from the bungling, unmanlike way that pistol was laid in the dead hand; the only question I had to answer was which woman – Fifi, Lady Stavornell, or this wretched little hypocrite. Here's your "little dark man" – here's the assassin. She made Stavornell think that she, too, was going to the fancy ball, and that the surprise Fifi had planned was for her to meet him as she did and travel with him. When the train was under way she shot him. Why? Easily explained, my dear chap. His death made her little son heir to the estates; during his minority she would have the handling of the funds; with them she and her precious husband would have a gay life of it in their own selfish little way!'

'Her what? Lord, man, do you mean to say that she and the Colonel—'

'Were privately married seven weeks ago, Mr Narkom. The certificate of their union was tucked away in Colonel Murchison's private effects, where it was found this evening.'

'How was the escape from the compartment managed after the murder was accomplished?' said Cleek, answering Narkom's query, as they whizzed home through the darkness together by the last up train that night. 'Simplest thing in the world, sir. As you know, the five twenty-eight from London Bridge runs without stop to Anerley. Well, the five-eighteen from the same starting point runs to the Crystal Palace Low Level, taking the main line tracks as far as Sydenham, where it branches off at the switch and curves completely away in an opposite direction. That is to say, for a considerable distance they run parallel, but eventually diverge. Now, as the five-eighteen is a way train with several stops, the five twenty-eight, being a through one, overtakes her, and several times between Brockley and Sydenham they run side by side – at so steady a pace and on such a narrow gauge that the footboard running along the side of the one train is not more than two and a half feet separated from the other. Their pace is so regular, their progress so even, that one could with ease step from the footboard of the one to the footboard of the other but for the horrible suction which would inevitably draw the person attempting it down under the wheels. Well, something had to be devised to overcome the danger of that suction. But what? I asked myself; for I guessed from the first how the escape had occurred, and I knew that such a thing absolutely required the assistance of a confederate. That meant that that confederate would have to do on the five-eighteen exactly what they had trapped Stavornell into doing on the other train – that is, secure a private compartment, so that when the time came for the escape to be accomplished he could remove the electric bulbs from the roof of his compartment, open the door, and when the two came abreast the assassin could do the same on the other train, and presto! the dead man would be alone. But what to use to overcome the danger of that horrible suction?'

'Ah! I see now what you were driving at when you enquired about the ironing board or the Indian canoe. The necessary sections to construct a sort of bridge could be packed in either?'

'Yes. But they chose a simpler plan – the cutting table. A good move that. Its breadth minimised the peril of the suction; only, of course, it would have to be pulled up afterwards (to leave no clue), and the added space would call for enormous strength to overcome the power of that suction: and enormous strength meant a powerful man. The rest you can put together without being told, Mr Narkom. When that little vixen finished her man she put out the lights, opened the door (deliberately locking it after her to make the thing more baffling), crossed over on that table, was helped into the other compartment by Murchison, and then as expeditiously as possible slipped on the loose feminine outer garments she carried with her in the brown portmanteau; the table was hauled up and taken in (nothing but wire rope for that, sir), and the thing was done. Murchison, of course, purchased two tickets, so that they might pass the barrier at the Low Level unquestioned when they left; but he wasn't able to get the extra ticket clipped at London Bridge because there was no passenger for it. That's how I got on to the little game! For the rest, they planned well. Those two trains being always packed, nobody could see the escape from the one to the other, because people would be standing up in every compartment and the windows completely blocked. But if— Hullo! Victoria at last, thank goodness; "and so to bed," as Pepys says. The riddle's solved, Mr Narkom. Good night.'

Headhunter

JAN CAROL SABIN

The Long Island Railroad from New York is one of the oldest, busiest and most crowded tracks in America. Each day it carries many thousands of commuters from several dozen suburban stations along the island to the heart of Manhattan. It is also one of the most notorious lines in America, for over the years it has been the setting for a large number of crimes, a great many acts of violence and as many as thirty murders. But all of these paled into insignificance on the evening of 8 December 1993 when a young man climbed aboard the packed 5.33 p.m. train at Penn Central bound for Port Jefferson and half an hour later took a 9mm semi-automatic pistol from his bag and proceeded to randomly shoot and kill commuters. Most of the passengers on the rush-hour train were wearily finishing reading their evening papers or asleep as the train wound across suburban Long Island when 'the massacre', as it was later described, took place. The gunman began calmly shooting just as the train approached Merillon Avenue station in Nassau County and he killed five people and injured eighteen more before three commuters managed to struggle through the chaos and bloodshed to overpower him. Police later found over 100 rounds of ammunition in the man's bag. The multiple murders so horrified America that, within days, it prompted President Clinton to launch a drive for tougher new gun controls.

With a reputation such as this, the Long Island Railroad has not surprisingly been featured in a number of novels and short stories, but perhaps nowhere with quite such a sense of tension and unease as in this next tale, first published in the February 1994 issue of America's premier crime fiction monthly *Ellery Queen's Mystery Magazine*. (Murder-on-the-rails stories were, in fact, nothing new to Queen who had earlier written a highly praised novel *The Tragedy of X* (1932) as well as a short story of skulduggery on a train, 'The Black Ledger', in 1954.) The author of 'Headhunter', Jan Carol Sabin (1952–), was for a number of years a resident of New York and regularly travelled on the Long Island Railroad during the rush hour and sometimes late at night, which gives her story an added dimension of authenticity. In 1980, however, she moved to Florida to continue her career in the entertainment business and there also began writing crime stories for *EQMM* – although it may come as a shock to some readers of 'Headhunter' to learn that Sabin is actually better known as a humorist and for her appearances on stage and TV as a comedienne! There is certainly nothing to laugh about in this story of a serial killer at loose on the Long Island Railroad, especially not its chilling finale.

***

She whispered. He listened. The shabbily dressed bag lady watched them out of the corner of her eye. They were completely oblivious of her. Only once did the young woman glance at her with penetrating eyes then went back to her conversation with her companion.

The well-dressed man entered the train-station waiting-room. He looked at the three people and took a seat. The small room was drafty and the howling night wind pierced the cracks. He drew his overcoat more snugly about him. The couple never glanced his way. The old woman adjusted her torn gloves and looked him over. He hoped she wasn't going to beg money from him. He unfolded the newspaper he had under his arm. Get engrossed in it, he told himself, and he would be left alone.

He read the first page and opened the paper up in front of him, completely absorbed in the story behind the headlines. The young woman glanced over at the crackling of the newspaper being opened. The headline caught her eye. The old woman followed her gaze to the paper: THIRD HEAD-LESS BODY FOUND.

The man behind the paper was appalled by the story of a maniac beheading his third victim in two months. One man and two women decapitated, and their heads never found. Their bodies were found in different locations along the Long Island Railroad tracks. The man noted that each one had left home to travel by train into New York City and had departed late at night from small stations on Long Island such as – this one.

The man finished the story, closed the newspaper, and laid it on the bench next to him. He then looked up at the ashen face of the young woman. Her eyes were fixed on the paper. The young man next to her was staring at him. It was then he noticed the large cooler sitting on the floor next to the couple. His curiosity was aroused. He hadn't seen anyone at this bleak time of year carrying a cooler into the city.

'Going to a party?' he asked. He looked at the cooler and then at the young man, who continued to stare at him, emotionless. 'Cold beer in March?' He smiled and shivered.

The young man said nothing and never acknowledged that he had even heard him. A smile played about the corners of the young woman's lips. She leaned forward.

'I wish,' she said. 'I'm afraid it's only loaded with food sent home with me by my mother. She lives in fear that I'm starving to death as a model in the city. Her weekly trip to my apartment brings the home-baked goods.'

The man smiled. He now noticed her fine features and

deep-set eyes. She was lovely. Perhaps, he thought, her companion was her live-in lover. He wondered if she would ever consider dating an older man, a stockbroker, like himself.

The bag lady moved her things close to herself. She rooted down into an overflowing bag of clothes. The man looked at the bag. It had plastic sticking out around the top. It looked as if she had it lined with a plastic garbage bag. He smiled, thinking of the commercial guaranteeing it not to pull apart, imagining the old woman endorsing it with a toothless grin, instead of the soft smile of the attractive model across from him.

'May I see your paper?' asked the young woman. 'It's a wonder my mother didn't make my father stay here with me after that headline.' Her long fingers nervously tapped her face.

The man smiled. He thought about saying something about her mother knowing she had an escort, but maybe they didn't know he was with her. As he leaned across the small aisle and handed the paper to the woman, he looked at the man beside her.

The young man was well built. He wore faded jeans, a worn jacket, and workman's shoes. His blond hair needed a good haircut and there was a stubble of beard on his face. The woman was well groomed, dressed in designer clothes: black loose-fitting jogging pants zipped up at the ankles, a heavy, multicolured jacket, and his brand of tennis shoes – expensive. The young man wasn't in her class.

She read for a few minutes and looked up. He saw her glance nervously at the man next to her. She stood and came over to sit next to the older man. She handed him the paper.

'I can't believe there are no clues,' she said. 'They all rode trains. You would think there would be a police officer stationed here at night. What do you think?'

'I would think so too.' He didn't want to disagree with

her. His ex-wife said he always took opposite sides with everything anyone said to him. He was like that – she had said.

'All the victims were found on the tracks near a train station,' she said. 'An officer should be here, right?'

'Exactly,' he said, and smiled at her.

'I'm worried about my father,' she said quietly. 'He has a heart condition. I just thought that maybe he wasn't feeling well, and that's why he didn't wait with me. There's a phone booth outside. I think I'll call home. I've this . . . funny feeling.'

She looked at the bag lady and leaned close to him. 'I slipped my purse in the cooler when she came in. Would you watch it?' She smiled slightly. 'And once in a while look outside to make sure I'm safe?'

He nodded and watched her go outside. A moment later she opened the door and called to him. 'I forgot I've no change. Do you have any? I live so close, I should really go home.'

The older man searched his coat pocket and found some change. He stood and brought it over to her. He held out the palm of his hand to her. She took the change, and his hand tingled from her touch. She leaned close and whispered.

'I really don't know the man sitting next to me. He arrived when I did. He helped my father bring in my mom's cooler. Now he makes me nervous.' She smiled weakly and went back out.

As the man turned to walk back, the old lady started shuffling through her bag. He knew she had been watching them. He glanced at her as he walked past. Something caught his eye in the bag. It was the rounded end of a club sticking out of the clothing. He pretended he hadn't noticed.

He sat where he could watch the young woman outside. The young man was staring hard at him with a look of contempt. There was no mistaking it. His heart pounded. He wondered what he would do if the young man decided to go outside. He knew he was no match for him. Then the blond man stood and looked towards the door. Through the glass window in the door, they both saw the woman leave the booth.

The young man moved quickly. He was out the door and almost reached the woman, but she dashed back into the booth and closed the door. The phone-booth light shone on her as she desperately pressed her hands against the door, trying to hold it against the intruder. The girl looked frantically towards the train station. The older man broke into a cold sweat. The bag lady was just sitting and staring at the couple.

He took advantage of the bag lady looking outside. He moved quietly, reached down into her bag, and pulled the club out. He held the club behind him as he ran outside.

'Getting excited, Pop?' the young man said, looking at him. 'Want a piece of the action, or do you just want to watch?' He laughed sarcastically and turned back to push on the door.

There was the sound of a thud as the club caught the young man on the head. He groaned and fell. The man dropped the club. 'Oh God,' he said, 'let me not have killed him.'

Then the woman was at his side, grabbing on to his arm. 'I was so scared.' Her voice quivered. 'Is he dead?'

'No, thank goodness. He just moved.'

She began trembling. 'Please, let's get out of here and get the police.'

'You phone the police, and I'll watch him.'

'I can't,' she cried. 'Something is wrong with the phone. I couldn't get a dial tone. We have to get away from here.'

He looked at the station door. Through the glass he saw the bag lady watching them. A cold shiver ran through him. The man on the ground began to moan.

'How close do you live from here?' he asked.

'Our house is across the tracks,' she said. 'But I have to get Mom's cooler. I slipped my wallet under the packages. Oh no, he's moving!'

He looked down. The man on the ground rolled on his side, moaning, and his jacket opened. There was a leather sheath on his belt. 'He's carrying a knife. You head for your house. I'll get the cooler and follow. Hurry!'

The girl gasped and ran. He watched her go past the platform and start across the tracks. He hurried into the station, lifted the heavy cooler, and headed past the bag lady. He turned at the door and looked back at her. She stood tall and straight. She seemed to transform before him. And her eyes . . . They weren't the eyes of an old lady. They were alert, cold and bright. Now he knew the truth.

He ran in the direction the young woman had gone. He knew without looking back that he was being pursued. He crossed the tracks. The woman was waiting anxiously for him.

'I was so worried. Thank goodness you're safe,' she said.

'We can't stop,' he said. 'We have to keep going.'

'Let me help carry the cooler,' she said, grabbing one handle. Before he could protest, the lid swung off and she bent down. As she stood a shot rang out, and the girl dropped. He turned and froze at the sight of the figure in the middle of the tracks. In the moonlight he could see the bag lady clearly, standing there holding a gun, and it was pointing at him.

'Steady, mister,' said the bag lady in a deep voice. 'Stand still. Now look down at the woman.'

Numbly he followed the instructions. The young woman was lying still. He knew she was dead. The front of her jacket was soaked with blood. He felt sick inside. Then he saw the large knife in her hand. He stared dumbfounded at it.

'I don't understand,' he stammered.

'That's a machete in her hand, and you just missed being decapitated. She pulled it out of the cooler before I fired. She was so intent on killing you, she never saw me.'

The man stood there in the cold wind and watched the bag lady shed her tattered clothes to reveal a masculine body in a sweater and jeans. It was as he had suspected in the station. The bag lady was a man, only now he was showing him a shield.

'I'm Detective Zimbrosky of the Suffolk County Special Investigation Task Force. We've been covering five railroad stations, waiting for this vicious killer's next attack. My partner is phoning it in now. He was hiding near the booth.'

'I don't understand . . . What about her father?'

'There was no father. She arrived with the cooler alone. The blond guy, a drifter, came in later. I heard them whispering. She made a big play for him before you arrived, that's why he went after her. She counted on you to rescue her. She knew the drifter and bag lady – me – would take off at the first sign of police. No witnesses.'

'Why did she do it? Why me and those other people?'

'What the paper didn't say was that expensive jewellery had been taken from each victim, like your ring and watch, plus their wallets with all those credit cards. Like yours.'

'Why the . . . heads?' He had to ask it.

'No head, no wallet, takes longer to identify. But I suspect with her, it could have been an added thrill.'

'What do you think happened to the – heads?'

The detective bent down and examined the large cooler. 'I heard her whispering to the young man that he should see her sculptures. We have, weighing down this cooler, a box of plaster of Paris and a container of water. Mix it, and it hardens fast . . . I imagine she did nice work with her long fingers.'

Escape to Danger

ERLE STANLEY GARDNER

The development of the railways since the middle of the nineteenth century has also resulted in the emergence of the long-distance commuter. The old, relatively short lines like those between London and Brighton, New York and Long Island, soon proved to be just the stepping-stones towards nationwide rail networks which made it possible for passengers to travel huge distances. This was especially true in America where the early lines that sprang up on the eastern seaboard in the middle of the last century had by the end of it been expanded to link every corner of the USA. One of the great innovations that made long-distance travel in the States not only possible but enjoyable was the invention of the Pullman carriage which made its maiden trip in May 1870 on the transcontinental train from Boston via the Rocky Mountains to San Francisco. Created by George Mortimer Pullman, these carriages contained sleeping berths, a dining car and bar, and comfortable seating – all aimed at 'promoting the ease of passengers', to quote a contemporary advertisement. Soon the Pullman was being introduced on to the railways in Britain, Europe and the rest of the world, making city dwellers everywhere feel they could now travel as easily for business as for pleasure. As one commuter journeying from Boston to New York observed just over one hundred years ago, 'Now all America is our home.'

The next two stories are both about long-distance travel in the USA where crime and death are fellow passengers.

Erle Stanley Gardner (1889–1970) needs very little introduction to crime aficionados for he is widely recognised as
one of the biggest selling writers of all time in the genre.
What is less well known is that he spent a lot of his
childhood on trains due to the fact that his father was a
mining engineer who was often on the move all over the
country to places like the Klondike, Oregon and California. Gardner himself took up the study of the law and after
qualifying in 1911 became a legal counsel in Oxnard,
California where he rapidly earned celebrity status for his
successful defence of a number of underprivileged people
engaged in disputes with authority and the business
community. In his spare time, Gardner also started to write
crime stories and by the early twenties was selling regularly
to the popular 'pulp' magazines under a variety of pen-
names. The old steam locomotives of his childhood
featured in several of these tales including 'Track to
Murder' (1924), 'Smokestack Revenge' (1927) and 'Death
to the Railroad Boss!' (1930). Having learned his craft in
the short story form, Gardner switched to novels and
enjoyed an immediate success with *The Case of the Velvet
Claws* (1933) which introduced Perry Mason, who is now
after eighty novels and innumerable films and TV series
probably the most famous lawyer in crime fiction. Despite
the success of Perry Mason, Gardner continued to write
short stories, at least three with railroad settings: 'Death
Rides a Boxcar' (1948), 'Round Trip to Murder' (1955)
and 'Escape to Death' (1960), which I have selected for
reprinting here. It is an example of Erle Stanley Gardner at
the top of his form as he describes the tense railway journey
of a young woman who has danger not only ahead of her
but also riding close beside in the train's club car.

* * *

Only once before had the woman in the club car ever known panic – not fear, but the real panic which paralyses the senses. That had been in the mountains, when she had tried to take a short cut back to camp and had realised she was lost. Now, surrounded by the luxury of a crack transcontinental train, she again experienced that same panic. Once more she felt an overpowering desire to run.

Someone had searched her compartment while she had been at dinner. She knew it was a man. He had tried to leave things just as he had found them, but there were little things that only a woman would have noticed. Her plaid coat in the little steel closet had been turned so the buttons faced the door, instead of away from it. A detail, but a significant one which had left her, for the moment, cold and numb. Now, seated in the club car, she strove to maintain an attitude of outward calm. Actually she was taking stock of the men who were in the car.

Her problem was complicated by the fact that she was a compactly formed young woman, with smooth lines, clear eyes and a complete quota of curves. It was only natural that every male animal in the club car should sit up and take notice.

The fat man across the aisle who held a magazine in his pudgy hands was not reading. He sat like a Buddha, motionless, his half-closed, lazy-lidded eyes fixed upon some imaginary horizon far beyond the confines of the car – yet she felt those eyes were taking a surreptitious interest in everything she did. There was something sinister about him, from the big diamond on the middle finger of his right hand to his ornate cravat.

Then there was the man in the chair on her right. He hadn't spoken to her but she knew that he was going to, waiting only for an opportunity to make his remark sound like a casual comment.

He was in his late twenties, bronzed by exposure, with

steely-blue eyes. His mouth held the firmness of a man who has learned to command first himself and then others. The train lurched. The man's hand reached for the glass on the little table between them. He glanced apprehensively at her skirt.

'Sorry,' he said.

'It didn't spill,' she replied, almost automatically.

'I'll lower the danger point,' he said, raising the glass to his lips. 'Going all the way through? I'm getting off at six o'clock on a cold Wyoming morning.'

For a moment her panic-numbered brain failed to grasp the significance of his remark. Then she felt a sudden surge of relief. Here, surely, was one man she could trust. She knew that the man who had searched her baggage hadn't found what he wanted because she had it with her, neatly folded, fastened to the bottom of her left foot by strong adhesive tape. Therefore the enemy would stay on the train as long as she did, waiting, watching, growing more and more desperate, until at last, perhaps in the dead of night . . . She knew only too well that he would stop at nothing. One murder had already been committed.

But now she had found one person whom she could trust, a man who had no interest in the thing she was hiding.

He seemed mildly surprised at her sudden friendliness.

'I didn't know this train stopped anywhere at that ungodly hour,' she ventured, smiling.

'A flag stop,' he explained.

Across the aisle, the fat man had not moved a muscle, yet she felt absolutely certain that those glittering eyes were concentrating on her and that he was listening as well as watching.

'You live in Wyoming?' she asked.

'I did as a boy. Now I'm going back. I lived and worked on my uncle's cattle ranch. He died and left it to me. At first I thought I'd sell it. It would bring a small fortune. But now

I'm tired of the big cities; I'm going back to live on the ranch.'

'Won't it be frightfully lonely?'

She wanted to cling to him now, dreading the time when she would have to go back to her compartment.

She felt the train officials must have a master key which could open even a bolted door – in the event of sickness, or if a passenger rang for help. There *must* be a master key which would manipulate even a bolted door. And if the officials had one, so would the man who had searched her compartment.

Frank Hardwick, before he died, had warned her. 'Remember,' he had said, 'they're everywhere. They're watching you when you don't know it. When you think you're running away to safety, you'll simply be rushing into a carefully laid trap.'

She hoped there was no trace of the tension within her. 'Do tell me about the cattle business,' she said . . .

All night she'd crouched in her compartment, watching the door, waiting for that first flicker of tell-tale motion which would show the doorknob was being turned. She was ready to scream, pound on the walls of the compartment, make sufficient commotion to spread an alarm.

Nothing had happened. Probably that was the way 'they' had planned it. They'd let her spend one sleepless night; then, when fatigue had numbed her senses . . .

The train slowed abruptly. She glanced at her wrist-watch, saw that is was 5.55, and knew the train was stopping for the man who had inherited the cattle ranch. Howard Kane, twenty-eight, unmarried, presumably wealthy, his mind scarred by battle experiences, seeking the healing quality of the big, silent places; the one man she could trust.

There was a quiet competency about him, one felt he

could handle any situation – and now he was getting off the train, walking out of her life when she most needed him.

Suddenly a thought gripped her . . . 'They' would hardly be expecting her to take the initiative. 'They' always kept the initiative, and that was why they always seemed so damnably efficient, so utterly invincible. They chose the time, the place and the manner, and with that advantage . . .

There wasn't time to reason the thing out. She jerked open the door of the little closet, whipped out her plaid coat, turned the fur collar up around her neck and, as the train eased to a creaking stop, opened the door of her compartment and thrust out a cautious head.

The corridor was deserted. She could hear the vestibule door being opened at the far end of the Pullman.

She ran to the opposite end of the car, fumbled for a moment with the fastenings of the vestibule door on the side next to the double track and got it open.

Cold morning air, tanged with high elevation, rushed in to meet her, dispelling the train atmosphere, stealing the warmth from her garments. The train started to move. She scrambled down to the step and jumped for the gravelled roadbed by the side of the track.

The train gathered speed. Dark, silent cars slid past her with continuing acceleration until the noise of the wheels became a mere hum. The steel rails gave cracking sounds of protest. Overhead, stars blazed in steady brilliance. To the east was the first trace of daylight.

She looked for a town. There was none.

She could make out the faint outlines of a loading corral and cattle chute. Somewhere behind her was a road. There was a car standing on it, the motor running. Headlights knifed the darkness, etching into brilliance the stunted sagebrush shivering in the cold north wind.

Two men were talking. A door slammed. She started running frantically.

'Wait!' she called. 'Wait for me!'

Back on the train, the fat man, fully dressed and shaved, contemplated the open vestibule door, then padded back to the recently vacated compartment and walked in.

He didn't even bother to search the baggage that had been left behind. Instead he sat down in the chair, held a telegraph blank against a magazine, and wrote out his message:

THE BUNGLING SEARCH TRICK DID THE JOB. SHE'S LEFT
THE TRAIN. IT ONLY REMAINS TO CLOSE THE TRAP. I'LL
GET OFF AT THE FIRST PLACE WHERE I CAN RENT A PLANE
AND CONTACT THE SHERIFF.

Ten minutes later the fat man found the porter. 'I find the elevation bothering me,' he said. 'I'm going to have to leave the train. Get the conductor.'

'You won't get no lower by gettin' off,' the porter said.

'No, but I'll at least get fresh air and a doctor who'll give me a heart stimulant. I've been this way before. Get the conductor.'

This time the porter saw the twenty-dollar bill in the fat man's fingers.

Seated between the two men in the warm interior of the car, she tried to concoct a convincing story.

Howard Kane said, by way of introduction, 'This is Buck Doxey – I'm afraid I didn't catch your name last night.'

'Nell Lindsay,' she said quickly.

Buck Doxey, granite-faced, kept one hand on the steering-wheel while he doffed a five-gallon hat. 'Pleased to meet yuh, ma'am.'

She sensed his tight-lipped disapproval.

Howard Kane gently prodded for an explanation.

'It was a simple case of cause and effect,' she said, laughing nervously. 'The compartment was so stuffy I couldn't sleep. So I decided I'd get out for a breath of fresh air. When the train slowed and I looked at my wristwatch I knew it was your stop and . . . well, I expected the train would be there for at least a few minutes. I couldn't find a porter to open the door, so I did it myself, and jumped. That was where I made my mistake.'

'Go on,' he said.

'At a station you step down to a platform that's level with the train. But here I jumped on to a slanting shoulder of gravel, and sprawled flat. When I got up, the step of the train was so far above me . . . Well, you have to wear a tight skirt to understand what I mean.'

Kane nodded gravely. Buck turned his head and gave Kane a quartering glance.

She said, 'Just then the train started to move. Good heavens, they must have *thrown* you off!'

'I'm travelling light,' Kane said.

'Well,' she told him, 'that's the story. Now just what do I do?'

'Why, you accept our hospitality, of course.'

'I couldn't . . . couldn't I wait here for the next train?'

'Nothing stops here except to discharge passengers coming from a division point,' he said.

'But there's a . . . station here. Isn't someone on duty?'

'Only when cattle are being shipped,' Buck Doxey explained. 'This is a loading point.'

'Oh.'

She settled back against the seat, and was conscious of a reassuring masculine friendship on her right side, a cold detachment on her left.

'I suppose it's horribly ravenous of me, but do we get to the ranch for breakfast?'

'I'm afraid not,' Kane said. 'It's slow going. Only sixty feet of the road is paved.'

'Sixty feet?'

'That's right. We cross the main transcontinental high-way about five miles north of here.'

'What *do* we do about breakfast?'

'In the trunk of the car,' Kane said, 'there's a coffee pot and a canteen of water. I'm quite certain Buck brought along a few eggs and some ham . . .'

She gave him her best smile. 'Would it be impertinent to ask when?'

'In this next coulée . . . right here . . . right now.'

The road slanted down to a dry wash that ran east and west. The perpendicular north bank broke the force of the wind and Buck stopped the car squarely in the ruts.

They watched the sun rise over the plateau country, and ate breakfast. She hoped that Buck Doxey's continued disapproval wouldn't communicate itself to Howard Kane.

When Buck produced a battered washing bowl, she said, 'As the only woman present, I claim the right to do the dishes.'

'Women—' Buck began and abruptly checked himself.

She laughingly pushed him aside and rolled up her sleeves.

As she was finishing she heard the motor of a low-flying plane. All three looked up. The plane, which had been following the badly rutted road, banked into a sharp turn.

'Sure givin' us the once-over,' Buck said, his eyes steady on Kane's face. 'One of 'em has binoculars and he's as watchful as a cattle buyer at a loading chute. Don't yuh think it's about time we found out what we've got into, Boss?'

'I suppose it is,' Kane said. Before her startled mind could counter his action, Buck Doxey picked up the handbag which she had left lying on the running-board of the car.

She flew towards him.

Doxey's bronzed, steel fingers wrapped around her wet wrist. 'Take it easy, ma'am,' he said. 'Take it easy.'

He pushed her back, found her driving licence. 'The real name,' he drawled, 'seems to be Jane Marlow.'

'Anything else?' Kane asked.

'Gobs of money, lipstick, keys and . . . Gosh, what a bankroll!'

She went for him blindly.

Doxey said, 'Now, ma'am, I'm going to have to spank yuh if yuh keep on like this.'

The plane circled, its occupants obviously interested in the scene on the ground below.

'Now – here's something else,' Doxey said, taking out a folded newspaper clipping.

She suddenly went limp. There was no use in further pretence.

Doxey read aloud, ' "Following the report of an autopsy, the police, who have never been satisfied that the death of Frank Hardwick was actually a suicide, are searching for his attractive secretary, Jane Marlow. The young woman reportedly had dinner with Hardwick in a downtown restaurant the night of his death.

' "Hardwick, after leaving Miss Marlow, according to her story, went directly to the apartment of Eva Ingram, a strikingly beautiful model, who had however convinced police that she was dining out. A matter of minutes after entering the Ingram apartment, Hardwick either jumped or fell from the eighth storey window.

' "With the finding of a witness who says Frank Hardwick was accompanied at least as far as the apartment door by a young woman whose description answers that of Jane Marlow, and the evidence that several thousand dollars were removed from a concealed floor safe in Hardwick's office, police are anxious once more to question Miss Marlow." '

'And here's a picture of this young lady,' Buck said, 'with some more stuff under it.

' "Jane Marlow, secretary of scientist who jumped from apartment window to his death, is now sought by police after witness claims to have seen her arguing angrily with Frank Hardwick when latter was ringing front-door bell of apartment house from which Hardwick fell or jumped." '

Overhead, the plane suddenly ceased its circling and took off in a straight line to the north.

As the car proceeded northwards Buck put on speed, deftly avoiding the bad places in the road.

Jane Marlow, who had lapsed into hopeless silence, tried one more last desperate attempt when they crossed the paved road. 'Please,' she said, 'let me out here. I'll catch a ride back to Los Angeles and report to the police.'

Kane's eyes asked a silent question of the driver.

'Nope,' Buck said decisively. 'That plane was the Sheriff's scout plane. He'll expect us to hold you. I don't crave to have no trouble over women.'

'All right,' Jane said in a last burst of desperation, 'I'll tell you the whole story. Then I'll leave it to your patriotism. I was secretary to Frank Hardwick. He was working on something that had to do with cosmic rays.'

'I know,' Doxey interrupted sarcastically. 'And he dictated his secret formula to you.'

'Don't be silly,' she said. 'But he did know he was in danger. He told me that if anything happened to him, I was to take something, which he gave me, to a certain individual.'

'Just keep on talking,' Buck said. 'Tell us about the money.'

Her eyes were desperate. 'Mr Hardwick had a concealed floor safe in the office. He left reserve cash there for emergencies. He gave me the combination, told me that if anything happened to him I was to go to that safe, take the money and deliver it and a certain paper to a certain scientist in Boston.'

Buck's smile of scepticism was certain to influence Kane even more than words.

'Frank Hardwick never jumped out of any window,' she went on. 'They were waiting for him, and they threw him out.'

'Or,' Buck said, 'a certain young lady became jealous, followed him, got him near an open window and then gave an unexpected shove. It has been done, you know.'

'And people have told the truth,' she blazed. 'I don't enjoy what I'm doing. I consider it a duty to my country – and I'll probably be murdered, just as Frank Hardwick was.'

'Now listen,' Kane said. 'Nice little girls don't jump off trains before daylight and tell the kind of stories you're telling. You got off that train because you were running away from someone.'

She turned to Kane. 'I was hoping that you at least would understand.'

'He understands,' Buck said, and laughed.

After that she was silent . . .

Overhead, from time to time, the plane came circling back. Once it was gone for nearly forty-five minutes and she dared to hope they had thrown it off the track, but later she realised it had only gone to refuel and then it was back above them once more.

It was nearly nine when Buck turned off the rutted road and headed towards a group of unpainted, squat log cabins which seemed to be bracing themselves against the cold wind while waiting for the winter snow. Behind the buildings were timbered mountains.

The pilot of the plane had evidently spotted the ranch long ago. Hardly had Buck turned off the road than the plane came circling in for a landing.

Jane Marlow had to lean against the cold wind as she

walked from the car to the porch of one cabin. Howard Kane held the door open for her, and she found herself inside a cold room which fairly reeked of masculine tenancy, with a paper-littered desk, guns, deer and elk horns.

Within a matter of seconds she heard the sound of steps on the porch, the door was flung open, and the fat man and a companion stood on the threshold.

'Well, Jane,' the fat man said, 'you gave us quite a chase, didn't you?' He turned to the others.

'Reckon I'd better introduce myself, boys.' He reached in his pocket, took out a wallet and tossed it on to the desk.

'I'm John Findlay of the FBI,' he said.

'That's a lie,' she said. 'Can't you understand? This man is an enemy. Those credentials are forged.'

'Well, ma'am,' the other newcomer said, stepping forward, 'there ain't nothing wrong with my credentials. I'm the Sheriff here, and I'm taking you into custody.'

He took her bag and said, 'You just might have a gun in here.'

He opened the bag. Findlay leaned over to look. 'It's all there,' he said.

'That plane of yours hold three people?' Findlay asked.

The Sheriff looked appraisingly at the fat man. 'Not us three.'

'I can fly the crate,' Findlay said. 'I'll take the prisoner in, lock her up and fly back for you . . .'

'No, no, no!' Jane Marlow screamed. 'Don't you see, can't you realise this man isn't an officer. I'd never get there. He—'

'Shut up,' the Sheriff said.

'Sheriff, please! You're being victimised. Call up the FBI and you'll find out that—'

'I've already called up the Los Angeles office of the FBI.'

Kane's brows levelled. 'Was that because you were suspicious, Sheriff?'

'Findlay himself suggested it.'

Jane was incredulous. 'You mean they told you that. . . ?'

'They vouched for him in every way,' the Sheriff said. 'They told me he'd been sent after Jane Marlow, and to give him every assistance. Now I've got to lock you up.'

'She's my responsibility, Sheriff,' Findlay said.

The Sheriff frowned, then said, 'Okay. I'll fly back and send a deputy out with a car.'

'Very well,' Findlay agreed. 'I'll see she stays put.'

Jane Marlow said desperately, 'I presume that when Mr Findlay told you to call the FBI office in Los Angeles, he gave you the number, didn't he?'

'Why not?' the Sheriff said, smiling good-humouredly. 'He'd be a hell of an FBI man if he didn't know his own telephone number!'

The fat man fished a cigar from his pocket. Biting off the end and scraping a match into flame, he winked at the Sheriff.

Howard Kane said to Findlay, 'Mind if I ask a question?'

'Hell, no. Go right ahead.'

'I'd like to know something of the facts in this case. If you've been working on the case you'd know . . .'

'Sure thing,' Findlay agreed, getting his cigar burning evenly. 'She worked for Hardwick, who was having an affair with a model. She followed him to the model's apartment. They had a quarrel. Hardwick's supposed to have jumped out of the window. She went to his office and took five thousand dollars out of the safe. The money's in her bag.'

'So she was jealous?'

'Jealous and greedy. Don't forget she got five grand out of the safe.'

'I was following my employer's specific instructions in everything I did,' Jane said.

Findlay grinned.

'What's more,' she blazed. 'Frank Hardwick wasn't having any affair with that model. He was lured to her apartment. It was a trap.'

Findlay said, 'Yeah. The key we found in his waistcoat pocket fitted the apartment door. He must have found it on the street and was returning it to the owner as an act of gallantry.'

The Sheriff laughed.

Howard Kane glanced speculatively at the young woman. 'She doesn't look like a criminal.'

'Oh, thank you!' she snapped.

Findlay's glance was patronising. 'How many criminals have you seen, buddy?'

Doxey rolled a cigarette. His eyes narrowed against the smoke as he squatted down cowboy fashion on the backs of his high-heeled riding boots. 'Ain't no question but what she's the one who jimmied the safe, is there?'

'The money's in her bag,' Findlay said.

'Any accomplices?' Buck asked.

'No. It was a combination of jealousy and greed.' Findlay glanced enquiringly at the Sheriff.

'I'll fly in and send that car out,' the Sheriff said.

'Mind if I fly in with yuh and ride back with the deputy, Sheriff?' Buck asked eagerly. 'I'd like to see this country from the air. There's a paved road other side of that big mountain where the ranger has his station. I'd like to look down on it. Some day they'll connect us up. Now it's an hour's ride by horse . . .'

'Sure,' the Sheriff agreed. 'Glad to have you.'

'Just give me time enough to throw a saddle on a horse,' Doxey said. 'Kane might want to ride out and look the ranch over. You won't mind, Sheriff?'

'Make it snappy,' the Sheriff said.

Buck Doxey went to the barn and after a few minutes returned leading a dilapidated-looking range pony saddled and bridled. He casually dropped the reins in front of the ranch 'office', and called inside:

'Ready any time you are, Sheriff.'

They started for the plane. Buck stopped at the car to get a map from the glove compartment, then hurried to join the Sheriff. The propeller of the plane gave a half-turn, stopped, then gave another; the motor spluttered and roared into action. A few moments later the plane was sweeping over the squat log buildings in a climbing turn before heading south.

Jane Marlow and Kane watched it through the window until it shrank to a speck.

Howard Kane said, 'Now, Mr Findlay, I'd like to ask you a few more questions.'

'Sure, go right ahead.'

'You impressed the Sheriff very cleverly,' Kane said, 'but I'd like to have you explain . . .'

'Now that it's too late,' Jane Marlow cut in indignantly. 'You've let him . . .'

Kane motioned her to silence. 'Don't you see, Miss Marlow, I had to get rid of the Sheriff. He represents the law, right or wrong. But if this man is an impostor, I can protect you.'

Findlay's hand moved with such rapidity that the big diamond made a streak of glittering light.

'Okay, wise guy,' he said. 'Try protecting her against this.'

Kane rushed the gun.

Sheer surprise slowed Findlay's reaction. Kane's fist flashed out in a swift arc, just before the gun roared.

The fat man moved with amazing speed. He rolled with the punch, spun completely round on his heel and jumped back, the automatic held to his body, his eyes glittering with rage.

'Get 'em up,' he said.

Slowly Kane's hands came up.

'Turn round,' Findlay said. 'Move over by that window. Press your face against the wall. Give me your right hand . . . Now the left.'

A smooth leather thong, which had been deftly knotted into a slipknot, was jerked tight, then knotted into a quick half-hitch.

The girl, taking advantage of Findlay's preoccupation, flung herself on him.

The bulk of Findlay's big shoulders absorbed the onslaught without making him even shift the position of his feet. He jerked the leather thong into a last knot, turned and struck the girl in the pit of the stomach.

She wobbled on rubbery legs, then fell to the floor.

'Now, young lady,' Findlay said, 'you've caused me a hell of a lot of trouble. I'll just take the thing you're carrying in your left shoe. I could tell from the way you were limping there was something . . .'

He jerked off the shoe, looked inside, seemed puzzled, then suddenly grabbed the girl's stockinged foot.

He reached casual hands up to the top of her stocking, jerked it off, pulled the adhesive tape from the bottom of her foot, ran out to the car and jumped in.

'Well, what do you know!' he exclaimed. 'The damn yokel took the keys with him . . . So there's paved road on the other side of the mountains, is there?'

Moving swiftly, the fat man ran over to where the horse was standing on three legs, drowsing in the sunlight unconcernedly.

'Come on, horse, I guess there's a trail we can find. If we can't, they'll never locate us in all that timber.'

Findlay gathered up the reins, thrust one foot in the stirrup, grabbed the saddle, front and rear, and mounted.

Jane heard a shrill animal squeal of rage. The sleepy-looking horse transformed into a bundle of dynamite, heaving himself into the air, ears laid back along his neck.

The fat man clung on with frenzied desperation.

'Well,' Kane asked, 'are you going to untie me, or just stand there gawking?'

She ran to him then, frantically tugging at the knot.

The second his hands were freed Kane went into action.

Findlay, half out of the saddle, clung drunkenly to the pitching horse for a moment, then went into the air, turned half over and came down with a jar that shook the earth.

Kane emerged from the cabin holding a rifle.

'All right, Findlay, it's my turn now,' Kane said. 'Don't make a move for that gun.'

The shaken Findlay seemed to have trouble orientating himself. He turned dazedly towards the sound of the voice, and clawed for his gun.

Kane, aiming the rifle carefully, shot it out of his hand.

'Now, ma'am,' Kane said, 'if you want that paper . . .'

She ran to Findlay, her feet fairly flying over the ground despite the fact that one foot had neither shoe nor stocking . . .

Shortly before noon, Jane Marlow decided to invade the sacred precincts of Buck Doxey's kitchen to prepare lunch. Howard Kane showed his respect for Findlay's resourcefulness by keeping him covered despite the man's bound wrists.

'Buck is going to hate me for this,' she grinned.

'Just open a can of something and make some coffee,' Howard said. 'And for heaven's sake don't try to rearrange his kitchen according to ideas of feminine efficiency!'

It was as they were finishing lunch that they heard the plane.

They went to the door to watch it turn into the teeth of the cold north wind, settle to a landing, then taxi in towards the low buildings.

The Sheriff and Buck Doxey started running towards the cabins, and it was solace to Jane Marlow's pride to see the look of almost comic relief on the face of the Sheriff as he saw Kane with the rifle and Findlay with bound wrists.

Jane heard the last part of Doxey's explanation to Kane.

'Wouldn't trust a woman that far, but her story held together and his didn't. I thought you'd understand what I was doing. I flew in with the Sheriff just so I could call the FBI in Los Angeles. What do you know? Findlay is a badly wanted enemy spy. They want him bad as . . . How did *you* make out?'

Kane grinned. 'I decided to give Findlay a private third-degree. He answered my questions with a gun. If it hadn't been for that horse . . .'

Buck's face broke into a grin. 'He fell for that one?'

'Fell off it,' Kane said.

'If he hadn't been a fool tenderfoot he'd have noticed that I led the horse out, instead of riding him. Old Fox is a rodeo horse, one of the best bucking broncs in Wyoming. Perfectly gentle until he feels it's time to do his stuff, and then he gives everything he has until he hears the ten-second whistle . . .'

The next day Jane was once more speeding east aboard the sleek streamliner, wondering why, although her mission was no longer opposed, she still felt vaguely disappointed.

She did not wonder long. A telegram – delivered when she reached Omaha – told her simply what was missing. It was from Howard Kane and read:

YOU WERE SO RIGHT. IT GETS TERRIBLY LONELY AT TIMES. HOLD A DINNER DATE OPEN FOR TONIGHT. YOU NEED A BODYGUARD ON YOUR MISSION AND I AM FLYING TO CHICAGO TO MEET YOU AT TRAIN AND DISCUSS THE WYOMING CLIMATE AS A PERMANENT PLACE OF RESIDENCE. MUCH LOVE, HOWARD.

Death Decision

WILLIAM F. NOLAN

This next story is also about a long-distance journey from the heart of Missouri to Los Angeles with murder as a fellow traveller. It is ostensibly the account of a small boy taking his first ride on a train – the sort of experience that should stay in someone's memory for ever. But it is no ordinary journey that young Michael is about to undertake with his sister, Lucy, and their father: for he is consumed with a deep and abiding hatred and the trip promises to be one in which something dark and violent and terrible will occur before the end of the journey is reached.

William Francis Nolan (1928–) is well-known as the author of a number of ingenious mystery and fantasy stories as well as the landmark novel *Logan's Run* (1967), co-written with his friend George Clayton Johnson, which was filmed in 1967 and subsequently made into a TV series ten years later. As a crime novelist, however, he has twice won the Edgar Allan Poe Special Award Scroll from the Mystery Writers of America and has also garnered the Maltese Falcon award for his pioneering work on the life of Dashiell Hammett which resulted in the definitive biography, *Hammet: A Life at the Edge*, published in 1983. Recently, he has been earning widespread praise for his series of hardboiled novels that began with *The Black Mask Murders* (1994), in which he has resurrected three of the great masters of the genre, Dashiell Hammett, Raymond Chandler and Erle Stanley Gardner, in stories of crime and murder.

Nolan is also the author of a number of comic fantasies

about Sam Space, a hardboiled private eye of the future, and Bart Challis, a Los Angeles sleuth who has been named among the century's best in critic Robert Baker's study, *Private Eyes: 101 Knights*. Nolan's enthusiasms and interests range far and wide, and it is no surprise to find railways among them. Among his best stories of this kind must be listed 'The Train', published in *Gallery* in 1981, in which a traveller waiting at a desolate station in Montana is unwittingly thrown into a series of horrific events when he finally gets aboard; and 'Death Decision' which has never been previously anthologised. It was written in 1981 but concerns a very different journey to destiny. The author's work has been deservedly praised by many of his peers, and Ray Bradbury neatly hints at what is to follow in this tribute: 'Nolan is able to create a real atmosphere of ultimate terror, causing the reader to live out his nightmares.' You have been warned!

***

Michael followed his younger sister up the sloping ramp, the heavy leather suitcase bumping his knee, the cool dusk of the station tunnel behind him – seeing the snake-length of train ahead of them, the gleaming passenger coaches waiting on the tracks in the glare of late afternoon sunlight.

He paused for a moment on the edge of the blazing white expanse of concrete and allowed the hot, unfamiliar iron-and-steel smells of the platform to envelop him.

His first train . . . his first trip outside the city . . . his first real adventure . . .

Then his father's hard voice probed at him sharply. 'Hurry along, Michael. And take sister's hand. We don't want the train to leave without us.'

The tall figure moved past him, a lean silhouette against the reflecting silver of the coaches, and Michael followed, switching the suitcase to ease its weight, taking Lucy's small hand. He thought: Lucy is too young to understand death. When you're seven, death is a dark fantasy you can't really believe in. But she was learning, thought Michael bitterly; she was learning all about death, as he had learned. Father was seeing to that.

Michael tried to imagine what they would find in Los Angeles, California; he tried to envision his mother lying starched and painted like a plaster saint in a flower-banked coffin with organ music playing softly in the background and people moving past her in a dreamlike procession, silent and tight-lipped. When his uncle had died of a heart attack it had been that way, with the flowers so sickeningly sweet that Michael had nearly become ill. He remembered it all, every detail.

But now it was different. He had not seen his mother in six years, not since he was eight, when she had gone away from them for ever, and it was impossible to imagine her lying cold and unmoving somewhere in a strange city. She still seemed alive to him; he could hear her repeating his name over and over again, the favourite name she'd had for him: 'Mikey, oh, Mikey . . .'

'Michael!' The lost voice of his mother became the hard, commanding voice of his father. 'I *told* you to move along.'

A round-faced, smiling porter took the suitcase from Michael as they mounted the iron coach steps and led them toward their compartment. The coach interior was cool, cooler even than the long station tunnel, and Michael moved behind his father with a feeling of having entered a new world, separated utterly from the city-world beyond the glass windows. He'd *seen* trains, heard them roar past in the night, but this was his first time on one. It was nothing like the bus that had taken them into Jefferson, here to the big station. Not like the bus at all.

His father gave the porter some change and the man disappeared down the narrow corridor, leaving them alone in their compartment. It was like a little room, with a silver wash basin over to one side and green velvet seats.

'Well, don't just *stand* there, Michael. Close the door and put away our things. What *is* the matter with you today?'

Mr Leonard Bair, Michael's father, was a tall man with a thin, corded neck and small black bird's eyes. He wore steel-rimmed spectacles which made his eyes look even smaller and more birdlike, and when he smiled, which was infrequently, his lips twisted up from porcelain dentures which seemed at least a size too large for his spare face.

Michael helped his father put away their coats and the leather suitcase. Then he sat down opposite him. Lucy pressed her nose flat against the cool glass of the windows. 'Will we be starting soon?' she asked, watching the pre-journey activity outside.

'I guess so,' replied Michael. He looked over at his father.

Mr Bair said nothing. He was shaking out the evening paper he'd purchased at the depot.

Michael said, I hate you, to his father – but the words were deep within him and Mr Bair did not hear them. I hate you for what you did to my mother and for what you did to me and for what you're doing to my sister. You sent my mother away and now she's dead in a strange city – and it's all because of you.

The evening paper rustled softly in Mr Bair's carefully manicured hands.

I hate you, the voice deep inside Michael continued, because you lied to me about my mother, told me awful things about her that I know are lies . . . all lies . . .

His father's voice lived again in his mind. And the words were there, the words he would never be able to forget: '*Your mother was sick, Michael. She had a serious illness which she could not control and which eventually destroyed her. She was a drunk, Michael, a lost and helpless alcoholic – and now she is dead, a victim of her own weakness.'*

You never loved her as I loved her, Michael silently accused his father; she went away because you drove her away. She was good and kind and never like you. Never like you . . .

Michael remembered listening, in darkness, from his bed next to Lucy's crib, to the violent quarrels they had, to the shouted terrible words ringing through the night rooms and entering his body like a series of small explosions – until he would begin to cry and bury his head under the pillow, trying not to hear . . .

'Watch sister,' said Leonard Bair, folding aside the paper. 'I'm going up to the front of the coach and get us a little something to eat. Don't you think oranges would be agreeable?'

Michael nodded and Lucy said, 'Yes, thank you,' softly, looking down at her lap. She sat primly on the green velvet seat like a solemn toy doll, serious and unsmiling.

'Very well,' said Mr Bair. 'I'll return shortly.'

When the compartment door had slid closed Lucy raised her dark eyes to Michael. 'Tell me about her again, please. Will you? *Will* you, Michael?'

The boy looked at his sister, at her large, clear eyes and pale face and he thought: She's older, too, like I am. Father's made her that way. She *looks* seven, but she's not like other seven-year-olds.

'Please,' Lucy prompted. 'Tell me, Michael.'

'Well,' he began, 'when you were a baby she'd pick you up and hold you for hours, just singing to you and rocking you in her arms.'

Lucy was silent, watching her brother. The train had begun to move, sliding out of the station over the steel rails, gathering momentum, but the little girl's eyes did not waver from Michael's face.

'She used to take you out for long walks and lots of times

she'd let me push your carriage if I promised not to run or bump you over kerbs. Don't you remember her at all?'

'No,' said Lucy in her soft child's voice. 'Not any. I wish I could, like you can, Michael. Oh, I *wish* I could.'

'Her eyes were like cool water,' he told his sister, 'deep and full of sadness. And she loved us, Lucy, I *know* she did. No matter what father tells you, she loved us both.'

The compartment door opened.

'Well,' said Leonard Bair, sliding it closed again. 'That didn't take long.' He handed an orange to each of them.

Michael began to strip away the thick rind, mechanically, not really wanting the fruit but knowing he must accept it. He repeated the process for Lucy.

'Can't understand why people choose to spend hard-earned money on an airplane ticket when a train will do nicely,' said Leonard Bair. 'My father *always* travelled by rail. Right to the day he died. Sensible. Civilised. Lets you see the country.'

Michael listened, and told himself, someday I'll fly in a plane. It must be wonderful . . . like a bird . . . free in the sky. I've never been free to do anything. Never.

Beyond the train window, the countryside was flowing past, city outskirts giving way to open farm country. A pattern of browns and greens checkered by, and the sun, moving rapidly down the western sky, was beginning to glare in solid yellow waves through the glass.

'Lower the shade, Michael,' instructed Leonard Bair. 'These windows should be tinted, but then we accept what we get. Ah, that's better.'

The tall man arranged a magazine on his lap and adjusting his steel-rimmed spectacles, settled into the velvet seat, his lips already moving almost imperceptibly as he read.

Michael studied his father's calm face above the magazine, thinking: You killed her and I know it. No matter *how* she died you killed her. She needed us and you sent her away. Why should I care what happens to you? Why should Lucy care? Michael's heart began to beat faster in his chest and he could feel its steady throb behind his eyes. An anger was building inside him, a deep and long-withheld anger which was only now, in the coach on this particular day, fully revealing itself.

The train changed things. The train was taking Michael away from the old world of fear and darkness; the small Missouri town of his childhood was behind them now, lost in gleaming rails and distance. It was easier not to care, here in his new world of the train.

It was easier to hate.

I saw him pack, thought Michael, and I know he didn't take along the gun. Or a knife, either. Only the bottle. That was all he took along – just the small, green bottle.

'May I please be excused?' Lucy asked, standing in the aisle between the seats.

'Go with sister, Michael,' said their father, his eyes still fastened to the print he was reading. 'But don't be too long.'

'All right,' said Michael, and pushed open the door.

The rest room was at the far end of the coach, and Michael braced one hand against the compartment walls to help balance himself in the swaying car.

'Here we are,' said Michael, reaching the rest room door. 'It's empty. You can go in okay by yourself, can't you?'

Lucy nodded and entered the small cubicle.

While he was waiting, another boy approached him, maybe a year or two older. Tall and blond and bored-looking. He started toward the door.

'My sister's in there,' said Michael.

'Okay,' said the blond boy. 'I can wait.'

A moment of awkward silence. Then Michael said, 'This is my first train ride.'

'Me, too. We always fly. You fly a lot?'

'I've never been on a plane. Are they fun?'

The boy looked at him oddly. 'Yeah . . . I guess so. Sure beats rattling across the country on this damn thing. How far you going?'

'Los Angeles.'

'LA's a good town. Too much smog, though. Been there before?'

Michael shook his head. 'I've never been anywhere. Is it big, Los Angeles?'

'Sure it's big. Takes all day just to get from one end to the other.'

'I see,' said Michael, but he didn't. He could never imagine a town that large. Jefferson had seemed enormous to him.

'I'm afraid of big cities,' said Michael.

'How come?'

'A big city can swallow you up. They frighten me.'

'How old are you anyway?'

'Fourteen.'

'Jeez,' said the blond boy, shaking his head. 'You sure don't know much.'

'I don't know anything,' said Michael honestly. 'I have to learn it all new.'

The rest room door opened, and Lucy came out. The boy darted in, closing it behind him. 'Jeez,' he said, faintly.

As he moved back down the coach aisle with his sister, Michael thought: to that boy I'm a fool. And he's right. I've got to grow up. It's time now. Time to begin acting like a man.

Why should I be afraid of a city? A city is really the same, big or small, familiar or strange. It can't, of itself, hurt you. People can hurt you, but only if you let them, only if you get in their way. He was good at staying out of people's way and so was Lucy.

Michael's heart thudded faster as he neared their compartment. I'm almost a man now, he thought, I'm very close to being a man. I must no longer be afraid.

Outside the window, the sun was nearly down and Michael felt the quietness of sunset here in the clicking train, which seemed to be hurrying faster and faster through the greying country, skimming over the endless tracks, keeping ahead of the night.

Back in the compartment, sitting stiffly across from his father, Michael watched him carefully. He always gets sleepy at this time of day; he and Lucy usually take a nap in the late afternoon. It won't be long now. They must *both* be sleeping. He couldn't do it unless they were both asleep.

He waited.

Lucy curled up near the window with a pillow under her head and was quickly asleep. Michael, too, pretended to drowse, with his head against the seat, eyelids down. But through the lacy slit beneath his lashes he watched his father, as a hunter watches for deer. Soon, he knew. Soon.

In the gentle, rocking motion of the train Michael watched his father's eyes close, the lids, sliding over the harsh, bright pupils; he watched the magazine settle lazily into the lap of Leonard Bair and he listened to his father's measured breathing.

Now!

No, not too quickly. Be certain; make no mistakes. He knew he would have one chance, one try at the bottle and no more.

He studied his father's face, the half-opened mouth, the lidded eyes. Then, slowly, Michael began to move.

The bottle was in his father's briefcase, which he had packed under the seat when they entered the compartment. Michael knew the briefcase was open, the small gold lock was broken as it had been for years.

Slowly. *Glide* your hands toward the briefcase, Michael told himself. Another few inches. That's it. Now you can reach it.

Michael's fingers closed firmly over the dark leather and

he eased the case from its place under the seat, his eyes never off his father's sleeping face. Swiftly he loosened the two worn straps and reached inside. Yes, there it was, the bottle, green and solid in his hands, the neat metal cap screwed tight over the white, grainy powder inside.

Well, don't sit there holding it, Michael told himself. You know what to do with it. Quickly!

Outside the darkening country flowed past. Lights were beginning to blink on in the dusk.

Michael slid the briefcase back under the seat and moved toward the door, the bottle safely in his shirt pocket.

'Michael, where are you going?'

The boy froze. Had his father been playing one of his terrible games? Had he *seen* Michael take the bottle?

'Answer me! I asked you where you were going.'

'Just to the end of the coach. I wanted to take a walk.'

'Well,' said his father, easing back, closing his eyes again, 'see that you don't leave the car. I don't want you wandering all over the train.'

'I won't,' Michael said, still facing the compartment door. He didn't want to turn; his father might ask about the bulge in his shirt pocket.

'Go along, then.'

Noting that Lucy still slept soundly, Michael slid open the door, and moved into the aisle. His heart was pounding against the wall of his chest. Could he do it? Could he *really*?

The rest room at the end of the coach was unoccupied. Michael stepped inside, throwing the latch, locking himself safely away from everyone. The small cubicle smelled of disinfectant, like a hospital room. It was cramped and ugly. A neatly lettered sign on the wall above the toilet said, 'Please DO NOT flush while train is in station'.

Michael took out the green bottle, unscrewed the cap and upended the contents into the bowl. Then he pressed the round silver foot pedal and watched the grainy white powder swirl and foam away.

Michael drew a small square of folded paper from his trouser pocket, opened it. He carefully funnelled the contents into the green bottle. White. Grainy. The same, but *not* the same.

The train was moving faster over the unseen rails below him. The steady clicking of the wheels beneath his feet seemed to be matching the rapid beating of Michael's heart as he made his way back to the compartment. It was evening now, and with the corridor lights on all the windows were dark, as if the glass had been painted black.

Mr Bair was sleeping soundly when Michael entered the compartment, and even the slight noise of the sliding door did not awaken him. Lucy, too, still slept deeply near the window.

In another few minutes it will all be over, thought Michael. His hands were trembling as he slipped the bottle back into the leather case and replaced it under the seat. There, now. Everything ready.

'Wake up,' said Michael, prodding his father's shoulder. 'Wake up.'

Mr Bair coughed, raising his head. He focused his eyes on Michael and frowned. 'I assume you have an excellent reason for disturbing my sleep. Disturbing it, I might add, for the second time this evening.'

'I have a reason, all right,' said Michael, sitting down across from his father and meeting his eyes squarely. 'I want to find out a few things, Father. A few things I've been wanting to know about for a long while.'

'Your behaviour is extraordinary Michael. I believe the train has upset you. Perhaps—'

'I want to know,' cut in Michael, 'why you sent Mother away.'

'This is neither the time, nor the place, to discuss—'

'*Answer* me,' said Michael, his voice edged in hate. 'You answer me!'

'You'll wake your sister!'

'No, I won't. Lucy can sleep through anything. Even this.'

'You'll go without supper tonight, Michael. I promise you that.' Leonard Bair's eyes glittered, coldly.

'You *drove* Mother away,' said Michael evenly. 'And she died because of you.'

'She died because she was a weak-minded alcoholic. And I sent her away because the court ruled her unfit to raise you and sister. Her drinking killed her. I had nothing to do with it.'

'You lie!' accused Michael. 'She drank because of you, because of the sick way you treated us, because of all the terrible things you said to her. And you're only going back for the money she left us.'

'I won't listen to this kind of talk,' snapped Leonard Bair. The veins on his corded neck stood out, taut with anger. 'You will apologise at once or—'

'Or what? Or you'll take out your bottle and use what's in it. Is *that* what you'll do?'

'Yes, Michael,' said Leonard Bair, in a quiet, steady tone. 'That is exactly what I shall do.'

The scene, for young Michael, was horribly familiar. It had been repeated over and over, with variations, a thousand times in his life. Whenever he or Lucy would seriously misbehave, whenever they would create a scene with Father, the threat would descend upon them. Sometimes a knife was brandished, held close to the flesh of his father's throat, when only the smallest movement would part the skin; sometimes it was a razor, held above a wrist artery; sometimes the gun, with the barrel inside his father's mouth . . . But, always, the threat was the same: 'Behave. Obey me or my death will be on your head. Tell me you'll be a good boy, Michael, and that you are sorry you troubled your father. Tell me, Michael, tell me . . .'

And he would always cry and say that he was sorry, that he would do as his father told him to do, that he would never misbehave again. Never again.

But now, in the train, it was different. Leonard Bair's threat could be challenged, put to the test that Michael had so often pictured in his mind's eye.

'Take it, and be damned!' urged the boy. 'Take it all. I *want* you to take it! Go on, what are you waiting for?'

Leonard Bair snapped up his briefcase, dipped his hand inside for the green bottle. 'Then I will,' he threatened. 'I will, Michael. I'll die, and all your life you'll remember *why* I died.'

At the window, her head deep into the pillow resting against the dark glass, Lucy stirred faintly, then lapsed back into sleep.

Leonard Bair moved to the small sink, set into the wall of the compartment.

Michael watched his father fill a paper cup with water from the silver tappet, watched him unscrew the metal cap and pour the white powder into the cup. 'You see,' said the tall man. 'I mean to carry out my word, Michael.'

The boy said nothing. He smiled coldly up at his father, who was swaying above the seats, the cup poised in his hand.

He *can't* do it, thought Michael. It's always been his sick way of establishing control over us, but he can't do it. But, if he does, then I'll have beaten him.

The cup hovered in the air near the mouth of his father. 'You still have time, Michael. Say the words and mean them. Tell me you're sorry.'

Michael continued to smile. He waited. Silently.

Leonard Bair lowered the cup. His face was ashen, his forehead finely beaded with silver perspiration.

'I – I'll give you one final chance,' he stammered, settling heavily into the seat. 'I'll wait for you to regain your senses. This trip has upset you, Michael. I'll give you one more chance.'

'Damn you, swallow it! I don't care any more. I *want* you to do it!'

'Then let my death be on your conscience!'

And tipping back his head, Leonard Bair emptied the cup down his throat.

And Michael thought, I've finally called his bluff. Now that I've forced him to do it, he'll try to find a way out, a way to pretend it was real. It will be more fun if I help, give him what he wants me to give him, what I've always given him: repentance.

'Father, I didn't really mean what I said! Shall I call for the conductor?' Michael stood up, looking frightened.

'No, that's not necessary, not if you promise me you'll never question me in this manner again, ever!'

'I promise.' Soft-voiced. Defeated. Head down.

'And you will always remember this?'

'Yes . . . always.'

'Very well then. Luckily, I brought along an antidote. It will reverse the effects of the poison.'

And Leonard Bair shook the contents of a small packet into the paper cup, added water, drank quickly. 'There. Done.'

'Not quite, I'm afraid,' said Michael.

'What?'

'It's not quite done. Not until you die, Father. Then it will be done.'

Leonard Bair stared at his son, as Michael continued. 'Too bad your antidote wasn't real. It could have saved you.'

'You're talking nonsense!'

'No, for the first time in my life, I'm talking honestly to you. I don't even hate you any more. Now that you're dying. You're like a cockroach that's been stepped on. One almost feels sorry for it. *Almost*.' And Michael smiled.

'What are you saying?'

'I'm saying that the fake antidote you took won't change anything.'

Bair was ashen-faced, beginning to tremble. 'Fake? What do you—'

'Fake . . . like the knife you never *really* would have used . . . or the gun, with no shells . . . or the stuff you had in the bottle. I wasn't absolutely sure until I tasted it, tasted your "poison" before we left for the train. Saccharine. Then I knew you'd never do it, never really kill yourself because of anything we did, Lucy and I . . .' Michael began to chuckle. 'But the joke's on you, Father – because you *have* killed yourself after all!'

Bair's face glittered with sweat; his skin was paper-white, his hands shaking. 'You – you put—'

'Real poison, Father. That's what I put in the bottle.'

And Leonard Bair fell forward, across the seat, eyes jittering, fluttering closed, glazing with death.

Michael watched him quietly.

Los Angeles was waiting for them beyond the depot – an immense city in which they could hide for ever. The tall buildings were waiting, and the endless rush of cars and the hurrying people, all waiting to engulf them, to swallow them up.

Michael was breathing hard when he stepped from the station doorway into the bright California sunlight; he could feel Lucy's small hand in his, clinging tightly. He paused on the edge of the concrete wilderness, afraid. Despite himself, afraid.

But they were free now, at last, and there was no turning back.

The people on the train had been so nice, so kind and understanding. A shame about his father. Man that age, should have had many good years ahead of him. But a heart can give out on anyone. Yes, Michael had agreed, on anyone.

Now he would have a *double* funeral to attend.

'Where are we going, Michael?' his sister asked him. 'Are we going to see Mother? Is that where we're going?'

'Yes,' said Michael, 'that's where we're going.'

And he stepped forward, under the hot noon sun, into the city.

Broker's Special

STANLEY ELLIN

Few other American mystery story writers have better portrayed the life of the everyday commuter than Stanley Ellin who has written a number of short stories dealing with the day-to-day grind of existence in the city and the pressures which can cause even the most good-natured individual to crack and even drive some to terrible acts of violence. Whether these people are long-distance travellers like Mr Willoughby returning from a rest-cure for over-work who is plunged into a nightmare situation in the club car of a train in the story 'Unreasonable Doubt' (1964), or the Wall Street broker Cornelius Bolinger who changes his normal evening train and finds himself confronted with infidelity and the urge for revenge in 'Broker's Special', all are immediately recognisable people who could be found on any train anywhere. Not surprisingly, Ellin has been described by *Atlantic Monthly* as 'the writer who can reveal the devil in even a little man in a frayed business suit carrying his briefcase to the train'.

Stanley Ellin (1916–1986) was born in Brooklyn and initially thought about making a career in engineering. But after periods of employment as a steelworker, dairy farmer, teacher and newspaper distributor, he turned to writing and in 1948 submitted 'The Speciality of the House' to *Ellery Queen's Mystery Magazine* which, with its hint of cannibalism, shocked and delighted readers in equal measure. It has since earned the reputation of being one of the most original and distinctive crime stories of modern times. Ellin's interest in railways first surfaced in his novel *The Key to Nicholas Street* (1952), but was made more evident in 'Unreasonable Doubt' and 'Broker's Special'. Several of Stanley Ellin's novels have been filmed, including *The Big Night* (1951) directed by Joseph Losey and *House of Cards* (1968) which starred George Peppard and Orson Welles, while a number of his horror stories have been adapted for television in series such as *Alfred Hitchcock Presents*. 'Broker's Special' is, in my opinion, long overdue for treatment by either medium.

***

It was the first time in a good many years that Cornelius, a Wall Street broker, had made the homeward trip in any train other than the Broker's Special. The Special was his kind of train; the passengers on it were his kind of people. Executives, professionals, men of substance and dignity who could recognise each other without introductions, and understand each other without words.

If it weren't for the Senator's dinner party, Cornelius reflected. But the Senator had insisted, so there was no escape from that abomination of abominations, the midweek dinner party. And, of course, no escape from the necessity of taking an earlier train home to the tedium of dressing, and an evening of too much food, too much liquor, and all the resultant misery the next morning.

Filled with this depressing thought Cornelius stepped down heavily from the train to the familiar platform and walked over to his car. Since Claire preferred the station wagon, he used the sedan to get to and from the station. When they were first married two years ago she had wanted to chauffeur him back and forth, but the idea had somehow repelled him. He had always felt there was something vaguely obscene about the way other men publicly kissed their wives goodbye in front of the station every morning, and the thought of being placed in their position filled him with a chilling embarrassment. He had not told this to Claire, however. He had simply told her he had not married her to obtain a housekeeper or chauffeur. She was to enjoy her life, not fill it with unnecessary duties.

Ordinarily, it was no more than a fifteen-minute drive through the countryside to the house. But now, in keeping with the already exasperating tenor of the day's events, he met an unexpected delay. A mile or so past where the road branched off from the highway it crossed the main line of the railroad. There was no guard or crossing gate here, but a red light, and a bell which was ringing an insistent warning as Cornelius drove up. He braked the car, and sat tapping his fingers restlessly on the steering-wheel while the endless, clanking length of a freight went by. And then, before he could start the car again, he saw them.

It was Claire and a man. His wife and some man in the station wagon roaring past him into town. And the man was driving – seated big and blond and arrogant behind the wheel like a Viking – with one arm around Claire who, with eyes closed, rested her head on his shoulder. There was a look on her face, too, such as Cornelius had never seen there before, but which he had sometimes dreamed of seeing. They passed by in a flash, but the picture they made was burned as brilliant in his mind as a photograph on film.

He would not believe it, he told himself incredulously; he refused to believe it! But the picture was there before him, growing clearer each second, becoming more and more terribly alive as he watched it. The man's arm possessing her. Her look of acceptance. Of sensual acceptance.

He was shaking uncontrollably now, the blood pounding in his head, as he prepared to turn the car and follow them. Then he felt himself go limp. Follow them where? Back to town undoubtedly, where the man would be waiting for the next train to the city. And then what? A denunciation in the grand style? A scene? A public humiliation for himself as much as for them?

He could stand anything, but not such humiliation. It had been bad enough when he had first married Claire and realised his friends were laughing at him for it. A man in his position to marry his secretary, and a girl half his age at that! Now he knew what they had been laughing at, but he had been blind then. There had been such an air of cool formality about her when she carried on her duties in the office; she sat with such prim dignity when she took his notes; she had dressed so modestly – and when he had first invited her to dinner she had reddened with the flustered naïvety of a young girl being invited on her first date. Naïvety! And all the time, he thought furiously, she must have been laughing at me, She, along with the rest of them.

He drove to the house slowly, almost blindly. The house was empty, and he realised that, of course, it was Thursday, the servant's day off, which made it the perfect day for Claire's purpose. He went directly to the library, sat down at the desk there, and unlocked the top drawer. His gun was in that drawer, a short-barrelled .38, and he picked it up slowly, hefting its cold weight in his hand, savouring the sense of power it gave him. Then abruptly his mind went back to something Judge Hilliker had once told him, something strangely interesting that the old man had said while sharing a seat with him on the Broker's Special.

'Guns?' Hilliker had said. 'Knives? Blunt instruments? You can throw them all out of the window. As far as I'm concerned there is just one perfect weapon – an automobile. Any automobile in good working order. Why? Because when an automobile is going fast enough it will kill anyone it hits. And if the driver gets out and looks sorry he'll find that he's the one getting everybody's sympathy, and not that bothersome corpse on the ground who shouldn't have been in the way anyhow. As long as the driver isn't drunk or flagrantly reckless he can kill anybody in this country he wants to, and suffer no more than a momentary embarrassment and a penalty that isn't even worth worrying about.

'Think it over, man,' the Judge continued: 'to most people the automobile is some sort of god, and if God happens to strike you down it's your hard luck. As for me, when I cross a street I just say a little prayer.'

There was more of that in Judge Hilliker's mordant and long-winded style, but Cornelius had no need to remember it. What he needed he now had, and very carefully he put the gun back in the drawer, slid the drawer shut, and locked it.

Claire came in while he still sat brooding at the desk, and he forced himself to regard her with cold objectivity – this radiantly lovely woman who was playing him for a fool, and who now stood wide-eyed in the doorway with an incongruously large bag of groceries clutched to her.

'I saw the car in the garage,' she said breathlessly. 'I was afraid something was wrong. That you weren't feeling well . . .'

'I feel very well.'

'But you're home so early. You've never come this early before.'

'I've always managed to refuse invitiations to midweek dinner parties before.'

'Oh, Lord!' she gasped. 'The dinner! It never even entered my mind. I've been so busy all day . . .'

'Yes?' he said. 'Doing what?'

'Well, everyone's off today, so I took care of the house from top to bottom, and then when I looked in the pantry and saw we needed some things I ran into town for them.' She gestured at the bulky paper bag with her chin. 'I'll have your bath ready, and your things laid out as soon as I put this stuff away.'

Watching her leave he felt an honest admiration for her. Another woman would have invented a visit to a friend who might, at some later time, accidentally let the cat out of the bag. Or another woman would not have thought to burden herself with a useless package to justify a trip into town. But not Claire, who was evidently as clever as she was beautiful.

And she *was* damnably attractive. His male friends may have laughed behind his back, but in their homes she was always eagerly surrounded by them. When he entered a roomful of strangers with her he saw how all men's eyes followed her with a frankly covetous interest. No, nothing must happen to her; nothing at all. It was the man who had to be destroyed, just as one would destroy any poacher on his preserves, any lunatic who with axe in hand ran amok through his home. Claire would have to be hurt a little, would have to be taught her lesson, but that would be done most effectively through what happened to the man.

Cornelius learned very quickly that his plans would have to take in a good deal more than the simple act of waylaying the man and running him down. There were details, innumerable details covering every step of the way before and after the event, which had to be jigsawed into place bit by bit in order to make it perfect.

In that respect, Cornelius thought gratefully, the Judge had been far more helpful than he had realised in his irony. Murder by automobile was the perfect murder, because, with certain details taken care of, it was not even murder at all! There was the victim, and there was the murderer standing over him, and the whole thing would be treated with perfunctory indifference. After all, what was one more victim among the thirty thousand each year? He was a statistic, to be regarded with some tongue-clicking and a shrug of helplessness.

Not by Claire, of course. Coincidence can be stretched far, but hardly far enough to cover the case of a husband's running down his wife's lover. And that was the best part of it. Claire would know, but would be helpless to say anything, since saying anything must expose her own wrongdoing. She would spend her life, day after day, knowing that she had been found out, knowing that a just vengeance had been exacted, and standing forewarned against any other such temptations that might come her way.

But what of the remote possibility that she might choose to speak out and expose herself? There, Cornelius reflected, fitting another little piece of the jigsaw into place, coincidence would instantly go to work for him. If there was no single shred of evidence that he had ever suspected her affair, or that he had ever seen the man before, the accident *must* be regarded by the law as coincidence. Either way his position was unassailable.

It was with this in mind that he patiently and singlemindedly went to work on his plans. He was tempted at the start to call in some professional investigator who could promptly and efficiently bring him the information he wanted, but after careful consideration he put this idea aside. A smart investigator might easily put two and two together after the accident. If he were honest he might go to the authorities with his suspicion; if he were dishonest he might be tempted to try blackmail. Obviously, there was no way of calling in an outsider without risking one danger or the other. And nothing, nothing at all, was going to be risked here.

So it took Cornelius several precious weeks to glean the information he wanted, and, as he admitted to himself, it might have taken even longer had not Claire and the man maintained such an unfailing routine. Thursday was the one day of the week on which the man would pay his visits. Then, a little before the city-bound train arrived at the station, Claire would drive the station wagon into an almost deserted sidestreet a block from the Plaza. In the car the couple would kiss with an intensity that made Cornelius's flesh crawl.

As soon as the man left the car Claire would drive swiftly away, and the man would walk briskly to the Plaza, make his way through the cars parked at the kerb there, cross the Plaza obviously sunk in his own thoughts and with only half an eye for passing traffic, and would enter the station. The third time Cornelius witnessed this performance he could have predicted the man's every step with deadly accuracy.

Occasionally, during this period, Claire mentioned that she was going to the city to do some shopping, and Cornelius took advantage of this as well. He was standing in a shadow of the terminal's waiting-room when her train pulled in, he followed her at a safe distance to the street, his cab trailed hers almost to the shabby apartment house where the man lived. The man was sitting on the grimy steps of the house, obviously waiting for her. When he led her into the house, as Cornelius bitterly observed, they held hands like a pair of school children, and then was a long wait, a wait which took up most of the afternoon; but Cornelius gave up waiting before Claire reappeared.

The eruption of fury he knew after that scene gave him the idea of staging the accident there on the city streets the next day, but Cornelius quickly dismissed the thought. It would mean driving the car into the city, which was something he never did, and that would be a dangerous deviation from his own routine. Besides, city tabloids, unlike his staid local newspaper, sometimes publicised automobile accidents not only by printing the news of them, but also by displaying pictures of victim and culprit on their pages. He wanted none of that. This was a private affair. Strictly private.

No, there was no question that the only place to settle matters was right in the Plaza itself, and the more Cornelius reviewed his plans in preparation for the act the more he marvelled at how flawless they were.

Nothing could conceivably go wrong. If by some

mischance he struck down the man without killing him, his victim would be in the same position as Claire: unable to speak openly without exposing himself. If he missed the man entirely he was hardly in the dangerous position of an assassin who misses his victim and is caught with the gun or knife in his hand. An automobile wasn't a weapon; the affair would simply be another close call for a careless pedestrian.

However, he wanted no close calls, and to that end he took to parking the car somewhat further from the station than he ordinarily did. The extra distance, he estimated, would allow him to swing the car across the Plaza in an arc which would meet the man as he emerged from between the parked cars across the street. That would just about make explanations uncalled-for. A man stepping out from between parked cars would be more in violation of the law than the driver who struck him!

Not only did he make sure to set the car at a proper distance from the station entrance, but Cornelius also took to backing it into place as some other drivers did. Now the front wheels were facing the Plaza, and he could quickly get up all the speed he wanted. More than that, he would be facing the man from the instant he came into sight.

The day before the one he had chosen for the final act, Cornelius waited until he was clear of traffic on his homeward drive, and then stopped the car on a deserted part of the road, letting the motor idle. Then he carefully gauged the distance to a tree some thirty yards ahead; this, he estimated, would be the distance across the Plaza. He started the car and then drove it as fast as he could past the tree, the big machine snarling as it picked up speed. Once past the tree he braced himself, stepped hard on the brake, and felt the pressure of the steering-wheel against his chest as the car slewed to a shrieking stop.

That was it. That was all there was to it . . .

He left the office the next day at the exact minute he had

set for himself. After his secretary had helped him on with his coat he turned to her as he had prepared himself to do and made a wry face.

'Just not feeling right,' he said. 'Don't know what's wrong with me, Miss Wynant.'

And, as he knew good secretaries were trained to do, she frowned worriedly at him and said, 'If you didn't work so hard, Mr Bolinger . . .'

He waved that aside brusquely. 'Nothing that getting home early to a good rest won't cure. Oh,' he slapped at the pockets of his coat, 'my pills, Miss Wynant. They're in the top drawer over there.'

They were only a few aspirins in an envelope, but it was the impression that counted. A man who was not feeling well had that much more justification for a mishap while he was driving.

The early train was familiar to him now; he had ridden on it several times during the past few weeks, but always circumspectly hidden behind a newspaper. Now it was to be different. When the conductor came through to check his commutation ticket, Cornelius was sitting limp in his seat, clearly a man in distress.

'Conductor,' he asked, 'if you don't mind, could you get me some water?'

The conductor glanced at him and hastily departed. When he returned with a dripping cup of water Cornelius slowly and carefully removed an aspirin from the envelope and washed it down gratefully.

'If there's anything else,' the conductor said, 'just you let me know.'

'No,' Cornelius said, 'no, I'm a little under the weather, that's all.'

But at the station the conductor was there to lend him a solicitous hand down, and dally briefly. 'You're not a regular, are you?' the conductor said. 'At least, not on this train?'

Cornelius felt a lift of gratification. 'No,' he said, 'I've only taken this train once before. I usually travel on the Broker's Special.'

'Oh.' The conductor looked him up and down, and grinned. 'Well, that figures,' he said. 'Hope you found our service as good as the Special's.'

In the small station Cornelius sat down on a bench, his head resting against the back of the bench, his eyes on the clock over the ticket agent's window. Once or twice he saw the agent glance worriedly through the window at him, and that was fine. What was not so fine was the rising feeling in him, a lurching nervousness in his stomach, a too-heavy thudding of his heart in his chest. He had allowed himself ten minutes here; each minute found the feeling getting more and more oppressive. It was an effort to contain himself, to prevent himself from getting to his feet and rushing out to the car before the minute hand of the clock had touched the small black spot that was his signal.

Then, on the second, he got up, surprised at the effort it required to do this, and slowly walked out of the station, the agent's eyes following him all the way, and down past the station to the car. He climbed behind the wheel, closed the door firmly after him, and started the motor. The soft purring of the motor under his feet sent a new strength up through him. He sat there soaking it up, his eyes fixed on the distance across the Plaza.

When the man first appeared, moving with rapid strides toward him, it struck Cornelius in some strange way that the tall, blond figure was like a puppet being drawn by an invisible wire to his destined place on the stage. Then, as he came closer, it was plain to see that he was smiling broadly, singing aloud in his exuberance of youth and strength – and triumph. That was the key which unlocked all paralysis, which sent the motor roaring into furious life.

For all the times he had lived the scene in his mind's eye, Cornelius was unprepared for the speed with which it happened. There was the man stepping out from between the cars, still blind to everything. There was Cornelius's hand on the horn, the ultimate inspiration, a warning that could not possibly be heeded, and more than anything else an insurance of success. The man swung toward the noise, his face all horror, his hands out-thrust as if to fend off what was happening. There was the high-pitched scream abruptly cut off by the shock of impact, move violent than Cornelius had ever dreamed, and then everything dissolving into the screech of brakes.

The Plaza had been deserted before it had happened; now, people were running from all directions, and Cornelius had to push his way through them to catch a glimpse of the body.

'Better not look,' someone warned, but he did look, and saw the crumpled form, the legs scissored into an unnatural position, the face greying as he watched. He swayed, and a dozen helping hands reached out to support him, but it was not weakness which affected him now, but an overwhelming, giddy sense of victory, a sense of victory heightened by the voices around him.

'*Walked right into it with his eyes wide open.*'

'*I could hear that horn a block away.*'

'*Drunk, maybe. The way he stood right there . . .*'

The only danger now lay in overplaying his hand. He had to watch out for that, had to keep fitting piece after piece of the plan together, and then there would be no danger. He sat in the car while a policeman questioned him with official gravity, and he knew from the growing sympathy in the policeman's voice that he was making the right impression.

No, he was free to go home if he wished. Charges, of course, had to be automatically preferred against him, but the way things looked . . . Yes, they would be glad to phone Mrs Bolinger. They could drive him home, but if he preferred to have her do it . . .

He had allowed time enough for her to be at home when the call was made, and he spent the next fifteen minutes with the crowd staring at him through the car window with a morbid and sympathetic curiosity. When the station wagon drew up nearby, a lane magically appeared through the crowd; when Claire was at his side the lane disappeared.

Even frightened and bewildered, she was a beautiful woman, Cornelius thought, and, he had to admit to himself, she knew how to put on a sterling show of wifely concern and devotion, false as it was. But perhaps that was because she didn't know yet, and it was time for her to know.

He waited until she had helped him into the station wagon, and when she sat down in the driver's seat he put an arm tight around her.

'Oh, by the way, officer,' he asked with grave anxiety through the open window. 'Did you find out who the man was? Did he have any identification on him?'

The policeman nodded. 'Young fellow from the city,' he said, 'so we'll have to check up on him down there. Name of Lundgren. Robert Lundgren, if his card means anything.'

Against his arm Cornelius felt, rather than heard, the choked gasp, felt the uncontrollable small shivering. Her face was as grey as that of the man's out there in the street. 'All right, Claire,' he said softly. 'Let's go home.'

She drove by instinct out through the streets of the town. Her face was vacuous, her eyes set and staring. He was almost grateful when they reached the highway, and she finally spoke in a quiet and wondering voice. 'You knew,' she said. 'You knew about it, and you killed him for it.'

'Yes,' Cornelius said, 'I knew about it.'

'Then you're crazy,' she said dispassionately, her eyes still fixed ahead of her. 'You must be crazy to kill someone like that.'

Her even, informative tone fired his anger as much as what she was saying.

'It was justice,' he said between his teeth. 'It was coming to him.'

She was still remote. 'You don't understand.'

'Don't understand what?'

She turned toward him, and he saw that her eyes were glistening wet. 'I knew him before I ever knew you, before I ever started working in the office. We always went together; it didn't seem as if there was any point living if we couldn't be together.' She paused only a fraction of a second. 'But things didn't go right. He had big ideas that didn't make any money, and I couldn't stand that. I was born poor, and I couldn't stand marrying poor and dying poor . . . That's why I married you. And I tried to be a good wife – you'll never know how hard I tried! – but that wasn't what you wanted. You wanted a showpiece, not a wife; something to parade around in front of people so that they could admire you for owning it, just like they admire you for everything else you own.'

'You're talking like a fool,' he said harshly. 'And watch the road. We turn off here.'

'Listen to me!' she said. 'I was going to tell you all about it. I was going to ask for a divorce. Not a penny to go with it, or anything like that – just the divorce so that I could marry him and make up for all the time I had thrown away! That's what I told him today, and if you had only asked – only talked to me—'

She would get over it, he thought. It had been even more serious than he had realised, but, as the saying went, *all passes*. She had nothing to trade her marriage for any longer; when she understood that clearly they would make a new start. It was a miracle that he had thought of using the weapon he had, and that he had used it so effectively. *A perfect weapon*, the Judge had said. He'd never know how perfect.

It was the warning clangour of the bell at the grade crossing that jarred Cornelius from his reverie – that, and the alarming realisation that the car's speed was not slackening at all. Then everything else was submerged by the angry bawling of a Diesel horn, and when he looked up incredulously, it was to the raging mountain of steel that was the Broker's Special hurling itself over the crossing directly ahead.

'Watch out!' he cried out wildly. 'My God, what are you doing!'

In that last split-second, when her foot went down hard on the accelerator, he knew.

Galloping Foxley

ROALD DAHL

Like Stanley Ellin, Roald Dahl is a writer who uses everyday situations as the starting point for the most surprising and often quite bizarre stories. Indeed, the best of these formed the basis of the long-running Anglia Television series, *Tales of the Unexpected* (1979–1984), in which every episode ended with a sting in the tall. Several of the episodes contained scenes on the railways – mostly featuring commuters on their way to and from work – and all had been modelled on Dahl's own early experiences as a Shell employee in the city. Certainly, the following pages are some of the most evocative of everyday business travel that I have come across. ('Galloping Foxley' was, in fact, dramatised by Dahl himself for the series in 1980 and starred two veteran British actors, John Mills and Anthony Steel.)

Roald Dahl (1916–1990) may well be best remembered as the most popular children's author of the past quarter of a century, but as a writer of crime and mystery stories he also had few equals for sheer ingenuity and shock value. Apart from the Anglia series, his stories have also been featured in *Alfred Hitchcock Presents* and the American series, *Way Out*, which he hosted and which went out on the same network as *The Twilight Zone*. It was C. S. Forester, the creator of the famous Captain Hornblower historical series whom Dahl met while living in America, who encouraged him to take up writing. The Welshman soon proved himself to be a highly imaginative storyteller with an evident penchant for the macabre. Apart from his short stories found in brilliant collections such as *Someone Like You* (1954) and *Kiss, Kiss* (1960); his comic novels, *My Uncle Oswald* (1979) and *The Witches* (1983); not to mention all the best selling children's books, Dahl also wrote film scripts including the James Bond movie, *You Only Live Twice* (1967). Even though his private life was blighted by a series of tragedies which affected his first wife, Patricia Neal, and two of their five children, Dahl never lost his sardonic sense of humour when it came to his writing, especially in stories like 'Galloping Foxley' (1953) about a commuter train bound for London and the extraordinary events that occur one seemingly ordinary morning.

***

Five days a week, for thirty-six years, I have travelled the eight-twelve train to the City. It is never unduly crowded, and it takes me right in to Cannon Street station, only an eleven and a half minute walk from the door of my office in Austin Friars.

I have always liked the process of commuting; every phase of the little journey is a pleasure to me. There is a regularity about it that is agreeable and comforting to a person of habit, and in addition, it serves as a sort of slipway along which I am gently but firmly launched into the waters of daily business routine.

Ours is a smallish country station and only nineteen or twenty people gather there to catch the eight-twelve. We are a group that rarely changes, and when occasionally a new face appears on the platform it causes a certain disclamatory, protestant ripple, like a new bird in a cage of canaries.

But normally, when I arrive in the morning with my usual four minutes to spare, there they all are, these good, solid, steadfast people, standing in their right places with their right umbrellas and hats and ties and faces and their newspapers under the arms, as unchanged and unchangeable through the years as the furniture in my own living-room. I like that.

I like also my corner seat by the window and reading *The Times* to the noise and motion of the rain. This part of it lasts thirty-two minutes and it seems to soothe both my brain and my fretful old body like a good long massage. Believe me, there's nothing like routine and regularity for preserving one's peace of mind. I have now made this morning journey nearly ten thousand times in all, and I enjoy it more and more every day. Also (irrelevant, but interesting), I have become a sort of clock. I can tell at once if we are running two, three, or four minutes late, and I never have to look up to know which station we are stopped at.

The walk at the other end from Cannon Street to my office is neither too long nor too short – a healthy little perambulation along streets crowded with fellow commuters all proceeding to their places of work on the same orderly schedule as myself. It gives me a sense of assurance to be moving among these dependable, dignified people who stick to their jobs and don't go gadding about all over the world. Their lives, like my own, are regulated nicely by the minute hand of an accurate watch, and very often our paths cross at the same times and places on the street each day.

For example, as I turn the corner into St Swithin's Lane, I invariably come head on with a genteel middle-aged lady who wears silver pince-nez and carries a black briefcase in her hand – a first-rate accountant, I should say, or possibly an executive in the textile industry. When I cross over Threadneedle Street by the traffic lights, nine times out of ten I pass a gentleman who wears a different garden flower in his button-hole each day. He dresses in black trousers and grey spats and is clearly a punctual and meticulous person, probably a banker, or perhaps a solicitor like myself, and several times in the last twenty-five years, as we have hurried past one another across the street, our eyes have met in a fleeting glance of mutual approval and respect.

At least half the faces I pass on this little walk are now familiar to me. And good faces they are too, my kind of faces, my kind of people – sound, sedulous, businesslike folk with none of that restlessness and glittering eye about them that you see in all these so-called clever types who want to tip the world upside down with their Labour governments and socialised medicines and all the rest of it.

So you can see that I am, in every sense of the words, a contented commuter. Or would it be more accurate to say that I *was* a contented commuter? At the time when I wrote the little autobiographical sketch you have just read – intending to circulate it among the staff of my office as an exhortation and an example – I was giving a perfectly true account of my feelings. But that was a whole week ago, and since then something rather peculiar has happened. As a matter of fact, it started to happen last Tuesday, the very morning that I was carrying the rough draft up to town in my pocket; and this, to me, was so timely and coincidental that I can only believe it to have been the work of God. God had read my little essay and he had said to himself, 'This man Perkins is becoming over-complacent. It is high time I taught him a lesson.' I honestly believe that's what happened.

As I say, it was last Tuesday, the Tuesday after Easter, a warm yellow spring morning, and I was striding on to the platform of our small country station with *The Times* tucked under my arm and the draft of 'The Contented Commuter' in my pocket, when I immediately became aware that something was wrong. I could actually *feel* that curious little ripple of protest running along the ranks of my fellow commuters. I stopped and glanced around.

The stranger was standing plumb in the middle of the platform, feet apart and arms folded, looking for all the world as though he owned the whole place. He was a biggish, thickset man, and even from behind he somehow managed to convey a powerful impression of arrogance and oil. Very definitely, he was not one of us. He carried a cane instead of an umbrella, his shoes were brown instead of black, the grey hat was cocked at a ridiculous angle, and in one way and another there seemed to be an excess of silk and polish about his person. More than this I did not care to observe. I walked straight past him with my face to the sky, adding, I sincerely hope, a touch of real frost to an atmosphere that was already cool.

The train came in. And now, try if you can to imagine my horror when the new man actually followed me into *my own* compartment! Nobody has done this to me for fifteen years. My colleagues always respect my seniority. One of my special little pleasures is to have the place to myself for at least one, sometimes two or even three stations. But here, if you please, was this fellow, this stranger, straddling the seat opposite and blowing his nose and rustling the *Daily Mail* and lighting a disgusting pipe.

I lowered my *Times* and stole a glance at his face. I suppose he was about the same age as me – sixty-two or three – but he had one of those unpleasantly handsome, brown, leathery countenances that you see nowadays in advertisements for men's shirts – the lion shooter and the polo player and the Everest climber and the tropical explorer and the racing yachtsman all rolled into one; dark eyebrows, steely eyes, strong white teeth clamping the stem of a pipe. Personally, I mistrust all handsome men. The superficial pleasures of this life come too easily to them, and they seem to walk the world as though they themselves were personally responsible for their own good looks. I don't mind a *woman* being pretty. That's different. But in a man, I'm sorry, but somehow or other I find it downright offensive. Anyway, here was this one sitting right opposite me in the carriage, and I was looking at him over the top of my *Times* when suddenly he glanced up and our eyes met.

'D'you mind the pipe?' he asked, holding it up in his fingers. That was all he said. But the sound of his voice had a sudden and extraordinary effect upon me. In fact, I think I jumped. Then I sort of froze up and sat staring at him for at least a minute before I got a hold of myself and made an answer.

'This is a smoker,' I said, 'so you may do as you please.'

'I just thought I'd ask.'

There it was again, that curiously crisp, familiar voice, clipping its words and spitting them out very hard and small like a little quick-firing gun shooting out raspberry seeds. Where had I heard it before? And why did every word seem to strike upon some tiny tender spot far back in my memory? Good heavens, I thought. Pull yourself together. What sort of nonsense is this?

The stranger returned to his paper. I pretended to do the same. But by this time I was properly put out and I couldn't concentrate at all. Instead, I kept stealing glances at him over the top of the editorial page. It was really an intolerable face, vulgarly, almost lasciviously handsome, with an oily salacious sheen all over the skin. But had I or had I not seen it before sometime in my life? I began to think I had, because now, even when I looked at it I felt a peculiar kind of discomfort that I cannot quite describe – something to do with pain and with violence, perhaps even with fear.

We spoke no more during the journey, but you can well imagine that by then my whole routine had been thoroughly upset. My day was ruined; and more than one of my clerks at the office felt the sharper edge of my tongue, particularly after luncheon when my digestion started acting up on me as well.

The next morning, there he was again standing in the middle of the platform with his cane and his pipe and his silk scarf and his nauseatingly handsome face. I walked past him and approached a certain Mr Grummit, a stockbroker who has been commuting with me for over twenty-eight years. I can't say I've ever had an actual conversation with him before – we are rather a reserved lot on our station – but a crisis like this will usually break the ice.

'Grummitt,' I whispered. 'Who's this bounder?'

'Search me,' Grummitt said.

'Pretty unpleasant.'

'Very.'

'Not going to be a regular, I trust.'

'Oh God,' Grummitt said.

Then the train came in.

This time, to my great relief, the man got into another compartment.

But the following morning I had him with me again.

'Well,' he said, settling back in the seat directly opposite. 'It's a *topping* day.' And once again I felt that slow uneasy stirring of the memory, stronger than ever this time, closer to the surface but not yet quite within my reach.

Then came Friday, the last day of the week. I remember it had rained as I drove to the station, but it was one of those warm sparkling April showers that last only five or six minutes, and when I walked on to the platform, all the umbrellas were rolled up and the sun was shining and there were big white clouds floating in the sky. In spite of this, I felt depressed. There was no pleasure in this journey for me any longer. I knew the stranger would be there. And sure enough, he was, standing with his legs apart just as though he owned the place and this time swinging his cane casually back and forth through the air.

The cane! That did it! I stopped like I'd been shot.

'It's Foxley!' I cried under my breath. 'Galloping Foxley! And still swinging his cane!'

I stepped closer to get a better look. I tell you I've never had such a shock in all my life. It was Foxley all right. Bruce Foxley or Galloping Foxley as we used to call him. And the last time I'd seen him, let me see – it was at school and I was no more than twelve or thirteen years old.

At that point the train came in, and heaven help me if he didn't get into my compartment once again. He put his hat and cane up on the rack, then turned and sat down and began lighting his pipe. He glanced up at me through the smoke with those rather small cold eyes and he said, '*Ripping* day, isn't it. Just like summer.'

There was no mistaking the voice now. It hadn't changed at all. Except that the things I had been used to hearing it say were different. 'All right Perkins,' it used to say. 'All right you nasty little boy. I am about to beat you again.'

How long ago was that? It must be nearly fifty years. Extraordinary, though, how little the features had altered. Still the same arrogant tilt of the chin, the flaring nostrils, the contemptuous staring eyes that were too small and a shade too close together for comfort; still the same habit of thrusting his face forward at you, impinging on you, pushing you into a corner, and even the hair I could remember – coarse and slightly wavy, with just a trace of oil all over it, like a well-tossed salad. He used to keep a bottle of green hair mixture on the side table in his study – when you have to dust a room you get to know and to hate all the objects in it – and this bottle had the royal coat of arms on the label and the name of a shop in Bond Street, and under that, in small print, it said 'By Appointment – Hairdressers To His Majesty King Edward VII'. I can remember that particularly because it seemed so funny that a shop should want to boast about being hairdresser to someone who was practically bald – even a monarch.

And now I watched Foxley settle back in his seat and begin reading his paper. It was a curious sensation, sitting only a yard away from this man who fifty years before had made me so miserable that I had once contemplated suicide. He hadn't recognised *me*: there wasn't much danger of that because of my moustache. I felt fairly sure I was safe and could sit there and watch him all I wanted.

Looking back on it, there seems little doubt that I suffered very badly at the hands of Bruce Foxley my first year in school, and strangely enough, the unwitting cause of it all was my father. I was twelve and a half when I first went off to this fine old public school. That was, let me see, in 1907. My father, who wore a silk topper and morning coat, escorted me to the station, and I can remember how we were standing on the platform among piles of wooden tuck-boxes and trunks and what seemed like thousands of very large boys milling about and talking and shouting at one another, when suddenly somebody who was wanting to get by us gave my father a great push from behind and nearly knocked him off his feet.

My father, who was a small, courteous, dignified person, turned around with surprising speed and seized the culprit by the wrist.

'Don't they teach you better manners than that at this school, young man,' he said.

The boy, at least a head taller than my father, looked down at him with a cold, arrogant-laughing glare, and said nothing.

'It seems to me,' my father said, staring back at him, 'that an apology would be in order.'

But the boy just kept on looking down his nose at my father with this funny little arrogant smile at the corners of his mouth, and his chin kept coming further and further out.

'You strike me as being an impudent and ill-mannered boy,' my father went on. 'And I can only pray you are an exception in your school. I would not wish for any son of mine to pick up such habits.'

At this point, the big boy inclined his head slightly in my direction, and a pair of small, cold, rather close together eyes looked down into mine. I was not particularly frightened at the time; I knew nothing about the power of senior boys over junior boys at public schools; and I can remember that I looked straight back at him in support of my father, whom I adored and respected.

When my father started to say something more, the boy simply turned away and sauntered slowly down the platform into the crowd.

Bruce Foxley never forgot this episode; and of course the really unlucky thing about it for me was that when I arrived at school I found myself in the same 'house' as him. Even worse than that – I was in his study. He was doing his last year, and he was a prefect – a 'boazer' we called it – and as such he was officially permitted to beat any of the fags in the house. But being in his study, I automatically became his own particular, personal slave. I was his valet and cook and maid and errand-boy, and it was my duty to see that he never lifted a finger for himself unless absolutely necessary. In no society that I know of in the world is a servant imposed upon to the extent that we wretched little fags were imposed upon by the boazers at school. In frosty or snowy weather I even had to sit on the seat of the lavatory (which was in an unheated outhouse) every morning after breakfast to warm it before Foxley came along.

I could remember how he used to saunter across the room in his loose-jointed, elegant way, and if a chair were in his path he would knock it aside and I would have to run over and pick it up. He wore silk shirts and always had a silk handkerchief tucked up his sleeve, and his shoes were made by someone called Lobb (who also had a royal crest). They were pointed shoes, and it was my duty to rub the leather with a bone for fifteen minutes each day to make it shine.

But the worst memories of all had to do with the changing-room.

I could see myself now, a small pale shrimp of a boy

standing just inside the door of this huge room in my pyjamas and bedroom slippers and brown camel hair dressing-gown. A single bright electric bulb was hanging on a flex from the ceiling, and all around the walls the black and yellow football shirts with their sweaty smell filling the room, and the voice, the clipped, pip-spitting voice was saying, 'So which is it to be this time? Six with the dressing-gown on – or four with it off?'

I never could bring myself to answer this question. I would simply stand there staring down at the dirty floor-planks, dizzy with fear and unable to think of anything except that this other larger boy would soon start smashing away at me with his long, thin, white stick, slowly, scientifically, skilfully, legally, and with apparent relish, and I would bleed. Five hours earlier, I had failed to get the fire to light in his study. I had spent my pocket money on a box of special firelighters and I had held a newspaper across the chimney opening to make a draught and I had knelt down in front of it and blown my guts out into the bottom of the grate; but the coals would not burn.

'If you're too obstinate to answer,' the voice was saying, 'then I'll have to decide for you.'

I wanted desperately to answer because I knew which one I had to choose. It's the first thing you learn when you arrive. Always keep the dressing-gown *on* and take the extra strokes. Otherwise you're almost certain to get cut. Even three with it on is better than one with it off.

'Take it off then and get into the far corner and touch your toes. I'm going to give you four.'

Slowly I would take it off and lay it on the ledge above the boot-lockers. And slowly I would walk over to the far corner, cold and naked now in my cotton pyjamas, treading softly and seeing everything around me suddenly very bright and flat and far away, like a magic lantern picture, and very big, and very unreal, and sort of swimming through the water in my eyes.

'Go on and touch your toes. Tighter – much tighter than that.'

Then he would walk down to the far end of the changing-room and I would be watching him upside down between my legs, and he would disappear through a doorway that led down two steps into what we called 'the basin-passage'. This was a stone-floored corridor with wash basins along one wall, and beyond it was the bathroom. When Foxley disappeared I knew he was walking down to the far end of the basin-passage. Foxley always did that. Then, in the distance, but echoing loud among the basins and the tiles, I would hear the noise of his shoes on the stone floor as he started galloping forward, and through my legs I would see him leaping up the two steps into the changing-room and come bounding toward me with his face thrust forward and the cane held high in the air. This was the moment when I shut my eyes and waited for the crack and told myself that whatever happened I must not straighten up.

Anyone who has been properly beaten will tell you that the real pain does not come until about eight or ten seconds after the stroke. The stroke itself is merely a loud crack and a sort of blunt thud against your backside, numbing you completely. (I'm told a bullet wound does the same.) But later on, oh my heavens, it feels like someone is laying a red hot poker right across your naked buttocks and it is absolutely impossible to prevent yourself from reaching back and clutching it with your fingers.

Foxley knew all about this time lag, and the slow walk back over a distance that must altogether have been fifteen yards gave each stroke plenty of time to reach the peak of its pain before the next one was delivered.

On the fourth stroke I would invariably straighten up. I couldn't help it. It was an automatic defence reaction from a body that had had as much as it could stand.

'You flinched,' Foxley would say. 'That one doesn't count. Go on – down you get.'

The next time I would remember to grip my ankles.

Afterwards, he would watch me as I walked over – very stiff now and holding my backside – to put on my dressing-gown, but I would always try to keep turned away from him so he couldn't see my face. And when I went out, it would be, 'Hey you! Come back!'

I was in the passage then, and I would stop and turn and stand in the doorway, waiting.

'Come here. Come on, come back here. Now – haven't you forgotten something?'

All I could think of at that moment was the excruciating burning pain in my behind.

'You strike me as being an impudent and ill-mannered boy,' he would say, imitating my father's voice. 'Don't they teach you better manners than that at this school?'

'Thank . . . you,' I would stammer. 'Thank . . . you . . . for the beating.'

And then back up the dark stairs to the dormitory and it became much better then because it was all over and the pain was going and the others were clustering round and treating me with a certain rough sympathy born of having gone through the same thing themselves, many times.

'Hey Perkins, let's have a look.'

'How many d'you get?'

'Five, wasn't it. We heard them easily from here.'

'Come on, man. Let's see the marks.'

I would take down my pyjamas and stand there while this group of experts solemnly examined the damage.

'Rather far apart, aren't they? Not quite up to Foxley's usual standard.'

'Two of them are close. Actually touching. Look – these two are beauties!'

'That low one was a rotten shot.'

'Did he go right down the basin-passage to start his run?'

'You got an extra one for flinching, didn't you?'

'By golly, old Foxley's really got it in for *you*, Perkins.'

'Bleeding a bit too. Better wash it, you know.'

Then the door would open and Foxley would be there, and everyone would scatter and pretend to be doing his teeth or saying his prayers while I was left standing in the centre of the room with my pants down.

'What's going on here?' Foxley would say, taking a quick look at his own handiwork. 'You – Perkins! Put your pyjamas on properly and get into bed.'

And that was the end of a day.

Through the week, I never had a moment of time to myself. If Foxley saw me in the study taking up a novel or perhaps opening my stamp album, he would immediately find something for me to do. One of his favourites, especially when it was raining outside, was, 'Oh Perkins, I think a bunch of wild irises would look rather nice on my desk, don't you?'

Wild irises grew only around Orange Ponds. Orange Ponds was two miles down the road and half a mile across the fields. I would get up from my chair, put on my raincoat and my straw hat, take my umbrella – my brolly – and set off on this long and lonely trek. The straw hat had to be worn at all times outdoors, but it was easily destroyed by rain; therefore the brolly was necessary to protect the hat. On the other hand, you can't keep a brolly over your head while scrambling about on a woody bank looking for irises, so to save my hat from ruin I would put it on the ground under my brolly while I searched for the flowers. In this way, I caught many colds.

But the most dreaded day was Sunday. Sunday was for cleaning the study, and how well I can remember the terror of those mornings, the frantic dusting and scrubbing, and then the waiting for Foxley to come in to inspect.

'Finished?' he would ask.

'I . . . I think so.'

Then he would stroll over to the drawer of his desk and take out a single white glove, fitting it slowly on to his right hand, pushing each finger well home, and I would stand there watching and trembling as he moved around the room running his white-gloved forefinger along the picture tops, the skirting, the shelves, the window sills, the lamp shades. I never took my eyes off that finger. For me it was an instrument of doom. Nearly always, it managed to discover some tiny crack that I had overlooked or perhaps hadn't even thought about; and when his happened Foxley would turn slowly around, smiling that dangerous little smile that wasn't a smile, holding up the white finger so that I should see for myself the thin smudge of dust that lay along the side of it.

'Well,' he would say. 'So you're a lazy little boy. Aren't you?'

No answer.

'Aren't you?'

'I thought I dusted it all.'

'Are you or are you not a nasty, lazy little boy?'

'Y-yes.'

'But your father wouldn't want you to grow up like that, would he? Your father is very particular about manners, is he not?'

No answer.

'I asked you, is your father particular about manners?'

'Perhaps – yes.'

'Therefore I will be doing him a favour if I punish you, won't I?'

'I don't know.'

'Won't I?'

'Y-yes.'

'We will meet later then, after prayers, in the changing-room.'

The rest of the day would be spent in an agony of waiting for the evening to come.

Oh my goodness, how it was all coming back to me now. Sunday was also letter-writing time. 'Dear Mummy and

Daddy – thank you very much for your letter. I hope you are both well. I am, except I have got a cold because I got caught in the rain but it will soon be over. Yesterday we played Shrewsbury and beat them 4–2. I watched and Foxley who you know is the head of our house scored one of our goals. Thank you very much for the cake. With love from William.'

I usually went to the lavatory to write my letter, or to the boot-hole, or the bathroom – any place out of Foxley's way. But I had to watch the time. Tea was at four-thirty and Foxley's toast had to be ready. Every day I had to make toast for Foxley, and on weekdays there were no fires allowed in the studies so all the fags, each making toast for his own study-holder, would have to crowd around the one small fire in the library, jockeying for position with his toasting-fork. Under these conditions, I still had to see that Foxley's toast was (1) very crisp (2) not burned at all (3) hot and ready exactly on time. To fail in any one of these requirements was a 'beatable offence'.

'Hey you! What's this?'

'It's toast.'

'Is this really your idea of toast?'

'Well . . .'

'You're too idle to make it right, aren't you?'

'I try to make it.'

'You know what they do to an idle horse, Perkins?'

'No.'

'Are you a horse?'

'No.'

'Well – anyway you're an ass – ha, ha – so I think you qualify. I'll be seeing you later.'

Oh, the agony of those days. To burn Foxley's toast was a 'beatable offence'. So was forgetting to take the mud off Foxley's football boots. So was failing to hang up Foxley's football clothes. So was rolling up Foxley's brolly the wrong way round. So was banging the study door when

Foxley was working. So was filling Foxley's bath too hot for him. So was not cleaning the buttons properly on Foxley's OTC uniform. So was making those blue metal-polish smudges on the uniform itself. So was failing to shine the *soles* of Foxley's shoes. So was leaving Foxley's study untidy at any time. In fact, so far as Foxley was concerned, I was practically a beatable offence myself.

I glanced out the window. My goodness, we were nearly there. I must have been dreaming away like this for quite a while, and I hadn't even opened my *Times*. Foxley was still leaning back in the corner seat opposite me reading his *Daily Mail*, and through a cloud of blue smoke from his pipe I could see the top half of his face over the newspaper, the small bright eyes, the corrugated forehead, the wavy, slightly oily hair.

Looking at him now, after all that time, was a peculiar and rather exciting experience. I knew he was no longer dangerous, but the old memories were still there and I didn't feel altogether comfortable in his presence. It was something like being inside the cage with a tame tiger.

What nonsense is this? I asked myself. Don't be so stupid. My heavens, if you wanted to you could go ahead and tell him exactly what you thought of him and he couldn't touch you. Hey – that was an idea!

Except that – well – after all, was it worth it? I was too old for that sort of thing now, and I wasn't sure that I really felt much anger toward him anyway.

So what should I do? I couldn't sit there staring at him like an idiot.

At that point, a little impish fancy began to take a hold of me. What I would like to do, I told myself, would be to lean across and tap him lightly on the knee and tell him who I was. Then I would watch his face. After that, I would begin talking about our schooldays together, making it just loud enough for the other people in the carriage to hear. I would remind him playfully of some of the things he used to do to me, and perhaps even describe the changing-room beatings so as to embarrass him a trifle. A bit of teasing and discomfort wouldn't do him any harm. And it would do *me* an awful lot of good.

Suddenly he glanced up and caught me staring at him. It was the second time this had happened, and I noticed a flicker of irritation in his eyes.

All right, I told myself. Here we go. But keep it pleasant and sociable and polite. It'll be much more effective that way, more embarrassing for him.

So I smiled at him and gave him a courteous little nod. Then, raising my voice, I said, 'I do hope you'll excuse me. I'd like to introduce myself.' I was leaning forward, watching him closely so as not to miss the reaction. 'My name is Perkins – William Perkins – and I was at Repton in 1907.'

The others in the carriage were sitting very still, and I could sense that they were all listening and waiting to see what would happen next.

'I'm glad to meet you,' he said, lowering the paper to his lap. 'Mine's Fortescue – Jocelyn Fortescue, Eton, 1916.'

The Second Passenger

BASIL COPPER

Retribution on a train is also the theme of this next story by English thriller writer Basil Copper. It is a tale of mounting suspicion and horror set on another of England's busiest suburban lines, between London's Charing Cross station and the Kent commuter belt, and is written by a man eminently familiar with the network having used it himself regularly during his working life as a journalist and newspaper editor. In fact, Copper lives in Sevenoaks where the denouement takes place, which gives an added sense of *frisson* to the terrible events it describes.

Basil Copper (1924–) is a practised exponent of both the crime and horror story genres. For many years he has enjoyed considerable success with his series of hardboiled novels about a Los Angeles private eye, Mike Faraday (now over fifty titles strong), as well as the half dozen volumes of adventures of London detective Solar Pons, a pastiche of Sherlock Holmes. Pons, who lives in Praed Street with his 'Dr Watson', Parker, makes frequent use of the railways during his cases. Copper has also utilised his knowledge of the English rail system in a couple of his horror novels, *Necropolis* (1980) with its haunting account of a ghost train, and *The Black Death* (1991) which provides an authentic picture of the railway system on and around Dartmooor as it was operated during the Victorian era. 'The Second Passenger', in contrast, has a more modern setting and is another example of why Copper is so highly rated as a writer of macabre fiction; he was recently praised by Colin Wilson for being 'one of the last of the great traditionalists of English fiction'. In the modern horror story genre, he can always be relied upon to tell an engrossing story without resorting to the excesses of 'butcher shop' blood and gore, a fact to which the following pages will bear eloquent and chilling witness.

***

Mr Reginald Braintree sat quite still in the corner of the fusty third-class compartment, with his feet up on the opposite seat and a copy of *The Times* spreadeagled on his lap. The carriage was quite empty and had been since he left Charing Cross so the liberty was pardonable. Outside, the blurred scenery of wood and stream whirled effortlessly by, the white-grey smoke from the engine fogging the windows and restricting the vision. The noise of the wheels went monotonously on and on, as though some tireless hand were rhythmically beating time in some fantastic computation.

Dusk was closing in and the carriage lights shed their yellow glare on to the wan face of Mr Braintree, making his usually pale features look macabre. They heightened the sombre effect of his never genial eyes, distorting them into black pits, from which his pupils gleamed, greenishly and balefully. His mouth was a mere slit in the twilight, the shadow underneath making it resemble a letter box which, metaphorically speaking, it was.

He was dressed in a faded suit of salt and pepper broadcloth. His stout brown shoes were scratched and worn but they did not look old; his hat was battered, yet it did not seem antique. In short Mr Braintree was a successful man who could afford to dress well yet did not choose to, a thing not entirely unknown among a certain class of businessmen.

His paper, stirred by some motion of the train, slipped unheeded to the floor, and he did not bother to pick it up.

His figure slumped at the sudden motion when the carriage rounded a bend and then he automatically recovered himself as it regained the straight. In a way the railway was something like the course of Mr Braintree's own career; it ploughed remorselessly on, unable to leave its designated route and when at length it came to a hill, instead of going round, it smashed an impetuous path through.

There were times when Mr Braintree lapsed into compassion but they were few for he did not care to make a cult of weakness, as he called it. His first day as an office boy in a stockbroking firm in Cheapside many years before had taught him the efficacy of force, a lesson he had never forgotten; and which ever since he had used to determine the course of his life. The occasion was common enough, yet it left an everlasting impression.

It appeared that it was the duty of a certain Samuel Briggs, also a species of clerk, to fill the inkwells and run the errands, in addition to his other multifarious duties. However, being the type of person who will never do a thing if he can get someone else to do it for him, he somewhat naturally chose the moment of the newcomer's arrival to assert his authority. Unfortunately, from his point of view, the other clerks were big and determined men, not at all disposed to run his errands for him, but the entry of the diminutive Braintree altered the picture completely.

His first commissions were executed willingly enough and without suspicion, but later, one of the other employees having let something drop, young Braintree began to see the true situation, and not having a vacuum where his brain should be, sought to escape from this unwelcome and decidedly irksome yoke. The first hint of mutiny was met with black looks and a clenching of fists which, although subduing Braintree for a time, did not permanently dampen his resolution to be rid of his bondage.

The next time the dapper young gentleman told him to

empty the wastepaper baskets and be quick about it, this spate of rhetoric being accompanied by a well-propelled kick in the rear, the younger's temper flared. Impetuously turning, he flung the contents of the inkwell he was carrying full into the sneering, weakly handsome face of the clerk before him. The next moments were somewhat hazy for he was picked up violently, shaken like a rat and, with a vicious back-handed slap in the face, hurled unceremoniously downstairs.

As he dazedly came to rest in the hallway he heard the malicious laughter of his contemporaries floating down towards him, and the sound was like gall to his already bitter soul. Spitting curses through the mask of blood that covered his features, he swore then and there to get even with his tormentor if it took him all his life. This resolve was interrupted by the appearance of the bedraggled form of Mr Samuel Briggs at the head of the stairway, wiping some of the ink off his mottled countenance and transferring it to a convenient towel.

But although defeated physically, Braintree had gained an enormous moral victory over his opponent, for the confidence of the bully had been shaken, and from then on his manner was less assured. The younger boy received fewer commissions and they gradually stopped. But his dark brooding spirit still rankled over the day of his degradation and the promise he had compacted with himself remained as implacable as ever.

As he grew older his feelings became more subdued and subtle, and it would have needed a very shrewd and worldly person to see that the two clerks who worked so amicably together were in reality deadly enemies, each determined to usurp the other in the estimation of their employer, should the opportunity present itself. If it were Braintree who arrived early one morning, filled the inkwells, tidied the office and waded through arrears of work, then one could be sure that it was Briggs who sat up half the night sweating over a mountain of paper.

Was it not Briggs who cycled five miles through the pouring rain to old Mr Steyning's house with some important documents that had been overlooked? And yet had not Braintree been just as meritorious in returning from a fortnight's holiday on his first day away, in order to tell Mr Steyning of an important business speculation which he had learned en route? Who ran for the doctor when Mrs Steyning was ill? Briggs, of course. And who summoned the courage to risk serious injury by rescuing the old man's daughter from the wheels of a bus? Braintree, naturally.

Finally, what cloak of generosity masked the actions of two unscrupulous men who eventually jointly subscribed the money needed to put the firm on its feet again? As sure as the earth revolves round the sun it was Briggs and Braintree, but that their actions were motivated by quixotic impulse is beyond imagination. Yet later it did not seem that they had been risking anything at all. For when their employer's anxiety with regard to the future of his organisation was allayed, he naturally turned to the men who had made this reversal possible.

The result was a junior partnership for both of them, an opportunity which neither of them neglected. From that time onwards their careers were set. With the passing of the years, while increasing in prosperity, they never forgot for a single moment that they were enemies, and though no one could have divined it, the germs of hatred were breeding and multiplying within their respective brains.

Things might have gone on like this for ever except for one fact. Mr Steyning was growing old, his business prospering and with two capable junior partners to all appearances contentedly running things, he saw no reason why he should not sit back and put the reins unreservedly into their hands. So he retired and sealed their fates by so doing.

Without the old man's restraining influence the two men immediately fell apart again, and although no one would have seen any outward difference between them, their consuming passions were more openly manifest than usual. Their morning greeting was elaborately polite, almost to the verge of irony, while now and again, the masks slipping, cutting remarks would whip about the office, to the bewilderment of those who heard them.

Everyone began to suspect that something was wrong, and the clerks, on the same stools which had accommodated their employers years before, to whisper and gossip among themselves. The business too, began to suffer. Each of the partners, in his eagerness to outdo the other, eventually deprived himself of the benefits of their transactions. With the curb of Mr Steyning's presence acting as a restraint to their impatient spirits they were safe; without him they were lost.

The affair swiftly progressed to an open rift, culminating in Braintree's discovery of Briggs's misdemeanours. The whole truth of the matter was never really discovered; some said women, some said horses were the reason, but the upshot of it was the Briggs had been spending above even his considerable income. Neither had families to tie them down in any way, for both men were bachelors, and thus there were no domestic questions.

For almost a year, considerable sums of money had been taken by Briggs and only covered by dextrous and skilful handling of the books. Perhaps it was a malicious and selfish ego that enjoyed and exulted in the fact of cheating a hated partner out of the money, or a pressing and desperate need, the step being taken only after long consideration; the truth will possibly never be known.

Discovery could not be postponed indefinitely; the misdemeanour uncovered some time. The denouement occurred on a cold March morning, when the rime sparkled on pavement and railing and fog hung like a thick yellow cloak over the city. Braintree was in an unusually foul temper, even for him, and strode through the outer office, looking neither right nor left, responding with a grunt to the chorus of salutations from the staff.

Briggs, a tall, sallow man with pock-marked cheeks was already seated at his desk sipping a measure of whisky from the cap of a silver hip flask, to take 'the nip off the air', as he explained it.

'It would be more to the point if you attended more closely to the firm's affairs, instead of indulging in that debasing practice,' Braintree sneered, for he was a strict teetotaller. The other, however, said nothing, which was unusual for him and the younger man commented on it.

Briggs's eyes were beginning to burn angrily and he half slewed on his seat, his right hand methodically screwing the cap of his flask; he twisted it savagely as though it were the thick head of his enemy. He opened his mouth to spit out a reply when the door was pushed back by the head clerk; he looked agitated and white.

'It's about the accounts, sir,' he jerked hesitantly.

Braintree excused himself and went off irritably; if there was one thing he disliked it was any interruption to the smooth routine of the office. He was away a long time and Briggs sat staring moodily at the swirling fog outside the window; he made no attempt to deal with the jumble of documents on the desk before him. He was still sitting there when Braintree came back. He glanced coldly at his partner before crossing to his desk. He took something from a drawer and then relocked it.

'I shall be some time,' he told Briggs in a hostile voice.

The door clicked to behind him. Briggs took another swig from the flask and re-stoppered it. He toyed idly with a bunch of keys, his hands suddenly sweaty. Perhaps he did not move into the outer office because he was already acquainted with what would be found there. The clock ticked away while he listened with straining ears. There was the confused murmur of voices, mingled with the jingling of keys and rustling of papers.

The whispered consultations were still going on when Briggs left for lunch; they went on throughout the afternoon and eventually night fell again. Instead of leaving for his home as he usually did Briggs remained behind at his desk. The fog passed sullenly against the window. He heard the outer office door close behind the last of the clerks, waited for the heavy footfall of his partner. It was nearly seven o'clock before the door of the inner office opened again.

The stocky form of the younger partner appeared. His manner was extremely mild when he spoke, yet the curious pose of his body suggested the coiling of a steel spring. Briggs had not moved; he gazed abstractedly across the office, as though trying to discern whether the Chinaman on the commercial calendar was grimacing or smiling. He felt like doing neither. He lifted his face, his forehead slightly shiny, and coughed; a nervous, startled cough, which sounded incongruous in the pregnant stillness.

'Well?'

It was Braintree who spoke. He stood by the back of the other's chair, his thick knuckles gleaming white where he clenched the woodwork.

'You know?' the other answered dully. 'You've found out?'

Braintree nodded. He kept remarkable control. His voice was dry and smooth, as though a life's ambition had been achieved. 'But twenty thousand, Briggs . . .'

He looked curiously at the still figure of his partner.

'How did you expect to get away with it?'

Briggs turned away from Braintree with a convulsive movement. He put his head in his hands.

'I wouldn't expect you to understand,' he said. 'What are you going to do?'

'Do?' said Braintree. He looked at his watch. 'I've already done it. I've sent Simmonds round with a note to the station. The police should be here in twenty minutes.'

'A bit premature aren't you?' Briggs sneered.

Red stood out in vivid patches on his cheeks and his breathing was becoming laboured.

'I don't think so,' said Braintree smoothly. 'It is a criminal matter, after all. Such a huge sum of money. And your personal accounts should tally with the discrepancy.'

He started back as Briggs got up with a sudden movement.

'You're enjoying this, aren't you?' said Briggs thickly.

Braintree declined to answer. He went to the window and watched the swirling fog. He toyed nervously with the heavy office ruler in his hand.

'I suppose it's no good asking you for an hour's grace?' said Briggs heavily.

Braintree shook his head. He had a sardonic smile on his lips. 'None at all,' he said. 'You should have thought of this before. I must advise you against attempting to leave. I should be forced to prevent it.'

He hefted the massive, metal-edged ruler in his hand uncertainly. Indeed, he was a somewhat incongruous figure and obviously ill-fitted for the self-appointed task. Briggs stared incredulously at him for a moment. Then he gave a short, barking laugh.

'I'm off,' he said. 'To blazes with you and your police.'

He strode impetuously forward, thrusting Braintree aside. The partner fell against the window; he felt a sharp pain as his hand broke the glass. The sudden shock stung him into action. Briggs was at the door when Braintree reached him. The two men began a silent struggle; then Braintree was thrown aside. He fell against the desk this time and barked his shin; this second, unexpected pain sent a spurt of anger through him. Galvanised into action he struck at Briggs again and again with the heavy ruler.

Briggs gave a hoarse cry. The big man turned. Braintree saw blood on his face, the eyes filmy and horrified. He felt sick. The older man fell asprawl with a crash. His head caught the edge of the desk with a horrifying crack. He lay still. Braintree bent over him, searched for the steady pump of the heart, failed to find it. His own heart stood still.

Then another sound sent the adrenalin flooding through his own system. He started dragging the body of Briggs along the floor towards the cupboard as heavy footsteps sounded on the stair.

It was nearly eleven before Mr Braintree reached the Essex marshes. It had been a long and tiring drive through East London and the little Morris was not behaving well. Braintree believed it might be the effect of the damp weather and one defective plug. He had not liked it at all when the vehicle had stalled completely at a traffic lights in Walthamstow.

But now he was clear of the more populous areas and he breathed more easily, the car positively humming along. The moon was up and its pallid light cast shadows across the humped form of Briggs on the back seat, covered by thick layers of motoring rugs. It had been a miracle that Briggs had driven his own car in from Surrey that day, Braintree reflected.

Once he had got rid of the police by telling them that Briggs had left, it had been fairly simple to bring the car to the seldom-used side alley and take the body down the back stair. Fairly simple, but how tiring, Braintree thought. Now, he had the perfect answer to the problem.

With Briggs's disappearance he had only to drive his car back to the nearest tube and abandon it. When it was found it would merely add substance to the circumstance that Briggs had been unable to face the music and had fled.

Braintree would have to stay in town tonight; that was the only flaw in his plan. By the time he got back to central London his last train from Charing Cross would have long gone and he had no desire to wait for the early morning paper train in this weather.

He must be careful, that was all; he had no luggage. He would simply register under another name, carefully choosing a small family hotel away from the city centre and tell them the truth; that he had missed his train. There must be many businessmen who were in a similar predicament, every evening. The more Braintree thought about it on his long, foggy drive, the more he liked it. He was free of the villages at last and making for a spot he remembered from years before. Unless it had been built up since then.

He took a rutted side road, the Morris protesting at the surface, and drove carefully along it. The fog had lifted with his clearing the city and he knew where he was. When he had driven as far as he could go, he left the car; the next hour, dragging Briggs's heavy form through the under-growth, was the most tiring he had ever known. When his feet began to squelch in mud he looked down; his prints were already beginning to fill with water. It was nearly time. He got his hands under Briggs's armpits and dragged him the last few yards to the top of the bank.

He was sweating as he gave the final push. The body rocked, sagged and then started to slide down the steep slope. The moon gilded the dead face as it slid to a halt; green scum parted, viscous mud sucked at the corpse. It began to sink slowly, bubbles of marsh gas bursting in foul, scummy pustules on the surface of the swamp. Mr Braintree waited for twenty minutes until the entire corpse had been consumed. The last thing to go was one of Briggs's hands. It seemed to wave a valediction at Braintree as the fingers slowly disappeared beneath the surface.

Braintree shivered. It was growing cold again. Or the effect of his exercise was wearing off. He waited a few minutes more and finally the bubbles stopped coming to the top. The green scum of the surface resumed its interrupted sway. Mr Braintree made his way heavily back to the road. No one would ever find Briggs now. That swamp was bottomless, he'd heard in years gone by; what it took it kept. He looked at his watch. It was already nearly one a.m. It seemed like a long drive back towards the city.

The train roared on through the night and still Mr Braintree sat comfortably sprawled with his feet up and his antique hat poised beside him. Presently there came the hiss of brakes and the carriage shuddered and was still. Came the burst of escaping steam and a nervous little pulse beat somewhere under the floorboards. Figures went by in the corridor and, after glancing at the uninviting figure of the stockbroker, their owners passed on.

Carriage doors were slamming and the hoarse, inarticulate cry of a porter drifted up wind. 'Sevenoaks, Sevenoaks.'

A railway employee came down the carriages, slamming the doors. He caught sight of Mr Braintree's recumbent form and slid back the door of the compartment, annoyance on his face.

'This train doesn't go any further, sir.'

Mr Braintree's body sagged, asprawl at an awkward angle.

The porter bent over him, hesitated. His nostrils were assailed by a loathsome stench. He saw then, in the dim radiance of the carriage lighting, a patch of damp green slime on the floor. It glimmered wetly and the stench seemed to come from this. Fighting his nerves the porter seized Mr Braintree by the shoulder.

The dead face fell forward and the man was conscious of the slime on the features; something like moss clustered round the nostrils and a thin driblet shuddered from the corner of the mouth. A shadow fell across the carriage and the figure of a tall, burly man passed in the corridor. The porter gave a hoarse shout and stumbled away from the corpse of Braintree.

'Just a minute, sir,' he called after the tall figure. 'There's been an accident.'

On the platform the big man marched forward under the lamps without stopping. At every footprint green slime seemed to spring up on the surface of the platform. The porter cursed as he almost sprawled on the muck. There was that disgusting smell again. The big man went on. The porter increased his pace.

'Stop him!' he bawled at a group of railwaymen who were gossiping at one end of the platform.

They looked up curiously as the form of the big man went steadily up the steps of the bridge. He did not seem to be hurrying but the porter was unable to gain on him.

He shouted again and this time the group was stirred into action. Its members ran up the stairs, searching for the tall figure. One of them turned as the porter came up.

'What was it? What was it?' he said, his eyes wide with fear. There were patches of green slime on the steps of the bridge. A putrefying stench came to them down the wind. But the tall, hurrying figure of the big man was never seen again.

The Green Road
to Quephanda

RUTH RENDELL

This final item in the book is also the most curious story in
the entire collection, featuring as it does the remnants of an
old suburban line that once served the commuters of
London and now lies forgotten, its tracks pulled up and its
stations abandoned and choked with weeds, yet still
remaining a magnet for people. It is a story which also
brings back memories for me: my wife and I lived in the
Highgate district where the story is set during the early
years of our married life and once overheard remarks about
an abandoned railway line in the vicinity which was
supposed to be haunted by a ghost train. It was, in all
probability, that same rumour which inspired this story
that mixes the prosaic and the fantastic in a unique way.

Ruth Rendell (1930–) was born in East London where
her parents were teachers in Limehouse, but she was
educated in Essex and began her working life as a journalist
on the *Chigwell Times* where one of her most notorious
stories concerned an allegedly haunted house. Our paths
may have briefly crossed there, for I started my own career
on the rival paper, *The West Essex Gazette*, where my
territory was also Chigwell. Later, when Rendell began
writing the psychological crime and detective novels and
short stories which have made her famous, she lived for a
time near Hampstead Heath, the setting of 'The Green
Road to Quephanda'. Although her main home is now in
rural Suffolk, she still follows the example of one of her
literary heroes, Charles Dickens, by walking long distances
around the streets of London, observing and remembering

all she sees – a fact which gives her books such a sense of atmosphere and realism. Rendell says that all her early attempts at novels were rejected by publishers and it was not until she hit upon the character of Detective Chief Inspector Wexford in *From Doon With Death* in 1964 that success at last came her way. The subsequent stories about the methodical policeman which have reached an even larger audience through television, have made her a household name, while similar acclaim has also been given to her second string of novels written under the pen-name Barbara Vine. 'The Green Road to Quephanda' is an evocative story of the railway's past – and one, I think, that provides a perfect finale to the journey we have taken through the pages of this book.

* * *

There used to be, not long ago, a London suburban line railway running up from Finsbury Park to Highgate, and further than that for all I know. They closed it down before I went to live at Highgate and at some point they took up the sleepers and the rails. But the track remains and a very strange and interesting track it is. There are people living in the vicinity of the old line who say they can still hear, at night and when the wind is right, the sound of a train pulling up the slope to Highgate and, before it comes into the old disused station, giving its long, melancholy, hooting call. A ghost train, presumably, on rails that have long been lifted and removed.

But this is not a ghost story. Who could conceive of the ghost, not of a person but of a place, and that place having no existence in the natural world? Who could suppose anything of a supernatural or paranormal kind happening to a man like myself, who am quite unimaginative and not observant at all?

An observant person, for instance, could hardly have

lived for three years only two minutes from the old station without knowing of the existence of the line. Day after day, on my way to the Underground, I passed it, glanced down unseeing at the weed-grown platforms, the broken canopies. Where did I suppose those trees were growing, rowans and Spanish chestnuts and limes that drop their sticky black juice, like tar, that waved their branches in a long avenue high up in the air? What did I imagine that occasionally glimpsed valley was, lying between suburban back gardens? You may enter or leave the line at the bridges where there are always places for scrambling up or down, and at some actual steps, much overgrown, and gates or at least gateposts. I had been walking under or over these bridges (according as the streets where I walked passed under or over them) without ever asking myself what those bridges carried or crossed. It never even, I am sorry to say, occurred to me that there were rather a lot of bridges for a part of London where the only railway line, the Underground, ran deep in the bowels of the earth. I didn't think about them. As I walked under one of the brown brick tunnels I didn't look up to question its presence or ever once glance over a parapet. It was Arthur Kestrell who told me about the line, one evening while I was in his house.

Arthur was a novelist. I write 'was', not because he has abandoned his profession for some other, but because he is dead. I am not even sure whether one would call his books novels. They truly belong in that curious category, a fairly popular genre, that is an amalgam of science fiction, fairy tale and horror fantasy.

But Arthur, who used the pseudonym Blasie Fastnet, was no Mervyn Peake and no Lovecraft either. Not that I had read any of his books at the time of which I am writing. But Elizabeth, my wife, had. Arthur used sometimes to give us one of them on publication, duly inscribed and handed to us, presented indeed, with the air of something very precious and uniquely desirable being bestowed.

I couldn't bring myself to read them. The titles alone were enough to repel me: *Kallinarth, the Cloudling*, *The Quest of Kallinarth*, *Lord of Quephanda*, *The Grail-Seeker's Guerdon* and so forth. But I used somehow, without actually lying, to give Arthur the impression that I had read his latest, or I think I did. Perhaps, in fact, he saw through this, for he never enquired if I had enjoyed it or had any criticisms to make. Liz said they were 'fun', and sometimes – with kindly intent, I know – would refer to an incident or portion of dialogue in one of the books in Arthur's presence. 'As Kallinarth might have said,' she would say, or 'Weren't those the flowers Kallinarth picked for Valaquen when she woke from her long sleep?' This sort of thing only had the effect of making poor Arthur blush and look embarrassed. I believe that Arthur Kestrell was convinced in his heart that he was writing great literature, never perhaps to be recognised as such in his lifetime but for the appreciation of posterity. Liz, privately to me, used to call him the poor man's Tolkien.

He suffered from periods of black and profound depression. When these came upon him he couldn't write or read or even bring himself to go out on those marathon walks ranging across north London which he dearly loved when he was well. He would shut himself up in his Gothic house in that district where Highgate and Crouch End merge, and there he would hide and suffer and pace the floors, not answering the door, still less the telephone until, after five or six days or more, the mood of wretched despair had passed.

His books were never reviewed in the press. How it comes about that some authors' work never receives the attention of the critics is a mystery, but the implication, of course, is that it is beneath their notice. This ignoring of a new publication, this bland passing over with neither a smile nor a sneer, implies that the author's work is a mere commercially motivated repetition of his last book, a slight variation on a tried and lucrative theme, another stereotyped bubbler in a long line of profitable pot-boilers. Arthur, I believe, took it hard. Not that he told me so. But soon after Liz had scanned the papers for even a solitary line to announce a new Fastnet publication, one of these depressions of his would settle on him and he would go into hiding behind his grey, crenellated walls.

Emerging, he possessed for a while a kind of slow cheerfulness combined with a dogged attitude to life. It was always a pleasure to be with him, if for nothing else than the experience of his powerful and strange imagination whose vividness coloured those books of his, and in conversation gave an exotic slant to the observations he made and the opinions he uttered.

London, he always insisted, was a curious, glamorous and sinister city, hung on slopes and valleys in the north of the world. Did I not understand the charm it held for foreigners who thought of it with wistfulness as a grey Eldorado? I who had been born in it couldn't see its wonders, its contrasts, its wickedness. In summer Arthur got me to walk with him to Marx's tomb, to the house where Housman wrote *A Shropshire Lad*, to the pond in the Vale of Health where Shelley sailed boats. We walked the Heath and we walked the urban woodlands and then one day, when I complained that there was nowhere left to go, Arthur told me about the track where the railway line had used to be. A long green lane, he said, like a country lane, four and a half miles of it, and smiling in his cautious way, he told me where it went. Over Northwood Road, over Stanhope Road, under Crouch End Hill, over Vicarage Road, under Crouch Hill, under Mount View, over Mount Pleasant Villas, over Stapleton Hall, under Upper Tollington Park, over Oxford Road, under Stroud Green Road, and so to the station at Finsbury Park.

'How do you get on to it?' I said.

'At any of the bridges. Or at Holmesdale Road. You can get on to it from the end of my garden.'

'Right,' I said. 'Let's go. It's a lovely day.'

'There'll be crowds of people on a Saturday,' said Arthur. 'The sun will be bright like fire and there'll be hordes of wild people and their bounding dogs and their children with music machines and tinned drinks.' This was the way Arthur talked, the words juicily or dreamily enunciated. 'You want to go up there when it's quiet, at twilight, at dusk, when the air is lilac and you can smell the bitter scent of the tansy.'

'Tomorrow night then. I'll bring Liz and we'll call for you and you can take us up there.'

But on the following night when we called at Arthur's house and stood under the stone archway of the porch and rang his bell, there was no answer. I stepped back and looked up at the narrow latticed windows, shaped like inverted shields. This was something which, in these circumstances, I had never done before. Arthur's face looked back at me, blurred and made vague by the dark, diamond-paned glass, but unmistakably his small wizened face, pale and with its short, sparse beard. It is a disconcerting thing to be looked at like this by a dear friend who returns your smile and your mouthed greeting with a dead, blank and unrecognisable stare. I suppose I knew then that poor Arthur wasn't quite sane any more. Certainly Liz and I both knew that he had entered one of his depressions and that it was useless to expect him to let us in.

We went off home, abandoning the idea of an exploration of the track that evening. But on the following day, work being rather slack at that time of the year, I found myself leaving the office early and getting out of the tube train at Highgate at half-past four. Liz, I knew, would be out. On an impulse, I crossed the street and turned into Holmesdale Road. Many a time, walking there before, I had noticed what seemed an unexpectedly rural meadow lying to the north of the street, a meadow overshadowed by broad trees, though no more than fifty yards from the roar and stench of the Archway Road. Now I understood what it was. I walked down the slope, turned south-eastwards where the meadow narrowed and came on to a grassy lane.

It was about the width of an English country lane and it was bordered by hedges of buddleia on which peacock and small tortoiseshell butterflies basked. And I might have felt myself truly in the country had it not been for the backs of houses glimpsed all the time between the long leaves and the purple spires of the buddleia bushes. Arthur's lilac hour had not yet come. It was windless sunshine up on the broad green track, the clear, white light of a sun many hours yet from setting. But there was a wonderful warm and rural, or perhaps I should say pastoral, atmosphere about the place. I need Arthur's gift for words and Arthur's imagination to describe it properly and that I don't have. I can only say that there seemed, up there, to be a suspension of time and also of the hurrying, frenzied bustle, the rage to live, that I had just climbed up out of.

I went over the bridge at Northwood Road and over the bridge at Stanhope Road, feeling ashamed of myself for having so often walked unquestioningly *under* them. Soon the line began to descend, to become a valley rather than a causeway, with embankments on either side on which grew small, delicate birch trees and the rosebay willow herb and the giant hogweed. But there were no tansy flowers, as far as I could see. These are bright yellow double daisies borne in clusters on long stems and they have the same sort of smell as chrysanthemums. For all I know, they may be a sort of chrysanthemum or belonging to that family. Anyway, I couldn't see any or any lilac, but perhaps Arthur hadn't meant that and in any case it wouldn't be in bloom in July. I went as far as Crouch End Hill that first time and then I walked home by road. If I've given the impression there were no people on the line, this wasn't so. I passed a couple of women walking a labrador, two boys with bikes and a little girl in school uniform eating a choc ice.

Liz was intrigued to hear where I had been but rather cross that I hadn't waited until she could come too. So that evening, after we had had our meal, we walked along the line the way and the distance I had been earlier and the next night we ventured into the longer section. A tunnel blocked up with barbed wire prevented us from getting quite to the end but we covered nearly all of it and told each other we very likely hadn't missed much by this defeat.

The pastoral atmosphere disappeared after Crouch End Hill. Here there was an old station, the platforms alone still remaining, and under the bridge someone had dumped an old feather mattress – or plucked a dozen geese. The line became a rubbish dump for a hundred yards or so and then widened out into children's playgrounds with murals – and graffiti – on the old brick walls.

Liz looked back at the green valley behind. 'What you gain on the swings,' she said, 'you lose on the roundabouts.' A child in a rope seat swung past us, shrieking, nearly knocking us over.

All the prettiness and the atmosphere I have tried to describe was in that first section, Highgate station to Crouch End Hill. The next time I saw Arthur, when he was back in the world again, I told him we had explored the whole length of the line. He became quite excited.

'Have you now? All of it? It's beautiful, isn't it? Did you see the foxgloves? There must be a mile of foxgloves up there. And the mimosa? You wouldn't suppose mimosa could stand an English winter and I don't know of anywhere else it grows, but it flourishes up there. It's sheltered, you see, sheltered from all the frost and the harsh winds.'

Arthur spoke wistfully as if the frost and harsh winds he referred to were more metaphorical than actual, the coldness of life and fate and time rather than of climate. I didn't argue with him about the mimosa, though I had no doubt at all that he was mistaken. The line up there was exposed, not sheltered, and even if it had been, even if it had been in Cornwall or the warm Scilly Isles, it would still have been too cold for mimosa to survive. Foxgloves were another matter, though I hadn't seen any, only the hogweed with its bracts of dirty white flowers, garlic mustard and marestail, burdock and rosebay, and the pale leathery leaves of the coltsfoot. As the track grew rural again, past Mount View, hawthorn bushes, not mimosa, grew on the embankment slopes.

'It belongs to Haringey Council.' Arthur's voice was always vibrant with expression and now it had become a drawl of scorn and contempt. 'They want to build houses on it. They want to plaster it with a great red sprawl of council houses, a disfiguring red naevus.' Poor Arthur's writing may not have been the effusion of genius he seemed to believe, but he certainly had a gift for the spoken word.

That August his annual novel was due to appear. Liz had been given an advance copy and had duly read it. Very much the same old thing, she said to me: Kallinarth, the hero-king in his realm composed of cloud; Valaquen, the maiden who sleeps, existing only in a dream-life, until all evil has gone out of the world; Xadatel and Finrael, wizard and warrior, heavenly twins. The title this time was *The Fountains of Zond*.

Arthur came to dinner with us soon after Liz had read it, we had three other guests, and while we were having our coffee and brandy I happened to say that I was sorry not to have any Drambuie as I knew he was particularly fond of it.

Liz said, 'We ought to have Xadatel here, Arthur, to magic you some out of the fountains of Zond.'

It was a harmless, even rather sympathetic, remark. It showed she knew Arthur's work and was conversant with the properties of these miraculous fountains which apparently produced nectar, fabulous elixirs or whatever was desired at a word from the wizard. Arthur, however, flushed and looked deeply offended. And afterwards, in the light of what happened, Liz endlessly reproached herself for what she had said.

'How were you to know?' I asked.

'I should have known. I should have understood how serious and intense he was about his work. The fountains produced – well, holy waters, you see, and I talked about it making Drambuie . . . Oh, I know it's absurd, but he *was* absurd, what he wrote meant everything to him. The same passion and inspiration – and muse, if you like, affected Shakespeare and Arthur Kestrell, it's just the end product that's different.'

Arthur, when she had made that remark, had said very stiffly, 'I'm afraid you're not very sensitive to imaginative literature, Elizabeth,' and he left the party early. Liz and I were both rather cross at the time and Liz said she was sure Tolkien wouldn't have minded if someone had made a gentle joke to him about Frodo.

A week or so after this there was a story in the evening paper to the effect that the Minister for the Environment had finally decided to forbid Haringey's plans for putting council housing on the old railway line. The Parkland Walk, as the newspaper called it. Four and a half miles of a disused branch of the London and North-Eastern Railway, was the way it was described, from Finsbury Park to Highgate and at one time serving Alexandra Palace. It was to remain in perpetuity a walking place. The paper mentioned wildlife inhabiting the environs of the line, including foxes. Liz and I said we would go up there one evening in the autumn and see if we could see a fox. We never did go, I had reasons for not going near the place, but when we planned it I didn't know I had things to fear.

This was August, the end of August. The weather, with

its English vagaries, had suddenly become very cold, more like November with north winds blowing, but in the last days of the month the warmth and the blue skies came back. We had received a formal thank-you note for that dinner from Arthur, a few chilly lines written for politeness' sake, but since then neither sight nor sound of him.

The Fountains of Zond had been published and, as was always the case with Arthur's, or Blaise Fastnet's, books, had been ignored by the critics. I supposed that one of his depressions would have set in, but nevertheless I thought I should attempt to see him and patch up this breach between us. On 1 September, a Saturday, I set off in the afternoon to walk along the old railway line to his house.

I phoned first, but there was no answer. It was a beautiful afternoon and Arthur might well have been sitting in his garden where he couldn't hear the phone. It was the first time I had ever walked to his house by this route, though it was shorter and more direct than by road, and the first time I had been up on the Parkland Walk on a Saturday. I soon saw what he had meant about the crowds who used it at the weekends. There were teenagers with transistors, giggling schoolgirls, gangs of slouching youths, mobs of children, courting couples, middle-aged picnickers. At Northwood Road boys and girls were leaning against the parapet of the bridge, some with guitars, one with a drum, making enough noise for a hundred.

I remember that as I walked along, unable because of the noise and the press of people to appreciate nature or the view, that I turned my thoughts concentratedly on Arthur Kestrell. And I realised quite suddenly that although I thought of him as a close friend and liked him and enjoyed his company, I had never even tried to enter into his feelings or to understand him. If I had not actually laughed at his books, I had treated them in a light-hearted cavalier way, almost with contempt. I hadn't bothered to read a single one of them, a single page of one of them. And it seemed to me, as I strolled along that grassy path towards the Stanhope Road bridge, that it must be a terrible thing to pour all your life and soul and energy and passion into works that are remaindered in the bookshops, ignored by the critics, dismissed by paperback publishers, and taken off library shelves only by those who are attracted by the jackets and are seeking escape.

I resolved there and then to read every one of Arthur's books that we had. I made a kind of vow to myself to show an interest in them to Arthur, to make him discuss them with me. And so fired was I by this resolve that I determined to start at once, the moment I saw Arthur. I would begin by apologising for Liz and then I would tell him (without revealing, of course, that I had so far read nothing of his) that I intended to make my way carefully through all his books, treating them as an *oeuvre*, beginning with *Kallinarth, the Cloudling* and progressing through all fifteen or however many it was up to *The Fountains of Zond*. He might treat this with sarcasm, I thought, but he wouldn't keep that up when he saw I was sincere. My enthusiasm might do him positive good, it might help cure those terrible depressions which lately had seemed to come more frequently.

Arthur's house stood on this side, the Highgate side, of Crouch End Hill. You couldn't see it from the line, though you could get on to the line from it. This was because the line had by then entered its valley out of which you had to climb into Crescent Road before the Crouch End Hill bridge. I climbed up and walked back and rang Arthur's bell but got no answer. So I looked up at those Gothic lattices as I had done on the day Liz was with me and though I didn't see Arthur's face this time, I was sure I saw a curtain move. I called up to him, something I had never done before, but I had never felt it mattered before, I had never previously had this sense of urgency and importance in connection with Arthur.

'Let me in Arthur,' I called to him. 'I want to see you. Don't hide yourself, there's a good chap. This is important.'

There was no sound, no further twitch of curtain. I rang again and banged on the door. The house seemed still and wary, waiting for me to go away.

'All right,' I said through the letterbox. 'Be like that. But I'm coming back. I'll go for a bit of a walk and then I'll come back and I'll expect you to let me in.'

I went back down on to the line, meeting the musicians from Northwood bridge who were marching in the Finsbury Park direction, banging their drum and joined now by two West Indian boys with zithers. A child had been stung by a bee that was on one of the buddleias and an alsatian and a yellow labrador were fighting under the bridge. I began to walk quickly towards Stanhope Road, deciding to ring Arthur as soon as I got home, to keep on ringing until he answered.

Why was I suddenly so determined to see him, to break in on him, to make him know that I understood? I don't know why and I suppose I never will know, but this was all part of it, having some definite connection, I think, with what happened. It was as if, for those moments, perhaps half an hour all told, I became intertwined with Arthur Kestrell, part of his mind almost or he part of mine. He was briefly and for that one time the most important person in my world.

I never saw him again. I didn't go back. Some few yards before the Stanhope bridge, where the line rose once more above the streets, I felt an impulse to look back and see if from there I could see his garden or even see him in his garden. But the hawthorn, small birches, the endless buddleia grew thick here and higher far than a man's height. I crossed to the right-hand, or northern, side and pushed aside with my arms the long purple flowers and rough dark leaves, sending up into the air a cloud of black and orange butterflies.

Instead of the gardens and backs of houses which I expected to see, there stretched before me, long and straight and raised like a causeway, a green road turning northwards out of the old line. This debouching occurred, in fact, at my feet. Inadvertently, I had parted the bushes at the very point where a secondary branch left the line, the junction now overgrown with weeds and wild shrubs.

I stood staring at it in wonder. How could it be that I had never noticed it before, that Arthur hadn't mentioned it? Then I remembered that the newspaper story had said something about the line 'serving Alexandra Palace'. I had assumed this meant the line had gone on to Alexandra Palace after Highgate, but perhaps not, definitely not, for here was a branch line, leading northwards, leading straight towards the palace and the park.

I hadn't noticed it, of course, because of the thick barrier of foliage. In winter, when the leaves were gone, it would be apparent for all to see. I decided to walk along it, check that it actually led where I thought it would, and catch a bus from Alexandra Palace home.

The grass underfoot was greener and far less worn than on the main line. This seemed to indicate that fewer people came along here, and I was suddenly aware that I had left the crowds behind. There was no one to be seen, not even in the far distance.

Which was not, in fact, so very far. I was soon wondering how I had got the impression when I first parted those bushes that the branch line was straight and treeless. For tall trees grew on either side of the path, oaks and beeches such as were never seen on the other line, and ahead of me their branches met overhead and their fine frondy twigs interlaced. Around their trunks I at last saw the foxgloves and the tansy Arthur had spoken of, and the further I went the more the air seemed perfumed with the scent of wild flowers.

The green road – I found myself spontaneously and unaccountably calling this branch line the green road – began to take on the aspect of a grove or avenue and to widen. It was growing late in the afternoon and a mist was settling over London as often happens after a warm day in late summer or early autumn. The slate roofs, lying a little beneath me, gleamed dully silver through this sleepy, gold-shot mist. Perhaps, I thought, I should have the good luck to see a fox. But I saw nothing, no living thing, not a soul passed me or overtook me, and when I looked back I could see only the smooth grassy causeway stretching back and back, deserted, still, serene and pastoral, with the mist lying in fine streaks beneath and beside it. No birds sang and no breeze ruffled the feather-light, golden, downy, sweet-scented tufts of the mimosa flowers. For, yes, there was mimosa here. I paused and looked at it and marvelled.

It grew on either side of the path as vigorously and luxuriantly as it grows by the Mediterranean, the gentle swaying wattle. Its perfume filled the air, and the perfume of the humbler foxglove and tansy was lost. Did the oaks shelter it from the worst of the frost? Was there by chance some warm spring that flowed under the earth here, in this part of north London where there are many patches of woodland and many green spaces? I picked a tuft of minosa to take home to Liz, to prove I'd been here and seen it.

I walked for a very long way, it seemed to me, before I finally came into Alexandra Park. I hardly know this park, and apart from passing its gates by car my only experience of it till then had been a visit some years before to take Liz to an exhibition of paintings in the palace. The point in the grounds to which my green road had brought me was somewhere I had never seen before. Nor had I ever previously been aware of this aspect of Alexandra Palace, under whose walls almost the road led. It was more like

Versailles than a Victorian greenhouse (which is how I had always thought of the palace) and in the oblong lakes which flanked the flight of steps before me were playing surely a hundred fountains. I looked up this flight of steps and saw pillars and arches, a soaring elevation of towers. It was to here then, I thought, right up under the very walls, that the trains had come. People had used the line to come here for shows, for exhibitions, for concerts. I stepped off on to the stone stairs, descended a dozen of them to ground level and looked out over the park.

London was invisible, swallowed now by the white mist which lay over it like cirrus. The effect was curious, something I had never seen before while standing on solid ground. It was the view you get from an aircraft when it has passed above the clouds and you look down on to the ruffled tops of them. I began to walk down over wide green lawns. Still there were no people, but I had guessed it likely that they locked the gates on pedestrians after a certain hour.

However, when I reached the foot of the hill the iron gates between their Ionic columns were still open. I came out into a street I had never been in before, in a district I didn't know, and there found a taxi which took me home. On the journey I remember thinking to myself that I would ask Arthur about this curious terminus to the branch line and get him to tell me something of the history of all that grandeur of lawns and pillars and ornamental water.

I was never to have the opportunity of asking him anything. Arthur's cleaner, letting herself into the Gothic house on Monday morning, found him hanging from one of the beams in his writing room. He had been dead, it was thought, since some time on Saturday afternoon. There was a suicide note, written in Arthur's precise hand and in Arthur's wordy, pedantic fashion: 'Bitter disappointment at my continual failure to reach a sensitive audience or to attract understanding of my writing has led me to put an end to my life. There is no one who will suffer undue distress at my death. Existence has become insupportable and I cannot contemplate further sequences of despair.'

Elizabeth told me that in her opinion it was the only review she had ever known him to have which provoked poor Arthur to kill himself. She had found it in the paper herself on that Saturday afternoon while I was out and had read it with a sick feeling of dread for how Arthur would react. The critic, with perhaps nothing else at that moment to get his teeth into, had torn *The Fountains of Zond* apart and spat out the shreds.

He began by admitting he would not normally have wasted his typewriter ribbon (as he put it) on sci-fi fantasy trash, but he felt the time had come to campaign against the flooding of the fiction market with such stuff. Especially was it necessary in a case like this where a flavour of epic grandeur was given to the action, where there was much so-called 'fine writing' and where heroic motives were attributed to stereotyped or vulgar characters, so that innocent or young readers might be misled into believing that this was 'good' or 'valuable' literature. There was a lot more in the same vein. With exquisite cruelty the reviewer had taken character after character and dissected each, holding the exposed parts up to stinging ridicule. If Arthur had read it, and it seemed likely that he had, it was no wonder he had felt he couldn't bear another hour of existence.

All this deflected my thoughts, of course, away from the green road. I had told Liz about it before we heard of Arthur's death and we had intended to go up there together, yet somehow, after that dreadful discovery in the writing room of the Gothic house, we couldn't bring ourselves to walk so close by his garden or to visit those places where he would have loved to take us. I kept wondering if I had really seen that curtain move when I had knocked at his door or if it had only been a flicker of the sunlight. Had he already been dead by then? Or had he perhaps been contemplating what he was about to do? Just as Liz reproached herself for that remark about the fountains, so I reproached myself for walking away, for not hammering on that door, breaking a window, getting in by some means. Yet, as I said to her, how could anyone have known?

In October I did go up on the old railway line. Someone we knew living in Milton Park wanted to borrow my electric drill, and I walked over there with it, going down from the Stanhope Road bridge on the southern side. Peter offered to drive me back but it was a warm afternoon, the sun on the point of setting, and I had a fancy to look at the branch line once more, I climbed up on to the bridge and turned eastwards.

For the most part the leaves were still on the bushes and trees, though turning red and gold. I calculated pretty well where the turn-off was and pushed my way through the buddleias. Or I thought I had calculated well, but when I stood on the ridge beyond the hedge all I could see were the gardens of Stanhope Road and Avenue Road. I had come to the wrong place, I thought, it must be further along. But not much further, for very soon what had been a causeway became a valley. My branch line hadn't turned out of that sort of terrain, I hadn't had to climb to reach it.

Had I made a mistake and had it been on the *other* side of the Stanhope Road bridge? I turned back, walking slowly, making sorties through the buddleias to look northwards, but I couldn't anywhere find that turn-off to the branch line. It seemed to me then that, whatever I thought I remembered, I must in fact have climbed up the embankment to reach it and the junction must be far nearer the bridge at Crouch End Hill than I had believed. By then it was getting dark. It was too dark to go back, I should have been able to see nothing.

'We'll find it next week,' I said to Liz.

She gave me a rather strange look. 'I didn't say anything at the time,' she said, 'because we were both so upset over poor Arthur, but I was talking to someone in the Highgate Society and she said there never was a branch line. The line to Alexandra Palace went on beyond Highgate.'

'That's nonsense,' I said. 'I can assure you I walked along it. Don't you remember my telling you at the time?'

'Are you absolutely sure you couldn't have imagined it?'

'*Imagined it*? You know I haven't any imagination.'

Liz laughed. 'You're always saying that but I think you have. You're one of the most imaginative people I ever knew.'

I said impatiently, 'Be that as it may. I walked a good two miles along that line and came out in Alexandra Park, right under the palace, and walked down to Wood Green or Muswell Hill or somewhere and got a cab home. Are you and your Highgate Society friends saying I imagined oak trees and beech trees and mimosa? Look, that'll prove it, I picked a piece of mimosa, I picked it and put it in the pocket of my green jacket.'

'Your green jacket went to the cleaners last month.'

I wasn't prepared to accept that I had imagined or dreamed the green road. But the fact remains that I was never able to find it. Once the leaves were off the trees there was no question of delving about under bushes to hunt for it. The whole northern side of the old railway line lay exposed to the view and the elements and much of its charm was lost. It became what it really always was, nothing more or less than a ridge, a long strip of waste ground running across north London, over Northwood Road, over Stanhope Road, under Crouch End Hill, over Vicarage Road, under Crouch Hill, under Mount View, over Mount Pleasant Villas, over Stapleton Hall, under Upper Tollington Park, over Oxford Road, under Stroud Green Road, and so to the station at Finsbury Park. And nowhere along its length, for I explored every inch, was there a branch line running north to Alexandra Palace.

'You imagined it,' said Liz, 'and the shock of Arthur dying like that made you think it was real.'

'But Arthur wasn't dead then,' I said, 'or I didn't know he was.'

My invention, or whatever it was, of the branch line would have remained one of those mysteries which everyone, I suppose, has in his life, though I can't say I have any others in mine, had it not been for a rather curious and unnerving conversation which took place that winter between Liz and our friends from Milton Park. In spite of my resolutions made on that memorable Saturday afternoon, I had never brought myself to read any of Arthur's books. What now would have been the point? He was no longer there for me to talk to about them. And there was another reason. I felt my memory of him might be spoiled if there was truth in what the critic had said and his novels were full of false heroics and sham fine writing. Better feel with whatever poet it was who wrote:

I wept as I remembered how often thou and I
Have tired the sun with talking and sent him down the sky.

Liz, however, had had her interest in *The Chronicles of Kallinarth* revived and had reread every book in the series, passing them on as she finished each to Peter and Jane. That winter afternoon in the living room at Milton Park the three of them were full of it, Kallinarth, cloud country, Valaquen, Xadatel, the lot, and it was they who tired the sun with talking and sent him down the sky. I sat silent, not really listening, not taking part at all, but thinking of Arthur whose house was not far from here and who would have marvelled to hear of this detailed knowledge of his work.

I don't know which word of theirs it was that caught me or what electrifying phrase jolted me out of my reverie so that I leaned forward, intent. Whatever it was, it had sent a little shiver through my body. In that warm room I felt suddenly cold.

'No, it's not in *Kallinarth, the Cloudling,*' Jane was saying. 'It's *The Quest of Kallinarth.* Kallinarth goes out hunting early in the morning and he meets Xadatel and Finrael coming on horseback up the green road to the palace.'

'But that's not the first mention of it. In the first book there's a long description of the avenue where the procession comes up for Kallinarth to be crowned at the fountains of Zond and . . .'

'It's in all the books surely,' interrupted Peter. 'It's his theme, his leitmotif, that green road with the yellow wattle trees that leads up to the royal palace of Quephanda . . .'

'Are you all right, darling?' Liz said quickly. 'You've gone as white as a ghost.'

'White with boredom,' said Peter. 'It must be terrible for him us talking about this rubbish and he's never even read it.'

'Somehow I feel I know it without reading it,' I managed to say.

They changed the subject. I didn't take much part in that either, I couldn't. I could only think, it's fantastic, it's absurd, I couldn't have got into his mind or he into mine, that couldn't have happened at the point of his death. Yet what else?

And I kept repeating over and over to myself, he reached his audience, he reached his audience at last.

ACKNOWLEDGEMENTS

The editor is grateful to the following authors, agents and publishers for permission to include copyright stories in this collection: Hughes Massie Ltd for 'Express to Stamboul' by Agatha Christie; the Executors of the Estate of Freeman Wills Crofts for his story 'Crime on the Footplate'; Victor Gollancz Ltd for 'The Man With No Face' by Dorothy L. Sayers and 'Murder on the 7.16' by Michael Innes; BP Singer Features for 'Dead Man' by James M. Cain; William Heinemann Ltd for 'A Curious Suicide' by Patricia Highsmith; Fleetway Publications Ltd for 'Jeumont: 51 Minutes' Wait' by Georges Simenon, 'The Coulman Handicap' by Michael Gilbert and 'Escape to Danger' by Erle Stanley Gardner; the Authors and Dell Magazines for 'Three-Ten to Yuma' by Elmore Leonard and 'Headhunter' by Jan Carol Sabin; A.P. Watt Literary Agency for 'The Aventure of the First-Class Carriage' by Ronald A. Knox; Methuen Publishers Ltd for 'The Knight's Cross Signal Problem' by Ernest Bramah; Mercury Publications Inc. for 'Once Upon a Train' by Craig Rice and Stuart Palmer; Hodder Headline Publishing Group for 'The Rhine Maiden' by Leslie Charteris and 'The Mysterious Death on the Underground Railway' by Baroness Orczy; Telegraph Publications Ltd for 'Murder in the Tunnel' by Brian Hunt; Chase Manhattan Bank, NA as Executors of Cornell Woolrich for his story 'Death in the Air'; Atlas Publishing Co. for 'Thubway Tham's Bomb Scare' by Johnston McCulley; *Evening News* and Chapman Publishers Ltd for 'A Midnight Train to Nowhere' by Ken Follett; Random Publishing Group for 'Oxford Circus' by Maeve Binchy; Abner Stein Literary Agency for 'Drink

Acknowledgements

Entire: Against the Madness of Crowds' by Ray Bradbury; the Author for 'Death Decision' by William F. Nolan; Little, Brown Publishers for 'Broker's Special' by Stanley Ellin; Michael Joseph Publishers Ltd for 'Galloping Foxley' by Roald Dahl; the Author for 'The Second Passenger' by Basil Copper; and Peters, Fraser & Dunlop for 'The Green Road to Quephanda' by Ruth Rendell. While every effort has been made to contact the copyright holders of material used in this collection, in the case of any accidental infringement concerned parties are asked to contact the editor in care of the publishers.